BOOKS 1 - 5

IVY BLACK

ISBN: 9798527556841
Copyright © 2021. All rights reserved.

It is not legal to reproduce, duplicate, or transmit any part of this document in either electronic means or in printed format. Recording of this publication is strictly prohibited and any storage of this document is not allowed unless with written permission from the publisher except for the use of brief quotations in a book review.

This is a work of fiction. Any resemblance to actual persons, living or dead, or actual events is purely coincidental.

Your Exclusive Access

From the bottom of my heart, thank you so much for your support.

To show my appreciation, I've created an exclusive VIP newsletter just for you. When you join, you'll immediately receive a free prequel you won't find anywhere else!
You will also receive bonus chapters, notifications of future releases, future discounts, and many more surprises!

Download the prequel, receive future discounts and other bonuses by visiting:
www.BookHip.com/NXQBZZ

See you on the inside,
Ivy Black

Table of Contents

Angel's Phantom	1
Devil's Bullet	143
Hard Bullseye	285
Huge Dynamite	443
Riding Shotgun	599

BOOK 1

ANGEL'S PHANTOM

Chapter One

Phantom

What had started out as the odd passing rumble had become a continuous roar with the setting sun, and the now raucous thundering awoke me from my sleep. I hadn't meant to doze off, but after nearly a month of running, it was difficult to stay awake if I stopped anywhere for longer than a few minutes.

I looked up at the setting sun and figured most of the day must have passed while I was out. It was stupid of me to fall asleep in such a vulnerable position, but it beat sitting there all day, just waiting.

A few tiny critters scattered as I rolled over in the shrubs that shrouded me and dared to poke my face out through the leaves. The bar across the street had been abandoned when I first arrived, but now, with the day giving way to the night, the place was coming alive. Patrons arrived one after the other, slowly filling the parking lot of the establishment and turning it into a showroom of motorcycles and hot rods.

Hoppa's Taphouse. It'd been a long time since I last saw it.

As a bike went roaring past with a familiar silver, dual-bladed sigil on the side, I recoiled into the bush as quickly and quietly as I could. My left bicep pulsated with pain as if the image had summoned it. The tattoo of a pit bull amidst a shattered chain was now hidden beneath poorly wrapped bandages. I should be thankful for the bandage, given that the tattoo would get me killed if anyone within a hundred-mile radius saw it, but it was difficult to be grateful that the flesh was burned nearly to the bone. I pushed the pain to the back of my mind in favor of getting my attention back on the bar. Patience had been the theme of my day ever since I pulled into Hoppa, and now that the Taphouse was open, all I had to do was wait to see the person I'd risked everything to find.

The bushes rustled as I used my hands to create a small window to peer through. The bike that had sent me hiding was parked in one of the silver-painted parking spots lined along the Taphouse wall. Its rider was already gone, and I whispered, "Fuck," as I realized that three additional bikes had already pulled in and parked beside it.

One by one, the remaining silver spots filled up, none of them bringing my saving grace along. There went all hopes of seeing each club member as they arrived. I officially had no choice but to watch the door in the hopes that a familiar face came out. Prayers that it didn't take all night whispered across my brain, but I didn't get my hopes up even as they did.

Time to get comfortable. I winced as I shifted, my left side starting to burn worse with each passing minute. My preference would have been not to move at all, but I'd pass out and miss her altogether if the pain got too much worse. Even though pulling out of my hiding spot while the sun was still in the sky was a bad idea, it was worth the risk. I braced myself on my arms and pushed backward out of the bush but opted to stay on my knees as opposed to standing up.

I crawled over to where my motorcycle was riskily catching the glinting orange of the setting sun. When the shine slid across my vision, a kaleidoscope of reds and oranges flashed across my brain, partnered with the song of flames crackling all around me. My stomach started to burn, my left side, my left leg. It was as if the fire was crawling up my body once again. It licked over the edge of the bed, ate away at my blankets so that it could bite at my skin.

With a shake of my head and a crack of my neck, I dragged myself back to reality. Being out in the open, this wasn't the place to be trapped inside my own mind. I closed the distance between myself and my bike and got to my feet. The cover of the bush was all I had as I reached into the carrying compartment on my bike's rear and snatched out the small bag within. I snapped the compartment closed and dropped back to the ground. The sudden revving of an approaching bike made me jump, and my head snapped over my shoulder. My heart pounded so hard that I thought it might leap out of my chest. The bike rushed down the street and turned into the Taphouse parking lot. It parked in the last of the silver-painted parking spots, and then the rider climbed off the bike, left his helmet behind, and walked into the bar.

"Focus, Colin." I brought my attention back to my bag and started to sift through it.

Pushing past the old and bloodied bandages that I was hanging onto for safe disposal later, I dug to the bottom of the bag in search of the pill bottle I'd managed to save on my way out of my house. A few rolled wads of cash—what was left of the reason I was running—faked me out a few times. Much like the pills that I was in search of, my cash supply was running short. Lack of meds and money in my condition wasn't good, and maybe that was why I convinced myself that coming back to Hoppa was a good idea when it clearly wasn't.

"Shit, where is it?" My fingers raked through the bag's contents until they slid across the gloss of the only picture I'd managed to grab. I carefully pinched the unburned corner of the photo and pulled it free of the bag. The entire bottom-left corner of the photo was charred and curling, but the important part remained untouched by the char. I smiled down at the reflection of my own face, though feebler and weaker.

Identical in the face but not in our circumstances.

The person in the picture was lying in a hospital bed with numerous IVs stuck into him, making him look remarkably similar to a marionette doll. Despite this, he had a huge, bright smile on his face. He always was better at being happy than I was.

"Hey, Caid," I huffed out loud, touching the face. "How's Germany?"

Caid's raspy voice snuck into my mind as I imagined him responding to me. He was probably blown away by the different landscapes or lamenting that he couldn't understand anyone around him. I hadn't heard from him yet, which was terrifying, but I had to have faith that he was getting the help he needed.

"Hey!"

A sudden voice barking out made me jump so hard that I dropped everything in my hands. The pill bottle I'd been searching for fell out of the bag and went rolling across the grass, just out of arm's reach. The wind started to push the photo of Caid away in the opposite direction, but I didn't move. My chest cavity had to be cracking from how hard my heart was pounding. I threw a hand to my mouth and slowed my breathing. I watched powerlessly as the Arizona desert winds pushed my photo in one direction and drove my pain meds in another. I bit the inside of my cheek until metallic swill filled my mouth.

"Squared!" another voice said.

The voice that had called out, startling me, responded, "Come on in here, you ass. I'm gonna kick your ass all over this pool table."

I took a deep breath in and held it while turning my head at a snail's pace over my shoulder. The fear that I may meet a set of eyes watching me made me sick to my stomach, but the Taphouse came into view, and whichever loud individuals had grabbed my attention were gone. As fast as a bolt of lightning, I crawled on my hands and knees over to the picture and snatched it up, then I crawled over to the bottle. The latter took me totally out of the bush's shade, but I didn't stop to see if someone was watching. I steadily moved until I collapsed back on the ground at the tires of my bike. I untwisted the lid of the bottle, dumped the remaining three pain relievers into my hand, shoved the empty bottle and picture back into my bag, returned my bag to the holding compartment of my bike, and then crawled back over to the nook I'd been bunkered in a few feet away from my bike.

With a sigh, I tossed the pills back and then fell down to my back. Sweat that wasn't from the heat dripped down my forehead, and my vision blurred and threatened to give out. I wanted to give up. I even considered just crawling out to the road and lying flat until something turned me into roadkill. I'd made it so far, though, and I'd been through so much. Just one more push was all it would take, and hopefully, I'd be home free.

Rolling to my stomach, I balanced myself, perched my face in the small window I'd made, and kept my eyes on the bar, patiently waiting for the one I needed to see. People flowed in and out, some hanging in, some hanging out, all with different drinks in their hands. I was grateful for the reprieve from my pain that the few pills I'd just popped would bring me, but I was jealous of the patrons' drunkenness. It'd been over a month since I'd tasted booze or experienced the forgetful naivety it could bring. I'd do nearly anything for release from the prison of fear in my own mind now, but I couldn't afford the risk.

Minutes bled into hours that felt like days as the sun descended further toward the horizon before it was hidden beneath it. Stars dotted the sky, and for as hot as the desert could get during the day, it could get just as markedly cold at night. I clung my leather jacket closer to my body in an attempt to negate the chill settling in my bones. I could imagine my old favorite jacket hanging in my coat closet back home, at least until it went up in flames. That jacket could keep me warmer than a seal's coat of blubber, but it also had the Unchained Dogs' emblem stitched on it. The warmth wouldn't have been worth the risk, but God, did I miss it as I shivered.

The moon was high in the sky when I started to calculate my next move. A few silver parking spots had emptied, but I still hadn't seen the person I came looking for. The cold was nearly unbearable now, and if I continued to lay in the grass with no warmth, water, or food, the burns covering the left side of my body wouldn't be the only reason I might die.

I knew Hoppa much better than I knew the other handful of cities that I'd stopped in on my run, and there were a couple of motels not far from the Taphouse. Spending the last bit of the money I had on a place to sleep wasn't ideal, but it was better than the alternative. All I had to do now was get to my bike, get on it, and get it started without raising any eyebrows.

Moving for the first time in hours sent my body screaming in pain, but I forced myself through it. A few feet felt like twelve yards as I crawled to my bike and used the handles to pull myself to my feet, but I felt better when I was finally mounting my bike again. I fished the keys out of my pocket and slid them into the ignition. Just as I was about to turn the key, I heard voices and froze in place.

"Come on, Val! Stay for one more round. I got you this next hand. I promise you that!"

A woman with auburn hair emerged through the bar's swinging front doors. "If I take any more of your money, Marianne is gonna have your neck and mine. Give it up."

A melody of groans and laughs rang out, but the woman just waved her hand and stepped out into the moonlight, a hulking pit bull at her side. Her curves swayed back and forth as she sauntered into the parking lot, and I couldn't help but smile.

"Beautiful," I whispered into the night.

She was recognizable as the person I once knew, but she was so much more beautiful than I thought possible. Her arms now held colorful tattoos that, if I got lucky, I'd get to inspect closer when I got the chance. Though still the same, gorgeous color, her hair now fell past her shoulders and down her back—much longer than she ever kept it as a kid. The teenager inside me was both delighted to be back in her presence and lamenting the time we'd lost. If the circumstances were any different, I'd charge in and make sure I didn't let life snatch her away from me again.

Unfortunately, I probably wasn't going to get that lucky.

She approached a sleek, modern Ducati. It was bright red, exactly her style. I grinned and watched as she loaded her vicious-looking pet into a rear carrier that had been affixed to the back, and then she mounted the bike and started it with a magnificent growl. I started my own bike in synchronization with hers to mask the sound and waited as she started to move. Just like the girl I once knew, she was fluid and smooth as she whipped it out of her parking spot and onto the road. She'd be a nice way to say goodbye to Arizona and America forever.

When there was a safe distance between us, I started up my own bike again, a more old school Harley-Davison. It was an old bike of Luther's that he'd let me dig out of a dumpster full of old meat and probably the rotting parts of his victims as an initiation. It didn't even work when I got it, but I worked on it painstakingly until it was in the pristine condition it was currently in. When I wasn't taking care of Caid, I was working on my bike. I wouldn't say that this little joke alone was the reason I was willing to steal from Luther, but it sure made it a hell of a lot easier.

I kept the distance of a few car lengths or more between us until we were clear of the bar, then I closed the distance bit by bit. At first, her driving was calm and smooth as she abided the speed limit, weaving at a leisurely pace between the cars on the road. I kept up without issue until she started speeding up, slowing down, and changing lanes suddenly. Following her actions, I tried to keep her in my line of sight without making it too obvious that I was following her. If she moved lanes, I would stay in mine for a few feet and then switch. If she sped up, I'd allow her to do so for a few minutes, and then I'd follow suit.

Trying to stay covert was costing me, though, and I was beginning to fear that I was going to lose her when she rode past a row of houses and then turned down an alley. My options ran a mile a minute through my brain. I could pass the alley, wait for her to come out, and try again, or I could roll the dice and follow her in.

She wouldn't sic her pit bull on someone on sight, right?

Shadows closed around me as I turned down the alleyway, and I immediately became confused at the sight of the red Ducati sitting at the end of the alleyway, still with the dog in it, still alive and rumbling.

I pulled my bike to a stop and cut it off. My experience had me reaching into my waistband for my gun, but then I stopped. I came seeking help, and I needed the person I sought to know that I didn't pose a threat. Relying on the hope that she didn't know where I'd been for the past fourteen years was already a calculated risk. I didn't need to make the situation any worse by pulling a gun.

With my hands in the air, I stepped carefully down the alley. The pit bull started to bark and growl as I approached, but I didn't flinch. A few dumpsters shielded the end of the alley, so I crept past them slowly and looked to see if she was hiding.

But there was no one.

I started to fear that maybe something bad had happened to her when the cold, heavy feeling of steel against the back of my skull snapped me into place.

A sweet but menacing voice huffed from just behind me, "You have thirty seconds to tell me why you're following me, or I'm gonna leave you in a puddle of your own blood."

I smirked. She'd always been a badass. "Tess," I said before turning my head slowly to give her a better look at my face. "It's been a long time. You look good."

Chapter Two

Tess

Lockjaw, my beefy, all-white pit bull, had gotten used to sensing danger whenever my gun clicked. The second I set the barrel to the back of the head of the man following me, Lockjaw let out a low, menacing growl. Unbeknownst to my pursuer, I'd unlatched Lockjaw's harness when I climbed off my bike, just in case. All it would take was one word, and he'd be out of his seat and latched onto whichever body part he could get to first.

Unfortunately for me, the typically simple task of speaking was eluding me for the time being. The confidence I'd just had when I slunk behind the alley's dumpsters to get the jump on my stalker abated in an instant. His dirty-blond hair was a bit longer, even a bit unkempt, and the clean, baby face I had etched in my brain was hidden behind a growing scruff of a goatee, but there was no denying the voice or those emerald eyes.

Colin, my childhood love, was the man at the other end of my gun.

I kept the barrel against his head as I sidestepped him slowly and paced to his front to view his face better. What wasn't covered in facial hair was covered in various scrapes and scratches, along with a couple of places that looked like someone had held a lighter against his skin. I studied him closely, making sure I wasn't projecting one of my lingering high-school dreams, but as I locked my eyes on his, it felt like being suddenly thrust backward in time.

It was him.

"Colin?"

He tilted his head with a crooked smile. "A decade made you forget me? It's CJ."

I furrowed my brow. I wasn't misremembering the name of the first guy I'd ever fallen in love with. I had half a dozen notebooks still packed in storage at my parents' house with his name scribbled all over them. The boy I was infatuated with was named Colin.

"CJ?" I asked.

"Yeah. Blue house four doors down. I accidentally broke your front window, trying to get your attention," he responded.

That was definitely Colin. I smiled as I remembered the silly, nine-year-old boy. A failed attempt to pull the romantic rocks-at-my-window cliché ended with a rather large stone in my living room and my dad loading up a shotgun because he thought someone was trying to break in. He was so terrified when my dad came storming out of the house that he bolted and jumped into a nearby trash can. I had to wait for my dad to calm down before I could go and coax him out. He was the cutest Oscar the Grouch I'd ever seen.

First name Colin, last name Jones. I would never forget it.

Colin's presence halted my typical tendency to fly on the defensive. Was it just because I was so happy to see him again? Were those intoxicating green eyes working me over the same way they always had?

I tried to understand the name change. Maybe he was abbreviating it for some reason? I'd known plenty of people who stopped letting people refer to them by a childhood name and picked a different name to live with for the rest of their days. CJ was different enough, I supposed, and it distanced him from his childhood, which I knew was rough.

It would also explain why I could never find Colin Jones on social media when I searched. If he'd stopped going by the name on his birth certificate in lieu of something more concise, he'd probably be using that name on social media. I wanted to continue to poke at it for the full truth, but my inner eleven-year-old was berating me for not already having kissed him.

I couldn't justify continuing to press when he seemed like he was on the verge of death. Gorgeous though his face still was, he looked worse for wear. It wasn't just the abrasions on his face, either. His clothes seemed ragged and looked like he'd been wearing them for multiple days in a row, and he was holding his left arm against his stomach, with blood-soaked bandages visible through the holes in his gloves. He was hurting—badly.

"CJ, of course," I said finally. "How could I *ever* forget?"

Colin smirked, seemingly unbothered by the state he was in. "No idea."

"Ten plus years will do that to you," I responded.

Colin eyed my gun before slowly turning his gaze to Lockjaw. "Are you gonna pull away your weapons?"

"Should I?" I let out a sharp whistle, and Lockjaw hopped out of his seat and bounded over to my side, his snarl worsening as he prepared to attack on my behalf. "Old friend or not, you were following me, and it's been longer than thirty seconds."

Colin's smirk pursed a little. It wasn't fear, but something else. Intrigue? "I need your help. My house caught fire, and someone is trying to kill me."

It was almost humorous that Colin tried to pass off such an outrageous statement as a satisfactory excuse without further explanation. Colin had always been laconic, but that was too much, even for him—or too little.

"That's all I get? Your house caught fire, and someone's trying to kill you?"

Colin shrugged and glanced down at himself as if to say, "It's obviously true."

"Why is someone trying to kill you?"

"I don't know," he replied.

I scoffed. "You don't know? People don't earn that much wrath without knowing who would do it and why, Col—CJ."

"I don't. I woke up to my house on fire. I didn't have a chance to ask whoever did it what their reasoning was. I got on my bike and ran."

"Did they chase you? How do you know that they don't think you burned up in that house?" I asked.

Colin swayed a little to the right and looked as if he was going to pass out. I clicked my teeth in irritation. There would be time for questions, but that time wasn't right now. If I didn't get Colin to a doctor, our reunion would be over as quickly as it began, and not because his mom packed him up and left. I pulled my gun back, and Lockjaw's growling stopped. He stayed standing at attention next to me, though, until I reached down and patted his head.

"Does *that* weapon have a name?" Colin asked.

I chuckled. "Lockjaw."

Colin nodded. "That's appropriate."

Lockjaw's tongue lolled out of his mouth as he leaned into my head scratches. "He's a good boy. I stole him."

Colin raised an eyebrow. "You stole him?"

"Yup." I walked over to my bike and whistled, and Lockjaw ran and leaped up into my arms. I settled him back in his seat and fastened him in, complete with his own doggy helmet. "I'll tell you *that* story when you fess up about why you're being hunted."

Colin smiled. "Fair."

"Can you ride?" I asked.

"I can always ride," Colin said with a chuckle.

"Good. Follow me. My place is not far."

Colin turned around and made his way back to his bike, and I noticed that he had a limp. Whatever had happened to him was definitely meant to kill him. It honestly didn't make much sense to me. Colin wasn't a bad guy and never had been. Despite that his mom was a raging drunk and drug user, and despite that she kept a rotating door for men, Colin spent his days with me and taking care of his sick brother. He and Colin were twins as far as I was told, but I'd never met Caid. He didn't leave the house. Colin was just a simple kid who wanted to take care of the people he loved. It was one of the things I adored about him. How he got caught up with someone trying to kill him was a huge mystery. I couldn't see him angering anyone that much.

I cut the engine on my bike for a brief moment so that I could pull out my phone and call one of the doctors I had on call. I was the vice president of my dad's motorcycle club, the Steel Knights. The club had been in my family for generations, and both my brother and I were officers and part of my dad's inner court. If the thrill of the danger and excitement of the club wasn't enough, I also had certain advantages, like paid-under-the-table doctors who would drop everything and come running the second I called to deal with any ailments or injuries any of the brotherhood had without asking any questions. There were a couple of doctors in the Steel Knights' pocket, but Dr. Xavier Marteau was skilled in the kind of down-to-the-bone injuries that it seemed Colin may have obtained.

"Good evening, Val," he answered, using the shortened version of my club moniker, Valkyrie.

It was a name I'd earned from my dad after taking his bike and riding into our rival gang's territory to steal Lockjaw when he was still a puppy. My dad walked outside in the middle of the night to see me perched against his bike, holding Lockjaw. My story impressed him so much that he didn't kill me for stealing his bike. He said that my story reminded him of a Norse Valkyrie riding into battle. That was the first time he considered me strong enough to one day prospect for the Steel Knights. It was one of the best days of my life. When I became a member, my dad presented me with a Steel Knights jacket with the name on the back. Most of the brotherhood shortened the name to Val when they weren't using *Bitch* or *Slut*.

Most of them didn't like me very much.

"Hey, doc. Can you meet me at my place? I've got a bad case. Burns, possibly broken bones, and a shit ton of other stuff."

"Of course. Give me ten minutes."

"Cool, thank you. Oh, and doc?"

"Yes?"

Colin's bike roared to life behind me, and I knew he was ready to get going. I held up my pointer finger to tell him to wait. "Discretion is key, so please come alone, and don't tell Squared."

Squared was my dad's official nickname because his legal name was Nicholas Nicholas.

"You got it, Val. See you soon."

"Bye."

I slid my phone into my jacket pocket and zipped it up, then pulled on my helmet and started my bike back up. My tires screeched as I spun in place, and I whizzed past Colin and out onto the street. The low rumble of Colin's bike let me know he was behind me, so I started to navigate the streets of Hoppa toward my house, which was more toward the edge of the small town. I never liked that my parents were right in the heart of everything. Hoppa wasn't insanely small—it had about sixty thousand people—but it was small enough that everyone liked to be in everyone's business. With my dad at the head of Hoppa's famous Steel Knights, more people looked at us.

I hated it. The second I was old enough to get my own place, I found a house as close to the edge of Hoppa as possible. I preferred the call of a coyote over the perilous whispers of nosy neighbors.

My place was a small, shotgun-style home made of rustic red bricks and topped with a dark brown terracotta roof. I had the mountains in my backyard and the stunning, expansive Arizona desert as my front view. It wasn't a mansion, but it was enough for Lockjaw and me. It didn't occur to me until we were approaching it that Colin was the first non-familial guest I'd had in a while. Poetic justice or dumb luck? I didn't know, and I didn't care.

Field rats scattered as I turned my bike into the driveway, and Colin pulled in next to me. The twin calls of our engines went silent as we powered down, leaving only a chorus of crickets, coyotes, and the distant hoot of owls.

I unfastened Lockjaw just as Colin was climbing off his bike, and Lockjaw quickly hopped off his seat and went to stand at the beginning of the L-shaped walkway that went up to my door. His pointed ears stood straight up, and he kept his golden eyes deadlocked on Colin as he moved.

I crouched in front of Lockjaw and petted his face with a loving scratch. "Who's Mommy's good boy? It's okay. He's a friend."

I stood up and stepped past Lockjaw, snapping my fingers as I did so, and Lockjaw stood up, allowing Colin to approach the door more comfortably. We followed the path, and I unlocked it before standing aside so that Colin could pass by me to enter.

Lockjaw stepped in, and I followed him, reaching to the left of the doorway to switch the light on as I went. I shut the door and tossed my keys down the kitchen island that divided my small, open kitchen from the living room and started down the hallway. Lockjaw plopped down into his living room dog bed and almost immediately fell asleep. It was well past his bedtime.

"Follow me," I called out, and I heard Colin's footsteps behind me in response. A long hallway led from the front of my house to the back. I stopped at the first door on the right but pointed a little forward to the first door on the left. "Bathroom's up there." I tapped the door I stopped in front of. "This is the guest bedroom. The door at the end is my bedroom."

I turned the doorknob to the guest bedroom and led the way in. It was a modest room, housing only my old queen-sized bed from before I upgraded to my king, and a small, totally bare desk. I didn't put too much effort into decorating the guest room. I rarely had guests, and the room usually served as a sleepover place for the odd friend too drunk to drive home.

"I imagine the doctor will need to take a closer look," I told Colin. "This will have to do."

I'd wandered further into the room than I planned, and when I turned around to flip on the light, I ran right into Colin. He winced in pain but still let out a light chuckle. With us standing so close, our size difference was more apparent. He had at least four inches on me, all of which I felt as his green eyes peered through the darkness to slowly paint my form. I abandoned going for the light and just allowed him to drink me in. It wasn't as if I was some idealist, thinking my middle school boyfriend was just gonna waltz back into my life and that we were going to live happily ever after, but if he wanted to make a move to give us a few hot nights together before he blew out of town, I'd be more than happy to oblige.

"Take your time," I said snidely.

Colin smirked. "You look good."

It was going to be hard to keep up my Tough Tess act when my gut reaction to Colin's presence was to swoon like a schoolgirl. "I know," I snipped back with a grin, and his smile got a little larger.

He walked further into the room, and I finally cut on the light.

"Ah, fuck."

I whipped back around to see that Colin was attempting to shake his jacket off but was struggling. "Want some help?"

Colin sighed. "Please."

I walked over, tucked my hands under the shoulders of his jacket, and slowly rolled it down. His arm and back muscles were firm under my hands, and I was curious about what lay beneath his shirt, but the way he grunted while I worked let me know that his torso was pretty damaged, too.

"So…" I started, finally getting his jacket off and tossing it onto the desk. "How's Caid?"

There was a quick flash of shock before it disappeared behind another twisted expression of pain when Colin tucked a finger into his mouth to remove his right glove. I grabbed his hand and pulled it down. "I'll do this. You answer my question."

"He's overseas." Colin kept his eyes trained on our hands as I worked the glove off. "His illness got worse, but there's an experimental surgery that could save his life."

"Wow. How long has he been gone?"

Colin didn't answer right away. I couldn't read his hesitation, but he eventually continued. "About two months."

"You must miss him." I freed the glove and set it on top of Colin's jacket before turning to the left. This hand was wrapped in bandages that seemed to go even further up his arm, indicating it was in worse shape than the other. I was slower and more careful, but it didn't stop Colin from clenching his jaw. "Sorry. Does it hurt?"

"I'm okay." His left hand balled into a fist, suggesting otherwise. "And yes, I do miss him. We haven't talked since he left."

"Why?" Again, Colin's answer didn't come right out. It was almost like he was choosing what to say and what not to tell me. It was borderline insulting. I didn't expect him to open up entirely after so many years apart, but I assumed that he came to me because he trusted me. "You know, before, you said it had been ten years since we last saw each other," I changed the subject.

"I rounded," he replied instantly, and I looked up to meet his gaze, which was already fixated on me. "It's been fourteen. Guess I'm trying to act like it hasn't been so long."

"It's easier for someone who hasn't been around, I suppose," I said. The glove reached a spot where my only choice was to yank it the rest of the way. "I'm sorry. This may hurt."

"It's fine."

I snatched the glove quickly a la ripping the bandaid, and I felt the bandage pull with it, no doubt dragging some of Colin's skin along. The dried blood had glued his hand and glove together, which was why pulling them apart was so painful. Why he even had a glove on, to begin with, was anyone's guess.

His hand instantly started to bleed. I wasn't prepared and raced from the room for the linen closet. The rattle of Lockjaw's chain collar let me know that he'd jumped up in response to my rush. He padded down the hallway, but I grabbed the first towel my hand found in the linen closet next to the bathroom, then jumped over Lockjaw to get back into the room. Colin was cradling his hand in his jacket to prevent the blood from getting on the floor. I wrapped his hand in the towel and then set his jacket aside once again. If I tossed it in the washer before I went to bed, I could hopefully get the blood out.

"Sorry. I should have warned you about that," Colin said.

"It's fine. The doctor should be here any second." I reached for the base of his shirt. "I'll help with this, too."

Colin backed away from me. "I can do it."

I scoffed. "No, you can't. You couldn't even get your gloves off. Let me help."

"It's fine, Tess."

"Will you stop being so damn stubborn?" I started to lift the shirt, and Colin jerked away from me so hard that he bumped into the desk and elicited a growl from Lockjaw, who was now standing in the doorway.

"I said, I got it!" Colin barked.

I held up my hands in defeat. "Fine."

The front door cracked, and Lockjaw raced out to investigate. He did not bark, and a few seconds later, Dr. Marteau rounded the corner into the room.

"Hey, Val." He looked at Colin. "Oh. Hello." Colin didn't respond. Dr. Marteau, an older gentleman with long brown hair and an outdated and greying soul patch, raised his eyebrows at me. "This is the case?"

"Yeah. He's an old friend. Can you help?" I asked.

Dr. Marteau shrugged. "I'll see what I can do." He looked at Colin. "It's probably best if you lose the shirt. Pants, too, so I can get a thorough look."

Colin looked at him first, then at me. "Can you step out?"

"Yeah," I said.

I wanted to argue, but things had already turned sour, and I didn't want to make them worse. I gave Dr. Marteau a tap on the shoulder and then stepped out into the hallway again, closing the door behind me. I whistled, calling, "Lockjaw." I waited a few seconds, but there was no response. I whistled again, that time throwing in a clap as well.

"Here boy." Again, nothing. "Lockjaw."

I walked down the hallway to make sure he hadn't escaped through the front door, but what I saw in the living room was much worse. There, sitting on my couch, petting an obedient Lockjaw on his left and with my brother, Taylor, sitting on the arm of the couch to the right, was the man I'd expressly asked Dr. Marteau *not* to call. Nicholas "Squared" Nicholas—my dad.

Chapter Three

Tess

Any excitement that Colin turning back up in my life gave me bled out when I saw my dad and brother. I deliberately asked the doctor *not* to contact my dad because I knew that there was a pretty good chance Taylor was still with him. I could explain certain things to my dad, not just because I was a bit of a daddy's girl, but also because I was his vice president and noted right hand. He'd listen to me if I told him to trust me and that I was taking care of an old friend.

Taylor, however—well, he was a different story.

I couldn't pinpoint exactly when Taylor lost his mind. Our mother died before either of us was really old enough to remember her, so my dad had raised us by himself and did a hell of a job at it. I distinctly remembered having a normal, loving brother as a little girl, but then it suddenly seemed like any guy that even looked in my direction got his head bitten off. Figuratively, at first, but as he got older, he started to get slowly more physical and violent. I tried to call his bluff with my first boyfriend after I pledged for the Steel Knights, and it turned out to be a huge mistake. Taylor broke into my house while we were having sex, dragged my boyfriend out into the backyard, and shot him before I could get a word in edgewise. My dad had it covered up like a break-in gone bad. To say it traumatized me would be an understatement.

After that, I committed myself to never doing anything other than letting the odd, wavering guy take me home for a one-night stand, and even those encounters were treated like such a big secret that they could have been stored in Area 51. I imagined Colin's crooked grin and green eyes, and my stomach twisted into a knot. Adulthood had been good to him, and he still had his brother to think about. I couldn't get him killed by trying to rekindle an old flame, even if he still looked at me like I was the most important thing in the world. Now that Taylor was aware he existed or would be aware soon, I had to make sure that nothing happened between us.

For a really long time, my dad tried to convince me that Taylor was just being overprotective—it's what a brother is supposed to do—but somewhere along the way, I realized that Taylor didn't have much other than blind aggression inside his body. Sometimes, I felt like he was doing it because he felt more like I was his property than his sister, and someone who touched his property had to die. Most of the time, though, I thought it was just because Taylor was crazy. Around five years ago, my dad had stopped defending his behavior and just tried to steady the waters. He was starting to realize his son was unhinged, too, even if he didn't want to accept it.

"Hi, Daddy," I finally greeted him. I reserved familial association for when we weren't around the other members of the brotherhood. Otherwise, I called him Squared or Nick like everyone else.

My dad, a man with short brown hair, a severe jawline, and several scars across his stubbled skin, gave me a smirk. "Hey, baby. Working late, I see?"

"A friend of mine needed some help," I replied. "I told Marteau not to bother you with it."

My dad chuckled. "You know good and well that everyone has orders to tell me *everything*. Big or small, if it's worth your time, it's worth mine." That was my dad's way of saying that he was paranoid about everything that happened without him, but I'd never dare say that out loud. "We were still at the Taphouse when he called. Taylor was right there with me, so we both decided to come and make sure you were okay."

I sat down in one of the armchairs that sat perpendicular to the couch and tapped my leg, and Lockjaw finally tore himself away from my dad and came to me, setting his head in my lap and waiting patiently for scratches.

I set a hand on his head and rubbed for a few seconds silently before continuing. "I'm okay, Daddy. Really. A friend came to me and was a little banged up, and I called Dr. Marteau to get him a little help."

Taylor raised an eyebrow immediately. "Him?"

"Yes. A friend from high school. CJ." I locked eyes with Taylor. "Just a friend." I decided to omit the fact that it was Colin from my childhood that was in the other room. I wasn't sure what my dad or Taylor would do if they knew it was my childhood crush, but I was hoping they wouldn't put two and two together so that I didn't have to find out. I shifted my gaze from Taylor to my dad. "I'd like a private audience."

Taylor was the spitting image of my dad apart from his auburn hair that was closer to mine. When he scoffed, he and my dad were nearly indistinguishable. "Aw, come on. We're all family here. Why the secrecy?"

"This isn't a family matter," I responded, but I directed the comment to my dad. "I'm asking for a private audience as your vice president."

The smirk that Taylor had turned into a scowl. "That's low."

My dad tapped his fist against Taylor's arm. "It's fine, Taylor. Why don't you head home? We'll talk tomorrow." Taylor didn't move. I shifted my attention toward him and saw that he was staring at me like he wanted to set me on fire. My dad cleared his throat and turned to look at Taylor. "Leave. Now."

I was surprised that the deep sigh Taylor let out in response didn't blow actual smoke out of his nose. He stood up off of the arm of the chair, glaring at me as he moved. He came to stand in front of my coffee table, staring at me over it, and suddenly, he brought up and threw down a fist into the glass, shattering it all over the floor. He was unbothered by his destruction as he stepped through the frame and over to the front door. He opened it and walked through, slamming it behind him.

"Brat," I hissed under my breath, staring sadly at my coffee table. I'd had to replace more than one piece of furniture due to Taylor's outbursts, but I really liked that coffee table.

My dad chuckled. "You know how he is. I'll replace the table."

I shook my head. "It's fine. I'll just redecorate."

He crossed his arms and looked at me, a little more relaxed, but also a little more business. "Now. Are you going to tell me what this is *really* all about?"

"I didn't lie," I replied quickly. "It *is* a friend from high school, and he *is* banged up, though that might be a kind way to put it. He looked like he was going to pass out any second."

"What happened?"

I scratched behind Lockjaw's ears, and he started to pant with satisfaction. "He said someone set his house on fire…with him in it. He thinks whoever did it is still after him."

"Why are they after him?"

"He doesn't know."

A scoff of disbelief skipped over my dad's lips. "How does he not know why someone would try to kill him?"

I smiled, remembering that I said something damn near identical. "That's what I said, but he's pretty shaken. I really don't think he knows."

"It sounds a little convenient to me."

"I'd swear my title on the guy. He's a good guy. Kind, well-liked. If someone *is* trying to kill him, I highly doubt he had anything to do with it. It must be a situation totally out of his control." Lockjaw walked away from me and over to his bed, allowing me to cross my arms to match my dad. "He's in rough shape. He'll need to stay for a week maybe, just until he's in good enough shape to be on his way. If trouble comes his way, can you protect him?"

My dad sat in silence while he considered this. He pondered my face, and I could tell that he could read my passion. I was glad that he didn't ask why I felt compelled to do something for Colin at all. The truth was, I didn't really know. I cared so much about Colin when I was still a kid, but more than a decade had passed since then. Plenty of people had neighborhood crushes, and plenty of people got over them. I never got closure from Colin, but I also never dated anyone that made me feel the way he had. Even if I couldn't keep him in Hoppa forever and chase what we once had, part of me felt inexplicably compelled to help him in any way that I could.

"You called an official audience, swore your title, and now you're asking me to protect him." My dad chuckled. "It's always interesting to see what lights your fire. It's so rarely burning." He sighed. "Still. The only ones I protect are the brotherhood. Anyone who isn't a Knight is outside my purview."

"So, make him a Steel Knight."

My dad let out a full laugh then, slightly condescending. "That's not how it works, and you know it. The bylaws are Taylor's fully loaded AK-47. If I tried to just make the man who showed up at your house and begged your help a Steel Knight without him prospecting, Taylor would likely finally snap all the way and kill us both before serving your friend to Lockjaw."

That sent a chill down my spine. He wasn't wrong, but if there really was someone hunting Colin, I'd need more than my Colt to protect him. If he was a Steel Knight, Taylor couldn't touch him, either, not without violating the bylaws. That option really did make the most sense.

"So, what if he pledged?" I asked. "If he's serving as a prospect, can we keep him safe until he's healthy enough to leave?"

That time, when my dad started to consider my question, he stared up at the ceiling. I could see the gears turning as he mentally flipped through the pages of bylaws to see if the loophole I was attempting to exploit was big enough to do so.

Finally, he looked back at me with a more serious expression. "If he were in my territory, acting on my behalf while serving as a prospect, I would consider that under the extension of my umbrella of protection. But if it turned into something too dangerous, I'd cut him loose and he'd be on his own. Do you understand?"

I nodded. "Yes, Squared."

"Good."

I relaxed a little bit, thinking that I could at least buy Colin some time to heal and chart his next move. "I really think you'll like him, anyway. He has this old-school, vintage ride. Just like you like."

My dad's presidential expression broke in favor of a childlike smile, complete with wide, sparkling eyes. "I saw it outside, the Harley. It's *so* pretty. Did he build it? It looks custom."

"I don't know, but that's kind of his style, so I bet he did." I smiled at my dad's excitement. Colin had always been known for being a charismatic guy, which was odd considering how little he spoke. If Colin could get on my dad's good side while he was around, it'd serve him all the better.

"The casing he put on it, it is—"

The phrase didn't get all the way out before we heard a series of crashes and bangs from outside. My heart dropped into my stomach. It didn't occur to me before that moment that I never heard Taylor's bike start after he left. With each resounding creak of breaking metal, I imagined Colin's beautiful bike taking damage.

I leaped up off the couch with my dad and Lockjaw right behind me. I flung the front door open and ran out onto the lawn, but I was too late. My bike had a series of dents, all of my dials were shattered, and Lockjaw's added seat had been knocked completely off. I wasn't as concerned about that, though. Taylor had damaged my bike before, but Colin's bike had been destroyed to the point of being inoperable. It was on its side, and Taylor had a lead pipe in his hand and was circling around the bike like a vulture over prey, taking the pipe to the gorgeous black casing and shining metalwork. The tires were flat, and Taylor used his own knowledge of motorcycles to slam his pipe against all of the most important parts of the bike.

I could see Lockjaw chomping at the bit to get the command to race over and stop Taylor, but I had no confidence that Taylor wouldn't shoot my dog. I started to walk over myself, but my dad grabbed my arm to hold me back. He strode past me calmly, always a man with the ability to keep a cool head in hectic situations and walked over until he was standing between Taylor and Colin's bike.

"Enough," he said simply. "Drop the pipe."

Taylor was in the act of swinging and had the pipe held above his head. For a moment, I imagined Taylor bringing it down across my dad's head. They stood there, inches from each other. Taylor held his weapon raised and was shaking with anger, and my dad stared at him like he was still a little boy who'd disappointed him. Minutes passed that felt like hours before Taylor finally tossed his pipe over into the grass.

"Get it, Lockjaw," I said, and Lockjaw ran over to where he'd tossed the pipe and retrieved it, bringing it back and dropping it at my feet.

Taylor side-eyed me briefly before turning around and heading out to where his bike was parked in front of my dad's on the street. He mounted it, started it up, and took off down the street without putting on a helmet or gloves.

I walked over to assess the damage, and I was already dreading explaining this to Colin. I looked up at my dad. "You owe him a new bike now, too."

My dad nodded. "Bring him and his bike by Hoppa's tomorrow. I'll see what I can do." He stepped up to me, kissed me on my forehead, and then walked over to his bike, climbed on it, put on his helmet, and left.

I looked at the ruins of Colin's old-school motorcycle and sighed. Hopefully, he wouldn't hate me when I told him what happened. I tapped my leg, prompting Lockjaw to follow me, and led the way back into the house. Just as I was closing the front door, the doctor walked out of the guest room, quietly closing the door behind him.

"What was all that commotion?" Dr. Marteau asked, and my heart thudded as I imagined Colin hearing all of that while he was afraid he was being pursued.

"You guys heard?" I rolled my eyes. "My brother lost his temper."

"I heard. CJ is out cold. I gave him the good drugs. He's in bad shape," Dr. Marteau replied. "He'll be okay, though. He'll have some permanent scarring, especially on that left arm. You'll need to regularly dress his wounds until they heal, but he doesn't require surgery. I left a burn cream and some Vicodin for the pain. I should see him again in a few days."

I nodded. "Thanks, doc."

"Of course."

I stood aside so that he could walk past me toward the front door. As soon as he was beyond me, I pulled my gun out of the back hem of my jeans and fired directly at Dr. Marteau's right shin. He hissed out a swear as he dropped to the floor. Lockjaw ran over and loomed over him, growling and snarling.

I walked over and crouched next to Lockjaw so that I could look Dr. Marteau in his eyes. "I thought I asked you not to call my dad, doc."

Dr. Marteau was groaning in pain, trying to pull himself to his feet, but every time he moved too much, Lockjaw snapped at him. "I have strict orders to always call your dad. He's a scary man."

"Well, I think you can now see that we're cut from the same cloth," I replied in a low, resonant voice. "Next time I tell you to do something, you'd better not disobey me. We can always find another doctor."

"Y-yes, Valkyrie."

"Good. Now get out of my house. Lockjaw will see you out."

Leaving Dr. Marteau to figure himself out, I stood and walked back into the guest bedroom. As Dr. Marteau said, Colin was passed out on the bed, starfish style, one leg hanging off the bed. He looked much better with a new white wrap of gauze around his left arm and crawling over his torso. I was able to see his bare torso now that he wasn't awake to freak out about it, and I let out a little groan. He'd taken great care of himself. Mind wandered briefly to what he could do with me with those full, thick arms, but I shook it out of my brain.

I had hoped to explain what happened with his bike sooner rather than later, but he'd have to hear the story in the morning. I pulled a blanket from the closet and pulled it over him, then left the room, ducking my head into the living room just long enough to see that Dr. Marteau managed to get out and that Lockjaw was already snoozing away in his bed. Then I turned around and went back into my own bedroom.

As I changed for bed, I couldn't shake the fear that Colin might be gone when I woke up the next day, but it wasn't like he could get far without his bike, anyway. I set my gun and phone on my bedside table where I could reach them both in case of emergency, and with the hope that I'd find *CJ* still in the guest bed in the morning, I climbed in my bed and quickly drifted off to sleep.

Chapter Four

Phantom

Usually, the sun on my face in the morning served as a frightening realization that I'd actually allowed myself to drift off, and feeling the morning light would send me into a panic. I woke with the need to make sure that my bike hadn't been stolen, that someone hadn't lifted me from wherever I was, or that someone wasn't preparing to kill me. For the first time in close to a month, I woke up in a warm and comfortable bed and felt totally at ease. Because I'd gotten actual drugs as opposed to my main medicine recently—booze—I didn't have the usual headache that came with waking up in the morning, and though my body was sore all over, it wasn't the barking pain I typically had to fight through before I could set out for the day.

When was the last time I got a good night's sleep? Even before I left the Unchained Dogs, my nights were usually plagued with worry over Caid, and thus also sleepless. Caid was in Germany and under the best care Luther's money could buy, and I was in Tess' house with my wounds finally having been tended to by an actual doctor. I felt the best I'd felt in a very long time, if ever.

I lifted my arms to stretch them above my head and was happy when they moved without too much protest. The white bandages coiled around my left arm were a painful reminder of the discoloration beneath that Dr. Marteau had told me would be permanent. It wasn't as if I was a shorts and t-shirt kind of guy, but Arizona heat was nothing to play around with. Regardless, I'd be creating a permanent wardrobe of long-sleeved shirts and jackets going forward. Vanity aside, I didn't want anyone linking my arm to anything that happened to me back in Rumble, and I didn't want anyone to think that I was too weak to handle myself.

Gathering my bearings, I realized there was a blanket pulled over me. I assumed that Dr. Marteau wasn't the romantic type, so I figured Tess must have come in and covered me up before she went to bed. She'd always been that way, quietly caring for me, doing the things I was too dumb to do for myself. Half the time, I'd neglect my homework, eating, or even sleeping when I took care of Caid back before we left Hoppa. Tess would help me get my schoolwork done, feed me some lifted leftovers from her family's dinner, and even soothingly run her hand through my hair until I couldn't hold my eyes open anymore. For someone so young, the way she took care of me was unbelievable. She clearly was still up to her same antics in that regard. It'd be difficult not getting caught up in her before I left. I didn't realize how much I missed her until I was talking to her again. It was almost enough to make a guy want to stay.

Almost.

I climbed out of bed, and my bladder made itself known almost instantly. Another luxury I'd forgotten all about was peeing in a place that didn't have a tick risk. I thought of the door Tess pointed out the day before, grabbed my long-sleeved shirt off the desk, and made my way to it. At the very end of the hallway, I saw the door that Tess had pointed out as being hers. I reached the bathroom door, but I couldn't drag my eyes away from Tess' bedroom. It was probably a bad idea, but the pull was too sweet, and I continued past the bathroom door and down to the end of the hallway.

Thankfully, the door was cracked, so I tipped it open just a bit further and peeked my head inside. Unlike the more subdued decoration in the rest of Tess' home, her bedroom was well designed and littered with pictures of her family and Lockjaw and tons of Steel Knights logos and sigils. Her bed was king-sized and covered in a dark blue comforter, and Tess was dead center in a nest of pillows. Her hair was spread across the bed above her head, and her sleeping face was perfectly calm and serene.

She was still the most exquisite sight I'd ever seen.

I could have stood there and stared at her forever if I didn't have to pee and wasn't concerned about her labeling me as a creep, so I snuck back out of the room and down to the bathroom to relieve myself. I pulled on the shirt when I was done and noticed for the first time how grungy and dirty it was. Hopefully, I'd be able to take some time to purchase a few new articles of clothing and take a long, hot shower before I had to get the hell out of dodge. As much as I wanted to stay and soak up more of Tess, staying in one place for too long was dangerous, and I didn't want my trouble to find Tess or her family.

I left the bathroom and walked into the living room. I was planning on helping myself to some coffee and working on getting Lockjaw to not hate me, but the sight I found froze me in place. The coffee table was completely shattered, and not far from it was a concentrated stain of blood, droplets of which spattered across the floor in a line toward the front door.

Shit.

I rushed to the front door and threw it open. My heart started to race as I ran out to the driveway where Tess and I had left our bikes, and though I was expecting what I saw, it didn't frighten me any less. Tess' bike was banged up, but mine was mangled beyond recognition.

How did they find me so fast? Did Luther honestly anticipate that I would hide amongst the enemy? I'd been careful to keep my association with Hoppa to myself while I was running with the Dogs. I'd already dragged Tess into my trouble. It was too late.

I needed to run. As much as it would kill me to leave my bike behind, it wasn't going anywhere in the condition it was in after the clearly ferocious beating it withstood last night while I slept. I could grab my stuff, hike out of Hoppa, and then see if I could catch a ride. Where I'd catch a ride to, I wasn't sure, but if I could just get out of Luther's purview, I could figure out my next step. With my wounds sufficiently patched, I could travel more than a few miles without needing to stop. I could start by getting out of Arizona.

But what about Tess? They knew where she was now. They'd caused all this damage as a way of leaving a message that they could find her if and when they needed to. If I ran and left her behind, Luther would have her head mounted on his wall by the end of the day. I couldn't have that. She'd be difficult to convince, but I needed her to come with me. Given a choice, this wouldn't be how I increased my time with Tess, but desperate times called for desperate measures.

I ran back into the house and down to Tess' bedroom door. Unlike my quietly creaking it open a few minutes earlier, I slammed the door open, sending it colliding against the wall with a resounding crack. It alone stirred Tess, but I still clamored over to her bedside and started to shake her awake.

"Tess. Wake up. We gotta go."

Tess stretched a little bit. "Huh?"

"We have to leave. They've found me. I don't know how, but they found me."

There were a few cracks as Tess twisted her head to one side then the other. She wasn't exercising the urgency I needed her to be. "How do you know that?"

"I'm so sorry, but they broke in. They broke your coffee table, and they destroyed our bikes, and there's blood on the floor. I don't know whose…maybe Lockjaw." It didn't occur to me until that moment that I didn't even stop to check for the dog. My stomach twisted, thinking that he'd be gone when I went back out—or worse, lying in his bed, gutted.

"Calm down," Tess grumbled.

"Calm down? Someone's trying to kill me!"

Tess looked at me with a mix of irritation for waking her up and pity for my fear. "Taylor broke the table."

"Who?"

"Taylor. My brother."

My fear abated. "Your brother?" That's right. Tess had an older brother named Taylor. I very rarely saw him when we were growing up. If it weren't for the fact that Tess mentioned him a few times when I would talk about Caid, I wouldn't even have known the man existed. "Why would he do all that stuff? The blood was his?"

"The blood was probably Dr. Marteau's," Tess said with a yawn, "and he did it because he's not playing with a full deck."

"What did he do to Dr. Marteau?"

"No, that was me."

I stood in silence for a second. Each additional thing she said brought the explanation further and further from anything I understood. "What?"

Tess snuggled one of her pillows closer to her and continued to look at me like it was just any other run-of-the-mill day. "I shot Dr. Marteau."

She said it so simply. I recoiled a bit, but not out of fear. I was almost more impressed than anything. "Why?"

"Because I told him not to call my dad, and he did anyway. They came over, and when I mentioned that the friend I was helping was a man, Taylor flipped his shit, broke the table, and destroyed the bikes. I had to send Dr. Marteau a message. Don't cross me. So I shot him in the shin and then left him to figure out how to get out of my house."

"Wow."

"I'm sorry about your bike, but we'll get it fixed, don't worry." She scoffed. "The blood probably stained, huh?"

I was still trying to calm the errant ricocheting of my heart. "I think so."

She tossed the covers back. "Shit. I'm gonna have to get it replaced again."

Again?

Tess kicked herself out from under the covers and climbed out of bed, and the temperature in the room doubled instantly. She was dressed in nothing but a lilac lace nightie and a matching thong. When I'd last seen Tess, she was just starting to grow her feminine curves. She certainly wasn't a little girl anymore. She had a form that rivaled some of the late 60s actresses like Marilyn Monroe. She wasn't stick-skinny, but she had a flat stomach that umbrellaed into a wider waist and full thighs. Her backside was a plump peach shape, and with her shirt and jacket from the day before discarded, I could see that she had a large bust. It was unfair. All those dumb phrases I'd heard as a kid made much more sense to me now. All that and a bag of chips. A pocketful of sunshine. Good enough to eat. However one chose to describe it, Tess was the kind of beautiful *and* sexy that someone should have to pay to see up close.

Though it felt like trying to force away two magnets, I managed to drag my gaze away from Tess as she sidled over to her dresser. Her near-naked image was already emblazoned on my brain, but that didn't give me the right to gawk; she deserved respect. I waited to hear her drawers open or for her to duck into her bathroom, but after a few seconds of silence, I felt a hand on my arm.

I glanced over, and Tess was standing there, still in her racy nightclothes, looking up at me with a begging, starved gaze. My mouth was suddenly as dry as if I had never drunk water before in my life.

I wanted her so badly.

"Why do you look away? I don't look good?" Tess asked.

I tried to stay tied into her intoxicating eyes. "You look amazing. I'm trying to be respectful."

"If I didn't want you to see it, I would have asked you to leave." She leaned forward a little bit, and I couldn't prevent my eyes from dropping down to take in her enrapturing chest. "That was a hint, you know."

I'd gathered. The problem was, I'd spent most of the night calculating any outcome of allowing myself to take even a small bite of Tess. There was no way I couldn't get attached. What would start as sex would quickly grow into something more because I had never gotten over Tess. She was the only person in my entire life that I'd allowed to see my mind, my emotions. Did I want to rip her nightie off and tackle her onto her bed? Sure. Would I then want to run away with her and act like I didn't have a sick brother in Germany and a madman hunting me? One hundred percent, yes.

"I'll meet you in the living room," I said, and the words burned coming out. "I want to say goodbye."

I turned to leave, but Tess' hold on my arm clenched tighter, and she pulled me back. "You're not going anywhere."

God, please don't make me have to verbally turn Tess down. I wasn't strong enough for that. "I'm still recovering," I managed to grumble out as an excuse.

"No. I mean you're not leaving Hoppa."

I furrowed my brow. "I can't stay here. If I stay in one place for too long, I'll get caught. It's dangerous."

"If you keep running, you'll never heal, and you'll get caught. That's more dangerous because you won't even be able to defend yourself."

"I have medicine, and the doctor treated my wounds. I can deal with it well enough from here on out."

Tess shook her head. "No. You came to me for help. This is me helping. You're staying until you're healed, and then you can go."

"That could be weeks, Tess." I imagined the scene from this morning and how convinced I was that Luther had found me. I should have known that he'd do much worse. I couldn't let him get his hands on Tess. "It's not safe for you either. I can't protect you if they show up."

Tess scoffed. "I'm not a damsel, I don't need you to protect me, and as far as protecting yourself goes, I've got that figured out, too. You're gonna prospect for the Steel Knights and get protection."

If I was a man who laughed, I would have at that suggestion. Sure, Tess didn't know that I was a former Unchained Dog, but she did know that I was a man she hadn't spoken to in fourteen years who had shown up out of the blue, burned to shit and asking for help because I was being hunted. That suggestion made no logical sense, and that was very unlike Tess. She was probably behaving on the same impulse that I was trying to resist. It would be a convenient excuse to be together, but the idea on its own wasn't smart.

"Tess, that doesn't make any sense."

"Of course it doesn't make sense," she replied. "None of this makes sense, but as long as you're in the condition you're in, you need to be stationary. Dr. Marteau said that he'd need to see you again in a few days and that you're even worse off than you're thinking. I get it. I get that you need to go, but if you try to leave now in your state, you'll die, and if you try to stay and just fly under the radar, we could both die. This way, my dad and the Knights can keep us both safe, and as soon as you're cleared, you can go. I won't stop you."

"I'm not about to drag you and your family into my mess."

Tess stepped closer to me, bringing my attention back to how scantily she was still dressed. "You know, Colin. The medical attention cost a lot, and it was a huge risk. My bike is even damaged. You owe me."

I clenched my jaw as the final three words hissed across her lips. I was painfully aware of how much I owed Tess for the last twelve hours. "I don't have any money."

Tess' hands drifted up to my stomach and slid up to my chest. "I don't want any money. I want a prospect."

"Why?" I said, standing stone still and begging my hands to stay put.

"My father's men don't like me very much. I'm the VP in title alone. I want someone on my side for once. Even just for a little bit. You're likable. Maybe they'll like me more because they like you."

Behind Tess' minx-like expression was something genuine and pleading. Maybe it was because I was a man of honor, maybe it was because I was weak to Tess standing in front of me naked for as much of her body that her clothes covered, or maybe it was because I'd struggle to make it beyond the city limits without my bike, but for the first time in my entire life, I was considering banking on the lowest probable outcome. There was a possibility, minuscule though it may be, that I could successfully become a Steel Knight, stave off or even kill Luther, and get to be with Tess. Maybe I was staring down a barrel no matter what I did. If there was a chance that Tess' plan could work or that I could at least improve her life a little bit before my inevitable end, wasn't that worth trying?

"Fine." I looked at Tess. "I'll stay."

Tess smiled. "Good."

My brain immediately started working on a new plan. Germany.

If I could successfully prospect and start earning a little money, I could buy a one-way ticket to Caid. That was my freedom, my mecca, my Graceland. Germany was my way out, and maybe…maybe I could convince a certain redhead to come with me.

I'd never been much of a gambler, but running wasn't looking much better than staying, and staying kept me near Tess. "Now," she continued. "Are you going to take these off, or am I going to have to?"

I smirked. Words couldn't express how much *I* wanted to take them off, but I couldn't risk it. "Like I said," I huffed. "I'll meet you in the living room."

I tried to ignore Tess' challenge-accepted expression as I turned my back to her, but as I walked away, I heard her low, taunting chuckles and knew that I was in trouble.

Chapter Five

Tess

A person with less resilience would be convinced that Colin didn't share my harbored feelings about our childhood love. I'd given him more than one opportunity to take me any way he pleased, but he didn't seem to be biting. His excuse that he was still recovering was just that, an excuse, and a weak one at that.

The only thing keeping me from thinking that Colin just didn't want me was the fact that I could feel the heat emanating off of him as he struggled to keep his eyes from drifting downward. The notable clench in his jaw and his balling of his fists were resistance tactics I'd seen before. My brother had half of Hoppa scared shitless to even look at me. People don't often consider it with women, but we have sexual urges, too. I'd used my wiles to lure more than one man back to my place who knew well what would happen to them if Taylor caught them in my bed. They pulled all the exact same things out of their bag of tricks. Clench their jaws to keep from speaking their true desires. Ball their fists to keep from reaching out. Colin's case was even worse. I could see it in his eyes. Hear it in his voice. He wanted me, too.

So why wouldn't he take me?

I suppose this could be the one reason that I didn't like Colin's sterling coat of honor. Was he just practicing some sort of gentlemanly code? If we only had a couple weeks to be together, I really wished he'd just hang it up, just for a little while. Even if Taylor didn't scare men away, none of them made me hot the same way Colin did. None of them made my heart race and skin prickle. I'd get to him, one way or another. If I didn't, who knew when I'd get something exciting again, if ever.

Lockjaw stood up and padded over to me as I walked into the living room. I reached down and patted his head, saying, "Morning, buddy." I looked up and saw Colin sitting on the couch with a collection of my supply of meat—cold cuts, hot dogs, and one of my specialty orders, prime cut steaks.

"That's a mighty big breakfast," I said with a snicker.

He pulled a piece of bologna out and whistled. "I'm making friends."

I raised an eyebrow. "Lockjaw can't be…"

I watched as Lockjaw traveled away from my side and back over to where Colin was sitting. Colin held up the slice of bologna and ordered, "Sit," and Lockjaw obediently sat, lolling his tongue out in anticipation of his treat. "Good boy." Colin dropped the cut, and Lockjaw snapped it out of the air, taking a few quick bites to gobble it down before eyeing the stash of meat and waiting patiently for his next orders. Colin looked up at me. "You were saying?"

I walked around the scene and into the kitchen with a smile. "Huh. I guess he is food motivated."

The truth was, Lockjaw was *not* food motivated because I'd painstakingly trained him not to be. I always thought that there was a possibility that someone would come to retrieve what I'd lifted, but during the bike ride from Rumble to Hoppa, I'd grown attached to my stolen pup. The first thing I did when I woke up the day after we got back home was start Lockjaw on a long, arduous path of loyalty only to me, in spite of any motivators. Female dogs in heat, the promise of a good fight, and yes, even all types and qualities of meat were paraded before him while I trained him over the next six months to respond to my commands perfectly and exclusively.

I knew I'd done my job the day I had my dad set a freshly grilled prime T-bone steak down in front of Lockjaw and tell him that he could eat it. Lockjaw didn't even blink. He kept his eyes on me with a cheery wag of his tail as if to say, "I'd like that steak, Mom, but I won't eat it unless you say I can." His reward was the steak, and my reward was the best security system a girl could steal.

The fact that Lockjaw was breaking the rules to take a few treats from Colin was an indicator that I wasn't the only one in the house with a weakness for Colin and that Colin was the amazing guy I always thought he was. They say dogs and babies can tell, and if Lockjaw liked you, you were good, and that was it.

"Well, you've given all the meat to the dog. What'll us humans eat for breakfast?" I opened the fridge and sifted through what was left. "Oh, you left some bacon. I could put that together with some eggs and fried potatoes?" When I didn't get a response, I glanced up over the fridge door. Colin was just staring at me, but it wasn't the lusty gaze I got in the bedroom. This was something calmer and sweeter, if not a bit conflicted. "What?"

"Oh, nothing," he replied. "I don't think I've ever had someone cook for me before."

"Never?"

He shook his head. "No. My mom didn't, and when Caid and I got our own place, I did all the cooking." He chuckled. "I never realized it before now."

I couldn't imagine. As much of a roughneck as he was, my dad always made sure Taylor and I were taken care of. "Well, there's a first for everything."

His smirk got a little wider. "Yeah. Thanks."

There was only the sizzle of the food in the pan as I cooked it while Colin continued to try to butter up Lockjaw. I'd have to walk him double to undo the severe spike in calories. Still, the silence was almost welcoming. Normally, I hated the silence because it made me anxious, but things just felt peaceful with Colin around. I didn't feel like I needed to fill it.

When the food was done, I made a nice-sized plate for Colin and brought it over. Lockjaw looked up at me. He usually got some of whatever I cooked for breakfast, but I shook my head at him. "Yeah, you've had enough for one morning, buddy."

I grabbed my own plate with a smaller portion and went and sat in the armchair perpendicular to Colin, the same one Taylor had been in the night before.

That's when I noticed for the first time that the floor was totally clean. "Oh my god." I looked over to where the bloodstains should have been, but they, too, were gone. I looked over at Colin. "Did you clean up in here?"

Colin's cheeks were so full he looked like a chipmunk. "Yeah."

"You didn't have to do that."

Colin finished swallowing down his food before speaking again. "It's like you said. I owe you."

I sighed. I *did* say that, though it was mostly a ploy to work on Colin's chivalry. It might have worked too well. "How did you get the blood out?"

"I was basically a parent to Caid. He would spasm and spill all the time. I had to know how to get rid of a stain." He took a bite of his bacon. "You seemed disappointed about getting rid of it."

"I was. I like this carpet." I smiled at him. "Thank you."

We finished breakfast and then made our way outside to head to Hoppa's Taphouse and meet up with my dad. Colin's bike was damaged beyond repair, so I helped him move it out of the driveway and over into the grass, and then I moved my own bike over to where his bike had been sitting so that I could open my garage door and pull out my car.

The Steel Knights were gearheads in general. Bikes were our bread and butter, but we had quite a few expensive, designer cars between us. In any situation, I'd prefer to get on my bike, but Colin's bike was busted, and my bike didn't have space for a second person due to Lockjaw's specialty seat added, so there just wasn't a way all three of us were going to make it to the bar without the use of a car.

Colin let out a whistle as the garage door lifted up. "Camaro. American muscle. What year?"

I led the way over to my army green, four-door Camaro and opened up the back door so that Lockjaw could jump in. "Brand new, 2020. I can never go longer than a year without upgrading."

Colin chuckled as he climbed into the passenger's seat. "Sounds about right."

I started the car, loving the roar of the engine echoing off the walls of the garage. Lockjaw let out a low growl to match, and Colin laughed as I backed the car out and headed down the road toward Hoppa. I liked to take the side-streets when I was on my bike to enjoy the ride a little more, but riding down Hoppa's main interstate, the Taphouse was only a five-minute drive away. I pulled into the bar's empty parking lot, seeing only a handful of other bikes and our bookkeeper Bullet's car.

I held the door open so that Lockjaw could hop over into the front seat and then climb out of the car, and I leashed him immediately while Colin unloaded out of his side and smiled over at me. "Just so you know, I don't do anything by halves."

"You think I don't know that already?" I asked. I coiled Lockjaw's chain around my fist a couple of times and started for the door. "I wouldn't expect anything less."

Colin grabbed the handle of the door and held it open, and I led the way in with him right behind me. The bar didn't have any of its non-Steel-Knight patrons inside yet because it was still early, but most of the Knights' members, as well as their three current prospects, were all seated inside, and all eyes fell on us as we walked in. The gazes were vile, at first, the ones I was used to, but when Colin entered behind me, they cooled. Some of them even looked a little confused.

"Who the hell is that?" the Steel Knights' Road Captain, Bernard "Bucky" LePall, barked.

I didn't get to answer before Taylor was out of his seat and already marching toward us. I could tell by the look in his eyes that he was intent on causing trouble, but Lockjaw moved to stand defensively in front of us, and I held up a hand. "Stop it. He's here to prospect."

Taylor stopped short. He glared at me, and the heat of it was so intense that I thought I may start sweating. "What?" he asked through gritted teeth.

I glanced back at Colin, and he nodded, saying, "I intend to become a full patch member of the Steel Knights."

The Taphouse erupted into laughter apart from our bookkeeper, Harry "Bullet" Booth, and our chaplain, Parker "Father" Piscatoni, who both looked at me with indifference. The three loudest jeers came from Hoppa's current prospects, Aaron, Vil, and Seth.

Aaron, the largest of these three, lifted himself off of one of the main bar's stools and ambled over to Colin. He approached until he was standing nose-to-nose with Colin and sniffed the air like he was a brutish warthog. "And what gives you the right to come in here and state any intentions at all?"

"Knock it off," I growled, but like most of the members, he didn't listen to me and held his ground.

Colin stared back at Aaron as unbothered as if Aaron weren't three inches taller than him and at least twice his size.

Vil and Seth ambled their way over from where they were standing and flanked Aaron on either side. Aaron cracked his knuckles, and a grin snaked its way across Aaron's face. My dad strictly enforced the no fighting rule, but these prospects, in particular, seemed to have a thirst for it. That might have been why Taylor found them so amusing and backed them all as soon as they showed up. The rest of us, however, could tell they were nothing but trouble.

All eyes were on Colin, waiting to see what his reaction would be, but with a half-lidded gaze and relaxed mouth, he looked more like he was waiting in line at the bank.

"What's with that stupid look?" Seth hissed. "The man asked you a question."

There was no response from Colin, and Vil let out a muted grunt. "Maybe we'll have to get an answer out of him by other means."

Aaron took a step closer, leaving just enough room to breathe between him and Colin. "Maybe."

I grinned as the bar's front door opened, and my dad came striding through, calling out, "Well, you're not causing trouble in my bar, are ya boys?"

Aaron held up his hands and backed away. "Nah, Nicky. Just meeting the new prospect."

Seth and Vil each threw my dad a sneer but followed Aaron's lead and backed off, all heading as a group to sit at a table in the far back of the bar.

My dad walked around Colin and turned to face him, not standing much further back from where Aaron was seconds before. "New prospect. Well, now, I always love getting some fresh blood around here. It helps to mix things up." He held out a hand. "I'm Nicholas. You can call me Squared, Nick, or Nicky."

Colin took my dad's hand and shook it firmly. "CJ."

There were some snickers around the bar, but Taylor took a deep breath. It seemed as though hearing the name satiated him for the time being.

"CJ," my dad repeated. "Nice to meet ya. Oh, and I don't know if Val here told ya, but I'm a man of honor. I'll be sure to replace your bike, which was damaged on my watch."

They released hands, and Colin's simply fell to his side. "I appreciate it, but I actually liked building it. You've given me an opportunity to do that again."

A sly smile crossed my dad's face. "Is that right? Tell ya what. I'll get the parts, and you can use my tools and garage. I might even join you since I gotta fix Val's bike, too."

Colin nodded. "It'd be an honor."

Taylor looked like a bull about to charge. His eyes were wild, and his nostrils were flaring. "We didn't discuss any new prospects."

My dad turned to face Taylor, and subsequently, more of the members. "I do believe the bylaws state that all prospects need the backing of a single officer in order to pledge." He crossed his arms. "CJ has got two."

"Two?" Taylor repeated.

"Two. The president and the vice president."

"You know this guy, Squared?" Avery "Bullseye" Pairings, our treasurer, asked.

"He's a friend of Val's from back in the day." He scoffed. "I didn't know I had to explain myself so much. Does anyone else have any questions they'd like to ask?" The members and prospects exchanged nervous glances, but no one said anything more. My dad nodded. "Good. Then, members, let's head back. I wanna get started so that we can make the best use of our day. Prospects, busy yourselves. We'll be back out soon with a task for you to take on."

I handed Lockjaw's leash over to Colin, and he took it with a look of pride. He walked over to a chair at one of the scattered tables and sat down, bringing Lockjaw to sit between his legs. He tapped him on the head a few times, and confident that they'd both be just fine in my absence, I followed my dad around the bar and through the swinging door in the back of the Taphouse.

Past the small kitchen and through a set of double doors was Hoppa Taphouse's warehouse. All of the non-perishable goods and bar materials were stored back there, and in the very middle was a large, round oak table with enough chairs situated around it for all the officers to sit.

We took our respective seats, and my dad leaned forward and folded his hands across the table. "Well, I'll cut right to the chase. We all know why we're here. We need to pick from our prospect pool. I'd really like to do it before MiD, in case the Dogs or anyone else plans an attack there. We need a few grunts to stay back and protect the bar while I meet with the Blazing Rebels and the Raging Vipers. I suppose I'll start with the obvious. Do any officers have a prospect who they'd like to enter into the pool?"

All eyes turned to me. Despite the scrutiny, I did my best to remain unmoved by their obvious disapproval. "Yes. I'd like to enter CJ into the prospect pool."

"CJ what?" Bullseye asked.

"Just CJ," I spat back, and he growled.

"Great. Did he state his intention to join the Steel Knights in full view and audible range of three or more officers?" my dad asked Taylor.

Taylor was quiet for a long time, but eventually grumbled out, "Yes."

"Then I'm entering a motion to enter CJ into the prospect pool," my dad said.

Not a single person responded, not that I expected them to. I raised my hand with a scowl. "I second the motion."

My dad slammed the table. "So moved. CJ will officially join the rank of prospects." He grabbed a folder from the compartment that he kept under the table for stashing his documents and brought it to rest on top of the table. He flipped it open and started reading over the top page. "What I need from these prospects is strength. Not just physical strength, but the mental strength it takes to stand up to the Dogs or anyone else that may come our way. We're growing in numbers, just like Hoppa, and people need to know that we intend to stand our ground. I don't want any flashy business, though. I like my muscle like I like my drinks, neat and dry. I've sent a few of the members out to a bar in uncharted territory about an hour away. I'm gonna send the prospects there and have the members pick a fight to see how they react. Whoever keeps a level head, I'm willing to consider for membership. Does anyone have a problem with that?"

No one objected. That was how the Steel Knights like to do things in general, under the radar and without much of a fuss. Apart from a few members who didn't know how to hold their liquor, the Knights dedicated themselves to being as smooth as steel. You barely knew they were there until they were driving into your gut. I smiled, imagining the ever-stoic Colin. If anyone could master what my dad was looking for in a prospect, it was him.

"Good," my dad said. "We're not going to be subjective here. We're looking for someone who ticks the boxes. I'm expecting straight shooting. The exact same way you were considered." There were varying affirmations, and my dad smiled. "All right. I'm gonna need someone to go out and view the prospect. I was thinking—"

Before he could get the words all the way out, he was interrupted by a series of bangs and grunts coming from the bar. The Steel Knights owned Hoppa's Taphouse, and no one should have been in there who wasn't an officer of the Steel Knights or there for the prospect test. We all sat in silence and listened for a minute. I, in particular, listened for Lockjaw to bark, but he didn't. Only the continued sounds of grunts and groans, with the occasional dull thud, reached us. My dad stood up, and the officers all followed suit, taking after him as he made his way back through the warehouse and kitchen and through the swinging door into the bar.

I walked in and made my way to a spot where I could see, but the scene that greeted me was confusing. Colin was sitting in the same chair I'd left him in, still absent-mindedly patting Lockjaw's head. Lockjaw didn't seem bothered or put out at all, but all three prospects were laid out across the bar, unconscious. Nothing was broken, they didn't appear to be bleeding, and Colin hadn't even broken a sweat.

"What the hell happened?" my dad asked.

Colin looked up at him and shrugged. "They said they wanted to fight me. So we fought."

I watched as a slow smile crept across my dad's face. "I fucking like this guy."

He paced around the bar and over to where Colin was sitting. Several expressions crossed his face in rapid succession. We all stood in silence while he stared down at Colin. Colin remained unmoving and unconcerned by my father's sudden approach. My dad crossed his arms, and the fingers of his left hand dug into the flesh of his right arm, something he typically only did when he was battling with an internal struggle.

"Squared?" Bucky started finally, but my dad held up a hand to silence him.

Finally, my dad sighed and released all of the tension in his shoulders. "This is the answer to our problems," he muttered quietly.

"What?" I asked.

Suddenly, my dad raised his hand. "I'm entering a motion to make Colin an immediate member of the Steel Knights."

"What!" Taylor barked. "Under what circumstances would we make someone an *immediate* member?"

I didn't say as much out loud, but even I was confused. Something like that had never happened before. Our current prospects had been pledged for close to a year.

What was he suddenly seeing in Colin?

"The Unchained Dogs could strike at any time. Currently, we have four prospects pledged, and based on the previous listed criteria of strength and stealth,"—he set a hand on Colin's shoulder—"he's the best choice. Traditions be damned. If the Dogs come tomorrow, we need to be ready." The room sat in tense silence in the wake of the sudden decision. "Are there any opposed?"

Taylor's hand shot in the air. "Opposed."

My dad ignored him. "All in favor?"

Every member's stare drifted to me, but despite the prevalent irritation on all of their faces, their hands slowly climbed into the air. I lifted mine, as well, and my dad held up his. He counted the raised hands as if it was even necessary. "That's five out of six." He smiled down at Colin. "Looks like you just became a Steel Knight, son."

Chapter Six

Phantom

The leers of the Steel Knights members wouldn't bother me so much if they didn't shift to Tess once they realized they weren't landing with me. Tess brought me to prospect for the Steel Knights, but I was a grown man who made my own decisions, and the same was true for Nick. The fact that he was willing to make me a member straight out of the gate because the other prospects couldn't control their tempers wasn't Tess' fault, nor was it mine. I hated people like them—those who couldn't just worry about themselves. As much as I hated working with Luther and the Unchained Dogs, that was one thing they had going for them. Minding your own business was in the bylaws. I'd seen Luther take off more than one man's head because they thought that it was somehow their business to help decide who he chose to add to their ranks. At least Nick allowed it to be a traditional vote. Luther was a wild boar and did what he wanted.

No wonder the Steel Knights had fallen to the Unchained Dogs in the past. Their minds were in the wrong place. That was no doubt why Nick's desires for his prospects had changed. He wasn't a dumb man. Evidently, he'd learned a valuable lesson during the Unchained Dogs' last raid—if his members were more worried about other people's shit than their own, they wouldn't do good work. I wouldn't be with the Steel Knights long, but if I could change their nosy dispositions even a little, I would consider my time here beneficial to someone other than myself.

"What the hell happened in here?"

I looked over to the door of Hoppa's Taphouse, and three men were making their way through the doorway. The man who spoke was incredibly tall and broad-shouldered, and he had a scruffy goatee encircling his mouth. He was looking at the three prospects that I'd made short work of. The other two men had already made their way over to the big one, Aaron, who'd started all the trouble, and were looking down at him.

Nick laughed, leaning over the bar. He nodded his head toward me. "Our newest member happened to 'em."

All three men's heads shot in Nick's direction. "New member?" the tall one asked.

"Yeah. Guys, this is CJ. CJ, that tall one's Paulie, but we call him Texas. The short one is Derek, or Small Fry." One of the other guys standing near Aaron stood at maybe five and a half feet tall, but he had enough scrapes to let me know that he wasn't afraid to fight. "And that's Jonathan Jones. We call him Jonesie."

The last of the men had brown hair falling down his back in a long braid, and he nodded as Nick introduced him. Derek and Jonathan both seemed to be fighting back comments, but Paulie's knitted eyebrows and pursed lips had already relaxed. He stepped over the unconscious bodies and held out a hand to me. "Nice to meet you."

I shook it. "You, too." Someone with a little more respect for Nick's authority was someone I could see myself liking amongst these guys.

Paulie walked up to Tess next and held out a fist, which she eagerly bumped hers against. "What's goin' on, Val? Did you get a good night's rest after ditching the rematch last night?"

Tess snickered. "Yeah, I stacked up all your money I'd already taken and slept like a goddamn newborn."

Paulie seemed to be one of the few who actually treated Tess like an equal. That was nice, at least. I imagined trying to pass a woman as a member back with the Unchained Dogs. They'd have emptied their clips into me before I even got her name out.

"Where's Stag?" Nick asked.

"Who knows," Jonathan grumbled back. "He was off his ass last night."

"You didn't let him drive, did you?" Tess asked.

Unlike Paulie, who had a kind demeanor, Jonathan sent a scathing look at Tess before he responded. "I'm not his fucking babysitter."

Tess looked at her dad. "So he could be wrapped around a tree."

"Call him, Jonesie. Tell him if he ain't here in an hour, that's his ass," Nick spat.

"All right, Nicky," Jonathan replied, throwing Tess another disgusted look before turning and walking back out of the bar.

Nick pulled a bottle of whiskey out from under the bar, followed by a line of shot glasses. He started pouring some of the dark liquid into each of the glasses and then motioned to his members to pass them around. When everyone had one in hand, Nick moved to sit in front of the bar and smiled at me.

"A toast to our new member!" He held his glass in the air, and everyone mimicked the action, apart from Taylor. "To 'Just CJ'."

The reception was lukewarm, but everyone said some form of "To CJ" before emptying their glasses. Tess grinned at me, and it sent a wave of electricity over my body. If the circumstances were different, I'd dedicate myself to chasing her smile. I suppose I'd have to settle for what I could get in a week's time.

"So. Have you been properly introduced to everyone?" Nick asked. "You know me. I'm the top dog around here." He nodded at Tess, who'd made her way over to the chair across from me at the table and reclaimed Lockjaw. "That's my vice president."

So I *had* heard that correctly. When Nick first said that I was backed by the president and vice president, I was certain I misunderstood him. For as much as these guys didn't seem to care for Tess, that she was the vice president was astounding. I didn't plan to ask Tess many questions next time we were alone, mainly because I didn't want her to ask me many, but I had to know how that happened.

Nick turned his head to look at Taylor. "The one with the scowl over here is my boy, Taylor. He's our Sergeant at Arms. He's married to the bylaws, so if you're thinking about acting up, I'd think again."

The family resemblance between Nick, Taylor, and Tess was strong. They all had the same almond-shaped gray eyes and auburn-colored hair. Tess' was long, flowing down her back, but both Taylor and Nick were giving her a run for her money. Taylor's was shorter, settling over his shoulders in unkempt waves, but Nick's was straight, fell down to his chest, and looked neatly brushed. The men both had more triangular jawlines as opposed to Tess' rounder one, but the only other thing that really distinguished Nick from his kids was the crow's feet in the corners of his eyes. He was clinging to his youth, and someone might think they were siblings instead of a parent and his kids if they didn't know any better.

"Speaking of the bylaws," Taylor started, "I still object to this new member."

"Oh, and why don't you tell me why?" Nick responded, grabbing the bottle of whiskey and refilling his glass.

"They explicitly state that any prospect must be in consideration for two or more weeks." He eyed me like he wanted to stick a knife in my forehead and drag it down until I was in two pieces. "CJ hasn't been in consideration for two or more minutes."

"I believe the two-week probationary period you're referring to is up to alteration for extenuating circumstances," one man that I had seen but hadn't yet been introduced to said. He had glasses settled on his nose and short brown hair that hung down into his eyes and curled down his neck, likely from a helmet sitting on his head regularly. "It's not strict."

Taylor's glare shifted to this man. "Don't quote the bylaws to me, Bullet. You worry about your books."

"I'd never misquote my books," the man spat back, unafraid.

A smile crept across Taylor's face, but he was not amused. "You wanna go?"

"There have been enough fights today," Nick growled before tossing Taylor a look of his own, but it was almost amusing in its indifference. He, too, was far from concerned with Taylor's attitude. "Are you questioning my decision?"

The entire atmosphere in the bar shifted at the question. The members exchanged looks, and Tess averted her gaze down to her prized dog. From what I could tell, I was the only one intently watching the interaction as it sucked the very oxygen out of the room with its heat. I wasn't sure how much time had passed, but finally, Taylor walked around the bar and to a table in the far back and threw himself down into it. Nick turned to look back at me and smiled.

"Now, where were we? Oh, yes." He pointed a finger out at the man with the glasses who'd made a comment to Taylor. "That's Bullet, our bookkeeper. I'm not gonna tell you his real name, because ya gotta earn it." I nodded at Bullet, and he nodded back. "He's our bookkeeper. I would say, next to myself, he's the one who takes his job the most seriously. There ain't a dollar comes in or out this place without him knowing. I once forgot to expense a three-dollar box of shot glasses—I thought he was gonna take me out."

There were some chuckles around the bar, but Bullet had a stone-serious expression. He stared at me as if to say, "They're laughing, but I'm not," and I read the message loud and clear. It sent a shiver down my spine as I thought about how easy it was for me to get fifty thousand from under Luther's nose. If he had a bookkeeper like Bullet, it probably wouldn't have happened. I probably should be relieved he didn't. If anything, I knew that there wouldn't be room for sticky fingers of any kind with the Steel Knights, not that I'd risk it anyway with Tess' reputation on the line.

Nick shifted his finger toward a man wearing a full suit and tie. When he became the center of attention, he smiled brightly at me as though we were at a sleepover. "That suit and tie there is our chaplain, Father. He's also a lawyer, so, needless to say, he gets shit done."

Father walked across the room and held out a hand to shake, which I did. "Father is fine, or my God-given name, Parker Piscatoni. The Lord smiles upon those who stand resilient against the darkness. If you ever need anything, just let me know."

Being near people like him made me more than a little uncomfortable. My mom had grown up in a strict Catholic household but was already a drunk and drug addict by the time she became a parent. She'd get wasted and quote bible verses at Caid and me. Whenever she beat me, she would tell me that my heavenly father wanted her to punch me in the face because snatching some bread and cheese from the kitchen to feed myself and my brother was a sin that he frowned upon. It didn't take a psychologist to know that events like that were why I ended up leaving religion in my past with my mom.

I settled for a simple, "Thanks," so that Parker would walk away from me, which thankfully, he did.

Before Nick could get to him, one of the other members stood up out of the chair he'd found and walked over to me. He slapped my back, and he was a heftier guy, so it nearly knocked me out of my chair. Tess chuckled.

"Name's Bucky," he said. "I mean, my mama called me Bernard, but who wants to go by that, ya know?"

"Bucky it is," I replied.

Bucky looked up at Nick. "I'm with you, Squared. I think I like this guy." He raised an eyebrow at me. "Sorry for that cold reception earlier. A guy just walks in, and with Val, no less. What's a guy to think?"

"Why would it matter who I walked in with?" I asked before I could stop myself. Even all these years later, Tess was still a hot button for me. Having sat in the bar and watched these guys glare at her for the past hour was trying my patience enough, let alone someone mentioning it like it was fine.

Bucky's wide grin faded some. "Well, ya know."

"I don't." I stared up at him. "Tell me."

"It's fine, CJ," Tess said, but I didn't shift my stare from Bucky.

Bucky held up his hands and just walked away, not providing an answer. I looked back at Nick, concerned that I had pissed him off by nearly picking a fight, but he had an even bigger smile on his face. He took a deep breath and then pressed on. "Last but not least, that heartbreaker there." He motioned to a man not quite as tall as Paulie, but he was up there. He was leaning against the wall behind the pool table with his arms crossed. "That's Avery Pairings, our treasurer. As you might have guessed, Bullet can't do his job right if Avery ain't doing his job right, so Avery's sharp as a tack, too."

Not only that but of all the men in the bar, Avery was the most fit-looking at a glance. I was certain that more than one of the Steel Knights had muscles hiding under their jackets, but Avery was wearing a tank top with the Steel Knights' sigil on it, and with his arms crossed, his biceps looked like they were about to split his skin. That probably had something to do with why people didn't play with the money in the Steel Knights' wallet—they didn't want to find themselves at the other end of Avery's fist.

"There's one other guy, but I guess you'll see him when you see him," Nick finished, chasing the sentence with a shot. "Did you get a hold of him, Jonesie?"

"Yeah." I didn't notice Jonathan walk back into the bar, but he walked past me to grab a barstool a few down from Nick. "I know you said get him here, but if he showed up like that, he'd just piss you off. I told him to go to sleep, and I let him know if he ain't in here tomorrow, you're gonna cut him open."

Nick nodded with a sigh. "Fine." He looked back at me. "In any event. We have some celebrating to do! We got us a new member. Let's get this place up and running." He pointed over at Avery. "And I'm getting you back for yesterday." He left the stool, tapping me on my back as he passed me, and made his way back toward the pool table.

After another hour or so, a few bartenders and waitresses showed up, along with a cook, and then around sundown, other Hoppa residents started to show up. I stayed sitting at my table and kept to myself. I didn't associate with many people outside of Tess when I had lived in Hoppa before, but I went to school and had to make occasional trips to the grocery store to make sure there was food around for Caid and me. The last thing I needed was for someone to recognize me and call out, "*Colin*," in the middle of this bar, revealing that the only piece of information I'd shared about myself was a lie.

Tess did her best to mingle, but she was not well received. After trying and failing to involve herself in a few conversations, she came and sat back down at the table I was at. "Why don't they like you?" I asked.

Tess dramatically reached up and grabbed her breasts. A few guys stopped to gawk at the sight, but I was quick to throw a gaze at them, and they looked away. She released herself and went back to the beer she was working on. "I'd say they're progressive in that they don't think women belong *only* in the kitchen. We're also allowed in the living room now."

"Hoppa's not the Women's Rights capital of the world," I said.

She shook her head. "No, it is not."

"How'd you become VP?"

"I fought hard as hell for it," she replied, and I could hear the insult in her voice. "No one gave it to me."

"You forget how well I know you, Tess. I know you didn't let your dad just give you the spot. If I thought that, I wouldn't have asked."

She side-glanced me and then smiled. "Right. Sorry."

"Wasn't there a vote?" I asked.

"Yep. My dad laid out all these criteria, and the old VP, he liked me enough. They said if a prospect ticks all these boxes, they should be voted in. None of 'em wanted me in, but I was the only prospect who ticked every single one of those boxes, and I made sure I did. As much as they didn't want to vote for me, they knew they'd be in violation of the bylaws if they didn't. So, I got voted in when the VP died." She glanced over at me. "It was a raid with some real bad guys, worse than the Dogs. He actually had a will written out because he didn't think we'd make it. He had me named as his replacement. My dad wanted that, too, and the bylaws say two officers, so…" She held out her arms in a presentation of herself.

It was irritating. If a former vice president who wasn't related to her at all had enough confidence in her to write her in his will as his replacement, why couldn't these guys respect her? I didn't press the issue any further because it was clear that Tess didn't want to talk about it. Instead, I observed the rapidly filling bar. Nick was laughing with some of his guys and the unrelated bar patrons in the corner. The other prospects, who'd come to about ten minutes before the place started to fill up, were all at a table, working on a round of drinks while staring me down. I gave them a nod to let them know that I saw them, then moved on.

Nothing got me too spooked, apart from Taylor. He was circling the bar like a kid on a sugar high. His jaw and fists would clench as he spoke to different groups of people, then all of their gazes would turn in my direction. What he was saying to them, I didn't know, but easily swayed people were the worst kind to be around. I'd have to be sure to always be on guard, especially when Taylor was around. Whether it was because I was a friend of Tess' or because Nick had made me a member on sight, he had it out for me. I made an internal promise never to let him stand behind me.

"Do you wanna leave?" Tess asked suddenly.

"Sure. Is there a motel or something around here?"

Her face screwed in response. "Is the bed you slept in last night that uncomfortable?"

"No. I don't want to impose."

She rolled her eyes and let out a long sigh, then handed Lockjaw's leash to me. "Let me go close out, then we can go."

"Fine."

Tess stood up and walked over to the bar, and the second she was gone from her seat, someone else sat down in it. I braced myself for trouble, but it was Bullet, the bookkeeper. He had a beer in his hand, and he took a long drink of it before he said anything.

"Enjoying yourself?" he asked.

I nodded. "It's fine."

Bullet looked over his shoulder, then back at me. "How do you and Tess know each other?"

Trying to take this guy's temperature was difficult. He was about as stoic as I tried to be, which meant he was hiding quite a lot below the surface. "We know each other from high school. I just recently moved back, so I looked her up."

He took another drink of his beer. "Well, look, from one guy to another, I'm telling you not to trust her. She's only worried about herself. She always has been."

"What do you mean?"

He shrugged. "Aren't all women only worried about themselves?"

It took everything in me not to deck him. "I'm sure there are countless selfless women."

Bullet looked at me out of the corner of his eyes. "I've never met one. I don't trust women, and I really think it's in your best interest to be of the same mindset."

"Maybe you shouldn't worry about what I do."

Bullet scoffed. "Fine. Don't say I never tried to help you." Just like that, he was up and gone from the seat. Whatever had happened with him and women had left a wide gash that was still bleeding profusely.

The Steel Knights were rather dented.

Tess came back to the table to collect Lockjaw, and then we left the bar without saying goodbye to anyone. It wasn't until we were in her car and already traveling down the road back toward her house that she said anything else.

"What did Bullet want?" she asked.

"He was warning me not to trust you."

She laughed. "Fucking asshole. I'd probably have an easier time working the rest of them over if it wasn't for him."

"Mommy issues?" I asked.

She shrugged. "Who fucking knows. I just wish my dad would stop keeping me from knocking his lights out." I didn't respond. I honestly didn't know how to. I couldn't imagine what it must be like, trying to lead a group of people who hated you. "Anyway, if it wasn't clear before, you can have my guest room for as long as you're here. It's rarely used, only when friends get too drunk and have to crash."

"Do you have a lot of friends outside of the club?"

She laughed. "I have to, don't I? They all hate me."

"Yeah, I could tell." I shook my head. "I promise I'll never do that."

Tess pulled her car into the driveway of her house and then turned it off. She looked over at me, and all of her haughtiness was gone, leaving only a gentleness behind. "Thanks."

As much as I knew I shouldn't sit and stare, I couldn't help myself. She was just too beautiful. "You're welcome."

I wasn't unaware of the way Tess lingered in the doorway of the guest bedroom as we both prepared to go to bed that night, but I bit the inside of my cheek and kept my temptations in check. I was happy to be around Tess again, but I needed to be sure not to complicate things by getting so attached that I lost sight of my end goal. Get my bike fixed, get some money, and get out. The sooner, the better.

"Well, I guess I'll see you in the morning," Tess said with a sultry rasp to her voice.

I nodded, smiling. "I guess you will."

Chapter Seven

Phantom

I stirred to the feeling of a heavy weight settled on top of me and warm breaths on my face. I groaned as I shifted—my still partially burned stomach didn't appreciate the extra pounds—but the weight only moved with me. Finally, I forced my eyes open and saw that Lockjaw was lying on top of me, his mouth wide open and huffing on me as he snored while he slept.

I heard a snicker from the doorway and looked over to see Tess leaning against the frame, watching us with a smile. "I swear, he's not usually like that with people."

She looked next to none in a pair of short jean shorts that strangled her thick thighs and a neon green tank top with a healthy swooping neckline. Her hair was up in a bun, allowing her intoxicating gray eyes to be the star of her face, and she had a cup of coffee held between her hands.

I tapped Lockjaw on his head. "He's a good boy."

"He is."

I tried my best to sit up in a way that wouldn't disturb the sleeping pit bull on my stomach. "Didn't you say you stole him?"

Tess smiled. "I did."

"From where?"

Tess shook her head. "Nope. I'm not telling you anything until you answer some of my questions."

"What questions?"

"Come on. I made coffee. Let's have a chat." She waved a hand before disappearing from the doorway.

I scrubbed behind Lockjaw's ear as an apology for disrupting him, then I moved him over so that I could climb out. He grunted, peeked a single eye open, and then settled back into sleep. Once I was out of bed fully, I could see some folded shirts and pants on the desk in the room. Whether Tess had snuck a peek at my tags or just guessed at my size, I didn't care. I grabbed the top shirt and pair of jeans and took them down to the bathroom. I took a brief but welcome hot shower, donned myself in the fresh clothes, and went out to the living room.

Tess was sitting at her kitchen island with a breakfast sandwich on a plate in front of her, and there was an identical one with a cup of steaming coffee sitting next to it. I stood motionless for a minute, just staring at the scene. Tess was scrolling through her phone. Lockjaw had no doubt followed the smell of bacon out into the living room and had been rewarded with a couple of pieces in his dog bowl. The morning Arizona sun glinted in through the front window and cast an angelic glow around the room. What a life that could be. I wouldn't mind waking up to Tess every day, starting my mornings with her smiling at me, enjoying a hot breakfast before climbing on our bikes to take a ride in the heat. Some people wanted millions of dollars, a big house, or fancy cars. Me? I'd be happy with just this. This with no worries of Luther hunting me down or not knowing how Caid was feeling. Just this.

Tess finally looked up with a raised eyebrow. "You gonna stand there all day? It's gonna get cold."

It was enough to shake me loose. I continued through the living room and over to the other barstool and sat down. "Thanks for the breakfast and the clothes."

"You're welcome for the food. Clothes were actually my dad."

"Seriously?" I asked.

Tess chuckled. "I was just as shocked as you were. He was here bright and early, dropping off a bunch of tools so that you two can work on the bikes later on. Brought the clothes, too. Said he could tell you needed 'em." She gave a little shake of her head. "He really seems to have taken a shine to you."

"I don't know what I did." I took a bite of the sandwich and let the salt of the melted cheese and bacon wash over my tongue.

"I don't either, but I wouldn't waste it. Trust me when I say, Nick Squared is a good man to have on your side."

"I believe it." I took a quick sip of my coffee before continuing. "So. You said you had questions?"

Tess took the last bite of her sandwich and then turned to face me properly. She kicked a foot out, and it slid briefly across my leg. Her ability to tease was unparalleled. Never mind being careful around Taylor and the other Knights. Tess was the real trouble that I had to keep an eye on.

"You gonna tell me why you're being hunted?"

My heart slammed a little harder in my chest. "I told you, I don't know."

"And I told you that I don't believe you." She crossed her arms. "Your urgency to get out of here, the fact that you stayed on the run so long when you were in such bad shape, and you taking out the other prospects without so much as a scratch. I ain't dumb, and I'd prefer you not treat me like I am."

I sighed. She had me pegged. It was stupid of me to think I could pull the wool over her eyes. She'd always been smart and observant. I calculated the risk of telling Tess everything, even about where I'd come from. Would she believe me if I told her I wasn't running with the Unchained Dogs anymore? That I truly picked her because I trusted her, and not because I was trying to get one over on the Steel Knights?

"Fine." I turned to face her, too. "Here's the truth." Tess took a deep breath, almost as if she knew she wasn't going to like what I had to say. "I stole some money. A lot of it."

Tess raised an eyebrow. "How much?"

"Fifty grand."

"Jesus!" she yelped. "For what?"

"For Caid."

She calmed a little. "So, the experimental treatment in Germany. That's all true?"

"Yes. He was getting worse by the second and was running out of time. The doctors here all said he wasn't gonna make it, but one of them recommended this treatment in Munich. Hadn't been verified yet, but it had a ton of success. He…" My throat burned a little as I thought of my poor brother, scared and weak in a hospital bed, strung up worse than Pinocchio. "He had asked me to kill him. He didn't want to be alive anymore. He was in so much pain."

Tess reached a hand forward and settled it on my cheek. That time, her actions weren't seductive, only comforting. "I can't imagine."

"It was his last hope, but I didn't have that kind of money. So, I stole it."

"From whom?" Tess asked.

Even if she believed that I was uninvolved with the Unchained Dogs, the truth was too intense to share just yet. "From where they keep lots of money." Half-truths had been working so far.

"So, the feds are after you," Tess said, drawing her own conclusion.

It was a split-second convergence from the plan, a sign that I should save at least some information for myself. "Yeah." I pulled out my cell phone and held it up. "I'm sure they can track me, but I can't get rid of my phone—"

"Because it's the only way Caid can contact you." She rubbed her face with her hands. "How'd you get burned? They didn't really set your house on fire?"

I rattled through a thousand feasible explanations in a matter of seconds. "I crashed the getaway car. It went up in flames, and I just barely managed to climb out."

"Shit. You're on the run from the cops for robbing a bank, and now you're in a motorcycle club that's into more than one illegal money maker. I can see why you didn't want to tell me." She grabbed my hands in hers. "I'm glad you did, though. You don't have to worry. Your secret's safe, and my dad has a few buy-outs at the station, so if they come looking for a Knight, we should be okay."

I did feel a little guilty. Tess had stuck her neck out for me in more ways than one, and I was still lying to her about the whole truth that had brought me back to Hoppa. Still, it wasn't advisable for me to tell Tess that I used to run with the Unchained Dogs. Until I completely lost management of that situation, I needed to keep that single gem to myself.

"Thanks, Tess."

She held up a finger. "One other thing." I nodded to urge her on. "Is that why…" She held up air quotes. "CJ?"

I snickered. I might have expected that wouldn't get too far either. "It's kind of dumb, right? It *is* just my initials."

She whacked my arm. "You honestly thought I was going to forget your whole name? I was crazy about you. I know your name."

I smiled, remembering those days when I could steal away from home for a few hours and just enjoy being around Tess. "I was crazy about you, too."

She leaned forward and set her hands on my face, and for the first time since I'd arrived, I wasn't able to bring myself to hold back. Tess set her lips on mine, and I leaned into her and let it happen. It was sweet, even sweeter than I remembered. Just like the beautiful scene of Tess sitting calmly next to a breakfast cooked for me, her lips felt too good to be true.

I was glad when she didn't elevate us but pulled away with a satisfied smile. "That wasn't so difficult, was it?" I just chuckled because the truth was that it was incredibly difficult. Not to kiss her but to stop. Every time I allowed myself to take a taste of Tess, I was only going to want more. "So. You wanna know how I got Lockjaw?"

"What unlucky jerk woke up to find his dog missing?"

A sly smile curled up Tess' cheeks. "The Unchained Dogs."

My stomach emptied out. "What?"

She giggled. "I know. I'd heard through the grapevine that they had gotten a new pit bull puppy as their mascot, and my dad had just told me that he wasn't gonna let me pledge for the Steel Knights. So, I woke up in the middle of the night, stole his prized old-school Harley, drove to Rumble, stole their dog, and left without them even knowing I'd been there."

It was difficult to keep my poker face. I remembered the day vividly. Not just because it was a huge deal that the puppy had been taken, but because I was the one who picked out and was responsible for it.

Luther had randomly decided that the Unchained Dogs deserved a live mascot and sent me to pick up a purebred pit bull puppy that he'd paid nearly five grand for. Because no one wanted to take care of a new puppy and because I was still only a year old in the gang at that time, I was put in charge of taking care of the dog. I couldn't bring him back to my apartment, so I had to leave him at the club overnight, and the next day when we got there, he was gone. Luther beat the shit out of me, and I had to give him half my dues for the next two years to pay him back.

"Wow," Tess said. "Are you that impressed?"

"Yeah." I looked over at Lockjaw standing near his bowl, hoping for whatever food Tess or I didn't eat. "Crazy." No wonder he was no nice to me when Tess swore he was usually only that loyal to her. I was his first caretaker. I believed I'd accounted for everything, but I had not accounted for a dog giving away my secrets.

"Okay, sorry. I came up with one more question," Tess said, bringing my attention back to her.

"What's that?"

She leaned forward and kissed me again. It took me so much by surprise that I didn't even have a chance to put my defenses up. My hands were on her thighs before I could stop them. Tess was leaning into me, deciding her first successful kiss was more than enough evidence that I wanted more. She wasn't wrong, as I lost control of myself and stood up, gripping Tess as I moved so that I could lift her up onto the island. My plate tipped, which Lockjaw was more than happy to clean up, and Tess' legs wrapped around my waist and locked behind me.

I was falling fast and hard down a slippery slope, unsure of how I would break free when a knock at the door saved me.

Tess let out a growl that would rival Lockjaw. "Go away!"

"Is CJ awake yet? We're losing daylight!" Nick called back.

Tess took a deep breath in and held it for a few seconds before letting it out. "I can't murder my father, right?"

I snickered. "I wouldn't." I wanted to hug him. I could already sense that I was fast approaching the point of no return, and I might have completely lost control just now if he hadn't turned up.

As difficult as it was, I unlaced my arms from Tess' side, and she hopped off the island and walked over to the door. I bent down and took the already clean plate from Lockjaw, getting a lick on the cheek as I did. I was praying that my unintentional peace offering would be enough for him to not rat me out in his own unique dog way.

Behind me, I could hear the door open. A moment later, Tess said, "Hi, Daddy. I thought you said you'd be back later."

"This *is* later." The sound of boot steps entering the house pulled me to attention. "Morning, CJ."

I nodded. "Hey, Nick."

"Did Val tell you I came by earlier?" Nick asked. "I've got a pretty nice set up for working on bikes at my place, but I figured it'd be more trouble than it was worth getting your bike over there. We'd probably hurt it worse."

I hadn't considered that, but he was right. "She told me."

"All right. Let's get started, then." Nick turned and kissed Tess on the cheek. "Can you open the garage door for us?"

Tess nodded, saying, "Sure," and Nick was out of the door a moment later. Tess turned and looked at me. "Well, that was shitty timing."

I smiled, the feeling of Tess' skin still burning against my hands. "Indeed."

She raised an eyebrow. "Finish later?"

I knew that I shouldn't, but she looked so hopeful, and I wanted it, too, so I smiled and said, "Yeah."

"Good." She grabbed her keys from the key rack next to her door and pointed it outside. A few seconds later, the rumble of the garage door lifting pierced the calm morning air. She chuckled at me. "Have fun bonding."

"One question," I said.

Tess closed in on me and quickly pecked me on the lips. I wasn't expecting it, but she pulled away quickly, keeping me safe. "I suppose you've earned one more question."

"Why does he keep calling you Val?"

Tess let out a loud, barking laugh that reminded me of her father. "Oh, you don't like it when someone else uses different names?"

I let out a huff, knowing she wasn't wrong. "Fine, don't tell me."

I started to walk around her, and she grabbed my arm. "Don't be a brat." She put her hand up and stroked my cheek. "My nickname at the club is Valkyrie. After I stole Lockjaw on the bike I'd stolen from my dad, he said I was like a fearless Valkyrie riding into battle and coming back with the spoils. Over time, they stopped saying the full name and just settled for Val."

I thought about the headstrong girl I knew back before I left Hoppa and the impressive one I'd known since I got back. "Valkyrie." I grinned at her. "I like it."

She walked past me. "Go before I tackle you and do something I'll regret doing while my dad is outside."

I'd started off toward the door when I heard the rattle of Lockjaw's collar. I looked down, and the pit bull had bounded to my side and was waiting patiently. I chuckled down at him. "I guess Lockjaw is coming."

"He's got a bed in the garage, too," Tess called before disappearing down the hallway.

I stepped out into the already blazing Arizona morning with Lockjaw at my side. I walked down the path and up the remaining length of the driveway into the garage, where Nick had already arranged both bikes and had a bunch of tools and parts laid out on a tarp, along with what I immediately recognized as the type of engine that my bike used.

"Hey," Nick greeted again. He followed my gaze to the engine. "Yeah. I'm a big Harley fan myself, and I thought that I had a spare engine. Turns out, I did." He rubbed the back of his head, and it was almost as if there was a touch of nerves there. "Taylor made sure the engine was destroyed. I'm sorry about him." The nerves faded in an instant, and he just laughed. "I guess fifty-percent success isn't bad, kid-wise, right? Don't get me wrong, I love my son, but he needs help. Help he's probably never gonna get."

"Maybe not, but you're doing the best you can as a dad, loving him regardless."

I thought about how quickly my mom discarded her responsibility to take care of Caid because of how sick he was. A good parent would have done anything they could to help, but my mom regularly complained about how she *didn't sign up* for taking care of Caid. I had respect for Nick, who could at least love Taylor, even if he didn't know how to help.

"Thanks," Nick replied. He held out a wrench to me. "Well, should we get started?"

I took the wrench from him with a nod. "Yeah."

The silence around us as we worked on the bikes was welcome and calming. The clink of metal and ratchets was a sound that often relaxed my mind and spirit. I thought back to when I first restored my bike after I fished it out of that dumpster. It took me close to two weeks to clean it enough to see what needed to be replaced and what didn't. Fortunately, I didn't have to clean human remains out of my bike this time, but Taylor had done a number on it. The casing was going to need to be replaced, but, fortunately, the exhausts were okay. The engine was totally busted, so it was a good thing Nick brought a replacement.

About halfway through dismantling my bike, Nick swapped from working on Tess' bike to helping me with mine, taking apart the pieces so that we could take out the old engine and replace the new one.

"So. You and Val knew each other from high school?" Nick asked.

"Yeah," I replied. "I wouldn't say we were best friends or anything, but we were close."

Nick nodded. "Well, I'm thinking she must have liked you. Tess always kept the guys she liked a secret from Taylor and me. For good reason. If Taylor found out, he'd flip." We worked together to slowly lift the top framing off the bike and set it to the side. Then we started working on undoing the mechanics so that we could disconnect the bad engine. "I see the way she looks at you. I see the way you look at her. I'm guessing I interrupted something earlier."

I stopped short and looked up at Nick, my heart pounding a little quicker. Suddenly, I was a nine-year-old boy again as Nick came stomping out of his house with a rifle in his hands. I wished I could run and jump in a trash can like I did then. Most people didn't frighten me, but something about the totally calm way that Nick approached subjects that would normally enrage someone else reminded me of how I liked to carry myself. I finally understood why it was so terrifying.

Nick laughed. "Don't shit your pants there, son. I know that Tess is a beautiful girl. Takes after her mother. It's been a *long* time since I've seen her look at someone like that, though. You'll have to forgive my eagerness. All a dad wants is for his kids to find someone great for them. It's been so long. I didn't think Tess would ever date again. Maybe I'm being dumb by acting on my gut, but it's never steered me wrong before. I have a good feeling about you. I think you'll be good for her. You'll be good for each other."

It was completely unexpected. I knew that I was probably worse at holding it together than I was hoping for. Every time I laid my eyes on Tess, my heart rate went up. It was only natural that it would show on my face, even if I was trying to remain stoic.

"I do like her," I admitted. I couldn't rightfully explain that, though I had feelings for Tess, strong ones, I'd never be able to act on them. "She's very important to me."

"That's good," Nick said. "Of course, I wouldn't be a good dad if I didn't say…" He stopped what he was doing with the bike, reached over, and opened up one of the toolboxes he'd brought. There were no tools or parts inside, just a single sparkling, silver pistol. He looked right into my eyes. "If you hurt my daughter, I'll put you in the ground."

"I wouldn't dream of it," I replied faster than I intended, especially considering it was a promise that I couldn't keep.

Nick slammed the top of the toolbox down again. "Good. Then we have no problems."

He leaned away from the bike and stretched his body out. He looked down at my bike and tapped it. "Well, what do you think we call it for today? We can get the engine in there, but it's gonna need more than that to get up and running again. It's not like we can do much without all the parts we need."

"I'm fine with that."

"Cool. I'll leave everything here. As soon as the parts come in, we can keep working."

We spent the next thirty minutes or so putting the bikes in a position where they'd be fine until we could resume work on them, and then I followed Nick up the pathway and through the front door, with Lockjaw right at my heels.

"I'm going, angel!" Nick called in.

"Already?" Tess came down the hallway, likely having been in her room up to that point. "I expected you two to be at it all day." She gave Nick a kiss on the cheek before reaching down to pet Lockjaw.

"Yeah," Nick responded. "Worse damage than we thought. I'm gonna need to order some more parts, and then we'll keep going." Nick slammed a hand on my shoulder, and it had some force behind it, not so subtly following up his earlier threat. "All right, I'm gonna get outta here. You kids be good."

He reached down to rustle Lockjaw's head and then was back out the door. A few minutes later, we heard his bike start, and neither of us said anything until the rumble was barely audible as he drove off down the street.

I shut the door behind me and walked all the way in, moving over to sit down at one of the barstools to think about what the past couple of hours had meant.

Tess crossed her arms. "How was that?"

I snickered. "Terrifying."

She laughed. "Nicholas Nicholas is nothing if not a horrifying man."

I smiled, remembering the love he had in his eyes when he talked about Tess. It actually made me a little jealous. "He's a good dad. He loves you."

"Yeah. He's a great dad." She stepped a little closer to me. "Don't tell me you have a crush on him now?"

A laugh caught in my throat. "He's not my type."

Tess closed in on me, and my arms moved up on impulse to wrap around her waist and pull her the rest of the distance to me. The taste of her lips was one I was quickly growing addicted to, and all of my fears of resistance were coming true. It was one thing to hold myself back when I hadn't given in yet, but now that I'd gotten my hands on her, I never wanted to take them off.

Tess smiled. "Get that shirt off. No more fighting like you did last time."

I grabbed the base of my shirt and prepared to pull it up over my stomach. Unfortunately—or fortunately, depending on the perspective—the shirt caught on some of my bandages. I froze, remembering the horrible scarring and discoloration that covered my entire left arm and some of my left pec and my stomach. I'd looked at it a couple of times in the mirror when I replaced the bandages over the worst part after my shower.

I didn't want Tess to see. I stopped short and put my shirt back down.

"What's wrong?" Tess asked.

My heart started to pound, and my throat tightened up. It'd been a couple of days since I truly thought about my scars. Tess was a nice distraction. But now my whole body was heating up as if I was lying amongst the flames again. I shook my head, trying to free myself from the thoughts, but it wasn't working.

"Colin?"

I looked up into Tess' concerned, gray eyes. All of my senses snapped back into place, along with remembering the reason why I couldn't. Nothing good happened on the other side of letting myself get attached to Tess. Only pain for us both.

"I don't think we should," I forced myself to say. "I won't be here long."

Instead of the look of annoyance Tess had gotten when I turned her down before, now she just looked heartbroken. "Maybe it doesn't have to be that way. We can figure it out."

"No." I stood up and pushed past her, putting distance between us. "I can't stay here. This isn't a good idea."

She stared at me for a minute, and then her expression went back to knitted eyebrows and pursed lips. "It's my dad. He got to you today. Did he tell you to stay away from me? Did he bring up Taylor?"

I thought of Nick's desire for me to be the one who saved Tess from his feared path of loneliness for her. "It's not that."

She scoffed. "You already lied to me once. Why should I believe you?"

I shook my head. "You shouldn't."

She glared at me for a long time before storming past me down the hallway, and a few moments later, I heard her door slam. I was hopeful that I'd effectively hammered a nail in that coffin. I could see myself falling into Tess again, and there were millions of reasons why that was the absolute *last* thing that either of us needed.

Chapter Eight

Tess

Colin and I didn't say much to each other over the next week. It wasn't that I was angry, more that I was confused. He continued to work on his bike, sometimes with my dad, sometimes alone, and while they seemed to be bonding, the wedge between Colin and me only seemed to be getting larger.

I didn't understand.

Before my dad showed up, Colin was gung-ho. If my dad hadn't shown up when he did, we probably would have ended up going all the way. It made sense to think that my dad had something to do with his sudden reluctance, but the looks didn't stop, the heat between us didn't stop, and he only seemed to be trying harder to resist it.

Had my dad developed Taylor's same penchant for scaring off men who I was involved with?

After a shower, I walked out of my bedroom, past the empty guest room, and into the living room, where I expected to see Colin, but he wasn't there. There was, however, a plate of eggs, fried potatoes, and fried ham sitting on the kitchen island. It was still steaming, along with the cup of coffee that sat next to it. I walked over and opened the front door, grabbed the plate and coffee, and walked outside toward the garage.

Colin was lying on the floor, working on his bike, and Lockjaw was curled up in the corner. When the pit bull noticed me, he hopped up and ran over, reinstating some of my confidence that I was still his number one, and I sat on the ground to eat my breakfast and watch Colin as he worked. If he noticed me come out, he didn't react, only continued twisting and turning his tools.

I was nearly done with my breakfast when Colin pulled away from his bike and finally looked over at me. "Good morning."

I smiled. "Morning. How's it going?"

Colin nodded, putting some of his tools away and grabbing others with an intention that I didn't understand. "Pretty good. It's functioning again. It's just cosmetic stuff now."

"That's good." I held up my plate. "Thanks for the breakfast. It's delicious."

"You're welcome. I've been waiting for the opportunity, but you always wake up before me."

"Did you used to cook for Caid?"

"I had to. Our mom didn't cook, and then when I finally got us out of her house, it was totally up to me." He used a cloth to wipe his head free of sweat. "Although, on Caid's healthy days, he made me let him cook. He preferred baking. Making fresh scones or cinnamon rolls. They were amazing, too."

"They sound good." I smiled, imagining a domestic Colin in a frilly pink apron, baking with his brother. I'd pay to see the sight. "Have you heard from him yet?"

Colin shook his head. "Not yet. I did get an admittance report from the hospital, though, so he's there. I just don't have any additional information."

"Can't you call?" I asked.

Colin went quiet for a minute as he considered the question. "I'm afraid that if someone's tracking me…"

"Right." I couldn't imagine the stress that the situation was putting him under. Maybe that was why he was so resistant to me. "Well, hopefully, he'll reach out soon."

"Hopefully."

As if intending to add tension to the situation, a phone did ring, but it was mine. I pulled it out of my pocket and saw that it was my dad. I answered it, handing what was left of my breakfast to Lockjaw. "Hey, Squared."

"Hey. Sorry to bug ya so early, but some of the guys are up to stuff this evening, so we have to move up our MiD meeting. Can you meet here in about fifteen minutes?"

"Sure."

"Thanks, pumpkin. I'll see you soon."

"See you soon. Bye." I hung up my phone and looked up at Colin. "A meeting got moved up, so I gotta go. Are you planning to just work on your bike?"

"That's all that's on my agenda," Colin responded, and even though it sounded like a joke, he was stone-faced as he set it.

"Good. Can I leave this guy with you?" I patted Lockjaw on his head, and Lockjaw slowly rolled over to his side, bearing his stomach for belly scratches, which I gave.

Colin smiled. "Sure."

"Thanks."

I gave Lockjaw a few more pets and then stood up, taking the plate and cup with me, and walked back into the house. Since I was free of a dog and a passenger, and since my dad had managed to fix the damages that Taylor caused to my bike within the week, I would finally get to ride my bike. I grabbed the keys and walked back outside, giving Colin another quick smile before climbing on my bike, starting it up, and roaring down the street.

I took the backstreets to Hoppa's Taphouse so that I could enjoy the long ride and the fresh air on my face. It'd been a while since I used my car for more than transporting groceries once every couple of weeks, and I'd forgotten how empty I felt when I couldn't ride my bike every day. It helped me clear my mind a little bit. I liked Colin. In truth, my feelings were probably a bit stronger than that. I wasn't ready to make any declarations, but my feelings had never really abated from when we knew each other as kids. I was crazy about him then, and I was crazy about him now. His rejections aside, I couldn't bring myself to stop wishing that things would eventually move forward with us. Perhaps I was going about it all wrong, trying to lead with sex. Did it make more sense to back off altogether, or was it hopeless regardless?

I pulled into the parking lot of Hoppa's, and Taylor was pulling in at the same time. He climbed off his bike and looked over at mine with a vile smile on his face. "Looks like Dad got you put back together."

"And I'd like to keep it that way." I rolled my eyes at him. "Please refrain from letting that temper of yours result in damages at *my* house."

Taylor shrugged. "Maybe." He looked around a little and then back at me. "Where's your friend?"

"Damned if I know." My dad and I were keeping it on the low that Colin was staying at my house. If Taylor knew, he'd be back with his bat, and he'd probably cause much more damage than busting up a coffee table and a pair of motorcycles. "Only officers are meeting today, right? It's a MiD meeting."

Taylor scoffed at me. The biggest problem with my brother's evil nature was that he was also incredibly smart. Between my parents, who were both intelligent, both Taylor and I had taken in their brains.

"I just thought dad might have invited him since he's clearly willing to bend the rules for him," Taylor hissed.

Taylor was observant and quick, which made hiding things from him next to impossible. He was probably fully aware that Colin was staying with me, but unless my dad or I could confirm it, he couldn't justify acting on it. It was the main reason why I kept Colin's bike holed up in the garage overnight. Originally, it was my hope that we could hide Colin until he left, but now I didn't want Colin to leave. I'd have to figure something else out.

"Last I checked, Dad hasn't bent any rules. He just didn't do things exactly as you would have him do it." I looked Taylor right in the eyes, letting him know I wouldn't be bullied by him. "Good thing he's the president and not you."

Taylor's jaw clenched as he leered at me. "I guess so."

A flurry of bikes approaching made it too loud for us to continue our conversation, not that I was at all interested in continuing it. The remaining three officers, Bullseye, Bucky, and Bullet, rode their bikes into the lot, parked them, and climbed off.

"Hey, Taylor," Bullseye greeted. "Val." The way he hissed my name was seething compared to the way he greeted Taylor.

"Hey," Taylor responded.

I didn't waste my breath. It was pointless to wait for any sort of pleasantries from Bucky or Bullet. Bullseye was typically the only one even willing to greet me, if even nastily, but neither Bucky nor Bullet was known for giving me the time of day.

I made my way into the Taphouse and straight back into the warehouse. My dad was already sitting at the table with a game of solitaire laid out in front of him. My dad had an affinity for card games, and we knew better than to interrupt him when he played. One by one, we all took our seats around the table and waited in silence while my dad finished up his game. It took about twenty minutes, but eventually, he was able to lay out what was left of his cards before swooping them all up back into a deck, and then he tucked the deck neatly back in his drawer under the table. He pulled out a couple of manilla folders at the same time as putting the cards away and set them up on top of the table.

"Okay. Thank you all for meeting early. Call me a softie, but I thought making sure that Bullet has an uninterrupted date this evening was actually worth it, given his general abhorrence to women."

Everyone's eyes shot over to Bullet. He rebalanced his glasses on his nose. "Please tell them the full story so that I don't sound like a fool."

My dad let out a laugh. "Fine, fine. Bullet and I were playing a little pool last night, and this woman slides up to him." My dad did a dramatic reenactment of the slide from his seat. "She was a stunner, too. A coke bottle frame. Real pretty face. Says she's been eyeing him for a few weeks now."

Taylor looked over at Bullet with his upper lip hiked slightly up. "Really?"

Taylor and I did not share the same feelings on Bullet's looks. He wore prescription glasses, but they were always thin-framed and gave him a sexy, studious look. He was a bookkeeper, but he was a bookkeeper in a motorcycle club, after all. His brown hair was around shoulder length, and what didn't fall in his face, he slicked back into a waterfall down his neck, which curled up slightly at the bottom because of how frequently he wore his helmet. His style was always understated, but though he tried to act aloof, he cared a lot about how he looked. His clothing was always coordinated from his shirt down to his boots, even if it was just making sure everything was the same precise shade of black. He boasted an impressive set of arms, and on one occasion, I'd seen his bare back, which was ripped, forever changing my perspective of the man. If it wasn't for the fact that he hated women and, by extension, me, I might have been tempted to take a run at him.

"So, I make him a bet. You lose this game of pool, you gotta ask her out." My dad held up his hands. "And I don't lose at pool."

Bucky laughed. "Bet you hate that whole man-of-your-word bullshit now, don't ya?"

"So, they're going out tonight, and I'm not about to let a little business stand in the way of true love," my dad said.

Bullet sucked his teeth. "Hardly."

"All right." My dad slammed his hand down on the table. "MiD. It's just a few weeks away, and we've still got a lot left to do."

MiD was the shorthand name for Music in the Desert, the huge music festival that we hosted along with our ally clubs, the Blazing Rebels and the Raging Vipers. Back when my great-grandfather started the Steel Knights, he didn't believe in allies—said you could never truly trust anyone—but during my granddad's regime, a nasty global gang called the Devil's Riders started encroaching on Arizona. In one night, the Devil's Riders had decimated the numbers of all three groups, including my grandfather, who died protecting his brothers.

As a result, that was the first thing my dad addressed as president. He forged an alliance with the Blazing Rebels and the Raging Vipers so that we could all work together to protect our territories, and they decided to remember their fallen brothers through the Music in the Desert festival. By day, it was a family-friendly music festival with food booths, carnival rides, and games, and by night, it turned into a bass-bumping rager. Screw Christmas or my birthday—MiD was my favorite time of any year.

Though the festival was always hosted in the same place, an exact midpoint between all three groups, the club that hosted it rotated each year. We split the profit three ways and invite our communities to come and enjoy it with us. It's a huge success every year, and this year was the Steel Knights' year to host.

"Obviously," my dad continued, "with the Unchained Dogs so quiet lately, my fear that they're planning something big is going up. They may be planning an ambush at MiD, so on top of our regular tasks, I want someone to go out there and make sure things are safe and solid." He looked at me. "Tess, you're gonna go, and you'll be taking CJ with you."

"What?" Taylor and I asked in unison.

My dad always left us out of MiD planning. He didn't trust Taylor's temper, but Taylor was even worse whenever I was involved while Taylor wasn't. It was the adult version of making sure both kids have the same toy to prevent fights. He always said that Taylor's and my main duties were to focus on the Steel Knights during event planning, but I knew the truth.

"Why would you send CJ instead of one of the older members?" Taylor asked.

My dad held up a hand and started counting off something unknown to us on the one hand, and then he looked at Taylor. "You know, Taylor. You've been questioning me a lot lately. Is there something you want to say?"

To my surprise, Taylor actually did a cursory glance of the table, almost as if he might puff up if he felt like he'd have support, but everyone was looking back at him like he was insane. His gaze shifted back to my dad, and they had another one of their tense, silent showdowns. This one didn't last as long, as Taylor had likely sensed the heat permeating off my dad. Dad didn't often get ruffled feathers, so when he did, it was time to back down.

"No," Taylor said finally. "I can adjust to change as much as the next guy. CJ is here to stay, so I might as well get used to it."

My dad smiled, but there was a poison behind it that served as a quiet threat. "Couldn't have said it better myself." He looked back at me. "You good with that?"

"Yeah." Honestly, a trip to the desert sounded lovely. "We'll go this afternoon."

"Great." The smile my dad gave me was one of his rare warm ones, and Taylor snarled.

My dad really did seem to like Colin more and more by the day, and the more my dad seemed to like him, the more Taylor seemed to hate him. Maybe Colin was just considering what I was overlooking. Taylor had proven that he'd stop at nothing to harm someone close to me. I'd like to think that our ironclad rule not to fight with other brothers would protect Colin in a pinch, but that might be giving Taylor too much credit. As much as it killed me to admit it, maybe it did make more sense to keep things professional with Colin. I didn't want to get him killed.

Though even as I thought it, another part of me was thinking that I'd be the one becoming murderous if Taylor tried anything, and I'd probably have my dad's support in the matter.

Taylor's evil glare didn't let up as my dad continued to hand out tasks to the rest of the officers. Bullet was on finalizing vendors, Bullseye was in charge of merchandise, and Bucky would work with my dad on marketing and ticket sales. When my dad finally called Taylor's attention to direct him to work with the non-officer members to follow up with the musicians and make sure they were all still on board, Taylor gave him a shallow head nod and nothing more as he continued to stare at me.

Finally, my dad dismissed everyone but Taylor, likely to give me a chance to escape without Taylor as a shadow, and I didn't pass up the opportunity. I was the first one out of the warehouse, and I nearly made it all the way out of the bar, but I stopped when someone called my name.

"Hey, Val." I had a hand on the door already, but I looked back over my shoulder, and Bucky, Bullseye, and Bullet were headed my way, with Bullseye leading the pack. He came to a stop in front of me with his arms crossed. "Grim's set to snap if you keep letting your dad run amok like he is."

Grim was the nickname given to my brother, though no one ever said it to his face. He'd earned the moniker after killing my ex just for being my boyfriend.

"What makes you think I have any control over my dad?" I said back. "He's my boss, just like he's yours."

"I told you this was pointless," Bullet hissed.

"You know that ain't true," Bucky said. "If you tell him to back off, he will."

I didn't respond, mostly because they were probably right. Unlike Taylor, I didn't question my dad. On top of being his daughter, I was also his VP. If I approached him and told him to stop favoring Colin, he'd probably listen. I didn't want him to back off, though. The closer Colin and my dad were, the greater Colin's chances were at survival. From cops, Taylor, or otherwise.

"If you all have a problem with the way my dad's calling the shots, the bylaws have actions you can take."

"Yep." Bullet shoved by Bucky and Bullseye until he was face to face with me. He looked me up and down before spitting at my feet. "Useless," he said and continued past me and out the door.

Bucky didn't say anything, just glared at me and walked by as well.

Bullseye shook his head. "If you were waiting for a window to earn some trust around here, Val, that was it." With that, he walked around me and left.

I stood motionless for a few seconds. It was hard to hear but even harder to believe. The second I started doing what they wanted under the false guise that I was earning their respect was the second I'd start losing myself. I wasn't gonna be anyone's puppet.

I stormed out of the bar and mounted my bike. Bucky, Bullseye, and Bullet were discussing something in the middle of the parking lot, so I made sure to rev up a lot and kick up dust to let them know what I thought of their little suggestion, then I blazed out of the parking lot and rode onto the highway, choosing to take the quick way home. I wanted to see Colin. He was the one person who saw me for who I was, and whether it was as friends or something more, I wanted to soak up as much of that feeling as possible.

I pulled into the driveway and saw that Colin was still lying on his side, working on his bike. Lockjaw was standing over him, grunting and licking his face in a continuous pattern.

I turned off my bike and got off, then walked into the garage. "You know, you can put him inside if he's being irritating." There was no response. "Colin?"

Lockjaw turned and barked at me, and I could see the urgency.

"Colin." I walked over, leaned down, and pulled on Colin's shoulder. He slumped over to his back without resistance. He wasn't moving, and he was burning up. "Fuck. Colin!"

Chapter Nine

Phantom

Thick, swamp-green shrubbery grew around me on all sides. It stretched up much further than my vision could carry and into a darkened void the likes of which I'd never seen before. Looking forward, I saw there were a dozen different paths I could take. I searched my brain for any sense of direction, but none came. Backward, forward—nothing was familiar, so I settled for just moving and hoping that it eventually came to me.

My pace was slow as I gathered my bearings, but the more I moved, the more I realized that I didn't know where I was or how to get to a place I knew. Though I preferred to keep a level head in any situation—panicking gets you killed—each corner I turned led me down a row with its own flurry of new roads to travel. Always turning right didn't seem to get me anywhere specific, nor did consecutively turning left. If I kept heading straight, I'd meet dead ends and be forced to turn around. Nothing made sense, and my heart rate quickened, my breath starting to run short.

"Where the hell am I?"

In no time at all, I was running. I didn't quite know how to explain it, but I couldn't shake the fear that my time was running short. What my goal was, I didn't know, but I had to get there quickly. I bolted in every direction I could find, quickly losing track of where I was going and where I had been, simply trying my hardest to move forward. It took active effort to bring myself to breathe, and my head started to fog.

Reaching a T-shaped intersection in the path, I looked to the left and to the right, but both were dead ends. The shrubbery rustled, and Tess stepped out from between the tall hedge wall. She turned and smiled at me, and it put me at ease. Something about her spirit started to slowly pull my heart rate down and make me feel more in control of myself and my situation.

"Well?" She held out a hand toward me. "Are you coming?"

I took a step forward, wanting to follow her anywhere she would take me.

"Colin."

A voice I knew all too well called out to me from the other direction. I looked back over my shoulder and saw a reflection of myself. My skin prickled, but the longer I stared at the image of me, free of tattoos, less muscular, slightly longer hair—it was Caid.

He held his arms out on either side of himself. "I look better, don't I?"

Twins though we were, he'd always looked more feeble than I had due to his illness, but though the man before me didn't have my full arms and thick calves, he looked leagues healthier than the frail man I'd put on a plane to Germany.

My brain created a response, but nothing came out of my mouth. Instead, I just watched as Caid held out a hand to me and grinned. "Come on. You're gonna love Germany."

I moved in his direction on impulse. Caid had always been my goal. His health and happiness had been the only things that I'd truly wanted to accomplish in my life ever since we were kids.

"Where are you going?" Tess' voice pulled me to a halt. I turned to look back at her, and her arm was still extended. "Let's go."

Caid and Tess both stood looking at me with their hands outstretched. If I were to go with Tess, I could find a life of my own. I could be with someone who truly made me happy and find a way to deal with my problems instead of running from them. If I went with Caid, I could see the culmination of years of hard work and finally enjoy life with my brother the way I'd always wanted. Both seemed too good to be true, and for as much as I wanted to take a step in one of the directions, I couldn't do it.

"Colin," Tess said.

"Colin," Caid said.

"Colin." The third voice sent a chill down my spine. It hissed from directly behind me and made my heart crawl to nearly a stop. Slowly, I turned around and looked right into Luther's cold, unrelenting eyes. "Hey, Phantom."

My gut told me to scream to Tess and Caid to run, but no words would come out. They stood in their respective directions, still just looking at me, waiting patiently with their open hands. My throat tightened while Luther stared me down, and when he lifted his left arm, it brought with it a black pistol with a silencer at the end.

"Which one of them should I kill?" Luther stepped forward and set the tip of the silencer against my forehead. "Or should I just kill you." *Kill me*—but no matter how hard I thought it, nothing left my lips. Luther's lips curled into an icy smile. "Time's up."

A bang had me shooting straight up. My head swirled from the sudden rush of movement, and my stomach churned.

"Oop."

I didn't get the chance to see who spoke, but fortunately, a trash can appeared before me a second later, just in time for me to stick my head in and throw up all of my breakfast. My head pounded as I leaned away from the garbage can, seeing for the first time that the other person in the room with me was Dr. Marteau, the same doctor who'd patched me up when I first got to Hoppa. It took a few minutes for me to really figure out what was going on, but as my nightmare slowly evaporated from my brain, it was replaced with the memories of me working on my bike out in the garage.

"Where am I?" Even as I asked, I knew the answer. The folded clothes on the desk, the sheets I'd rustled just earlier that day—I was back in Tess' guest room.

"You are in bed," Dr. Marteau responded, "on the precipice of a lecture from your doctor, who would seek to remind you that 'take it easy' does not mean go perform hard labor in a hundred degree heat with no water to speak of."

"Yeah."

Dr. Marteau shoved a glass of water into my right hand before pulling the trash can off the bed and turned his attention back to my bare left arm. "As far as this goes, you shouldn't have much more use for bandages. Everything's close. Now you need to allow it some space to breathe."

"Okay." There was a scratching sound that had registered as white noise at first, but it became more prominent as my faculties returned. "What's that noise?"

"I imagine the dog." Dr. Marteau turned to walk toward the desk where his supplies were, limping as he walked. "He's been like that since we carried you in here."

"Who carried me?" I asked.

"It was a combined effort between me and Tess."

My heart slammed hard. "Did she see—"

"No, no. I told her to leave before removing your shirt. I remembered that preference from last time." He hobbled back over to me and started to rub an ointment on my arm that cooled my skin the instant it made contact. "Although, I must say, I'm a little surprised she hasn't seen this already." He stopped working for a minute and looked up at me. "This wouldn't happen to be a fear of her seeing the scars, would it?"

What was this man, a physical doctor, or a mental one? "No."

"Hm." He went back to working on my arm. "Well, I'll just say this. These scars aren't going away, and it's not very attractive or logical to always have sex with a sweatshirt on, so unless you plan on becoming a eunuch, I suggest you make peace with it. Val's not shallow, and she seems to care about you a lot." He glanced up again. "In few words, don't be stupid."

I nodded. "Thanks, doc."

Dr. Marteau's hands moved in rhythm up and down my arm that seemed practiced, and my muscles were starting to relax and loosen with each pass. Finally, he stopped what he was doing, pulled off the gloves he had on, tossed them into the trash can, and then started to pack up his things. Mid-movement, he grabbed a shirt and handed it over to me, which I took and pulled on before kicking my legs over the side of the bed so that I could sit up.

"You can come in," Dr. Marteau called out.

The door opened almost immediately, and Lockjaw was the first into the room, racing across and jumping up onto the bed. He licked up my cheek, and I patted his head. "Good to see you, too, bud."

"He was worried about you." Tess was standing in the hallway. She took a couple of steps into the room and then backed out and situated herself right inside the doorway. I wanted to ask, but I decided it was probably better if she was finally staying away. "How's he doing, doc?"

"He's okay. Just a little heat exhaustion and dehydration."

Tess raised an eyebrow. "Can't I trust you to take care of yourself for a few hours?"

I shrugged. "Evidently not."

Dr. Marteau lifted up his bag and looked at Tess. "Call if you need anything else, but he should be fine."

Tess nodded. "Thanks."

Dr. Marteau slipped past Tess and left the room, and we stood in silence until we heard the front door open and shut. Lockjaw curled into a ball next to me on the bed, and I started to pet him as Tess crossed her arms and placed a warm smile on her face. "Glad you're not dead."

All I could think about was Tess holding her hand out in my dream and how badly I wanted to go to her. "Me, too."

"Your bike is operable again, right?"

"Yeah, just cosmetic stuff now."

"Feeling up to a ride?"

Suddenly, Caid flashed into my mind. His outstretched hand and the promise of seeing him healthy and happy in Germany. Was the way my dream laid it out the reality? The closer I got to Tess, the further I got from Caid? "I'm not sure."

"Okay," Tess sighed. "Is this because you don't feel up to going out, or because you're trying to maintain this weird distance between us? If it's the latter, you don't need to worry. My dad asked us to do this."

"Really?"

"Yeah. We have this big music festival every year. We and our allies do it together, and every year, the club hosting it rotates. It's our year this year, and my dad wants us to go check out the venue. It's this open plot in the desert. We built this clubhouse out there for all of our members, and there's a meeting space where my dad will have his annual meeting with the presidents of the other two clubs. He wants me to go and asked that I take you."

At first, I wasn't entirely sure how to respond. Tess was aware of the distance between us, and as much as I needed that distance, it didn't make me feel any better that she might be feeling hurt by it. If only I could reach out for her hand. If only there wasn't the need for me to get to Caid or Luther's impending threat.

"Okay. I'll go."

She nodded. "Good. I'll be in the living room. Just come out when you're ready. Take your time." With that, she was out of the room.

I dropped my head to my hands. Maybe coming to Hoppa had been a huge mistake, after all. Any way I looked at it, I knew that I'd overestimated my ability to resist Tess. Dr. Marteau's words skidded across my brain and ran down my left arm in a chill. She probably wouldn't think twice about the scarring. It was an excuse.

Crickets rhythmically called out in chorus just outside the bedroom window, and I used the sound as a cycle to breathe with—deep breaths in and deep breaths out. More likely than not, I was just overthinking things. More than one person had accused me of possessing that trait, and for as much as I tried to convince myself and others that it was a good thing, at the end of the day, I often lost a lot of the world as I sat in one place, trying to calculate all of the possible outcomes for any situation I found myself in. Tess gave me a feeling of freedom that I typically only felt when I was on a bike. It was time to give in to that feeling. Just a little bit, just enough.

"Come on, Lockjaw."

I stood up off the bed, and Lockjaw quickly hopped up and jumped down to follow after me. Tess was sitting in the living room exactly where she said she would be when I entered, and when she noticed me, she looked up and smiled.

"Ready?" I asked.

"Yeah. Let's go."

It had only been a week since I had last been on my bike, but it felt like years. The chilled air rushed against my face, and my whole form got lighter. For the entire two-hour ride, I disconnected from my reality and enjoyed the feeling of the pavement beneath me and the colorful blur of cars as I raced by. I kept Tess' bike in my sights while she led the way, and after what felt like too little time for me to have fully enjoyed the sensation of being back on my bike, she pulled off the main road and onto a plot of empty, desert expanse.

Apart from a chain-link fence wrapped around the area and a single building in the far distance, the place was entirely evacuated. Animal footprints in the dirt indicated that a few critters had made the property their home, but that aside, it looked undisturbed.

Tess pulled her bike to one side and turned it off, and I followed suit. We'd left Lockjaw at home for the trip, a decision I was grateful for when I saw the flurry of small rodents and birds skittering around. Trained or not, he'd likely be chomping at the bit to get out and chase them, and I highly doubted that we'd be able to catch him if he broke loose.

The lock on the fence gate rattled as Tess stuck a key in and undid the massive padlock on the front, then I helped her grab one of the big gate doors and pull it enough to the side that we could walk in.

"Pretty cool, huh?" Tess asked.

I led the way through doors, and Tess followed, shutting and locking the gate behind her. "My dad bought it forever ago. We pay reduced land fees because he promised not to build anything permanent on the property, and so it is considered protected land in Arizona." She pointed toward the single building on the land, a white barn with a black, slatted roof toward the back. "The barn was here when he bought it, but we flipped the inside and made it a clubhouse. I made him keep the loft in the top, though. I love it. Come on. I'll show you."

As we made our way toward the barn, we did a careful sweep of the open land. There were divots in the sand where booths and other temporary structures had stood in the past, but the fact that there were also little lizards rushing around was proof enough that the land had been undisturbed enough that creatures could live without issue. They'd be in for a hell of a party in a few weeks, but then they could go back to their usual routines.

When we reached the clubhouse, Tess used a different key on the same ring as the front gate key to unlock it. A beeping started immediately, and Tess reached to the right of the front door and entered a code into a security system hanging there, after which, the lights all cut on automatically. There was a thick layer of dust, but aside from that, the inside of the barn had a sleek, simple, modern look. A small kitchen nook had a fridge, stovetop, and a few units of cabinets and countertops, and a bunch of small sofas and chairs were scattered around, with a big white wooden pool table sitting in front of a fireplace. The pool table's legs were decorated, one with each of the Steel Knights, the Blazing Rebels, and the Raging Vipers' sigils, and the fourth had *MiD* painted on it.

To the right of the small kitchen nook was an open door that looked like it led into a bathroom, and next to that, another door was shut and was marked with an Authorized Personnel Only sign. Tess walked over to the shut door and used a third key to unlock it, then she opened it. I remained standing in the main room while she walked into the room that she had to unlock, but her head poked back out after a few seconds.

"What are you doing?"

I pointed at the sign on the door. "I'm not authorized personnel."

"Yeah, you are. Nick specifically wanted you to come and help me check things out. He knows you'll be in here, so just don't go snooping."

Her explanation was enough for me, and I walked over and entered the room. It reminded me of the meeting space in the warehouse back at Hoppa's Taphouse. A single round table sat in the middle of the room with a dozen or so chairs placed around it. The table itself was divided into three colored sections that I assumed correlated with each of the clubs. The Steel Knights' section was silver, the Blazing Rebels' was orange, and the Raging Vipers' was red. There was another fridge in this room, but there were no windows or additional doors, and there were a few tall filing cabinets stacked against one wall.

Tess started to creep along the walls, feeling her hand on the surface and carefully checking it for anything strange, so I dropped to the ground and crawled under the table. When I was still with the Unchained Dogs, stealth was my forte. Not only was I skilled in getting in and out of a place without being seen, but I also had to know the best spots to hide weapons and cameras for any covert missions. My paranoia tried to convince me that Nick somehow knew that, but the conversations we'd had thus far were an indicator that he didn't. He just trusted me, something I was both happy and sad for.

I ran my hand over the wood of the table and all the nooks and crannies, and when I was confident that there was nothing hidden under the table, I moved over to the filing cabinets and slid them aside to make sure there was nothing strange behind them, and then I did the fridge.

"Do you have the keys to the cabinets?" I asked Tess. "Not snooping, just if I was trying to hide something in an inconspicuous place, that's where it would be."

Tess didn't respond verbally, but she walked over to the cabinets and used yet another key on the ring of keys she had. She opened the drawers one by one, and I kept a safe distance so as not to seem like I was trying to see anything as Tess thumbed through the files and felt her hands under them to make sure there was nothing unusual.

When she finally shut the final drawer, she turned and looked at me. Sweat drenched the edge of her hairline, but her eyes still had a calm stillness to them. "Looks like we might be okay."

"Yeah." We walked back out of the office and then did a careful sweep of the main room, but I didn't see anything that seemed like it would lead upward. "Didn't you say there was a loft?"

Tess' eyes widened, and a smile shot across her face. "Yeah." She passed by me and walked out the front door. I followed her out, and she walked around to the back of the building, where there was another door. She used the last of the keys on her ring to unlock it and opened it, revealing a white ladder leading up. "After you."

I stepped up to the ladder and started to climb. Some dust floated off the wood after not having been disturbed for a year, but I continued on until my head poked out of an opening at the top. My hands itched as I placed them in the hay at the top to hoist myself up, but I was too distracted by the vision to pay attention to it. There wasn't a ton of space at the top, enough for two or three people max, and if I stood up all the way, I'd probably hit my head. It looked as if it still had most of the barn's original framework and coloring. Hay covered the ground, and on the wall opposite the one the ladder led up to, there was a window with a makeshift bed in front of it. Next to the bed was a smaller round bed with a dog bone in it. Strings of lights hung across the banisters that must have been illuminated along with the rest of the building's lights when Tess turned off the alarm. No wonder she loved it. It was amazing.

Tess crawled past me and over to the bed and threw herself down onto it. She stretched out, and even though I fully expected some sort of pass, she turned away from me and looked out the window. The sun was setting and was perfectly framed in the window like a work of art, rivaled only by Tess haloed in its glow.

"Pretty cool, huh?" She didn't look back when she asked.

I did my best to commit her visage to memory. "It's beautiful."

She kicked the wall that separated the loft from the rest of the clubhouse. "I wanted the whole upper level, but my dad said we needed the space. I was still a teenager when he remodeled it, so he didn't consider that I'd grow eventually, but I kind of like how cramped it is. Makes it cozy." She pointed out the window. "It faces the festival, so after I've done my rounds, I get some food and crawl up here and stay here for the rest of the night. I watch the music and partying and…" She sighed. "It's my favorite."

Shit.

The kid that had been trying to claw his way out of me and go after his childhood love was getting dangerously close to the surface. Being alone with Tess was getting harder and harder with each passing day. The resolve I had when I told myself it was best to keep my distance was thinning, and it was just a matter of time before I decided that being with her was worth any risk. I could say I was in love, but in truth, I never really fell out of love. They say that you'd eventually realize that the people you thought you were in love with as kids were just crushes—puppy love.

Not Tess.

The way I felt about Tess was freeing, enlightening, calming. Emotions I rarely ever felt. It was as if she carried a part of me with her, and the fractured piece that was still inside me was pulling toward her peace like a high-grade magnet. I didn't want to deny it anymore.

My heart started to beat a little faster. "Um."

"We should go." The bed rustled as Tess climbed off of it and crawled past me again.

She tossed me a quick smile before kicking her legs into the opening and bracing herself on the ladder before starting her descent. Disappointed wasn't a good enough word to describe how I felt, but I followed her. I climbed down the ladder and backed out of the door, and Tess shut it again and locked it. Then we walked around to the front of the building again so that she could arm the alarm and lock those doors.

We made our way back to the front gates and out to our bikes, where Tess finally stopped and turned to face me again. "Thanks for coming. I think my dad will feel good knowing we did such a thorough job."

"Of course." For whatever reason, I reached up and lightly punched Tess' arm. "Anytime."

She snickered. "Oh, are you gonna call me Sport next?"

Yeah. I couldn't blame her for that response. "No. I don't know why I did that." The desert venue was vast, but I could only imagine how chaotic and congested things would become in the coming weeks as the event approached. "You know, I was thinking. If I was really trying to pull one over, I'd be more likely to come when all the stalls and stuff were getting set up. The risk of someone bugging the place will probably go up as the event gets closer."

"That's a good point," Tess replied. "I'll talk to Nick about it. See what he wants to do."

She turned and was getting ready to get on her bike when I suddenly said, "I'd be willing to come back every day and do a sweep."

Tess stopped short and looked over her shoulder at me. "What?"

"Yeah." My hands went into the pockets of my jeans, a nervous tick of mine. "It's not a long drive, and I love being on my bike. I could come by every day and make sure things were good."

"Are you…" Tess started, but then stopped. She opened and closed her mouth a few times and then just smiled. "Okay. I think my dad would like that. I would, too."

I smiled back at her. "Let's plan on that, then."

"Yes." Tess' smile got even bigger. "Let's plan on that."

Chapter Ten

Tess

It was probably a good thing that motorcycles were best ridden with helmets and at high speeds because it meant that Colin couldn't see me smiling like an idiot as we rode back into Hoppa. I wasn't sure what had done it, but something changed. After a week of talking about how he couldn't stay in one place for too long and how he had to get out of Hoppa as soon as he could, he was suddenly committing himself to stay at least through MiD. For all of my considering that it might be best to pull back and stay professional with Colin, he'd sucked me back in again in just a few words. Call it love or stupidity, but I wanted to be with Colin, and if he was going to be staying in Hoppa and if my dad liked him so much, why couldn't I be?

We went right to Hoppa's Taphouse once we were back in the city because I knew that my dad would want to hear about how the trip had gone, and I honestly needed a drink to try to even out all of my excited energy. Colin parked his bike next to mine, and we powered them down and climbed off at the same time. He motioned toward the door, and I walked past him. As I did, his eyes quickly traveled down and up my form. When his eyes locked back on mine, he gave me a wink, and I thought I may pass out. If I thought he was handsome before, with him seemingly lowering his guard and opening up a little bit, he was downright *irresistible*.

"Hey, Val!" my dad called over from the pool table when I passed through the front door. "Hey, CJ."

"Hey, Nick," I greeted.

"Hi," Colin added on.

My dad waved us off. "Go ahead and take a seat and a drink. I'm gonna finish up this game, and then I'll head over."

Colin found a table about halfway between the bar and the pool table and sat down, and when I had to decide between the chair directly next to him or the one on the other side of the table, I decided to experiment. I picked the chair next to him. To my extreme delight, Colin's smile grew a little larger, and my heart skipped.

What the hell had changed?

"Hey, Val." One of the waitresses, Cara, had made her way over and was standing at our table. "Want a drink?"

"Just a beer." My mind was already wandering toward trying to make a move on Colin again, given his new attitude, so something muted was probably best. That way, I could keep my wits about me and not do anything stupid.

Cara nodded, then looked to Colin. Her stance changed a little bit, and she kicked out one of her hips. "What about you, gorgeous?"

"A beer, please." Colin only made what contact was necessary, then turned his attention to me. "Do you regularly leave Lockjaw at home?"

"Not often. He's probably pissed," I said with a chuckle. "He'll survive."

"You're the new guy, right?" Colin and I looked over to one of the high-bar tables directly behind Colin, and a few of the women who frequented the bar were all sitting together with their eyes on Colin. One of them asked, "What's your name?"

"CJ." Immediately after he said it, he turned back around. It was borderline rude. Colin was a quiet person in general, and even more so in mixed company. He didn't like to waste words, but even this was odd for him. "Is he bad when you leave him at home? Does he chew up your stuff?" he asked, resuming our conversation as if he hadn't been distracted at all.

Cara came back and set our drinks down on the table, and I took a sip of my beer before continuing. "No. He's really well trained. Although one time—"

"Hey." It was the same table of women beckoning to him. Colin looked back, even if his gaze thinned a little bit. "I'm Maxine," the one speaking, a blonde with a large bust in a *Bikers 4 Lyfe* shirt, said.

Colin nodded, saying, "Cool," then turned back to me. "Sorry, you were saying?"

"One time—"

"Okay." My dad slammed himself down at the table, and I was beginning to think he was interfering with us on purpose. "Made short work of those idiots. Do we need to take this in back?"

Colin and I locked eyes, and then I shook my head. "I don't think so. Wasn't super eventful." That wasn't entirely true, but it wasn't as if I could tell my dad, "I might get laid tonight," so as far as he was concerned, nothing eventful. "We checked everything out, a thorough check, too. I think we're good."

"Excellent." My dad lifted one of his large hands and slapped it on Colin's back. "Thanks for going."

"No problem. Actually." Colin gave me a brief look, but I nodded, so he turned his attention back to my dad. "I told Val that if it would be helpful, I'd be willing to go out there every day. Just to make sure no one settles in between now and MiD."

My dad's eyes widened, and the grin that sewed across his face was one of the largest I'd seen in a while. "You sure? That's a long drive back and forth."

"I gotta start earning my keep sometime," Colin replied.

My dad pounded on the table and smiled at me. "He's good."

I nodded, locking eyes with Colin. "Yeah, he is."

"Well, I ain't about to turn down a deal like that!" My dad suddenly swatted my arm. "You go, too."

My smile dissipated. "What?"

"You should go with him. You're the only one who has the keys. I like the guy, but I ain't stupid."

I tried and failed a few times to start a sentence. In truth, I didn't know exactly how to frame my thoughts on the matter. Trips to the desert every day with Colin seemed lovely, but why all of a sudden? "Really? You don't need me here?"

My dad shrugged. "Nah. We'll be all right." I didn't know quite how to take that. In the past, my dad had all but insisted that the VP be around frequently because my duties to and for the club were important. All of a sudden, he was okay with me being gone every day for three weeks? My dad sighed. "What, Val? I see those gears turning."

"Are you trying to get rid of me or something?" I asked.

My dad recoiled a little. "What? No. You're just the only one who I trust to make sure things are on the up and up, and I trust you to handle it yourself if things aren't." He leaned in a little. "I mean, I know Taylor could handle himself if shit hit the fan, but I think we all know I'm not about to send him out there." He leaned back. "Tess, you know I think your role around here is vital. Where's this coming from?"

The sincerity in his eyes made me feel as if I'd jumped the gun, accusing him of anything untoward, but the fact that it still didn't make a whole lot of sense to me kept me paused. Whether it was trust or something else, it wasn't like I could do much about it. "Okay."

"Yeah, come on." He was boisterous in a way that let me know he'd been drinking already.

He didn't abuse liquor like my grandad did, but on occasion, he let the guys get a little too much in him, and he suffered for it. His hangovers were not pretty. My dad put a finger in the air and nodded, and a few minutes later, Cara was back at our table with a glass of whiskey. He knocked back nearly half the glass in one shot and then slammed it back on the table.

"So, CJ. Is the bike back up and running?" he asked.

Colin nodded. "Yeah. It's in the lot right now. Got some cosmetic changes to make, but that's the easy stuff."

My dad snickered. "Yeah. I always hate that part. The nitty gritty, I like, but then I usually dump mine at a body shop to be bea-u-tified." He let out a roaring laugh as if he'd told a hysterical joke, then threw back the rest of his whiskey.

"Dad, maybe you'd better relax, or you're gonna end up like Grandpa."

My dad winced. "Oof. Hit me where it hurts, why don't you, pumpkin?" He pushed his glass away. "Fine. I'm on water for the rest of the night."

"And a ride home?" I replied.

"And a ride home," he mocked in a grumbling voice.

"Good." I looked at Colin. "Are you ready? I'm tired."

He nodded back at me. "Sure. Let's go."

"Actually." My dad tapped his fist lightly on Colin's shoulder. "Can you hang out for a little bit longer? I'd like a chance to speak with CJ." He narrowed his eyes. "Alone."

Colin and I exchanged glances, but he seemed just as lost as I was. "Um."

"Ah! Don't be so clingy!" my dad barked. "Just a quick card game."

"We had a five-hour round trip, Dad."

"It's okay," Colin said. "I can spare a few minutes. Especially if it's for cards."

My dad laughed. "I knew I liked this guy." He stood up from his chair. "Come on. Join me in the back."

He didn't wait for Colin before he started off for the bar, and after a few minutes of hesitation, Colin stood up. I watched him, but he avoided my gaze as he walked around the table, followed my dad behind the bar and through the doors, and moved out of sight. If I wasn't already uneasy, the fact that, when I turned back around, I had an unobstructed view of a seething Taylor in the back corner of the bar was the nail in the coffin.

Chapter Eleven

Phantom

He's just a man, I told myself over and over, *just another man.* Yes, Nicholas Nicholas was just another man, but in my life, he was several different men. He was the boss of my current motorcycle club, the boss of my former motorcycle club's rival, and definitely the man who would murder me if he found out who I used to run with. On top of that, he was the father of the woman I was rapidly reigniting my love for and the only man keeping his rabid dog of a son from slitting my throat for that love. Running through the multitudes of reasons why Nick would suddenly invite me back to his warehouse for a one-on-one chat, my brain refused to settle anywhere other than on the possibility that Nick had figured out who I was.

That sent me into panic mode.

Thanks to Tess distracting me, I hadn't done a careful enough sweep of the bar's patrons. Apart from the few women who'd been bothering me, I didn't notice how many other club members were actually *in* the bar. The people who Nick was playing pool with weren't club members, so any number of them could be waiting in the warehouse to jump me as soon as I got through the doors.

Was there any other way out?

We walked through the small kitchen between the warehouse and the front of the bar, and I did a scan, but there were no other doors in sight. There had to be a back door, something that led to a dumpster or alleyway. I kept my eyes on a few of the cooks, but they all threw their scraps away in trash cans scattered around the kitchen, and when one of them happened to notice that the can he was going for was full, he just found a different one to discard his items in. The reality of the situation was obvious. If a building has a warehouse, the back door was probably in it.

So as much as my body was leaning toward the *flight* in fight or flight, I pressed on through the kitchen and followed Nick through the swinging door that led to the warehouse. He pushed it aside, and when I swung it out so I could walk through, I fully expected all of the Steel Knights members to come out of any shadow that could conceal them.

But they didn't.

I watched in shock as Nick walked over to his table, sat down, and brandished a pack of playing cards from under it. Did he seriously just want to play cards?

Nick motioned to a chair a couple down from him at the table. "Come on, sit." My legs carried me forward despite the alarm bells going off in my head. Nick started dealing out a game while I pulled out the chair he'd indicated and sunk into it. "You know Gin Rummy?"

"No." There was a nervous, gravelly quality to my voice that had me wincing as the word fell out. I cleared my throat and tried again. "Sorry. No, I don't."

We didn't play cards a whole lot back in Rumble. Darts were Luther's bar game of choice, and no one ever liked playing with him because he was a shitty loser, so we mostly just hung around and watched him.

Nick chuckled. "Relax, CJ. Jeez, you're jumpier than a bullfrog around me."

"Force of habit," I replied.

"I know what you mean. Taylor and Tess' mom, Kelly, her dad was like a dad right out of a movie or something. Like full blown. I showed up for our first date, and he met me at the door with a shotgun. Opened the door, cocked it, pointed it at me, and told me to come in. I couldn't move. Damn near shit my pants. Every time I was around him after that, he could click a pen, and I would jump like he was cocking that shotgun." I forced out a laugh, thinking back on the rock and garbage can incident. "All right, here's how you play. It's real easy."

Over the next twenty or so minutes, Nick carefully explained the game, and when he was confident that I understood the rules, he shuffled the deck of cards and dealt out fresh hands. We played the entire first round in total silence. Every now and again, I would see Nick glance up over his hand and watch me with eyes that didn't only seem to attempt to discern if I had a good hand, but when our eyes would lock, he'd take his attention back to his hand. The lack of conversation was almost worse than whatever I thought he was going to say when he got me back here. There was the faint droll of music and intermingling voices coming from the bar, but that aside, the only sound in the warehouse was that of cards shuffling as Nick and I played out our game.

"I'm out," Nick said finally, setting down the last of his cards and ending his round. He counted his points and then looked up at me. "I got one-fifteen. What'd you get?"

I surveyed the cards still left in my hands and deducted the point totals from those I managed to get out on the table. "Sixty."

Nick let out a hollow whistle. "That's not a bad first round, considering I went out first." Nick scribbled the points down on a piece of paper and then gathered all of the cards and began to shuffle them. "You're still nervous."

I wasn't the type of person to admit to fear, but honesty was probably the best policy in the situation I'd found myself in. "I'm not entirely sure what we're doing."

Nick snickered. "We're playing cards and talking."

"We haven't done much talking."

Cards slid across the table as Nick dealt new hands. "True indeed, true indeed." He lifted his cards into his hands and started to move them around. "You're from Hoppa, right?"

Men like Nick didn't ask questions without intention. Thanks to my past with the Unchained Dogs, I knew better than to trust his questions for what they were, but I was also in no position to refuse to answer. "I am, but I didn't meet Tess until high school."

Nick nodded as he took in the answer. "So, are you two the same age, then?"

I furrowed my brow. "I'm a year older," I lied. "We met at one of the football games."

A snicker skipped across Nick's lips. "She always *was* a bit of a tomboy. Here I thought she was going to the games for the boys, so I decided to go with her one time, and she wasn't even paying attention to the guys. They all wanted her attention, but she was just there to scream plays at the players."

For the first time, I smiled in Nick's presence. "That sounds like Tess."

"So, you two were close?"

"Quite." I swallowed, opting for a moment of vulnerability, hopefully, in exchange for some trust. "I was pretty smitten."

"Well, she's got her mother's charm. Really, I can't take much credit for Tess. She got her mama's beauty and her mama's brain. She got my eyes, I suppose."

"And your love of bikes."

Nick slammed his hand down on the table with a wide smile. "That's for damn sure!" He laid down a spread of aces. "So, if you're a year older, that makes you twenty-six, or have you not had your birthday yet? When's your birthday?"

I swallowed hard, quickly trying to do math in my head. "I'm twenty-six. My birthday is March twelfth."

In truth, I was a touch younger than Tess. Her early summer birthday was in June, whereas mine would be coming up in just a few weeks on August fourth. The hope was that if Nick was going to try and use the information I was giving him to run some sort of check on me, that he wouldn't be able to unearth my true identity, but even as I sat there listening to him, I couldn't shake the feeling that he was up to something else altogether.

"Ah, we missed it. Well, we'll have to have a big celebration next year!" Nick waited while I took my turn in our card game before asking, "You got any siblings? Where are your folks?"

Tess and her dad were close, and even though I knew she was protecting the integrity of the story I'd started, that my name was CJ and that we were friends from high school, not elementary school, I didn't know if she would have mentioned that I had a brother. "I had a brother. He died a few years ago due to complications from an illness he had all his life." My throat clenched as I said the words. All too often had I stared down that reality. Compared to saying those words and having them be true, I gladly took on fifty grand worth of Luther's wrath. "Never knew my dad, and I haven't talked to my drunk of a mom since the day my brother died."

"We got more in common than I thought, kid," Nick replied. "My mom stayed away from booze, but that was probably because my dad lived on it. He used to beat the hell out of me and my older brother. Gave my brother a hemorrhage to his brain that killed him when we were just teens."

"I'm so sorry."

"The crazy thing is, I still find myself admiring the man. Is that dumb?" He chortled. "Beat the ever-loving shit out of us, but I still regard the day that he told me he wanted to take his place at the club someday as one of the best days of my life. When he died…" Nick's fingers squeezed into the cards he was holding, causing them to crinkle a little. "That shit tore me up."

"He was your dad," I responded. "Maybe he wasn't the best one, but he wanted big things for you. That's enough for a kid to love their dad."

Nick nodded. "I think so." He laughed a little harder. "Listen to me, pouring out my heart to some kid I barely know."

It was time to throw caution to the wind. "Why are you doing that?" I held up a hand. "Don't get me wrong, I appreciate that you are, but what did I do?"

"I've been trying to figure that out myself, if I'm being honest." He laid out a couple of spreads of cards and discarded one of two remaining in his hand. He was close to winning. "I just get this feeling about you. I got it the second I laid eyes on ya. This club. It's been in my family for generations. My grandad started it, then my dad took over, now me. It's part of the Nicholas bloodline, but I'm at an impasse because I could never hand it over to Taylor, and I'd give my right arm to hand it over to Tess, but the boys would never go for it. I can only flex so much muscle as president. When it comes down to bylaws and votes, the odds just aren't in her favor."

All the distant sounds completely faded out, and I just watched Nick. The game didn't matter anymore, and when I didn't start my turn, Nick didn't push. "She can't go up?"

"Not by normal means," Nick responded, "but, if she were, I don't know, married to the president, and she was VP, they could run things as a team." Nick's eyes flew up from his hand and locked into mine. "I've just been waiting, CJ. Waiting for Tess to bring along someone that made me feel like they could hold her up. Give her the door she needs."

When I opened my mouth to respond, no words came out. We barely knew each other. How could he offer me everything he had? "Um."

"Now, look, I'm not telling you what to do. Shit, it's all up to Tess at the end of the day because you and I both know she ain't going for no patriarchal, giving-her-away bullshit."

"No."

"But if she did pick you, and you picked her, I'd be happy with that." I didn't move or speak. Nick waited a long time, just watching me patiently, but when I didn't say anything else, he nudged my hand. "I'm just spit balling, kid. Don't worry about it. It's your turn."

"Why?" I finally managed to mutter out.

Nick shrugged. "Because I think I can trust you. With my club and my kid. Whatever your relationship with those things might be."

"I can't make any promises about my… involvement, but I can promise you this." I made sure to look Nick right in his eyes as I spoke. "I promise I would never do anything to hurt the Knights or Tess."

Nick stabbed a finger at me. "It's that resolve, right there. You showed it to me back when we were working on the bikes, too. That's what got me thinkin', 'Maybe this kid's the real deal.' You seemed so sincere, and honestly, I can't remember the last time someone made me a sincere promise."

Though it didn't feel like the conversation had reached a natural conclusion, I took my turn, and Nick took his turn, and we let the conversation lay to rest. After a few hands of back and forth grabs for points, I somehow managed to win, prompting Nick to growl, "Beginner's luck." He waved a hand. "All right, you can go back to her. I know she's itchin' for you to get back."

"Thanks."

The laugh that came out of Nick at that was a mix between a grunt and a sneer. "Don't thank me, just don't make me regret this." There was a hint of bass behind his words that hadn't been there up to that point.

"I won't squander your or Tess' kindness."

"Good. Oh, and, uh, let's keep this little chat between us, huh? I mean, I know you're gonna have to tell her something, but save her the gory details."

I nodded. "Of course. She wouldn't get any benefit from knowing them."

"Right." Nick started to collect the cards and shuffle them. "All right, kid, I'll see ya around."

"Yeah."

My mind was a haze as I turned around and left the warehouse, slightly unsure of what had just happened. Wherever it came from, or whatever feeling Nick had developed about me, it was all too complacent, and it made me sick to my stomach. Less because of what he said, and more because, as he said it, I found myself longing for it.

I navigated the kitchen and stepped out from behind the bar, where Tess was sitting at the same table where I'd left her, drinking a beer and talking with Avery. As soon as I reached the table, Avery stood up, patted my back, and walked away, and Tess leaped up from her seat.

"Everything okay?" she asked.

"Yeah. I'll explain more at home."

Lockjaw went nuts as Tess and I crossed the threshold into her house after taking the short ride home. I scanned the room, fully expecting it to be destroyed, but apart from some manic energy, the dog was just fine, and so was the house. Go figure.

"Okay?" Tess threw her keys and bike gloves down on the counter and then turned and leaned against it, crossing her arms as she did so. "What'd he say?"

My heart thudded as the conversation played on repeat in my head. "I think I just had *The Talk* with your dad."

Tess' eyes bugged out. "What?"

"Yeah. All the parts and pieces. He likes me but isn't afraid to kill me." Lockjaw was relentlessly clawing at my boots, so I reached down and gave him a few scratches on the head. "He also taught me how to play rummy."

Tess' head fell to one side. "Ironic, isn't it?"

"What do you mean?"

She shrugged. "All that talking, and it isn't like there's anything going on, anyway. You know, I think I might—"

Which part of my brain ordered my feet to move, I wasn't sure of, but mere seconds passed before I'd stepped up to Tess, cradled her head in my hands, and set my lips on hers. She was rigid in my hold, but she didn't pull away, and as I bled my lips over hers, delighting in the sweet taste of her Chapstick, she relaxed and grabbed my sides. Nothing in me wanted to pull away. All of the logic I'd mustered over the last week to keep myself at bay had left me in the lurch. Some things were worth risking everything for. I'd done it with Caid, so why couldn't I do it with Tess, too?

Was I getting greedy?

Tess let out a huff of disappointment when I finally managed to peel myself away. She tried a few times to say something, but only additional puffs of air came out.

"I just need time," I said.

"Okay," Tess responded in an airy tone. "Take all the time you need."

I risked my resistance to reach out and stroke the back of my hand along Tess' cheek. She leaned into it, so I quickly retreated back to my room, closing the door behind me. The bed was warm and welcoming as I flopped face down onto it, and I couldn't stop a smile from etching from cheek to cheek. Between offering to stay in Hoppa long enough to get to MiD, having the conversation I just had with Nick, kissing Tess, and asking for time, I'd somehow run smack dab into something that made me happy enough to discard my dedication to not getting attached. I faded from consciousness as the thoughts rolled across my head.

There has to be a way. I just have to find it.

Chapter Twelve

Tess

The couple of weeks that elapsed between Colin telling me that he needed more time and the week of the MiD event passed in the blink of an eye. On the one hand, it felt like things had taken a giant step forward between Colin and me. The mornings typically involved kissing of some kind, sweet touches, or lingering hugs. Any verbal interaction between the two of us could only be considered flirting, and when it came right down to it, we were behaving like a couple. After about a week, we were sitting on the couch watching a movie, and Colin grabbed my hand and held it firmly.

"What's this about?" I asked.

Colin blinked a couple of times at me. "Does it have to be about anything?"

I shook my head. "No."

Then he lifted my hand to his lips and kissed the back of it. "Good."

Our daily trips to the desert brought lots of alone time, and we'd gotten into the habit of driving out first thing after lunch, and after taking a couple of hours to do a sweep of the land and clubhouse, we would sit in the loft and talk until the sun was setting or until Lockjaw was grumbling at us to go get food on the days we brought him along.

On the other hand, it felt like we were stuck. The kisses, handholding, and flirting were all well and good, but whenever it felt like things may push past amorous, Colin would pull back. The marks he often left behind when he had to forcefully claw himself off me indicated that he wanted me as much as I wanted him.

How much time did he need?

I'd never been one to talk out my feelings, being more of a boots-and-beer kind of girl, but I'd give anything to know what was going on inside Colin's brain. Why was he holding back?

"Whoa."

Colin's voice pulled me from my thoughts. We were just getting off our bikes at the MiD location in the desert, but unlike the abandoned plot we'd found every day for the two weeks prior, the area was now drowning in vendors. A few bikes parked off to our side belonged to the Raging Vipers, based on the sigils on the side, and I recognized a few of the guys floating around and talking to some of the vendors.

"Wow," I huffed. "They always show up a few days before the event. I guess I didn't realize we were already so close."

"Who are they? I thought that Nick said the vendors weren't going to start showing up until the day before."

"Our vendors," I responded. "Even though it was the Steel Knights' year to host the event, the Blazing Rebels' hometown of Mascid and the Raging Vipers' hometown of Collinstown always include a few booths directly from their towns in order to make their town's residents feel more welcome. It's best for them to get in first so that, when our vendors start piling in, there's space for everyone."

"Makes sense." There was a gravelly quality to Colin's voice that made me look in his direction. "What?"

"Is everything okay? You sound weird."

"It's just a lot of people. It's gonna make ensuring that this place isn't bugged a little more difficult."

Colin's consideration for things that no one else would think about was almost supernatural. "It'll be okay. Now that the Rebels and Raging Vipers are around, too, it's safer. Come on. Let's check the clubhouse."

We passed through the fence's gates surrounding the desert plot and passed through the people, bound for the clubhouse. Those Raging Vipers who I recognized as I passed, I nodded hello to, but Colin's pace was too rushed for me to stop for any proper conversations. He suddenly seemed much more erratic than he had been. Was he that nervous about the influx of people?

When we reached the clubhouse's door, I reached out to unlock the door but stopped and faced Colin. "Hey, are you sure you're good?" Colin's head was on a swivel. He was folding up and releasing his fingers in a continuous pattern. It was the most unsettled I'd seen him since the day he arrived. "Colin."

I grabbed his face and turned it toward mine, and he immediately leaned in. Never one to turn down a kiss from him, I mirrored his actions, and our lips met. His lips had a slight tremble to them. I pulled back and unlocked the door to the clubhouse, pulled him inside, and shut the door behind him. He didn't resist when I brought him back in for another kiss. In fact, his arms wrapped around my waist and pulled me closer.

This kiss reminded me of the one we shared right before Colin asked for more time. He dragged me as close to him as he could, like he was afraid he may lose his grip. Whatever comfort he was taking from our connection, I wanted him to feel secure about, so I held on tight and worked him through it. Finally, he pulled away.

"Sorry."

My head was shaking before I could stop it. "For what?"

"I don't like large groups of people." He bobbed his head a little. "I don't like large, uncontained groups of people."

When I pulled on Colin's hand, he relented, and I dragged him over to one of the clubhouse couches. We sat, and I flicked him on his forehead. "You probably should have brought that up before now."

"Yeah." Colin's hands tightly held on to mine. "It didn't really occur to me until I saw everyone."

"Well, MiD isn't a small event. Are you gonna be okay?"

He nodded. "I will. It just needed to hit me, that's all."

"Okay. Are you sure? My dad's probably gonna be leaning on you a little this weekend. He trusts you."

One of Colin's hands drifted up to my face and stroked my cheek. "Yeah. I'm sure. Sorry."

With a chuckle, I pecked Colin on the lips. "It's okay not to be a superhero all the time, you know?"

Colin let out a laugh to match mine. "I'm hardly a superhero."

I left it at that because arguing with him about that particular fact was hardly worth it. We stood up and gave the clubhouse the traditional sweep. Then Colin mustered up his courage, and we started to cover the grounds. Even though he claimed to be okay, Colin stuck to the stalls' shadows, and on more than one occasion, I completely lost track of where he was. More than enough trust existed between the two of us, but every time I seemed to lose him, my heart would race a little quicker until I found him again.

In just the little bit of time that we'd been in the clubhouse, most of the Raging Vipers and vendors left, leaving their locked booths behind for the big day, and those who were still hanging around left while we were walking around. Once everyone was gone, Colin's head stopped whipping around so much, and his stalking movement abated, leaving a more normal pattern of movement behind.

Due to the little hiccup in Colin's habitually confident demeanor, and since the grounds now held about a dozen vendor booths, the crawl across the grounds took longer than usual. The sun was already setting by the time we were done with the sweep. Colin and I would usually climb into the loft to relax and talk at this point. Even though his actions had become more normal in the time elapsed, his energy still felt a little unsettled. I didn't want to give up our time in the loft, but he seemed like he could use a drink.

"Wanna head back?" I asked. "It's hot out here, and a beer sounds great."

He nodded. "Sure."

"Okay. You head to your bike. I'll go lock up and—"

"I'll come with."

I flipped around and stabbed a finger out toward him. "Hey! Don't fucking damsel-in-distress me. I can take care of myself."

Colin's jaw dropped. "I, um… no. I just…" He sighed. "Never mind. I'll meet you at the bikes."

"Okay." My auburn hair whipped around as I turned again to head to the clubhouse, and I immediately felt bad. If he was uncomfortable and just wanted to stick by me, that wasn't bad. "Fuck," I grumbled out loud to myself as I walked. I was too impulsive. Colin was good at thinking before he spoke. I needed to try that sometime.

With the lights off and alarm set at the clubhouse, I made my way back over to the bikes. Colin was already on his, and when I walked back out of the gate and locked it, Colin's bike roared to life. I hadn't even made it back to my bike when Colin revved his to life a few times and pulled out onto the street, starting off down the road without me.

All of me that felt bad before faded to being irritated. "Brat."

Maybe I only had myself to blame for upsetting him, but he didn't have to act so childishly about it. I got on my own bike and started off down the road after Colin. Trips between Hoppa and the MiD desert were usually really calming, but all I could think about was how to make nice with Colin. After the fractions of steps forward we'd taken, the last thing I wanted was to take a massive step back because I was so used to having to puff out my chest.

A small thought in the back of my mind told me that Colin may go straight home, but fortunately, he did stay on the highway past the exit to my house, and we took the exit for the Taphouse. When we were on the side road on the way to the bar, Colin's pace slowed, and eventually, I was riding at his side again. We pulled into the parking lot and parked our bikes, and that time it was me who rushed him. I hopped off my bike, raced over to his side, and threw myself into a hug.

"I'm sorry. That was out of line."

Fortunately, Colin didn't pull back from me. "I'm sorry for—"

"No. You…" My words were getting all muddled in my brain. When it came to Colin, it often felt like I couldn't think straight. "You don't treat me like that. It was just an impulse."

Colin squeezed me a little tighter. "I'll never not worry about you." He smirked. "Especially when mixed up with a guy like me."

My heart fluttered at his smile. "Well, I meant what I said. I *can* take care of myself, you know?"

"I know, Tess," Colin said. "You've always been a badass." He ducked his head, and the logical part of my brain short-circuited. I tilted my head up and took the kiss he was offering, regretting it only when another bike's rumble rocketed behind us.

"Shit." I whipped my head over my shoulder. Any other member of the Steel Knights could have been rolling into the parking lot, and I would have felt okay.

But fate isn't kind.

The bike that rolled into the parking lot while I was still trapped in Colin's arms was Taylor's chrome-plated cruiser. We wasted no time in pulling ourselves away from each other, but the way Taylor pulled his bike into the spot directly next to Colin, got off, and glared at Colin as he sauntered toward the front door was telling.

"That's not good," I muttered.

Colin ran a hand through my hair. "I'm not worried. Come on."

By the time we got inside Hoppa's, Taylor was already in his back corner, strangling the neck of a beer bottle with both hands. Our eyes instantly met, and Taylor kept his eyes on us while we picked a table and sat down. Before I knew it, we were locked in a continuous stare that neither of us was willing to break. I didn't feel safe taking my eyes off Taylor for a second. And given the fact that he kept his eyes locked on me, I was warranted in my feelings.

"You all right, pumpkin?" The screech of a chair was enough to break my gaze. My eyes shifted toward my dad as he settled into a chair at our table. "You seem out of sorts."

"I think that's my fault," Colin said. "Got a little jumpy in the desert today."

"The Raging Vipers were there," I tacked on. "The Collinstown vendors are in."

"Ah," my dad responded. "That's my bad for not saying anything. I got word they may come in today, but I forgot to mention it." He pounded a fist against Colin's shoulder. "Good on you for keeping your eyes open, though. I knew I was right to trust you two with that mission."

With a lift of his arm, my dad called over a waitress and ordered a round of drinks. As I watched him chatter away with Colin, I couldn't help but smile. He'd been hanging around much more ever since Colin showed up. It was nice to get a warm feeling when I was in the club as opposed to the cold, neglected one I had before. If Colin really did leave one day, I'd be hard-pressed to go back to the way things used to be.

"Drinks on me," my dad said. "I whooped Bullet's ass in rummy earlier. He was talking a big game and put money on it, money that I won."

"I'd like to thank you for teaching Colin, by the way. He makes me play it all the time."

My dad chortled. "God, I knew there was a reason I liked this kid."

We were all smiles until the door of Hoppa's flew open. Everyone came to a screeching halt and looked over at the door, and the Steel Knights' resident drunk, Adley "Stag" Johnson, came ambling in.

"Shit," my dad growled. "Stag, I told you not to come up in here wasted anymore!"

"Stag?" Colin asked.

In the few weeks since Colin joined, we hadn't seen Stag once. His drinking had been getting progressively worse as of late, and with MiD planning underway, my dad had given Stag the task of working with the prospects, exclusively in liquor-free environments. Clearly, he'd found his way to some booze.

"A non-officer member. Dad's been keeping him out of the bar because he can't handle his liquor." I held out a hand in his direction. "As you can clearly see."

Stag ambled over to the table and looked down at my dad. "I'm a grown ass man, Nicky. I'll do what the fuck I want."

My dad didn't flinch. "You're drunk. Get out."

Suddenly, Stag's gaze turned to me. "What the fuck are you looking at, Val?"

"It's like he said. You're drunk. Go home."

Stag nearly went down as he turned to face me. His beer belly poked out at me, and his long, braided beard whipped around as he turned to face me. "I'll go if you go with me, pretty girl."

"Adley, knock it the fuck off," my dad growled, actually raising his voice. "I really don't want to have to kick your ass."

I reached into the back pocket of my jeans, pulled out my favorite pair of brass knuckles, and slid them on my hand. "Oh, really?" I replied to my dad. "I'd love to."

Stag let out one chuckle, then a second, and then started a gurgling string of barking laughter. Nothing in me thought that he was dumb enough to do anything stupid other than run his mouth, so when he reached a meaty hand out, took my hair into his fist, and yanked me toward his crotch, I was too stunned to react.

"Suck my dick, you bitch!" he barked.

My dad tried to slide out of his chair, but he wasn't quick enough. I didn't even hear Colin's chair move, but suddenly, he was between Stag and me with his hand clutched around Stag's throat. Although Stag was at least twice Colin's size, Colin hunched and lifted Stag clear off his feet until he was about a foot off the ground. With impressive force, he flipped Stag sideways and drove him down onto the floor.

People screamed, and tables and chairs screeched as patrons slid out of the way, anticipating a fight, but Stag could barely move, and even if he could, he probably wouldn't dare take Colin on with the piercing, horrifying gaze Colin pinned him with. All of the Steel Knights had converged on the altercation in an instant, but getting in between Colin and Stag wasn't necessary. Colin walked over and settled back into his seat as if nothing had happened.

Bucky and Texas hiked their arms under Stag's arms and dragged him off the ground. They both peered past me, and I followed their gazes over to Taylor. As the Sergeant at Arms, he was the one who made decisions about how members were punished for violating the bylaws, and they were waiting for an order. Taylor's eyes were bouncing between Colin and Stag, but finally, they landed on Stag. He motioned his head toward the back, and Bucky and Texas pulled Stag behind the bar and through the doors toward the warehouse. Not much time elapsed before Taylor rushed back there himself, followed by the rest of the Steel Knights' members.

"Maybe you two should get out of here for the night," my dad said. "Let things calm down." After that, he got up from the table himself and disappeared behind the bar.

"I'm fine with that," Colin said.

"You go," I replied. "I need to check in with Taylor."

Part of me expected Colin to protest, but he wasn't dumb. "Understood. I'll see you at home."

He stood up from the table and was out of the bar a moment later. He trusted me to take care of myself, and he didn't deserve how I treated him in the desert. Another apology would be in order when I got home.

I waited for some of the patrons to calm a little bit, and then I stood up and made my way behind the bar, through the kitchen, and into the warehouse. If a fight had taken place, it was over already, and Stag was already gone. My dad was nowhere to be seen, but Taylor was sitting at the meeting table, perfectly calm and looking as if nothing had gone wrong. A few of the non-officer members were floating around, but I wasn't sure what they were up to. It made more sense to ignore that in favor of calming Taylor down before he did something outrageous, so I walked over and sat across from him at the table.

"Where's Dad?" I asked.

Taylor shrugged. "Dunno. He left."

"What about Stag?"

Taylor's gaze crawled up to me, empty, a void where emotions should be. "What about him?"

"I'm fine, so don't do anything dumb." As I looked around, Taylor quietly chuckled.

"What's so funny? Where is he?"

Taylor cracked his knuckles. "Parts of him are in a car on their way to Phoenix." My heart sank, and he grinned. "The rest of him is on the way to Rumble."

"Taylor." Rage boiled inside of me. I never wanted to be responsible for someone's death again. "That was an overreaction."

"You know the rules," Taylor hissed. "No one touches what belongs to me and gets away with it." His eyes narrowed. "No one." The last two words were laced with a warning.

The chair I was in sent a screaming screech across the floor as I backed it out. "I'm not your property."

Taylor didn't respond, not that it would have stopped me from bolting out the back door and rushing toward my bike if he had. He'd already taken care of Stag, which meant, without a doubt, that Colin was next.

Chapter Thirteen

Phantom

Blaming myself for the way I acted in the bar didn't do me any good, but I couldn't help it. Never before in my life had I acted so impulsively, but seeing that man put his hands on Tess sent an unknown rage coursing through my blood. My anxiety was already heightened after seeing the Raging Vipers in the desert—more of a chance that I could be recognized—but when Adley reached out and grabbed Tess' hair, I turned into someone I didn't recognize. It was a good thing that I didn't have a gun on me at the time because I might have put a bullet through his skull. Tess could take care of herself, and I knew that, but it didn't stop me from wanting to jump to her aid when certain threats arose. I just wanted her to be safe.

My leather jacket was the first thing to go when I was safely behind the door of Tess' guest bedroom, and I damn near ripped the black long-sleeved shirt off. It had the musty smell of the desert clinging to it, and it was covered in sweat from handling the glacier of a man that was Adley. The stack of clean shirts on the desk was calling out to me, but a cold shower would help me calm down. Tess wasn't back yet, which was good. I owed her an apology for playing knight again, but I'd rather do it while I was clean.

As I was unloading my pockets, the door of the guest bedroom burst open. My back was to the door, and I froze in place. I hadn't heard Tess' bike approaching, but Lockjaw's lack of barking was concerning. Whoever opened the door wasn't speaking, and I was debating whether or not to grab my gun before turning around.

"The burns."

Relief and anger battled for domination in my mind. I flipped around and saw Tess standing in the doorway, staring at my bare torso. My hand flew to the desk to grab a clean shirt, but Tess reached out and snatched it from my grip.

"Tess," I growled, "give me the shirt."

Her stare finally left my arm and came up to meet my eyes. "Is *this* why you've been so weird?" She clung the shirt tighter when I attempted to grab it back, and when I turned to try and grab a different one, she shifted toward the desk to stand between me and it. "Answer me. You've been hiding this from me? Why? Do you think I'm that shallow?" The discoloration on my left arm, my left pec, and left half of my stomach were screaming. The overexposure was difficult to deal with, and I was beating back my fight or flight response with a mental stick.

"Colin. Answer me."

"No," I responded finally. "I know you're not. It's me."

She lost some of the stiffness in her body. "Well…" She scoffed. "There's nothing wrong." She stepped up to me and stuck out a hand, dropping the shirt on the floor and leaving it behind. Her fingertips grazed across the permanent scarring, and I rigidified. "Does it hurt?"

"No." Not physically, at least.

Her hand settled a little more against my arm and started to smooth its way down. Tess' hands felt on my skin burned in a different kind of way. It was a welcome heat, unlike anything I'd experienced before. I stood still and watched as she methodically trailed her hand over all of the discoloration. For a brief minute, her hand slipped up toward the only bandages I still had on, those covering my Unchained Dogs tattoo. My heart and mind both started to race as I imagined what I might say if she pulled off the bandages and saw it, but eventually, her hands slid away and continued down my pec.

As her hands grazed over my stomach, her lips pursed into a hard line. "I hope they never come for you," she said before looking up at me. "Cops or not, I'm gonna struggle not to kill them for hurting you like this."

My heart was pounding in my chest, and I looked directly into Tess' eyes. "I hope they never come."

Tess swallowed hard, and her hands started to shake. "Well, if this is what was holding you back, I've seen it now." The hope in her eyes was almost too much to bear. "Do we have to wait any longer?"

The blood coursing through my veins was a loud, rhythmic thrum in my ears. Wanting to hide had been a reason, and not wanting to get attached had been a reason. Those things were gone now, so what was I waiting for?

"No. We don't."

Tess' shoulders lifted, and she leaned toward me. I brought my hand to her face and cupped it. Excitement rocketed through my body that felt like I'd finally let a wild animal out of a cage that had been too small to contain it. I leaned in to set my lips on hers, and it was at that exact moment that the doorbell rang.

"I swear to fucking God, Colin, if that's my dad, I'm gonna chop his head off."

I gritted my teeth. "I'll hold him down."

Tess turned around and tossed the door to the bedroom back so hard that it left a crack in the wall. As much as I hated to do it, I reached down and grabbed the long-sleeved t-shirt that Tess had dropped to the floor and pulled it over my body. I spent a few extra minutes in the room, letting my visible excitement die down, then I walked out into the living room where Tess was sitting on the couch next to—who else but—Nick, who was quickly becoming known for his supernatural ability to show up at the worst possible time.

Tess shook her head and rolled her eyes at me, and I smirked. "Nick, hello."

"Hey, sorry to drop by so late," Nick replied. "I assume Val told you what happened?"

I locked eyes with Tess. "Uh."

"We hadn't gotten that far. I rushed home to make sure the trouble hadn't moved this way," Tess said.

My heart thudded in my chest. "What trouble?"

"Taylor killed Adley after his little display today." Nick sighed, running a hand through his hair. "I can't fucking deal with this right now. I'm gonna need to pull from the prospects now. The week of MiD. God, this is a cluster fuck."

"He killed him?" Lockjaw hopped out of the armchair as I walked toward it, and I sank down into it. "Why would the trouble move this way?"

Tess looked over at me. "He said to me, and I quote, 'No one touches what belongs to me and gets away with it.' He made sure to emphasize, 'No one'."

My mind traveled back to when I kissed Tess in the parking lot at Hoppa's, and I remembered Taylor riding in to see us at that exact moment. That was an oversight on my part. "I'm not worried about him."

Nick snickered. "You're not easily spooked, are ya, CJ? You're like a fucking phantom." The racing in my heart doubled. I'd been called that nickname before—it was my moniker back when I was still with the Unchained Dogs. It could have just been a coincidence, but it was a little too close to home for comfort. "That's good if you can keep your head on straight around him, but it doesn't change the fact that we have a murder on our hands now. He's got a goddamn wife and kids. We can't deal with this shit right now."

"Well, we have to. It's way too close to MiD for rumors to start flying around. For now, we need to just treat him as a missing person," Tess said. "So just relax, and let's think this through."

"I don't want to overstep," I started, "but can I make a comment?"

Nick's eyes were weary when he looked up at me. "Please."

"If it comes down to it, just pin it on me."

Both Nick and Tess' jaws dropped. "What?" Nick barked.

"Everyone saw me slam him in the bar today. If rumors start floating around that he's been killed, the natural conclusion will be that I did it. Just let them go with that."

"What if the *police* come for you?" Tess asked, and it was clear that she was concerned about the version of my story that I'd told her.

"You said you have plants there, right?" I asked. "As long as they can give me a heads up, I can be gone before they even know I was here. You guys just pretend not to know me, and let it roll off your backs."

"You…" Nick's words died in his mouth.

Tess put a hand on her dad's back and the other one on my knee. "Let's not get ahead of ourselves. We can cross that bridge *if* we come to it. For now, none of us know what happened to Stag. He was a useless drunk, and it'd be easy enough for someone to believe that he wandered into the desert and got eaten by a coyote or something."

"They'll eventually find a body, Tess," Nick said.

Tess' expression darkened significantly. She looked directly at the floor, and her eyes glazed over. "No… they won't."

Silence filled the room as we all pondered this notion individually and what it meant.

"Daddy, where did you go when you went back behind the bar?" Tess asked. "I assumed you knew."

Nick's bottom lip poked out as he shook his head. "Nope. He told me that Texas took Adley out to the desert to kick his ass. I rode about twenty minutes out of town looking for 'em when it finally hit me that he'd given me the run around." He drove another hand through his hair, this time stopping at his skull to scratch a bit. "The bar's being flipped and cleaned right now, but fuck. We've never had to deal with shit like this before. I didn't think he'd take it that far. It was one thing when he beat your ex to death. It was just an accident, and I could cover it up."

"It wasn't an accident, Dad."

"It…" Nick shook his head. "I never thought he'd get this bad."

Both Tess and Nick had warned me that Taylor was off his rocker, but I hadn't realized that it was *that* bad. What a terrifying human being. Why would Nick keep him around if he was that bad? Just because Taylor was his kid? That was a kind of parental love that I had never once experienced in my life.

"He's been getting worse by the day," Tess responded. "He may be beyond our influence now."

Nick didn't respond. There was a little glisten in his eyes. It had to be difficult to realize that one of your children was outside of your reach. Parents, good ones, anyway, hang onto any hope that their children won't travel down a bad path, even after the parents themselves are long gone. There was nothing in Taylor's future except prison or death. I watched as that thought occurred to Nick, blended with the conversation that he and I had about Tess having hit a glass ceiling. He was probably feeling like he was terribly out of options.

"What's next?" I asked. "MiD is at the end of the week. You need to pull prospects?"

Tess tossed me a warm grin before looking back at her dad. "We can do that first thing in the morning. We could take 'em all, really, and stack the deck. The guys aren't gonna mind."

"They aren't trained," Nick said.

"So, I'll train 'em," Tess replied.

"No. I need you and CJ in the desert. I'll put Bucky and Bullseye on it. We'll call it a fast-track to membership if they put in a few long days to get ready for MiD."

"That's good," Tess said. "I'll keep my mouth shut so that it'll blow over without a problem."

Nick nodded. "Yeah. Sorry."

"Don't apologize. We don't have time for that now."

"You're right. The Dogs could show up anytime. We have to be ready."

It was as if there was a fifteen-car pileup in my body. My heart screeched to a halt, and my head started to swirl. "Is… is there a threat of them coming?"

"They've been quiet for a little too long for me. Whenever they get quiet like this, it's always right before they strike."

There was truth to his words, and I knew it because I'd been there. Luther always got the calmest right before he flipped. That was exactly why I didn't suspect that he'd figured out that

I was the one who lifted the fifty grand. It was why I was lying in bed as if nothing was wrong when my house went up in flames. I tried my hardest to mask my fear, but inside, I was boiling. If Luther was coming and if he found me here in the process, he wouldn't leave until every house in Hoppa was in ashes. He would leave no one standing.

"We've got it under control," Tess said. "We're gonna talk to the Blazing Rebels and the Raging Vipers at MiD and make sure they're in if things go wrong, and in the meantime, we've got an entire fucking music festival to worry about." Tess rubbed her hand up and down her dad's back. "He thrives when we get bent out of shape, Dad. We have to just go about it business as usual. He can't see us sweating. We've got this."

Nick nodded. "Yeah." He looked at Tess. "We do." He stood up. "All right. Thanks, both of you. I'm gonna go check in with everyone and make sure the cleanup is coming along."

"I don't know who Taylor got to… dispose, of Adley, but he said part of him was on the way to Phoenix and the rest was on the way to Rumble."

Nick nodded. "Fucking great. Night, kids."

Tess stood up and walked her dad over to the door, gave him a big hug, and then saw him out. When she came back, she closed the door and leaned back against it. "That probably ruined the mood, huh?" I glanced up at her, and she nodded. "Yeah."

"Just a little more time?" I asked.

She shrugged. "I've waited this long." She didn't come back into the living room, but instead, she turned and started off down the hallway. She stopped to tap her leg, and Lockjaw hopped up from his living room dog bed, and with one more quick, warm glance back in my direction, she continued down the hallway and out of sight with her pit bull right behind her.

My head fell to my hands as the fear that Luther was coming consumed me. It took all the willpower in my body to get me off the couch and into the guest bedroom. I fell down on my back on the bed and closed my eyes as if I was going to sleep, even though I knew good and well that I wouldn't.

Chapter Fourteen

Tess

Seeing my dad in such a state of anguish made it very difficult to want to kill him for interrupting Colin and me yet again. Whether it was the impending threat of facing off against the Unchained Dogs or that Taylor had scared Colin more than he was letting on, Colin seemed genuinely freaked out by our conversation. He was good at hiding his true emotions, but I'd known Colin for a long time, and the past month had only brought us closer together. As much as he tried to put on a brave face, I could see his hyper-logical brain calculating all of the ways out, and regardless of whether the conversation was a mood killer on its own, I knew after seeing my dad out that Colin and I wouldn't be going at it.

Again.

After that night, things kicked into high gear as we got ready for MiD. My dad stationed Colin in the desert permanently until the event. Though I was hoping that my dad would send me, too, he was still so freaked out by what had happened with Taylor that he kept me in Hoppa with him to help him clean up Taylor's mess and help finish the minutiae for MiD. It'd been four long days since I last saw Colin, but tonight was MiD, and I'd get to see him again. If I was lucky, we would finally take things where they needed to go.

My dad left for the desert early that morning while I stayed back to make sure that the new members were taken care of and prepared to take care of the Taphouse in the event that someone showed up there instead of the festival.

One of the new members, former prospect Aaron Rell, kicked a chair in frustration. "I don't get why we have to miss all the fun."

"Keep your mouth shut. Didn't you hear what happened to Adley?" another prospect-come-member, Vil Simmons, hissed.

"Both of you keep your mouths shut," I barked. "Don't bring up Adley, and don't complain. This is a job that new members do every year. You got to go last year when you were barely a speck in our eyes, and you'll get to go next year once you've earned your keep."

Seth Hardy, the last of the new members, stepped toward me, and Lockjaw snapped at him. He backed up with a string of swear words hissed under his breath. "I was just going to say thank you."

"Sure you were." I grabbed my dad's small black lockbox from behind the bar, twisted it open with the key that he left with me, and opened the lid. "Keys."

Whenever my dad had to leave someone in charge of the bar, he had a relatively fool-proof system to make sure that those left in charge didn't screw us over.

He took their keys.

I'd bring the lockbox with me to the desert and would bring it back tomorrow when the festival was over. The most important thing to any self-respecting member of a motorcycle club was their bike, and part of the contract that they all signed when they became members was an agreement to this particular practice. My dad was very aware of the fact that most people have multiple copies of their keys, which is why he requested all copies of the keys. He made sure to mention that since he had a copy of their keys, if they stabbed us in the back, he'd use his copy of the keys to steal their bike if he ever saw them again, and when they came to get their bike back, they'd have to face him.

No one had ever turned on my dad with this rule in place.

Seth and Vil stepped up right away and dropped their bike keys in the box. Seth dropped in three copies, and Vil dropped in two. I shifted my gaze to Aaron, but he wasn't moving.

"Are you violating your contract?" I asked.

The look Aaron gave me threatened to melt my skin off. He pulled his gun out of his waistband as if that would scare me, then stood up and walked over to the box. He pulled out a set of his keys and dangled them in my face above the lockbox. I just sat there waiting, and in an action that could only be described as flat out stupid, he slammed the keys into the lockbox so hard that the box slammed into my arms.

"Fuck!" I yelped as I stumbled.

And that was all it took.

Lockjaw leaped from my side and made good use of his name. He opened his mouth and bit down on Aaron's arm, and his jaw locked in place over the flesh. Aaron pointed the gun in his hand at Lockjaw, but Seth hopped up from his seat and yanked the gun from his hand. Vil stood up and swept Aaron's legs from under him, and Aaron tumbled to the ground, giving Lockjaw all the leverage he needed to maul him without hesitation. The bones in Aaron's arms crunched, and Aaron screamed.

I looked at Seth and Vil. "You made a good choice. I'll be sure my dad knows."

Seth nodded. "Thanks, Val."

A small grin found my face. It felt like I actually may have earned a little respect. I let out a hollow whistle, and Lockjaw released Aaron's arm, leaving it bleeding profusely. "Take care of him or leave him there. It is up to you." With a growl, I snatched Aaron's keys out of the box and chucked them directly down at his face. "Consider your membership revoked."

The lockbox lid clicked as I snapped it shut, and with a final nod at Seth and Vil, I stepped over Aaron's screaming, writhing body and left Hoppa's. Lockjaw hopped up into his seat, and I made sure to ruffle his ears a bit to thank him for a job well done. "Who's Mama's good boy?" His tongue rolled out of his mouth, and he panted happily, so I kissed his nose. "Should we go see Colin?"

Lockjaw's ears perked up a little bit at the mention of Colin's name, and I laughed. I never would understand why Lockjaw had attached to Colin so quickly, but it wasn't as if I didn't understand. Colin was pretty great.

With a deafening roar, I started my bike and started off for MiD.

My stomach flipped as I pulled into MiD. The empty desert that I'd been visiting daily up until a week ago was now unrecognizable. Colorful booths selling everything from food to merch were lined in rows, and at the far end of the desert was a massive stage with an electronic backdrop and tons of flashing lights. One of the more popular, family-friendly Arizona bands was playing. All of the headliners would perform during the night party, but people were still partying it up now. On either side of the stage, orange, blood-red, and steel-silver banners hung with the faces of our fallen members from the Devil's Riders' attack of the past.

On either side of the entrance gate were the different posters that Hoppa and Collinstown designed for the event. The event, originating with the name Music in the Desert, was depicted in a simplistic poster with waves of tan across the bottom, a music note in the center, and the Steel Knights', Blazing Rebels', and Raging Vipers' emblems across the top. The promotion for the rager part of the night was displayed on a poster with an electric purple bottom, a state emblem across it, and stars dotting a black sky, with a few of the stars being the Steel Knights, Blazing Rebels, and Raging Vipers symbols.

The entire place was packed with people, and I could see the bright red and orange Blazing Rebels and dark red Raging Vipers emblems floating around all over the place, not just on the jackets of the members, but on the Mascid and Collinstown residents as well. Hoppa wasn't to be outdone, as nearly half of the attendees seemed to be wearing the Steel Knights' sigil in a sterling silver color that was reflective and caught the sun's light perfectly.

Unlike the front where Colin and I had been parking our bikes, the clubhouse had members-only parking, and I followed the closely guarded backroad around to where the bikes were all parked, along with Colins. Just seeing his bike sent a jolt of excitement through me. I'd gone fourteen years without seeing him, and now after just four days, it felt as if it had been fourteen more years. I parked, climbed off, and pulled Lockjaw out. Normally, I'd leave him off-leash since he was very well trained, but I kept him on a short chain while at MiD for others' peace of mind. Though I thought he was cute as a button, everyone else saw a terrifying pit bull. I leashed him up and then walked into the club room.

The place was packed with the intermingling members of the Steel Knights, Raging Vipers, and Blazing Rebels. Some were playing pool, some were drinking and laughing, and some were just sitting on the couches, catching up. I did a quick scan of the room, but I didn't see Colin, my dad, or Taylor.

"Hey, Val!" I turned and looked over my shoulder, and the Raging Vipers' lean but unexpectedly strong Sergeant at Arms was walking in behind me.

Way back when I'd first met the Raging Vipers' officers, Saddle approached me as if I was no different from any of the men in the club. It took me by surprise, at first—that and his thick Russian accent—but when I mentioned to him that the guys in my club didn't necessarily like me, he playfully quipped, "Oh, I was unaware that men disliked having beautiful women around." It was a comment that fell right inside his hard sense of humor, strained with a tinge of seriousness. Whenever he was around, it felt like I got more respect. Maybe it was just because he loomed over everyone and because it felt like he could see into your very soul, but he was one of the main reasons I loved MiD.

"Saddle!" We threw ourselves into a hug. "How are ya?"

"Can't complain. You know, things never stay calm for too long in Collinstown. Gunner sees to that."

A chuckle slipped out before I could stop it. Raging Vipers Sergeant at Arms Adrian "Saddle" Ivanov was much more the troublemaker between him and their vice president, Gunner, but he tended to foist it off on others. "I'd take some of that over watching Nick play cards every night."

Adrian punched my arm. "Hey, be careful what you wish for. Things are always calmest before the storm."

That's what had my dad so spooked, after all. "I know that's right. Hey, have you seen him?"

"Squared?" Adrian asked. "Yeah, he and a few of the other Knights were standing around the beer stand a bit ago."

"No shock there. Thanks."

Adrian tapped my arm as he continued inside. "No problem. Good to see ya, Val."

"Bye." I shook Lockjaw's chain a bit. "Come on, buddy."

We walked back out of the clubhouse and started to wander around the desert grounds. As I walked around, I saw Bucky, Bullseye, Texas, and Bullet, but my dad, Colin, and Taylor were nowhere to be found. For half a second, I got a little nervous that maybe something had gone wrong between Colin and Taylor, but then the unexpected happened.

"Val." Lockjaw let out a quiet growl at the person beckoning me, knowing that it was unusual for Bullet to approach me in a way that wasn't hostile.

"Hey, Bullet. You enjoying yourself?"

Unlike the normal aggression between us, he seemed slightly tepid, if not somewhat pleasant. "Yeah. You know, MiD's always a good time."

"It is," I responded. "Are you… feeling okay?"

He looked at me, his thin-rimmed glasses making his cynical expression even more pronounced. "Yes. Why?"

My hands flew into the air defensively as I laughed it off. "No reason. We just don't talk much."

"Yeah. Is it a problem?"

"No." I shifted uncomfortably from one foot to the other. "How are things going around here? No big threats, I imagine?"

Bullet shrugged. "Squared's been like a chicken with his head cut off, but other than that."

"Do you know where he is?"

He nodded his head off toward the end of the desert plot opposite the clubhouse, behind where the bathrooms were usually situated. "Last I saw him, he was over there. Been dragging Colin everywhere with him, too."

Of course he was. It could be considered a good thing that my dad liked the guy I was into, but I didn't want to have to fight with him for his attention. "Cool. Thank you."

"No problem." I'd started to walk away when Bullet started up again. "Hey."

"Yeah?" Even Lockjaw seemed confused, standing next to me halfway between ready to attack and wanting to sit and be patient.

"Uh…" He rubbed the back of his head. "Can I ask you a question?"

If only I didn't get struck by lightning first. "Sure."

"There's this… woman."

There was no stopping the smile that immediately found my face. "Okay?"

"She's a…" He opened and closed his mouth a few times, trying to find words before finally settling on, "Challenge."

I snickered. "The best women are."

"How do I… I mean, what do I…" He shook his head. "Never mind."

Before I could stop him, he shuffled away from me and out of sight. I looked down at Lockjaw, my only nearby friend, with my jaw agape. "Did that just happen?"

Lockjaw just stared back at me, and all I could think about was getting to anyone who would listen to me. I made my way back toward the clubhouse with a pep in my step, knowing that Colin was okay. I figured it was probably best to just wait for them to come back. I joined up in a game of pool with Bucky as my partner and even stole a moment to tell him what happened with Bullet.

"Oh, yeah. Your dad didn't tell you?" Bucky said. "Apparently, he's, like, into her."

My jaw fell open. "He *hates* women."

Bucky shrugged. "Evidently not this one."

"That's the power of breasts," one of the Blazing Rebels' members, Hector "Ink" Vicario, joked. I glared at him, and he held up his hands. "Or, maybe she has a great personality."

Everyone laughed, and we continued to enjoy our game and pleasant conversation. Between what had happened with the prospects back at Hoppa's, having a conversation that wasn't scathing with Bullet, and actually mingling and feeling like one of the gang in the clubhouse, my feelings toward my role in the Steel Knights was slowly shifting. Maybe there was hope that things could change, after all.

The pounding bass of music from outside the clubhouse was the sign that the party was switching from kid-friendly to an all-out rager. One of the country's most famous bands, an Arizona original, The Flying Cardinals, was the headlining act, and they were already getting the crowd going. The clubhouse slowly emptied as everyone went to enjoy the growing party outside, but I stayed behind with Lockjaw, Adrian, and the Blazing Rebels' Sergeant at Arms, Elias "Iron" Serrano. We'd all be meeting once the party was in full swing, after which time I would hopefully be able to steal up to the loft with Colin and Lockjaw.

Over the next twenty or so minutes, the rest of those who would be present at the meeting turned up. Oliver "Tank" Ingram and Isaac "Wrench" McIntyre showed up together with their hands full of the gourmet hotdogs that one of Collinstown's booths sold every year. They were the Blazing Rebels' president and vice president, respectively, and their favorite thing to do was enjoy the cuisine that the other two cities had to offer.

Not long after they arrived, the Raging Vipers' president, Dustin "Brewer" Johnson, and Alex "Gunner" Thomas arrived, both seeming a little tipsy, but nothing that would interfere with the meeting.

Last but not least, my dad entered the clubhouse with Colin at his side. A wide smile crossed my face when I saw Colin. Not only was it good to see him again after being apart for a few days, but he was wearing a short-sleeved t-shirt, allowing the world to see the discoloration from the burns on his left arm. That level of acceptance was a subtle hint that he was dealing with it and that it wouldn't be a stopgap between us anymore. The excitement that gave me was almost unparalleled, except for the fact that Lockjaw leaped up from where he was sitting on the floor and bolted over to Colin.

Colin crouched to meet Lockjaw, scratching behind his ears, and then his gaze slowly crawled up to me, deep with admiration and a hint of seduction that actually made me blush.

Adrian stood up and plopped down on the couch next to me. "Oh! You finally found one that likes you?" I raised an eyebrow at him, and he let out a barking laugh. "Atta girl. Now if we get the rest to not be stupid, we're in good shape."

"I'll hold my breath while you work on it," I huffed back, and Saddle laughed.

"Hey, baby," my dad greeted.

I stood up and walked over to him and gave him a kiss on the cheek. "Hey."

He raised an eyebrow at me. "Heard you're making friends."

My already present smile got bigger. "It's been a good day."

"Glad to hear it." I slid over to Colin's side, and my heart leaped up into my throat when he reached out, took my hand, and kissed the back of it. It was like I was a schoolgirl again.

What the hell had happened in the last four days?

"What's goin' on, Squared?" Brewer greeted. "You must think you're slick shit, puttin' on the best MiD yet, huh?"

My dad shrugged. "Well, what can I say. I don't do shit by halves."

"No, you don't," Brewer replied.

"Well, thank you all for agreeing to meet. I won't waste too much of your time." My dad turned and tapped Colin's shoulder. "Folks, I want you to meet one of our newest members, CJ. He's gonna be joining us if it's all right. I guess he's been my go-to guy as of late."

My eyes widened, and I could tell in the shocked expression on Colin's face that he wasn't expecting that. My dad looked at Colin with a grin. "That work for you, son?"

Colin nodded. "Yeah."

"Good." He motioned toward the meeting room. "Let's get it started. If I keep Gunner from that party for too long, he might take me out."

Gunner nodded dramatically. "That's for damn sure."

Everyone started to file into the meeting room, so I took the transition to pull my dad back. "Where's Taylor?"

He looked over his shoulder at me. "Let's just say I think some hierarchical changes are in order, so he's out enjoying the party." With that, he headed off to the meeting room, and Colin started to follow, pulling me with him.

When I stayed frozen in place, Colin stopped and faced me. "You okay?"

"No," I said. "If Taylor gets out, he's gonna kill you."

As if he'd been summoned by the mention of his name, Taylor came striding through the door. On impulse, I dropped Colin's hand, but Taylor didn't even give us a second glance. He went storming into the meeting room, and I was close behind, watching as he sat down at the meeting table.

I looked at my dad, but he was unphased, maybe choosing not to deal with it while we were in the presence of the Blazing Rebels and the Raging Vipers. I walked inside and sat down in my chair, and Colin sat in the chair next to me.

Taylor eyed Colin. "What's he—"

"All right," my dad cut him off. "Let's get started."

Chapter Fifteen

Phantom

It wasn't difficult for everyone at the table to tell that there was tension between Taylor, Nick, Tess, and me. Taylor was glaring at me like he wanted to take my head off my shoulders.

Nick and I had been together for most of the day. He claimed that it was just because I was the one who'd been overseeing the desert while MiD was in planning, but all throughout the day, it was more like he was a dad breaking in his future son-in-law. We enjoyed the different food stalls, played a couple of games, and spent some time talking and listening to live music. Nick asked me flat out if I was in love with his daughter, and I had to tell him the truth.

I was in love with her now, and I always had been.

Even though it was more foreboding for me, it made Nick happy, and the somber mood he'd had ever since Taylor killed Adley started to slowly evaporate. We bumped into Taylor more than once, and Nick had even asked him to join us, but Taylor refused, always glaring at me before walking away.

Needless to say, Taylor and I wouldn't be making each other friendship bracelets anytime soon.

Still, part of me had to wonder if Nick was intentionally pitting us against each other or if he was just exploring, through me, the father-son relationship he'd missed out on with Taylor. Whatever it was, he wasn't improving the situation. Inviting me into a high-officer-only meeting with Taylor, who saw that Nick was about to commence the meeting without him, wasn't a good thing. Tess' fears were valid, despite that they didn't frighten me.

For the first time in my life, I had something for myself I wanted to hang on to. My relationship with Nick, having someone around who felt like an actual dad who wanted me to succeed, I didn't realize how much I was missing it until I had it. Being with Tess, someone who continued to care for me despite all the baggage I came with and who gave me multiple chances when my multitude of emotional issues got in the way, was amazing. I wasn't about to let some petulant kid with several screws loose come in and take it from me. If he wanted to fight, he knew where to find me, and until then, I would enjoy my new life without fear. I'd protect it.

"I want to thank you all again for meeting with us," Nick said, starting the meeting off finally. "Tess, Taylor, and I have been speaking at length about the Unchained Dogs' silence as of late. As you all well know, groups like them are only quiet when they're about to bark, and my fear is that they're planning a raid. I wanted to get through MiD, but I plan to send some spies into Rumble. We don't just want to be sitting ducks."

Goosebumps covered my skin as Nick said the words. It was a terrible idea.

Luther had everyone in Rumble from the postal workers to the mayor under his thumb. There was a reason that the Unchained Dogs were nearly impossible to penetrate—it was because Luther's umbrella extended far past the Unchained Dogs' members. If Nick sent Steel Knights into Rumble, not only would they be killed, but all that rage would come back to Hoppa, and the Knights would be short on men when it did.

"My hope is that you all could be something of a rumor mill for us. I'd like to try and plan an ambush right here, once MiD is over. Make it seem like we have a big meeting planned here, and when they show up to try to take advantage, we'll get the jump on them," Nick continued.

The inside of my lip hurt from how hard I was biting it. Luther didn't leave Rumble without his army, and they were twice the Steel Knights' size. If Nick went for that plan, he'd probably get himself killed and take out all the Knights with him. I imagined him bringing Tess, and I imagined Luther mowing her down. It made me sick to my stomach.

I'd have to find a way to tell Nick that his ideas were not good ones without tipping my hand, but that was going to be difficult, and it definitely wasn't good to do it in front of the Raging Vipers and Blazing Rebels.

"You know we've got your back," Eric, the Raging Vipers' president, replied. "When's the ambush?"

"I'm hoping for two weeks from now," Nick said. "The twenty-second."

Oliver, the Blazing Rebel's president, said, "Mascid's on the interstate. Lots of gossip travels in and out. We'll be able to get it out fast."

Nick nodded. "Good, thank you. What about backup? Could some of your men help out?"

Eric and Oliver agreed almost in unison. "You know we've got you covered, but in exchange, we're gonna need you to be ready to help us," Eric continued. "We've gotten word that The Devil's Riders may be back on the hunt."

"Shit," Nick said. "Seriously?"

"It's not confirmed," Alex, the Raging Vipers' vice president, said, "but my sources are reliable."

Next to me, Tess shifted. The Devil's Riders, whatever their history was with these three groups, seemed to make her very nervous. "They got our blood, too," she added. "We won't hesitate if we hear they're back in town."

"Damn straight, we won't," Nick added. "You didn't even have to ask."

"Good. Let's all agree to stay in regular contact, then," Oliver said. "We can set up some meetings in the near future, just in case. I'm beefing up my member-count, too. I'd suggest you all do the same."

"We just pulled three," Nick said.

"Two," Tess replied.

Nick looked at her. "Two?"

"Yeah. One wasn't up to the task."

Alex let out a low whistle. "Your VP doesn't play, does she, Squared?"

Nick laughed. "No, she doesn't."

"We're planning to beef up, too," Eric said. "The meetings are a good idea."

"I can have Bucky reach out to both your teams and get some things on the schedule. It's good to stay in contact, regardless," Nick said. He let out a breath. "All right. That's good. I feel better. When the Dogs start gettin' quiet, it gets me jumpy."

"We've got you covered," Eric said, and Oliver nodded in agreement.

"Good. Well, I won't take up anymore of your time. Go! Enjoy the party! Celebrate our fallen comrades!"

There were some resounding affirmations, and then everyone started to get up from the table. The thoughts of Nick bungling an interaction with Luther and the Dogs terrified me to my core, but I refused to only dedicate a passing thought to that concept. It would take some dedicated thought and the careful laying out of all of my options, which would definitely need to happen on a day other than MiD. Everyone was off to enjoy the night, and I already had some things of my own planned.

No one even stopped at the clubhouse. They all walked straight through the main room, and out the front door, bound for the thundering party outside. Nick started to walk out but then looked back at me standing next to Tess and smiled before leaving. Taylor lingered in the main room, his eyes locked on mine. Never in my life had I been a pushover, and I wasn't about to start. I nodded at him to let him know that I saw him there, then I took Tess by the hand and led her out through the front door.

"God, you must have a death wish," she whispered to me as I pulled her around the back of the barn that the clubhouse was built into.

I laughed. "I told you already." With a step toward her, I pinned her between me and the wall, placing my arms on either side of her. "I'm not worried." Then I set my lips on hers. Only when Lockjaw started to paw at my feet did I remember he was there. "Oh." I looked at Tess. "I'll be right back."

I walked Lockjaw back to the main part of the clubhouse and opened the door so that he could walk in. Taylor was already gone, and there was no one left, so I tapped one of the couches for Lockjaw to hop up onto, and then I scratched his ears. "Sorry, buddy. I don't need a third wheel. We'll be back." I stood up and gave Lockjaw a firm, "Stay." I was happy that when I started to walk away from the couch, he didn't move but dropped his head to his paws and drifted off.

With quickness, I made my way back around to the back and saw that the door was already open and the ladder was exposed. My heart started to race as I climbed, knowing what awaited me on the other side, and when I crested over the top, Tess was already lying on the makeshift bed, looking back at me. The hay crunched beneath my feet as I crawled over and laid down next to her, and I was glad when she didn't rush anything. She only moved to rest her head on my chest.

"I missed you," she admitted.

"I missed you," I said. "It was only four days, but it felt like—"

"Fourteen years?" Tess finished.

My hands laced into Tess' hair to caress her head gently. "Yeah."

Tess pointed up to where I'd pulled away some of the roof slats, offering a view of the night sky dotted with stars. The existing window offered a good view of the concert outside, and the new skylight allowed us to enjoy nature's beauty as well—a perfect backdrop for what would hopefully be the first of many nights together.

"I'm sorry," I said finally.

Tess tilted her head up to look at me. "For what?"

"It took me so long to just let go." My left arm was wrapped around her waist, and I twisted it, letting the discolored scarring shine in the moonlight. "I was so afraid of getting attached to someone, but the more time I spent with you, the more I realized that I didn't have a choice. You were already such a big part of my life, and when we reunited, it became clear that I don't want to let that go again."

"Me, too." Tess sat up on her forearms and looked down at me. "So, stay. Stay here. My dad can keep you safe. We'll figure out things with Caid. When he finally makes contact, we can figure out how to get him back here to Hoppa. We could get a bigger house so that he can live with us, too. Lockjaw would probably like him because he looks just like you."

That life sounded so perfect to me. It was everything I ever wanted, all wrapped up and topped with a bow. The truth was, I'd never been a lucky person, and I probably wasn't about to start.

But why couldn't I dream?

"Okay."

Tess' eyes widened. "Okay?"

"Yeah, okay." My thumb rubbed over her cheek as I admired her beautiful face, framed by the sea of stars behind her. "I don't want to leave you again, Tess. I…" I took a deep breath. "I'm in love with you."

A smile exploded across her face. "Well, look at you, sharing your feelings." She leaned down and kissed me. "I love you, too." At that point, her hands did snake under the hem of my t-shirt. "Does that mean we're done waiting?"

Bracing my foot on the hay, I held tight to Tess' back and flipped her until she was underneath me. I grabbed the base of my shirt, pulled it over my head, and tossed it aside. "Yeah, Tess." My breath was shortened and deep from the anticipation. "We're done fucking waiting."

Chapter Sixteen

Tess

Keeping my breath even while Colin slid his hands under my shirt and over my stomach was difficult. The many times we'd gotten close in the last few weeks skidded across my brain, but with his lips on mine and the weight of him pressed against me, there was no denying that we'd be interrupted no more.

His lips worked from mine down over my cheek and across my jaw. He got to my neck and took a hungry bite, following it up with a series of soft kisses, and I couldn't bring myself to be worried about the mark that would probably be left behind. Colin had very boldly taken me by the hand right in front of Taylor. That was as clear a sign as any that he wasn't threatened by Taylor, which was astounding but not unwelcome. If there was anything to be gained from Taylor's manic, possessive behavior, it was that it kept me single until Colin made his way back to me, not that I could ever thank him for that to his face.

Colin left my neck behind in favor of working his way down my cleavage, and he slid his hand up to meet his mouth at my breasts. I helped him along the way by pulling my shirt up and off, and I was glad that I'd made a last-minute decision to throw on a set of deep purple lingerie. A bustier top held my breasts like trophies on display, and the lace was a perfect overlay for my tan skin.

With his hands smoothing down my sides, Colin buried his face between my breasts and sent a trail of kisses down until he could lick over an awaiting nipple. I let out a moan, and my hands instinctively clawed into his hair to pull.

He lifted his head with a grunt. "I'm sorry, this is so sexy, but I don't want anything covering you up."

I grinned, my face hot, my heart thundering. "Do whatever you want."

It was all the permission he needed. I sat up enough so that he could unzip the bustier and unwrap it from my torso, and he appreciated my exposed chest like it was the best present on Christmas day. He peppered kisses along my collar bone, over my nipples, across my sternum, and down my stomach. When he got to my jean shorts, he popped the button and pulled him down, continuing his descent between my legs.

Coiling his arms around my thighs, Colin pulled me to meet his face, and I let out a drawn-out breath of relief as his tongue danced over me. Any ability I had to think logically fled from my body as I arched myself into the feeling of Colin below. With an expert mix of his mouth and his fingers, in no time at all, he made me a mess of incoherent sounds and shudders. One of my hands rested on the back of his head while the other grasped the sheets around me as if I needed to hold on to keep from floating up and out of the loft into the collection of stars above us.

"Colin," I moaned. "Don't stop."

And he didn't.

The desperation in my voice must have kicked him into overdrive. He buried his face even deeper, and his alternating licks and sucks got more fervent and hungrier. My legs shook as a strong orgasm reached out from the edges of my body, all corralling for my middle. The scream that left my mouth was louder than it was meant to be, but when I put the hand that wasn't fastened to Colin's head over my mouth to stifle my sounds, he brought a hand up to pull mine away.

He snaked his way up my body until he was hovering above my face. "Don't be quiet."

"We could get caught," I managed to respond.

"I don't care."

He ducked his head in and pressed his lips against mine, and though I could taste myself in the connection, I couldn't be bothered to care. I pushed against Colin's body and rolled him onto his back.

"My turn," I hummed.

Since we were clearly marking each other, I placed my lips on the spot right beneath the back left side of Colin's jaw and fastened myself there, licking and sucking as my hands snaked down to undo the buttons on Colin's jeans. I reached in and rubbed over the sheathed member and was delighted to feel that there was a lot of him just barely managing to stay contained within the fabric of his boxer shorts.

Lifting from the spot on Colin's neck, I grinned down at him. "You grew up."

Colin reached up and squeezed one of my breasts. "I'm not the only one."

So, time had been kind to us both.

With excited anticipation causing me to shake as I moved, I made my way down Colin's body. I made sure to take a little bit of extra time to kiss all of the discolored burn marks on Colin's left arm, chest, and stomach. He still had a few bandages wrapped around his bicep that were there earlier in the week, as well, but given that the discoloration was darkest there, I imagined that it was where the worst of the burns were. I kissed the top of the bandages and made a silent vow to myself to increase his confidence to the point that he could show me even that. The truth of the matter was, I found the scars kind of sexy. They gave him a uniqueness, and he wore them like a medal of honor—a sign that he was willing to do anything for the people he loved. Not wanting to disrupt the moment, though, after giving him that touch of attention, I made my way south.

The scarring near his hip continued past the hem of his pants, and for a brief second, I imagined him half-engulfed in flames. The part of my mind that told me that the police were just doing their jobs when they chased after Colin was forced beneath the part that wanted to hunt and kill the people who'd hurt him so badly. I kissed his hip and forced the thoughts out of my mind before turning my attention to his hard, waiting self.

I popped it out of his boxer shorts and grinned at the size. Whatever God had punished me with Taylor's unrelenting possessiveness was apologizing now with Colin. As if it weren't enough that he was good looking, smart, cool, and well-liked by my father, he was also well endowed. It was almost unfair. With my tongue outstretched, I leaned in and licked the tip. I marveled in Colin's immediate response, him opening his mouth and letting out a huff. I took my time, giving the outside of his length some attention, working my way up one side and down the other until Colin's hands combed into my hair. The way his dark, blown-out eyes were looking back at me when I looked up at him sent chills down my spine. Maintaining eye contact, I lowered myself, and his eyes drifted closed.

It'd been a while for me, but any concerns that I had that I wasn't doing a good job were quickly abated by Colin's sounds and gentle thrusts. I kept a hand fastened to his base and worked it up to meet my mouth as I worked down, and I enjoyed the taste of Colin's enjoyment filling my mouth.

When I started to pick up the pace a little, Colin pulled at my head to take me off him. He laughed. "Not yet."

"Are you sure?"

I tried to pull down again, but he dipped a hand under my chin and pulled me up. I straddled his waist, teasingly keeping my core floating just above him. Though I fully planned on teasing him a bit more, I looked down at Colin's face and got goosebumps. His eyes instantly locked on mine. My nakedness be damned, Colin was staring directly into my eyes, with his hands sliding slowly up my back. He wasn't smiling or smirking, and there wasn't even lust behind his eyes for a moment. He just watched me, and the longer we sat there, the more overexposed and out of control I felt.

"Why are you looking at me like that?" I finally asked when the silence became too much.

He shook his head. "I don't get it."

"Don't get what?"

"You." There was a breathless quality to his voice. "How? You're so… perfect."

My throat clenched, and my nose started to burn. Never in my life had someone looked at me that way before, spoken to me that way before—years of always just getting by.

It wasn't me who was perfect.

I reached behind myself, grabbed Colin's shaft, and guided it carefully to my entrance. With a slow pace, I lowered my hips and let Colin slide inside until I was seated against him with him fully inside. We let out a pair of matching moans. My eyes fluttered shut, and my head tossed back as I started to rise and fall. Colin's hands curved against my sides, and his fingers dug in. There was nothing in my brain that I could compare the feeling to. It was falling, and it was flying. It was fireworks against a night sky and white, fluffy clouds against a bright blue one. It was loud and, at the same time, silent. Heavy and, at the same time, light. I lifted myself and dropped myself, and it settled into a rhythm that my body quickly memorized and looped subconsciously, allowing my brain to take all of it in.

Years of Colin, both of knowing him and being without him, collided. He was beneath me. It was really and truly him. I wasn't aware of how much I missed him until he was back in my life, and just like that, I hinged myself inexplicably to him. Nothing, no one, would be allowed to come between us. He was my future. The deep connection as he thrust up into me was a premonition of things to come.

As the party roared on outside, Colin and I kept at it until both of our bodies were exhausted. How many minutes had passed? How many songs had played outside the window? When exactly did we stop and start again? When exactly did I drift off? When did I come to with his hands all over me, willing me into another round?

When I finally collapsed against Colin's chest, the number of orgasms I'd experienced past what I could keep track of, it was both too soon and just soon enough to keep me from passing out entirely.

Colin snickered in my ear. "Wow."

My head fell onto his chest as I attempted to catch my breath. "Yeah."

"It's not usually like that, right?" Colin asked. "I've had sex, but I've never had *that* before."

"No," I replied with a smile on my face. "It is *not* always like that." I craned my head to look up at him. "I blame you."

"Funny," he replied, twisting his head to look down into my eyes. "I was about to blame you."

His lips found mine in the moon-illuminated darkness, and my heart leaped up. If I had any stamina left, I might have tried to get us going again, but my legs were already sore. We'd done enough for tonight, and now that I knew he was staying, we had plenty of time.

Outside, a new band started playing, one of my favorite lesser-known bands from Hoppa. "Hey, wanna head to the party?"

"You expect me to dance after this?" Colin yelped.

"Maybe just sway?" I started to sit up, and my back screamed at me. "Oof, yeah. Definitely just swaying."

He grinned and placed a hand on my cheek. "We can do whatever you want."

Despite what both of our bodies were attempting, we managed to avoid falling back into each other again long enough to get dressed and then, slowly and carefully, descended the ladder to the clubhouse. The desert air was much cooler now that the sun had set, but the rager roared on despite that. Hand in hand, we walked back around to the front of the clubhouse, only stopping when I glanced toward the door and remembered Lockjaw.

"Oh, let me check on my dog," I said.

Colin released me, and I skipped over and opened up the clubhouse door. All the bliss I felt ran away when I saw Taylor sitting on the couch, petting a sleeping Lockjaw. I glanced up toward the wall that divided the bulk of the clubhouse from the loft. Though the ceilings were high and there was a lot of distance between the couch that Taylor was sitting on and where Colin and I were in the loft, I had no awareness of just how loud we'd been or if it could be heard from where he was.

"Hey," I greeted. "I was just coming to get Lockjaw." I had planned to get Lockjaw some food and water and leave him behind, but I had no idea what Taylor might do.

"He's pretty comfortable," he replied. "Why don't you just leave him here with me?"

"No." My head was shaking before I could stop it. "He probably wants to get out. Pee and stuff." I smacked my leg. "Come, Lockjaw." Lockjaw immediately hopped to attention and tried to jump off the couch, but Taylor held him down. Lockjaw struggled against Taylor's hold, even snapping at Taylor's hand to try and get free so that he could come to me. "Taylor, let him go."

Tears were already filling my eyes when Taylor lifted his arm, allowing Lockjaw to jump off the couch and rush over to me. I didn't give Taylor another look, only led Lockjaw back out the door. By the time I got to Colin, I was sobbing.

"Tess?" Colin rushed forward, but his attempts to grab me failed when I crouched to wrap my arms around Lockjaw. Colin knelt next to me and put his hand on my back. "What happened?"

"He definitely heard us," I said. "I thought he was gonna hurt Lockjaw." My mind tortured me, showing me images of Lockjaw and Colin cut up into pieces like Adley. "I'm afraid he's gonna hurt you." I hugged Lockjaw close, and he licked my face.

"Taylor?" Colin asked, and I nodded. He wrapped an arm around me and one around Lockjaw and pulled us close to him. "I told you already. I'm not afraid of him."

"You may not be," I sniffled, "but I am."

Chapter Seventeen

Phantom

All the mornings previous to that one, waking up alone either in my bed back in Rumble, in some shitty motel while I was on the run, or even in Tess' guest bed didn't even come close to the feeling of waking up in Tess' bed next to her. My arms were curled around her stomach, holding her close to me, and the smell of her coconut shampoo and the lingering scents of her sweet perfume wrapped around me and made me lightheaded in the best way.

She still had her eyes closed and was breathing in and out softly. There wasn't a thing in the world I wouldn't do for her. The night before was playing on repeat in my head, and not just the amazing lovemaking, but how quickly we left MiD after Taylor freaked her out about Lockjaw. My eyes drifted down to where the dog was curled at the foot of the bed, also snoozing away. For the fact that he was a dog, I'd grown quite attached to him, too. The way Tess panicked was understandable, and I was more than happy to bring her back home early and make love to her until Taylor's threats were far away from her mind. I just wished I could protect them permanently. Keep them out of his insane clutches.

After giving Tess a gentle kiss on the shoulder, I flipped back the covers on the bed and started to climb out. At first, I just sat up, but then I stood, being followed almost immediately by Lockjaw, who stirred and hopped down in response to my movements.

I crouched down and scratched Lockjaw's ears. "Morning, buddy." He stretched, sticking his butt in the air first as he stretched backward, then leaned forward, craning his neck up. "Want some breakfast?"

Lockjaw sprang into action and was out the bedroom door before I even stood back up. My neck cracked as I twisted my head to either side, and my back followed suit. Comfortable though the bed was, running around with Nick the whole day prior and then going at it with Tess more times than I could count after finally opening those flood gates had left my body more than a little sore. Baths weren't really my thing, but one might be in order to get my muscles back in line.

With a sigh, I took a step toward the doorway to go and get breakfast started, but my arm was snatched, and my weight gave as I was dragged back into the bed. Tess crawled until she was on top of me and kissed me before speaking.

"Where do you think you're going?" she asked, a sultry huskiness to her voice.

"I *was* going to go get breakfast started."

She lifted her satin, spaghetti-strap pajama top off and tossed it to the side. "Breakfast is right here."

There wasn't a world or parallel universe in which I would complain about that. I braced my hand on Tess' back and flipped her over until she was between the bed and me, and her hands were a flurry of movements over my already bare chest and stomach while we made out in earnest.

It'd been such a long time since I'd done something without the fear of rushing or what came next. Even though it was just a morning romp, I didn't worry about getting to breakfast, rushing off to Hoppa's to meet with the club, or anything that didn't involve drinking in as much of Tess and her beautiful body as I could.

When we'd finally finished, Tess started to laugh. It was a sweet sound, and I couldn't help but join in.

"What?" I asked.

"It's just so ironic," she responded. "For, like, a whole fucking month, getting you into bed was like pulling teeth. Now all I have to do is touch you, and"—she snapped her fingers in the air—"you're in."

I turned my head so that I could kiss her cheek. "That was *before*-Colin. I don't know what his problem was."

She looked at me. "Thank God we got rid of *that* guy."

"Good riddance." A gruff bark from the direction of the doorway brought our attention to a very irritated Lockjaw. I snorted. "Sorry, bud."

That time, when I tossed back the covers, Tess didn't stop me. I leaned down over her to give her one more kiss and then fought to drag myself out of the room and start breakfast. Lockjaw got his dry kernels first, but he ate them while staring at me as I cooked, having not gotten the additional cooked meats he usually got when the humans had their breakfast.

"He's such a brat," Tess said as she walked into the room. She bent over and looked down at him. "You *do* realize that most dogs aren't as spoiled as you."

He looked back at Tess as if to say, "What does that have to do with me?" and continued crunching away at his food as if we'd given him a servant's gruel for breakfast.

Tess and I enjoyed a light conversation while we ate the bacon and eggs that I made for us, then after getting a little distracted taking a shower, we finally found ourselves dressed and on our bikes, headed for Hoppa's.

It seemed like most of the club had already arrived when we were finally pulling into the lot, so we were intentional in not lingering. We headed straight in to convene with the club for the after-MiD meeting. Tess would probably have to attend some specific officer meetings, but I also had to find some time to talk to Nick about the Unchained Dogs and about the information he was working with that was sure to get them all killed. No truly good plan had occurred to me about how to get the information to Nick in a way that wasn't suspicious. The only best way I could think to get the knowledge across to him was to tell him the truth, and I was heavily considering it. I'd been living half a truth in Hoppa for long enough, and if I was planning to stick around, at the very least, Tess and Nick needed to know the truth. They both trusted me, and I trusted them. Surely if I told them the truth, they'd understand why I'd hidden it from the beginning, right?

Though they both needed to know the truth, who to tell first was a bigger conflict than I was expecting it to be. On the one hand, having Tess know before Nick could serve as a backup plan for when I told him. However, if Nick reacted badly and found out that Tess knew, as well, he could take it out on her, which was the last thing I wanted.

Tess would probably never forgive me, but I needed to come clean to Nick first. Only then could I tell her the truth. She wasn't an unreasonable person, and I was confident that if I could just get her to listen to me, she'd understand. The bigger battle was getting in and out of a conversation with just Nick, and I prayed that the truth didn't get a bullet in my brain the second that I said it. As soon as I had an opportunity to pull Nick aside, it was finally time to come clean.

"Hey!" Nick greeted Tess and me as we walked in. "You're late."

"Yeah, sorry. We overslept. Partied a little too hard," Tess explained.

Across the room, Taylor was glaring at us, and his glare was new. The hatred behind his eyes had his pupils dilated wider and looking much darker than normal. The only thing that really scared me about Taylor was that he was going to do something that I was going to have to kill him for. If he truly tried to hurt Tess, Lockjaw, Nick, or myself, I'd have no choice but to end him for good. Things in Rumble had been a little more murderous for me than I would have liked. I didn't want that life in Hoppa, but if Taylor continued to pose a threat to the new family I was building, I wouldn't stop until he was under the ground.

"Well, MiD went amazingly. Best turnout we've ever had and," he said and paused as he held up a stack of envelopes that he tapped against his hand. "Dues are the best they've ever been."

One by one, Nick went around the room, handing envelopes to Avery, Bernard, Bullet, whose real name I still hadn't learned, and Taylor. When he got to where Tess and I were situated near the bar, he handed an envelope to Tess, and then he held one out toward me.

So as not to insult Nick, I took the envelope despite the glares I was getting, and when Nick walked away, I leaned toward Tess. "What's this?" I whispered.

Tess took her envelope and tucked it into her back pocket. "He just said it's dues, weirdo."

Fortunately, only officered club members were around because it probably would have gone worse than it already was going with all of the officers looking at me like they wanted to chop my head off.

"I thought only officers got paid," I replied.

She side-eyed me. "Dad gave you a very specific and important role in preparation for MiD. He kept you by his side almost the entire time and had you join our exclusive, high-officer meeting. What do you think you are?"

It didn't take a bylaw expert to know that the treatment I was getting from Nick was far outside the realm of what was normal or accepted, but though I was nearly tempted to return the money and ask Nick to start treating me more normally, when I flipped through the earnings in the envelope, my eyes nearly came tumbling out of my skull.

There was close to five grand in the envelope.

I quickly folded the top down again and moved it to my back pocket as well. There was no way for me to know if everyone else got the same amount, or if Nick's preferential treatment was extending even to this, but there wasn't a single day when I was with the Unchained Dogs that I got more than a grand in a single sitting. It was more than enough to get me to Munich, and even enough to get Caid and me situated once I got there. Glancing over at Tess with Lockjaw at her side, my brain started to wander.

It was even enough for a second passenger and her animal companion.

"Jeez, you look like the man just offered to give you a prostate exam," Tess joked. "If you really don't want it, I'll take it."

I opened my mouth to respond, but Nick's voice cracked out and interrupted me before I could. "Okay. Now that the money's all squared away, let's talk about how the meeting went with the Raging Vipers and the Blazing Rebels." Avery's hand shot into the air, and Nick pointed at him. "Yes, Bullseye?"

"Squared, you know I'm not about to start questioning you, but this is getting a little out of hand." He motioned over toward me. "CJ isn't an officer. Payment, fine. He did a lot to help us get ready, but someone who's barely been around a month shouldn't get such sensitive information."

"CJ was in the meeting," Taylor said suddenly from the back of the bar.

"What?" Barnard barked. "Why? He's not an officer. Even we are not allowed in those meetings."

"I decided that having our new secretary in the meeting was important," Nick responded.

Secretary? Although his words flipped me upside down internally, I held my best poker face as everyone, Tess included, turned to look at me with shock.

"Secretary?" Tess asked before turning to look at her dad. "This may sound like a shock coming from me, but we didn't vote on that."

"Exactly!" Avery barked. "The bylaws say—"

"All officers must be nominated by an existing officer and voted and approved by a majority vote," Taylor finished. "All of which, CJ was not."

"I like CJ, obviously," Tess said, "but there's a certain way that we're supposed to do things."

The fear in Tess' voice was similar to that when her dad first invited me into the meeting the night before at MiD. In this situation, I agreed with her whole-heartedly. Nick's blatant disregard for the rules was going to get me killed.

"I'm fine with earning my position," I said.

"Nicky," Bullet started.

Suddenly, Nick pulled a gun out of his waistband, stuck it straight up in the air, and shot. The bullet pierced the bar ceiling with a deafening crack and sent splinters of wood flying everywhere. With just as much calmness as he might have if he were doing laundry, Nick set the gun down on the bar's corner and crossed his arms.

"I'm the fucking president," Nick said. "I know what's best for us." He pointed at me. "CJ is a new era that's going to take our club to the next level." The hushed tone in his voice was still terrifyingly loud in the silent room. "But, I understand your concerns, so let's do things the right way." He glared around the group. "I'm nominating CJ for the currently vacant position of Secretary of the Steel Knights. All in favor?"

Tess looked at me, and with a sigh, slowly raised her hand. "Aye."

Nick turned and tossed a leer down at Bullet, who, after a long stare off, raised his hand into the air. "Aye."

Bernard was next in Nick's crosshairs, and he held out for much longer than Bullet but soon realized Nick wasn't planning to relent. He held his hand up, not even extending his arm to do it. "Aye."

Nick's gaze shifted to Avery, but Avery had already caught on. He held up his hand. "Yeah, aye, Nicky," he said, but he shook his head and rolled his eyes.

Finally, Nick stared over at Tayor. "That's a majority vote."

Taylor glared back at his father. "So it is."

I locked eyes with Tess, and I knew that we thought the same thing at the same time.

This isn't good.

Suddenly, all of my plans were shifting dramatically. Nick was a great guy. He'd welcomed me into his club and his family, and he had treated me better than anyone ever had in my entire life. That didn't change the fact that he was forcing me into a position that wouldn't be good for me, him, or Tess.

He was making it so that staying wasn't an option.

The confidence that I had that I could tell Nick the truth about where I'd really come from and not have him behave irrationally was abating fast. He was becoming a wild horse, and if his brotherhood's reactions were any indicator, he'd never been like that before. I had to leave, and it had to be soon so that things could return to normal before everything he and those before him had built came crumbling down.

"So, with that sorted, does anyone have any objections to getting on with what I fucking wanted to get on with?" No one responded, so Nick grabbed his gun, slid it back into his waistband, and then continued. "Good. We spoke with the Blazing Rebels and the Raging Vipers last night, and they're going to help us in a few different ways, the main of which will be helping us plan an ambush. That will only happen after we've done some reconnaissance. One of you will take one of the members into Rumble to see what you can see. Is there a volunteer?"

When my hand went up, it was met with a melody of scoffs and gasps of disbelief.

Nick pointed at me. "CJ?"

"I don't think that's a good idea."

Nick recoiled a bit. "You don't?"

Luther was a paranoid psychopath who kept more guards stationed around Rumble than the Secret Service kept around the White House. If two people he'd never seen before came wandering into Rumble, he'd know within minutes, and if they weren't Oscar-worthy liars, he'd blow their brains out before they were a hundred yards inside the city limits.

"No. The plan you laid out about the rumor, that's good, but we shouldn't do it in the desert, and we shouldn't wait…" I didn't want to sound too knowledgeable, but I knew Luther had rushed off impulsively toward an enemy more than once, mostly because he was a lunatic who loved to fight. "If it were me, and I suddenly heard that my rival gang was battling with itself, I'd try and take immediate action, maybe even before I could rally all of my allies to help. I would assume there was enough conflict that I could take advantage with just a few men." I cleared my throat. "That's just me, though."

"So, you think we should use the rumor mill, but we shouldn't plan it out? We should have it happen immediately?" Nick asked.

"And here. It wouldn't make much sense if we weren't agreeing with one another to not be on our turf."

"He's right," Tess added. "The most believable story is if we're here."

Nick nodded. "Okay. I like it. The bar could suffer some damages, but it'd be worth it to keep those Dogs at bay. We'll get word out to the Rebels and Raging Vipers and have them tailor the rumor mill."

Nick seemed to be accepting of my suggestions as nothing more than just intelligence on the situation, it seemed, and as I scanned around the bar, staring with Tess and making my way around, the looks in my direction were indifferent, but there wasn't suspicion in anyone's eyes.

And then I locked eyes with Taylor, who, slowly but surely, developed a wide, ear-to-ear, evil, and malicious grin.

Chapter Eighteen

Tess

Weighing the options in my head, it almost seemed like it was the best idea to just get Colin out of the bar for the time being. My dad had, not so subtly, exerted a threatening dominance to get the club to vote Colin in as an officer, and that couldn't have improved his station in their eyes. Colin finally agreed to stay in Hoppa, and now my dad was pulling stunts like that, and it wasn't helping anyone.

As terrified and angry as it made me, Colin seemed unphased if not completely lost while thinking about something else. Whatever it was, I'd have to ask later. My goal at the moment was to give Colin and the other officers some time apart. Hopefully, once they got to know Colin better, they'd see that my dad was just doing what he thought was best, even if he strong-armed the club into doing it.

"Hey," I said to Colin once the MiD meeting was over. "Do you wanna take Lockjaw and head home?"

"Tess," Colin replied. "I've told you already—"

"I know." Though I wanted to put my hand on his face to help drive home my point, I didn't want to piss anyone off any more than they already were. "It's less about you and more about them. This is unlike my dad. Give them some time to take it all in and get some booze in 'em, then come back this afternoon. You may have to play a couple of games of pool to make up for it."

Colin rolled his eyes. "Do you think that would help?"

"I do, but only after they've had some time to cool down." With a foot on Lockjaw's rear, I scooted him a little forward. "Go do some male bonding or something."

"Okay," Colin said. "Text me later?"

"Of course."

Colin didn't linger after that. He tapped his leg, and I watched as Lockjaw bounded after him, and they both left the bar. Colin didn't have a special seat for Lockjaw like my bike did, but his bike was also more equipped to carry another rider, even if that rider was a meaty pit bull. They'd be fine getting home, at least.

Once Colin was gone, I tried to figure out what I needed to do first. The guys already didn't like me, and even if Bullseye did his best to treat me normally, and even if Bullet had lost himself for a second and asked for a bit of dating advice, I highly doubted that my involvement in the apparent coup my father was pulling was helping tip my needle in the right direction. They wanted me to interfere with my dad long before now, so if I knew them all, and I did, they were probably all blaming me a fair amount.

So that left talking to my dad. At first, I thought he just liked Colin, but I'd never seen that kind of aggression out of the man before in my life, at least not toward people he cared about. He loved the club and the guys in it like a family. I'd been blind to some of the stuff he'd already pulled because I love Colin and wanted him to be safe, but it was as if a shroud had been lifted. Colin would be okay regardless, but what my dad was doing was going to make it pretty goddamn difficult for either of us to get a leg up.

"Hey."

The way I jumped when Taylor's voice growled out behind me was borderline embarrassing. For God's sake, he was my brother, even if he had been losing it a little more as of late.

"Hi," I replied. "Sorry, I was thinking. You scared me."

"I'm requesting a formal audience," he said.

My eyebrows knitted together. "With dad? Just go ask to talk to him."

"With you."

If my heart could have fallen out of my chest, it would have. "Why do you want an audience with me?"

"Are you declining?"

The language was specific. Taylor knew the bylaws like some people knew the Bible. There was probably some fine print that required the president and vice president to hear out any requested audiences or something, so even though I would have rather jumped into the Grand Canyon than been alone with Taylor, I shook my head.

"Not at all. In the back?"

Taylor didn't respond, only led the way back behind the bar, past dad without saying anything to him, and back into the warehouse. All of me was shaking despite my best attempts to keep myself still, so I was glad when I was finally sinking down into a chair at the table. I could at least clench myself together and attempt to seem unafraid.

Taylor sat across from me and crossed his arms before leaning back in his chair. "How are you?"

"What do you want?"

A deep smile curled from one end of Taylor's face to the other. "You know, I was just thinking about when we were kids. Do you remember?"

His angle was a mystery, and it was terrifying. "Sure."

"I know I was much more of a homebody, but you… you were always so popular. Everyone loved you."

I cleared my throat. "I don't know about all that. I had friends."

Taylor leaned forward suddenly, his eyes bugging out and his smile growing impossibly larger. "That's right! You *did* have friends! Didn't you have one in particular? A boy."

My stomach collapsed in on itself, and I thought I was going to throw up. "Um, I knew several boys."

"No, no, no. You had one in particular. One who you were always following around like a little puppy dog. What was his name?" Taylor stared to the sky, and I said a silent prayer, but he snapped his fingers, and I knew it fell on deaf ears. "That's right! Colin. Colin Jones."

"Did I?" I stuttered. "Maybe? It was a long time ago."

"It's so interesting," Taylor said. "Don't you think that CJ could be short for Colin Jones?"

"CJ is CJ, so I don't know what you're insinuating."

Taylor nodded, leaning back in his chair. "That's good. It's good that it's not short for Colin Jones. It's good because I think we'd be in real trouble if it were Colin Jones."

I hunched my brow. "What do you mean?"

He shrugged. "Well, it doesn't matter. I looked up Colin Jones, but if CJ is not Colin Jones, then we don't need to be worried about Colin Jones, do we?"

I had no idea what he was talking about, but it was the most manic I'd ever seen Taylor, and I wanted out of the room as quickly as possible. "No. We don't have to worry about him."

Taylor smiled wide. "Well, good, then. That's it."

"That's it?" I asked.

He nodded. "That's it."

"Okay."

With quickness, I got up from the table and rushed out of the warehouse using the back door. I did need to talk to my dad, but that was going to have to wait. The fear coursing through me was too much to bear, and I just needed Colin. To look in his eyes and have him tell me that everything was going to be okay.

The dust kicked up as I kicked a leg over my bike and prepared to leave when some of Taylor's words ambled across my brain.

I looked up Colin Jones, but if CJ is not Colin Jones, then we don't need to be worried about Colin Jones, do we?

The feeling that I'd done something inexplicably dumb wouldn't shake away from my mind. Why didn't I do a quick search for Colin after he first showed up, claiming that his name was CJ and not Colin? I was suspicious by nature. My default assumption was that someone was lying to me, but ever since Colin showed up, I was able to take everything he'd said to me at face value.

But it was Colin. He loved me, and I loved him. That was what mattered.

I started my bike and pulled out of the Taphouse, bound for home. All I could think about was curling up with my boyfriend and my dog and just forgetting about the day's events. Hell, maybe we needed to plan a vacation and just get away from it all for a bit.

I think we'd be in real trouble if it were Colin Jones.

There was nothing troublesome about Colin. The urge to pull over to the side of the road and do a search on Colin from my phone was hard to resist, but I did it. I trusted him. He wouldn't lie to me, certainly not about anything major. Whatever Taylor said was said specifically to psych me out, and I wasn't going to let him get to me that way. Home was just a block away, and once I was there, I could forget all about Taylor.

That's good. It's good that it's not short for Colin Jones.

Why?

By the time I was pulling my bike into the driveway in front of my house, the curiosity had burned a hole straight through me. Before even unmounting my bike, I dragged my phone out of my pocket and opened it to a web browser. I typed in Colin's name, and for some reason, my heart was pounding. The search seemed to take longer than it should have, almost like it was preparing me. When the results splashed across the screen, I immediately felt sick to my stomach.

Unchained Dogs' Colin "Phantom" Jones goes free again with no evidence to tie him to the latest murder.

Phantom Jones is the real ghost story Rumble citizens are afraid of.

The Unchained Dogs' sharpened teeth are president's assassin, Colin Jones.

To be safe, I clicked a few of the articles, but they all returned images of Colin. Some of them were mugshots, and some of them were shots of him standing alongside the Unchained Dogs' President, Luther.

Biting back my emotions, I climbed off my bike and walked into the house. Colin was standing in the kitchen, making a sandwich, and Lockjaw was patiently waiting next to him, hoping for dropped spoils.

"Hey," he greeted me with a smile when I walked. "I wasn't expecting you back so soon. Want a sandwich?" My throat felt tight, and my nose burned. Tears were already rising to my eyes, but I held them back as much as I could. "Tess?" Colin asked.

"When you left Hoppa, where did you go?" I asked.

Colin froze. "What?"

"You heard me," I said. "When you left Hoppa, when your mom took you from here, where did you go?"

He stood staring at me for a long time, then finally sighed. "Rumble."

What a simple question I never thought to ask before that moment. "Ah," I responded. "What'd you get up to while you were there? Any jobs? School?"

Colin shook his head. "How'd you find out?"

My hand went to my mouth. "It's true? You're with the Dogs?"

"No," Colin responded quickly. "I'm… not anymore."

"Anymore!" I yelped. "You were with the Unchained Dogs! My family's rival motorcycle club?" My heart sank. "Oh my god. Are you here infiltrating us?"

"No, Tess." Colin walked around from behind the kitchen bar and attempted to approach me, but I quickly pulled my gun and held it on him. He stopped and held up his hands. "Tess. I swear. I'm not still with them."

"Why would I believe you? You've been lying to me this entire time!" I started to laugh. "Fuck! I'm so dumb! Of course, you've been lying to me. You didn't just show up out of the blue. You came here with a purpose."

"Please, please, just let me explain."

"Explain!" I cocked my gun. "You're lucky I don't bury bullets in you right now."

"Tess."

"Get out."

"Please, Tess."

"Get out!" I snapped my fingers. "Lockjaw." Lockjaw looked up at me, and his ears folded back over his head. He started to whine and back away from Colin. "What are you—"

"He's mine," Colin muttered.

"What?" I said.

"Lockjaw. I was his first owner."

Tears streamed down my face. No wonder he seemed to take to Colin differently from anyone else. "Please, just get out."

Colin opened his mouth to say something but then closed it. He grabbed his wallet and keys off the kitchen counter and rushed out the door. I stayed frozen in place while I listened to his bike start and rumble out of the driveway, and it wasn't until the rumble of his bike had totally faded from sight that I collapsed on the floor, tears flowing as I sobbed. Lockjaw whimpered as he timidly approached me, but when I held out my arms, he came into them fully and licked my face.

How could I have been so blind?

Chapter Nineteen

Phantom

"Room 208. I'd take the staircase on the left. The right's closer, but it's busted."

The keys scraped as I slid them across the dingy motel reception desk counter. "Thanks."

"Hey, you seem pretty down. You need some company tonight? I can get you a girl. Fifty bucks for a nice one. Twenty-five if looks don't matter."

Tess' pristine body, beautiful curves, auburn hair, and sparkling eyes cracked across my mind. "There's not a single person you could offer that would satisfy me."

"What? Like a guy? I got guys, too."

I turned my back to the motel clerk, followed his instruction down the row of motel rooms and up the staircase on the left end, then walked down to my room. The lock let out a dull thud as I turned my key in it, and when I opened the door, I actually let out a groan at the state of the room. The bed was covered in a coat of dust, and the television was already sparking like trying to turn it on would get me electrocuted.

On the run again.

Tossing my bag onto the bed, I walked over to the bathroom nook near the back of the room and peered into the mirror. My facial hair had gotten longer, but I quickly noticed something else.

There was a darkened hickey on my neck.

My stomach turned as I touched it and did my best to remember the feeling of Tess' soft lips on the spot. God, had I fucked up. I started to count my chickens before they hatched. All I had to do was come clean on my own, ease Tess into it, or say something to Nick before he started going haywire. Better yet, I shouldn't have come to Hoppa at all. I'd selfishly dragged Tess, Nick, and all of the Steel Knights into my mess.

Tess would have to tell Nick the truth eventually. It killed me to think that he would believe I betrayed his trust. I made a sincere promise never to hurt his club or his daughter, and I did both. Maybe one day, once everything had blown over and I was safely within Munich, I could call him and explain everything. He may not believe me, regardless, but I'd sleep better at night if I knew that I'd at least apologized to the man. He was willing to trust me with everything and even risked isolating himself inside his own club.

Someone who would do that did not deserve what I had done to him.

What I couldn't figure out was how Tess had come across the truth, to begin with. When I left her at Hoppa's not ten minutes earlier, she was none the wiser. Had she just broken down the advice I gave and figured it stemmed from somewhere?

The sound of shrill ringing brought me back to attention with a jump. It'd been such a long time since I heard my phone ring. Well, it had been before I left Rumble. Tess and I would text when we weren't together, but that wasn't very often since we'd been attached at the hip for the most part. I walked over to my bag on the dusty old bed and pulled it out. My heart dropped into my stomach.

It was a foreign number.

"Hello?" My attempts to keep my tone even as I answered failed.

"Colin?"

Dust drifted up as I fell down to sit on the bed. "Caid."

"Hey!"

Tears came to my eyes immediately. He sounded so healthy, so strong. "Hey. You…" I laughed. "You sound great."

He chuckled from the other side of the phone, and I couldn't stop myself from fishing out that old, burned picture of Caid in his hospital bed that I'd saved. The voice I was hearing sounded nothing like one that would go with the feeble body in the picture.

"The treatment is going really, really well. I feel the best I've felt in my entire life. I've been walking round the hospital all on my own. Well, my nurse walks with me, but I can keep myself up."

All of the times that I had to brace Caid on my shoulder and carry him from place to place flashed across my mind. To hear that he was walking on his own two feet was nearly too much to bear. "That's amazing."

"Yeah. I'm sorry I didn't call sooner, but, well, I was kind of nervous. I knew that things weren't great when I left, so I was afraid I might learn… bad news."

As much as I tried to shield Caid from my life, eventually, he caught on. Though he was holed up in a hospital for most of his life, he could still read my mind like it was his own. Mix that with the fact that he worked on his brain for every day that he couldn't work on his body, and one day he flat out asked me if I'd joined the mafia.

Close.

"Yeah. It was wild for a while, I'm not gonna lie to you, but…" I sighed. "I came back to Hoppa, and I reconnected with Tess. She's kept me safe."

"Wow! That's an old, old flame. Or is it rekindled now?"

"It was. I fucked it up."

"Don't tell me, you focused a little too much on your brother and didn't live your own life?" he spat back.

"I… no." Everything that had happened was a result of the fact that I lied to Tess and Nick, a lie that was necessary because of the money I stole—the money I stole so that I could take care of Caid. "Well, maybe a little."

He growled on the other end. "Listen. There's no more of that happening. I'm getting better by the day, so when I get back to the states, I'm helping you fix it. You were always crazy about Tess. You should be with her and be happy."

I remembered how quick Tess was to work Caid into her plans for our future. They barely even knew each other, and they were considering one another. If only I could have it all. "It's not really that easy anymore. Things got really complicated, and I bought a ticket to Munich earlier today."

"Seriously? You're coming here? Are you sure?"

"Yeah. We don't have to stay in Munich, but it's like you said, things are bad here. We'll be safer on your side of the pond."

"So, bring Tess with you," Caid said. "Munich's housing rules are really lax, and I'm sure we'd be able to get a place that we'd all be comfortable in. I'll give you two lots of private time, I promise."

For as sad as I was, a smile rose to my face. "I miss you."

"Gross. Don't be sentimental."

"Brat."

"Look, whatever you did wrong, just apologize. Lay out all your feelings one last time and let her make the final call. If she rejects you again, then yeah, just come to Munich, and we'll drown your sorrows in some good old-fashioned German beer.

"After the week I've had, that sounds good."

"Fine, but only if you make a valid attempt first."

I set the picture down and put my phone on speaker so that I could still hear as I navigated to my email to look at the confirmation for the tickets to Munich I'd purchased—one each for Tess and myself, and a companion ticket for Lockjaw. After leaving Hoppa's, making a run for it felt like the best option, so I purchased the tickets right away. My plan was to come clean to Tess and ask her to come with me that night, but she beat me to the punch.

"I'll try," I said. "I don't think she's gonna go for it."

"For once, fight for yourself. You don't have to fight for me anymore," Caid replied.

A grin crossed my face. "Yeah. Thanks."

"No problem. This is my new cell number, so call me when you land."

"I will." I gently tucked the picture back into my bag, excited for an opportunity soon to take a newer one. "Bye."

"Bye."

The line went dead, and I just sat looking at the Munich tickets on the screen. Tess' name on her ticket was enough to make my stomach burn. I'd gotten so excited, imagining starting a life with her. My mind was already traveling to things I'd never considered before—marriage, kids, a real and true life, and sharing myself with someone else in a way that I never had before.

Caid had been sick for our entire lives, so I never once thought that I'd have the opportunity to have something that wasn't taking care of him. Then, even when I did start to dream of it, it was always just that, dreaming. I knew my lot in life, and Tess always felt like a just-for-now luxury. She felt like something I could have for just a little while until I had to hang up any chance of happiness forever. Whether my life was ending with me running off to Munich to spend the rest of my days caring for Caid or dying with Luther's gun down my throat, I refused to let myself think that it could be anything other than just what I had to do to get by.

Somewhere along the way, I forgot my cynicism. It was almost as if I'd taken on some of Tess' impulsive, fiery nature and decided that I would just let the cards fall where they may. I lost myself, but at the same time, I found myself. The happiness I'd long since written off was, all of a sudden, in the palm of my hand. Days spent with Tess, evenings drinking at the Taphouse, early mornings working on my bike with Lockjaw curled up nearby—it was real, and it was happy, and it was mine.

I didn't want to give that up.

Quickly, I slid my phone into my pocket and grabbed my bike and room keys. A cabinet in the chipping wooden entertainment center was a perfect place to stash my bag, so I opened the cabinet and shoved my bag in, then left the room, locking the door behind me.

Forgetting the advice that I'd given, I took the right staircase down and nearly killed myself as I hopped over the broken slabs of stairs, but I was too anxious to care. My bike sent birds and other critters scattering as I started it up and sped out onto the street and back onto the highway toward Hoppa.

Caid was right.

I would lay everything out in front of Tess, the truth, and pray that she would see the truth in my words and give me one last chance to seize the happiness I suddenly wanted so badly.

Chapter Twenty

Tess

My fingers skated back and forth across Lockjaw's fur in a rhythmic pattern. He was lying on the bathroom floor next to the bathroom, which was barely illuminated by the lights of the candles I'd lit and scattered around before running a piping-hot bubble bath and climbing in. My head was pounding, a feeling that was only paralleled by the continuous cracking in my heart. Every time it panged in my chest, I rubbed the spot as though it were merely an itch I could scratch away.

Colin had only been with me for about a month's time, but my place already reminded me of him. I never wanted to be one of those people who had to replace everything they owned and move to an entirely different place after a breakup, but that might be in order. My bathroom smelled of the body wash that he'd purchased not long after he arrived, the body wash that he's used every day, twice a day. A couple of men's razors were balanced on the edge of the tub and sink, and there was a black towel hanging next to my purple one on the rack against the wall.

All of his clothes were still in the guest bedroom, and the spare pair of boots he'd worn was still askew by the front door. When he left, I tried sitting on the couch, but having sat there almost exclusively with Colin at my side for the past month sent a flurry of painful twists through my stomach.

Even my bed smelled like him, so when I face planted on it to cry my eyes out after I tried and failed to do so on the couch, the pain just got worse. Even Lockjaw seemed to have the wind knocked from his sails, and eventually, the only thing I could think to do was pour myself the largest glass of wine, climb into a bath so hot that it was all I could think about, and pet my poor dog until he went to sleep and could stop worrying about never seeing his first master again.

Again.

It turns out, Lockjaw and I had even more in common than I realized. We both had bad tempers, we were both meat-eaters, and we'd both had to say goodbye to Colin more times than we wanted to. Just like Colin's mom had taken him from me when he was a kid, I took Lockjaw from Colin in the same way. At least we could bond over this heartache, or so I hoped, anyway.

With the bathwater getting tepid, there was no reason to stay in it, so I used my foot to kick out the stopper, and the hiss of the draining water stirred Lockjaw. I climbed out of the tub and reached out for my purple towel, and at the last second, I grabbed Colin's. I wrapped it around myself and took a deep breath, letting his comforting smell wrap around me. Was it stupid? Yes, but I did it anyway.

Tucking the towel around me and putting my hair up in a bun on top of my head, I motioned Lockjaw out of the bathroom, and he padded out with me right behind him. Food was probably a good idea, though all I felt like doing in the wake of Colin's revelation was to just go to bed and try to forget that any of it ever happened. My plan was to call it a summer fling and pretend that I didn't let a huge blind spot land me madly, head over heels in love with a man whose real story I didn't even know. I would probably never find someone who made me feel the way he did. I could only survive knowing that I had to go back to my fear-ridden life where Taylor controlled my every action if I lied to myself and said that Colin was nothing more than a way to pass the time.

A great way to pass the time.

I turned to the left out of the bathroom and made my way down the hall toward my bedroom. Lockjaw's claws clacked against the wood floors as we moved, and I was just about to climb into bed when I heard a knock at the door.

"Well, now, who do we think that could be, boy?" I said aloud to Lockjaw.

My go-to gun was with the rest of my stuff on the kitchen counter, so I grabbed my back up from the top drawer of my nightstand and crept my way down the hallway toward the door. The second I lifted my gun to hold it out as I reached for the door handle, Lockjaw started letting out a low, warning growl for whatever poor soul was on the other side.

"Who is it?" I called out.

"Tess."

My heart dropped into my stomach as Colin's voice broke across the threshold. Lockjaw stopped growling in an instant and started to whine as he scratched against the frame of the door. With my gun still pointed, I grabbed the door handle and twisted it, slowly pulling it aside and filling my vision with Colin once again.

His eyes immediately danced down and up again, and I tried to ignore the way my body immediately ran hot. "You're wearing my towel," he said.

"What do you want?" I growled.

"You deserve the truth. All of it," Colin responded. "Caid told me to just come here and lay out all my feelings and let you decide. So that's what I'm doing."

I scoffed. "Oh, you spoke with Caid? So, he was also part of the lie?"

"No," Colin responded. "Caid called. I just got off the phone with him. It was the first time I've talked to him in two months. I can show you the Munich phone number."

I raised an eyebrow. "Show me."

Colin dipped his hand into his pocket and pulled out his cell phone. With a few quick clicks, he was to his phone log, and he turned the phone to face me so I could see it properly. The last number was in a format that was a little bizarre and had an international calling code in front of it.

I stood to the side so he could come in. "I'm keeping my gun pulled."

"I understand." Colin passed me as he entered the house, and Lockjaw bounded happily next to him. Colin walked over and sat on his spot on the couch and motioned to mine. He still had a pull on me that was hard to deny, and I found myself drifting over to sit, even if it was ill-advised. "Thanks for hearing me out."

"You've got about ten minutes," I spat back.

"Understood. I swear, after this, you'll never see me again."

Even with my gun outstretched in Colin's direction, hearing those words broke my heart all over again. I was so angry with him, but still, so much of me couldn't make peace with never seeing him again. "Fine."

"First of all, and I swear this is not meant to be an excuse, not everything I told you was a lie," Colin began.

"How nice," I replied flatly.

"My drunk, high mother dragged Caid and me out to Rumble, chasing one of her suppliers promises to make her rich. To this day, I have no idea what she believed he was going to do for her, but he really just wanted her in Rumble because it was his turf and he could dope her up double that way. Any money that came into our household was wasted on drugs, and with as sick as Caid was, that was a problem. I had no choice. I wandered into the Unchained Dogs' club and asked for a job. I dropped out of high school and started running with them. I was just an errand boy, at first, responsible for shit like securing and raising the new mascot pit bull puppy."

I looked over at Lockjaw, who was staring at Colin with his tail wagging back and forth. "I took him from you."

"And I got the shit beat out of me for it, too, because he was fucking expensive."

"You want an apology?" I hissed.

Colin shook his head. "No. You don't owe me anything. He probably had a much better home here than he would have had with Luther's crazy ass." He sighed. "Anyway, they started to pay me, and Luther kept offering me more if I would do more shit. Eventually, I ended up working for him as an assassin. If I got caught trying to take someone out, I got hell for it, so I was careful. In and out, quietly. As little damage as possible, and as quick and painless as possible."

"Just like those prospects."

Colin actually chuckled. "Yeah. They were easy pickings."

I furrowed my brow. It'd be much easier to be angry at him if he weren't so good looking. "Did you really steal money from a bank?"

Colin stuck out a finger. "I never told you I stole it from a bank."

"Yes, you did."

"No. I said I took it from a place where they keep a lot of money."

Though he was right, his reliance on semantics made me angry. How many other carefully phrased sentences had he thrown me in the past month? "You must want me to blow a hole in your head."

"I'm sorry." Colin shook his head. "No, I stole it from Luther. They don't have anyone like Bullet, and I realized that they were keeping their books really loose. Caid and I heard about this experimental treatment that could potentially cure his condition, but not only did it require him to fly to Germany, the treatment alone cost forty-five thousand dollars. I stole fifty."

"That's insane."

"I didn't have a choice! Caid was getting worse. He was gonna die, Tess."

The sincerity in Colin's eyes was similar to what I'd seen before. When he first told me he loved me, his eyes were the same. "So, they were the ones chasing you when you crashed."

"No," Colin grumbled. "I didn't crash. They set my house on fire. With me in it."

"Jesus."

"I really didn't think that he would figure it out so fast, but Luther's smarter than I thought. My plan was to get Caid situated, earn a few more pay checks, and then leave for Germany. Even when I came here, that was always the plan."

"So, you always planned to leave me?" I asked, my stomach knotting at the phrase.

"Tess." The seriousness in Colin's voice brought my gaze up to his. "When I first came to Hoppa, I thought, 'Yeah, I'll get some help and be gone in a week.'" His hand drifted past my gun to settle on my face. "That was all it took for you to fuck everything up."

"Me?"

"Yeah. Being back with you again, it was like everything that I didn't know I was dreaming of. I talked to your dad, and he…" his voice trailed off.

Finally, I set my gun down on the coffee table. "What, Colin?" He shook his head, and I stabbed a finger into his face. "Hey! You told me you were going to tell me the whole truth."

He looked into my eyes. "I did, but I don't want you to get hurt."

The scoff that left my mouth was so loud that it made Lockjaw jump. "I think it's a little late for that."

"Yeah," he replied. "I spoke with your dad. He told me he wanted to turn the club over to you but that the guys would never go for it. He was hoping that he could one day hand it to me, and then you and I could lead it together."

Any wind left in my sails was knocked clean out of me with that gut punch. "He wasn't even gonna try?"

"It broke his heart, but…" Colin shook his head.

"Wow. Turns out all the men in my life are complete bullshit." I swatted Colin's hand away from my face as I stood up and walked away from the couch a few feet. "So, what? You were gonna do that?"

"I honestly didn't know what I was gonna do, but then your dad pulled that stunt today, and I knew I couldn't stay here. As soon as I got home, I bought a ticket to Munich."

"What? Were you just gonna ghost? Truly live up to the name Phantom?"

"I should have been more specific." Colin lifted his phone up again, clicked through it, and then held it out toward me. With a few careful steps forward, I grabbed his phone and stepped backward. Looking down at the screen, I could see a confirmation that there was a ticket under Colin's name to Munich, but there were two others with it. There was a ticket for me and one for Lockjaw. "I wanted you to come with me."

Colin stood up and walked across the room to me. He brought his hands up to cup my face, and as much as I wanted to push him away, I couldn't. When it came to Colin, I was powerless.

"I'm not asking you to forgive me, but I needed you to know how much I love you. How much all of my plans got screwed up the second I laid eyes on you again. I don't want to go back to a life without you in it, but if you say that's what you want me to do, I'll do it. I don't want to hurt you any more than I already have."

Thoughts raced through my mind at a mile a minute. Had I reached a ceiling within the club? I was never going to be president, or even get a shot? Colin had wanted, maybe still wanted, to take me with him to Germany. If there was nothing left for me in Hoppa, why wouldn't I start over with the man of my dreams in Germany? Then again, it seemed like every time I took a chance on someone, they let me down.

What was the right answer?

Colin leaned in and gently set his lips on mine. He didn't linger. His kiss was barely there, and then he was away from me again. "Thank you for listening. I'll go."

He pulled his hands away from me and turned his back to me, and I panicked. The thought that Colin may walk out that door and that I would never see him again broke me. When I was with Colin, I didn't feel like there was nothing left for me.

A future in Germany? One where I could start over and grow? That was what I wanted.

I reached out, grabbed his arm, and pulled him back to me. In a swift motion, he wrapped his arms around me and lifted me off the ground. Our lips smashed together, and my hands clawed helplessly at him, trying to find something to take away the feeling of free-falling that he gave me. He lowered me onto the bed, quickly discarding the towel that was the only thing keeping me hidden from his hands, and I made quick work of removing his shirt and unbuttoning his pants, which he pulled down with his boxers and kicked aside.

I stood and pushed him to sit on the edge of the bed, and then I crawled on top of him. He hooked a finger under the hair tie that held my hair up and yanked it out, and as I pressed my lips back to his again, he guided his already hard self to my entrance, and I lowered over. I curled my arms around his shoulders and held on tight as I moved in a rhythm of rising and falling.

Colin's hands slotted into the curves of my waist, and his fingers clawed into me with the same desperation with which my hands had moved earlier. How was it possible for one person to destroy me so much and, at the same time, build me up? His lips worked away from mine and down my neck, and before I could stop them, tears were slipping down my cheeks. When Colin noticed them, he tilted my head down so that he could kiss away the drops.

"I'm so sorry for hurting you and lying to you," he said. "I'll never do it again."

"You'd better not," I huffed back. "Or I really will shoot you."

He grinned. "I accept the terms." He cupped my chin in his hand. "I love you."

He didn't necessarily deserve to hear it just yet, but I couldn't stop myself from responding, "I love you, too."

I lost track of time as we poured into each other again and again and again. It seemed that

Colin was dedicated to kissing every inch of me, feeling every inch of me. I couldn't have strung coherent sentences together if someone had offered me millions of dollars to do so. Instead, I let myself slip safely beneath the surface of Colin's waters, drowning in him and letting him be my air when I ran out. Even when the rising sun started to peek through the window, we didn't stop, not until it was the only option we had left.

"When are the flights to Munich?" I asked, and I was legitimately impressed that I was able to say it.

"Not until tomorrow. I have a motel room, though. It's disgusting, but it's outside Hoppa. We can stay there until it's time."

"What do I tell my dad?" I asked.

"Oh, that's not something you'll have to worry about." Colin's and my heads whipped toward the bedroom door, where Taylor was standing in the doorframe. "I'll take care of telling him *everything*."

Chapter Twenty-One

Phantom

Tess and I were sitting ducks when we realized that Taylor had gotten into the house. We were both totally naked, and neither of us had guns within arm's reach. It was dumb of me to get caught up in her when we were still in Hoppa, but when she pulled me back, any resistance in me dissipated. That small indicator that she was willing to forgive me took all the logical, methodical parts of my brain and scattered them across the desert.

"Taylor," Tess said.

Taylor shook his head like a disappointed dad. "I honestly expected more from you, Tess. I handed you the truth on a silver platter. Did you not figure it out, or are you so dumb that you're going to look past it?"

"Colin's past has nothing to do with his present," Tess replied.

Taylor's face lit up at that response. "Ah, so you did figure it out."

"You," I hissed.

Taylor was how Tess figured out the truth about me. In truth, I only had myself to blame. Taylor had been an issue from the beginning, and though I knew he was around back when Tess and I were friends, I never saw him much, and I was hoping he wouldn't remember me. It was a possibility I didn't see, or rather, one I didn't want to see. A hole that large would have willed me away from Tess before I even followed after her when I first came to Hoppa. Whether consciously or subconsciously, I put that fear out of my mind and pretended like it wouldn't be an issue.

Well, now it was, and that's what I got for ignoring my better nature.

"You should have left Hoppa when you had the chance," Taylor said. "Now I get to kill you, and I'm going to do it in full respect of the bylaws." He turned his back and waved a hand through the air. "See ya later."

Neither Tess nor I was in any position to get up and run after him, so we both just sat in stunned silence, each letting out a sigh of relief when we heard Lockjaw's distant growls before the door opened and slammed shut, followed by the sound of Lockjaw's claws on the floor as he came to investigate.

"We have to go now," I said. "The motel is about an hour out of Hoppa. Take only what you need. We can replace our stuff when we get to Munich."

I sprang up out of bed, but Tess reached out a hand and took my arm. "Colin, we can't run."

"We have to. Your dad is going to order him to kill me. In a straight up fight, I can defend myself, but if all the Knights are holding me down, I don't stand a chance."

"He wouldn't do that," Tess yelped. "My dad likes you. Hell, he considered giving his entire fucking club to you. He knows that Taylor is batshit. He'll listen to reason."

"I was an Unchained Dog, Tess." I crouched on the bed and took her head into my hands. "I love you so much, but if I go back there, I won't leave."

"He'll listen," Tess said. "Please, just trust me."

There was nothing about what she was saying that made any logical sense. I needed to get out of Hoppa, not go to the epicenter of where I'd committed the most transgressions. Still, Tess had given me the benefit of the doubt more than once, and so did Nick, for that matter. She deserved a little bit of faith. If we could solve this one last problem, Caid and a brand-new life awaited us in Germany.

"Okay, baby," I said finally. "I trust you."

She kissed me. "Thank you. Get dressed. We'll leave in five minutes."

My fight or flight told me to flee, so the closer I got to Hoppa's Taphouse, the closer I felt to a meltdown. Tess clung tightly to my hand as I drove us in her car to the Taphouse and parked in one of the designated Steel Knights spots. My stomach did backflips as we walked through the front door and nearly emptied out when we walked into the bar and saw Nick standing there, waiting with all of the Steel Knights, Taylor included, behind him like a pack of wolves that were ready to pounce.

He locked eyes with me. "Is it true? You're a Dog?"

I held my head up high. "I used to be. I stole a shit ton of money from 'em, and there's a hit out on me."

Nick's jaw clenched, and in all of the tense interactions I'd seen him have with the other club members, nothing compared to the way he bore into me. "I trusted you." He looked at Tess. "Both of you."

"This was all me," I said. "Tess had no idea."

"She knew you weren't CJ," Nick said. "She wagered her position on you. She knew what she was doing, and she will pay with the loss of that position."

Even though we were planning to leave, Tess deflated next to me when Nick said the words. "I understand."

"As for you," Nick said. "Your actions break more than one of our bylaws. Hiding your true identity is strictly forbidden, as is having served for a rival club. The latter of these is considered betrayal in the highest regard and is punishable in our bylaws by death." He shook his head at me before turning to look at Taylor. "As Sergeant at Arms, the task will be Taylor's."

"Daddy!" Tess barked. "You're not even going to hear him out?"

"There's nothing to hear," Nick replied, but there was desperation and sadness in his eyes when he looked at Tess. "I've been outvoted."

"Our bylaws give anyone who has been punished with execution twenty-four hours to get their affairs in order," Tess spat back. "Colin's owed that."

"He's owed nothing," Taylor said. "He lied."

"Fine," Nick said. "He can take his twenty-four hours."

"Nicky, don't be stupid," Bernard said. "He'll just run."

"I won't run," I said. "I'll accept my punishment as I've earned it."

"These aren't bent rules, Bucky. She's right. Our bylaws explicitly state that." He looked back at Taylor. "Correct?"

Taylor glared at me. "They do." He looked at Bucky. "Let it go. This will be the last of Dear Old Dad's favoritism."

"Get out, both of you," Nick ordered, and neither Tess nor I hesitated.

We turned and rushed out of the bar, and the second we got outside, Tess started to panic. "I'm sorry. I'm so sorry. I honestly thought he would listen."

"He wanted to," I said. "He ran out their patience."

"I never should have made you come." She grabbed my hand and pulled. "Come on. We gotta go."

We climbed back into Tess' car and took the fastest route home, speeding while we were at it. Tess packed a few of her essentials while I grabbed a couple of changes of clothes from the guest bedroom and grabbed some of Lockjaw's dog food.

"We'll take the car," I told her. "We can leave our bikes in the garage and leave the lights on so that they think we're here if they come by."

Tess let out a deep sigh. "Okay."

"I know. I don't want to leave them, either, but it'll be better this way." I kissed her on the forehead. "Let's go."

We didn't spend more than five minutes in her house before we were back in the car with me at the helm. We both spared longing gazes at our bikes as I backed out, but then we turned onto the road headed out of town, leaving our bikes and, unfortunately, our Hoppa lives behind.

The motel I'd secured was about an hour outside of Hoppa. It wasn't any place I would ordinarily want to bring Tess or Lockjaw, but we were making do with what we had. It was just one night. By tomorrow afternoon, we'd be on a plane on our way to Munich.

We got in the dingy and dirty room, and Tess immediately worked to make the place as comfortable as possible. She took her time, cleaning as much of the dust—and God knew what else—off every surface in the room using a rag that she found in the bathroom. In truth, her efforts were pointless. Her cleaning seemed more like a nervous tick than anything else, so when I caught her trying to clean the exact same spot over and over, I grabbed her and pulled her over to the bed to lay next to me.

"I'm sorry, Tess. I never wanted it to be like this."

"Maybe this is always how it was meant to be," she replied. "I was always hoping that if I just stuck it out, things would change, but ten years is a pretty good indicator that's not the case, eh?"

"Some people just don't want to change," I said. "I'm just sorry that it took me coming here, lying to you, and disturbing your life for you to realize it."

Tess' fingers gently caressed the side of my face. "You still have a lot of making up to do for those lies, by the way."

"Oh, yeah?" I looked down at her. "We do have a lot of time." She rolled over and straddled me, and my hands were already sliding up under her shirt when I heard a sound that made me sick to my stomach. I clung onto her to stop her moving. "Shh. Do you hear that?"

Tess twisted her head a little and listened, and her face registered a fear that let me know she could hear it, too. We could both hear the distant roar of multiple motorcycles, and it was getting louder.

I carefully set Tess to the side and climbed out of bed. The door unlatching was louder than I might have liked it to be, but I ignored that fact and poked my head out the door. The open layout of the motel rooms allowed me to look right out onto the road, and as much as it made my stomach knot up to stand there and wait for the sound to reach me, doing anything other than that didn't make any sense. I stood in wait, staring up the road toward Hoppa, waiting to see the Steel Knights come cresting over the horizon.

"Is it them?" Tess asked, but I just shook my head and remained quiet.

And then came the only thing worse that could possibly happen. The bikes' rumble finally reached the motel, but it wasn't Steel Knight bikes heading out of Hoppa. My heart and head pounded unbearably as I watched a familiar sleek, gray and black, modern street bike go flying past the motel. Even though the rider was wearing a helmet, his long blond hair blowing out of the back in the wind was unmistakable.

"It's Luther," I huffed.

"What!" Tess yelped, and a second later, she was at my side, looking out the window.

We watched in horror as at least a dozen Unchained Dogs' bikes rode past the motel. Any relief that I had that they weren't turning into the motel abated in a flash. I wasn't their target.

Hoppa was.

"They're going to the Knights."

"Fuck," Tess said. "What do we do?"

It was my fault. I was the one who gave Nick the idea to start a rumor mill to bring the Unchained Dogs to Hoppa sooner rather than later. Luther acted impulsively, exactly as I expected. The ten or twelve bikes he had with him weren't a nick in his total army, but I'd originally planned to be there when the Unchained Dogs arrived.

"We have to go back," I said.

"What?" Tess said.

She grabbed my arm, pulled me back inside the motel room, and shut the door. "You want to go back?"

"They need us, Tess," I said.

Her eyes shimmered with concern, but I could see the gears turning in her head as well. "We may not leave Hoppa if we go back."

"I know."

Tess reached into her back pocket and pulled out her go-to brass knuckles. "All right. Let's go."

Chapter Twenty-Two

Phantom

All I could think about as Tess and I drove at top speed back into Hoppa was how, for the first time in my entire life, I was truly happy that I'd left my bike behind. All it would have taken for the Dogs to stop to investigate was for one of them to glance to the right and see a pair of bikes. Luther would have recognized my bike without an issue. Bless my logical brain because Tess and I would be face down in a ditch instead of on our way back to Hoppa if I hadn't thought to take the car.

It was almost poetic justice. All I'd done for the past two months was try and put as much space between the Unchained Dogs and myself as possible. In any other circumstance, I'd be cutting my losses and living up to my name, Phantom. Tess and I could have well left the Unchained Dogs and Steel Knights to battle it out instead of hunt us down, and by the time the dust cleared and anyone was on our trail again, we'd be sixty thousand feet in the air.

But something about the last month I'd spent in Hoppa just wouldn't let me leave things that way.

Nick had taken me in like a son, and whether or not they agreed with my presence there, the Steel Knights accepted me. With more time, things might have been different—for me, at least. In a year or two, I could have had people looking at Tess the way she deserved to be looked at.

Unfortunately, time just wasn't something I had.

I still felt obligated to help defend the club that had kept me hidden and safe for a month, and maybe I was looking for an opportunity to face Luther again, too. Maybe I was looking for a final battle with the man who'd built me and broken me down. If Tess and I could make it in and out of this fight alive, we could put this world behind us and start a new life somewhere where no one was looking for us, where no one was judging us.

This seemed like a fair final obstacle before my happy life.

In the time that we were driving, we never caught up to the bikes, so the fear that we were too late slowly washed over Tess and me the closer we got to the Taphouse. As we were crossing the city limits into Hoppa, Tess slid on her brass knuckles and pulled out her gun. A few minutes later, we turned onto the block where the Taphouse was, and we saw that all of the Unchained Dogs' bikes were parked haphazardly outside.

Two of the Dogs were standing in front of the door with their arms crossed. I looked over at Tess, expecting her to be afraid, but she had a wide grin on her face. She twisted her head to one side, and her neck cracked. "I'm so fucking ready for this."

She looked so sexy as she geared up for a fight, and it sent a jolt of excitement rushing south, but we had no time for that. Instead, I laughed and parked the car outside the Taphouse, and we climbed out. We walked up to the front door, and I could see that the men standing out front were two of Luther's watchdogs, a pair of burlier men who insisted on vests with no undershirts, Fred "Bedrock" Marcus and Anthony "Fat Cat" Kirio.

"Fuck," Bedrock growled when he saw me. "Is that fucking Phantom?"

Fat Cat looked right at me, and the fear that flashed across his eyes gave me a needed boost of confidence. He looked back toward the Taphouse and then back at me. "I ain't letting you in there."

"No?" I asked. "Then meet my better-half, Valkyrie."

Tess didn't stop in her stride. She marched right up to Fat Cat and decked him in the face. Bedrock went for his gun, but Tess quickly kicked him in his groin and sent her brass-armed fist crashing against his face.

"Go," Tess said. "I got this."

There was no reason for me to hesitate. I stepped over her—she was easily handling Fat Cat and Bedrock—and passed through the front doors of Hoppa's. Unexpectedly, the place was totally empty, but I could hear scuffling coming from the warehouse. I used both hands to hoist myself onto and over the bar. I rushed through the door into the kitchen and then through the door into the warehouse, where all hell was breaking loose. Unchained Dogs were battling Steel Knights left and right, and though no one seemed to have the upper hand, there was one Unchained Dog that had the better of the Steel Knight he was up against.

Luther was looming above Nick, who knelt on the ground with a gun pressed to his forehead.

"Where's that pretty daughter of yours?" Luther asked Nick. "I was *really* hoping to see her, Nicky."

I took a few steps into the warehouse so that I could clearly be heard when I yelled, "How about me instead?"

Everyone stopped in their tracks and turned to look at me. Luther's head turn was slow like he was savoring the moment. To my relief, he completely turned his back to Nick and faced me.

"Well, now isn't this an unexpected treat," Luther started. "You sure do know how to get around, I'll give you that."

Nick's eyes widened. "CJ! Watch out!"

Though Luther was nowhere near me, I heeded the warning and ducked, shuffling to the side as I did so. What just narrowly missed my head was a large, wide machete blade. The wind of it brushed through my hair as I dodged to the side, and when I finally got my bearings, I looked up into Taylor's cold, unrelenting eyes.

"Oh, looks like you've made friends all over the place," Luther said with a laugh. "Maybe

I'll save this one, and we can kill you together. Just let me finish things off here first."

Luther started to turn back toward Nick while Taylor advanced on me. I perched myself into a crouch and waited for Taylor's next swing. His blade caught the edge of my shirt and managed to slice through some of the skin underneath, but I got out from under him. I tackled Nick backward under his meeting table and used a boot to kick it over so that it shielded us from the fray. Looking to my left and right, Avery and Bernard were holding their own, and a couple of the Unchained Dogs were already down. The Steel Knights had the upper hand, but between Luther and Taylor, there was more than enough to tip the balance.

I reached over the table and fired, narrowly missing Luther, who immediately fired back. When I ducked back down next to Nick, he laughed. "You're well-liked."

"Yeah, I like to leave an impression." Once again, I lifted my head up, but that time, Taylor had advanced and swung, nearly getting me. "Shit. Your son is batshit."

"Yeah, I'm learning that. Crawl."

Following Nick's orders, I crawled forward, and he pulled the table, keeping it blocking us like a shield. "Thank God I invested in the strongest wood." The table collided with the wall, creating a sort of nook in which we were positioned against the wall, leaving us less exposed due to the tabletop blocking the majority of the fighting. "CJ, why are you here? I gave you twenty-four hours so that you could run."

"We saw them coming and had to come back," I replied.

"We?"

"Yeah. Tess is outside, putting in work."

"You guys gotta get out of here," Nick said. "Grab Tess and go."

"We'll see this through to the end."

Nick shook his head. "As long as Taylor is here, neither of you will be safe. You gave us the edge we needed by showing up and surprising 'em, but now you gotta go." He put a hand on my shoulder. "Trust me. Get out of here. Take care of my girl."

I nodded. "I will. I promise."

Nick pulled his gun out, and I held mine up, and at the same time, we crawled out of the sides of the table and jumped into the insanity. Nick went for Luther, and because Luther had his eyes on me, Nick was able to get the jump on him. They wrestled around a bit, both of their guns knocking free, and though Nick was older, it wasn't long before he got the edge over Luther and had beat him down to the ground. Bullet, Avery, Bernard, and even the prospects were holding their own. Nick was right. They had what it was going to take to defend themselves. It was what I was hoping for all along. With Nick's blessing, we could go in peace.

That is, we would if I could escape.

Suddenly, someone backed into me, and I went flying across the room. I was prepared to turn and fight, but I looked up, and Paulie was ducking away from an angry Taylor.

"Pay attention, rookie!" Paulie yelled.

Little did he know, but he saved me from Taylor. With his huge machete held high over his head and bloodlust in his eyes, my next course of action was going to be somehow dodging Taylor. He'd never let us out without a fight. The warehouse was awash with the Dogs and

Knights, along with the debris of several broken items scattered around. Some of the crates in the corner that held some of the bar's cooking items had tipped, and a few bags of flour were spilled on the ground. It was a long shot, but I turned and ran straight for the crates, jumping into them and using my feet to kick up the flour.

The more mess I could make with the flour, the better. The flour created a hazy shroud around me. I could barely see any way out, but I was pretty well oriented and was hopeful that I could get to the back door. Taylor was advancing, trying to see through the haze, and when his blade swung down, slicing into another bag of flour, I slipped to the right. Every time there was a burst of noise, I moved behind an adjacent stack of flour, and relief covered me when I noticed Taylor turn in the other direction and start fighting his way through the mess I'd created.

It was as clear a window as I was going to get. I slunk along the wall, passing unnoticed behind a few of the fights happening near the back door, and took my time to press the button on the door carefully so that it didn't make much noise.

When I was out in the setting sun, I raced around to the front and saw Tess sitting in the car with Lockjaw. The keys were still in the ignition, so I started up the car and moved at a slow, quiet pace as I pulled back out onto the road, where I picked up the pace and left Hoppa's behind.

"What happened?" Tess asked. "What about my dad?"

"Your dad's fine, and the Knights are gonna be fine, but Taylor..." I shook my head. "He tried to kill me."

"He just doesn't know how to leave it well enough alone. We came back. What more does he want?"

"My head," I responded. I kept looking into the rearview mirror, afraid that Luther or Taylor may catch on and follow me, but after about ten minutes, I still saw no one coming. The pounding in my heart finally started to slow, and I immediately felt dizzy.

"Colin?"

The car veered as I steered, and I knew I wouldn't hang on much longer. I quickly pulled us over onto the shoulder and pulled the car to a stop. My eyes were starting to cross, and it felt like I might throw up or pass out at any second. I opened the door of the car and stumbled out, hoping that maybe a bit of fresh air would help. It was difficult keeping my feet straight as I walked around the car to the safety of the embankment, but as soon as I was out of the street, I collapsed. My lungs were burning like they were going to give out, and it was only then that I noticed the searing pain in my side.

"Colin!"

Tess ran over just as I was rolling over onto my back, and my head was barely able to focus on the beautiful sight in front of me.

"Fuck, he got you." Tess' hand was on my stomach then, lifting my shirt and causing my side to scream out in pain. "It's not too deep, but you lost a lot of blood. Do you have extra tape?"

I nodded. "In my bag."

Tess rushed over to the car and threw herself into the back. My vision was waning. Though

I wanted to open my mouth to say something else, the strength in my body was quickly falling away. I lifted a hand and peered at the sight of Tess through splayed fingers. I imagined Caid in Germany. He sounded so great. I would have given anything to see him in his new, healthy state.

Each time I blinked, my eyes threatened not to open again.

The last thing I saw was Tess turning around and running back toward me, with the blurry image of an approaching motorcycle wavering behind her as I blacked out.

"Colin!"

Chapter Twenty-Three

Tess

"Shit. No, no, no, no."

My hands were shaking as I tried to work some of the bandages that I got from Colin's bag around his side. He was heavy, so getting the wrap under his back was a trial on his own. The blood from his side soaked through the first few layers of the bandages, but by the time I was giving him a fourth wrap, not as much was getting through. I did my best to keep my breathing under control, knowing that he likely just passed out from the sudden blood shortage. If he could have a few minutes of rest, he'd be okay.

Then Lockjaw started to bark.

I looked over my back, and my heart dropped into my stomach like a lead weight. A bike I'd come to fear and dread was pulling off the road onto the shoulder, with Taylor sitting on top of it with his machete resting on his shoulder like some sort of desert devil. He left it on his shoulder as he climbed off his bike.

Lockjaw, who was still in the car, was standing up on the backseat, barking and snarling. If I let him out, he'd protect me, but he'd also probably get sliced in half by Taylor. Looking back at Taylor, I saw that he was taking slow steps toward me, and I knew that this vision of him would probably haunt my nightmares for years.

Next to me, a gun discharged and made me jump. A bullet went flying from just behind me toward Taylor. Looking back, Colin had come to, but he was still looking worse for wear. If he tried to fight now, he would probably die. If Taylor wanted a fight, he was going to have to take me on. I wasn't going to let him control me anymore.

With a deep breath, I got to my feet. I pulled my brass knuckles out of my pocket and slid them on my hand. The dried blood of the Unchained Dogs I'd beaten was still caked and dried on the front, and though I promised that I would never use any weapons against my own family, Taylor wasn't a man I knew anymore. It'd been a long time since he was.

He chuckled. "What are you doing?"

"I'm not gonna let you hurt my family, Taylor," I said.

"I *am* your family." He fanned his arms out, his machete extending his wingspan on the right side by a couple of feet. "This is your flesh and blood."

"I don't know you," I growled back. "I never wanted to have to face you this way, but it's clear that you don't plan on changing any time soon."

I had to free myself and those I loved from Taylor. I was willing to give up love when he killed my first boyfriend, but I'd only been a scared girl back then. Maybe no one else was willing to give me credit for it, but I'd been training just as much as anyone else. Never was I going to be someone's poor helpless woman, but I let Taylor control me like I was. It was time to end that by ending Taylor.

My hands balled into fists. "I'm done with you."

To my surprise, Taylor tossed his machete to the side. "Fine. I'll drag you back to Hoppa unconscious. My family is just that—*mine*. You won't be going anywhere with him. I'm gonna bury him in this desert. Don't worry. I'll make sure he gets the dog."

With my blood boiling, I advanced on Taylor. My mind went back to all of those days I spent demanding that my dad treat me with the same respect he gave Taylor. For years I had to chase acceptance, all until I rode into Rumble and stole Lockjaw. That was the first time my dad truly accepted that I had the strength to be part of the club, and I'd hoped that I'd have more moments like that with the members or even Taylor, but it wasn't meant to be. Colin was the only one willing to see that I had strength. When he needed help, he came to me.

I wouldn't let him die out in this desert for the risk that he took.

When I got to Taylor, I swung out my right fist, but he ducked out of the way. He tossed a left jab back, but I ducked it and shuffled forward with alternating punches, landing one across his jaw. He tried to throw a right jab after that, but I twisted out of the way and sent another round of successful punches right into his face. Even without the brass, the hits would be doing damage, but his face was quickly bruising underneath the force of the knuckles.

Confidence was flooding into me as I turned and landed a hard hit right into Taylor's side. He doubled over, and I kicked out my right leg, but he grabbed it and lunged, sending me crashing to the ground. Lockjaw's barks were getting louder and more aggressive from the car, and a quick glance over let me see that the window was cracking. I wanted to shout for him to stay, but Taylor stood over me, pulled his right fist high above his head, and sent it down toward my face. I was able to turn out of the way so that I didn't take it straight in the face, but it still slammed against my cheek. It stung, and I could immediately taste metallic blood in my mouth, but now wasn't the time to get squeamish.

I tucked my legs against my stomach and threw them out at the same time, making hard contact with Taylor's stomach. He flew backward and crashed into the sand of the desert. We were evenly timed in getting to our feet, but I was faster getting to Taylor, and he was just stabilizing when I threw a haymaker that crashed into his face, then I uppercut with my left hand and sent him flying off of his feet and back to the ground.

Pulling the back of my hand across my mouth, I wiped away a bit of the blood that was pooling there and spit some of it out on the ground. I watched Taylor writhe around on the ground, and I was starting to feel confident that I'd win the fight when the sound of shattering glass erupted behind me. I looked over my shoulder, and Lockjaw had broken free of the car and was racing across the desert.

"Lockjaw! No!" He didn't listen. He crashed into Taylor and locked down on Taylor's leg, using all of his strength to quite literally drag Taylor around. Taylor was screaming, and I ran over and started to clap in Lockjaw's face. "Let go! Let him go!"

But Lockjaw wasn't listening. Taylor fumbled around, trying to get at his waistband, and the inevitable was quickly approaching. My gun was burning against my back, and tears filled my eyes as my hands instinctively went for it. Whereas I'd been hoping to just put Taylor out and call my dad to come and collect him, that option was no longer existent.

Taylor dragged his gun out just as I got mine out, and the second he pointed it at Lockjaw, I fired. The bullet flew forward and pierced Taylor's arm, but he didn't drop the gun. He started to lift his arm again, which should not have been possible, but that time, he was aiming just past me in Colin's direction.

The resolve was painful to watch. Taylor would never stop.

Almost as if he knew it was happening, too, Lockjaw released Taylor's leg and lunged at the arm that held the gun. With Taylor's arm pulled away from his face, there was only one option left. I swallowed hard, pointed my gun at Taylor's head, and fired. Almost in slow motion, I watched the bullet leave the gun. As Lockjaw pinned down the arm that held the gun, the bullet from my gun pierced through Taylor's forehead, and his arm fell to the dust, sending the gun in his hand clattering to the side.

His body went limp, but Lockjaw continued to claw at him until a hollow whistle filled the air. "Lockjaw!" Colin bellowed.

Finally, Lockjaw released Taylor's motionless arm, ran over to me, and looked up. He whimpered and whined, looking almost apologetic. I dropped to my knees and hugged him. "No, it's okay. You were a good boy."

Boots shuffling through the desert brought my attention up, but it was just Colin, having gotten to his feet. Though he was limping, he looked okay.

"I didn't want to kill him," I said, tears filling my eyes. "He was gonna kill you."

"I know." He set a hand on my head. "I know."

We both looked over at Taylor's lifeless body, and though I should have been sad, the relief coursing through me was almost sickening. Never again would I have to look over my shoulder. Never again would I have to fear him taking away someone I loved. He was my brother, but he was also my greatest nightmare.

Both were gone now.

"I need to call my dad," I said. "Can you figure out how to deal with… that?" I pointed at the shattered window on the car.

"Yeah." Colin tapped his leg, and Lockjaw obeyed the command, following after Colin as they both made their way to the car.

I pulled my phone out of my pocket and dialed my dad's number. As it was trilling, I walked over to Taylor and kicked the gun further away from his hands. I folded his arms over his chest, which was probably far more than he deserved, and closed both of his eyelids.

"Tess?" my dad answered. "Are you okay?"

"I am," I responded. "Taylor is not."

My dad sighed. "CJ killed him."

"No, Daddy." I swallowed hard. "I did. I had no choice. He was gonna kill Colin. He was gonna kill Lockjaw."

"Where are you?" he asked.

For a while, I hesitated. Who knew what my dad's level of discernment would be without Taylor looming behind him, but regardless of it, I was leaving to start a new life with Colin in Germany. If the club still wanted Colin's head, we couldn't stay, and though I loved my dad, I didn't want to risk it.

"We left already. If you drive west along Highway 40, about thirty minutes out of Hoppa, you'll find him. I'm sorry."

"Val," my dad said, and there was a crack in his voice that immediately brought tears to my eyes. "I love you."

"I love you, too, Squared."

The line went dead immediately after that. I stood staring down at Taylor long enough for the sun to set and the stars to begin peeking out. It was only once Colin came and covered him with a blanket from my trunk that I could drag myself away. He pulled me into a hug and held me in place for a few minutes.

"I'm sorry. We have to go."

"Yeah," I replied, sniffling in my emotions. "Are they gonna let us keep a pit bull at our side in the airport."

"I have no idea," Colin responded, "but somehow, that seems like a really trivial problem."

I nodded. "It does, doesn't it?"

"To Germany?" he asked before kissing my lips.

A smile found my face without my permission. "To Germany."

Epilogue

Phantom

My fingers pressed into my skull, and my blood started to boil. "No. Po-ta-toes."

The woman on the other side of the counter furrowed her brow and poked out her lip. A string of words in a language I was still learning hissed back at me, and even if I didn't know what she was saying, the sting in her voice made it clear that she wasn't inviting me over for afternoon tea.

"What'd you say?" I barked.

An arm extended out in front of my chest and pushed me backward. Although we were identical twins, Caid and I looked very different these days. I'd chosen to let my facial hair grow out a little bit, due in part to the fact that my fiancée loved it and also because, even after almost a year, I still wanted to distance my image, at least a little bit, from how I looked in the past. Who knew how many people were still trying to find me. I figured it was at least a little bit harder with some longer hair. Caid, however, had a cleanly shaven face, and his body was still lean, even though he was pretty much free of his illness.

"You can't get mad at her because *you* don't understand her," Caid growled.

"She called me a bitch or something. I know that much," I spat back.

Caid handed the woman some euros, and her scowl turned into a smile. He said a series of things to her in German, and his accent sounded almost natural. She reached behind her, grabbed a bag of some of the store's specialty potatoes, and handed them over to Caid, and he nodded with a "Danke", and then turned to walk out.

"Bitte," the woman sang back, then her scowl returned as she looked me up and down.

She hissed out another series of words, so I hoped that a middle finger would translate and stuck it up at her while following Caid out.

"You're a brat," Caid said simply.

"You've only been here two months longer than me. How did you learn so much faster than I did?" I asked.

"I'd already been learning it before I came here, then once I got here, it was all I did every single day for two months. Besides, you're not really trying."

We turned out onto a road with the sun shining above us and people happily chattering as they walked by. "I'm trying."

"Tess is better than you," Caid replied. "Lockjaw's better than you."

"Hey!" I barked. "Lockjaw is *as* good as me." Lockjaw wasn't learning German, per se, but Caid had been teaching him German commands over the past year, and he'd gotten pretty good. "Whatever. You can just do all the talking forever."

Caid brandished his copy of the key to our high-rise complex and opened the door. I walked through with the other groceries I was carrying. We took the elevator up to the top floor, and I used my keys to let us into the apartment. Lockjaw jumped up from his dog bed in the corner near the wall-to-wall, ceiling-to-floor windows that overlooked Munich and ran over.

"Hey, bud." I crouched so I could give him proper head pats. "Where's Mama?"

"In here!" Tess' voice called back. "Come in here, both of you. Tell me how this looks."

Caid and I dropped the groceries off on the dining room table and walked through the huge open living room to the left, which was Tess' and my wing of the apartment. We passed the bathroom on the left but didn't go as far down as the bedroom. Instead, we turned into the guest bedroom, which was in the process of being converted.

I walked in and saw that Tess was balancing a huge box against her waist. "What are you—" I snatched the box away from her. "That's dangerous."

"I'm fine, Colin," Tess said. She turned, leading with her eight-months pregnant belly, and leaned in for a kiss. "Brat."

"I just called him a brat five minutes ago," Caid said, almost as if he was proud.

Tess poked his cheek sweetly and then turned around and motioned to the room. "What do we think?"

Under the windows was a white crib that Caid had built from scratch and painted, and the room was decorated with all of the white bunny stuff that we'd been collecting since we found out that Tess was pregnant.

"I like it," I said.

"And." Tess turned and motioned toward the small dresser that was also something Caid built. She lifted a picture of her and her dad from back in Hoppa. "So that she gets to know her grandpa."

Her face immediately saddened, and I felt bad. It felt like we'd been living in Germany so much longer than a year. Tess had, not surprisingly, built herself a successful dog training business with Lockjaw as her right-hand-pooch, and Caid and I co-owned a furniture business. It turned out that the meticulous way I liked to work on bikes translated, and after years of watching me, Caid had developed a love for it, too.

Wrapping an arm around Tess' back, I pulled her close to me. "That's wonderful."

A few tears always came to Tess' eyes as of late every time she thought about how her dad wasn't going to be involved in our baby's life. It was something I couldn't relate to. I didn't know, nor care about, where my mom was. Caid was my family, and he had gotten to be here every step of the way.

All of a sudden, I felt selfish. I wanted a happy life so much, one I thought I deserved, but I didn't realize how much Tess was giving up just so that I could have it.

She hadn't complained once in the year since we had moved to Germany. She met Caid, and the two became peas in a pod almost instantly. Though Tess and I connected in almost every possible way, she and Caid leaned toward being a little dorky and bonded over things that I didn't understand. Caid taught us German, and he was probably right when he said that Tess was doing better than I was. After years of needed laser focus, when I was finally able to relax in Germany, my attention span got incredibly short.

"Like a chair?" Caid asked.

"Yeah." Tess and Caid's conversation, the beginning of which I missed, brought me back from my thoughts. "A chair would be good, or maybe even a chest. Like a little toy chest?"

"I can do that," Caid responded and then gasped. "I can make a little bunny chest! The belly can open and close and be the door for the toys, and it can be a giant white rabbit!"

"That sounds amazing!" Tess yelped. She looked up at me. "Doesn't it?"

"It really does," I said. "Uh, you guys talk about that. I'll be right back."

I kissed Tess on the cheek and walked out of the room. I grabbed my phone off the dining room table and walked over to the small table with a drawer in it that sat by the front door. I opened the drawer and pulled out my old cell phone and wasn't shocked that it didn't turn on when I pressed the power button. I dug out a charger to plug it into, then walked to the opposite end of the apartment, where Caid's room was. I plugged my old phone in, and when it was charged enough, I powered it on. I left it on long enough to get a phone number from my contacts, then I powered it off again, even unplugging it for good measure.

After picking up my new phone and navigating to where I could make an outgoing call, I dialed the number I just got from my old phone and pressed the green *call* button. I patiently waited while it rang, and when a voice answered on the other line, I couldn't keep from smiling.

"Hello? Tess?"

"Almost," I replied with a chuckle.

"CJ!" Nick said. "How the hell are ya, man?"

"I'm good, Nicky. Started up a company with my brother. Got a nice apartment out here in Stuttgart. It's going well." We were, of course, in Munich, but old habits die hard. "How are things there? You guys recovering okay?"

"Recovering?" Nick said. "Oh! After the attack, you mean? Hell yeah, we're recovering! Thanks to your advice, they didn't know what hit them. I missed the chance to take Luther out, but once he saw that we'd stiffed everyone else he brought, he wised up and ran. I imagine he'll retaliate at some point."

"He will," I warned. "Luther is viciously vengeful. Keep your eyes open."

"That's the only way I live," Nick replied. "We've got allies, too. We're good."

"How are things now that Taylor's gone?" I asked.

Nick let out a long sigh. "I know he had a few issues, a few *big* issues, but it's never easy for a parent to bury their kid."

"I'm sorry, Squared."

"Nah. Thinking back, I made more than one mistake. All of a sudden, I saw this future for Tess and the club, and I think I went a little crazy."

"A little?"

He chuckled. "Hey, pipe down. You went there with me, boy."

"You're not wrong."

"How's my baby girl?"

"She's good! She's…" I took a deep breath, knowing the weight of what I was about to tell him. "She's pregnant."

There was no response for a really long time. I might have thought Nick hung up if it weren't for the breathing on the other end—catching in spurts, almost like he may have been fighting to hold back tears.

"Nick?"

"She's pregnant?" he said. "How far along?"

"Eight months."

He whistled. "Wow. Poppin' any day. Now, tell me you're gonna to do right by her, CJ. I really don't want to have to hunt you down."

"She was engaged before it happened," I responded. "Uh, sorry. We're not married yet, though."

"Hey. I'm not some prude. I know how these things go. As long as you're gonna be there for them both, I'm happy."

"I'd be dumb to give up someone like Tess." Her sad face when she looked at the picture of Nick flashed across my brain. "Hey, listen. Nick. If I turn myself in, would you pardon Tess?"

"What?" Nick said. "Where's this coming from all of a sudden?"

"She misses you, and I know that she hates that you can't be in your granddaughter's life."

"Granddaughter?" Nick repeated, and I could hear the smile. "A little girl?"

"That's what we were told."

Again, Nick went silent. Nick was a man who liked to talk, so when he went quiet, I knew he was thinking deeply about something. "A pardon's probably not in the cards, I'm afraid. She killed one of our own and chose you over us. That kind of thing just doesn't go over well."

"Nick—"

"But you know," he continued. "I've got some work to do over in Germany. Maybe it's time I made a trip soon. Maybe in a month or so. In Stuttgart, as a matter of fact."

"Munich," I replied.

Nick scoffed. "You never change, do ya, kid?"

"I could say the same about you."

"Well, if I were to come to try to find two of the Knights' at-large criminals, surely the club would understand," he said. "Is there a particular date I should be sure to be around?"

"August seventh."

"I'm gonna be a Pop-pop," he said. "Or do I go with Papa?"

"I'll leave that up to you, Tess, and Annelise."

"Annelise!" He laughed. "Hold on, baby! Grandpa's coming!" The phone line went dead, and all I could do was grin. He had my new number, so the specifics could be decided later. Making contact with Nick might have been a mistake, but I had a feeling it wouldn't be.

"There you are," Tess said, walking into the room. "What are you smiling at?"

"I took calculated risk," I responded to her. "Sounds like we'll have a visitor around the seventh."

Tess walked into the room and sat down next to me on Caid's bed. "The seventh?" she growled. "Why would you invite a visitor on my due date?" I unlocked my phone and handed it to her, showing her my most recent contact. Her eyes widened, and her jaw dropped. "My dad? Are you sure it's okay?"

"His biggest concern was whether or not he would be Pop-pop or Papa."

Tess started to laugh, and tears rose to her eyes. "My dad's gonna be here when Annelise is born?"

"As long as you don't go early," I said before directing my attention to her stomach. "That's not a challenge, by the way," I added because I had a funny feeling that this little girl was going to be a lot like her mother.

Lockjaw padded into the room and set his head on Tess' stomach. "I can't wait to see him handle being a big brother," Tess said, and then she put her hand on my face, "but I'm even more excited to see you handle being a father."

I kissed her. "With you by my side, it could only be perfect."

"I love you," she said. "Well, should we go start the rest of our lives?" she asked.

I nodded. "Let's."

BOOK 2

DEVIL'S BULLET

Chapter One

Bullet

The sound of bullets piercing their targets was my favorite sound in the world. Something about the hollow hiss, just before the dull pinpoint of the heated metal sinking in was like music to my ears.

"Bullet! Fucking fire!"

My finger flexed against the trigger and the gun vibrated in my hand as the bullet fled from it with a mission in sight. I recoiled back but smiled as the bullet found purchase. I sighed with satisfaction as the remains of my quarry splattered out and hit the floor below.

"That'll teach you to challenge me," I growled.

I rubbed the barrel of my gun free of any stippling with a rag and grumbled at some of the evident soot on my shirt. A change of clothes would be necessary, no matter how much I tried to avoid it.

"That's why they call ya 'Bullet'," Avery said, pointing his gun out in front of him, peering over it like a hunter cornered on its prey, "but you know what they call me?" I smirked as he pulled the trigger and his bullet released, but it faded down to a frown as I watched his bullet shoot straight through the center point on the target in front of him, skirting mine which was one ring outside the center. He looked over at me and winked. "Bullseye."

"Fuck." I stared down the row of ten targets, each with one bullet hole near the target and all with one straight through it. Not one of the direct hits was mine. "Load up another ten. I'm *gonna* beat you."

"Dude," Avery groaned. "We've gone five rounds already. Give it up. You are *not* going to beat me."

"I'll pay for it, just go tell them to load up another ten."

"Stop. What's wrong with you?" Avery lifted his goggles, letting his blue eyes catch in the overhead halogen lights of the shooting range. "I know you like a good shoot-off, but this is weird, even for you."

"Nothing's wrong. I just wanted to get some shooting in before the meeting," I replied. "Are you scared?"

Avery snickered. "Do you honestly think I'm that childish, I'd fall for that? You've known me since college, and I've known you, too, and I know something's wrong." He pointed his gun at me, knowing full well the one bullet in it had already been discharged at the target. "You fucking tell me or I'm calling Cameron."

"Do what you say or you're gonna tell my dad? How old are you?"

"Take it or leave it, Bullet. I ain't shooting another ten targets just because you have a bug up your ass about something." He raised an eyebrow at me. "Is it that date you had?"

The question knocked me sideways just a bit. Avery's nickname was Bullseye for two reasons as far as I was concerned. One, because he could hit a dead shot at midnight with one eye closed, and the other because he could take one look at me and know exactly what was going on in my brain.

"That date was weeks ago," I barked. "Why would it be that?"

"Exactly, it was weeks ago. You were asking people for advice and you wouldn't shut up about her for a few days there, then all of a sudden you just stopped talking about it."

Grabbing the cloth again, I cleaned my gun off one more time, engaged the safety, and shoved it into the back of my waistband. "I stopped talking then, and I'm done talking now. Let's go, we have a meeting."

Avery let out a low whistle and then a gruff chuckle. "Aw, man. Doesn't go out on a date in how long, six months? Seven?"

It had been closer to a year, but who was counting. "Shut your mouth."

"Fine. Party Pooper."

"It's not like you have women falling outta your house," I snapped back.

"Don't you worry about me, bud. I do just fine."

He could say that, but I knew Avery was a romantic. He hadn't had a woman on his arm in any permanent capacity in at least as long as it had been since my last date; it had to be getting to him. "Anyway, Celia is hardly a concern of mine."

"Celia," Avery repeated. "That's her. That tall, hot chick right?"

I didn't respond. "Tall" and "hot" were descriptors that objectively described Celia, but she was much more than that. In the one meal we'd shared, we went tit for tat like a tennis match. She took everything about me in her stride, and we shared one amazing night together.

Then I never heard from her again.

"Isn't that the one Nicky set you up with?" Avery asked.

I rolled my eyes. "He didn't set me up with her so much as he forced my hand."

"Yeah, but you went."

We checked out of the gun range, I paid for the targets we'd shot, and then we walked out into the fresh fall morning and over to where our bikes were parked. "You took her home, too," he laughed, "because you walked into the club the next day like you had springs in your shoes."

With lightning speed, I reached over and smacked him across the back of the head. "Shut the fuck up."

"Fine!" Avery yelped, rubbing his head. "Fuck, you try and joke with your best friend a little and look what it gets me."

We each climbed on our bikes and a moment later, the rumble of them starting up pierced the quiet air. Birds and squirrels scattered from nearby as I twisted my handle to rev a couple of times, then with a screech, I spun my wheel to kick a little dust up at Avery, and then fired off, out of the parking lot and onto the main road.

Nothing in Hoppa was too far from the next thing over. Anyone who lived here long enough could draw the entire town map from memory, and it made it easy to get from A to B. Of course, this was bittersweet for motorcycle riders. By the time we really got going, we were already arriving at our destination. Back in the day, I might have spent a little time taking the long way around, maybe even ditching Avery and taking a ride down the highway and back before the meeting, but history had taught me that keeping a trusted ally by your side was a good idea and that, sometimes, long rides lead to trouble.

I was first into the parking lot at Hoppa's Taphouse, the meeting grounds of the Steel Knights Motorcycle club. Apart from being Hoppa's premiere drinking spot, it was no mystery that we ran our operations there. A large Steel Knights banner hung from the roof down the side of the building, overlooking the parking spots that were painted with the same sigil to symbolize that they were designated for club members only. Only two of the spots were occupied when Avery and I pulled in, so I parked in the next one over and then Avery next to me.

The rumble of our idling bikes filled the air for a few brief seconds until we powered down, leaving us in a deafening silence.

"It's weird isn't it?" Avery said. "Just four officers. I'm not paranoid like Nick, but even *I* know this isn't good."

A few different thoughts crossed my brain, but I opted to keep them to myself. After everything I'd been through with the former Vice President and Nick's daughter, Tess, and our brief, President-forced Secretary, Colin, my feelings on their sudden absconding together were complicated, to say the least.

"How many spots does it leave open?" Avery asked.

"Three, including Grim's spot. We're out a VP, a Sergeant, and a Secretary."

Avery sputtered out a chuckle as he climbed off his bike. "I didn't even know Secretary was a position."

"Quite a useful one," I said as I unmounted my bike and tucked my helmet away in the back compartment. "Though I can admit, it wasn't until Nick suddenly nominated CJ to that spot that it even occurred to me that we didn't have one."

"How come?" Avery asked.

"That I don't know." With a tap on Avery's shoulder, I started for the front door. "But I intend to ask."

The front door to Hoppa's jingled as we walked through it, and as expected, only two other people were inside. It'd been a few weeks since everything had gone down with our rival gang, the Unchained Dogs, and Tess, Colin, and Taylor came to blows which ultimately ended Taylor's life, but we'd been sort of ignoring and skirting the issue. Today was the first official meeting our President, Nick, had called since then, and I had no idea what to expect. All I knew was that it was a strange feeling not seeing Taylor, Nick's late son, throwing me a psychotic gaze from the back corner, while I attempted to keep my own hateful glare from settling too long on his sister, Tess. Despite my thoughts about the former Vice President and Sergeant at Arms, there was no denying that their departures had left a couple of wide, deep crevices in the Steel Knights battalion, and Nick had done little to close them yet.

"Hey, y'all," Bernard "Bucky" LePall called over from the pool table that sat in the back-left corner of the bar. He was hunched over, aiming his stick at the white pool ball. "I'm *just* about done kicking Nick's ass, then we can get started."

I looked to Nick, expecting a colorful jeer or counterstrike, but he looked more like a ghost sitting on a stool against the wall with a pool stick balanced between his legs. He was staring at the table, but it likely wasn't what he was seeing. His short brown hair had, in the span of just a few weeks, started to sprout patches of gray, and though he normally kept his face shaven, he'd grown a budding goatee, which also had gray hairs poking through.

Nodding my head in his direction, I called out, "Hey, Nick."

It was almost as if he didn't hear us enter or hear Bucky address us. "Oh, hey." He looked around the empty bar with sunken-in eyes and pursed lips. "I guess this is it, huh?"

"For officers," Avery said as he walked around the bar and pulled a couple of bottles of water from the small cooler that sat against the back wall. He tossed one to me before leaning over the bar and opening his own. "How ya holding up there, Nicky?"

He shrugged. "I'm still here, ain't I?"

"Eight ball, corner pocket." Bucky finally took his shot on the pool table, smacking the white pool ball, knocking it into the eight ball, which flew into the pocket he'd called. He chuckled with satisfaction. "That's how it's done, Squared."

Nick hardly seemed fazed. He set a few bills on the pool table, then hung up his stick and walked over to the bar. He sat down on one of the bar stools and I sat on one a few down from him. "Get me a whisky, Bullseye. Neat," he said.

Avery side-eyed me quickly, no doubt because Nick was requesting a drink, but I just shook my head, and Avery shrugged before pulling a bottle of whisky out from below the bar, along with a glass to pour it into. He filled the glass up about halfway and slid it over, but Nick didn't drink it, rather just pulled it up to his nose and smelled it a bit, before setting the glass back down on the counter and just staring into the liquid.

After a few seconds of silence, he took a deep breath and stood up off the stool with the glass in hand. "All right. Let's head back."

No one protested as Nick walked around the bar and Avery waited for him to pass through the door to the kitchen first, before following after him. I stepped just ahead of Bucky behind the bar, but he was right on my heels, and we filed through the kitchen and followed Nick through the heavy, swinging metal door in the back of the kitchen into the warehouse in the back, in the center of which was our round meeting table. There were still several chairs situated around the table, but no one made mention of that as Nick sat in his regular chair and the rest of us situated ourselves at equal intervals around the table to not make it feel so empty.

"First of all, gentlemen," Nick started, "I need to apologize. Not just for these past few weeks of uncertainty, but for the way I behaved after Colin first arrived. I could try and make excuses for what happened, but the truth is, I let the fact that I'm a father overshadow the fact that I'm your President. I was nervous about things with the Unchained Dogs, yes, but I embarked on a course of action that was in direct conflict to our bylaws and dwarfed your jobs as members, simply because I liked Colin and wanted him to be close at hand." He snickered. "I'm not gonna lie to you guys, I *still* fucking like him. He loves my daughter and I know he's gonna take care of her, wherever the hell they are. I wish things had worked out differently. This all may be a different story."

"He was an Unchained Dog," Bucky grunted.

Nick nodded. "He was, but a little flip-flopping isn't entirely unheard of in our world, though I might have trusted him less. Though maybe not, too. I don't know. He's a weird blind spot for me, that's all I can say."

"He's like you," I interjected. "The last couple of months notwithstanding, you're typically much more like him. Reserved, not super flashy, silently tough. You saw yourself in him."

A small smirk cracked across Nick's face. "That was pretty insightful of you."

I shrugged. "I have my moments."

He crossed his arms. "You're probably dead on there, Bullet. He felt like family already. Maybe that's why. In any event, none of it is worth the way I behaved, so I apologize. As President, I have the responsibility to offer up my position. I believe any of you would have exercised better judgment than me, so if any of you would like to vie for this spot, I would respect that nomination."

Avery, Bucky, and I exchanged looks, and then I looked across at Nick. "Don't be so dramatic," I huffed. "No one is asking you to step down, just be a little more mindful next time."

The small smirk curved wider across his face. "Thanks, guys. I don't want to step down, but… you know…" He shrugged. "Anyway. We'll get through this, and I promise, I'm bylaw-bound from here on out." The tension in the room immediately dissipated. Nick was wearing the stress of losing his kids like a brightly colored coat, but he at least seemed to be in a better place as far as the club was concerned, and that could only bode well for us. "Which brings me to our next topic of discussion. Obviously," he motioned to the empty chairs, "we're down a few bodies. Tess has left the VP position vacant, Colin left the Secretary position wide open, and Tay—"

Just like that, the tension was back. We all watched as Nick rapidly deteriorated. Tears quickly welled up in the corners of his eyes, and his jaw clenched. Despite his best attempts to keep his emotions back, a couple of tears broke loose and slid down his cheeks. Apart from when he announced that Taylor had fallen to Tess, Nick hadn't brought up his son once. Signs of stress aside, it seemed like he was holding it together well, but suddenly he was shaking and barely managing to hold himself up.

Bucky held out his hand timidly and set it on Nick's shoulder. "Hey, Nicky, we know. It's okay, man."

Nick wiped his eyes and then took a deep breath. "Sorry."

"Don't be," Avery said. "It was your kid."

Nick cleared his throat a few times. "Yeah. I know he was off his rocker a little, but—"

"Nick," I cut him off. "I'm not like a therapist or anything, but I don't think it's wrong of you to mourn your kid."

Nick nodded. "Yeah. Thanks." A few more tears escaped his eyes, and he slapped his hands against his cheeks and shook his head. "Wow. Sorry. Okay. Well, you guys know. I mean you were fucking there. Point is, we have the VP, Secretary, and Sergeant at Arms positions to fill, so there's going to be some changes internally probably. We have our member pool to pull from, but promotions from within isn't off the table either and we do need to do some recruiting."

"Can I ask a question?" I asked. "The Secretary position, why didn't we have anyone in that position before? We have careful records. I know because I've used them. Who was doing that?"

After first taking a deep breath in and then out, Nick replied, "Well, we kind of did. I was breaking the rules a little bit before you guys, but this one I can't take entirely on myself. You guys wouldn't really *let* Tess do the VP stuff. None of ya." He looked at Avery. "Well, hardly any of ya. Thanks, Bullseye."

"No problem, Nicky," Avery replied.

"Most of you wouldn't take Tess seriously. She didn't know as much, but in order to make sure she was actually doing stuff here, I gave her the Secretary duties as well. She was the one keeping all of our records. Actually, she went off and documented us to the best of her ability, all the way back to when my grandpa established us."

Bucky let out a hollow whistle and my jaw dropped as well. "That must have taken forever."

"Yeah, she worked on it for a year or more," Nick said.

Knowing how many times I'd referred to our club history for spending habits and audits, that realization was bittersweet. Tess and I didn't really… get along. It wasn't so much anything she'd done personally, but more my personal distrust for women. My experiences drove my feelings, but they hadn't steered me wrong yet, so the guilt I'd slowly been developing regarding Tess was disconcerting, to say the least.

"Well, hopefully, we'll get a chance to thank her someday," Avery said.

Nick nodded. "Yeah. Hopefully." He cleared his throat again and continued. "Anyway. I'm working on a plan right now. Got a few things in mind, but I really want to bang it out solidly before I present it, so have a little patience with me. I hope to have things chiseled out soon. If any of you have any thoughts though, please talk to me. Obviously, time is of the essence, but we're gonna do it right this time. I do think we're gonna have to go for open enrollment, though. The bylaws call for this, and my old man did it a lot, but it's not my favorite method. I prefer recommendations from existing members, but shit, we lost three officers, plus Stag, the poor bastard."

Bucky turned his head down. "He had it coming, grabbing Tess the way he did, though. Dumb drunk couldn't get out of his own way."

"He's dead, Bucky, Jesus," Avery hissed.

"What?" Bucky replied. "Rest in peace and all that, but we were all smart enough not to piss Grim off *that* bad."

"He did *not* play games when it came to Tess," Nick said. "I suppose, if nothing else, he looked after her, but she wasn't really able to live her life." He shrugged. "Truth be told, though, if Taylor hadn't ended him, I was going to for putting his hands on my baby girl."

"A prospect didn't make it through, too, right?" Avery said. "Didn't one of them go toe-to-toe with Tess right before MiD?"

MiD stood for Music in the Desert, the fundraiser The Steel Knights and our allied clubs hosted in the desert every year. I'd heard that one of the prospects got cut the day of, but I never knew the details.

"Yeah, Aaron. I guess he tried to get snippy, so Tess cut him loose. Seth and Vil backed her up, so I respected her decision," Nick explained. "That's only happened once before." He locked eyes with me. "Hopefully, it doesn't go as bad as it did last time."

I shook my head. "I'm not worried."

He smiled. "Glad to hear it." He crossed his arms and leaned back in his chair. "Anyway, I'm probably gonna get some posts out on social media and just see what comes walking through the door. We'll have to vet everyone carefully, but I'm thinking we can pour a little booze into 'em and see who shows their true colors and go from there. Sound good?" Avery, Bucky and I all let out our own sounds of affirmation and then Nick finally broke out one of his typical, good ol' Nick smiles. Everyone let out sighs of relief and then Nick clapped a hand against the table. "Well, does anyone else have anything else we need to cover?" No one responded so Nick clapped the table again, as if he was hitting it with a gavel. "All right then; meeting adjourned."

We all lingered for a few minutes longer, breathing in the silence of Nick's words, but eventually, Bucky gathered himself up from the table. "Well, I'm starving. I know it's only about eleven, but let's go find someplace to hole up and eat."

Nick nodded. "I could go for that."

Avery and I looked at each other and then Avery nodded his head with a smile. "Yeah, we're in."

Bucky and Avery led the charge out of the warehouse, while I stayed behind after noticing that Nick hadn't moved. He was just sitting in place, smelling the glass of whisky in his hand. "You good, Squared?" I asked.

"He liked whisky most," Nick said, "Taylor did. Got that habit from me. Weird thing is, I haven't brought myself to drink it since then. Keep pouring glasses and just..." He took a big sniff in and let the sentence die out. I didn't say anything else. Loss wasn't something I dealt with in the healthiest way, so I couldn't really offer any sound advice. Eventually, he set the glass down on the table and looked up at me. "Hey. You ever thought about applying for a higher position?"

Math and finances were something I'd always been good at. I went to college for it and loved being a bookkeeper. "No."

Nick didn't press. He nodded his head as he stood up from the table. "Let's go then. I'm starved."

We left the warehouse and made our way back into the main room of the bar, where the two newest and also youngest members of the Steel Knights had arrived and were packing up a game of pool. Seth and Vil had prospected for months before Colin showed up, and his fast track pulled them into membership a bit before they were meant to be. For those mistakes, they'd turned out to be worth their weight in gold. They were strong, not easily ruffled, and had been good additions to the club thus far. In short, I liked them.

"Hey, Nicky," Vil greeted, slapping hands with the man as he walked around the bar.

Nick smiled. "There he is, Knuckles!"

"Knuckles?" Avery asked.

Nick slapped Vil's shoulder. "These boys got nicknames last night," he announced. "Vil here's a bit of a scrapper, and a few disrespectful idiots wandered in at bar close and got a taste of his fists. I've never seen hands flying so fast. Called him Knuckles and it just stuck."

Vil smiled. "I acted fast." He flipped over his left arm and revealed the new moniker tattooed down the inside of his forearm.

"Whoo!" Nick said. "Look at that!"

Bucky hooked an arm around the much more stoic Seth. "This one here, we call him 'Dynamite' now. He's always off in some corner quiet as a bird, but the second those guys caused trouble—BOOM!"

"True members now," Avery said. "Welcome to the family." Both Seth and Vil smiled at that. "To start, I need you young bucks to school Bullet over here."

I furrowed my brow. "I don't need to be schooled on anything," I sighed, rolling my eyes. "Can we go? I'm hungry."

Avery's eyes narrowed. "Come on. You still have a snit up your ass about that girl." He looked at Seth. "He went out with this chick, right? Really liked her, but he hasn't heard from her since."

Seth looked over at me. "Have you called?"

My nostrils flared with frustration at the sudden intrusion into my business. "Of course I've called. "

Vil raised an eyebrow. "Was she talkative leading up to when you guys went out?"

I crossed my arms. "Yes." Seth and Vil looked at one another and then back at me. "What?" I yelled.

"Did you take her home?" Vil asked.

My body burned all over instantly just thinking about it. "Yes."

Vil's lip turned down at the corner. "And how long has it been since you guys spoke?"

"The last time I talked to her was when she left my house the morning after," I replied, "about three weeks ago."

Seth frowned. "Sorry, Bullet," he said with a sigh. "It sounds like you were ghosted."

Chapter Two

Bullet

The sound of shattering glass sent my Calico cat, Chatterbox, skittering out of the kitchen, mewling as he went.

"Sorry, Box," I grumbled out loud, wincing at the shattered pieces of coffee mug now scattered across my kitchen counter. Very little had managed to abate my anger since Seth and Vil explained to me what it meant that I was being ghosted.

Used and discarded? Who the fuck did I look like?

I opened the cabinet under the sink that held a pull-out trash can and pulled it up to the countertop so I could swipe all the broken glass in. In my rage, I accidentally slammed the mug down on the countertop and destroyed it, fortunately before I had poured my morning coffee in at least. My head throbbed, thanks to the amount of liquor I drank at Hoppa's the night before, trying to wash away my frustrations. Coffee was certainly needed if I was going to get through an entire Monday without crashing.

Carefully, I pulled down another coffee mug, and Chatterbox peeked his head around the corner to see if I'd calmed down. I stopped preparing my coffee long enough to pull down a bag of his fish-shaped treats and the second I did, he came traipsing back into the kitchen and hopped up on the counter. I sprinkled a few of the pieces on the countertop and then when he walked up to nibble them, I scratched the top of his head.

"Sorry, buddy."

While Chatterbox worked on his treats, I finished pouring coffee, skipping the cream to really help knock the edge of my hangover off, and carried the mug into the living room. I used my phone to play some calming, ambient lo-fi music, and forced myself to relax in the calmness of the morning. Eventually, Chatterbox made his way over from the kitchen and up into my lap, and the call of snuggles was enough to draw out the shyer of my cats, a spotted Bengal named Jingle. He walked from the hallway toward the back bedrooms and hopped up onto the couch and curled up next to me.

With only one free hand, I had to alternate between petting each feline, which was fine for Jingle, but every time I stopped petting Chatterbox, he let out a series of loud, disgruntled meows.

"You are such a brat," I chided. "Your brother doesn't scream about it."

Chatterbox's only response was to lean heavily into my hand as I switched back to petting him, and with Jingle curled up and purring at my side, I continued to stroke Chatterbox to keep him quiet.

I stayed like that for about an hour, letting my cats and the warm coffee soothe my soul, and made my peace with putting Celia behind me. Next time someone tried to set me up, whether it was the President of the motorcycle club or not, I would be sure to decline. My mom, the judge handling my case, and now Celia. All they'd done was let me down, and I was too old to continue being taken advantage of.

If it was just me and my furry friends for the rest of my life, so be it. I wasn't about to be treated like an idiot.

At exactly seven-thirty AM, my alarm went off on my phone, coaxing me to get up and start my day. Thanks to learning I'd been shiested, I hadn't gotten much sleep and was up well ahead of my alarm, but the blaring disturbed the cats, who both got up and walked off to go find a quieter corner to curl up in, which meant I could get up and do what was left to do before leaving for Hoppa's. I packed up my laptop, did another pass through the kitchen to make sure all the glass was cleaned up, filled up the boys' dishes for them to eat later, grabbed my helmet, keys, and wallet, and left the house.

Eight in the morning was considered pretty damn early for my brood. No one, not even Nick, got to the Taphouse that early, mainly because they didn't need to. The Taphouse didn't open to the general public until three PM, and even then, the bulk of the crowd didn't start to arrive until well after five. Those of us who had "desk" jobs as officers could come in as late as eleven AM and still get done what we needed to get done for the day.

I, however, liked to work without distractions.

A true, blue early-bird, I preferred to get to the club as early as possible so that I was already done working by the time everyone else started showing up. Nick had gotten sick of me bothering him to let me in and eventually had a set of keys made for me. His kids were the only other club members with keys to the building, so with them gone it was just Nick and me.

Once I was inside and back in the warehouse, I used my phone once again to connect to the sound system and play more of the lo-fi music, and then pulled out my books and got to work. Thankfully, my job was pretty easy. The money was a mess when I first joined the Steel Knights, but I'd kept a tight leash since then. People did what they were supposed to so I could track the money effectively, so my daily tasks mostly involved reconciling purchases and tracking payables and receivables. Easy.

Just like any other day, I was working on the books, and hours had passed without my noticing. I hadn't even looked at a clock until I heard the warehouse door opening, and I looked up to see Nick walking in. His face was back to being shaven and it looked like he'd trimmed his growing hair, too, though the grays were still present.

"Morning," I said.

He nodded at me. "Good morning. Early as usual."

"You know me," I replied, turning my attention back to my books.

Nick kicked around the warehouse doing different things that I didn't really have much interest in, but eventually, he came to sit down across from me at the table. "How we lookin' over there?"

"Not bad at all. Last quarter was really good. Bucky's really running 'em in," I said. "I imagine we're going to stick with this new business venture then?"

"We'd be dumb not to," Nick said. "Although, I'd be lying if I said I wasn't just a hair uncomfortable with him doing border runs without Taylor."

"You should talk to Bullseye about taking his place," I suggested. "He's stealthy and pretty charismatic, like Bucky."

He smiled. "That's not a bad idea. I've always liked that decision-making quality in you, Bullet."

"Thanks?"

He chuckled before his face faded to seriousness again. "How much did we lose when Taylor fell out?"

"I hate to…" I sighed. "We're doing better now that it's just Bucky."

Nick let out a long, deep sigh. "That doesn't surprise me. It's not just because Bucky is more charismatic, but I think Taylor was dipping into the supply. It wasn't consistent, but on occasion, I would find we were getting less than I ordered. I'd ping-pong between who I had handle the coke, and whenever it was Bucky, not an issue, when it was Taylor, I was coming up short."

I glanced up, letting my eyes peer at Nick over the top of my glasses. "How long did you suspect that?"

He held up a hand, nodding his head knowingly. "I know, I know. I should have said something, but I didn't really have any proof beyond the hunch, and then before I could really dig into it too much, we had to start prepping for MiD. I had Bucky do those runs all himself with Texas and Jonesie so that we didn't get fucked in the desert and then, well… it wasn't an issue anymore."

"Look, Nick, this is *your* club, and I'm in no position to tell you how to run it—"

"On the contrary," Nick cut in, "you run the money. I may be President, but whoever has the money, has the power. You know that."

"Well, I don't really see it that way, but let me say this. We have potential to grow. You've been talking about it for years, adding officers, getting a facility of our own, but it won't happen if you continue to side-step obvious shit like this."

"Yeah." Despite the fact that I was lecturing him, Nick developed a smile on his face. "I got it, Bullet. I'm gonna rein it in, I promise."

"Good."

He peered over. "So, we really have potential?"

"With the border runs going as well as they have been and Vil and Seth getting the product out the door like good car salesmen, yeah, we do. We could even be looking at something by the end of the year if we really wanted to," I told him.

"Wow."

"At least begin talking about it. Building something or buying something and having it remodeled." I looked around the warehouse that was stacked, not only with our filing cabinets of paperwork, but with Hoppa's bar supplies. "I'd appreciate an office."

"Okay. Well, look at this..." Nick reached under the table, into the cubby where he kept all of his papers, and pulled a notebook out. He flipped it open to a page with a tree of boxes and arrows on it and turned it to face me. "I wanna start here."

I tilted my head to the side as I read. It didn't look like Nick's handwriting. "What is this?"

"It's Tess' model."

My eyes went wide as they shot up to look at Nick. "Really?" I wasn't going to insult her to her dad's face, but I honestly didn't think she had that in her.

"Yeah. She knew I wanted to expand, and she was annoyed that I would never actually pull the trigger. This was among the stuff she was working on behind my back—wiley woman that one. I haven't gone through most of her stuff yet, I haven't been able to bring myself to do it, but I made it this far at least."

My gaze drifted back down to the map, and it was all there. Twice as many officers as we usually had, higher salaries, and there were notes that seemed to refer to additional money sources as well. Nick may not have gotten through more of Tess' plans, but they were definitely out there.

I… was impressed. "So, we wanna get up to twelve titles?"

"Yes. Pay-ins for those bottom two levels is pure income, because they get nothing out of it." He pointed to the bottom two squares, inside of which the words "Friendly" and 'Regular" were written. "It's basically all the people that fucking pay around the Taphouse, and they can 'donate' to be able to say they have an affiliation. That fucking kid of mine, I swear."

"Yeah, this…" I looked up at Nick with a smile. "This could work."

"We'd need salaries for every officer, obviously, and the stipends for the members, which we're seeing a return on anyway because of dues."

I flipped through the pages of my books, looking at our trajectory for profit by the end of the year. "We could do this going into next year, Nicky."

"For real?" he asked.

"For real."

"How about you head it up, then?"

My eyes shot up to him. "What? Why would I do it? It's something the new VP should do."

"Exactly," Nick said.

There was silence between us for a moment before I plainly said, "I'm not interested in being VP."

The excitement that had gone into Nick's face as we spoke about the new plans evaporated in a second. "Fine." He reluctantly pulled the plans away and tucked them back into the cubby, muttering, "We can't really expand until I find a second-in-command," then got up from the table and wandered away.

I didn't like that it seemed like I added to his stress, but that kind of position just wasn't for me. My life was fine exactly as it was. Shaking it up never seemed to work well for me, and

I was good at what I did, so why change it? We *were* going to find a VP, and there were several men in the club who'd been there longer than me that Nick could choose from, so why he seemed to have his mind set on me, I wasn't sure. Whatever the reason, I had no plans of buying into them at all. Even if he went for Avery or one of the younger guys, I was meant to be the Steel Knights' Bookkeeper, nothing more.

Things got progressively louder over the course of the next few hours, and just as I was finishing my books for the day, I could hear the kitchen firing up as Hoppa's prepared to open. The other members floated in and out of the warehouse, knowing better than to bother me while I was working, but eventually, Avery walked over and sat down in the chair next to me. He handed me over a band of receipts, with a grin. "The monthlies."

I added them to my book for reconciliation tomorrow. "Thanks."

"So, did you see what's going on out there?"

"Huh?" I was jotting down my last numbers and notes for the day and was mostly not listening.

"Did you see all the people?"

Finally, I stopped and looked up at him. "What do you mean?" It was only then that I realized it was as loud as I would expect it to be at eight or nine at night, but it was still just after opening. "Wait, what's going on?"

"*All* that commotion," Avery said, "is hopefuls."

My jaw dropped. "What?"

With that, I finished up what I was doing, put my books away in the locked drawer where I kept them, and made my way out to the bar with Avery at my heels. I shoved my way through the swinging doors and when I passed into the bar, I froze.

There were *dozens* of people scattered around, all talking excitedly.

Nick was standing behind the bar with a wide smile on his face. "They're *all* here to pledge?" I asked.

"Most of 'em," Nick responded. "So, we're gonna spend tonight whittling 'em down, and you know who I think *you* should start with, Bullet?"

"Who?"

Nick pointed out and I followed his finger to someone who took my shock away and replaced it with rage. In the center of the bar, mingling with the different hopeful prospects, and in an outfit that unsubtly showed off her assets, was Celia.

Chapter Three

Bullet

By the time the evening had rolled around, Hoppa's Taphouse was standing room only. Nick had already made Seth and Vil start pilfering chairs from the bar one by one and taking them back to the warehouse because they were taking up too much room, and many of the occupants had poured out into the parking lot. The music was pumping at a louder volume than usual so that even those overflowing outside could still hear it, and inside, the bar was backed up and had already stopped serving any kind of food to ensure everyone who wanted a drink could get one without too much wait.

After collecting all of the members in the warehouse and giving a quick briefing on what to look for, and telling us he would be refraining from nominations as further punishment to himself for what he pulled with Colin, Nick sent us off to mingle with the possible prospects, who were all wearing a silver flag pinned to their jackets, and figure out who might be a good addition to the club. These were still just hopefuls, and no one was *ensured* membership, but with us already being down so many men and Nick's expansion plan in the back of my mind, I was thinking that we collectively needed to find seven to ten possible prospects to really fill our new ranks out.

But I was distracted.

First, I wasn't much of a "mingler". "Hello," I said to one of the possible prospects. "What's your name?"

"Mario Boone." He stuck out a hand and I took it and gave it a brief shake before letting it go. "You?"

"Just call me 'Bullet'," I replied.

"Bullet," he repeated. "Nice to meet you."

"You, too. So…" I glanced over at Avery and Bucky who were floating through the room without a care in the world, talking and laughing with nearly everyone in the bar. "Uh, why do you want to pledge?"

"I've been a bike rider my whole life. Literally, my dad first took me out on his bike when I was just six months old. Ma nearly divorced him."

I chuckled. "Sounds like my dad."

"Oh yeah? You two close?"

My throat tightened a little bit. "We were. He died when I was young."

"Oh, man, I'm sorry," Mario replied. "I... God, that was stupid."

"It's okay. We were very close. I'm also very close with my foster father. He's still alive, so that's safe territory." Mario stared back at me nervously and I chuckled. "Sorry. I have a dark sense of humor. It's true though, I'm close with him, too."

"Cool. Does he ride bikes?" Mario asked.

"No, he's a four-walls, both-feet-on-the-ground kind of guy. He doesn't even like to fly."

Mario chuckled. "My dad is a high-risk, high-reward type, so if adrenaline is involved, he's into it. I inherited it from him for sure."

"So, you would say you aren't afraid of a little danger then?" I asked.

He shrugged. "We're all dying, it's what we do with the time we have that counts."

"True indeed."

The only thing worse than starting a conversation with a stranger, was ending it. Both Mario and I stood in silence for much longer than I would have liked before I finally just decided I didn't care to be awkward and just walked away. I kept my eyes out for those the other members were talking to and tried to pick out those it didn't seem they'd crossed, but it seemed like they were covering the bases. Thanks to that, my attention kept getting siphoned by the other distraction present for me that evening.

Celia.

Fortunately, she wasn't there to pledge, but she was floating around, flirting with all of the different prospects like it was her job. Her long, curly black hair was like a magnificent mane flowing down her back and she somehow kept finding a place to stand that cast a perfect spotlight over her pristine, honey-colored skin. Her hazel eyes flashed every time she laughed at what someone was saying, and every now and again, she would flick out a hand and run it along the arms or chest of whoever she was talking to. It was taking me an active effort not to stand there staring at her like an idiot. She hadn't so much as looked in my direction since she arrived, yet she was always right in my eyeline when I looked up.

Was she doing it on purpose, or was my brain just betraying me?

That ship had sailed regardless. I'd spent a minuscule amount of time thinking that maybe, just maybe, she was going to be the one who pulled me out of my cage.

Damn, I hated being wrong.

To drag myself away from her, I scanned the room for Avery, planning to join him in whatever conversation he was locked in. I found him, along with Bucky and Vil, talking to one ridiculously tall man, with slicked-back black hair and a thick, bushy horseshoe mustache. They were all so captivated by him, that I had to walk over and see what all the fuss was about. Sifting through the crowd, I eventually came to stand at Avery's side just as he was finishing speaking.

"The second cow says, 'Wow. Good thing I'm a helicopter!'" Everyone listening to the guy speak erupted with laughter, except for me, because I missed the joke. The guy in question noticed my lack of response and jutted out his hand immediately. "Oh! Sorry, I didn't see you sneak up on us. I'm Joey."

I took Joey's hand and shook it just as Avery put his hand on my shoulder. "Oh, this is the guy I was telling you about, Bullet." He looked at me. "Joey's a huge Age of Logic fan!"

My eyes widened. Age of Logic was a lesser-known, Arizona-bred band who played at MiD every year. "No kidding?"

"Aw, yeah, man! I first saw 'em with a bunch of my friends back in high school and I've loved them ever since. I went on a huge, cross-country trip last year following them to all their concerts, and it ended with the Steel Knights desert concert. I saw you guys, the fellowship, and how much fun you guys were having, and I said, 'Shit, I gotta get with them somehow.' I just moved to Hoppa a couple weeks ago and saw the call for prospects yesterday."

"Wow. So, you've wanted to join long before today?" I asked.

"For like a fucking year!" He smiled. "I'm gonna do whatever it takes to prove I belong here."

Bucky let out a husky chortle. "Isn't this guy great, Bullet?"

"Seems pretty great," I said. "Do you think…"

Behind Joey, Celia walked back into my field of view. When I first looked up, it almost seemed like she was looking over at me, but when I focused on her, she was talking to someone else, not looking in my direction in the least.

"Uh…" Joey chuckled. "Did he run out of juice or something?"

Avery looked in the direction I was staring in and then rammed his shoulder into mine. I cleared my throat and shook my head. "Sorry. I lost my train of thought there."

"Yeah, booze'll do that to ya," Joey said. "Don't touch the stuff."

"Really?" Avery asked.

"Oh yeah, don't get me wrong, no judgment or anything, I've just seen a lot of stupid people do a lot of stupid shit. I do enough stupid shit *without* the influence of liquor, so I try not to tip the odds any more than my mama did when she pushed me out."

Everyone laughed, and even I broke into a chuckle, but I was distracted by Celia in the background once again. "Excuse me for a second."

"Sure."

In an instant, Joey turned his attention away from me and went back to entertaining the crowd surrounding him, and I threaded my way through the people until I was able to slip behind the bar, through the kitchen, and back into the much quieter warehouse. I wasn't shocked to see Seth hiding out back there, too. He hadn't been in the club long, but he was less of a social person, much like me.

"Running away, too?" I asked as I walked over and joined him at the table in the middle of the room. "This is why we need a legit clubhouse so we can just escape somewhere when Nicky packs the place."

Seth snickered. "That'd be nice for sure, but then I'd probably never talk to anyone."

"You and me both." I crossed my arms. "Did you see anyone noteworthy out there?"

"A couple of guys. Some guy named Travis and a real thick, beefy guy named Kyran I think? Neither of 'em seemed like big brain types, but we're a leaner group of individuals. I think we could use some real muscle, especially since we lost Stag. Texas and Bullseye can't hold us down all alone."

I side-glanced my own bicep. "I mean… I'm no slouch."

Seth held up a hand with a laugh. "Nothing personal, man. Listen, we can take a punch collectively, but did you *see* that one guy that came with Luther when they raided us?" He didn't have to get too into explaining him for a vision of the behemoth that joined Luther and the other Unchained Dogs when they came to bother us. He was stacked, damn near seven feet tall, and with enough muscle to lift a bus. "We need a guy like that."

"That couldn't hurt," I replied. "I chatted up a couple guys, too. That one guy everyone seems to like, Joey, and some guy named Mario. Biking's in his blood."

Seth nodded. "That's the fundamental we're looking for."

"Yeah," I replied. "I think he could be good. The prospect trail will tell."

The door swung open and Nick's head peeked in. He looked over at Seth and I sitting at the table and sighed. "How did I know I'd find you two hiding out back here?"

"You know what you get with us," I quipped.

"Well, knock it off and get out here, we're gonna nominate some prospects."

He didn't stick around to see if we listened or not, just left, and I looked across at Seth. "We each have a couple names, so I think we're good."

Seth chuckled. "No one can say we didn't do our job."

Together, we walked out of the warehouse and back into the bar. Everyone had been quieted and had packed in along the tables and was waiting. Nick climbed up on the bar, not without a little bit of waver, and held his arms out.

"Hey, everyone, I just want to thank you all for coming tonight!" All the patrons started to cheer or raise their glasses to Nick. "Tonight, we're doing something we haven't done since my old man was running the joint, and we opened prospecting for the Steel Knights. Ordinarily, I like for my members to come recommended, but if I've learned anything tonight, it's that *everyone* in Hoppa is a worthy prospect!"

More hoots and hollers screamed out and I found myself scanning the crowd for Celia, but she was nowhere to be found. After a pass in both directions, I finally stopped trying to find her, figuring she must have gone home. It wasn't all that surprising. She wasn't there to see me regardless, so why would I give a damn if she stayed or left?

From the front of the crowd, one of the Steel Knights' non-officered members, Derek "Small Fry" Myers, cupped his hands on either side of his mouth and shouted out, "Let's get to nominatin'!"

People clapped along and cheered, and Nick held out his hands to quiet the crowd. "All right. Can I have all the *members* of the Steel Knights come stand behind the bar please?" Seth and I were already standing behind the bar, and another member, Jonathan "Jonesie" Jones, was sitting right at it and just hoisted himself up and over, and the rest of the members, Avery, Bucky, Texas, Small Fry, and Vil all walked around and packed in alongside us. "All right, gents, remember, prospects need a nomination and a second to qualify. Let's hear your nominations."

To my surprise, Seth's hand was first in the air. "I have a nomination."

Nick looked down at him. "Let's hear it."

He'd told me about the two guys he spoke with, Travis and Kyran, but he cleared his throat and said, "I nominate Colt Hardy."

"Colt?" Nick called out, and a man excused his way through the crowd and stepped to the front. He was a bit shorter than Seth, and looked younger as well, but the resemblance between the two was uncanny. "Uh, there's gotta be a relation here, right?"

"Yes," Seth replied. "Colt's my brother."

Everyone shifted uncomfortably behind the bar. In the wake of what had happened with Colin, not to mention Nick's preferential treatment of his kids, everyone was no doubt thinking a familial nomination was probably not the best idea.

"Uh, look..." Nick started, but before he could finish, Bucky's hand went into the air.

"I second," he said, and then looked up at Squared. "These boys are cut from the same cloth, Squared. Colt shows real promise."

"Well, okay then," Nick replied. "I'm holding you both to this one though."

Seth offered a silent nod, compared to Bucky's very boisterous, "Fine by me, Squared! I have another nomination. Joey Williamson."

Half the members behind the bar started to hoot as Joey made his way from the back of the bar near the pool table to the front. Avery, Vil, and Small Fry's hands went into the air, and even though they didn't need the numbers, I put mine up as well.

"I second," Avery got out first.

"Third," Vil said.

Small Fry followed with, "Fourth."

And I rounded us out. "Fifth."

Nick let out a whistle. "Well, Joey. Seems you're liked around here! All right then!"

A few people near Joey tapped him on his shoulder to congratulate him.

"I have one," I said with my hand in the air. "Mario Boone."

Near the door to the bar, Mario was standing, and his eyes had widened with shock. Perhaps no one else really got the chance to talk to him throughout the night, but then Avery put his hand in the air and yelled, "I second."

Mario walked over and stood with Colt and Joey, still with a surprised expression on. "Thank you," he said.

Over the course of the next fifteen or so minutes, nominations continued until we had seven people standing in front of us. Along with Colt, Joey, and Mario, the rest of the members nominated a shorter, but stockier man named Karl Collier, with long blond hair falling down his back, a man named Marshall Roman, who had a purple heart patch sewn onto his jacket, and the two guys Seth had mentioned to me, Travis and Kyran.

"Well now, this looks like quite the array," Nick said with a wide smile on his face. "Are there any other nominations, or is this it?" Directly behind Nick, Texas cleared his throat. Nick looked back over his shoulder at him. "Yes?"

"Uh, yeah. I do have one more nomination." He took a deep breath in, held it for a few seconds, and then let it out. "I'd like to nominate Seneca Villetrio."

A body shifted in the crowd, and then a woman side-stepped her way through the group. She had bronze skin, a short, black haircut with the right side of her head shaved and the rest brushed over and hanging down the left side of her head and a little in front of her face, and striking gray eyes.

"Whoa," Avery whispered next to me. "She's been here all night?"

I hadn't even noticed. Apart from the couple of guys I'd spoken with, the only *woman* I noticed was Celia.

The crowd murmured and muttered to themselves as Seneca came to a stop at the front of the crowd, and she just stood there, patiently waiting for anyone to second. The room was silent, and for as dejecting as that had to have been, she stood there with a look of confidence that was shocking, to say the least.

Nick waited, not closing the nomination for as long as he could, but then he lifted his hand into the air. "Well, I'm sorr—"

Then Seth's hand went up. "I second." Everyone's gaze shot to him. "I talked to Seneca for a bit. She's never even driven a car before, just bikes. That's…" He chuckled. "That's pretty cool."

Vil's hand went up after that. "I third." He smiled. "She's a punk rocker like me, plus she's tough as nails."

After that, Small Fry's hand went up. "She beat Bucky in an arm wrestle," he snickered. "Fourth."

"No," Bucky spat out, "she's pretty strong though, I'll give her that." His hand went up. "I'll fifth."

I felt conflicted. If so many of them had positive experiences with her, why had no one nominated her before now?

As if they'd all heard my thoughts, all the members turned to look at me. "What?"

"I'll defer to you," Nick said to me.

"Why me?"

"Because of Tess," Nick said simply.

That was a shattering statement. Seneca was a woman, and my trust issues with women created more than one issue with Tess. Was I prepared to take on the full responsibility for the way she was treated? No. But, if we were to say who had the biggest problem with her…

"She only needs two," I replied. "A nomination and a second. She had that four votes ago."

Nick's nervous expression melted into a smile. "That she did." He turned to face her again. "Well, congrats! Do we have anyone else?"

No one said anything and a few of the other silver-flag-wearing people in the crowd deflated. Nick must have seen it, too, because he clapped his hands a few times. "Hey. I'll have none of that. There was a shit ton of people here tonight and this isn't the end all be all. If you think the Knights are right for you, come by and see us more often. Who knows, you may find yourself nominated yet."

This seemed to brighten spirits and as Nick climbed off the bar, the music started up again, and everyone went back to talking, drinking, and dancing. The chosen prospects continued to stand as Nick made his way over to speak to them.

"I'm surprised you cleared that," Avery said.

I frowned. "It wasn't up to me."

Avery tapped my back. "Sure it was."

With that, the rest of the members walked out from behind the bar and threaded back into the crowd, but I'd had enough excitement for one night. I walked back through the warehouse and used the back door to leave the Taphouse, walking around to the front at a slow, tired pace to get to my bike. I got to the side of it and started to pull my helmet out of the back when a finger tapped me on the shoulder.

I turned around and my heart started to beat faster than I was comfortable with. Celia was standing there facing me, her hip kicked out to the side and a seductive grin on her face.

"Aw, were you just going to leave? Without even saying goodbye?"

Chapter Four

Celia

It turned out to be a better idea than I realized, staying away from Harry until that night. The whole point was to keep him hanging on by a thread, but if I'd seen him prior to that night, I might have lost sight of my goal.

"I know you saw me in there," I hummed. "I'm surprised you didn't say hello. Especially after that night we had."

The memory of it burned over my skin as it fought to recall all the places Harry had touched me. He was just a means to an end, but what a sexy one he was. If it wasn't the muscles that I knew were hidden under his reserved jacket and jeans, it was the glasses that sat in front of his golden eyes, with the few wisps of his brown hair hanging down in front of them. If my target had been any less attractive, I wouldn't be struggling so much.

"How have you been these past few weeks?" I asked.

Harry was standing next to his bike with his helmet in his arms. He looked at me with something between a curious gaze and a harsh glare. "You're kidding, right?"

I pushed out my bottom lip, doing the best I could to achieve faux innocence. "What do you mean?" Instead of answering me right away, Harry climbed on his bike. He watched me, almost like he was waiting for me to say something else, and for a moment, it seemed like an invitation. "Oh, do you want me to come?"

"Do I look like an idiot to you?" he asked. "We go out, and I actually thought we had a good time."

"We did. In fact, that was one of the best nights I've ever had."

"So then, why haven't I heard from you? I called you. I texted you. Was it just about the sex? If it was, that's fine, but I'm not interested in wasting my time, so you can go find someone else to spend the night with."

"Call me clueless but given that someone else had to convince you to go out with me at all, I'm a little surprised that you're the 'all or nothing' type." I set my hands on my hips and intentionally stuck them out to accentuate the curves that Harry's eyes kept flicking to, no matter how hard he was trying to keep them straight. "So I wasn't trying to marry you after a single date. That makes me a bad person?"

"I didn't say anything about marriage," Harry replied, "but I had a certain expectation that you'd at least answer my phone call if I tried to contact you again, not just completely ghost me. If you weren't interested in anything more than spending the night together, you could have said that so that I wasn't left wondering."

To say I was surprised by Harry's position would be an understatement. He simply didn't seem like an emotional guy. The point was to lead him on, but I didn't think it'd be so difficult. Was he really only going to give me one chance?

"Listen, I thought everyone enjoyed a little cat and mouse. It's not like I'm the only one who played hard to get."

"Yeah," he said, "but once I agreed to go out with you, you didn't have to try anymore. I wasn't so lucky." I opened my mouth to retort, but before I could get any words out, Harry started up his bike, cutting me off with its loud rumble. "There are plenty of people in that bar who would be happy to have you. Go play around with someone else."

With that, he pulled his helmet over his head and revved his bike a couple of times, then he pulled out of the parking spot and roared away without looking back.

Insulted would be putting it mildly.

Our first night together was one for the history books. Why would anyone turn down the opportunity to have *that* again? With my arms crossed, I watched Harry pull out of the parking lot and ride off down the street until he was out of sight. I knew I had to go home, but I didn't want to face what awaited me there.

Did I wait too long to contact Harry again? Did I mess everything up by playing it a little too cool?

With nothing left to do, I fished my keys out of my pocket and made my way over to my car. I got in, and even waited a few additional minutes to see if Harry was going to double back, but he didn't. Defeated, and unsure of how I was going to explain my failure, I finally left Hoppa's Taphouse and made my way home.

Part of me was hoping that the late hour would save me as I pulled up to my godfather's house, but pulling into the driveway, I could see the lights were on and the television was flickering in the living room. I let out a sigh and slowly crawled my car into the garage. I turned the car off before dropping my head to the steering wheel in frustration.

"Sorry, Daddy," I said out loud.

There was nothing to be gained from continuing to linger in the car. He heard the garage door open; he knew I was home.

It was time to just face facts.

I climbed out of the car and made my way through the door that led from the garage into the kitchen. I hung my keys on the hooks next to the door and waited to see if I heard any sounds.

"Celia?"

I dropped my head. "Yeah, it's me."

The next thing I heard was the sound of wheels squeaking their way across the carpet. It wouldn't help to move or run, so I just waited and eventually, my godfather, Darrien, entered the kitchen in his wheelchair. His curly, brown hair was a mess and there was already a look of fervent disappointment in his green eyes.

"I didn't expect you home tonight," he said in a tone that was as judgmental as it was accusatory. "I thought you were going out with Harry again."

"Yeah, uh, things didn't quite go as I expected them to," I explained.

"What do you mean?"

"I think I may have waited a little too long to strike again. He was… less than thrilled to see me."

At this, Darrien rolled over to the fridge where he kept an article about his accident hanging. He smoothed a finger along the edge of it, brushing specifically over the words "paralyzed" and "dead". "Well that's unfortunate. Isn't there anything a smart girl like you can do?"

"He was pretty pissed off," I replied. "I told him I was just trying to be coy, but he wasn't going for it."

"That doesn't surprise me, knowing him. Still, it's nothing a little hounding can't fix. You said he seemed to really enjoy himself. Surely, if you continue to dangle the fruit, he'll take a bite at some point."

"Dangle it how?" I asked.

He looked up at me. "Don't let him loose so easily. Call him. Text him. Contact him on social media. Tell him you just want a chance to explain yourself and lay it on thick that you're still really interested. Eventually, he'll take the bait, if for no other reason than to get you to leave him alone, and in that moment, you reel him back in."

Darrien's finger on the article on the fridge glided under the image of my dad. One of the last smiling pictures he took before he died. "You owe this to your dad, don't you think?"

"Yeah."

"You don't just want him to get away with what he did to us, do you?"

I shook my head. "No, I don't."

"Good. So, figure it out. You can do this."

"Yeah. I'll figure it out. I promise."

"Good." He wheeled back a little and opened the fridge and I could see that the dinner I'd made him was still inside. I glanced over and saw the pills he was supposed to take were still on the counter as well.

"Why haven't you done any of this yet? It's after midnight," I asked. "You'll be uncomfortable all night now."

He waved his hand in my face. "Don't worry about me. You just worry about how you're going to get back in Harry's good graces. We're not messing up this opportunity."

"Fine."

With that, I stepped around Darrien and made my way up the stairs to the second floor. I spent some time prepping his bed, including powering the machines which would help get him from his wheelchair into his bed, and then I went into my bedroom and changed into more comfortable clothes. I climbed into bed and pulled out my phone and navigated to Harry's number. Now having to beg him to see me again left a sour taste in my mouth. I didn't want to have to beg anyone for anything, and I could only imagine my dad wouldn't want that either.

Still.

My dad would still be with me if it weren't for Harry. Darrien was right. I couldn't waste the opportunity I had. So, I swallowed my pride and pressed the button to call him, my skin sizzling with anger when it only rang once before going to voicemail, but I took a deep breath and tried again.

And again.

And again.

For the next couple of weeks, it felt like that was all I was doing. I started out just calling and texting. Everything from sexy innuendos to blocks of text of me trying to explain away why I ghosted him, but nothing seemed to work. Eventually, he blocked me so I couldn't call or text, and he didn't have many social media outlets, just one, which I was blocked on before I even got to that method.

Which left showing up at the bar.

The new prospects that the Steel Knights had nominated the first night I went back had the place regularly packed with new people and a fresh, electric energy. Harry wasn't wrong, more than one man approached me looking to have some fun, but I had to keep my sights set on the prize. I would buy him drinks, try to coax him into a corner with me, even straight-up challenge him to a game of pool or darts, but he flat out ignored me.

Finally, I threw caution to the wind and approached one of the other club members, looking for some advice. I'd heard them calling him Dynamite, and he was closer to being my age than Harry was, not that it made much of a difference.

"Oh, you're the one who ghosted him?" Dynamite asked.

Word had spread. "I wasn't trying to," I lied. "I just got busy and I thought a little push and pull was sexy."

"Sure, maybe for *anyone* else, but you're lucky he even went out with you to begin with," Dynamite explained. "Harry hates women."

I raised an eyebrow. "What?"

"Yeah, I know it sounds kind of shitty to just say it like that, but that's what it is. He has, like, *no* respect for them. Don't get me wrong, he doesn't attack them or hurt them or anything, more like he just ignores them." He took a sip of his beer. "When we heard that he agreed to go out with you, we were *all* shocked."

"I never would have guessed from our date that he didn't like women."

Harry did everything from pull out my chair to try and convince me to wait to let him take me home. He was a perfect gentleman. Well, until we got back to his place, then he was perfect in other ways. If he did have a hatred for women, it wasn't evident that night.

"You got lucky. *Real* lucky," Dynamite said. "The fact that he went out with you at all is crazy. He gave you a shot and you blew it, so you can forget about ever talking to him again."

Harry was sitting at the bar talking to one of the bar's patrons as I spoke with Dynamite. His broad shoulders and straight jaw were a sight to behold and something about thinking I'd never get to be with him again bothered me.

A lot.

Without saying anything else to Dynamite, I stood up and walked over to where Harry was sitting. I slipped in between him and the person he was talking to, facing the other person. It was an older man, probably Harry's same age if not a bit older, and there was nothing impressive about his look, but he wasn't unattractive.

"Hi," I greeted, setting my hand on his chest. "I'm Celia."

His eyes nearly bugged out of his skull. He grinned back at me, letting one of his hands come up to skirt along my hip. "Well, hello there. I'm Mark."

"Mm, Mark," I replied. "That's an easy name."

"Easy?" he said.

"Yeah," I replied, "to scream."

Mark's jaw dropped and he looked all around him before bringing his eyes back to mine. "Am I being pranked or something? Did one of my friends put you up to this? There's no way you're real."

"I'm very real," I replied. "I'd love to show you."

"Uh." Mark downed everything that was left of his beer in one large gulp before slamming the bottle on the bar. "Hell yeah."

I took Mark's hand and turned around, but to my shock, Harry was still sitting there, though he had his back turned to me and was speaking to someone else on his other side.

"They could take it all the way this year," the man he was now talking to, said. "The Suns are looking nice already."

"You keep telling yourself that, Bucky," Harry replied in his gruff voice, and it sent a shiver down my spine. I still had dreams about him from that night we were together. That voice in my ear. "I'm gonna go with the Celtics, just like I do every year."

The other guy, Bucky, laughed. "Yeah, yeah, yeah. Damn traitor."

"Let's go," Mark said in my ear. "I can barely hold back right now."

We continued past Harry and Bucky talking, but Harry didn't even look up. It was frustrating and irritating. I was throwing everything I had at the man and he just wasn't picking it up. The thought that, after everything, I might have blown my one shot being a little too arrogant was enough to make me want to pack up, leave Hoppa, and never come back, but I simply couldn't give up. Not just yet.

So, Mark got lucky. At least at first. I let him take me home, more as an outlet for my frustration than anything else, but he wasn't even half as good as Harry and I ended up leaving halfway through. I didn't feel like sitting under my godfather's disappointed stare, so I went to crash with my old college roommate Laura. She was used to me coming, and even left my room in the apartment the same, so I used my key to enter, walked right past her on the couch, and went into my old bedroom and plopped down on the bed.

"Rough night?" Laura asked from the doorway.

I didn't look up from my pillow to respond. "You have no idea."

"What happened?"

Laura didn't know what I was up to. "I… like this guy."

"Seriously?" she yelped. "What's his name?"

"Harry."

"Wow. I wouldn't have expected it from you. You do the whole 'no strings attached' thing. So why the long face?"

"I tried to play hard to get," I said, "and I failed."

Chapter Five

Bullet

I got the last of my beer down just as Nick shut and locked the front doors.

"Whoo, we've been packin' the place ever since the prospects started up," Nick said. "Y'all sure know how to attract a crowd."

The timer on my phone beeped to let me know it was three in the morning. On occasion, I'd get a little too caught up in hanging out at the Taphouse and forget I had two cats at home that got really angry when I came home too late. I slid my empty beer bottle over to one of the bartenders who was cleaning up and then stood up from my barstool.

Turning around and looking at everyone who was still left in the Taphouse, I did feel a little better about our numbers. With all of the members there, plus the seven new prospects, we were actually starting to look like a proper club again. Nick had been so opposed to open enrolment, but it seemed to be going okay. The prospects were taking on their tasks with pride and completing them without issue. At first, I was thinking at least half of the prospects would drop or fail out, but so far, they were all proving themselves worthy.

Open enrolment just might be the way to fill ourselves out permanently.

"You outta here, Bullet?" Nick called over when he noticed me standing.

"Yeah. I'm exhausted."

"Hey, what was ol' girl up to tonight?" Bucky asked. "That was her, right? The one Nicky set you up with. She slid in and started talkin' to that guy right in your face."

"I don't know what she's doing lately," I replied. "One day she won't even return my calls, next day I could use her incessant texts as morning alarms. She'll buy me a drink and then turn around and mess with that guy." I shrugged. "I don't know, but I damn sure don't have the energy to try and figure it out."

"She asked me about you," Seth said. "Was wondering why you weren't giving her the time of day."

"What'd you tell her?"

"That she fucked up," he replied simply. "I told her that it was a surprise at all you even went out with her so she could pretty much forget you talking to her ever again."

He wasn't wrong, but something about hearing it laid out like that left a sore spot in my stomach. I guessed that *was* what I was doing, ignoring her to get her to leave me alone, but did

I really plan on never talking to her again?

I looked over at Seneca. She was sitting at a table near the back with some of the other prospects, and though she wasn't looking in my direction, she was quiet, and I could tell she was listening.

"What do you think?" I asked.

Everyone followed my gaze back to her, and then Joey, who was sitting across from her, nudged her and she looked over at me. "Me?"

"Yeah."

"You want *my* opinion?" she said. "You realize I'm a woman." The tone of her voice was thickly sarcastic, and slightly dark.

"I'm aware of that. I'm wondering if you have any idea why she's acting the way she is?"

Seneca stood up out of her chair. She had a bottle of water in her hand, but it was empty, and she squeezed, crinkling the plastic. She walked through the bar, over to where I was and came to stand very close to me. Avery was sitting at the stool next to where I was, and turned to face her, but he didn't move or say anything, just watched.

"I've heard all about you," she said. "I've been a fan of the Steel Knights for a while, but I never came in here because I'd heard all about the guy who hates women. Hates 'em so bad that he wouldn't even respect the Vice President."

Deep in me, my blood started to boil. "Whatever."

I made as if I was going to walk away, but Seneca stepped to the side, staying in my path. "That's true, isn't it? Everyone followed your lead and you fucking ran her out of here."

"I didn't run her out of anywhere. She left with a traitor."

"Interesting version of that story," she remarked before scanning the bar. "I've heard it a few different times from a few different people and the only one who tells it that way is you."

I looked around at the other members of the club, eventually at Nick who looked down at the ground, and then Avery who turned his attention back to his beer. "So this is all on me?" I said out loud. "Shit going sideways with Tess, that's *all* because of me?"

"It's not," Bucky said. "We all played our part, it's just... You know, CJ wasn't that bad."

"Yeah, and I truly think if Tess thought she had somewhere to go here, she would have stayed," Small Fry added.

"Where is all this coming from? None of you ever said this before?"

"What do you want from us?" Avery asked from next to me. He was the only one who ever refused to play into my energy about Tess and always treated her with kindness. "Would you have listened?"

"You want my honest to God opinion about why that chick is acting the way she is?" Seneca said, pulling my attention back to her. "It's because you deserve it. After all this time of treating women like shit, you should have expected that someone would come along and return the favor. So, don't be so surprised. This is what karma feels like, *Harry*."

With that, Seneca turned around and walked out of the bar, leaving us in complete, intense silence. A total stranger felt that strongly about me, and the entire club was hiding their true feelings from me because of how strongly I'd projected my dislike.

That was never what I wanted.

"Women have never been anything but horrible to me," I said. "I'm not about to apologize for that." It wasn't entirely what I wanted to say, but apart from not wanting to apologize when I didn't really think I'd done anything wrong, I just felt misunderstood. Avery tried to put a hand on my shoulder, but I pulled myself away. "Don't." And with that, I walked out of the bar, glad to see that Seneca was quick in leaving, and carried myself home as well.

I didn't get a wink of sleep that night.

I'd already been thinking that I made a mistake with Tess since Nick showed me some of her plans, but after Seneca's accusations, I couldn't see straight.

Was she right? Was Celia just toying with me to get back at me for the way I'd treated other women?

My alarm going off to coax me out of bed was interrupted by the sound of my phone ringing. It was early, and it was hard to ignore the sense of actually hoping it *was* Celia, but when I lifted my phone, it wasn't her number, but my foster father, Cameron.

I pressed the button to answer the call and then immediately hit the speaker button. "Hello?"

"Hey. Oh, don't worry. It's just me, your father. The one who loves you and took care of you when you were sick. Paid for your field trips and packed you lunches. You wouldn't know that by how little you've called me, but don't worry. I'm okay. It's me, Cameron. Your father."

"Are you done?" I replied.

"I mean, I also got you a puppy, but who's counting?"

"I prefer cats."

He laughed. "That's cold, Harry."

I laughed back at him. "Hey, Dad."

"Hey. Sorry to call so early, but I was wondering what you were up to today? Wanna come over for breakfast?"

Technically, I had to work, but the club would be fine for one day without me. I could make it up whenever. Nick wasn't overly stressed about schedules. "Yeah, I could do that. Do you want me to bring anything?"

"Nah. I got all the stuff for omelets yesterday. Bacon and sausage just like you like. You know, because I'm a good dad."

"You're sure to win the Oscar, Dad."

He laughed again, this time louder. "Yeah, yeah. Just get over here. That dog that you would have rather had a cat misses you."

"All right. I'm on the way."

"Cool, bye."

"Bye."

Already, my mood was lighter. I wouldn't be the man I was if Cameron hadn't come along. He'd been my foster dad from the time I was eleven years old and had loved me like I was his own. It was hard at first, treating any man like my dad other than the man who'd raised me, but Cameron told me he was probably looking down on me, happy I was out of my mom's clutches.

He'd want me to have a good parent still.

Thanks to Cameron, I did.

Milton, the Dachshund that Cameron had bought me as a puppy not long after I came to live with him, came ambling up to the door as soon as I walked in. His brown fur was graying all over, and he didn't move with the same vigor he used to, but at damn near thirteen years old, that he was still alive at all was a miracle.

Sure, I preferred cats to dogs, but Milton was a therapy dog and had helped me through many rough nights, so I sat on the floor as he walked up and let him wander into my lap. "Hey, buddy."

Cameron walked down the hallway from the kitchen and smiled down at me. "He still sleeps in your old room, you know?"

"Are you *trying* to break my heart?" I asked.

"You could take him. Don't get me wrong, I love the old guy, but he clearly would rather be with you."

I scruffed the sides of Milton's face. "I don't know how well he'd get along with the cats."

"He gets on fine with Marty," Cameron replied, and as if on cue, Cameron's huge, gray Maine Coon came wandering into the hallway from the living room. He snuggled against me and immediately started to purr, so I held out my arm so he could crawl up as well, though he took up much more space than Milton.

Cameron sputtered out a laugh. "You and animals, I swear."

"They like me, what can I say?"

"Well, get off the floor before you get too much hair on you and come eat."

As soon as I moved to get to my feet, both Milton and Marty let out their individual grunts of dissatisfaction, but both followed as I walked down into the kitchen. Looking over at Cameron, I laughed, noticing for the first time that he was wearing a yellow, frilly "kiss the cook" apron, which looked even more hysterical against his dark brown skin and bald head.

"That's a unique look," I said as I dropped down into a chair at the kitchen table.

"Yeah," he laughed awkwardly. "It was a gift."

He used a spatula to move an omelet onto a plate from one of the pans at the oven and then he brought it over and set it down in front of me. On top of being an amazing father, Cameron was an out-of-this-world cook. He never went into the field professionally, which was a shame, because it was *obviously* his calling. He grabbed some orange juice and milk from the fridge and set them down in front of me with a glass and then returned to the stove to finish off his own omelet.

"Who gave you that as a gift?" I asked, settling into my food, the hot spices and juicy meat easing my stress from the night before.

"Uh… We'll get to that, but first, why do you look so tired?"

It shouldn't have surprised me that he noticed. "I didn't sleep well last night. Rather, I didn't sleep at all."

"How come?" He finished his omelet and moved it over to a plate, then came and joined me at the table. "Work?"

"Kinda." I looked up at him. "You know how you always told me the way I felt about my mom was justified?"

That took him back a bit. He looked up at me, worried. "Yes?"

"And that judge and cop. You always said it was understandable the way I felt about them, too."

"It was. They favored your mother when they shouldn't have, and it could have spared you a lot of pain."

"Is it fair that I distrust women?" I asked finally.

"Fair is an interesting word to use," he replied. "I understand why you distrust women. I think anyone would, given everything you went through, but I don't know that I would consider it fair."

"How come?"

"Well, because not all women are like your mother, or even that judge or cop who looked the other way when you were being abused or when your father died." He cleared his throat. "There are some really good women out there."

People like Celia and Seneca came to mind. "I may have recently learned that total strangers hate me because of my reputation, and even a bunch of guys at the club don't agree with my philosophy."

"Well, most people love their mothers. Or they have sisters, girlfriends, even wives that they love and believe in. It's like I said, there are really good women out there. You just got dealt a really bad hand. You've struggled to trust women and I couldn't blame you, but I did try and snap you out of it. There were a lot of women who *did* care about you. You had teachers that were worried about you, and my mother loves you like her own grandson."

"Yeah," I replied.

"It's not as if you just pulled this stuff out of thin air though, Harry. If you're feeling bad about it now, that's good, but don't expect it to all go away in one day. Just work with it, you know? Think about it this way; you have a sibling out there somewhere, right?"

"That's what I'm told."

Cameron pointed his fork at me. "What if it's a sister? Would you be okay knowing someone was out there treating her how you've treated some women in the past?"

My birth father was a man who honored women above everything. Even for all the abuse he endured from my mom, he never once put his hands on her. I made sure I was never abusive toward women, because I knew how disappointed he'd be if he were still alive. But there were times I went out of my way to spite Tess. I even approached Colin when he first arrived and told him not to trust her, too.

"No," I said finally. "I wouldn't be okay with that."

"So keep that in mind. Treat women how you'd want her to be treated," Cameron said.

"Yeah," I replied. "Thanks."

"By the way, I spoke to the detective yesterday, but still no new news. Do you want to keep him on retainer? It's sucking your settlement dry."

"Yep," I responded immediately. "I want him to keep looking until he finds my mom and we can save my little brother or sister."

"You got it. I'll send over the next wave of payments then."

As far as silver linings were concerned, mine came in the form of an accident I'd been in about six years ago. For all the injuries I'd suffered, the settlement I got from the accident was large enough to support the hunt I'd been on for about seven years after learning my mom had another kid after I was finally removed from her care. Knowing my mother, that child was abused as I was, and I wouldn't stop until I found them so I could save that poor kid from my fate, or worse, my father's.

"Thank you, and thanks for this talk, too. It helped."

"Actually, uh," he snickered uncomfortably again. "It's kind of interestingly timed."

"What do you mean?"

"Well, there's a reason I called you over. I mean, I wanted to see you, too, don't get me wrong, but I had to discuss something with you." He pulled out his phone, flicked through it a little bit, and then passed it over to me. On the screen was a picture of a woman with rosy peach skin, short black hair, and a bright smile. "That's Marisha."

"Okay?" I said. "You're trying to set me up on a date?"

His nose wrinkled up violently. "No! I'm… I'm dating her. Well, more than that. She's my girlfriend."

"Oh…" I said. "Wow."

"Yeah. I deliberately didn't date when you were growing up, for the aforementioned female-trust issues, but I met her at a gas station of all places. I'd just bought my new car and didn't know where the stupid gas button was. She saw me struggling and came over. All I had to do was push it, so I felt *pretty* dumb, but I got to meet her, so it all worked out."

My brow furrowed at the story. "Your new car? You bought your new car like a year ago." His gaze drifted downward and my shoulders slunk a little bit. "Oh."

"Yeah. She's so amazing. Really, Harry. I know you have your hang-ups or whatever, but I really do think you'd like her. She's been talking about moving in together and I…" He sighed and then reached into the pocket of his apron and pulled out a little black box and set it on the table. "I'm madly in love with her, bud. Like the kind that's in movies. I want to propose, but I don't want to do that without you meeting her. I'd love it if you approved of it. She'll be your new mom, kind of."

I was quiet for a really long time. All the words fluttered around my brain and I wasn't sure which ones terrified me more. "Meeting her", "Approved", "New Mom". They were all scary.

But Cameron had done so much for me and had given up a lot. I owed it to him to give it a shot. "Okay," I told him.

"Yeah?"

"Yeah, I'll meet her. There's a lot going on at the club right now, we just got a bunch of new prospects, but as soon as new officers are in place and stuff, things should calm down. Can we do it then?"

He nodded. "Of course!" A wide grin crossed his face as he took his phone back and looked down at the picture. "I can't wait."

Chapter Six

Bullet

It was annoying the way all conversation ground to a halt as soon as I walked into the warehouse for my meeting at Hoppa's the next day. The sparse remaining officers were situated around the table and all zipped their lips as soon as they saw me. All that could be heard was the echo of my steps as I walked over to the table and sat down, and when I sat, Avery leaned over toward me.

"Hey, man, you okay? That was a rough show the other night."

"I'm fine," I replied. "Seneca…" I let what Cameron and I had talked about and the idea that my missing younger sibling was a little girl weigh heavy in my mind. "She was right to respond the way she did toward me. I wasn't fair to Tess."

"What?" Bucky barked. "Did you just… agree with her?"

"Yeah," I snapped, "got a problem with it?"

"No." Bucky looked over at Nick who shrugged and looked toward the rest of us.

"Well, thanks for coming, guys. I know you've been waiting for me to make some decisions about how things are going to go around here, and with the new prospects looking good so far, I think I'm ready to let you know exactly what I've been planning on." He reached under the table and pulled out a long piece of legal paper, which he laid out on the table and appeared to have a hierarchy tree, similar to the one that Tess had created in her book.

"Whoa," Avery said. "There's a ton of open spaces. Are we really that short?"

"Well…" Nick looked across at me. "This is an expanded plan. I don't just want to fill our empty spots, I want to start expanding. We're growing and I want to meet that growth head on. This new plan will give us ten officers, plus two new titles, Friendly, and Regular. These titles will be applied to people who are associated with us and Hoppa's Taphouse, but don't have any pull in the club."

"Using the city to fluff ourselves," Bucky said. "That's sick."

"Exactly. That's the way the Unchained Dogs helm their entire city. I want all of Hoppa under our umbrella. Here's what I'm thinking." He flipped the page over and it was the exact same tree but with all the boxes filled in. He looked across at me. "I wanna nominate Harry to VP."

Bucky and Avery both turned to look at me and my jaw dropped. "I… said…"

"I know what you said. We'll talk about it more. Let's just move on for now." He pointed back at the paper. "Harry for VP. Bucky," he looked over at him, "I'm nominating you for Sergeant at Arms."

Bucky smiled. "Really?"

"Yeah. I think you and I both know that's what it should have been anyway. You had to babysit Taylor a lot, and I know you know the bylaws. I think you'd be good for it."

Bucky nodded. "Thanks, Squared."

Nick looked back at the paper. "Bullseye, you'd stay in the treasury position, overseeing Seth as the new bookkeeper. He's got experience in accounting and is good with numbers." Something about hearing someone else's name associated with bookkeeping made me immediately uncomfortable, but I *did* like Seth. We were very similar. "I'm thinking Jonesie will replace Bucky as the Road Captain, and Small Fry would be the Secretary. That man's got a memory like I don't know what."

"Yeah!" Avery yelped. "I've noticed that. He's weird that way."

"Then we need an enforcer, and I think you all know who I'm thinking for it," Nick said.

"Texas," we all said in unison.

Nick laughed. "He's a fighter, and he'll keep us in line for sure, and I'll fucking hunt down Father and see if he still wants to be Chaplain."

"He did *not* take well to all that crazy shit going down when CJ was here, did he?" Bucky said.

"No, he did not." Nick pointed at a lower box. "Then Vil will be in charge of whipping the prospects into shape and keeping track of the Friendlies and Regulars."

"This is a solid plan," Bucky said. "I like it. A lot."

Avery looked over at me. "Given Bullet goes for it."

How was I, all of a sudden, the wrench in the plan again? Nick, Bucky, and Avery were all staring at me patiently and I didn't know what to say. I tried a couple of times to come up with something, but nothing came out.

Finally, Nick held up a hand. "Look, you don't have to decide right now. The whole club has to vote on it, so we can talk about it. Actually..." He looked at Bucky and Avery. "Can you guys give us a minute?" Neither Bucky nor Avery replied, just stood up from the table and walked away, excitedly chattering about Nick's new plan. When the heavy metal door swung, signifying they'd exited, Nick looked over at me. "All right," Nick started. "You want the truth?"

I leaned back in my chair and crossed my arms. "That'd be good. I'm pretty confused."

"The truth, the honest to God truth, Harry, is I don't fucking trust anyone. Not one of 'em. Not Bucky, not Bullseye, not even you to be completely honest." His fingers combed into his hair. "Fuck, I haven't even taken the time I need to mourn my Goddamn kids. My son is in the ground, my daughter's off to who knows where. It's been about two months and she hasn't called. I'm supposed to be running the Steel Knights and, honestly, I don't even know what I'm doing. Taylor was the one who helped me with the bylaws, Tess helped me make all my decisions. I got fucking nothing here anymore, Bullet. I need a VP, but who do I make VP out of a whole bunch of people I'm just now realizing I barely fucking know?"

"I don't know, but I don't get why it would be me out of everyone? Avery brought me here, Bucky's more enthusiastic, plus him, Texas, *and* Small Fry have all been here longer. Why me?"

"Because I gotta start somewhere," he said, "and my daddy taught me a really important lesson super young in my life. You can *always* trust the man who manages your money."

"The night before, last I found out that you *all* think I'm responsible for what happened with Tess."

"That's not what we think," Nick replied then he flew his hand out. "It's a bunch of fucking guys out there with this new woman who they all think is pretty Goddamn great, but also a little terrifying, and she's asking questions about why they'd treat Tess like that, they gotta point the finger at someone." His hand came back to his chest as he got more impassioned. "Shit, I told Colin like three weeks after he got here that I would *never* recommend Tess for President. Basically, told him that she'd hit a ceiling here. We wanna talk about the real reason she left? That's why! Because Colin knew she wasn't going anywhere fast. I could have kicked your ass or at least kicked you out of the club for the way you treated her, and I didn't. That shit, Harry, keeps me up at night."

"I'm sorry," I said.

He folded his hands together and his voice calmed. "This expansion is so much more than that. We have to just start over. Scrap what we've been in the past and build something that can actually sustain its own weight."

"I agree."

"I knew you would," Nick said. "That's why I want you on my right side, because this shit is gonna get real crazy, and I need your level head to get us through it. I'm not even expecting you to take your hands off the money. I'm just thinking you could be more of a manager instead of a teller." I opened my mouth, but he held up a hand. "Don't say anything right now. Just, you know, sit with it for a little bit. The reason these guys all swayed with you is because they respect you—a lot. And yeah, if you're gonna pull that woman-hater shit with Seneca or any future members, it's obviously not gonna work, but I heard what you just said about her."

I nodded my head. "Yeah."

"I saw it in your face when she was telling you off the other night, you feel bad. Not just about her, but about Tess, too. I'm right there with ya." He stabbed a finger down at the expansion plan. "This is our ticket to redemption. We build and we go up and we leave that shit behind us."

The allure of it was evident. I had a great respect for Nick, and if he believed, out of everyone there, that I was the one he could trust most, I didn't want to squander that. However, I was comfortable where I was. I was happiest working with the books, and in truth, the responsibility of the VP position terrified me. It wasn't just because I saw how Tess got ripped to shreds, because most of that was on me, it was more about the height of where Nick wanted to go. He was finally ready to take the club to new heights, and I wasn't sure I was ready to take on the responsibility that entailed.

Then again, what else was I doing?

"I'll think about it. I promise," I said.

Nick nodded. "Thanks, Harry. That's all I'm asking."

Despite the place of uncertainty Nick and I had left in, the bar was buzzing with the energy of Nick's plans. Word of his ideas to promote and fill out spread quickly, and by the time the evening rolled around, the guys were toasting to the promoted members and expanded positions. Nick was quick to remind everyone that nothing would be official until that month's members' meeting where everyone could vote on the plans, but it didn't seem like he'd get many objections.

After a while, the prospects arrived and Nick tasked them with getting to know all the existing members, teasing that he may be drilling them in the near future, and the different conversations that erupted after electrified the bar from the inside out. Unfortunately for me, I couldn't enjoy the energy. All I could do was focus on the conversation Nick and I had.

"You all right there, Bullet?" I looked up from my beer and one of the new prospects, Karl, was sitting next to me. "My name's Karl, in case you forgot."

"I didn't," I replied.

He pointed at the bottle in my hand. "You've been holding that bottle halfway to your lips for about ten minutes, but it looks empty to me." I looked down at the bottle and saw that he was right, so I set it down on the bar so that one of the bartenders could scoop it up. Karl held up a hand to flag one of them down. "Hey, can I get another one for Bullet here?"

I waved my hand through the air. "No, no. That's okay. I'm calling it an early night anyway."

"You sure?" Karl said. "The round's on me."

"No, no, that's fine. If Nicky asks you what you learned about me, I have two cats named Chatterbox and Jingle."

Karl sputtered out a laugh. "Lemme guess, that's a test, right?" He saw my plain expression and frowned. "Wait. Seriously?"

"Yeah, Chatterbox is a Calico and Jingle is a white Bengal." After that, I stood up from the bar. "See ya."

With Karl still staring at me in stunned silence, I turned my back and made my way out of Hoppa's Taphouse through the front doors. The parking lot was filled with additional patrons, some of whom greeted me on my way, and I found myself absent-mindedly tracking some of the people that would be considered "Friendlies" and "Regulars" in the future. I nodded and waved, nothing so inviting as to get me caught in a conversation, and then walked over to where my bike was parked. I climbed on immediately but sat for a few minutes and enjoyed the chatter and fresh, cool night. It turned out to be my downfall, as after a few minutes, a ghost stepped into my field of view.

"Hey, Harry," Celia said. She wasn't wearing her typical layer of sass, and instead just had her hands shoved into the hooded jacket she was wearing. "Nice night out."

"It is," I replied. Behind Celia, I saw a few people stop and look over at me. In the center of them was none other than Seneca, with her arms crossed, waiting to see what would happen next. "How are you doing?" I asked.

That made Celia smile. "Not bad. You?"

"Can't complain."

"You know, I don't like being ignored," Celia said.

I nodded. "Yeah, doesn't feel good, does it?"

That seemed to strike a chord of understanding with her. "No, it doesn't. Look…" She rolled her eyes a little bit, but when they settled back into mine there was a genuine warmth, "I'm sorry for going ghost after our first date. You want to know the real truth about why I hit the bricks? It's because things went *too* well. I've never been with someone like you before and it scared the hell out of me."

"Someone like me?"

"Yeah, someone who just feels so…" she said as she bobbled her head and she searched for the right word, "…good."

I remembered the feeling all too well. As much as I tried to ignore it, Celia hadn't left my mind for a second. Her touch still lingered on my skin the way her voice lingered in my ears. "I know what you mean."

"Yeah? Then why? I'm *trying* to put myself out there. Why do you keep shutting me down?"

"Don't act as if I'm just some jerk not giving you the time of day. I was the one who called *you* back, remember? You did this first, not me." I crossed my arms. "The truth is, I don't really like wasting my time."

"And you don't like women," Celia tacked on.

I glanced past Celia to Seneca, who could at least hear enough of the conversation to hike her eyebrow as if to say, *"I told you so."*

"My relationship to women is unique. We probably would have covered it at some point during a second or third date."

"You're right," Celia said. "I should have called you, but I'm here now."

"Why now? Why all of a sudden?"

"Because…" She flopped her arms on either side of her body. "Because I've been dating, and no one does it for me like you do. Not just in bed, but in general. None of my conversations have that much depth or meaning. No one really seems to connect the same way you did. What do you want from me? I'm having—" She snickered. "Ghoster's remorse."

I couldn't keep my own chuckle from coming out and Celia smiled at me. "Look, I'm not about to do a back and forth with you, but, if you're saying you want to try, that's different," I told her.

"Would I be here making an ass of myself if I didn't?"

"I'd hope not." My eyes traveled up and down her form, reminding me of *just* how stunning she truly was. "Then what are you doing Saturday night?"

The small smile on Celia's face got infinitely wider. "I'm doing whatever you want to do."

Chapter Seven

Celia

Laura squealed as I finished tying the sash on the grape purple wrap dress she was loaning me for my date with Harry. I could see her reflection in the body-length mirror I was looking into, shaking her head with a knowing pride.

"I *told* you that dress was gonna look amazing on you. It's perfect with your skin tone." She crossed her arms. "You may thank me now."

Instead, I just rolled my eyes and started to fiddle with my hair. In most cases, I preferred to keep it totally out and wild, but I wanted to send a message to Harry that I was opening myself up for the night and being more vulnerable. The more he believed I was committed to developing something real with him, the more damage would be dealt when I threw him off again.

With one hand, I slicked back a portion of my hair and pressed it firmly against my head, and then I used the other hand to slide a bobby pin in to hold that section back. Behind me, Laura raised her eyebrows. "Whoa. You're putting your hair back for this guy. Must be serious."

"You are sending my nerves into overdrive," I admitted.

"That wasn't a denial."

"No," I responded, "it's not."

"Wow." She sat down on the edge of her bed and crossed one leg over the other. "How long before I'm allowed to put this revelation on Twitter?"

"You are *not* allowed to put anything on Twitter."

"Oh, come *on*," Laura whined, reaching out and pulling on my arm as she did so. "Stay-single Celia pinning back her hair. I feel like I need to memo the President."

"You're being overdramatic."

She flopped back on her bed. "You're being underdramatic. You never told me about how your first date with this guy went," Laura said.

"It was a date."

She scoffed. "Whatever. Tell me, come on. I loaned you that bangin' dress, you owe me."

I turned around and sat down on the edge of the bed next to Laura so I could pull on the white, strappy, platform heels I was wearing with the dress. "It was really nice. He took me out to a sort of ritzy club where we could have dinner on the mezzanine and then go down to the main floor for dancing. He's light on his feet. I guess his dad liked to dance a lot and it was just something he picked up." I smiled, remembering Harry spin me around the dance floor. "The food was delicious, and we ended up talking forever and ever about damn near everything."

Laura sat up and kicked her legs over so that she was sitting right next to me. I continued reminiscing. "We stayed there literally until the club closed, but we weren't done yet, so he invited me back to his place. He asked if I wanted coffee, I said yes." My face started to warm as I imagined Harry walking back out of his kitchen after he'd put the coffee on and the sudden impulse I had to jump him. "For all I know, that coffee is still sitting in that pot."

Laura giggled. "Wow. Sounds wonderful."

"It was, it really was." My eyes flitted up and I caught a glimpse of the stupid smile on my face in the mirror. I wiped it off quickly and cleared my throat, doing my best to shake away the memories. "I mean, it was a date, you know? I've had better."

If I wasn't careful, I was going to let Harry's unconventionally handsome looks and straight-shooting personality sweep me away. I had a goal in mind, and I needed to achieve it. My dad would be rolling over in his grave if he thought I was falling for the man who killed him.

Which I wasn't, of course. It was all an act.

"Here we go," Laura said. "You're already opening that door of doubt. I should have known."

"I don't know what you're talking about." The shoes were secured so I stood up and walked into the living room to start packing up my clutch with my phone, keys, cards, and cash. "Please quit stressing me out. He'll be here soon."

"Why aren't you having him pick you up at home again?" Laura asked.

I used the chain on the clutch to sling it over my shoulder. "You know how weird my godfather gets about me dating and stuff. I figured it didn't make sense to get him all riled up about nothing."

"Yeah, I guess that makes sense." She slumped down on the couch and I couldn't stop her from taking a picture. I opened my mouth to protest and she held up her hand. "I'm not posting it anywhere. I'm just taking it, you know, like a 'just in case'."

"Just in case of what?"

"In case, you know..." She shrugged with a coy grin on. "He's the one."

In case he's the one? It made my heart compress just to think about. "You're leagues ahead of yourself, Laura."

She chuckled. "I'll remind you of that when I'm framing it for your wedding."

I left that comment where it sat. Marriage simply wasn't something I thought much about. Could I see myself marrying someone *like* Harry? Sure, but he wasn't the one.

He couldn't be.

As if to save me from the uncomfortable conversation, my phone finally buzzed. I'd instructed Harry not to come up, but just text me when he arrived, and I'd come down. When I noticed the text come through and given that I couldn't deal with the heft of the conversation anymore, I nearly ran out the door, despite Laura trying to say goodbye in a more friendly way.

I gave her a quick, one-armed hug, and rushed down to the stairs leading down, slowing only when I was well outside of Laura's influence. I took a few deep breaths and then lingered for a few minutes so it didn't seem like I was bolting out to him, and when I was convinced I'd communicated "aloof" effectively, I walked out the front door where Harry was parked on his bike, waiting patiently.

I took a few minutes to take in the sight. He was wearing a white t-shirt underneath a black button-up, that was unbuttoned and rolled up to his elbows. A pair of simple dark blue slacks were on his legs, and brown Doc Martens were on his feet. It was oddly designer for such a muted guy, but thinking back on it, he wore a similar look to our first date. He was leaned back and had his helmet off and balanced against his hip, and when he saw me, a sly smile slipped across his face. It made me burn all over in an instant.

"Hello," he greeted. "You look amazing."

"Thank you." I leaned in and gave him a kiss on the cheek, letting it linger and then pulled away. "You do, too." With a smile, I scanned his rumbling bike. "I get my first ride on the monster, huh?"

"Is that okay?"

"Of course. I've been anxiously awaiting the moment."

He reached into the back compartment and pulled out a spare helmet. "Would have been sooner if you'd answered my phone calls."

A laugh skittered out of me before I could stop it. "How long am I gonna have to hear about that?"

He handed the helmet over. "I don't know. Maybe you'll have to earn your way out."

I raised an eyebrow. "Don't challenge me."

A wild excitement flared through his eyes. "Why not? I want to know if you're up to the challenge."

Lifting the helmet above my head, I said, "You'll regret that," and then pulled it down over my head and straddled the bike behind Harry. I wrapped my arms around his stomach, reminding myself of the muscles that were waiting just beneath his clothes, and off we went.

Unlike our first date which was in a more electric environment, Harry opted for something much calmer for date number two. He drove us a little outside Hoppa to a piano bar with orders designed to share food and a wide array of themed drinks for notable jazz musicians.

I hadn't intended to show my appreciation for the location choice, but as we were sitting down at the table, Harry chuckled at me. "I take it you like the place."

It was only then that I realized the stupid smile I had plastered on my face. "Yeah. Jazz music is my favorite. My dad used to listen to it every morning when he'd drive me to school. While most of my friends were jamming out to Panic! At The Disco or Post Malone, I found myself enjoying Etta James and Dizzy Gillespie."

"Can't go wrong with those two," he said, "Etta and Dizzy are good, too."

My eyes widened and my jaw dropped and then I let out a much harder laugh than I wanted. "Is that the elusive Harry Booth sense of humor I hear?"

He set the table's provided glass of water to his lips. "Maybe," he hummed before taking a sip. "My dad, my birth dad, was a major jazz head. In the basement of my childhood home, he built this huge cabinet that was packed with old records, and sometimes we would just sit down there for hours and listen. He had all of Lippa the Bird's records. I got to take them with me when I left and they're all I listen to."

My heart slammed in my chest. "She's my favorite."

Harry recoiled a bit. "Lippa the Bird's your favorite jazz musician? She's so unknown, whenever I mention her, people look at me like I'm nuts."

"When I was eleven, my dad and I drove all the way to Minneapolis to see her play live at First Avenue."

Harry's jaw fell so wide it looked like it was going to detach from his face. "I was at that show! My foster father took me because I wouldn't shut up about it! I wore all gold because *Painted in Gold Dust* is my favorite song of hers."

My hands flew to my mouth. "Oh my God." I leaned halfway across the table. "I *saw* you! You were only like two rows back on the main floor."

"Yes!" He started to laugh. "Holy shit, I can't believe this. Looks like we were destined to find each other."

"Looks like it." A soreness emanated from my cheeks from how hard I was smiling.

Harry cleared his throat and sat back in his chair a little, and all I could think about was how unbelievably cute he looked, getting extra excited about something. He was ordinarily such a quiet and reserved person. I wondered what other topics would open him up like that.

Our food came to our table not long after we ordered it, and conversation carried us through our date like a well-practiced symphony, exactly as it had done the first time.

"You mentioned that you work at Hoppa's Homelessness Organization?" Harry said.

"I do. I got super lucky and snagged an entry-level position in their youth division out of college, and unfortunately for HHO, they're overworked and understaffed, so I got moved up quickly to help manage the load. I'm still just a junior social worker, but I get to work hands-on with the kids, which is cool."

"They did a lot for me back in the day."

I raised an eyebrow. "They did? Were you homeless?"

"In a way," he replied. "I won't get into the details of it, but I didn't want to be at home. I spent a lot of time out in the streets and whenever I needed a meal or a place to sleep, I'd go there, but then they'd always send me back home."

"Yeah. That's one of the things I'm working on right now. I love the organization, but their rule to just blindly send runaways back home is a little harsh to me. Some kids have very legitimate reasons to not want to be in their homes."

Harry took a quick sip of his wine, and I saw his eyes flash with a painful memory for a brief moment. "Trust me, I know."

I decided not to push that topic. If he wanted to bring it up, he would, maybe once we got closer.

Not that we would be getting much closer, because this was all just a ploy.

It was only after a shared plate of cheesecake, another glass of wine, and then a handful of cups of coffee that we finally had to approach the topic of ending the date. When I mentioned it, Harry looked up at me and then rolled his eyes.

"What?" I asked.

"Nothing."

"Tell me."

He shook his head. "No."

"Hey," I snipped, "you can't roll your eyes at me and then not tell me what you're thinking."

He waited for a few minutes and then locked his eyes directly into mine. "I was just thinking about how much I want to take you home again."

The resonance in his voice washed over my skin and left goosebumps in its wake. "So why don't you?"

"It didn't work out so well for me last time, did it?"

If I hadn't ghosted him on purpose, I *might* have taken offense. "Still draggin' that one out, huh?" I leaned as far across the small table as I could and danced my fingertips across the back of his hand. "Didn't you say I'd have to earn my way out?"

Harry considered me quietly for a minute and then said, "You're not gonna ghost again are you?"

I perked an eyebrow and flashed him a seductive gaze. "Give me a good reason to hang around."

That was the straw that broke the camel's back. Harry quickly paid for our meal and then in the blink of an eye, we were back on his bike and blazing back into Hoppa. We tripped and fell our way up the sidewalk, already tangling into one another, but when we were finally behind the front door, there was no holding back. It didn't take a genius to know that sleeping with Harry was only going to confuse my feelings. Not only was he one of the sexiest men I'd ever been with, but there was something about the way he looked at me. Something about the way each place he touched burned as if his hands were made of fire. It threw logic out the window. It had me pulling at him like I was starved and he was the only food available as he pushed up against the door with his hands sliding down my sides, journeying lower to the base of my dress.

His lips found mine in his unlit living room, sliding over them and pressing with his tongue, requesting I let him in. I sent mine forward to meet him and they twisted into one another. I let a quiet moan escape my lips, giving Harry the confidence to go further, because his hands wrapped around my thighs and he lifted me from my feet. He kept me fastened between himself and the door, reminding me exactly how strong he was behind his glasses and quiet charm. His button-up shirt, though unbuttoned, was struggling to contain his thick arms, so I did us both a favor and pulled it free.

"We're not even in the bedroom yet," Harry said with a snicker, and that same resolve was back but it had a depth to it that made me glad it wasn't on me to stay on my feet for the moment. There was a beast inside Harry, one I'd met at the conclusion of our first date, and I was glad to meet it again. In most circumstances, he chose to keep that beast at bay, but now he'd released the leash and it was running rampant, letting his lips and hands go anywhere he wished.

I clawed along his back, pulling the t-shirt that had been under his button-up further up his stomach. He rested his head against my neck and licked a line up the side. I dragged the shirt further and further up until it was at his shoulders. He pulled his head back enough for me to get his shirt over his head, leaving his torso bare. I groaned at the well-cut abs and firm pecs, partnered by his biceps, flexed slightly as his arms did the job of keeping me up. The man I'd slept with in a petty fit of rage a few nights ago cracked across my brain briefly. Not one ounce of that experience had been as satisfying as the one I was having now.

And we were still in the front hall.

"Bed," I growled, but Harry shook his head.

Through the shield of his glasses, he looked at me and I realized I'd stepped right into a trap I didn't even see set there. "You said you'd earn your way back, so don't rush me. I'm going to treat this as if I won't see you again."

He kissed me again and this time when he did it, he pinched my bottom lip in his teeth. His fingers dug into my skin, reminding me of my dress that still kept our skin apart, but his hands felt so hot against me, it was like they were ignoring that fact. Excited for what could be, I relinquished control. The more inches I gave Harry, the more feet he took.

What awaited me on the other side was equal parts terrifying and exciting to imagine.

I did what I could to anchor myself to the *real* reason I was there. My mission was important, and I kept having to repeat it internally in a weak attempt to keep myself from falling too deep into Harry's spell.

But then he would hiss my name.

"Celia."

And it was as if the arousal deep in my body was begging me to forget anything other than my carnal desires. I gripped the back of his head, fighting to catch my breath, and looked into his eyes. "How long are you going to make me wait?"

"Tsk, tsk, tsk," he tutted. "You made me wait."

My fingers dug a little deeper. "Punish me for it then."

He pulled me away from the door and turned. As if he were carrying a sack of feathers, not a person, he carried me down to his bedroom. He moved with an ease, but a quickness that had the moisture between my legs doubling. I wanted, *needed*, him. Maybe I was impatient. I'd never had someone demand so much of me before. I felt inexplicably compelled to give it.

He dropped me down to the bed and stood over me. His normally light eyes were much darker now and wide with lust. They took several trips up and down my form and my body temperature increased.

"Stop staring."

"No," he replied immediately, and it was the best kind of gut punch. Who knew Harry was *that* kind of alpha? I'd never experienced anything like it. The way he let his eyes bore over me, I had to resist the urge to physically bare my neck. "You're too beautiful not to stare at." His hands moved to his pants to unbutton them. "I told you already, I'm behaving as if this is the last taste of you I'm going to get. Don't expect me to hold back…"

I swallowed hard. My heart was thundering through me and my head was fuzzy. "I don't want you to."

His hands moved away after freeing his button and pulling down the zipper, giving me a teasing view of the bulge that rested within. It seemed larger than I remembered, but the thoughts disappeared as his hands went down to my legs to unwrap my dress and pull it away from my body. He left it to rest beneath me and wrapped his arms around my thighs and pulled, dragging me to the edge of the bed as he knelt. His eyes fluttered closed and he placed soft kisses all along the inside of my legs, trailing down until he was almost at my core, before hopping back up the top of the other legs and starting down again.

"Stop teasing me," I growled.

His eyes flicked open for a moment, landing in mine. "No."

I was terrified of him. Of how quickly he made me forget everything that wasn't him. I'd spent my entire life always keeping some semblance of control over myself, but Harry made me feel like I was falling from the top story of a skyscraper.

And I liked it.

I dropped my head back, and Harry returned to kissing my legs. Kisses turned to nibbles and then to bites. I gasped as his teeth sunk in. His breath caressed my skin as he chuckled at my reaction and his hands moved forward off my thighs, just enough to grab the edges of my underwear and drag them down my legs. The exposure was frightening but exciting, and I was rewarded for my lack of complaints by Harry's head finally pushing in to lick.

I whined and writhed as he set to work, taking as much of me below as he wanted. I pulled the blanket beneath me into my hands and squeezed, but it did little to keep me holding on. "Harry," I moaned, but it only encouraged him, increasing his focus on my sweetest spot. My mind went blank and my ears hummed with a quiet white noise as an orgasm pulsed through me. It started small but grew into the greatest feeling I'd ever experienced. If sound was coming out of my mouth, I couldn't hear it, only feel the pleasure as it rocketed over me.

Harry pulled up, and my cheeks burned at the sight of him licking his lips. The more time we spent together, the more convinced I was becoming that he knew my plan all along and was trying to drive me from it. He had to be using something supernatural. How had he helmed so much control of me in such a short period of time? What did it mean?

But then Harry's hands were back on my sides, and it didn't matter. They slid around my back to pull apart the clasp of my bra, and then he blanketed himself over me and landed a kiss against my neck as he pulled it free.

He stepped back again and smiled down at me, shaking his head. "Unbelievable."

Alarms of all kinds were going off in my mind. I'd put in so much hard work building a wall between Harry and myself that would keep him close enough to hurt, but not close enough to hurt me, but in he waltzed with a sledgehammer and was knocking shit down left and right. Anything he could find that stood between him and me was destroyed until his skin against mine felt more permanent, and more real than anything that had ever touched me before. He pulled down his pants and boxers, doing away with what clothes remained between us, quickly snaking a condom from his pants pocket before releasing them fully.

He set the wrapper between his teeth, and all the places he'd bit me up to that moment pulsated with memory. As he rolled the condom over, I put on a sly smile. "I'm ready."

"Good," he replied.

He grabbed my legs and pulled them up against his chest, and then a hand moved down to guide himself inside. My hips bucked and insides swirled, both rushing toward and away from the intense feeling. It wasn't just that my most recent sexual experience had been *so* unsatisfying, it was that Harry was profoundly different from anyone I'd let near me before. He crossed a physical threshold, but he was inserting himself into me on a deeper, more ethereal level. He worked himself into a rhythm, letting out quiet, sexy grunts of his own as he did, and I opened up as much as I could, not even recognizing the lurid noises I was making as a result.

His hands slid into the grooves in my hips and mine wrapped around his wrists for leverage as we moved against each other in a bowing pattern that made each thrust feel like ten. Each bead of pleasure burst like a piñata and rained bottomless rapture down over me.

"Fuck." It was all I could get out before my whole body started to shake.

He held onto me tighter and I shuddered as my very bones rattled inside of me. Now, I could hear myself, crying out, trying to form words, but nothing coming out besides incoherent sounds, but Harry didn't slow. He used his strength to lift me up again and flipped us until I was straddling over him, riding him instead. My body moved on instinct, up and down, finding any angle or speed I could to keep my skin searing hot and latched to Harry. Even though I could feel sweat dripping down my skin, I continued, going faster and faster, because before I knew it, I was at the finish line again. How many laps had it been? Harry's grip on me got tighter and tighter, until I knew there would be marks there the next day, and finally, he slammed all the way into me and shuddered as he came, a sexy, animalistic growl roaring out of him as he did.

He released, and I collapsed on top of him. His chest rose and fell under me just as mine did, while we both struggled to catch our breath.

"I have to apologize," I said, in a moment of raw honesty. "How I *ever* didn't return your calls is beyond me. You are far and away the best I've ever had." It wasn't a lie.

"Yeah. I've never been with anyone like you before," he responded and then groaned. "I know we have to move, but I don't want to."

"So, let's not." My eyes were already growing heavier and heavier, worsened by Harry wrapping his arms around my back and tracing gentle circles along the small of it. "I'm gonna fall asleep if you keep doing that."

"So, fall asleep," he said, "or are you afraid of still being here in the morning?"

In truth, I was. Not because it was all just a ruse, but because if I stayed, I was afraid it'd start to feel less and less like one. "No," I lied. "I was hoping for round two."

He laughed. "We'll get there. Don't you worry." He kissed the top of my head. "It's okay to sleep here, you know."

"I know," I said, and then glanced up at Harry. His eyes fell into mine and it took my breath away. I set my head back down on his chest and closed my eyes, trying to still the thrumming in my heart.

The last thought that crossed my brain as I fell asleep was that I was in serious trouble.

Chapter Eight

Bullet

Every part of me truly expected Celia to be gone when I woke up, so when I peeled my eyes open and she was still nestled against me with my hand resting over her slender hip, I smiled. Even with her hair a mess from the raucous lovemaking we'd engaged in well into the early hours of the morning, she was still stunning, and I found myself staring. I'd be lying if I said I understood what was going on in my life at the moment. Between Nick trying to promote me at the club and Celia and I suddenly dating again after what happened the first time, it felt like things were more happening *to* me versus me making an active choice. What was I meant to do with it all?

Next to me, Celia started to shift and stretch in bed and then her eyes drifted open. "Morning."

"Good morning," I replied. "Sorry, I've been staring. I'm shocked you're still here."

She snickered. "Oh, you really are planning to get a lot of mileage out of that, aren't you?"

"Why shouldn't I?" I responded and then leaned down and kissed her.

In truth, I wasn't a man who thought much about the future. For a large chunk of my life, I never even knew if I was going to make it from day to day. Between being abused for most of my childhood and up through my bad accident of a few years ago, my goal was always just "make it to tomorrow". When Nick first asked if I'd ever thought about moving up in the club, and when the younger members first talked about me being ghosted, I realized I was being forced to think beyond tomorrow.

What did I want to do with my days beyond tomorrow?

Celia's hand went up to my cheek and brushed along it. "What are you thinking about? You've got this really scrunched-up look on your face."

"Just life," I said.

She sat up a little, holding herself up on her forearms. "What do you mean?"

I shrugged. "Don't worry about it. Are you hungry? I'll make us some breakfast."

Celia recoiled a bit but nodded. "I could eat."

Leaning over and taking one more kiss from her, I climbed out of the bed and walked down the hallway and turned into the kitchen. Both Chatterbox and Jingle were there in an instant, both no doubt angry that I'd slept in and denied them their timely breakfasts, so I grabbed a bag of treats from the cabinet and dropped a couple on the counter for each of them while I filled their bowls.

"Oh, hello," Celia said, turning into the kitchen and seeing the cats. "Who do we have here?" Jingle was gone in a flash. He wasn't a social cat, and the presence of someone new was never something he approved of. "Rude," Celia joked.

"Sorry. That was Jingle. He's not a people person."

"I see. This one, however..." As Celia was talking, Chatterbox walked over to her and started to nuzzle himself against her arm, begging for any head scratches she had to offer, complete with a begging meow. "He's talkative."

"Well, that's why his name is Chatterbox," I said.

Her jaw dropped. "Is it really?"

"Yep."

"Does he like being held?" she asked.

"Loves it."

Celia curled her arms under Chatterbox and lifted him up from his spot on the counter, and Chatterbox nuzzled his head against her neck. I smiled at him, understanding his affection toward her, and loving the adorable way she giggled as he snuggled her.

"I suppose this is what I miss when I cut and run," she said.

I started chopping up some potatoes and green onions to fry. "It is. Unlike his brother, he loves making new friends. Hang around long enough and he'll never leave you alone."

"I think I'd be okay with that." She walked over and looked down at the bowls on the counter. "This is their food, I assume?"

"Yeah," I responded. "Chatter will go for his when you two are done cuddling and Jingle will starve before he comes in here with you standing here."

Celia lifted the bowls from the table and walked into the living room and sat down on the floor. She crossed her legs and set the bowls on the floor in front of her. The second she set Chatterbox down, he walked over to his bowl and started to munch, but the other bowl sat untouched. I continued to prepare breakfast until I heard Celia clicking her tongue and tapping her leg. I looked back over and saw that Jingle was curled up under the dining room table, looking over at her. She took a handful of his food kernels from his bowl and set them in a line leading from about halfway to the table, and the bowl, and then returned to her spot.

"Come here, Jingle. I won't hurt you." She tapped her leg. "Come on. Come get your breakfast."

All breakfast preparation stopped as Jingle slowly stood up from where he was and started to tentatively step out. He approached the first kernel in the line and chomped it up, then took to the next piece. He continued through the line until he finally got to the last one, and to my utter surprise, he dove into his food with Celia sitting just behind the bowl. She stuck out her hand and he sniffed it a few times, then continued eating as she began to nuzzle his head.

"Wow. I'm... truly impressed," I said. "He doesn't usually take to people. Even my dad he stays away from."

"Well, I have a certain knack for dealing with the difficult," she responded.

"Was that a comment on me?" I asked with a smirk.

She just shook her head but there was amusement on her face. "I don't know what you're talking about."

I made us a couple of omelets for breakfast, after which point Celia went to go and take a shower. With her in the bathroom, I went out to my backyard where all of my workout equipment was setup so that I could get a good workout in for the day before I got distracted by the beautiful woman hanging around.

"Ah, so here's your personal gym." I was bench pressing when she walked out and stopped so I could sit up and look at her. The way her eyes flared at my bare, sweat-covered torso left an excited feeling in the pit of my gut. I was right to plan for her distracting me again. "I knew you had to have one with *those* muscles."

"It always surprises the guys at the club when I tell them I have a gym at home. Just because I'm an accountant, they see more of the intellectual side of me than the physical side."

Celia put her hands on her hips and shook her head. "Doesn't it suck when people see you for your brain and not your body? It's like, come on, be a little more shallow please."

With a snicker, I grabbed a towel to wipe my face, and Celia walked over and straddled the bench of the bench press, facing me. She let her fingers dance along my pecs for a moment before trailing them up my shoulder and eventually behind my neck. With a little tug, she pulled me to her, and I relented, leaning in to bring our lips together. My hands slid under the base of her dress, exactly as they had the night before and she laughed against my mouth.

"What?" I asked.

"Nothing," she said. I squeezed down on her thigh and she yelped. "Okay! I was just thinking it's kind of crazy how quickly you get me going. I have to leave for work, so I was like 'Don't let him get you, Celia,' but here we are."

I frowned. "Work? It's a Sunday."

"Yeah, and it's a homeless shelter," she replied. "They don't stop being homeless on Sundays."

"I guess. Still, don't go to work. Stay here."

"What? Just ignore my job and stay here with you all day?" she asked. "Even if it weren't about the job itself, I need the paycheck."

"Eh, I'll take care of you, it's fine." It was meant to be a joke, but Celia's face got a serious expression all over it and her eyes blinked a few times. At first, I was afraid I'd gone too far, but then a smile crossed her face. "What?" I asked. "Sorry if that joke was too much."

"No, it…" Her smile grew a little. "I'm always telling the kids at work, 'It's okay to let people take care of you. It's okay to let people take care of you,' but I'm kind of a control freak."

"I never would have guessed," I said flatly.

"Hush," she snipped back. "Anyway. I take care of my godfather, and I take care of the kids at work. I don't really let anyone take care of me. I thought I didn't like it, but when you said it just now, I don't know, I felt like I could really let you."

"If you'd let me, I'd do it. Not in that intense, drop-everything-you're-doing-and-let-me-take-care-of-you kind of way, but I'll make sure you're happy. You know, I'm not a romantic, but at the end of the day, when you've exhausted all your energy caring about everyone else, then I'll care about you."

Celia didn't respond. She sat staring back at me, and the expression in her eyes was searching, if not a bit scrutinous, like she either thought I was lying or wanted to think that I was. Whatever she'd been through that led her to such a place of mistrust, I wasn't sure, but I liked her a lot and found myself hoping that she'd let me break that barrier down.

Eventually, after about five minutes of just looking at me, she pecked my lips and said, "So you don't work weekends? I'd have thought a motorcycle club is on twenty-four-seven."

"Well, technically it is," I responded, allowing her to change the subject, "but all of the business Nick likes to take care of is during the week. Weekends are mostly for hanging out with the bar regulars, running the prospects, fellowship." Nick also reserved the drug runs to the weekends mostly, but that wasn't information Celia needed. "I'll probably go by the bar later. You're welcome to come, although if I'm being totally honest, I'd welcome an excuse not to go."

"You don't want to go there? How come?"

"It's not that I don't want to, but Nick's trying to promote me, and I haven't really thought it out yet. I know he's looking for an answer, I just don't have one yet."

"He's trying to promote you?" Celia said overdramatically. "How dare he!" I squeezed her thigh again and she giggled. "Seriously, though. What's to consider with a promotion?"

"It's not accounting. He wants to make me VP."

Celia's eyes widened. "Wow. That's a huge responsibility."

"Exactly."

"So that's it then? You don't want the responsibility?" she asked. "No offense, but you seem like the responsible type. That's probably why he wants you."

"Maybe, I just don't know that I'm the man for the job. There are other guys who have been there longer."

"Do you not care about the club that much?"

That question rendered me speechless for a second. "I care about the club a lot. It means the world to me. It's not just my job, those guys are like family. I spend more time there than I do at home."

"Then I don't get it," Celia replied. "If you're up to the task of taking on the responsibility, and you care about the club, and it's a better job, why wouldn't you do it?"

Again, I was left without a great answer. What had been so unclear just moments ago suddenly had much more clarity. In the grand scheme of things, Celia and I didn't actually know one another all that well just yet, but it felt like we'd been together for years. She simply spoke to a part of me that I didn't think anyone else had access to but me.

It was slightly terrifying.

"So you think I should do it?" I asked.

She shrugged. "I don't know why you wouldn't."

For me, nothing in life had ever been that simple. Maybe it was because Celia was younger, or because she worked in the field she did, but it put her in a much better place to just allow things to be that clean-cut. "Okay," I said. "I think you're right. I think I should do it."

She grinned. "Congratulations."

"Thank you." I wrapped my arms around her and pulled her even closer to me. "I know how I want to celebrate." I didn't wait to set my lips against the side of her neck.

Celia let out a soft moan but placed her hands against my shoulders and made a weak attempt to push me off. "I really have to go to work, Harry."

"No, I don't think you will."

As if on cue, Celia's phone rang. She slipped it out of her pocket, and I didn't stop kissing along her neck and jawline as she answered it. "Hello?" My hands slid even further up her dress and she used her free hand over the back of her mouth to keep from making too many noises with whomever she was talking to. "Yeah, turns out I don't feel so well. Can I swap for Thursday?" A smile of victory crossed my face as Celia said, "Thanks. Bye." She hung up her phone and glared at me. "You'd better make it worth it."

I stood and lifted her up with ease, slinging her over my shoulder. "Don't be silly. You know it will be."

Chapter Nine

Celia

The smile on my face was permanently affixed. My arms wrapped around Harry and his bike rumbling beneath me combined with the day we'd had together, I had to admit I didn't want to leave Harry behind. The last twenty-four hours had been some of the best I'd ever had in my life, and if it wasn't Harry absent-mindedly telling me he'd take care of me, it was snuggling with him on the couch with his cats curled in our laps. It all felt so *domestic*, but it felt amazing. When I finally convinced him to let me leave and bring me back to my old roommate's apartment, it was not without some mutual disappointment. He made everything worse by throwing on a tight-fitting black t-shirt and light blue jeans with combat boots; he looked good enough to eat.

"If you don't get off, I'm gonna ride away with you attached to me," Harry said.

My gut reaction was to tell him to do it. I could go to Hoppa's with him, spend the rest of the night with him there, and then go home with him. Just thinking about it made me inexplicably happy, but my godfather was waiting for me, and had been calling me nonstop for the past few hours, so I had to at least make an appearance and calm him down.

Despite my body desperately fighting against me, I released my hands from around Harry's waist and dragged myself off his idling bike. I tried returning his spare helmet, but he pushed it back into my hands.

"Keep it. Hopefully, you'll be wearing it a lot," he said with a smile.

It was like I was a teenager in high school again and my crush had just given me his letterman jacket. Butterflies fluttered through my stomach as I walked up the path and through the front door of the apartment complex. When I was safely inside, I watched Harry pull his own helmet back on and roar off down the street. I missed him the second he was gone, but my phone rang again in my pocket and snapped me back to attention.

Laura was probably out for the night, so I didn't bother going up to her apartment, and instead walked out back to the complex's parking lot and got in my own car to head home.

My cheeks hurt from the smile on my face, but I didn't think anything of it until I was walking into my house and my godfather was staring at me with a snarl.

"What?" I asked.

"What's that smile? Don't tell me that's because of Harry?"

Although I was something of a practiced liar, hiding anything from my godfather was borderline impossible. Still, I murmured, "I don't know what you're talking about," as if it was going to work, but the second I tried to pass him, he wheeled into my path, nearly running me over in the process. "Hey!"

"Have you forgotten what we're doing here?" he asked. "Everything we're fighting for? Your poor father? How do you think he'd feel knowing you're falling for the man who murdered him?"

"I'm not falling for him."

He shifted in his chair, a little more than I thought possible, but it was probably just my rising frustration. "I've never seen that look on your face before. Do you think I'm dumb? That I don't know what it looks like when my own godchild is developing feelings for someone? You're normally even-toned, smirking just like your dad. I've seen you around other men before, and none of 'em make you smile like that."

"So, what, you want me to be miserable?" I spat all of a sudden. "I *have* to do this. I'm doing what we have to in order to get back at him, can I not have a little fun as I do it?"

"Fun?" Darrien asked. "Are you having fun?"

The thick judgment in his voice knocked any cheer straight out of me. Was I having fun? With the man who killed my father? What was I thinking? "No…"

Darrien wheeled his way over to the kitchen counter and picked up a box that already had emotions rising in my throat. He set it in his lap and opened it briefly to pull out an article and handed it over to me. I'd read it half a dozen times or more, but that never stopped it from hurting as I looked down at it. It was my father's obituary, the one that had been published in the wake of the accident that had killed him.

"*Road rage ended a good man's life,*" was written in bolded letters at the beginning of the obituary. The thing was, I'd been on Harry's bike a lot in the past few days and he was an even more patient driver than I was. It almost would have *helped* to see Harry's road rage act out while we were together, but he didn't often put himself in road rage situations.

Of course, that could be because the last time he let his emotions get the best of him, my father died.

"Our car flipped over nine times," Darrien said. "Your father was dead before they even pulled us out of the car. He was talking about you right before we got hit. How proud he was of you and how he knew you were going to do big things with your life. Poor guy didn't even get to be here to see you succeed. He raised you alone after your mother left and this is how you're repaying him? By sleeping with the enemy?"

"The point is to sleep with the enemy," I said back, handing the article back to him.

Darrien returned the obituary to the box and instead pulled out a stack of white papers and waved them in my direction. "These are all of my medical bills that are *still* unpaid. I can't bring myself to pull from your father's settlement and I used mine to send you to school. After all of our sacrifices, are you still going to turn your back on us?"

"No." Tears slid down my face. "That's not what I'm doing."

He returned the papers to the box and set it off to the side, then he rolled his chair up to me and took my hands in his. "I don't mean to make you cry, Celia, but I had to remind you of what's at stake here. You aren't just doing this for me, you're doing it for our entire family that was ruined that day. We're going to be broken forever. You have to remain focused."

"You're right," I admitted. "I was losing myself. I'm sorry."

"I want you to be happy. Of course I don't want you to be miserable, but the sooner we destroy him, the sooner we can get on to bigger and better things," Darrien said. "We're so close."

"I didn't completely forget," I said. "I convinced him to take a higher position at the club."

Darrien's head ticked uncomfortably to the side. "They offered him a higher position?"

"Vice President."

"What happened to Tess?" he asked.

I didn't know what he was talking about. "Who?"

There were a few minutes of silence between Darrien and me and then he shook his head and cleared his throat. "Nothing. So, they offered him that position? Things are going well for him."

"The stakes are higher," I replied. "Now when we ruin him, we can get him kicked out of the club for good. I just have to wait for a moment to strike. We're getting closer. Eventually, he'll trust me enough to let his guard down and then I'll make my move. We just have to be patient."

Darrien started nodding with a smile rising to his face. "There's my smart girl. Now you're thinking."

"He wasn't going to take the position, but I convinced him to take it." I looked over at the picture of me and my dad that hung on the fridge. "The higher he is, the harder he'll fall, right?"

"That's right, Celia." His hands clasped around mine and squeezed even harder. "I know that it feels terrible, but he deserves it for everything he cost us. Can you do this?"

"I can," I said. "I will. For my dad. I'm going to make Harry pay for what he did. Guaranteed."

Chapter Ten

Bullet

Waking up without Celia in my bed was much less enjoyable than waking up with her in it. She was a drug I could easily get addicted to if I wasn't careful. For the fact that I *still* fully expected her to ghost me again, we'd spoken on the phone or texted every single day since our first rekindled date, sometimes both. She did simple things like ask about the cats, and I made sure she didn't get in *too* much trouble at work for calling in sick because of me. We met up for coffee before work a couple of times and it truly felt like we were actually dating.

It was nice.

It was only now that Celia and I were finally behaving as if we were actually trying to make something out of our relationship that I realized I'd never really been in one before. I'd been with women and I'd even dated someone for an extended period of time, but it was always just the baseline, first stage stuff. The light dates a few times a month, sex on occasion, but I'd never even dated someone that I cared to keep in regular contact with. I wasn't inhuman, and there were times where I would sit on the couch alone and wonder what it might be like to have someone else there, but thanks to my trust issues, getting to that point with a woman always seemed like more trouble than it was worth. With Celia in my life, I was suddenly thinking about it more, dreaming about it even.

Avery sputtered out a laugh so loud in my ears that I nearly punched him in the face. "Look at our little Bullet. You're glowing or something."

Seneca was sitting next to him at the table we were all seated around at Hoppa's Taphouse and laughed down into her glass of water at him. It was still early afternoon, and the members and prospects were just hanging out on Thursday before the bar crowd started showing up.

I was also officially being voted in as Vice President.

"Don't say stupid shit," I griped.

"It must be going well," Avery said, then he looked over at Seneca. "He wouldn't be acting like this if it wasn't going well."

A brief period of eye contact between Avery and Seneca had them both blushing lightly and I furrowed my brow. A pettier person could deflect easily if they wanted, but I had no interest in involving myself in someone else's romantic life. If there was something between them, good for them.

"So, you've never really dated women before?" Seneca asked.

"I have," I replied. "Just not seriously or for an extended period of time."

"There was this girl in college," Avery started, and I rolled my eyes, knowing where the story was going. "She was *crazy* about him. Beautiful, smart, funny. He took her out on a handful of dates and then ended it with her. He told her, to her face, that it just wasn't worth it." He started laughing and slamming his hand on the table, but Seneca was looking at him like he was a swamp monster. Finally, she threw me a disgusted look, threw him one, and then got up and left the table. He watched her walk away, all the humor fading from his face. "What did I say?"

"I'm the one who doesn't deal with women, how are *you* so clueless?" I asked.

"I'm not clueless, I just don't know why that story made *me* look bad," he replied.

"Maybe because you thought it was so damn funny." I took a sip of my soda. "Which I've told you isn't. Multiple times. You should stop telling it."

He looked truly disappointed that he'd upset Seneca. "I guess so."

"Gentlemen!" Nick announced as he entered the bar, then he looked at Seneca. "And lady, we've got a packed day ahead of us, so let's not waste any time."

"He says that like *he* isn't the one who's over an hour late," Small Fry grumbled to Texas.

"First of all, I heard that," Nick said, "second of all, yes, I'm late. I overslept because for the first time in months, I'm actually sleeping, so fucking sue me."

"Nah, that's great, Squared. You seem a little better," Bucky said, slapping a hand on Nick's shoulder.

Now that he mentioned it, Nick did look better. The sallow quality his face had taken on was thickening out, and he'd gone back to being cleanly shaven. A cut had his hair sitting shorter on his head, and his clothes were starting to fit well again. Not only was he getting more sleep, but he appeared to be eating normally again as well.

Almost as if he could read my thoughts, he looked over at me. "I have Bullet to thank for that."

That took me aback. "Me? I didn't do anything."

"You did," Nick said. "You accepted my offer and now when I can't sleep at night, it's from excitement of what we're gonna turn this club into. I just know it, Bullet, we're gonna take the Steel Knights to the next level. I can't wait, but first things first, members, let's head back. We've got some voting to do."

The members gathered from their different spots across the bar, bidding the prospects adieu as they did, and then we made our way back to Nick's rounded table in the back. There were more chairs around the table now, as a majority of the Steel Knights' current members had been promoted to some officered position, but a few people still had to stand. Nick pulled out his gavel, and the new Secretary, Small Fry, called an official meeting to order.

"There's only one matter on the agenda today, boys," he said, looking across at me. "I'd like to formally nominate Harry "Bullet" Booth to the position of Vice President."

Avery stuck his hand in the air immediately. "Seconded."

Seth's hand went in the air next. "Third."

And one by one, all of the members of the club unanimously voted to promote me to Vice

President. The bright look on Nick's face was enough that I *had* to smile as he announced, "So moved. Bullet, you are hereby designated to the position of Vice President, effective immediately. Congratulations!"

The members all started to clap and somewhere between humility and discomfort, I nodded my head in thanks and remained quiet.

"I believe that's all we had to cover today. We've got the prospect stuff this evening. Bucky, I'll need you and Bullet's help with that, but we can discuss that later. For now, I'd like some time alone with my new Vice President if we have nothing else?" No one else brought anything up, so Nick knocked his gavel on the table. "Great! Meeting adjourned then."

The members took their time filing out, each of them shaking my hand, patting me on the back, or fist-bumping me as they exited, and eventually it was just Nick and me.

I looked across at Nick with a smile. "Thanks again, Nick. I'm gonna work hard, I promise."

He let out a loud laugh. "For someone who resisted it for so long, I should be thanking you."

"Why didn't you just let it go?" I asked.

"I knew you were the one. Our visions for the club are aligned and I think we're gonna take things to the next level. I was prepared to offer the position to Bucky if you didn't shape up, but that was a worst-case scenario. Not that Bucky would be bad, but he's a bit too much of a yes man. You'll call me out on my shit, and I need that. Tess was like that, too. Speaking of which…"

He stood up from the table and started over to the lockers lined against the back wall of the warehouse. He moved until he was standing in front of the one that Tess had occupied back when she was there, then he looked back at me and motioned me over. Reluctantly, I stood up from my chair and walked over to where he was standing. He grabbed a pair of bolt cutters down from the top of the lockers and handed them out to me.

"What?" I asked.

He chuckled. "Well, I'm not asking you to solve for X here, Harry. I think it's pretty obvious what I want."

"I'm not breaking into her locker. Even if it wasn't a huge invasion of privacy, I'm the very last person she'd want going through her stuff."

"I know, but I can't do it, I told you," Nick said. "All I had was her notebook and even that was difficult for me to flip through. Just seeing her handwriting makes me miss her like crazy. I know wherever she and Colin are, they're happy and…" He shoved the bolt cutters against my chest. "They ain't comin' back. If those plans in Tess' notebook were even half of what she had going on in her head, there's probably a lot in this locker we need to see. First order of business as VP, I need you to go through everything in the old VP's locker."

Nick stared at me with a stone serious expression for long enough that I finally took the bolt cutters, and when I did, he turned and started to walk away.

"Wait," I said, grabbing his arm. "You're not staying."

"Bullet, you and I both know this is gonna make me cry and I'm not about to be reduced to a blubbering mess when we've got so much going on today. I'm gonna go and chat with the prospects, and you're going to go through Tess' locker." He slapped a hand on my shoulder. "Please?"

I wanted to protest, but the look on Nick's face told me it would be fruitless. Desperation and determination were a terrible mix, and I simply didn't have the arsenal to battle against it. With a roll of my eyes, I nodded, and Nick pulled himself away and walked out of the warehouse, leaving me alone.

Setting the bolt cutters to the lock on Tess' locker, I took a breath to steel myself, and then I busted the lock and removed it from the loop. I'd have to go and buy a new one for when I was storing stuff in there, but for the time being, I set the bolt cutters and broken lock on top of the lockers and then opened the locker door.

The inside of the locker was oddly simple. Tess had a flair for the dramatic, not unlike her father and brother, so though I didn't know what I *was* expecting, it was a mostly empty locker with a jacket hanging inside, a few miscellaneous papers and journals, and a file box on the bottom. I pulled the jacket out and slung it over my arm, then pulled the file box out and carried them both over to the table. The jacket I wrapped around Nick's regular chair, then I set the box down in front of my chair and returned to the locker. I pulled out what was left of the papers and journals and carried them back to my spot, then sat down to start going through it all.

First, I went through the journals. Nick had already given me the notebook he had of Tess' back when I first agreed to take on VP, and the journals were more of the same. It was a detailed account of Tess' work. She had research on some other motorcycle clubs that we considered allies like the Blazing Rebels and the Raging Vipers, as well as our rival gang, the Unchained Dogs. All their hierarchical information led her to the final hierarchy she'd been planning on introducing for the Steel Knights.

It blew me away. It was meticulous and well thought out.

In her file box, she had a variety of things including quotes for several locations for the club to relocate to outside of Hoppa's Taphouse. The bar had always been the home base of the Steel Knights, but with the club growing as it was, a bigger facility was definitely needed. Amongst these plans, were the detailed blueprints for a club to be built from the ground up. It included an office for each of the officers, a club room for the members and prospects, and even some secret rooms for when we were doing our less legal work. On top of all of this, there was a bar, not unlike Hoppa's Taphouse, with pool tables, dartboards, a stage for live bands, and a circular bar that would sit in the middle. Next to this part of the blueprint, she had a Post-it Note stuck on that read "Regulars and Friendlies only" and I smiled. It was genius. Give non-members the feeling of membership by having an exclusive bar just for them. I could already imagine the hype when one of the Steel Knights invited someone from Hoppa's Taphouse back to our exclusive bar.

She had plans for merch, plans to expand the underground business, and even a list of the pros and cons of each member for us to chart out the best way to use them all.

This went beyond Vice-President thinking; Tess was planning to be President one day.

The words of Seneca, Nick, and Avery filled my mind:

"Everyone followed your lead and you fucking ran her out of here."

"I told Colin like three weeks in that I would never recommend her for President."

"What do you want from us? Would you have listened?"

Yeah, I understood the role I played in Tess leaving. It wasn't just me, but my part was larger than everyone else's. I could sit there and say if I'd known what Tess had in her head, I might have been nicer to her, but the truth was, I never would have heard her out to begin with. Seeing everything she had up her sleeve was as enlightening as it was painful. Celia was changing me, not just because I liked her, but because she was my gateway to seeing that there had been women around me all along who weren't as bad as the ones who ruined my life. Tess, Seneca. Even some of the older members were married and their wives had never been anything but respectful to me.

For the first time ever, I was realizing how badly I'd messed up.

"I'm sorry, Tess," I said aloud. "I'm gonna do what you were not allowed to do."

It was as good an apology as I could muster for the time being, until I hopefully got the chance to apologize to her face.

Chapter Eleven

Celia

It hadn't occurred to me how much Harry's sourpuss attitude changed the atmosphere around Hoppa's Taphouse until I was walking in and it was totally gone. Everyone was laughing, people were dancing and exchanging loud stories over drinks, and the thing I most noticed:

There were many more women hanging around.

A few of the members of Harry's motorcycle club whose names I didn't know, had women on their arm and were enjoying their time with them present, and a few more biker girls were flirting their way around the younger, more eligible members. Harry didn't seem as bothered by their presence, and unlike the way he was standing in the corner brooding the first time I'd ever met him, he was playing a game of pool with the club's President, Nick, and a couple of other members, and he seemed totally relaxed and happy.

At first, a smile found my face and I just stared at him happily, but then my godfather's voice snuck into the back of mind, bringing with it images of my father's obituary, pictures from the accident, and Darrien's exorbitant medical bills and I physically smacked my own face to knock myself out of it. What I had with Harry *wasn't* real, at least for me it wasn't. I had to remain focused.

"Hey, VP!" A man I *did* recognize as Harry's former college roommate and now fellow club member, Avery, called out. "Your girl is here!"

In any other situation, the possessive phrase might have irritated me, but the way Harry immediately stopped what he was doing and crossed the bar to greet me had my stomach flurrying again. Something about being *his* girl just sounded so good to me.

No. I couldn't do this again, I couldn't get caught up.

"Hey," Harry said as he got to me. The arm that wasn't gripping a pool stick laced around my waist and he pulled me toward him in a kiss. Several of the people standing around started to hoot, inspired by Avery who kicked it off, but Harry whipped around and glared at him, and he calmed down. "Sorry about him."

"It's okay," I said. "How are you?"

"Much better now. I'm glad you came."

"You told me you wanted to see me and that was enough for me." This earned me another quick kiss.

He pointed over his shoulder at Nick standing at the pool table. "I'm just finishing up a game of pool with Squared and the guys. Wanna grab a drink and a table and I'll join ya when I'm done?"

"Sure," I replied, and with yet another quick kiss, Harry finally let me go and made his way back to the pool table.

Originally, I set a course directly for the bar, but decided against it. I was already struggling to keep my inhibitions in check around Harry without the aid of liquor. Instead, I scanned the bar for a free table, and though the place was packed, there was one small table in the furthest back corner away from all the action, that everyone seemed to have abandoned in the interest of being closer to something entertaining. I walked over and took a seat at one of the chairs and was glad for the clear shot it gave me of Harry and the others playing pool; that was, of course, until a body blocked my view. I looked up and Avery was standing above me with a pair of water bottles in his hand.

He held one out with a smile. "I saw you do a complete one-eighty from the bar, so I'm guessing you don't wanna drink tonight."

I took the other bottle, though tentatively. "Yeah. Thanks."

"Can I join ya?" he asked.

The only other seat at the table was intended for Harry, but I supposed once he got there he could just tell Avery to move. "Sure." Avery sat down in the other chair and grinned over at me. He was borderline dopey despite his good looks and I needed not wonder why none of the bar's increased female population seemed to have their sights set on him. He was kind of intimidating by just *how* cheerful he seemed. "Avery, right?" I asked.

"Or Bullseye, whatever you prefer," he said. "Harry's an introvert at his core, so he probably doesn't consider me his best friend. I am though."

It was almost sad sounding. "He does," I assured him right away. "He actually talked about you quite a bit on our first date. Said you brought him to the club and all that."

That seemed to improve Avery's mood even more and I was becoming increasingly more nervous he was going to start shining like a light bulb. "Aw man, that's awesome. Yeah, he's like family to me, so I thought it was time you and I had a chat."

"So that's what this is?" I asked. "You're sussing out the girl dividing your friend's attention?"

He was mid-drink, and he choked a bit on the water. He coughed to clear his throat and then started laughing. "Damn, Harry was right, you aim straight. I like it."

"I find beating around the bush doesn't get you many places.".

Avery let out a hum of approval. "No truer words. Well then, I'll aim straight." He looked over at me and his bright expression darkened significantly. He was still smiling, but it was as if he'd stepped out of the light and into a shadow. "Harry doesn't really trust women a whole lot. Actually, he doesn't really trust people in general. He's more himself now than ever, and I can tell if you were to try and ghost him again, it'd crush him, so give it to me straight, since that's what you're good at. Is this just a game for you? If it is, end it now."

My heart started to slam in my chest. I hadn't said more than a handful of words to the man, but it was like he could see straight through me. "This isn't a game." It wasn't. My motives may have not been clear, but nothing about what existed between Harry and I was a game, it was serious, if even for a different reason. "I know that Harry and I got off on the wrong foot, but we're doing good. I'm not going anywhere."

"Is that right?" Just like that, his expression went light again. Either the guy was crazy, or there was a dark side to him that he was trying incredibly hard to keep at bay. "Good then. I just had to make sure, you know, 'cause Harry's my guy."

As subtly as I could, I slid my chair a few centimeters further from Avery. "Of course. Hey, since we're bonding, can you tell me what Harry's hangup is on women? Did he get burned in a bad relationship or something?"

"Harry's never been with anyone the way he's been with you," he said, and it cut through me. Who was playing it straight now? "I've never known the details though. Something from when he was a kid, but he doesn't like to talk about it."

Harry had mentioned that he was homeless for a while because he didn't want to be at home, but I also knew he lost his birth father at some point and had lived with his foster father for many years.

Was it his mother?

I wanted to ask a few more questions. Get any information out of Avery that I could, even if it were details *he* didn't think were important, but I could use to piece his story together, but before I could ask, Harry shook hands with Nick and then started making his way over to the table.

Avery stood up as soon as Harry reached the table, tapped his shoulder, and walked off without saying a word. Harry settled in where Avery had been and looked over at me. "You were talking to Avery?"

"Yeah. He was doing the whole protective best friend thing," I replied. "It was cute."

"He's kind of a dork that way. He was always dragging me around through campus and stuff. Making sure I ate, making sure I socialized. He's kind of a mom."

I chuckled. "Pretty good mom."

He nodded. "He got the job done, that's for sure."

"Well, I think I passed," I said. "He said he was happy for us."

"Oh, did he?" He leaned over to me. "Congrats on getting past my mom."

Our lips melted together like they belonged that way and Harry's hand found my leg under the table. A heat boiled up in the pit of my stomach that sizzled its way up to my ears and had them burning inside of ten seconds. "Let's get out of here," I huffed.

"You have no idea how badly I want to," Harry said back, "but I have to hang around just a *bit* longer. We have a prospect test today, and I'm one of the benchmarks."

"What does that mean?"

"Prospective members get tested on a variety of things over the course of six months to a year to make sure they're up to the task of joining the Steel Knights. It's a bunch of different stuff, but tonight, Nicky wants to make sure the prospects have the skills to handle their bikes. Bucky and I are two ends of the spectrum. When I open up, my handling gets better, when

Bucky opens up, his gets more erratic, so we're the benchmarks Nicky is gonna gauge the prospects against in a bike race."

"Your handling gets *better*?" I asked in disbelief, forgetting for a moment that Harry wasn't aware that I knew about his accident from a few years ago.

"Yeah?" he said. "My life and my bike are about the only things I protect with everything I've got, so when I'm really putting the pedal to the metal, I home in to make sure neither are at risk."

That didn't make sense to me. Darrien had told me multiple times about the accident, and he always said it was Harry's erratic handling that caused it. "I'll be interested to see it," I said.

"Lucky for you, the race is starting in about five minutes." He stood up from the table and stuck out his hand. "Come on. I'll need my good luck charm there if I'm gonna win."

My heart stuttered, looking up at Harry's gorgeous face backlit by the bar lights, but I ignored it as I reached out and took his hand and let him lead me from the bar and out into the night air. Word of the race must have spread because the bar's patrons were spilling outside in throngs as the prospects were already pulling out their bikes and lining up on the street. Harry yanked me toward him with a strength that burned me up, kissed me, and then left my side to go and get his bike. He and the other member, Bucky, joined the line of bikes on the road, and Nick walked over to see them off.

"All right kids, let's be safe out there." He pointed down the road to where the gas station about a mile down could just barely be seen. "You're going down, circling the BP, and coming back. First one back wins, obviously, but it's not all about winning, it's about showing me you know how to handle your bike. Harry and Bucky are gonna be watching as well, so show us what ya got." He pulled a gun out of the back of his waistband and stuck it in the air. "On your marks..." All the bikes rumbled up. "Get set..." A few of them throttled to showboat, and then Nick fired the gun and the roar the collective bikes let out was almost too much for my eardrums.

They fired up, kicking up dust as they did, and blasted down the road. Whether he did it on purpose or not, I wasn't sure, but Harry immediately dropped behind. He wasn't behind for long though, as he ducked down and picked up the pace. He started to close in on one of the prospects and cut in front of him with expert precision. He slid his bike in and out of the other racers like he was threading a needle and my jaw dropped.

He was right, his handling was astounding.

For as long as I could, I kept a watch on Harry until he was over the hill and out of sight. Everyone standing around started to murmur about who they thought was going to win. The rumble of the racing bikes could be heard for the duration of the race, but they couldn't be seen for a few minutes. Eventually, however, the roar started to get louder again as the bikes came thundering back down the street. It was the only female prospect who was leading the back, and right behind her was Harry. He was like a bullet. He didn't veer or waver at all. Despite the fact that he was probably going ninety or more miles per hour, he was driving perfectly straight and he was gaining on the other driver fast.

It wasn't enough though, as she went blazing back past Nick at lightning speed, with Harry a few seconds behind her. They both went flying further up the road, as they worked to slow themselves down safely, and I watched as Harry decelerated at a much higher rate of speed than the other driver, and flip his bike around as if he'd been doing it since he was a child.

My whole body shook with fear and rage and every other negative emotion I could muster.

How could someone with handling skills of that caliber cause an accident that had made a car flip nine times? He had to just be driving recklessly for no reason. So it wasn't even that it was an accident or a matter of road rage, when it came to that day and that car, Harry must have made an intentional decision to drive in a way that was dangerous for Darrien's car. He didn't seem like such a reckless and careless person, but as much as I wanted to confront him right then and there, I was shaking too much to do it. I got in my car and used the crowd gathering around the returned bikers as a distraction to make my escape.

I didn't want to play around with Harry anymore. If I never saw him again it would be too soon.

Chapter Twelve

Bullet

It's been a few days since that night. I keep checking my phone despite how angry Celia leaving made me. I'd texted and called Celia a handful of times, but she never responded. I haven't been sleeping right because I was so worried. People around the bar remembered seeing her get in her car and leave that night, but no one knew *why* she left. Before the race started, she was chomping at the bit to get out of there and go somewhere private with me, so what the hell happened between when we last spoke and when the race was over to send her off?

There were no responses from Celia, so I threw down my phone and flopped back on my bed. I glanced over at the empty space and let out a frustrated grunt. Looking forward to coming back with her got me through the night; I just wished I knew why the sudden distance.

Was she ghosting me again?

I could draw a normal conclusion that it wasn't *me* who upset her. She was fine when I started the race, and she was gone when I got done. Did she just panic? She'd mentioned being wary of commitments, and the last time her feelings got the better of her, she ran off.

Maybe it was best to just leave her alone.

No part of me was constructed to be a complicated guy. Everything growing up was complex and unknown for me. In truth, I hadn't really spent all that much time thinking about a relationship in my life, but even I could determine that I wasn't a guy who could deal well with a flighty woman. Not knowing what was going on in her head, not having any clue what was going to set her off next and have her ignoring me—I just wasn't built for that. My time with Celia was nice, but even as wonderful as she was, it wasn't worth the stress. Trust issues with women or not, I was not about to be taken advantage of.

Although this certainly wasn't improving my trust in women.

I threw back the covers of my bed, trying not to let Celia get to me in that way. She'd wasted enough of my time, and after the breakthroughs I'd had after looking through Tess' notes, or even talking with Seneca, I wanted to try and stay on a path to redemption.

Not all women are like that.

Maybe just the ones I invest any real emotions into?

Whatever.

The cats were scratching at the door, so my time to mull it over was gone, just like Celia. I climbed out of bed and went through my morning routine, feeding the boys, taking a shower, eating breakfast and eventually leaving for the club.

To my surprise, when I got there, Seth was already there waiting. It was rare that anyone arrived earlier than me on any given day, but I was growing to like Seth quite a bit, so it didn't bother me much to see him.

"You're up early," I said as I approached the front door, fishing out my keys to let us in.

"Nicky said you were always here at the crack of dawn, so I figured I'd better start getting used to it," he replied.

"Used to it?" I questioned, then it dawned on me. "Oh, right, you're taking over the bookkeeping." Between everything with Celia, it completely slipped my mind that everything was different starting today. I was officially the Vice President now, and Seth was taking over bookkeeping. "You have experience in it, right?"

"Yeah. I never went to college formally or anything. Honestly, school has just never been my thing, but I've always been good with numbers. My mom was an accountant and I'd help her out, and I actually tutored kids in high school. Then my job up until I was offered this position was an office manager at this construction place. On paper, I wasn't the accountant, but I was the only one there doing any accounting, so you tell me."

I let us into the Taphouse and led Seth back to the warehouse, grabbing a couple of bottles of water on the way. If only I hadn't gotten so caught up, I may have actually formulated some sort of training plan. Winging it wasn't my strong suit.

"What did you have to do that was related to accounting?" I asked.

Seth pulled out a chair at the big meeting table and sat down. "Well, every month I reconciled all the credit cards. I had to manage inventory. I ran all of the month-end reports and zeroed them out against our income and expenditures."

"Wow. You did all that without any formal training?"

"Yeah. When I got there, some other lady was doing it, but she wouldn't even show up to work half the time. It was causing trouble for everyone, so I sort of just taught myself how to do it. I'd ask questions of her here and there to try and learn more, but I think she thought she was indispensable and that was why she acted like that, so she didn't want to share any trade secrets if you know what I mean."

"Didn't work out well for her, did it?" I said.

He let out a snicker. "No, it did not."

"Well, good. If you've done all of that then this stuff should come pretty easy to you, but don't fret if it takes a little bit. Also, do you drink coffee?"

"Uh, no," Seth replied. "I mean I have before, I'm just not a coffee guy."

"You may want to become one. Nick's on this whole kick of expanding things around here, and so I expect the bookkeeping part of this job is about to get a *little* more complicated. I'll be here to help out whenever I can, just don't be shocked. He's energetic about it, so if he comes rambling to you at eight in the morning, you'll want some caffeinated backup."

Seth nodded. "Got it. What kind of plans?"

"Well, I don't wanna get too into it without Nicky's approval, but the main thing is that we're going to be looking into building our own clubhouse. A place where the club can really hunker down and grow and thrive. A lot will be involved, as you know."

Seth held out his arms as if he had it *all* figured out. "I *do* know. I managed a construction office."

All my senses went dull for a second and then I let out a loud laugh. "Holy shit! You *did* just tell me that. I didn't even put two and two together! You're gonna be the fucking M.V.P."

He gave a slightly arrogant, proud smile. "Anything I can do to help, Vice Pres. I left on really good terms with my old company, too, so I bet I can get us the friends-and-family discount if we go with them."

"Can you set up a lunch or something and you, me, Nicky, can then talk it out and get a quote?"

Seth nodded excitedly. "I'm all over it."

How lucky did we get? There was no way Nick knew the specifics of Seth's accounting background, otherwise, he would have been twice as excited. Something in me shook a little with anticipation at dropping the good news. Part of Tess' frustration with Nick, at least according to him, was that he always talked a big game, but never pulled the trigger. With Seth in such a good spot with a construction company, I could get the gears moving before Nick could throw a wrench in it and save him from himself. We could be breaking ground on the new clubhouse before the year was over.

Seth started to snicker, and then clapped a hand over his mouth to prevent me from seeing. "What?" I asked.

"Nothing, I just don't think I've ever seen you excited like this before," he said. "I mean, I know we haven't known each other that long, but it doesn't seem like this is something you do a whole lot."

He wasn't wrong. In no time at all, I was already having fun in my new position, which was a little frightening. It helped that it couldn't just stop returning my calls like *some* people I knew, but it made me realize how much investing in something new freaked me out.

"Yeah, it's new for me," I admitted to Seth. "It's good though. I'm excited."

We spent the next few weeks working on the club expansion while simultaneously training Seth up on the books. I was impressed with how much Seth was able to take on each day, and the more we worked together, the more it felt like we were working side by side as opposed to me training him in my former profession.

I never heard from Celia, but for some reason, it didn't make me as angry as it did the first time she ghosted me. Maybe it was because I was operating with the expectation that she would disappear again at some point, but it made me sad more than it made me angry. I wished I could have been the one to break her out of her flighty, commitment-fearing phase, but it seemed it wasn't meant to be.

"It's a good thing, you know?" Avery said as we discussed it. "They say some people come into our lives for a short time but to teach us important lessons. She was able to get you to stop seeing women in such a negative light, and the fact that you are able to look back on it openly rather than blame her and shove her into the same box as women from your past is a sign of growth." Me, Seth, Nick, and Bucky all looked at Avery with our brows furrowed. "What?" he asked.

"Maybe I need to make Bullseye the club therapist," Nick joked.

"That intelligence is definitely fleeting. I wouldn't trust it," Bucky said.

Avery punched his arm. "Fuck you. I'm very smart."

Avery actually was one of the smarter people I knew, but I didn't realize he was that insightful. It made me feel better to think that something good had come out of my relationship with Celia. I just wished it was actually her and I being together, not some cosmic lesson that needed to be learned.

Oh well.

"So," Nick said, redirecting our attention back to the club. "Is it true? Do you really have a number for the expansion?"

"Yep," Seth replied. "Hoppa's Construction Company can handle the entire thing as a general manager. They'll take care of securing all the different subcontractors and help us get this thing built from the ground up. We just have to pick a spot. Based on everything we decided for the blueprint, the contract comes out to two-hundred-and-fifty-thousand with a twenty-percent upfront cost to break ground, so we'll need to hand over fifty grand to get it started."

"Do we have it?" Nick asked, looking at me, then at Seth.

"Not quite yet," I said. "It'd be better if we did it out of our fourth-quarter profits right before flipping over the year to avoid the least damage to our bottom line. We can cut a check sometime in October or later."

"Still, that's only a couple months away," Nick noted. "We have a lot of work to do if we're going to be breaking ground on a new place *that* soon. We're going to have split attention for a while, so we need to lay out a prospect plan for Dynamite to follow and make sure that the border runs are situated, although..." He looked at Bucky. "You've been killing those lately."

Bucky elbowed Avery. "Well, I've had some help. Treasurer says that now he's got *two* accountants breathing down his neck, he wants more money, so he set up more in-roads. Discreet midnight runs make for fast transportation and I think we're close to doubling up."

"It shows," Seth said, tapping the reconciliation book. "It's buying our new facility."

Nick folded his hands together with a smile on his face. "Man. I miss my kids, but if *this* is what a well-functioning operation feels like, I hate that I cost us this for so long."

"It's like you said," I cut in, "we're putting that behind us and starting from scratch."

He nodded. "Right you are. I'm excited, boys. This is gonna be huge for us."

"By this time next year, we'll be moving into our own facility, and it changes everything. You three," I said to Bucky, Avery, and Seth, "are gonna be integral in keeping the members in line as we move forward and making sure to tighten the ranks. The new era of the Steel Knights is going to completely change the landscape of Hoppa, and we can't let it fall behind us."

"Hoo hoo!" Bucky yowled. "Now *this* is what I joined up for!"

Nick smiled at me. "Things are about to get fun."

Chapter Thirteen

Celia

The pan sizzled as I dropped the eggs in, filling the kitchen, once again, with the smell of spices and butter. I imagined the way Harry liked to make his eggs in my mind and replicated the process because they were so good, but I didn't like the pit it left in my stomach. It was more than just anger or frustration, it was a longing.

I missed him.

There was more than one reason to stop playing around with him. Getting vengeance for my dad was all well and good, but it wouldn't mean anything if all I did was fall for the guy and get no revenge and end up getting hurt myself. There wasn't an *actual* future for Harry and me—there couldn't be. After all, once he learned who my godfather was, that the men who were in the car he flipped with his reckless disregard for others were the same ones I'd called "Dad" in my lifetime, all of my lies and deceit would come spilling out.

It was best to go our separate ways. My dad would understand, and my godfather would just have to get over it. It'd been close to three weeks since I last spoke to Harry, and about two since he stopped trying to contact me. It bothered me more than it should, but I just had to remind myself that it was for the best and move on.

"Good morning," a groggy voice grumbled into the silence.

"Morning," I replied.

Darrien rounded the corner in his wheelchair and made his way up to the fridge. He opened the door, blocking most of the view I had of him, and I didn't think twice about it until he shut the door with the orange juice in hand. I was fairly certain that I'd put the orange juice on the top shelf of the fridge, as I often mistakenly did, resulting in his inability to reach it, but maybe I'd subconsciously put it back where he could get to it. The small conspiracy that tried to sneak its way into my brain was snuffed out as Darrien rolled over to just below the kitchen cabinet where we kept the cups and used his grabber to open it and sat struggling for a couple of minutes trying to get a cup down.

"Are you just going to stand there watching me struggle?" he snapped.

"Sorry!" I yelped.

I scuttled over from my pan and pulled a cup down and set it on the counter, then pulled the orange juice carton from his hand and poured some into the cup. When I opened the fridge door, I started to put the carton back in a spot along the doors where Darrien could reach it, but then stopped and intentionally put it back on the top shelf. Just to see what happened next time he needed orange juice.

Darrien made his way to a spot at the kitchen table against the wall and I returned to my pan to pull out the eggs I'd made. "Do you want some toast?" I asked.

"Sure," he replied.

I scooped the eggs out of the pan onto a plate and set the plate on the small kitchen peninsula that jutted out from one wall and separated the kitchen from the eating area on the other side where the table was. Then I turned my back to grab the loaf of bread from on top of the fridge and slide two pieces of it into the toaster. I cracked a couple of fresh eggs into the pan to start cooking them for myself, and when I heard the toast pop, I flipped around to grab and butter the slices.

With the toast in hand, I flipped around to drop them on Darrien's plate, but it was gone. I looked over to the table and the plate was sitting in front of him and he was already working on the eggs. "Um…" I started. "Did you grab that, or did I give it to you?"

"I grabbed it," he responded. "Why?"

Darrien's wheelchair wasn't a quiet device, and more than that, the place I'd set the plate on the island was almost dead center, where it'd be difficult for Darrien to reach from the edge.

Was I losing my mind?

"I didn't even hear you move," I said.

His brow furrowed. "How is that possible? I haven't even oiled my wheels recently." His words were steeped in such genuine confusion that it was enough to convince me I was just distracted and not thinking clearly. "Is something wrong?" he asked.

"Maybe. Sorry."

I buttered Darrien's toast and brought it to him, then returned to the pan to finish my own eggs and put in some toast of my own. When my plate was done, I grabbed a bottle of water from the fridge and went to sit down across from Darrien. He was swiping through his phone, not really focused on anything in particular, but I couldn't stop staring at him.

There was no way he was able to get out of his chair. I had to change him. We'd paid thousands of dollars ramping his home so that he could get around. The more I thought about it, the more insane the idea seemed. Having Harry on the brain was having an adverse effect on my mind.

"So how's work going?" Darrien asked. "Any word about that promotion?"

My bosses had been talking about moving me up again for a couple of months now, and I'd made the mistake of mentioning it to Darrien, who never missed an opportunity to remind me how much more money we need coming in to make ends meet. I had about forty grand left of the settlement my dad got for the car accident, but Darrien didn't like making me use that money on him or anything he needed. Even with that considered, I used the money each month to pay the mortgage and utilities at his house, plus cover my student loan payments each month. The settlement money seemed like a lot but wasn't for how quickly those things were eating into it.

"Yeah, they are telling me that I'm gonna get it, but it probably won't happen until after yearly reviews," I said. "As long as my first review goes well, I should get it and a nice raise."

"When are reviews?"

I took a sip of my water before saying, "They'll happen in December, right before the holidays."

I took a bite of my eggs and was immediately filled with warmth. I'd only gotten breakfast out of Harry a couple of times before I decided to cut him off again, but it reminded me of his smile, and our passionate nights, and his adorable cats. All things that gave me a fuzzy feeling in my stomach that I rarely got. Suddenly, I was playing out the scenario of showing up at the Taphouse again. Approaching Harry and apologizing for going ghost and starting us up again. I could probably get him to forgive me again. To take me back to his place. My skin was already burning, imagining his hands on it, his lips on my neck, his arms lifting me with ease…

"Hey!" I jumped at the sudden yell and looked across the table, and Darrien was glaring at me. "Why aren't you answering me?"

"Sorry," I said. "I didn't hear you."

"Then pay better attention. I'm sitting five feet from you. Are you sure nothing's wrong?"

"Nothing's wrong," I replied.

"It has nothing to do with the fact that you haven't seen Harry in a few weeks?" he asked, and my eyes got a little wider. "Yeah, I know, Celia. I'm not stupid. You've been coming right home after work, hanging around here on your days off, plus I can tell that you miss him, even though you *swore* you weren't developing feelings."

"I'm not."

He rolled his eyes. "Please don't treat me like an idiot. You know I hate that."

"I'm not!" I repeated. "I don't have feelings for him."

"Celia, you walked around here glowing like the star on top of a Christmas tree, then all of a sudden, there was nothing." He shrugged. "I suppose it's better anyway. You clearly weren't up to the task of doing what had to be done, so I'll have to come up with something else."

"I'm not weak just because I don't want to be heartless with someone. I get that Harry ruined our lives, but…" I stopped myself shy of saying that he didn't seem like a bad guy. He didn't, but I doubted Darrien wanted to hear that. "I don't want to do this anymore. That doesn't make me crazy."

"You're right, I was wrong to assume you'd do anything to honor your father's memory," he replied. Rage was burning in my blood. I was a daddy's girl from the bottom of my heart. He'd raised me alone and losing him destroyed me. "Do I need to tell you the story again?"

"I don't want to hear the story," I said.

"Your father and I were out running errands, picking up things for *your* birthday. He was so excited to celebrate his princess turning sixteen in a few weeks and was planning a huge celebration for you," Darrien started.

"I said I don't want to hear the story."

Darrien continued regardless. "We were just minding our own business when Harry came blazing onto the road. He had *reckless* disregard for other drivers. He was swerving in and out of traffic. Cutting people off, tailgating, driving between cars in nonexistent lanes. You name it. If it was illegal, he was doing it."

I imagined the times I'd ridden on Harry's bike, and what I'd seen during the race. What I'd experienced was so vastly different from Darrien's story. "He's always safe when I've seen him on his bike."

"Well, I'd like to think so with someone else on it. At least he has a little bit of regard for someone else's life. Then again, maybe that was just because you were sleeping with him."

My ears burned, half from embarrassment and half from anger. "No…"

"He just picked us out randomly," Darrien said. "We weren't doing anything to him, didn't even know who he was. He just looked over at me, actually he locked eyes with your dad first. He told me this psycho biker was trying to challenge us, so I slowed down, just trying to get away from him. He wouldn't leave us alone though. He matched our speed and then when he had a window, he swerved toward us. I had to veer to the left just to keep from crashing with him. He laughed at us! He thought it was funny! He was trying to kill us!"

In my mind, I was seeing a cartoonishly evil version of Harry with a thin, evil guy mustache. Darrien and my dad were sitting in a toy car, and Harry was driving at them like a bullet from a gun, trying to flip it.

It just didn't seem real to me. "I don't want to hear the rest," I said. "I get it."

"You don't want to hear the next part?" he replied darkly. "About how he finally got the hit that he wanted? He smacked the side of my car with his back tire, right against your dad's door. I lost control of the car and it flew to the left and hit the guard rail, flipping up over it. He lost control, too, at least, but I didn't see what happened to him as my car started to flip and flip—"

"Okay!"

"And flip and flip and flip. It slammed down on your dad's side every single time it hit the ground again."

"Okay! Stop!" I screeched. Tears were sliding down my face as I imagined my dad dying and hitting the ground over and over. "Stop. I get it."

"I don't mean to upset you, Celia, but this is important. I don't know how to make you understand. You are the only one who can change things. The only one who can break him so much that he never hurts anyone like this ever again. It's not just for your father or for me, it's for every person he's ever put at risk. Don't you want to stop him?"

That was the first time Darrien had ever framed it like that. Like we were doing it for the greater good. Was I capable of breaking Harry that much, that he'd *never* get on a bike again? The women in his past, whoever they were, drove him to hate women just from what they had done. Didn't that mean I could also exercise that level of influence over him?

"I do want to stop him," I said. "I want to make him pay for what he did to us."

"I don't think you do," Darrien said. "You've told me that before."

"I swear." I used the back of my hand to wipe my tears away. "I want to. I won't give up again. I'm going to do it."

"This is our last chance, Celia. You can't mess this up again. If we screw up this opportunity, we won't be able to get close enough to him again to do what we need to do, and he could get worse."

That thought terrified me more than anything. Darrien was right. If I continued to upset Harry, he could have another dark night that could cost someone else their lives.

I didn't say anything else to Darrien and he didn't stop me as I stood up from the table, leaving my half-eaten breakfast behind, grabbed my purse and left the house. Without even thinking, I picked up my phone and tried to call Harry, but it rang once and then went to voicemail. I couldn't blame him for ignoring me. It was going to take a personal visit in order to get him to let me back into his life, and some good coffee never hurt anyone.

There was a coffee shop halfway between my godfather's house and Harry's house, so I stopped for a couple of lattés. Coffee made everything better and I was hopeful I could warm Harry's soul enough to hear me out as I gave him more lame excuses.

"Celia?" I looked over my shoulder, and Laura was sitting at one of the tables with her laptop. "Hey."

"Hi." I held up my finger and quickly placed the order for a couple of lattés and then went and sat down across from Laura while I waited. "How are you?"

"Good. I haven't heard from you in weeks though. I thought you were going through another one of your moody phases. Did you break up with Harry or something?" she asked.

"Uh… Kind of. I ran for the hills and now he won't talk to me. Hoping the coffee will help smooth that over."

"Damn commitment-phobe," she growled.

"I am not," I said. "It's just… It's complicated."

"It doesn't have to be. How do you feel?"

It wasn't that easy. I knew how I felt, but I also knew that I had no business developing feelings for Harry when he was the man that killed my father. Between the pressure from Darrien and my desire to do the right thing, I didn't know *how* to describe what I was feeling.

"I like him," I said. "He scares me."

"He scares you *because* you like him," she replied. "Don't overthink it. Don't try and figure out what's going to come next, just live in the moment. We're all still young and have time to let the pieces fall into place, but if it feels good, don't run from that."

"Yeah."

"I realize you're a control freak and that's not easy for you though, but try your hardest," she joked.

"Celia?" the barista called out.

I stood up and collected the lattes I ordered and then swung back by Laura's table for a brief moment just to say goodbye. I kissed her on the cheek, and she smiled up at me. "Be breezy, girl, and stop ignoring me, because if you do, I'm gonna hurt you."

A chuckle escaped my lips, the first real one I'd had in a while. "Got it. See ya."

"Good luck!"

With the coffees in hand, and Laura's advice in my mind, I got back in my car and made my way to Harry's. Laura was right, and even though she didn't mean it to, the advice was going to help me trick Harry successfully this time. No overthinking it. Just taking it day by day. That was my road to victory.

Harry's bike was parked out in front of his house, so I put my car in park and made my way up to the door with the coffees in hand. Using my elbow to ring the doorbell, I took a deep breath and tried to ignore the way my heart was racing with anticipation at seeing Harry again.

"Coming!" Harry called, and his gruff voice sent a wave of goosebumps rushing over me. The door opened and my heart jumped.

I forgot to remind myself how good-looking he was.

"Hi," I said, pouring as much guilt into my voice as I could.

Harry leaned against the frame of his door. "Hey."

Surprisingly, he didn't seem angry like I expected, though his apathy wasn't much more inspiring. "How are you?" I asked.

"Pretty good. Things are going well in the new position. You?"

I was awkwardly standing there with both coffees in hand. "Good. I suppose my presentation of coffee first thing in the morning is pretty obvious that I'm here to apologize."

Harry shook his head. "You don't have to apologize."

"I… I don't?"

"No. You told me upfront, well mostly upfront, that you struggle with serious things and that deep emotions scare you. When you ghosted, I wasn't all that shocked. Hurt, but not shocked," he explained honestly.

"Oh." I couldn't tell if *this* response was better or worse, but instead of thinking about it, I just extended one of the coffees. "A latté as a peace offering? Maybe I could come in and we can catch up."

Harry made no attempt to grab the cup. "I understand the position you're in, but I don't think that's a good idea," he replied. "I think we're just in different places. I'm not necessarily looking to get married and have kids right away or anything, but just like you were honest with me, I was honest with you. I don't want to just date for the sake of it and not know if and when you're gonna hit the bricks. I'm not angry, I just don't think we're meant to be."

It hurt to hear. I was the one toying with him, but it felt like he was breaking up with me. The thought of never seeing Harry again didn't sit well with me and not for the reasons it should. It wasn't a fear that I was going to miss out on my final opportunity to carry out my plan, it was a fear that I was going to lose him.

"I'm not," I started slowly, "in the business of begging, but I'd be willing to get pretty close to fix this. I shouldn't have disappeared again. I told you that I wouldn't and then I did anyway, but I'm just scared. Between my dad dying and taking care of my godfather, I just haven't dated a whole lot or really had many relationships of any kind. I have my best friend Laura, but literally, she just yelled at me in the coffee shop because she's been trying to contact me for a few weeks and hasn't heard from me." I let out a forced chuckle. "So, if it makes you feel any better, you aren't the *only* one being ghosted." Harry's expression didn't change, but I could tell he was legitimately listening to me, so I continued. "When I saw you on your bike, all of a sudden I realized, 'Oh shit, I really like this guy,' and I panicked. I'm sorry."

"I'm not unsympathetic, Celia, but I've heard that before. It's like I said, I don't think it's meant to be. I assume, at some point in your life, you'll meet someone that just changes all that commitment stuff for you and you'll want to look past everything else to make it work with them. Or maybe you won't and that's fine, too. Either way, I don't think I'm that guy."

"You are though," I yelped, and I hated how desperate I sounded. It was a gut reaction. What Harry was describing, and what Laura said about not running from something that felt good, that *was* the way I felt. "You're that guy, that's why I'm here. I've never gone back to a guy before. Usually, I ghost and then I'm gone, but then I go home and lie in bed at night and I'm angry at myself for messing it up with you. Harry, I mean it, I… want to be with you."

"Not just in a friendly, just-dating-for-fun kind of way?" Harry asked. "Not in a ghosting-me-again-in-a-week kind of way?"

"No," I said. "I want to do this. I told Avery that this isn't a game, and it isn't. I just need a little more patience than the average bear. I'm sorry. I *am* trying."

Harry didn't respond right away. He just looked me up and down with gears turning. Behind him, Jingle slunk out of the shadows of the house and sat staring up at me. Harry looked down at him and then back up at me, and then finally reached out and took the coffee. He stepped to the side so that I could enter, and I smiled as I walked past him, feeling like I'd won, but not for the right reason.

All it took was being invited back in, and I was already off track.

Chapter Fourteen

Bullet

I hated to admit it, but every time I sent Celia a text message or called her and she didn't answer, I thought it was happening again. Just a few minutes could have me panicking into thinking I was getting ghosted again, and then the sense of relief I felt when she *would* respond was hefty. Still, I knew I couldn't become *that* guy, and with each additional day that passed without her disappearing, my confidence was growing. It'd been about two months since we started dating yet again, and apart from work hours, our communication had been normal and reassuring.

However, Celia's fear of commitment was starting to show itself in other ways. She still very rarely stayed the night, she didn't talk a whole lot about her past apart from what I already knew, and she'd never invited me up to her apartment. I didn't know if that was a fear of wanting me to be her roommate or just trying to keep me at a distance again, but it made me nervous.

But I liked Celia. A lot.

The more we saw each other, and the more time we spent together, the more I was beginning to feel like I could be falling for her. It wasn't just the things we had in common, but it was also the things we didn't. She wasn't afraid to call me on my shit when I got in a very introverted and isolated mood, and she did a good job of coaxing me out of my shell. I didn't want to push too hard given that she'd already told me about her hangups and insecurities, and I wasn't the kind of guy to pressure someone, but I couldn't shake the odd feeling that I was investing more time into this relationship than I was going to get out of it.

I smiled at the good morning text I got from her just before getting to the Taphouse for the morning. It was just a simple, "*Looking forward to our date tomorrow. Hopefully you like thrills, good lookin',*" but it was enough to have me smiling from ear to ear. Yeah, I was falling for her for sure, I just wish I knew more about how to have the kind of conversations that would provide clarity.

"That's a happy smile," Avery said as I walked into the Taphouse. I looked at my phone, confused. Had I gotten to work later than I thought? Seth had been getting there earlier than me lately, but Avery didn't believe in times earlier than eleven AM. "Things must still be going well with Celia then?"

"Have you been replaced by a body snatcher?" I asked. "Why are you here so early?"

"No reason," Avery said, but almost as if she was summoned by our musings, the

Taphouse door opened behind me, and Seneca came walking in. Avery sat up a little and smiled. "Hey. Good morning."

"Good morning," Seneca said with a sweet smile. "Squared back there?"

"Yep! Head on back," Avery replied.

"Thanks." Seneca walked around the bar and through the swinging door toward the warehouse.

I looked back at Avery with an eyebrow raised. "So, you came early to see her?"

Avery shook his head. "No. It was just a coincidence."

"Sure." I sat down at the table across from him. "Well, since she's here, maybe you can help me with something. Do you think you could convince her to go out to coffee with me? Maybe even today?"

Despite his insistence that he wasn't at the bar so early to see her, Avery crossed his arms and furrowed his brow. "Uh. What about Celia?"

"First of all, you're not very good at hiding your true feelings, second of all, I don't want to go out with her romantically. I actually was hoping to talk to her about Celia. It's hard to get a beat on her and I thought maybe Seneca's perspective would help. She helped before, though unintentionally. I want to just talk to her."

"Oh," Avery said. "Okay. Yeah, I can ask for you."

"Thanks. I still don't think she likes me very much, but you two seem close."

That brought a smile to Avery's face. "I guess. Maybe."

We held a light conversation for about twenty minutes and then Avery stood up and walked back into the warehouse. I waited for an additional ten-ish minutes, texting Celia on my phone and researching the theme park we were planning on going to tomorrow, and then eventually, the door behind the bar swung open again. Seneca walked out and locked eyes with me immediately.

She seemed a little uncomfortable, but still walked up to me. "Uh, Avery said you maybe wanted to get coffee and chat?"

"Yeah," I replied, equally as uncomfortable. "Is that okay?"

"Sure. Wanna just head up to Mocha Loco?"

"That sounds good."

It was a little awkward, but I stood up with a smile and walked out of the bar. I could hear Seneca's bootsteps behind me, so I continued out and got on my bike. There was a gentle tap on my back as Seneca passed me to get on her bike and she threw me a smile, which I took to mean *relax*. For sure, it was me making things so tense, so I dropped my shoulders, took a deep breath, and smiled back, then we both started up our bikes with a pair of loud roars and made our way down the street to one of Hoppa's local coffee shops, Mocha Loco.

The shop was still pretty empty inside given how early in the day it was, so it wasn't difficult to find a table. I grabbed one near the door and prepared to ask Seneca what she wanted, but she set a hand on my shoulder and said, "What would you like?"

"Just a regular latté with an extra shot, please," I replied.

She nodded. "Got it. I'll be back."

Sitting down at the table, I tried to organize my thoughts while I waited for Seneca. I didn't want to immediately go into asking for help regarding Celia because I didn't want it to seem like I had no interest outside of personal gain. My best friend skated into my mind, and I smiled, wondering if she would talk to me about him if I asked. I was dangerously curious, and it could be a nice way to just get to know her better.

Seneca came back with the coffees and sat across from me, setting my latte down in front of me as she went. "Thanks," I said. "Round two is on me."

"Oh?" Seneca replied in a light tone. "I get *two* coffees with you? I'm lucky."

"Well, I don't know that I'd call it lucky, but sure, let's go with that," I replied. "Really, I feel lucky that you'd be willing to stay here for two coffees."

"I mean, it's not every day that Hoppa's hardass invites people out for coffee," Seneca said. "I wasn't about to throw away the chance."

"Thanks, and that's a great segue into what I wanted to discuss first, which is a heartfelt apology. I know we've kind of been butting heads ever since you came on as a prospect and I also know that a lot of that is due to my unique relationship with women. It shouldn't have been on every woman I met to bear the issues that I faced in the past, and if you hadn't come along, I may not have realized that. So I'm sorry and also, thank you."

"I just call it like I see it," she said. "I guess it was also a little frustrating because it seemed like you were really cool and then when I heard the rumor, I was really disappointed. Call me a dreamer, but I wanted to kind of snap you out of it, if nothing else."

"Well, you did. I mean, dating Celia has helped a lot, too, but that would have fizzled out entirely after the first time she ghosted me if you hadn't gotten real with me. She's amazing and I wouldn't be with her if it wasn't for you." I let out a snicker, only realizing as I said it how true it was. "Again, thanks."

"You're welcome. I'm glad my being a blunt asshole could benefit you."

"Blunt assholery is something we have in common," I replied.

She laughed. "So I've noticed."

"I'm sorry, too, that you didn't get to meet Tess and vice versa. She would have loved you, I think. Maybe she'll come back one day, and you'll get your chance."

"That confident that I'll become a member, huh?" she asked.

"If I have anything to do with it, yeah, and it has nothing to do with my making amends with women, and everything to do with the fact that you're badass and we'd be lucky to have you."

"If you don't mind my asking, why the problems with women? What'd they do?" she asked.

"It all started with my mom. She was abusive when I was a child. She killed my dad."

Seneca was mid-drink in her coffee and nearly choked on it when I said the latter half of the statement. "She *killed* your dad?"

"Yeah. She was super abusive toward him, but he just took it all in his stride so long as it was him and not me, but then one day it turned on me. He tried to take me and escape into the night and she killed him. The police were called, but she claimed it was self-defense and they just believed her. Even though I said it wasn't. Even though I said she used to hit my dad, they said it was different because she was a woman. The judge was female, and the cop that reported to the scene was female, too, and really laid it on thick in my mom's defense. Said I was crying for my mom when my dad was trying to take me away and a bunch of other stuff that just wasn't true. They sent me back with my mom and she beat the hell out of me for an additional four years until a teacher at my school finally noticed and called someone. They pulled me out of her house and put me with my foster dad."

"Wow," Seneca said. "I…" Her cheeks puffed up as she blew air out. "I would have trust issues, too. Just in general."

"To be fair, I *do* have your general, run-of-the-mill trauma-induced trust issues, but women just always put me in the mindset of my mom. It wasn't fair, I admit that." I shook my head. "That's probably also why I have no idea what I'm doing when it comes to women."

"Hitting another rough patch with Celia?"

"Not so much a rough patch as a long, flat path and I'm not really sure where the pitfalls are," I replied. "She ghosted me a bunch right there in the beginning, but we've been fine for a couple of months now, I just feel like I don't know if I'm still grasping at straws, expecting her not to bounce again."

Seneca took a sip of her coffee. "Do you get the sense that she will?"

"That's the thing, I don't really get *any* senses. Not in the romantic sense, like I know I like her, and I know she likes me, but the rest of her is sort of an enigma." I ran a hand through my hair. "She doesn't give any signs that it's serious or that it isn't. She's just kind of even-mannered. I don't want to be *that* guy, but I wish I just knew for sure that I wasn't wasting my time. That going ahead with her a third time wasn't a mistake."

"So, you just have to ask her," Seneca said. "Not just women, but people in general, are *far* more receptive to honesty than you might think. Don't be weird about it, just tell her you're checking in, want to know if she's still feeling good about you guys, and be honest that her ambiguity freaks you out a little. We can only expect our partners to meet our needs if they know what they are."

"That makes sense. So, I just say it? I don't have to say it in any special kind of way?" I asked.

"Nah. I've only seen Celia a few times, but she doesn't strike me as a fluffy kind of lady. Straight to the point is best. Don't be cold about it, just be upfront."

"Okay, I can do that. Thanks," I said.

"Yeah."

"So…" A smile found my face. "You and Avery?"

She recoiled. "Whaaat?" Her voice got an octave higher and I couldn't help but laugh. "Shut up."

"So, you like him, too?" I asked.

"Too?"

Ah, shit. I'd end up paying for that slip-up at some point. "I mean, he hasn't confirmed it to me or anything, but I know him pretty well. I see the way he looks at you, and believe me when I say this, Avery doesn't even know that hours before lunchtime exist. I saw him at the bar at seven AM and I nearly fell over. Then you came waltzing through the door and it all made sense."

She chuckled. "Well then, today is just a good day for me all round."

"So, how long before we can double date?" I asked.

Again, she sputtered on her coffee. "I'm gonna go with never, but thanks."

"Never? Why?" I asked.

"Because, at the risk of sounding like your girl, I'm not really a commitment type. Relationships just don't go well for me. It's not even that I don't trust men or anything like that, it's just that nine times out of ten, I don't get what I see. I develop feelings for someone thinking they're one way, then they turn around and they're the complete opposite. It just got exhausting trying to navigate. I gave dating apps and stuff a try and it was more of the same. Finally, I just gave up. It's easiest for everyone if we get what we need and get out before anyone gets hurt."

It was an odd sentiment coming from someone who had just given me sound long-term relationship advice, but her lack of good experiences had colored her view when it came to herself. "Avery's not like that," I said. "I've never met someone who presents a more genuine version of themselves, and honestly, I think he's just a little too thick to do anything other than that. Don't get me wrong, Avery is incredibly intelligent, like it'll shock you, but he's also kind of a dope. That's why the only thing he can do is present his most honest self. It just comes naturally. I think it's a virtue more than a flaw."

"You know, I kind of got that sense with him," Seneca said. "Maybe that's why I'm staying away from him. If he's so good at just purely being himself, the last thing he needs is for jaded ol' me to come in muddying things up."

"Well, I'm in no position to give advice, so I won't, but if you ever need someone to put in a good word for you with him, I've got you covered."

She smiled at me. "Thanks."

We sat for a few more hours, enjoying a couple more cups of coffee, and then we decided to go our separate ways for the day.

"This was fun," Seneca said. "Can we do it again sometime?"

"Yeah," I responded, "I'd like that a lot."

With that, she kicked on her bike and pulled off onto the road, leaving a wake of good old-fashioned Arizona dust behind her, bound for the bar for a long day of prospecting, and I decided to play hooky and go home to rest for my date. It wasn't just going to be a fun-filled day of rollercoasters and junk food, but I was actually going to try my hand at Seneca's relationship advice and see exactly how Celia felt about us.

Chapter Fifteen

Celia

Due to the fact that Hoppa, Arizona was a smaller town, there were no theme parks located within the city limits. Bars and restaurants were about all one had for entertainment there, although there was also a mall and a movie theater, but anyone looking for any actual thrills had to travel to the nearest big city. Hoppa was about three hours from Phoenix, Arizona's capital, but about halfway between Hoppa and Phoenix, was the smaller, but still bustling city of Anukasan, which meant eagle in Lakota. It had just debuted a new theme park and Harry planned a date to go and check it out.

That meant two things for which I was very excited.

The first, was that I was going to get to saddle up against Harry for a little over an hour as we made our way to Anukasan. I was well aware of the fact that it was Harry and his bike that got my father killed, but whenever I was on his bike, he handled it like a champ and there was little I loved more than the wind in my hair while I had my arms wrapped around Harry's waist. Most rides in Hoppa felt too short to me since everything was so close, so the long ride would be refreshing and welcome.

The second was the fact that we were going to a theme park specifically. I was a thrill-seeker by nature, but Hoppa didn't have many thrills. Harry had been a huge thrill for me the past couple of months, but I was excited for a chance to turn my guts inside out. It'd been since before my dad died that I had been to a theme park and I was really looking forward to it.

When we were finally pulling into the parking lot of Thrills and Spills, the electric energy was buzzing all over me. We were greeted with a sprawling image of their headlining attraction, a massive rollercoaster called The Underworld that spanned from one side of the theme park to the other and featured a terrifying, upside-down trip through a submerged segment of the ride. My stomach bottomed out looking at the cars at the top of the coaster taking almost a straight vertical dip from the summit of the ride above the theme park sign, and down until they were disappearing beneath the earth.

Harry pulled into a parking spot and turned off his bike, looking back over his shoulder at me as he did it. "I can't wait to ride that fucking thing."

"You and me both," I screeched. "Let's go!"

After getting tickets at the front gate, we passed into the bustling amusement park. There was jubilant music barely audible over the distant screams and hums of people chattering all around. Harry took my hand and locked our fingers together, kissing the back of my hand as he did it, and my heart leaped. I closed my eyes for a quick moment to resolve myself.

I could not get caught up in Harry the way I tended to.

I'd even packed a picture of my dad in my purse to keep me on the right track. Harry had a way of striking right to my center, and if I wasn't careful, I'd find myself getting swept up in enjoying the day and forget my goal: to find a way to destroy Harry.

"Okay, do we just head straight to The Underworld to start out?" Harry asked. "It's probably got a long wait time, and if we start out there, we can double back for a second ride before we leave."

"Absolutely," I said with a laugh, and we were off.

I'd look for a way to destroy Harry for sure, but I was going to enjoy some amazing rides while I searched.

As expected, the wait time for The Underworld was close to an hour. I knew it'd be worth it because just as we were approaching, a group of people were deboarding the ride, and at least half of them turned around and got right back in line. It made my skin sizzle with anticipation. Harry pulled me into the line, and once we had moved far enough that we weren't constantly walking and more standing, he brought me around to stand in front of him. He wrapped his arms around my stomach and dropped his head to my face to give me a kiss on the cheek. On instinct, I turned my head so that the kiss would strike me on the lips instead. I burned at the gentle feeling of his tongue brushing just against my bottom lip before we parted.

He smiled as he pulled away. "You tricked me."

"You act as if you don't like it," I replied.

He shook his head. "I'm not acting like that at all. I liked it. Let's do it again."

He leaned in and kissed me again, and then I leaned my head back against his shoulder as we slowly crawled our way through the line. We discussed a few different things during our wait, including everything going on at the club with the expansion.

In an attempt to keep myself from getting *too* attached to Harry, I was choosing not to tell him too much about myself, but I found that I loved watching him talk just as much, so it wasn't really helping. If I was going to find some way to destroy Harry, I was going to need to do it soon. Being with him felt too good, and within the hour that we had to wait to ride The Underworld, I'd completely lost sight of my mission and was just happily enjoying my date.

The Underworld was as terrifying and exhilarating as we'd expected, and the fun continued. From tilt-a-whirls, to rollercoasters, to flying swings rides, Harry and I did loops around the park, riding everything we could get to. We stopped for food here and there, but we were like children in that we barely wanted to stop long enough for anything other than the rides.

About two hours into our trip, Harry managed to convince me to get on the slow-moving boat ride through one of the mountains that the theme park was built at the base of. It didn't seem like his speed, but once we were on the ride, he slid close to me and kissed me on the lips before quickly moving down to my neck.

"Do you think they have cameras watching this ride?" he asked in a dark, seductive tone, and heat seared through my body instantly.

He didn't wait for a response, but instead ran a hand up my leg, under the base of my shorts. Gathering the gist of where he was going, I threw my leg over his and moved my hand over to start undoing the button of his jeans. The ride was just long enough for giving one another hand jobs.

Or so we thought.

Harry had already pulled an orgasm out of me, but my divided attention left me behind the ball bringing him to one. We could see the light of the end of the ride approaching, and it was looking like I wasn't gonna get him to the end before the ride ended it for us.

"Just stop before we get caught," he huffed as I pulled.

"Nope, you started it," I replied, then after looking around to make sure no staff were watching us immediately, I bent over and closed my mouth over him.

In the back of my mind, getting him finished before we re-emerged into the light of the day was key, so I moved at a fast pace. His hands found the back of my head, and after already getting him close with my hands, it didn't take long. I enjoyed the taste of him for as long as I could before he let out a quiet groan and exploded in my mouth. I made sure I'd properly cleaned my mess before coming up, then tucked him away and buttoned his pants. Our boat coasted back into the light and my heart was beating faster than it ever had. We *just* made it.

"Holy shit," I said, setting my hand to my mouth and laughing. "I've never done anything like that before."

He fell out laughing next to me. "I did *not* plan for you to go down on me." He started to smack his own face. "Fuck. I need to stop thinking about it or I'm gonna be walking around hard the rest of the night."

Neither Harry nor I could stop laughing as the ride docked back at the start and we were released from the boat. We took the fact that we weren't approached by any security guards as confirmation that we hadn't been caught being naughty, and linked hands to make our way to the next ride. Harry dragged me to him and wrapped his hand around my waist and gave me a kiss on the forehead. It was almost unfair how happy I was.

I'd never had so much fun in my entire life.

"Celia?"

I looked over my shoulder and there was a group of people walking in the opposite direction. They turned to face me, and I noticed it was a bunch of my friends from college, including Laura. She hadn't mentioned going to the theme park, but then again, neither had I.

"Wait," one of my friends, Bryce, said. "Are you… Is this… Is this guy your *boyfriend*?"

"Celia with a boyfriend?" another, Anna, added. "No way."

"Yeah, come on, Celia doesn't date. Not seriously anyway," my friend Sharee told them.

Laura gave them all different glares before looking back at Harry. "Don't listen to them." She stuck out her hand. "Hi. I'm Laura, Celia's roommate. I've heard a lot about you."

Harry shook her hand. "Nice to finally meet you. I've heard a lot about you as well." He looked at me. "Hey, spend a few minutes catching up with your friends. I'm gonna run to the bathroom."

"Okay," I said, and Harry turned around and walked toward the nearest bathroom.

"All right, spill," Sharee said. "When you dumping this one?"

"Yeah. I'm shocked you're even out in public with him," another of my friends, Cydney, said. "Is it like a sugar daddy situation?"

"No, idiot, sugar daddies are *way* older or ugly or something," Bryce snipped and then laughed. "If he's young and good looking, it's not sugar daddy, it's just… daddy."

Everyone fell out laughing and my face burned with embarrassment. Harry meeting my friends was *not* part of the deal. I wanted him to know as little about my actual life as possible.

Because this was all just a ploy. Nothing real.

"He's not really much of anything. I don't have to dump him because it's just casual to begin with," I explained.

Laura crossed her arms. "Are you *still* on this?"

"I'm not on anything. Harry is great, but it's not like… *a thing*. We're really closer to being friends with benefits than we are to being anything else."

My heart sank as a body stepped up and stood next to me. I looked over and Harry had returned from the bathroom, much quicker than I was expecting.

He definitely heard me.

"Well," Laura said, "we'll go and let you guys get back to your… time. Call me later, C."

"Okay, bye," I replied. Bryce, Sharee, Cydney, and my other friends said their goodbyes and then they all walked away. I could feel the anger permeating off of Harry, but instead of addressing it, I pointed off toward a ride we hadn't been on yet. "Should we head down this way next?"

"Celia," Harry started, and I knew I was in trouble. "Let's find a spot to sit."

I got a horrible, sinking feeling in the pit of my stomach. "Okay."

We walked to a bench nearby that wasn't occupied and didn't have many people standing right nearby and sat down. Harry was quiet for a long time, and I didn't press the issue because I was already worried. Why did I feel dread like my boyfriend was about to break up with me and shatter my heart? I wasn't in love with Harry. My relationship with him wasn't real. He was a means to an end. That was what I kept telling myself, but I couldn't shake the feeling away.

"Why did you say that to them?" Harry asked. "That we're closer to being friends with benefits. Is that really what you think?"

"N-no…"

"Then why did you say that? Are you embarrassed to have me meeting your friends? You know my friends. You've had whole conversations with Avery."

"No, I'm not embarrassed of you," I replied.

"Then what? I don't understand why you would say that, aside from it being true," he said. I was struggling to find an answer, and he took advantage of my silence to keep going. "Look… I was going to wait to ask you this until after the date, but I've been getting this feeling from you. *That* feeling, that what you said to them is exactly how you feel about us. I'm not trying to pressure you or anything, I just need to know that we're, you know, going somewhere. That I'm not just a friend with benefits."

My throat knotted up. What I wanted to say to Harry, more than anything in that moment, was that he was *so* much more to me than a friend with benefits, but he shouldn't be that, so I didn't. My mind reeled for something better to say, but nothing came to mind. I opened my mouth to just try and force something out, anything out, but nothing came.

Harry's head dropped in defeat and I knew that I'd messed up. "Harry…"

He held up a hand. "Don't. At least you didn't ghost me this time."

Ouch.

"I don't—"

"Can you get a ride home with Laura and your other friends?" Harry asked.

Despite the fact that I was trying my hardest to keep them back, tears gathered in the corners of my eyes. "Yeah, I can."

"Okay. See ya."

Harry stood up and I watched in pain and frustration as he walked away from me. When he was gone and I was convinced he wasn't coming back, I pulled out my phone and called Laura.

"Hi," she said, and the tone of her voice suggested she already knew things had gone south. "I'm guessing that conversation didn't go so well."

"Nope," I responded. "Do you have room in your car?"

"Yeah, of course. Where are you?"

"I'm back by where we were all standing," I said. "On a bench."

"Okay, sit tight, I'm on my way."

I watched all the other couples walking around as I sat, and it made me sick to my stomach. What was I doing? This was why I wanted to end things with Harry to begin with. The more time I spent with him, the more I liked him, but I wasn't supposed to be liking him. Opening the flap of my purse, I reached in and fished out the picture of my dad. His smiling face sent a wave of emotions washing over me.

Was this really what he wanted? Would he be happy knowing what I was up to? If I told him I was falling for the guy who killed him, what would he say?

"Hey." I quickly shoved the picture back into my bag as Laura approached and sat down on the bench next to me. My head dropped to her shoulder and hers fell onto my head. "We had enough cars that the people who rode with me could go with others, so we can leave whenever you're ready."

"Okay, thank you," I replied.

"What happened? Why did you say that stuff? You know it's not true. I've *never* seen you glow the way you have been these past few months since you met Harry. You're *obviously* falling for him. Why are you resisting it so much?"

I couldn't tell her the truth, but even the truth didn't feel totally like the truth anymore. "I don't know."

"What did I say about not running from it if it feels good? Does it feel good?"

"Yeah," I said.

"Then what's the problem?"

No words came out of my mouth. There were so many problems, I couldn't quite put my finger on the one that was causing me the biggest issue. I'd have to figure out a way to patch things up with Harry and then once I did, I'd have to bring this thing to a head before the situation got any worse. I was so close to falling in love with him, that every additional day I spent with him risked me throwing everything away to just be with him for real.

And my dad and godfather deserved better than that.

"Can I bring him to your place?" I asked.

"I already told you that you can. I'll leave and you can use your key to get in. I'll go out with Cyd that night so you can have the place to yourself."

"No," I replied. "Well, yes, if things go well and you could make yourself busy, that'd be good, but I want you to be there at first. Have dinner with us. I want him to know I'm not embarrassed for him to know the people I care about."

Laura smiled. "Deal."

Chapter Sixteen

Bullet

Hoppa's Taphouse had a happy, electric energy flowing through it as I rode my bike into the parking lot around eight o'clock. There were people spilling out of the bar and into the parking lot, and tons of couples were dancing, flirting, and enjoying themselves.

I hated it.

Frustration must have been emanating from me because everyone I got within fifteen feet of, stopped having fun and just stared at me quietly. In my mind, I was keeping my cool pretty well, but the second I pushed through the door to enter the bar, everyone nearby, including several of the members all stopped what they were doing to turn and look at me.

"What's going on, Bullet?" Nick asked from his seat at the bar. "Bad night?"

In order to take attention off myself and hopefully get the bar back to the state it was in when I arrived, I went and took the stool next to Nick and sat down. Sally, one of the bartenders slid me a beer without my even asking for it, but I needed it so I didn't complain. A few people were murmuring around me, but I had no one to blame for my reputation but myself, so I did the best I could to ignore it.

"Yeah," I said. "Bad night."

Nick didn't ask anything else, which I was glad for, because I was fully prepared to just drink my woes away. I couldn't get Celia off of my mind any more than I could get her saying we were just friends with benefits out of my ears. Was that *truly* what she thought? That was all these past couple of months had meant to her? Just sex? Had I just misinterpreted our relationship? I'd expected that maybe Celia was moving slower than I was, but I had no idea she wasn't getting *anything* else out of it.

That was disappointing to say the least.

Even though I probably wouldn't have answered even if she had, I was even more upset to see that Celia didn't call or even text me after I left the theme park. Part of me wanted to do the gentlemanly thing and make sure she'd successfully met up with Laura and was able to get a ride home, but if I did that, I wasn't sure what I might say. She wasn't a damsel in distress by any means, so I left it alone.

"So, uh," Avery said, sitting down next to me about an hour after I arrived, "I'm gathering by the multitude of beer bottles that your big date with Celia didn't go so well?"

"We bumped into a bunch of her friends and she told them we were just friends with benefits," I said.

"Ouch. This girl just doesn't let up, does she? One thing right after the other."

I shook my head. "She's a little ruthless."

"That wasn't the vibe I got when I talked to her," Avery said. "Not only considering the fact that she looked me straight in the eyes and said she wasn't just playing games with you. Either she's one hell of a liar, or she's conflicted about you."

"What's conflicting?" I asked. "We have an amazing time when we're together, she obviously isn't complaining about the sex if that's the only thing she's willing to admit to. Until that happened, we were having the best time at the theme park. I just don't get what the issue is."

"I mean, Nick had to force you to go out with her in the first place," Avery said. "Maybe there's a 'hates men' situation hidden somewhere that you don't know about and you just have to unearth it and get rid of it. Once that barrier is broken then you should be okay, right?"

"I don't know how to unearth it. She won't open up to me at all and shit like this keeps happening." I finished the latest of my beers and flagged down Sally to give me another one. She was reluctant but passed it over after a glare that I quickly grumbled, "Sorry," for and then, "Thank you."

"Are you getting drunk?" Avery asked. "I haven't seen you drink this much since college."

The theme park date kept playing over and over in my head. Cuddling in the lines for the rides, enjoying all the delicious food, getting heated in the dark ride. All up until we bumped into her friends. We were having the best time we'd had since we started dating. I very nearly started to admit how serious my feelings were starting to get for her, and I felt like it was the same for her. Was it dumb to wish that her friends just hadn't shown up? I could have lived in ignorant bliss for a few more hours at least.

"I just don't want to think about it," I replied to Avery finally.

"Well, I'm about to leave, but don't drink yourself stupid, all right?"

I waved my hand and grunted at him like a grumpy old man, and he chuckled and walked away.

And I did not listen.

Every time my beer emptied, I asked for a new one. Each time, Sally got more nervous about giving it to me, but did anyway, either because she didn't want to cross the Steel Knights or because I rarely got drunk. Either way, it didn't matter to me. I just wanted to be a haze of memories and so drunk that I'd be unconscious as soon as I got to my bed.

"Bar's closin' up," Sally said after giving me the last of my beers and collecting the other bottles to discard. "You're not driving, right?"

That was a good question, one I hadn't thought of. "No. I'm way too drunk."

"Understatement of the year, Bullet."

She shuffled away and I fished my hand into my pocket to pull out my cell phone. As I was dragging it out, it got caught on the fabric and dropped to the floor. I let out a loud groan before hopping off my stool to bend over and get it, but in doing so, I bumped into the next guy over at the bar. He had the last of his drinks in his hand and it spilled all over his shirt.

"Oh, shit, I'm sorry," I slurred out and resumed trying to grab my phone. As if to make things worse, when I finally was able to claw my phone up, I bumped him again as I stood up. "Damn it. So—"

"What the fuck is your problem?" he growled at me. "If you can't hold your liquor, don't drink."

"Okay, *Dad*," I hissed. It was odd that he was coming at me at all on the Steel Knights' turf, but I was too tipsy to be worried about it.

I started to return to my seat so I could finish my last beer, but the man reached over and tipped the beer over intentionally, spilling it across the bar.

"What the fuck, man?" I barked.

"What? You spilled mine, I spilled yours," he responded.

"Mine was an accident."

He looked back at me stone-faced. "Oops."

I definitely felt a gut urge to sock him in the face but resisted. After the night I'd had, I didn't want any more frustration, so I rolled my eyes, climbed off the barstool again, and started toward the door, but not without grumbling, "Dick," under my breath.

"What the fuck you say?" Objects on the bar clattered as he stood up, but I didn't even stop and turn around. "Hey! Get back here."

Waving my hand through the air, I pushed through the front door of the Taphouse and walked out into the fresh, evening air. The cool air felt good against my heated face and I was hopeful that after letting the air bring down my drunkenness a little bit, I could call for an Uber. However, I didn't get that far because the brute I'd bumped into came ambling out of the bar.

"You made a mistake turning your back to me," he growled.

"Yeah. I'm *super* scared," I replied flatly. "Just go about your business. You're gonna get caught in the middle of something you aren't prepared for."

"Oh, are you a big man now?" He rolled up his sleeves. "Come on then."

My head was pounding, and I really didn't want to get going with this guy, but he was advancing on me and I could tell that things weren't going to go my way. He took a few steps toward me and swung on me. I swiped my head backward away from his hand and then as his head came forward with the momentum of the swing, I slammed my head back forward, cracking it against his. There were a few people in the parking lot turning to watch us as he grabbed his head, and I could feel blood sliding down mine. He wasn't deterred though, and he advanced me again, this time fooling me with a fake hook that he then bailed out of and gave me a hard uppercut to my stomach. I grunted as I crumpled around his fist, and my drunkenness swirled around me. My disadvantage in this fight was that I *was* drunk, and barely able to stay on my feet.

As he pulled his fist back, I dropped to my knees. He stood over me and grabbed me by the shirt and dragged me up to my feet and pulled his fist out to punch me, but then someone else grabbed his shoulder, flipped him around, and punched him in the face instead. As a reflex, he let me go, and I wobbled but was able to stay on my feet. I threw a punch out and struck him across the face, and as he dropped to the ground, I saw that the person standing on the other side of him that had helped me, was Seneca.

"You okay, VP?" Seneca said in a much more formal voice than I'd heard her use before. "Want me to rough this guy up?"

"Fuck, you're a Knight?" the guy grunted on the ground.

I was so drunk that I hadn't realized that because I'd come straight from my date, I didn't have my jacket on me with my colors on it. "The Vice President," I replied, wiping some of the blood from my head. "Get the fuck out of here." The man scurried up from the floor and walked off, hissing a line of swear words under his breath. I looked at Seneca and probably would be embarrassed if it wasn't for how blitzed I was. "Thanks."

"You're welcome," she replied. "Are you drunk?"

"Would something like twelve beers get you drunk?"

She laughed. "Yeah, Bullet, it would."

"Then yes, I am *definitely* drunk."

She tapped a hand on my back. "Come on then. I'll get you home."

"Thanks."

Hoppa's was a safe place to leave my bike overnight. Nick certainly wouldn't have it towed, and with it parked in one of the Steel Knights' designated spots, no one would dare mess with it, and we had cameras if they were dumb enough to. I'd catch an Uber back the next morning to collect it. I followed Seneca over to her bike and she climbed on, then I climbed on behind her and wrapped my arms around her waist.

"I'm just gonna use your back to keep my head from falling off," I joked.

"Good idea," she called back.

My head fell to Seneca's back and the grumble of her bike as she started it up was comforting and my eyes felt heavy. I was able to keep myself awake enough to give Seneca directions to my house, which, fortunately, was only about five minutes from the bar. She parked her bike in front of my house and actually helped me off and up to my house. Fortunately, the ride back had been sobering enough to help me be able to get my keys out with minimal effort, and as soon as I opened the door, the cats started to meow angrily at me.

"I know," I murmured.

"My dogs hate it when I'm gone all day, too," Seneca said. She reached around the doorframe to get me in my house and then flipped the light on and then stood aside so I could pass her to cross the doorframe. "Are you good from here?"

"Yeah. Thank you for your help. I swear I don't normally get shitty drunk."

"Happens to the best of us. Was it Celia?" she asked.

"Yeah. That advice you gave me was great, but she decided to just reduce our relationship to fuck buddies before I even got that far."

"If she's a commitment-phobe, that's pretty one-o-one. I wouldn't give up just yet."

I gave something between a shrug and a shake of my head. "Whatever. The ball's in her court. I'm so exhausted with it at this point."

"If she calls, just know you're on the edge of a breakthrough and hang in there," Seneca told me.

"Really?"

"Yeah. She claims to be afraid of commitment but keeps coming back. Must be something about you that she's into."

Celia had said something similar when she showed back up after the last time she ghosted me. "Here's hoping."

"See ya, Bullet," Seneca said, turning around to head down the walkway.

"Harry," I called after her, and she looked back at me. "You can call me Harry. Or Bullet. Whichever."

She nodded. "Cool. See ya tomorrow, Harry."

I kept watch as she mounted her bike. As long as my godfather and I had been looking for my younger sibling, I'd been hoping that it would be a younger brother, but Seneca was making me wish for the opposite. A little cutthroat girl to keep me in line that I could protect didn't sound half-bad. Seneca gave me a final wave after pulling her helmet on and then rode off. I shut the door and trudged back to my bedroom. My bed felt like clouds as I face-planted it, immediately followed by the feeling of tiny paws stepping all over my back and head.

"I'm not the floor," I grumbled into my blankets, but neither cat seemed to care.

I was just fading from consciousness when my phone rang. It took some doing to get into my pocket in a way that didn't disturb the cats now curling up on my back, but I finally got it out and my heart leaped when I saw it was Celia. Despite knowing I should probably play a little harder to get after today's display, I was more relieved to hear from her than anything, and I answered.

"Hello?"

"Hi," Celia said back.

"Hi."

She was silent for a few minutes and then said. "Harry, you obviously mean more to me than just a friend with benefits. I mean, we *do* feel like friends and there are *certainly* benefits, but I see you as… a boyfriend."

The word shot straight to my heart. "Really?"

"Yeah. I just freaked out in front of my friends, and I don't know why, but I've never really introduced anyone to them before. Plus, they make it harder by being nosy and judgmental. I like that no one's really in our business, but I also understand that what I said was upsetting. It was entirely inaccurate."

"Okay," I replied.

I wanted to ask her what I *did* mean to her. If I was the kind of boyfriend that you hang around with for a few months and then ditch, or if I was the kind of boyfriend that you hope might turn into something more someday, but it felt stupid to ask.

"Are you done with me?" Celia asked.

"I don't want to be. It's really up to you. Would I be wasting my time to continue seeing you?"

"No, I don't think so," she said. "I want to prove it."

"Prove it? How?"

"Saturday is my next night out. I'm going to plan the date this time. I'll make all the arrangements, pick you up, all of it. I want to show you that I'm in this for real."

A smile curved onto my face. "Okay."

"Okay," she said, and there was relief in her voice. "I'm sorry again, for today."

"That's okay."

"Can… Can I come over?" she asked.

I very nearly said yes, but then I remembered how drunk I was, and I didn't want to seem that desperate. "When you prove it, you can."

She let out a little snicker. "Fair enough. I'll see you Saturday then?"

"Yeah. I'll see you Saturday."

"Okay. Bye."

"Bye."

We hung up the call, and almost immediately, my phone rang again. It was Cameron, and a pang of guilt rushed over me. I'd been selling him excuses about meeting his girlfriend for two months now, but it was probably long overdue that I met up with him and did what I told him I would.

That would have to wait until the morning when I was far less drunk, though, and before I even had the chance to change into anything more comfortable or even pull my phone out of my hand, I passed out.

Chapter Seventeen

Bullet

For a minute, I thought a fire alarm or something was going off, but it was just my phone. It was still fastened in my hand from when I was holding it the night before, and the cats were still curled up on my back like I was some kind of luxury cat bed. I pulled my phone over to my face and saw that it was Cameron again and groaned. I really did have every intention of calling him back, but I was hoping to deal with my hangover first.

With a grunt, I pressed the button to answer the call and then set it on speaker and dropped it next to my head. "Hello?"

"Oh *hi*," Cameron started, immediately melodramatic. "It's me, your loving father. The one who saved you from the very brink of destruction. Who took you into his home and cared for you as if you were borne from mine own loins."

"Don't go Shakespeare on me, you weirdo," I said.

"Your father who only loves you to the depths of his being. Who knows your favorite colors, your favorite foods, and your favorite shows. I even know your favorite brand of pen. Oh, how many pens of that brand I bought you because I love you so."

In spite of the headache threatening to shatter my skull, I started to laugh. "You are so fucking dramatic."

"Me," he sang in a high-pitched voice, "who once dressed up as an actual power ranger because I knew it would make you feel better?"

"It made me feel better because the outfit finally matched the man," I said.

He gasped and then sighed. "Goddammit, Harry. My soliloquy didn't call for you to randomly say something so sweet."

"Sorry," I replied.

"Are you okay? You don't sound good."

"I may be slightly hungover," I said.

"Hungover? You never drink like that."

"Yeah, it's kind of a long story. I'll explain more next time I see ya." Shaking my back a little so that the cats knew I was about to move, I slowly started to sit up on my arms, and once I felt both cats hop off my back, I stood up and started by stripping away my t-shirt to get a little cooler and then I picked up my phone and walked into the kitchen.

"When would that be, by the way," Cameron asked. "Because I've been trying to get you over here for like, oh I don't know, two months. You said you were going to meet Marisha."

"I am. It's just been hectic with the—"

"I know, I know, the expansion and the promotion and the new members and you're dating again, and you know, I'm really happy for you, but I also want you to continue being my kid."

He sounded so genuinely hurt that I wanted to punch myself in the face. I started a pot of coffee and filled up the cats' dishes. "I know, Dad, I'm sorry. Really, I didn't mean to neglect you."

"I've been getting the feeling that you don't want to meet Marisha. I meant what I said that I have no intention of proposing to her until you've met and approved of her. Is it that you know I won't that you're staying away? You don't want me to marry her?" he asked.

"No, Dad, I swear. I wasn't trying to prevent that at all. In fact, a lot has changed in these past couple of months and I want to meet her more than ever. Let's do it soon. I'm serious. When do you want to do it? I'll be there."

"How about Saturday?" he asked, and I felt stupid.

"Okay, no, sorry. I have a date on Saturday."

"Oh, that's okay, son. No, really. That's fine. I'll just die an old lonely man. I'll starve with no spouse to cook for me."

"You're a chef," I said. "Also, I know you're still seeing her, she's probably there right now."

"Noooo," a woman's voice called from the background.

"Exactly," I said. "Also, I swear that wasn't my intention. Can we do it Sunday? Let's do it Sunday."

"Sunday, really?" Cameron responded. "Like *this* Sunday? Not next Christmas?"

"No, Dad, not next Christmas. This upcoming Sunday. The next one on your calendar."

"Okay. Really, you'll come?"

Cooking wasn't the most exciting idea to me in the world, so I popped some toast in the toaster. "Yeah, I'll come."

"Okay," Cameron replied in a soft voice that made me even sadder, because quiet though it was, it was filled to the brim with excitement. "I'm looking forward to it. Marisha is, too."

"Me, too. Really. I'm sorry that it took this long."

"It's fine." His tone was completely back to normal. "I had a bet going with Marisha that it wouldn't be until December, so you owe me the dinner I now have to buy her."

"Please don't bet on my character flaws with your girlfriend," I said, and Cameron fell out laughing. "I'm going to go tend to my hangover now. I love you."

"I love you, too, kid. See ya Sunday."

"Yep."

The call ended, and even though I was relieved that I'd finally made the arrangements, I was also nervous. I'd never met a partner of Cameron's before and I didn't know his type. He was intentional about not dating, or at least not bringing women home, when I was still there, so I had no idea what his type was. He'd shown me a picture of her, but that was all I had to base it off of. It was less about the fact that she was a woman and more about the fact that she was dating someone who was so important to me. She had a hard, uphill climb to earn my acceptance. As far as I was concerned, Cameron was no different from my *actual* father, and my father deserved the best.

With that behind me, I decided that I should probably get dressed and head to the bar for the day. Even though being around liquor made my stomach twist, there was still work to be done, and even if there wasn't, I didn't have much else to do for the day. I ate my toast, downed a whole cup of coffee before pouring an additional one in a travel mug to bring with me, gave the cats a little bit of love and then left.

As expected, Nick and Seth were already at the club when I arrived, but Avery was also there again for another early morning. Nick and Seth were just heading to the back for a conversation about the expansion when I arrived, so I let them go in the interest of talking to Avery about this unique change in behavior.

"Hey," he said as I walked in.

"Hi." Unlike the other day when he was there early, just not doing much of anything and waiting for Seneca to show up, he had a few papers in front of him and was reading them over and making notes. One of the pages was a map with some highlighted routes, so I guessed he was expanding the drug runs. "So, are you just an early riser now, or…?"

He chuckled, looking back down at his paper. "Something like that."

"Is it Seneca?" I asked.

He looked up at me. "Can't a man just want to start actually putting in some real effort at work?"

"Sure, but you were doing that just fine in the afternoon hours. This is the second time in a week that I've seen you here as the sun's still coming up. I was your college roommate, remember? I used to have to leash and drag you to any classes that took place before noon. So, if it isn't Seneca, what is it?"

"I don't know, I think your hard-working attitude is rubbing off on me. You're running around, working on the expansion, fraternizing with the prospects, and still somehow dating. Call me jealous," he replied.

"Dating?" I said. "I am, but what does *that* have to do with *this*? Unless this is a little bit about Seneca?" He didn't respond, but just shrugged and went back to working. "I guess I'm a little offended. I thought I was your best friend. Expected you'd want to talk to me about her if you were into her."

Avery set his pen down and looked up at me like he was about to conduct a job interview. "Okay, Harry," he said. "What do you want to know?"

"I'm not asking for intimate details or anything. I just want to know if you like her."

"Yes, okay? Yes, I like her." His tone was dull and even, as if he was annoyed by that fact.

"Why do you say it like that? She's pretty cool, at least I think so. She killed the bike race, and yesterday after you left, I pissed some guy off bumping into him and she kicked his ass and made sure I got home. She's obviously beautiful, but she also seems really nice and smart, plus she's a biker chick. I mean, you being into her isn't a big shock nor a bad idea."

"She is cool. I think she'll become a member for sure down the road, so she'll be hanging around, I just don't necessarily know that it's a good idea to date her, that's all. I've talked to her a little bit, flirted, but I get the sense that it would be a bad idea, that's it."

I didn't exactly know what his hesitation was. Sure, Seneca had mentioned to me that getting into relationships wasn't really her thing, but it also just felt like she hadn't found someone of substance yet. Seneca and Avery seemed like they would be a perfect match to me, plus they clearly liked each other, so I couldn't quite put my finger on why they wouldn't just go for it.

"All right, I won't bug you about it anymore. Just let the record show, I'm Team Seneca," I said.

Avery nodded with a snicker as he returned to his work. "Noted. If I'm done being grilled now, you seem like you're in a better mood than last night."

"Yeah. I talked to Celia, and we worked it out, at least as much as things can be worked out with her, so I'm seeing her on Saturday."

"Good luck with that." Again, his tone was jaded.

I couldn't blame him though. Things with Celia and I had been very back and forth. Internally, I made a decision to discuss Celia less around the bar until things were a little more stable for us. Avery at the very least, but probably also Seneca at this point, had invested some interest in my happiness and well-being and didn't need to hear about all the push and pull. They'd still see us hanging around whenever Celia came to spend time with me here, but I could practice being a little more aloof until I was more confident about where we were going.

"Bullet." I looked over and Seth was standing in the doorway behind the bar. "Can you come here for a sec?"

"Sure." I stood up, tapping Avery's back as I went, and made my way back to the warehouse. Nick was sitting at the table and there were papers spread out everywhere. I walked over and took my usual seat as Seth sat down as well. "Hey, Nicky."

"What's up?" he replied. "I hope I didn't interrupt."

"Nah, just shooting the shit with Avery. It's weird seeing him when the sun's up," I said.

"I know what you mean. He's getting us more money though, so I'm fucking glad to see him doing it. Anyway, I wanted to run something by you that Seth found." He shifted one of the reconciliation books toward me. It used to be my daily work, but I hadn't actually looked at it in about a week with Seth working like he was. "I know we were trying to shift funds around and not get a check cut for another couple of weeks still to start the project, but I'm itching. He thinks we can shift some things around by paying some expenditures in bulk, six months or a year at a time, and it would free up some money to cut the check in the next few days. What do you think?"

I looked over Seth's work and was impressed with the ways he was identifying to flow money in and out that didn't leave the club in such a tough spot each month. It was the take-the-big-hit-all-at-once versus smaller hits throughout the year and was actually a much better method. There were notes with quotes and his communications with our vendors already, and it seemed like he had it all worked out.

"Yeah," I said. "This seems like it'll work just fine."

Nick slapped Seth's arm. "There ya go, buddy. You're killing it. This is working out even better than I thought it would."

A smile crossed my face as I looked across at Seth. "This is good work."

"Thanks, Bullet."

Nick, Seth, and I discussed a few more money-related things, then we split up to do our own work for the next few hours. Eventually, the rest of the members and prospects showed up, and then the bar was already starting to fill up as early as late afternoon. It was a typical bar night, and there was nothing too exciting to stick around for, so once Nick had settled into a game of pool for the night, I snuck over to Avery and invited him to grab dinner somewhere quieter. He was talking to Seneca at the time, who we invited along as well, and Seth seemed bored by the crowd, so I grabbed him, too.

We left the bar and went to one of Hoppa's hole-in-the-wall diners and ordered the best of their greasy food.

"Man," Avery said. "It feels like it's been forever since I've done this. It's the club or home for me lately."

"Same here," Seth said. "I love my new job, don't get me wrong, but I'm a little tired. It's nice to just come get some food and the fact that my ears aren't ringing from the constant murmur of the bar is nice."

"This is where a clubhouse will come in really handy," I said. "There will be tons of places where we can go to escape the music and chatter. I'm with you guys, I'm not a people person, so getting away for a little bit is nice."

"You're not a people person?" Seneca said in a high-pitched, overly dramatic voice. "I *never* would have guessed."

"Ha ha," I responded.

"So, wait, *all* you guys do is hang around the bar?" Seneca asked. "No rival-gang trips? No heated battles in the desert?"

For myself, and for Seth and Avery as well, that probably brought our most recent run-in with the Unchained Dogs screaming back to us. "Well, we don't seek that stuff out, but it has a way of finding us," I said.

"Listen," Avery told Seneca, "you don't *wish* for interactions with the Unchained Dogs. Their president is loony toons. If we didn't have CJ when he showed up last time, whoo, that might have not gone so well."

"CJ?" Seneca asked.

"Colin Jones. He was running with the Unchained Dogs but went on the run from them and came here because he and Tess were friends as kids. They fell in love and ran off to God knows where," Seth explained. "He was tough though, and fucking terrifying."

"You got your ass kicked by him, right?" Avery asked.

Seth frowned. "That's an understatement. You all weren't there, but we collapsed on him and he turned into a Goddamn tornado. You think I'm dynamite, that guy went from zero to sixty. The crazy thing was, it didn't take him long, and he didn't even break a sweat. That was when I was first like, 'All right. I'm not fucking with that guy anymore'."

"So, Tess ran off with him? That's kind of sweet, bad news for Nick though," Seneca remarked.

"Well, I'm to blame for that mostly," I said. "Thanks to my oppressive behavior, the club followed suit, even Nicky. When it came down to going with CJ or staying with us, she picked him because there was nowhere left to go here."

"It's unfortunate. Tess was actually a good person," Avery said.

"I've been working from her notes from when she was VP, she's damn smart." I bit the inside of my cheek, feeling bad. "I wish things hadn't happened the way they did. She should have had a chance here. I'll never forgive myself for that."

"Hey, don't take it so hard," Avery told me. "Yeah, if she came back, I'd be stoked, but I'm also happy for her that she no longer has to deal with Taylor's insane ass or live in her father's shadow. I'd be willing to bet, wherever they went, they're really happy."

"I hope so. I really hope they reach out to Nick again one day, too," I said. "He doesn't deserve to lose both his kids."

For the rest of dinner, we took turns filling Seneca in on the insanity of the months prior to her showing up, and it gave us renewed appreciation for just being able to sit and enjoy a meal with no stress. Once we were full, we said our goodbyes and parted ways for the night, promising to hang out again soon, and I went home to rest up, looking even more forward to my date with Celia.

Chapter Eighteen

Celia

Laura and I moved back and forth across my old room, arranging things in a way that made it look nice and neat, but also like it had been lived in. There weren't many clothes in the closet, so we hung some of hers up inside. We swapped out the bedsheets and scattered some shoes across the floor in the corner, anything to make it look like it was someone's current bedroom.

"So, he doesn't know that you don't currently live here," Laura said, "and you've mentioned that you take care of your godfather, but you haven't mentioned who he is or where you actually live at all?"

"Right," I replied, pulling some of the things out of my purse out and setting them on the dresser.

"Why? What's the point of that? Why aren't you just honest with him?"

"Because my godfather is weird, and I don't need to mix those two up just yet, and besides, there's nothing really all that sexy about bringing a man back to the same place where you change a different man's diapers."

It was partially true. Laura didn't know anything about the lies I was feeding Harry or why, and I knew I couldn't bring Harry back to Darrien's place, because he'd recognize him and begin to figure out something was up. This plan only worked if Harry believed I was falling in love with him, the same way he was falling for me, and a woman who is falling in love brings their guy around their friends' and back to their place. Harry wasn't striking totally off mark when he called me out for downplaying our relationship. I was keeping him at a distance on purpose. I was still trying to tread a line between something casual enough that I didn't feel bad, and serious enough to trick him.

But I needed to go all in.

If I was going to carry out my plan with Harry, I needed to turn up the heat, mainly because if I continued to see him, the feelings I was already developing that I knew I shouldn't have were only going to get worse and everything was going to get more complicated. So as gross as it felt, I was pulling a wild card to truly convince Harry that I was in this for the long haul, so that when I suddenly pulled a switcheroo it would crush him. I had to do it hard and I had to do it fast.

I was running out of time.

"I suppose that makes sense," Laura said. "You'll tell him eventually though, right? Or better yet, just move back in with me, then it's not a lie."

She flashed me a toothy grin and I laughed. "Do you have any idea how much I would love to live with you again? I miss you so much. Even though I was having a really good time with Harry at the theme park, when I saw you guys, I was a little jealous that you were all together and I didn't even know you were going."

"Yeah, I'm sorry, I probably should have mentioned something, but you'd already told me you were going out with Harry, so I didn't," Laura explained.

"It's okay. It's my fault for never being around."

"Well, you're taking care of Darrien and you're working really hard, plus now you're seeing Harry, too. You're juggling a lot. It just made me happy to see you out and laughing. I feel like you do that so rarely. I'm glad he brings that out in you. Kind of like he's taking care of you after you're done taking care of everyone else."

That sent a wave of chills through me. Harry had said that to me once, that he would take care of me that way. It felt good to hear and even better to experience. Once things were all said and done with him, I hoped I could find someone else like him who would be willing to take care of me in that way. In a way I needed.

"He's kind of good at that," I told her. "It feels nice and I feel like I take it for granted sometimes. Hopefully, this dinner will be a nice way of saying thank you."

"Speaking of which," Laura said, "I need to go check on the chicken. I'll be back."

"Okay."

Laura walked out and I dropped down to sit on the bed. I glanced around the room, looking like I'd never left, and I had a twinge of frustration. It was such a simple room in a simple apartment, nothing like Darrien's four-bedroom, three-bathroom house that I now had almost total reign of now that he couldn't get to most places in his wheelchair, but even I had to admit that things were cold there. I distinctly remembered living with Laura during college and it was so much fun to have a friend nearby and not be pressured by this need for vengeance. Part of me wished I'd never agreed to do it in the first place, but I wanted my dad to rest easy knowing that his killer wasn't going to just walk around unchecked for his behavior.

So even though it was hard, and even though I was developing feelings for Harry, I had to stay committed to the plan. I'd come too far to let it all fall by the wayside now.

I stood up off of the bed and walked out into the living room. "Okay. I'm gonna go get Harry."

"Okay," Laura called from the kitchen. "Dinner will just be getting done when you get back!"

Harry's house was only about fifteen minutes from Laura's and unlike our regular trips on his bike, I was picking him up in my old Altima. I smiled as he walked out his front door and made his way down the path toward me, and my stomach was already fluttering. He was wearing a very simple jeans-and-t-shirt look with black boots, but it all went together perfectly and looked amazing on him.

"Hi," I said as he got in the car. He leaned over and kissed me, and my heart leaped up. I thought it would take a little more effort getting intimacy from him after the theme park, but he seemed as happy as ever to see me. "I'm glad you're letting me do this."

"Me, too. I missed you."

He missed me? How could he say things like that so simply and have me backtracking any resolve I'd built up? What was this mysterious power he had?

"I missed you," I responded. "I'm sorry I made things weird between us again."

He set his hand on my cheek and leaned across again and kissed me. "Let's leave it behind us."

I nodded. "Deal."

"So, where are you taking me?" he asked as we pulled off.

"Somewhere special."

I'd purposely not told Harry he was coming to "my" apartment for dinner. I wanted him to see that I wasn't embarrassed for him to meet my friends and I wasn't afraid to show him more of my life.

At least convince him that I was all in.

We pulled up in front of the complex and parked, and Harry looked over at me. "Here?"

"Yeah," I said. "Come on. I'm told dinner should just about be ready." We climbed out of the car and I led Harry inside, up the stairs, and down to Laura's apartment. The door was left unlocked, so I opened it and led the way inside. "Honey, I'm home!" I called out.

Laura poked her head out of the kitchen with a smile. "Hey! I'll be there in just a second, I'm just pulling the chicken out."

Harry looked around the place, touched a jacket of mine he spied on the coat rack, looked at some of the pictures of Laura and me and our friends that were still hanging from when I lived there.

"Uh, yeah, so this is my place. It's not a whole house like you have, but it gets the job done," I explained.

"I like it. It's way nicer than any of the apartments I lived in before I bought my house."

"And…" I walked around the house a little bit until I found Laura's lazy cat Meatloaf and pulled him out. He was a fluffy, brown mixed breed who could be chucked across the room without blinking. "This is Meatloaf."

Harry's eyes lit up like a kid on Christmas morning, and he held out his arms, so I set Meatloaf inside. As expected, the cat gave Harry a little nuzzle before curling up and just allowing himself to be held, and Harry seemed perfectly fine to continue holding him.

Laura came twirling out of the kitchen, stopping by the dining room table to set a couple of bowls down, then she walked over to Harry and me. They'd already met at the theme park, but I still held out a hand toward Laura and said, "Harry, this is my roommate and best friend Laura. She put up with me during college and now I won't let her escape. Laura," I motioned to Harry, "this is Harry, my boyfriend."

Harry looked at me and then a large smile grew on his face. He then looked back at Laura and nodded. "Nice to see you again."

"Nice to see you, too. I see you and Meatloaf aren't going to have any trouble getting along," she said.

"Harry's a cat person," I informed her.

Laura nodded. "I knew I liked you. Well, come on, dinner is ready. I'll get it all dished up."

"This is my favorite restaurant in town," I said as Harry put Meatloaf down on the couch on the way over to the dining room table. "Laura's training to become a P.O., but she cooks in her spare time, and by spare time I mean to feed me."

Harry laughed. "That was kind of my foster dad, too, although he's a legit chef now."

We sat down at the table and Laura served up the baked chicken and potatoes she'd made, along with a salad. After serving the food, she took a picture of its nice display, and then moved her phone up to aim at Harry and me sitting close on one side of the table. She snapped a pic, and even though my gut reaction was to tell her to delete it, I saw another opportunity to bolster Harry's confidence.

"You gonna post it?" I asked her.

"Can I?"

"Yeah, as long as you mention he's mine. I don't need any of your thirst trap friends going after my man," I snipped back.

"Yes!" she said, pumping her fist, then she sat down at the table and started furiously typing. "'Celia and her boyfriend, Harry. I get to have dinner with him first, suck it losers. B.T.W. Meatloaf approves.' And send."

Under the table, Harry squeezed my leg, and I knew I'd been successful in my ploy. The smile on his face was enough to make anyone blush, and I was happy to start eating to give myself a chance to calm down.

All throughout dinner, Laura kept the conversation afloat, sharing silly stories about me from college. Harry was happy to hear more about me from the past, something he'd said on a number of occasions, and it didn't feel nearly as difficult to let him in a little as I thought it would be. He and Laura got on like they'd been best friends for years, and as the night carried on, the happier and more relaxed Harry seemed.

It made me feel good.

When the meal was all done, and only after laughing about how many of my friends seemed shocked that I had a guy on my arm, Laura announced her departure.

"Dinner was so good," Harry said. "Thank you."

"Thank *you*," Laura replied. "Celia tells me her new boyfriend is coming over and needs some of my home cooking, I'm gonna do that, *obviously*."

"Well, I appreciate it," I told her.

"I'm meeting up with Cyd for drinks in like twenty minutes, then I think we're just gonna do some bar-hopping. I won't be home until later so…" She winked. "You kids enjoy a little privacy."

"Thanks," I said.

She stood up from the table, pointed out the bottle of wine she'd been pouring from in the kitchen, then kissed me on top of my head and left.

"She seems really awesome," Harry said.

"Yeah, I like her. The funny thing is, we *hated* each other when we first met. Call it a fight for dominance or whatever. We were assigned as roommates freshman year and I couldn't stand her. She seemed like one of those prissy types to me, and I'm so… not that, but then she opened up, and I opened up. We realized we have a lot in common, we're both in social work, and now she's like my sister."

"That's cool. It reminds me of Avery," Harry said.

"Right."

"And…" Harry grabbed my hand and stood me up out of the chair and led me into the living room. We sank down onto the couch and he put his hands on either side of my neck and looked right into my eyes, it covered me with goosebumps and set my heart to racing double-time. "Thank you. I know that the commitment thing kind of scares you, but hearing you call me your boyfriend and letting her post the picture and stuff, it just…" He leaned in and kissed me. "I like that. Thank you."

"Thank you, too," I replied. "I know dinner with someone you barely know, let alone a woman, and without even knowing that's what was happening might have been a little difficult for you, but you're—" Harry leaned in and kissed me again before I could get the sentence out. "What was that for?"

"I was worried," he said. "I was worried that this didn't mean as much to you as it meant to me, and I was worried that I was beginning to fall for you and you didn't even see me as more than a friend. Hearing you say that you knew this was uncomfortable for me, it means you *are* learning more about me and care… I know I sound cheesy right now, but I'm just so happy."

I couldn't stop the smile from coming to my face. Harry was like a little puppy that had been given a new toy. I could damn near see a tail wagging. It didn't take all that much effort, just letting him in a little. If that would make him so happy, I'd do it more often.

"Me, too," I said. "I'm happy, too." This time, it was me who leaned in and kissed Harry, and I was glad when one of his hands broke loose from my neck and slowly started to slide down my back. I pulled away from him just enough to say, "Do you want a house tour?"

Harry furrowed his brow, looking around. "Uh. I've pretty much gotten the lay of the land."

"Most of it," I replied, then I stood up and walked over to my bedroom door and opened it. "Let me show you my bedroom."

He dropped his head in defeat before starting to laugh. "That was smooth. I hate that I didn't see it coming."

"Well, get over here then," I said.

Harry was off the couch in no time flat. "You don't have to ask me twice."

He hooked my waist as he reached me and backed me into the room, kicking the door shut behind him. His lips found mine and my hands slid up his chest to lock behind his neck. I gasped a little as he slid his hands down my legs and behind my thighs so he could lift me from my feet. I hooked my ankles behind him as he lowered me down to the bed.

One hand trailed down between my legs while the other worked its way under my shirt. His lips on mine continued to taste, sucking my tongue and making me dizzy, while his hands worked simultaneously to remove my shirt and pants.

Once unbuttoned, he pulled my pants down just enough to slink his hand underneath and between my legs. A finger flicked under my underwear to slide along my wetting middle, skipping over the sensitive bud there and causing me to moan. Those fingers worked me below while Harry finally lifted his head from my lips and joined the hand of his that was under my shirt. He expertly used one hand to lift my shirt and I took over to lift it up and over. He popped out one of my breasts and leaned down to close his mouth over it.

Between his hand massaging me below and his tongue licking me above, my mind was losing focus on anything that wasn't Harry. For whatever reason, I was just now smelling his marvelous cologne and it was adding to the euphoria that enveloped me. Harry lifted from my chest and continued to rub between my legs, slowly increasing his pace. He looked down at me and held my eye contact as he brought me closer to climax. Part of me wanted to look away, but there was also something enrapturing about him that kept me glued to his face as he stared down at me with his dark, lusty expression.

"Don't stop, baby," I hummed.

He moved even faster then, rubbing until I was shuddering and exploding. My moans were louder than I wanted them to be, but Harry was pleased with himself as he massaged me with a sly smile.

I reached my hands out and said, "I want you, Harry."

He didn't hesitate. Leaning back, he pulled off his shirt and threw it aside and then moved to his pants. I bit my lip watching him slowly work his way out of his pants, stroking his hard length. There was something enticing about him standing at attention. And remembering the taste of him that I got when we were at the theme park, I crawled forward and reached out to grab him. Laying on my stomach as he was kicking his pants off, I dragged my hand back and forth over his member, and then he eventually stepped up to me so I could pull him into my mouth.

He let out a sexy sigh as I closed around him, and his hands dropped to my head. He held it in place gently as he started to thrust into me, and I loved the length of him sliding all the way down my throat. He tilted my head back and I looked up at him as I sucked.

"So beautiful," he hummed, and it drove straight into me.

We continued to lock eyes as I moved up and down his shaft, feeling it elongate and leak into my mouth. His gentle thrusts blended with his natural scent and drove me wild. It would be so much easier to detach myself from Harry if I wasn't blown away by everything about him. His taste, his smell, the sound of his voice and the feeling of his hands. All that he was seemed to fit perfectly against all that I was and made it difficult to keep fact from fiction. When I was with Harry, he was all I could think about. I wanted to believe I could keep my composure around him and keep from getting too attached, but in truth, it was probably too late already.

Finally, Harry cupped a hand under my chin and pulled me up to let him go. I dropped him from my mouth and came up to my knees so he could drag another kiss out of me. His hands slunk around my back in order to unclasp my bra and drop it away.

He leaned a little back from me and huffed, "Turn around."

And I did just that.

Turning my back to Harry, I leaned over onto my hands and knees and Harry closed in behind me. He bent down over me to give my back a few kisses, and then I felt him poking at me. Farther from my mind than I was sure it really was, I heard him opening a condom wrapper, and his hands brushed against me as he slid it on. He set his tip just inside me then and braced his hands on my hips as he pushed in at a teasing pace. Inch by slow inch, he got deeper and deeper until he was seated inside. I expected his slow pace to continue, but almost immediately, he started to move in and out of me at an ever-quicker pace.

My mind went blank as I was struck repeatedly by Harry inside me. His hands burned across my hips and he slammed over and over against my sweet spot inside, dragging me closer to the edge once again. With a force that lit me on fire, he slammed a hand on the small of my back and forced my torso down against the bed, so I was flat apart from my ass in the air. He brought himself up onto the bed on his knees and repositioned until he was sawing directly down into me, I let out a scream as an orgasm snapped across me before I even felt it coming. My eyes watered and my hips were throwing back of their own accord to meet Harry's movements.

"Ah, don't do that," he commanded. "I'm trying to last back here."

"I'm sorry," I whined. "It feels too good."

Harry engorged inside me even more then, and his thrusts started to partner alongside animalistic grunts. His noises of pleasure made me lightheaded, and if I was moaning, I couldn't hear it over the sound of him.

"Fuck," he hissed, "I'm—"

He groaned and slammed as deep in me as he could go and then let out a series of loud, final growls as he finished, stuttering against me.

When he was done, he collapsed on top of me, still resting inside. "Shit," he grunted. "I didn't want that to be over that fast."

I let out a dark chuckle. "Oh, don't you worry. You and I are just getting started."

Chapter Nineteen

Celia

The bliss I'd found myself in was borderline unfair. My bed felt like a million soft, fluffy clouds wrapping around me, mixed with the warmth of Harry's arms wrapped around me. My entire body felt like jelly after the night we'd had, and he was still snoozing quietly in my ear. I could have laid there for two more hours or ten and been perfectly happy. I didn't really plan anything for Sunday, but I knew I wanted Harry to be a part of it. Being around him eliminated stress from my life and just made me feel like I could be myself. It was rare for me and I loved it.

My bladder had plans other than me staying in bed, however, so as much as I hated it, I unwrapped myself from Harry and climbed out of bed. He grunted as I left his arms, but then quickly settled back into a slumber. I lifted my phone and took a sneaky picture of him asleep. It was too cute, and I couldn't resist.

After that, I walked out into the living room and across to the hallway where the bathroom was. I went in to use it and chuckled at the image I caught of myself in the mirror, there were a few places along my chest where Harry had gotten a little possessive, but seeing the darkened spots made me happy, even if it meant I'd have to wear some higher-collar shirts to work for a few days.

As I came out of the bathroom, I heard some movement in the living room and I walked out with my stomach twisting excitedly to see Harry, but it was just Laura sitting at the dining room table dressed for work.

"Oh," I said flatly, and she fell out laughing.

"Oh? You brat! Don't sound so disappointed to see your amazing best friend who alley-ooped you a great night," she snipped.

I walked over and leaned down over her to hug her. "You're right, you did, and I'm so grateful to you."

"Boots by the door," Laura said, "so he's still here?"

"He's sleeping. When do you have to leave?"

"Another hour."

"I'll make you some breakfast then, as recompense," I said, and she nodded in agreement.

Walking into the kitchen, I got a pot of coffee started, and then pulled out some eggs, the leftover baked chicken, cheese, and onions. My skills in the kitchen were nothing like Laura's or even like Harry's who had picked up some tactics from his dad, but I was passable. I had to be to make sure Darrien ate. I worked over the next twenty minutes getting a few omelets made with the chicken and cheese and threw in some onions for crunch and flavor.

The smell of the food must have been enough of a draw, because I heard my bedroom door open, followed by Laura brightly saying, "Well, good morning."

"Good morning," Harry said. I was wearing his shirt, so as expected, when I looked out through the kitchen doorway, he was shirtless, but Laura didn't seem to mind, apart from her eyes bulging a little bit at how fit he was. He passed Laura and walked into the kitchen, coming up behind me and looping his arms around my waist. "Smells good in here."

"Hope you like omelets," I said.

"They're my favorite. You stole my shirt and none of yours fit me."

"Oh, please tell me you tried though?" I replied and he chuckled before kissing me on the neck. "Stop that, I'm cooking, and I won't get my security deposit back if I burn the place down."

"Fine." Harry pulled away from me but gave me a quick swat on my ass before leaving and heading down to the bathroom.

"Um, oh my God," Laura called into the kitchen once the bathroom door was closed.

"Yeah. He's real."

I carried our completed omelets over to the table as Harry walked back out of the bathroom, and then poured us each a cup of coffee and brought those in as well. We ate in silence for the first few minutes, then Laura looked up and asked, "So, what are the plans for today?"

"I don't know," I said, looking over at Harry. "I wanna spend more time though." He frowned at that. "Oh, I don't like that expression."

"Sorry, it's not you. I want to spend more time with you, too, but I'm having dinner with my dad today. I'm meeting his girlfriend. I'm supposed to go over a little early so that I can get to know her."

Harry's dad had a girlfriend? He hadn't mentioned that to me. Maybe he was feeling a little uncertain about her. "Oh, well that's okay," I said. "We can see each other this week again though, right?"

"Yeah, of course," he said. "Just try and keep me away from you."

My heart jumped up again. "I wouldn't dream of it."

"All right," Laura said. "You guys are too cute and it's making my sadly-single ass jealous, so I'm leaving for work."

"You work weekends, too?" Harry asked.

"Yup. Training to be a parole officer. Crime doesn't take Sundays off," she quipped.

Harry nodded. "So I've heard."

"I'll clean up the plate," I told Laura. "You go."

"Thanks, babe, see you later. Harry, this was lovely," she said.

"It was. Thanks again for the amazing dinner," he called after her, then she collected her things, slipped on a pair of her black heels, and left. "Hey, you know what?"

"Hm?" I replied.

"Why don't you come with me today?" Harry asked.

"With you… to your dad's?"

"Yeah. You brought me to meet Laura, I'd like you to meet my dad. Besides, I could really use the backup. It's like you said last night, me, dinner with strangers, especially strange women… you pretty much hit the nail on the head."

Harry wanted me to meet his dad? That felt so heavy and definitive, but for some reason, it didn't freak me out. A smile rose to my face and I nodded. "Yeah, okay."

He suddenly backed off a little. "I don't want to pressure you or, if that feels like too much, you don't—"

"Harry," I cut him off. "I'd love to come."

He relaxed then. "Okay. Good. I'll call my dad and let him know. Do you mind if we leave here sooner rather than later? I need to change and take a shower and stuff."

"Of course. I'll just go pick out something to wear and we can leave."

"Cool, but uh…" He pointed at me. "I'll need that for the trip."

"Obviously." I then grabbed the shirt and pulled it off, revealing my naked body underneath. I handed it over with a sly grin. "Here you go."

Harry sat in stunned silence for a minute, then stood up out of the chair. "Okay." He lifted me up out of the chair and flung me over his back, before carrying me back to the bedroom.

So, we didn't leave for another couple of hours.

When we were finally done gallivanting, I took a quick shower of my own before donning one of Laura's pink day dresses that was hanging in my closet for dinner, then we left and made our way back to Harry's. He plugged his phone up to charge in his living room and left me there while he went to take a shower and change, and eventually, both cats found me to get some cuddles.

We quietly listened to music and waited for Harry until his phone suddenly started to buzz with notifications on the table next to me. It was just one at first and I ignored it, but then there was another and another and another. Purely to make sure there wasn't an emergency, I looked over at the phone, and it appeared to be someone from Harry's work named Seth. I couldn't see all of the messages, but he appeared to be asking about the books at Harry's job, and cutting a check.

Whatever it was about that moment, it all came slamming back into me. For at least four hours, I'd been operating as if Harry really *was* my boyfriend. He had dinner with my roommate, we had an amazing night together, I made him coffee and breakfast, because that was what I felt like I should do as a good girlfriend, and when I whined about not wanting to be apart from Harry today, it was for no reason other than the fact that I truly didn't want that.

But none of this was supposed to be real. I was supposed to be looking for a way to destroy him…

And this was it. The books, the money, his new promotion. I saw the way people treated him once he became VP. His job was the window to truly crush him and take everything from him.

It needed to happen, and it needed to happen today. I was falling in love with Harry, drowning, and I needed to get out.

"Hey." I jumped sky-high at the sudden sound of his voice, jolting both cats. "Whoa, sorry, I didn't mean to scare you."

"That's okay. Your phone has been going crazy," I said. I looked up at him, but he was wearing a light blue button-up shirt, with a white t-shirt underneath, and navy slacks. He looked so good, and I couldn't focus my attention there, so I averted my gaze back to the cats.

Harry picked up his phone and scrolled through it a little before grumbling, "Shit."

"What?" I asked.

"They need me to stop by the bar and sign off on this check for the expansion." He looked down at me. "I'm sorry, but do you mind running with me there?"

A golden opportunity. "No, not at all."

"Okay then, we'll leave straight from there for dinner."

He finished getting ready, then we packed up and took his bike to Hoppa's Taphouse. The regulars were already starting to file in for the day, as it was late afternoon, so Harry took me around back and used a key to walk us through the back door. There was only one member of the club back there, and he was sitting at a table looking over some paperwork. When he looked up and saw me, his head tilted, then he smiled.

"Celia, right?" he asked.

"Yeah," I said.

He stood up and walked over. "Seth, nice to meet you."

"What's going on?" Harry asked.

"Nicky wants the check cut, but had to make an emergency run with Bucky, so I need you to sign off on it."

"Okay. I have dinner at my dad's in an hour, so let's hurry," Harry said. He kissed me on my cheek, said, "I'll be right back," and walked over toward some filing cabinets with Seth.

They stood with their back to me, talking quietly so as not to have me overhear what they were discussing, but what they weren't worried about were the books that were open on the table. One of them specifically, looked like a book for reconciling cash in and cash out. I looked over at Harry, and there was a little bit of resistance in my head. Once I did this, there was no going back.

But that was what I wanted.

I sneakily picked up the pencil and flipped the book backward until I got to the months before Harry took over VP. I erased some of the numbers, just the second digit or third digit, something unnoticeable and replaced the numbers with smaller ones. Numbers that looked similar were my target, changing 9s to 8s, 3s to 2s, anywhere I could, then I flipped back to today and changed a number from an 8 to a 3 by erasing the sides of the 8. I set the pencil down and stepped back from the table to where I'd been and started flicking through my phone.

Finally, Harry and Seth walked back to the table and they both started looking through the book. My heart started to pound, afraid that they were going to notice my change, but neither of them seemed to. Harry wrote out a check, for fifty-thousand dollars I spied, and then signed it, Seth signed it, and then he packed it into an envelope.

"Thanks, Bullet. Sorry for calling you in while you're with your lady," Seth said.

Harry walked over to me and put his hand behind my back. "No worries, right?"

I smiled and nodded. "Right."

"I'm pretty sure this girl and I could sit and watch paint dry and enjoy ourselves," Harry said. "It was really just an excuse to drag her around with me more."

My stomach turned a little and I experienced a tinge of remorse. It really was going to crush Harry when he realized this was all just a ploy.

It would be hard to go back to life without him for me, too.

"Well, I think that's all I needed, so unless you need anything from me, you guys can head out. I'm done wasting your time," Seth explained.

"Just make sure you get a copy of it, and don't hand the check over until you get the copy of the signed contract by *both* parties," Harry said.

Seth nodded. "You got it, boss."

"All right. See ya later, Dynamite."

"Bye."

Harry linked his fingers with mine and pulled me back out of the warehouse through the back door. Just before we got on his bike, he dragged me toward him. I was anticipating a kiss, but he just stood there, staring at me for a while.

"What?" I asked.

"Nothing," he replied, then he did kiss me, passionately and deep, in a way that shook me down to my toes. "You ready?"

"Yeah," I answered breathlessly.

"Cool. Let's go."

Chapter Twenty

Celia

Harry held up a bottle of wine. "Is this a good enough kind? I don't want to seem cheap."

"Yeah, I think that's good," I said.

We'd swung by a grocery store at my behest to get a bottle of wine and flowers for dinner. It was the kind of decorum that I had learned from my dad who was something of a stickler for manners. Maybe it was because he was born in Athens, Georgia, which was a bit of a debutante city, but practicing good gentlemanly and ladylike behavior was something he preached until his dying day. I no longer felt the need to put on airs or pretend as if I wasn't enjoying my time with Harry or looking forward to dinner. It was all going to fall apart at the seams soon anyway, why not give us both one last night of fun?

"I have no idea what kind of flowers she likes," Harry said as we perused the floral section.

"It's less about her specifically, and more just about flowers for the house. It's a sign of being grateful for the invitation." I pulled out a bouquet of sunflowers. "These are always good. They're pretty and not overly difficult to maintain if they want to."

"Okay," Harry said. "If you think sunflowers are the way to go, let's do sunflowers."

We took the flowers and wine to the front to checkout and standing next to Harry in the grocery store line felt oddly domestic yet comfortable. Thinking about what I wanted from my life, that was it. Someone that I didn't feel the need to constantly be talking to or regularly entertaining, but we could just be in one another's space and be okay.

Was I wasting my luck of ever finding something like this by intentionally torpedoing things with Harry? What we had seemed rare. I hoped there was someone else like him out there for me.

We got back on his bike after carefully packing the wine and flowers into the back compartment where they'd be safe, and then made our way to Harry's dad's house. He actually lived a little outside of Hoppa, which Harry explained was so that Harry wasn't regularly triggered by being near to where he grew up. He had a nice home, and it somehow fit who Harry was. I was hoping to get a few stories of young Harry running around while I was there, maybe even seeing a picture or two.

Harry parked his bike in the driveway, and we got off. The front door was already opening, likely called by the roar of the bike, so we pulled out the wine and flowers quickly and made our way up. Before we even got to the door, an older-looking dog came rushing out of the house wagging its tail with excitement. Harry bent down and lifted the Dachshund up from the ground with one hand and held him out toward me.

"This is Milton. He was my therapy dog."

I rustled Milton's ears. "Nice to meet you, sir."

We walked through the open front door and came face to face with a fairly attractive man with caramel skin and warm eyes that reminded me of my dad, and next to him was a tall, peach-skinned woman with short black hair and pristine blue eyes.

"Dad," Harry said, "this is my girlfriend, Celia."

My heart jumped up into my throat. It was the first time I'd heard him phrase it like that and I *loved* the way it sounded. I was suddenly feeling like I might have made a mistake. Maybe Harry and I could have come to some sort of understanding. He did kill my dad, but… maybe there was something I was missing.

It was too late. I'd already fudged his books. It was just a matter of time.

The man stuck out his hand and I took it. "Nice to meet you, I'm Cameron."

"Nice to meet you," I replied.

Cameron put his hand behind the back of the woman next to him. "This is my beautiful girlfriend, Marisha. Marisha, this is my kid, Harry."

I saw the shake in Harry's hand as he stuck it out to take Marisha's. She must have noticed it, too, because when Harry's hand got into hers, she closed over it with her other hand to calm him. She gave him a warm smile and said, "It's so lovely to finally meet you."

"Yeah, sorry about it taking so long. I'd give some excuse, but really I think I was just procrastinating," Harry admitted.

"I'm glad you brought backup then," Cameron said, winking at me. "Well, come in, dinner is on the table already, and we can get started."

Harry had mentioned that Cameron was a chef in the past but had definitely downplayed how amazing he was. He could have easily been a famous chef in New York or California with the way he presented freshly roasted brisket, perfectly cooked, over rice pilaf and a bed of greens. The red wine Harry and I bought just so happened to go perfectly with it, so we popped it open and poured everyone a glass, then settled down to eat it.

"So, Celia, how's it going dating my boy?" he asked.

I looked over at Harry and smiled. "Sometimes I feel like I don't deserve him."

"Right?" Cameron said. "I never had kids, but then Harry came into my life and it was like 'Wow. How did I get so lucky?'" He looked at Harry while pointing at me. "I like her."

"Me, too," Harry replied.

Cameron gushed about Harry and Marisha over dinner, clearly going the extra mile to make sure they liked one another. What he didn't see, but was plain to see for me, was that Marisha and Harry were silently bonding over how much they both loved Cameron. Every time he told a story or laughed, they exchanged a quiet glance of understanding, and each time it happened, things at the table got more and more relaxed. It was surreal to be around, and I felt honored to experience it firsthand.

"Have you heard from the private detective?" Harry asked Cameron after a while.

"Private detective?" Marisha and I asked at the same time.

"You didn't tell her?" Cameron and Harry asked each other in unison and then we all laughed.

"I kept it to myself because it's not my place to share," Cameron said.

"Yeah, I guess we never really got around to talking about it," Harry said. "I have a younger sibling out there somewhere. Living with my mom. We haven't really talked about it all that much, but she's the reason I had my, you know, trust issues. I've been using some money I got from a settlement to fund searching for him or her so that, hopefully, I can save them before my mom screws them up like she did me."

Settlement. "Were you in an accident?" I asked.

"Yeah," he said. "A handful of years ago. Four, maybe? Five?"

"Six," Cameron said.

"What happened?" I asked.

"It was not long after I joined the Steel Knights. I was on the road headed to the club, and this guy started up with me," Harry explained.

"Darrien Pescoe," Cameron hissed. "I'll never forget the name. The man who almost took my son from me." Marisha put a hand on Cameron's wrist, and he calmed a bit. "One day I get this call that a car ran Harry off the road, flipped his bike, and he was in the hospital."

"I guess the guy had pledged for the Steel Knights, but didn't make it," Harry said. "When he saw me in my colors, it pissed him off and he tried to race me. Although it was less like a race and more like a demolition derby. I felt bad for the other guy in the car, he was clearly trying to get him to stop, but he wouldn't listen."

My heart started to beat faster and faster. "He hit you?"

"Yeah, he tried to just nudge me, I think, but he had no control over the car. I was flying, trying to get away from him, so he had to be doing like a hundred or more in a car with low handling. I tried slowing down, speeding up, this guy just would not let it go. Finally, he scooted over and hit my tire, and we both lost control."

"If it hadn't been for the way Harry handles his bike, he would have died," Cameron said. "He at least had the frame of mind to get sideways so that he didn't flip and go flying. At that speed, his trajectory…" Cameron started to get emotional and then he reached out and put a hand on Harry's face. "I thank God every day that he survived."

"What about the car?" I asked, even though I already knew the outcome to the story."

"It flipped," Harry said. "A bunch of times. I lost consciousness and it was still flipping. I never knew his passenger's name, but I know he died. I only ever knew Darrien's name because it was in all the settlement paperwork."

Nothing made sense. If the accident was Darrien's fault, what money was I living off of? I'd always wondered why Darrien didn't have settlement money, too, if my dad did, but he always claimed he used it to cover my college tuition, although it didn't cover all of it because I still ended up taking loans and having payments.

"So Harry's using that money to find his sibling," Cameron added. "He's already said he's prepared to become a dad if he can hunt them down."

"I learned from the best," Harry said, then he looked at me. "Sorry, I guess I probably left that out for now so that it didn't apply too much pressure to us."

It had to be wrong. I had to just be hearing their slant on the story. Even if Harry's control of his bike always left me wondering how something like that could happen. Even if certain things happened with Darrien that made me question his story, I always wrote it off.

It can't have been a lie. There's no way.

"Did someone find you, Harry?" I asked. "You said you passed out."

"There were dozens of witnesses," Harry replied. "That's why we were able to settle out of court, because there was no way in hell that he was going to be successful in defending a case. All he asked was that it stay out of the papers, and I was fine with that because I didn't want the club getting any bad attention."

The only newspaper clipping Darrien ever showed me was my father's obituary.

"I remember just sitting next to his hospital bed, wondering why so much bad kept finding my son. He deserves a happy life."

"He's been careful not to tell me too much, Harry," Marisha said, "because your father respects your privacy, but do you mind telling me the story of what happened with your mom? It'd be nice to understand it better so that I know what lines not to cross and stuff. Of course, you don't have to if you don't want to."

"No, it's okay. I haven't talked about it with Celia either, so there's no time like the present," he replied.

"Thank you," Marisha said sincerely.

I watched Harry as he took a deep breath and started to tell his story. "My mom was always abusive to my dad when I was a kid. My dad was always very respectful of women and just took my mom's abuse in his stride, but she was vicious with him. She'd hit him, abuse him verbally, talk down to him, all of it. My dad had always said, as long as it wasn't me, he was fine to take it, but then one time at my birthday party, I spilled ketchup on my shirt and she lost it. All the other kids' moms started talking about it, and my mom got embarrassed."

"That's awful," Marisha said.

"Yeah," I replied. "That's stuff kids do."

"Yeah, well, she took it personally for whatever reason, and that's when the abuse against me started." Cameron shifted uncomfortably as Harry talked, and it was clear he struggled to listen to the story of someone hurting the boy he'd come to love as his son. "My dad wouldn't go for that though. He was always willing to take it, but the second it was me, he had to step in. One night, he tried to take me and run from her, but she caught us trying to leave. She…"

Harry hesitated and I could tell that even all this time later, it was hard for him to tell the story. I put my hand on his back, knowing that I'd made a huge mistake and my time to comfort him was running short. "It's okay."

He smiled at me and continued. "She shot him in his back, while he was trying to load me into the car to leave her for good. He didn't take any of the furniture or anything, even left his entire life savings for her to live off of, but she didn't care. She killed him and then called the police and said she did it in self-defense because he was trying to kidnap me."

"The cop that arrived on the scene was a woman, and one of those 'protect all women' types. It's not a bad thing, but it blinded her when she met Harry and his mom," Cameron explained. "She fudged some of the story to make sure that Harry's mom didn't go to prison for the murder, made it seem like it was self-defense. The judge, another female, took Harry's mom's side even after Harry testified that she'd murdered him. Then as Harry got older and ran away a lot, that judge kept getting his case and kept forcing him to go back to his mom."

"No wonder you don't trust women," Marisha said. "Harry, I'm so sorry that happened to you."

"Between that and the accident, I just wanted my kid to catch a break," Cameron told us.

At that exact moment, Harry looked up at me and smiled. "I did."

My heart shattered into a million pieces. I forced a smile back, tears gathering in my eyes, and all I could do was wrap my arms around him and hug him. He'd go back to hating women for sure when he realized what I'd done. Hell, he'd probably just start to hate everyone. Emotions burned in my nose as I realized I'd made a grave mistake, and worse than that was the fact that I had absolutely no clue how to fix it.

Chapter Twenty-One

Bullet

I was surprised when Celia suddenly decided to go back home after dinner with Cameron and Marisha. At first, I was terrified that I'd scared her with my story about my parents and mentioning that I was searching for my younger sibling, but she swore that wasn't it and said she just needed to take care of something. Because I was really and truly falling in love with Celia, I didn't want to push her to stay, but while I was waking up in bed alone, I was kind of wishing I'd tried at least a little harder. I'd have to work today, and she probably would, too, but it would have been nice to have her in my arms for at least a few minutes.

She promised to call me and that we'd see each other in the week, so as much as I nearly wanted to roll back over and go to sleep, the cats were scratching at my door, so I got up. I took my time traveling through my morning, giving the boys their food and eating breakfast myself, then I grabbed my phone and went into my living room to relax for a little bit before getting ready.

It was just after eight, and I was aware of the fact that I was slowly passing the time at which I'd typically be leaving my house and heading in, but I was early every single day. One later day wouldn't hurt anything.

Or so I thought.

As the nine o'clock hour came and went, I started to get one call from the club right after the other. First Nick, then Seth, then Avery, then Bucky. I'd only been the VP for about a month, why was everyone all of a sudden ringing my phone off the hook? I reluctantly stood up and trudged back to my bedroom, prepared to get dressed and head to the bar as soon as possible so everyone would calm down, when I suddenly got a string of texts from Avery.

"Harry, if you get this, you need to call me ASAP."

"Something is wrong with the books."

"Nick thinks you stole some money. Well, a lot of money."

"I need you to call me right away."

I stood staring at my phone in shock. Did Seth forget to notate the check or something? I was just there yesterday, how did I all of a sudden come to be accused of stealing? Smacking the call button on Avery's text feed and putting it on speaker, I ran around my room, finding anything to wear so I could leave and go to the club, and then Avery picked up.

"Hello?" He sounded frantic.

"Avery, what the fuck is going on?" I barked. "What do you mean Nick thinks I stole money?"

"The books are off. Really off. They aren't saying much to anyone about it, but Nick's on a fucking rampage around here, saying he made a mistake. You gotta get here and get this cleared up fast."

"Okay, I'm on my way."

The line went dead without me even saying goodbye and I finished getting dressed and made my way to the club as fast as I could get there. It was a particularly hot day in Hoppa, and between that and the anxiety I was suddenly feeling, I was drenched in sweat as I walked in.

Which even I had to admit, didn't look good.

All of the members were sitting around the bar and all their gazes shot in my direction as I walked in. In all of their expressions, in a way that made me feel sick to my stomach, I could see that hint of consideration that I'd actually done what Nick was accusing me of. All except for Avery who jumped up and ran over.

"Hey."

"Where's Nick?" I asked.

"In the back with Dynamite. I'd be careful heading back there, man. Nicky's blowin' a stack."

"I can't believe he would just blindly think I was stealing without talking to me first," I replied.

"That's what we all said, that he needs to talk to you first. Just head on back, but keep your wits about you, and holler if you need some help."

Some help? Did they all know something I didn't know? Was I about to be bum-rushed by a man who wasn't even going to give me a chance to defend myself, or was there some kind of damning evidence that already had them all convinced? It made no sense to linger in the front anymore, so I walked around the bar, through the swinging door, and back into the warehouse.

The tension in the room as soon as I entered was oppressive. Seth was sitting at the table with the books unfolded in front of him, and Nick was sitting in his regular spot, glaring back at me.

"Hey, Harry," he greeted. "Come. Sit."

"Nicky," I said as I started over. "I don't know what's going on, but you know I would never steal from you." I side-eyed Seth. Was he setting me up or something? Was his nice-guy act just a facade? "What's going on?"

"Show him," Nick said.

Seth turned the books to face me. He pointed to the column that had all the numbers in it from yesterday. "See anything wrong here?"

I scanned the numbers from all the different vendors, and the fifty-k check that we'd written out, and the bottom line showed a fifty-thousand dollar hit from the check we'd written, but that was it. "No?"

"Look again," Seth said.

At that, I started to slowly add up all the numbers in the column. When I got to the bottom, before the fifty-k check, I was already fifty in the hole, but then the check made it a hundred k. "These numbers don't add up," I said. "There's an extra fifty... missing." I looked up at Nick and felt conflicted. I didn't want to blame Seth for anything that wasn't his fault either, but I still had to ask the honest question. "Why is an imbalance in the books that he's handling lead you to believe that *I'm* stealing?"

Seth flipped a bunch of pages of the book, taking it back to about a month and a half ago when I was still handling the books personally. He had a bunch of columns highlighted and I looked through them and saw that there was a similar issue. They all looked as if someone had reconciled the books, and then gone back after the fact to make it look like we had certain amounts under what we had. The bottom lines all had numbers that showed less than we had, almost as if someone was skimming off the top and fudging the numbers to match.

"Okay," I said. "I get how this looks, but I didn't do that. First of all, it's sloppy. Second of all, you would have realized it before now, Squared. You saw the books every week."

"Yeah, but I trusted what you told me, that everything was lining up the way it needed to."

"And you didn't want to cut the check until the end of the year," Seth added. "Right as all the numbers would be rolling over and it would be easy to take more without anyone noticing. We cut the check for the expansion and I reported these earnings. We're now short fifty grand that we needed to cover bills and payroll."

"I'm not stealing money from the club," I spat.

"Show me your bank account," Nick said.

My heart stopped. "What?"

"Right now. Show me your bank account on your phone. You wouldn't have fifty grand in there."

Fuck.

Now I was realizing that it wasn't just some random, shit luck. Someone set me up. "Okay... I *do* have fifty grand in my account right now, but it's not money from the club. It's what's left of my settlement from the accident."

Nick crossed his arms. "The settlement from *years* ago?"

My skin was boiling with anger. I couldn't blame Nick for the conclusion he was coming to, outside of being angry that he would honestly believe that I'd do anything like that. "Yeah. I've been saving it because I'm searching for my missing younger sibling."

"You've never mentioned a brother or sister before," Nick remarked.

"Yeah, because I don't like talking about it here," I said back. "Nicky. You know me. You know I would *never* steal from you. This club means more to me than anything. I'm taking my job seriously, *and* I would never be that messy!"

"So, I should believe it's not you because you got caught and you would never get caught?" he asked.

"No..." I let my head fall back. "Nicky—"

"Oh, fuck..." Seth murmured. "Shit, Harry..."

"What?" Nick and I said at the same time.

"I didn't see this at first, but this number was changed recently. I wrote a copy of these vendor numbers and I wrote an eight here and not a three. Someone had to have changed it yesterday while you and I were writing the check."

"While we were writing it? How do you know?" I asked.

"Because I wrote the vendor numbers right before you walked in, and we were together the whole time. You couldn't have changed the number, and after I cut the check, I closed up the books, maybe five minutes after you left."

But that would mean…

Nick looked over at Seth for a second and then flung his arm out and punched him square across the jaw. Seth fell backward out of his chair and crumpled onto the ground.

"Have you lost your fucking mind?" Nick snapped. "You told me he stole it! I just fucking accused him of stealing fifty thousand dollars!"

"I'm sorry!" Seth yelped. "I really thought he did!"

"Fuck!" Nick screamed and then looked across at me. "Harry, I'm…"

I held my hand up. "No, don't apologize to me. At the end of the day, this is still my fault."

The scene played over in my head. Celia and I walked in and then Seth and I completely turned our backs to her while we discussed the check. I made sure to have us step away from her so that it wasn't like she could listen to what we were saying, and then I went and sat right back down at the books as I wrote the check out, without looking to make sure that Seth's math was all correct. No wonder Celia suddenly wanted to go home last night after the time we'd had together. No wonder why I hadn't gotten a call or text from her yet that morning.

She stole fifty grand and did so in a way that made it look like it was me.

To say I was crushed would be an understatement. If she had come back to my house with me, there wasn't a doubt in my mind that I would have ended up telling her I loved her. I *did* love her. After Saturday with her roommate and Sunday with my dad and Marisha, I was so sure that she was the woman I wanted to be with, that I'd fallen for her.

How could she do this to me?

"I brought Celia back here when I came in to write the check yesterday afternoon. I didn't want to go through the bar, because I knew we'd get distracted and we had to get to dinner with my dad and his girlfriend. Celia was standing here with the books on the table. Nothing in me didn't trust that she'd just leave everything alone. I don't know why she did this, but it doesn't matter, I never should have compromised our information by bringing a non-member back here."

"She was just using you to steal from us?" Nick said. "That's cold."

It was hard to believe. Everything played back in my head. The jazz bar, the theme park, dinner with Laura, dinner with Cameron. All the coffee dates we'd had or dumb times I spent doing nothing but texting her like some lovestruck teenage boy. All of it had been a lie? All of it?

"I've got fifty grand," I said. "I'll go withdraw it tomorrow and bring it in to cover the debt. We already gave the check for the club expansion, and I don't want to go back on that now."

Seth had gotten back up in his chair and was holding his face, while looking at me sadly. "What about your sibling?"

We'd been searching for months with no luck anyway. Maybe this was the world's way of saying it was time to give up on that. "I'll figure something else out."

I stood up and pulled my jacket off and hung it around the chair. "I'd like to nominate Seneca for membership. When the time comes, consider it my last act as VP. She's good with her bike, she can fight, and she has honor that's hard to find. She'll be a good addition to the club."

"Come on, Bullet, don't do this. I'm sorry. I should have made absolute certain before I blew up. Don't leave the club," Nick pleaded.

"I put all of our hard work at risk. I don't deserve this role." I looked over at Seth. "Don't let this throw you off. You're a good accountant. Anyone would have missed that."

With a final look at them, I made my way over to the back door of the warehouse. I didn't want to face anyone else at the time and could just say my goodbyes later. Before I got on my bike, I sent Celia a text telling her to call me immediately and then drove myself home to sit and wait.

Chapter Twenty-Two

Celia

I was sitting at the kitchen table, waiting for Darrien to come up for the day. In front of me, still unopened, was the box of things that Darrien often referred to when he was trying to guilt-trip me about the accident he'd been. I hadn't yet opened it, because I wanted to see if he would be truthful with me first, but that didn't stop me from staring down at it and wondering what was inside. A few of the things I knew, the ones he always threw in my face, like my father's obituary or his medical bills, but what else? He never allowed me to go through the box myself, but always kept it off to the side on the kitchen counter as a reminder. He banked on me being stupid enough never to look in there myself.

And I was.

"Good morning," Darrien said as he rolled up the ramp from the split-lower floor of the house where his bedroom was. "I'm surprised to see you home." He rode into the kitchen and up to the dining room table, but then sniffed the air and realized nothing was cooking. "Are you not working on breakfast?"

"No," I said. "I'm not."

"What's wrong?" he asked. "You seem angry."

I decided to start in the easiest place to start, with the truth. Pulling out my phone, I unlocked it and it was still sitting open to the article that I had looked up the night before, after I got home. Once again, my uncle had done a great job of convincing me that he was telling me the whole story so there was no reason to go in search of the contrary. I never even thought to look anything up on my own, because in my naivete, I truly believed my godfather would never lie to me about something like that. He told me that researching articles about the accident would show me marred images of my father and only bring me pain, and I believed him. If only I'd let my curiosity beat out my fear. All it had taken was a quick Google search and an article on a small news website popped right up.

One that confirmed Harry's side of the story.

I slid my phone across the table to him, and he picked up and then his eyes slowly started to widen. He swallowed hard before looking up at me. "Where did you find this lie?"

That made me angrier. He was prepared to lie to my face. To act as if I couldn't see what was right there. "That's just one article of fifty I found," I said. "Don't. Don't lie to me anymore." I set my hand on top of the box and he lurched forward a bit. "What's in here?"

"You already know," he replied. "Your dad's obituary. My thousands of dollars in unpaid medical bills."

"How was I so goddamn dumb? Is it because you've been lying to me since I was fifteen? I just didn't put the pieces together?"

"What are you talking about?" he asked.

"You're lying," I said. "About all of it. Medical bills are usually paid in car accident settlements, aren't they? In situations like yours, people can be paid out extra for anticipatory medical costs."

"All the money I got I spent on—"

"That's a lie!" I screamed. "I called my school, they told me they've *never* received any large payments on my student loans. I thought I was paying back twenty-thousand dollars but I'm actually paying back sixty-thousand dollars. You told me you got a settlement, that my dad had gotten one, too. What money do I have if it's not a settlement from the car accident?"

"It is," Darrien lied again.

"No, it's not." I folded my fingers under the lid of the box to lift the top off, and to my complete shock, Darrien jumped up out of his chair. He came to stand on his feet and my jaw dropped. "You're not paralyzed."

Darrien froze for a second before slowly lowering back down into his chair. "I have some mobility, but not full mobility."

"You jumped up!" I screamed. "I've changed you! I've bathed you! I've given up the last six years of my life taking care of you and you're not even paralyzed?" Tears started to streak down my face, but whether they were from sadness or anger, I wasn't sure. "I can't believe this. I'm so dumb. I thought you loved me."

"I do, Celia," he replied. "I've taken care of you this whole time."

"No," I said. "I've taken care of *you*."

I opened the box lid and started to drag out the contents one by one. There were medical bills inside, though they were the unpaid bills from my father's emergency care before he was legally declared dead.

I'd been told he was pronounced dead at the scene.

His obituary was in there, but it was folded behind an article of the accident, the true story of the accident that I saw on the internet, how Darrien had caused it and my father had died for it. Harry's words skidded across my mind about how my dad was begging Darrien to stop, but he wouldn't listen.

"*You* killed my dad."

"No. Harry killed your dad," Darrien said.

Inside the box as well were the legal documents containing my father's inheritance. He had a will and life insurance, so when he died, that money came to me. Darrien told me it was a settlement. He also had told me there was only sixty-thousand dollars, but the paperwork detailed a two-hundred-and-fifty-thousand-dollar life insurance policy.

"Where's the rest of the money?" I asked.

"I used it for the funeral," Darrien replied.

"You gave me sixty and funerals cost a few thousand," I spat back. "Where is the rest of my dad's money?"

"It's gone, I don't know what you want me to say!"

"You wanted me to get revenge on Harry because you weren't allowed into that motorcycle club?" I said. "You're that childish?"

"I should have been let in! I was a better biker than any of them! Who the hell was Harry, just some dumb kid who followed the rules and was a little bit better with numbers than the rest of us? Fuck that. They think they can give him my spot, then he had to prove to me that he was worth it."

"My dad died because of you!" I screamed. Continuing to sift through the box, I found a letter buried near the bottom. The envelope was worn and tattered and had been opened despite the fact that it had my name on it. "What's this?"

"It's nothing," Darrien said. "It'll only hurt you to read it."

I shook my head. "How can you still lie to me after everything? Haven't you hurt me enough?"

Sliding my finger into the already cut-open slit across the top, I pulled out the note inside. It was just as tattered and old as the envelope and had clearly been handled a few times.

Celia,

The doctors just came in and told me that my chances for survival are not high. I want you to know that I love you more than life itself, my beautiful girl. You are smart, and kind, and funny, and I want you to achieve all of your wildest dreams. Do it and know that Daddy's up in heaven cheering for you.

Please don't blame your godfather for what happened to me. He's just misguided, but he needs your love more than ever, now that I'm gone. Take care of him for me and have him do the same for you.

Use my life insurance to pay for college and go change the world, baby girl! Daddy believes in you.

I love you,
Daddy

My throat was tight with emotions and tears were streaming out of my eyes. "How could you not give this to me? The last thing my dad ever wrote me? Just because it incriminated you? You are the most selfish, careless man I've ever known." Just as I was about to tear into my godfather even more, my phone buzzed. It was still in Darrien's hand and he looked down at it and then glared up at me. "Give me it."

Though I should have known he wouldn't. He pulled back his hand, gave me one last evil look and then threw it against the wall, shattering it. Part of me wanted to get angrier, to scream more, or run over and punch him in the face, but all I could do was stand up.

"I'm so sad for you," I said. "I'm moving out. Enjoy your life alone."

"Celia," Darrien said, but I ignored him and continued for the door. "Celia! Get back here. Celia!"

I left the house, knowing I'd probably need to bring a cop back when I came to collect my stuff. There was still about forty-thousand dollars of my dad's settlement left, which would be enough for me to move back in with Laura and cover my expenses for a while, but I'd have to make those arrangements later. For now, I needed to talk to Harry and I was really hoping he was at his home.

I drove straight there, praying that what I'd done hadn't been discovered yet. Whether he forgave me or not didn't matter, if I could tell him what happened before anyone saw it, maybe he could fix it.

His bike was parked in front of his house, and I was relieved that he hadn't been to the bar yet for the day. I was trying to work out how I was going to explain everything was running through my mind, but I was thinking more than anything, that I just needed to tell him the truth from the beginning.

If I told him it was all meant to be a ploy, but I fell in love along the way, would he believe me?

"Harry?" I said as I knocked on his door. "It's me."

Very near the door, I could hear a weight settling, followed by footsteps getting closer to the door. It opened, and I was immediately hit with a feeling of dread. The look on his face could peel the paint off the walls. Neither of the cats were anywhere in the vicinity.

"Come in," he said without even looking at me. "We need to talk."

Shit. He knew.

"Okay." I stepped into the living room and walked over to the couch and sat down.

Harry walked over and sat down in the armchair perpendicular to the couch and folded over, setting his arms against his legs and balancing his head in his hands. "I'm confused, Celia."

"Yeah," I said. "That's fair."

There was a heaviness in the air that was suffocating. I wanted to wrap my arms around Harry and just beg him for his forgiveness, but the situation required me to hold back.

When he looked up at me, even with the sadness in his eyes, I was reminded of how good he looked. "Are you going to explain yourself?" he asked.

"Yeah," I said. "Um…" I took a deep breath. "Remember that car accident that you were in?"

He recoiled at that. "Yeah? What does that have to do with this?"

"I'm Darrien Pescoe's goddaughter."

Harry's eyes widened. "You're what?" He stood up. "You're what? Celia, that man tried to kill me!"

"That's not what he told me!" I cried. "He told me *you* killed them. He told me you killed my dad!"

"Your dad?" He dropped back down into the chair. "The other man in the car was your dad?"

"I was doing it for revenge. All of it," I said. "This was all just a ploy to destroy you for ruining my family."

Harry folded his hand over his mouth. "It was all fake?" he asked.

"At first," I said, and a toxic sludge knotted itself in my throat as I continued to speak, "but I fell in love with you, Harry. For real."

Harry shook his head. "No."

"I swear," I said.

"No, I don't believe you. You stole money from the club."

"I didn't!" I said. "I only fudged the numbers so that it would look like you were stealing."

"Well, it worked, so congrats. You pulled off what you wanted to," he said. "The numbers got reported as you wrote them, so now we're fifty grand in the hole for this month. I've got to use what's left of my settlement money to pay them back."

"What about looking for your brother or sister?" I asked.

"Well, I guess I'll have to stop that for now, won't I? Hopefully my mom doesn't kill them between now and when I can afford to pick the P.I. up again. It'll be hard, since I'm no longer VP at the club, but hey, I'm sure Hoppa is just full of lucrative jobs."

"I'll go to the club," I begged. "I'll tell them it was me and not you."

"They know that, and we were able to figure it out, but I stepped down because it was my fault you were there. The trust between Nick and me is all fucked up now, and it was sketchy to begin with, but none of that is as bad as the fact that I really did fucking fall in love with you. I was sitting at that dinner table thinking, 'Damn this is what I want my life to be like'. And you weren't even serious."

"I was!"

"How can you say that when you *just* fudged the numbers. If you loved me, how could you do that to me?" I opened my mouth to respond, but nothing came out. There wasn't a good answer. "Exactly," Harry said. "Now you need to get out."

"Harry, I—"

"Get out. Now."

I stood up from the couch, my heart breaking and breaking with each step. As I opened the door, I saw the cats peeking out from the kitchen, and I gave them a little wave before walking out, closing the door behind me

Chapter Twenty-Three

Bullet

I was struggling to do much of anything for the rest of the day, but I knew that I had to get the rest of the money and get it over to the club so that they were all set for bills. Unfortunately, my money was listed in both my name and Cameron's so that he could use it as he saw fit, meaning I had to involve him in pulling the money out, and explaining why. I flopped down to my bed, laying on my back, and trying to figure out how I didn't see the signs. Obviously, Celia didn't really care about me. There were so many red flags, I just chose to ignore them because I loved her and didn't want it to be true.

How dumb could I be?

There was no time for moping. Cameron and I were going to need to pull out the money, and I was battling between just calling him or actually going to see him in person, when my phone rang.

It was Cameron.

"Hey," I answered, and even I could hear how exhausted I sounded.

"Where are you right now?" he asked. "Are you at your house? I'm almost at your house."

The cats scattered from around my feet as I sat up. I hadn't even realized they were there. "You're coming to my house?" I asked. "Why?"

"Because I have *huge* news. Come let me in," he said, and then the line went dead.

"Okay," I replied to no one, then slid my phone into my pocket and stood up out of bed.

With the cats leading the way, I made my way down the hallway and up to the front door, and as he said, Cameron's car was pulling up in front. He parked and was out of the car in a flash. He ran up the sidewalk and had a huge smile on his face.

"Hey!" he said, throwing his arms around me in a hug. "Is Celia here?"

It burned my throat just to hear her name. "No."

"Okay, well let's head in and I'll give you the good news!"

We walked back inside the house and sat down at the dining room table. I grabbed a couple of bottles of water from the fridge and went and sat down across from Cameron.

"Okay, guess what?" he said.

"What?"

"You have a little sister!"

"Marisha's pregnant?" I asked.

Cameron shook his head. "No! *Your* sister! The private investigator found her and your mother living in South Florida!"

My stomach emptied out. "Are you serious?"

"Yes!" Then he frowned. "Now, it's not all good news. He found her because another C.P.S. case got opened, but this is kind of a final strike situation. Your mom is being arrested and your sister is being removed from the home. It'll be kind of a long battle, but as long as we can fund it, we shouldn't have any trouble getting custody of her."

Tears gathered in the corners of my eyes. "What's her name?"

"Ruby."

I smiled. What a cute name. "Wow. This sucks."

Cameron furrowed his brow. "Sucks? Why?"

My head dropped into my hands. "Everything with Celia was a lie, Dad. Her godfather is Darrien Pescoe."

Cameron's eyes widened. "What?"

"She lied to me, about everything. Apparently, it was all part of a plan to get revenge. Her dad was the passenger that died."

Cameron deflated. "I can't believe that. She really seemed like she was crazy about you."

"She tried to tell me that she fell in love throughout the process, but I struggle to believe her because yesterday, before we came over, we swung by the bar. She fucked with the numbers in the books to frame me for stealing. They wrote a check based on the bad numbers and now they're short fifty grand. Guess who has to repay it?"

"Not you, right? You didn't know she was going to do that. Make her pay for it."

I shook my head. "She doesn't have any money. Besides, I'm the one who brought her back there. She only had the opportunity to do it because I was blind and didn't pay attention to what she was doing when she was there."

"Fifty grand is like, all you have left," Cameron said. "This is going to be an expensive process. We'll have to pay a lawyer, pay for traveling costs, and I remember when I wanted to foster you, I had to shell out like fifteen-thousand dollars just to make sure my house was up to code, and you'll probably have to do the same thing. You need that money for Ruby."

It was so much more painful knowing her name. When she was just a concept, it was much easier to think about. Now, she was a real person out there who needed me, and I wasn't able to help her. It was killing me.

"I don't have any other choice. I'll find a way to make more money, or maybe I can take out a loan, I don't know. For now, I need you to come with me to get the money so I can bring it to the club. I don't want things to get any worse."

"If there's really nothing else we can do…" Cameron said.

"There isn't," I assured him.

"Okay. Let's do it then, I guess."

"Can you drive?" I asked, heartbroken about Celia and heartbroken about Ruby. "I probably shouldn't be driving anything right now."

"Yeah," Cameron said. "Let's go."

Chapter Twenty-Four

Celia

The wind blew through my hair as I got out of my car in front of Hoppa's main cemetery. It'd been a long time since I had been there, probably because I was avoiding it until I was able to get the revenge that Darrien convinced me my dad deserved. All this time I'd been chasing the ghost of something and I didn't even know the real story.

My dad must be so disappointed in me.

Instead of the typical flowers I used to bring, I instead chose to bring some birdseed to scatter around my dad's grave. He was always a huge fan of birds, and I figured having some hanging around would be a good way to ensure he'd forgive me for what I had done. I grabbed a blanket from my car, the birdseed I'd purchased, and made my way into the cemetery. The afternoon sun was just cresting over the mountains in the distance, and I remembered the times my dad used to bring me out for picnics on days that weren't too hot.

It was time for another picnic with my dad.

There were a few people dotted around the cemetery, but none of them looked up; people typically didn't. I made my way back to where my dad was buried and unfolded my blanket in front of his headstone. My heart ached to look at it as I remembered his warm smile and big, bear hugs.

"Hi, Daddy," I said. "I'm gonna invite some birds, okay?" I sprinkled some squirrel-friendly birdseed behind the headstone where they could get to them without bothering me too much, and almost as soon as the seed hit the ground, some nearby birds scurried down from the trees and helped themselves. I returned to the blanket I'd spread out and sat down. "How are you? I miss you. I'm sure you've been watching the trainwreck I've been becoming over the past few months, so I'm sorry about that."

One bird hopped closer to me. It got closer and closer until it finally hopped up onto my leg. I didn't move, hardly breathed, but it didn't seem super skittish. I tilted my head to the side and looked at it and it tilted its head to the side and looked back at me.

"Am I silly for thinking that's you in there?" It hopped a bit around my leg, and I smiled. "Okay. I'll take that as a yes. What do *you* think of Harry, huh? Probably should have listened to my heart instead of my gut on this one. Darrien convinced me that you would want vengeance, but I can't blame it all on him. At the end of the day, I think I was hoping if I did it, I would feel better about losing you, but I don't. If anything, I feel worse. You're probably not proud of what I've been up to these past few months."

The bird on my leg bounded a little further up until it was close to standing on my thigh. It probably could have been the fact that people often fed the birds at the cemetery, but when I reached out and tried to pet it and it let me, I chose to believe that was because it was my dad in there. I stroked the feathers on its head, feeling how soft they were under my fingertips and smiled.

"I'm gonna fix it though. I wanted to come and apologize to you in person, or in bird, for hurting someone in your name. Harry didn't deserve that and neither did you. I only have about forty grand of your inheritance left, and I'm going to give it to Harry's boss to help pay his debt so that Harry can use his money for his sibling. I was gonna move it for rent, but Laura said that she'll cover rent for a couple months if I want to move in, so I'm going to move in with her. I hope Harry will forgive me one day. Do you think he will?" The bird hopped around a few times on my leg and then fluttered off and I nodded. "Yeah, I don't think so either."

I spent a little more time enjoying the fresh air and just sitting with my dad, and then when the sun started to crest over toward the horizon and begin its descent, I stood up, taking my blanket with me, and made my way back to my car. The thought of going to Hoppa's made me nervous, but it had to be done. I swung by the bank to pull out everything that was left of my inheritance money from my dad, packed it into an envelope and then set a course for the Taphouse.

The bar was packed with people, which was a good and bad thing. Those members who saw me walk in, immediately looked at me, and the entire energy shifted as I crossed the threshold. Nick was in the back, playing pool, and when he noticed me, he stood upright and glared at me from across the room.

Boldly, and though everyone was staring at me, I made my way through the crowd and over to the table. Nick was there, along with Avery, and another shorter member that I hadn't been introduced to before, and they were all giving me the stink eye. Part of me wanted to run, but I knew that I owed it to Harry to stick it out, so I cleared my throat.

"Nick, can I talk to you in private, please?"

Nick looked at Avery and then nodded toward the back, and then they both stopped playing pool and headed toward me. "Follow me, and if you touch anything, you'll be sorry," Nick said.

I'd seen Nick a handful of times around the bar and he always had a welcoming, jubilant energy. That was gone now that I was an enemy of his club. He led the way toward the bar, and Avery saddled up behind me, keeping an eye on me as I followed Nick. He led me around the bar and through a swinging door that led into the kitchen in the back of the bar. No one bat an eye as we walked through, and then Nick pushed through another swinging door that led into the warehouse Harry had brought me to before.

Nick walked over to the table and grabbed a chair and moved it to the middle of the warehouse. "Sit." I did as I was told, sitting down in the chair, and I could feel Avery looming behind me. Nick crossed his arms and shrugged. "Okay? What'd you wanna talk about?"

"I have some money for you," I said, handing over the envelope with the cash in it. "It's not the full fifty, but I can pay that off with my next couple of paychecks, or I can work the bars on my day off, whatever you want." Nick reached out for the envelope and I pulled it back. "Can you answer a question for me though?"

A scoff blew out of Nick's nose. "You're bold. Sure."

"Can you tell me about Darrien Pescoe?" I asked. "He prospected here but was turned down."

"Yeah," Nick said. "I remember it vividly. He was a lunatic. Short-tempered, especially in competitions, and when he did the bike race, he nearly killed himself and another one of the prospects just trying to win. He was reckless with his bike, so much so that it was steaming by the end. There was no way I was gonna admit him after that."

"Why do you ask?" Avery said from behind me.

"I'm his goddaughter," I replied, and Nick took a couple of steps back. "He wanted me to get revenge, just like what he was trying to do, and we both hurt Harry. He told me the accident was Harry's fault."

"Have you *seen* Harry on a bike?" Avery asked.

I nodded. "I know. I fucked up." I held out the envelope. "Please don't take that money from Harry. He needs it."

Nick snatched the envelope from me, handed it over to Avery and then knelt down in front of me. "I won't take any more money from him, but I'm not done with you yet. You hurt my club and my members and now you're gonna have to pay for it."

Chapter Twenty-Five

Bullet

Cameron and I sat in the waiting room at the bank, and I couldn't get my mind off of how badly things had gone, and how quickly. Just twenty-four hours ago, I was the happiest man in the world, and now, all of a sudden, I was the most lost I'd ever felt in my life.

Ruby.

My brain refused to let her go. What did she look like? What did she act like? I didn't even know how old she was. Would we get along or would she hate me? How would she feel about being moved from Florida all the way to Arizona? I didn't know any of the stuff I needed to in order to take a kid in. I didn't know what school I'd enroll her in or how to design a bedroom that she would like. On top of that, I'd avoided women for most of my life and knew very little about them. As she grew up, who was going to teach her all of the things that I couldn't teach her? Would she forgive me for being a dunce when it came to some of the stuff she'd need to know?

"What are you thinking about?" Cameron asked.

"Ruby," I said. "I wish I could go get her."

"Yeah. You know what I was thinking?" Cameron said. "I have some money saved up. It's not as much as we have now, and we'd probably have to add to it, but it'd be enough to get us started. I was going to use it to buy Marisha a ring, but she'll understand. She doesn't want a big wedding, she's always talked about just tying the knot at the courthouse, so it wouldn't take me too long. Another six months maybe?"

After everything he'd already given up for me, my father was still so selfless. "I can't allow you to do that. You've already waited so long to be with Marisha. Even longer than you wanted to because I dragged my ass about meeting her. You're ready to propose and now you can't again because of a mistake I made?"

"First of all, I'm not letting you take this all on yourself. You had no idea Celia was doing what she was doing. You didn't know she was going to take money from the club, and you certainly have no control over your mother making more children that she can't take care of. You're just doing your best, Harry, and I'm your dad. if I want to help you, let me. There's a little girl out there who needs us, needs you. Marisha and I can wait. It'll be worth it."

I bit down on the inside of my cheek to keep from crying. The thought that my dad would be willing to continue to make sacrifices for me was an emotional thing. "I'll pay you back every dime, I swear."

He smiled. "I'll send you the link for the ring. If we can just get there, that's all I care about."

I nodded. "Deal." I wrapped my arms around him and gave him a huge hug, and a few tears did slip out. "I love you, Dad."

"I love you, too." We released ourselves from one another just as a banker was walking up to us. She looked a little uncomfortable, gathering that she'd approached at a bad time, but Cameron waved her off. "Just sharing a hug with my kid. You're all good."

"Great, well come on back and I'll help you guys get this withdrawal processed."

We followed her back into a private office, and because of the size of the withdrawal, we had to sign some paperwork saying that we intended to pull out the amount that we did, to verify our identity, and to ensure we were both approving the withdrawal, as both of our names were on the account the money was in. It was much more paperwork than I was happy with. I was hoping to get to the Taphouse before sunset so I didn't bump into too many people dropping off the cash and my keys, but the sky was already turning to night, and it seemed I wouldn't be getting that wish.

We were nearing the end of the transaction when I got a phone call. I ignored it, thinking that the only person who could call me that I cared about overwhelmingly at the moment was Cameron and he was right next to me, but the second the phone stopped ringing, there was a brief pause, and then it rang again.

"What the heck?" I pulled it out and saw that it was Nick calling me. "Sorry," I said.

"That's okay," the banker replied.

I stood up from the chair and walked out into the lobby of the bank, which was mostly empty, as the bank was near closing. "Hello?"

"Hey there, Bullet. Got a visitor here that you might be interested in," Nick replied. Immediately after that, I could hear kicking and screaming, followed by a hollow shout of my name before the voice got cut off, it sounded like, by someone covering their mouth. "Recognize anyone?"

"What are you doing to Celia?" I growled.

"It's simple, really," he replied. "She wandered in here with a wad of cash, but it only covered some of your debt. She begged me not to take any money from you and told me she'd do whatever it took to pay off the other half. I'm wondering what you think we should do with her."

"Nick, don't, I'm getting your money right now. Don't hurt her. I'm begging you." It was uncharacteristic for Nick to be so brutal, but he'd shown us that he was capable of it if the situation called for it. I didn't think some fudged numbers would upset him so badly, but maybe he was finally cracking after losing his kids. "Please, just give me another hour."

"Oh, Bullet, I just don't think that's gonna work. See, I keep doing this thing where I trust people and go easy on people, and I keep getting walked all over. This one here..." There was another round of screaming before her voice got cut off again. "She cost me fifty grand *and* my

VP. So, the way I see it, she needs to pay for her meddling."

"Nick, don't you—" The line cut off before I could finish. "Shit!" I bolted back into the bank, snatched my dad's keys off the desk, and ran out. "I'll pay for your Uber. It's an emergency!"

"Harry!" Cameron called after me.

"Just get the money! I'll call you later!"

I ran out to where his car was parked and was relieved that I thought to bring my gun with me when we left the house. Celia was dead center in my mind, and I was cursing her quietly for going there alone. Maybe she was trying to make up for what she did, but these guys weren't just friendly office coworkers. If anything happened to her, I didn't know what I would do, and I was grateful for a cop-free highway as I zoomed down the road to get to the Taphouse.

A loud screech emanated from the car as I whipped it into the Taphouse parking lot, circling around to the back. I still had my keys, so I used mine to get the back door open, cocked my gun, and ran in. Celia was sitting in a chair in the middle of the warehouse, tied to the chair with rope, and with her mouth bound by duct tape. She started trying to call out to me the second she saw me but couldn't. I ran toward her, but when I got close enough, Nick stepped out from the shadows and stood behind her.

"She sure is pretty, Harry," Nick said.

"Look, I'm getting your money, you don't have to do this," I said.

"No, I think I do, Harry. If I don't make an example out of someone, people are just going to continue to do what they want around here, and I can't have that. We're expanding, we're getting bigger, and if your little lady here is going to cause problems for that, she's gotta be stopped."

"She won't cause problems," I said. "Let her go."

"I don't think I will," Nick replied.

I pointed my gun straight at him and Celia's eyes widened. "You're *going* to let her go. Your money I can get, but if you hurt her, I won't stop until you and every single member of the Steel Knights are dead."

Nick looked back over his shoulder. "Did you get that?"

Avery stepped out from behind some filing cabinets with his phone in hand. "Got it, Squared." He walked over and showed his phone to Nick. "Wait, look at this part again. Look at his face."

Nick and Avery stared down at the phone and I could hear my own voice playing back, threatening to kill Nick. "Yeah, that's good. You know, Harry, you could have had an illustrious career as an actor." I looked down at Celia, but she just shook her head at me. Nick looked up, saw my gun outstretched, and waved a hand. "All right, put that thing down before you hurt someone." He leaned down and untied the rope binding Celia to her chair, then she brought her hands up and slowly peeled the duct tape off. "Sorry about that, sweetheart. It had to look believable."

"What's going on?" I snapped. Celia jumped up and ran over to me and I took an arm to push her behind me. "What is this?"

"An intervention maybe? I don't know. What would you call it, Avery?" Nick asked.

"I liked intervention," Avery said. "It's true."

"From one emotionally constipated person to two others, you needed some help. You obviously love each other, and yeah, she got a little misguided because of her crack-ass godfather, but he's contagious that way. Trust me, I know. Just…" He walked a little closer to us. "I lost my kids, you lost your dads," he said to Celia and me. "We don't need to lose anyone else. We gotta stick together in this world."

"So, Celia is free to go?" I asked.

"Yeah, I'm not crazy. Well, I am, just not in this specific situation," Nick replied.

"I don't know, Nicky," Avery said, "this was a little nuts."

"Eh, maybe, but I could tell these two were going to continue to be idiots. Hey." Nick held an envelope in the air, "I *am* keeping this money though," he said to Celia then looked at me, "and you're not quitting as VP, so go home and fuck or do whatever you have to do to get over that shit." He lifted my jacket off the chair and tossed it over to me. "You also owe me ten stacks."

"I'll bring it tomorrow," I grumbled.

"Good. Come on, Avery, let's go show everyone that video," Nick said.

"I think I can figure out how to cast it to the television," Avery said as they walked out.

Fair punishment.

Celia turned and faced me. "Wow. You really ran in here all heroic like and saved me."

"Yeah, well," I looked into her eyes, "I'm in love with you, so what are you gonna do?"

"Harry, I don't expect you to forgive me, but—"

Celia didn't even get the full statement out before I took her face in my hands and kissed her. For a minute there, I really thought Nick was going to hurt her and I panicked. I was so glad she was okay that it pushed everything out of my mind.

"I love you," I said. "I'm not sure what all this means for us, but I know I don't want to give up on this."

Celia shook her head. "All I've wanted is to just be with you without this ugly thing between us. I love you, too." She kissed me again and then pulled away. "Do we have to stay here?"

"No," I replied. "I also kind of stole my dad's car and left him at the bank, so I need to rectify that."

"Oh, let's do that," she said, "then let's go back to your place so you can re-enact busting in with your gun out to save me, because…" She smiled and licked her lips. "I need to be able to undress you immediately after you do it."

"Let's go quickly then."

I took her hand in mine and dragged her out of the warehouse through the back door, and we smiled, knowing that after the shit we'd been through together in just a few short months, surviving the rest of our lives should be a breeze.

Epilogue

Bullet

For the fact that a courthouse wedding was just that, it was far more beautiful than I expected it to be. Hoppa's City Hall was nestled right at the base of the mountains, so when standing outside, the backdrop was a picturesque scene of the sun kissing the peaks, and the red sand spanning the desert floor. The sun was setting, and I couldn't stop myself from taking a thousand pictures as Cameron and Marisha stood face to face, holding hands, and beaming as the pastor performed his small ceremony.

Cameron was wearing a suit and Marisha, a white sundress that was flowing in the evening wind. They looked so in love, it brought a tear to my eye and I was happy I'd met Marisha when I did so that she and my dad didn't have to spend another single day apart. He'd proposed within a month of my approving of her, moved her in a week later, and just shy of a six-month engagement, the two were tying the knot at the courthouse. They had their license, now they were just exchanging a few vows before making it official.

Celia and I were standing hand in hand a few feet back from where Cameron and Marisha were. Close enough to hear, but far enough for them to have their moment.

"I don't want to do that," Celia said. "I want a big, expensive wedding."

I side-glanced her. "Really?"

"Yeah. I've changed a grown man's diapers. When that day comes, I want it to be all about me and my future husband, and I want it to be the most luxurious thing we can afford." She looked back at me. "That's not a dealbreaker, is it?"

I smiled at her. "Nope. If a big, expensive wedding is what you want, a big, expensive wedding is what you shall have. I guess I'd better start saving up, huh?"

"What makes you think I'm marrying you? I barely even like you," Celia joked, and I rolled my eyes. She laughed. "In all honesty, as corny as it sounds, I wouldn't really care what we did."

"What do you mean?"

She shrugged. "I'm not going to be able to focus on much else besides you."

It made my heart skip a beat. "You have traveled far from being afraid of commitment."

"Well, I wouldn't have stuck with you for this long if I wasn't committed to it. It's not like our one-year anniversary is too far away," she replied.

"What date are you basing it off of, the very first one, the one we went on after you ghosted me, the one we went on after you ghosted me the second time, or the one we went on after you told all your friends we were just fuck buddies?" I asked.

She glared at me. "Are you done?"

"No, I'm legitimately curious."

She scoffed. "For your information, I'm not basing it off of any of that."

"No? What are you basing it off of then?" I asked.

A small grin brushed across her face. "I'm basing it off of the first time you told me you were falling for me. The night we had dinner with Laura."

"Ah. "So, the date we had after the fuck buddy incident."

"I'm gonna walk away from you," she snapped.

I laughed and pulled her a little closer to me. "Nope, I won't be letting go of you ever again."

The pastor declared Cameron and Marisha married after they exchanged their vows, and we congratulated them, signing their wedding certificate as witnesses, and then took a few pictures together to celebrate the moment. Cameron looked the happiest I'd ever seen him in his life, and I was glad after everything he'd given up that he was finally getting his happy ending.

"You guys gotta head to the airport soon, right?" Marisha asked. "What time does Ruby get here?"

"Three PM," Celia and I replied in unison.

"Are you nervous?" Cameron asked.

"Yes," we said in unison again.

"Oh, you guys are going to be great," Marisha said. "Ruby is going to have two wonderful new role models, and the happy life that every ten-year-old deserves."

"I helped Harry and now he's gonna help his younger sister, that makes me so happy," Cameron said.

"You know, she's my sister, but I'll kind of be raising her like my kid, which means you two are the youngest, hottest grandparents around."

Marisha rubbed Cameron's chest. "Ooh, sexy grandpa."

Celia nodded. "And with that, I think it's time for us to go."

We gave the newlyweds a final round of hugs and kisses before heading off to the airport. We were taking Celia's car to be able to fit Ruby and her luggage, but I was hopeful I'd be able to get Ruby out for a safe ride on the bike once she got settled and comfortable.

"I didn't lie," Celia said. "I'm *super* nervous. I have to be a good influence on this kid. I don't even think I know *how* to be a good influence."

I laughed. "You're gonna be fine, it's me I'm worried about. I don't know anything about little girls. Do ten-year-olds already have their periods? What do I do when that happens?"

"You call me, and never, ever, ever, try and talk about it with her," Celia said, "or tell her to calm down, because if she bites your head off, I will applaud her."

"It's gonna change things for us, too, you know?" I said. "I'm a dad now, kind of."

"Yeah, well, it'll be good practice." Celia quickly threw up her finger. "For way down the road, I'm talking *way* down the road, and besides, we're good. I'm not going anywhere. You know that. We talked about moving in together around a year, and I'm… still okay with that plan."

"Good," I said. "What about Darrien?"

Celia shook her head with a little shrug. "I'm officially cutting him out of my life. I tried making peace with him after I moved back in with Laura, but he's committed to staying in that damn wheelchair like he's actually paralyzed and blaming you and the Steel Knights for his issues. Last time I saw him, he said it's a choice between him or you, so I chose you. It wasn't a tough choice."

But I knew that was a lie. Despite what he'd done to her, Darrien was Celia's only remaining family and memory of her dad. She'd tried her hardest to make amends with the man after things calmed down, because deep down, I knew she didn't want to lose him.

"Well, obviously we can't have him around Ruby, but I'm okay continuing to try," I said. "I know you love him."

Celia smiled at me. "Your kindness is so much more than he deserves, but yeah. I'd like to try at least a little more before I give up entirely. Thanks."

"Yeah."

We parked our car and made our way into the airport that Ruby was flying into in Phoenix. We were a little early, so Celia dragged me into a gift shop to buy a stuffed animal and some flowers to greet her with. Ruby and I had spoken over the phone a few times, and I'd seen a picture of her. I thought she'd seen one of me as well. Flight staff were getting her from the plane to the gate, so all I had to do was wait there. Both Celia and I were shifting nervously, until finally, someone called out.

"Harry?" said a sweet, young voice.

Celia and I looked over, and all of my fears went flying from my body. Walking with the flight staff was a girl so much more adorable than the pictures I'd seen. She had shoulder-length auburn hair and glowing violet eyes. She looked a lot like me.

"Oh wow, she's so cute," Celia whispered.

I walked up and Ruby pulled away from the flight staff and ran toward me. Such a warm welcome was far from expected, but I wasn't about to turn it down. I opened my arms, and she ran right into them, squeezing me.

"Thank you for adopting me," she said. "I'm happy."

It broke my heart a little, imagining what my mom must have done to her to elicit that kind of response, but it didn't matter. My mom was behind bars for a long time, and I was going to see to it that this little girl got everything in the world that she deserved.

"I'm happy, too," I said. "Hey, can I introduce you to someone?" I held out an arm toward Celia. "This is Celia, my girlfriend."

Ruby's eyes widened. "Wow. She's so pretty!"

Celia melted. "Hey, Harry, remember that one year we talked about?"

"Yeah," I said.

"Yeah, I'm not gonna make it that long."

It hadn't taken long for Ruby to have us eating out of the palm of her hand. "Well, then I guess it's time for us all to head home...." I kissed the top of Ruby's head and Celia's cheek. "Together."

BOOK 3

HARD BULLSEYE

Chapter One

Bullseye

"Move!"

"No way, man! No freaking way!"

"No!"

Looking down the sight of my gun, I find the bullseye, exhale softly, and then, closing my eyes and firming my grip on my Ruger twenty-two, I squeeze the trigger.

Bang!

There it is. That delicious rush of adrenaline with a chaser of pure bliss. The smell of metal and the sound of casings hitting the concrete lull me into a state of peace. This, even more than being on my bike, is the one feeling that helps me forget the date and that night. Even if it's just for a fraction of a second—point-zero-seven seconds to be exact—when I'm shooting my Ruger with a muzzle velocity of a thousand-and-seventy feet per second, a distance of twenty-five yards.

Damn. I need to get laid. It's been way too long.

But what's getting laid going to do? Yeah, maybe a woman—the right woman—could set me straight for an hour or two, but nothing compares to the range long-term. And where am I going to find the right woman, anyway? Sure as hell not in Hoppa, Arizona. And that's okay. Hoppa has other things to offer. Like the fact that it's over two thousand miles away from New York City, and it's the home of the Steel Knights.

Just thinking of the Knights brings a welcome calm over me, which is good because today is September thirtieth, and that date is making me damned jumpy.

Taking a deep breath of the heavy, metallic air calms my brain. I don't bother looking at my target; no doubt it's a bullseye. They always are. Instead, I stay motionless, with my eyes closed, my feet still in a hips-width position, my arms bowed slightly for greater flexibility, commanding my heart rate to slow and the "fight or flight" instinct to quell. It doesn't matter that I've shot for nearly all of my twenty-six years of life, or that the guys call me "Bullseye…"

Every single time I squeeze that trigger is like the first time all over again.

Like I'm a damned virgin.

A stupid kid.

"Move!"

"No way, man! No freaking way!"

"No!"

Stupid kid.

What the hell was he doing there? And in the middle of a Bordono mob hit? The image of that damned kid, huddled in a corner, crouching down on the piss-soaked rug with his hands stuck to his ears like they were plastered there, will never leave me.

That one night, it was like everything moved in slow motion. Why was the kid even there? He must have been brought in by Mikey and Tony. I was commissioned to work alone, and I was only supposed to scare the scrappy, punk druggy who owed the Don a hell of a lot. Standing in the hallway outside the door with my gun drawn, I knew something was wrong. I could taste the acid in my mouth and feel the swirling unease in my gut. But what choice did I have? This was a favor for Don Bordono.

Sliding in through the cracked open door, I nearly doubled over from the smell of piss and feces. Forcing my stomach to calm, I saw them in the next room—the damned target, begging for his life, with Mikey and Tony laughing as they pointed their guns at him.

Whimpering pulled my attention off of the target—a cardinal sin in my old line of work—and that was when I saw the kid crouching in the corner.

Bang!

Even with a silencer, Mikey and Tony's guns were deafening in the small apartment. Don Bordono was going to be pissed.

"Police!" They were rushing up the stairs. It would only be a matter of seconds…

Damn it. A bad hit all around. Panicking, Mikey and Tony tossed their weapons at the foot of the kid.

"Kid!" I whispered as the police barreled in behind us. I was going to tell him to go, to jump out the window—risk the damned broken ankle—and run, but it was too late. Placing my piece on the floor, I raised my arms high in the air. I was going to go down, so there was no sense fighting it. Especially since I was there for Don Bordono, and once he knew what was happening, he'd be sure to fix it.

But Mikey and Tony decided to split. Scrambling across the floor in that pigsty on St. Mark's, crawling over needles, roach clips, spoons, and bongs that cracked under their weight, they clawed their way to a window. They were like two rats gnawing at each other so they could get off a sinking ship.

Maybe if that stupid kid had run and not sat there shaking with the literal smoking guns at his feet, maybe he'd be out today, too and not in for a murder he certainly did not commit.

I'm sorry for him, but it's not my problem.

Christ. My brain's a cluttered mess. I'm no good at handling a crapload of thoughts at once. No man is. The way a woman can multitask like Tess did, Nick's kid, our old VP, is astounding. She brainstormed the expansion of our organization while handling a world of shit, and frankly, that would just be impossible for most men. At least it is to a guy like me. I see straight and shoot straight.

Pushing the damned image of that night and the kid from my mind, I set up to unload my magazine. Forget the rush of hormones, unloading twenty-five rounds will feel damned near orgasmic.

I need the release because today is September thirtieth. The day Mikey and Tony are freed. The last time I saw them, I was walking out of Sing Sing, free after only six months on my three-year sentence. I'll never forget the look in their eyes as they peered out from their cages…

"Avery Fucking Pairings," they snarled and spat as I hurried past, a free man, thanks to the fact that Don Bordono likes me and called in some favors.

"One day, when we're out of here and find you, you'll wish you were still in this hellhole." Mikey sneered. His fleshy cheeks covered most of his eyes when he smiled.

"That's a promise," Tony added, flipping me the bird on the hand with only four fingers. He'd lost his pinkie during an initiation into the Bordono family.

An unease churns in my gut.

Yeah, okay, Mikey and Tony don't scare me. They're low-level thugs who work directly for a dealer, Ironclad, who works for *my* old boss and my father's boss, Bordono. But… small men with big vendettas can do stupid things. And they swore to me they'd seek vengeance on me and anyone I loved.

That's why I'm hiding out here, in Hoppa. Fortunately—and unfortunately—"anyone I love" doesn't mean my old man so much anymore, since he's still back on Long Island and on Mikey and Tony's turf. But even if they did come looking for him, my old man is in so deep with Bordono, he's mostly untouchable.

However, "anyone I love" does mean Nick, the founder and President of the Steel Knights, Harry, my best friend since college, and the guys at the club. Yeah, the guys can sure as hell take care of themselves if they have to. They've proven that just with this last raid from the Unchained Dogs when the scum tried to hit us on our turf. Sure, we had injuries, but we held off and chased them back.

But now that we're down men—and woman, counting Tess—we're in a tough spot. I don't care that some of the guys, including Harry, didn't like her much, I thought she had some good ideas. And her guy that she brought in—CJ—may have once been a Dog, but damn, the man could fight. He was a good man to have on our side. Even Nick's son, Taylor, who was a total psychopath, was at least another body—and one who was happy to kill.

So, now we're light. That's why, even though opening up the club to new prospects can be risky, it's the only way. We need members.

Boom! Boom! Boom!

What the hell? Spinning around, but still behind my partition, I glance at the lane on the opposite side of the range. Who the hell is that? Jackson, the guy who runs this range, promised I'd be here alone. I'm always alone at this hour.

Glancing farther around the partition, I see her. Wow. No wonder Jackson let her in. Even in her mandatory goggles and ear protection, she is all female. She's got short wavy hair that falls to one side, and in her deep purple fitted shirt that covers her from neck to waist, hugging all her impressive curves, she is damned sexy.

Boom!

Fighting to hold back a chuckle, I can't help the traitorous grin that escapes. Starting at one corner of my mouth, it spreads like wildfire across my lips, but I've got to control it. It's my usual charming smile, the one that gets me out of trouble more often than it gets me in, but still.

No, I don't know her in the least, but something tells me this is not a woman to mess with, especially when she's holding a loaded pistol. Yet I want to see more.

"Never step out of the lane with your finger on the trigger. Stay put." My father's words are swimming in my brain. He's right. You never put yourself, or anyone else, at risk by stepping backward or worse, forward around the partition. And you never move with your finger on the trigger.

Of course, as I grew older, I learned that saying was actually Bordono code for, "Stay put." Thankfully, since I ran to Hoppa, I haven't had any need for the Bordono crime family's codes or sharpshooting. And I intend to keep it that way.

And I also intend to catch some more of her…

Placing my pistol on the table with the muzzle toward my mark, I step back around my partition and hang just in the hallway, where I can get a better look at her.

From the safety of the hallway, I watch her. Her body isn't all that thin, but it's lean, and strong, and toned. *Boom!* When she shoots, her arms are ramrod straight, but that's an easy adjustment to make on an experienced shooter, and, looking down her lane to see she's hit her target multiple times, it's obvious she is that.

My gaze drops to her butt in her skintight black leather pants. Firm and high and round… Yup, I was right. All female. As she squeezes the trigger, her—

"Hey!" Whipping her head around, but keeping her gun on the target ahead of her, she catches me. I'll be damned, the entire side of her head is shaved.

This girl is hot shit.

"Don't be a perv," she snaps, and turning her head forward once more, she unloads the rest of her magazine.

Chuckling, I step back into my alley. Standing behind her in my long-sleeved black shirt and black jeans with black high combat boots, I probably did look like a perv.

Picking up my piece, a cocky grin sweeps across my face. She's a pretty good shot. But now, it's time to school her on how a master marksman shoots. One who's grown up on the fringes of a crime family, with a sharpshooter for a father.

Gripping the gun high on the backstrap, I wrap my left hand around the remainder of the grip. With the backs of my hands interlocking like a puzzle piece, and my feet at hips' width, I lift my arms and peer down the sight. None of these checks are necessary, this is all second nature to me now. I'm like a professional athlete when I shoot a gun, but something about being near *this woman* makes me want to go through all the motions.

Lining up my mark, I take a deep breath and, on my exhale…

How tight is that little body? And what color are her ey—

Bang!

What the…? I missed.

Looking down the alley, I shake my head in disbelief. No, most people may not care that I nicked the first ring outside of the splatter target's bullseye, but I'm not most people.

When I was in with the Bordonos for that year straight out of college, a mistake like this could have meant life or death. *My* life or death. What if my mark was more than seventy-five feet away, and I only had a second to kill him or be killed?

I let myself get distracted by a sexy woman, and it could have cost me my life. And that is the reason I can never be involved with a woman long-term. Women are a distraction I don't need. And more than that, I can't drag a woman into my world. Yeah, sure, I'm clean and my record was wiped, which was how I cleared the background check when I pledged with the Knights but is anybody ever really out? What happens if my old man needs something or stumbles deeper into debt, and Bordono decides that I need to work it off?

No. *Focus, Bullseye, focus.*

Staring down the sight again, I take another shot.

Bang!

Holy Mother. I missed, again. And this time it's outside the line. It'll be even harder to make it seem like I did it on purpose.

"Well, well, well…"

Placing my gun down, I wheel around and catch Clyde, a member of our filthy rival group, Unchained Dogs, waltzing in, clapping and howling over my missed shot.

"Nice shot, Bullseye!"

Warmth creeps up my spine, and I growl under my breath. A fail is bad, but a fail in front of this guy, and her, is unbearable.

Glancing quickly at the door to see if any more of his pack is with him, I consider keeping my weapon. Since he's alone, I put it down. When this standoff is over, Jackson is sure going to have a hell of a lot of explaining to do…

"What the hell do you want, Clyde?" I ask through gritted teeth. The tension in my jaw is creeping down into my shoulders, and I take deep breaths to fight it back. "What are you doing on Knights' turf? You got a death wish?"

Stepping into the hallway, I fight against my concerns as a bead of sweat trickles down my forehead. Was I just played? Did I let myself get sidetracked? Did the damned Dogs send this goddess in here to distract me?

Glancing at her in her lane, she's changed. Her stance is less confident, and she suddenly appears smaller and weaker. She stays as still as she can, like she's trying not to draw attention to herself. She's nervous. Does she know something's about to go down? Or have the two of us intimidated her?

"I asked you a question, Clyde." My voice is calm, and I keep it steady.

If I'm getting ambushed, might as well let them know who they're playing with.

She begins packing up her gear, and relief washes over me, like a million pounds fall away. She's not part of the sabotage, if that's what this is. But now, that means I have to protect her. Yeah, she's just some random girl at my range, albeit a sexy as hell girl, but women deserve our respect, and it's up to men like me to protect them from scum like the Unchained Dogs.

"I came with a message." He's chewing something stuck in the side of his cheek.

"Here?" Holding up my hands, I stand up to my full six-feet-three frame.

"You got a better place?"

In his colors and jacket, he's definitely here on official business. Being thin and at maybe five-eleven, Clyde's significantly smaller than me, and with the streaks of gray he has lining his full beard and long, wavy hair, he's also significantly older. It would be an easy fight for me, but these damned Dogs can't be trusted. All I need is for him to pull out a blade and try to slit my throat for fun.

"How about Hoppa's Taphouse?"

Clyde looks down at the ground and spits a wad of tobacco. "You expect me to go waltzing into the clubhouse of the Steel Knights? Shit." He jams the floor with the toe of his boot. "I'd never get past the parking lot with the insignia of the Dog in broken chains on my bike."

"That's true. You would have had the crap beaten out of you before you made it to the front door. So? You're here now. What's the message?"

"In a moment, I think I'm going to take in the scenery first."

Turning, he leers at the woman who's standing to the side of her lane and licks his lips. "That is one hot piece of ass…" Grinning, he steps closer to her. "Hey, why don't you come over here and sit on my lap—"

Before I know what I'm doing, I grab Clyde by the collar of his jacket and lift him into the air, holding him a good foot off the ground.

"Storytime is over. Now, you're gonna talk, while I beat the shit out of you."

Chapter Two

Wildfire

I'm a stalker now. There's no other way to look at it. Great. I'm adding stalking to my ever-growing list of winning behaviors.

I heard through the grapevine that Avery "Bullseye" Pairings shoots at this range, and I came to find him, even though he has no idea who I am and what I want. But being the new kid in town leaves me no choice. I just didn't expect to get lucky enough to catch him my first time out.

I also didn't expect him to look like *that*. With wide shoulders, a tall, lean body, short dark brown hair, and from this distance, what looks like light-colored eyes, I'd heard he was straight-up, old-school handsome.

Handsome is one thing. This is hot.

And okay, so maybe I'm not being completely upfront, but today, September thirtieth, may qualify as an emergency, and extreme times call for extreme measures.

Getting in here wasn't difficult. The guy, Jackson, who runs the place, gave me the once-over, told me Bullseye was here, and sent me in. Not such great security, but looking at Avery, I'm assuming he really doesn't need protection. He could handle anything that's sent his way.

Maybe even me. Seneca "Wildfire" Villetrio.

No. *Focus, Seneca. You're here for one reason, to impress him with your shooting skills and then convince him he needs to let you pledge for the Steel Knights.*

The Steel Knights, Avery's club, has a good rep with how they treat women—certainly in comparison to their rivals, the Unchained Dogs, or any of the clubs back home that are run by that asshole, Ironclad. There's no nasty, sexist initiation for women, and we're not considered property to be handed off or traded. Not that I'd put up with that crap.

Yeah, there's talk that the Steel Knights has a member who has the President's ear, and this guy hated the past VP, Tess I think her name was, but apparently, he hates all women. Well, I'm sorry for him, because that sure as shit won't keep me away.

As discreetly as I can, I glance at Avery and my confidence soars. Yes, he's just the Treasurer, and that doesn't make him a decision-maker per se, not like their President, Nick Nicholas, or "Squared," as they call him, but rumor has it that Avery is the one who really likes women. As in, respects them. If I'm going to play in the big leagues and get a club to allow me to pledge, this guy is the way in.

However, I've also heard that he's so damned charming, he can get a woman to flop onto her back just by smiling at her. So, I'm going to walk a straight line. The last thing I need is the complication of a man.

Staring into my gear bag at my singular pistol, that damned melancholy feeling washes down over me. *No, no, not now!* Since I left my parents' house and Matt was sent to jail, a cloud of depression has followed me everywhere. I am completely alone, worrying about him.

The only time I've come close to not thinking about Matt is when I'm riding. Turning the throttle and releasing the clutch, the roar of the pipes drowns out my anxious mind. As I sail faster and faster over gravel and dirt, holding—no, *commanding*—the bike to do as I say, for those few moments, my mind is at peace.

But as soon as my feet hit the ground, I see Matt, first at twelve years old, jumping his prize-winning horse, and then now, at twenty-two in a brown jumpsuit stamped with, "Ossining Inmate." How did this happen?

No. There's no time for this now. I can't let that affect me. Not before a performance.

Opening my bag and popping the top of the case reveals the gun pointing toward me. Uh-uh. I may be here to show off, but I'm not stupid. Spinning the bag in a one-eighty, I remove my weapon from its case and run a quick safety check. Aiming the piece away from me and Bullseye over there, I check the safety is on. Tapping the magazine floor plate and using my dominant hand, I release the slide and then let it return.

This is my chance. Who knows when he'll see me ride? With the speeds we move and the zigzagging in and out of traffic, I may lose him, leaving him in my dust before he even notices me.

Taking a deep breath, I release it slowly through my nose. Shooting isn't as natural to me as riding, but I'm still pretty good. Word is the Knights have had some recent trouble with the Dogs, and they could use a shooter like me. Adjusting and securing my ear protection, I take a few more cleansing breaths to slow my racing heart. Then, I lift and point at the target. It can't be more than twenty-five yards away. I can do this.

This is your chance, Seneca. You need this club. You need this protection.

Maybe it's selfish to come into a club carrying so much baggage, but right now, feeling how I do on this particular day, I just can't worry about that. I need them. Besides, it's not like I come empty-handed. I bring skills. Not only can I ride like the wind and shoot, but I can fix anything on two wheels.

It's time for Bullseye to see almost all of what I have to offer. Steadying myself with a deep breath…

Boom! I follow up one shot with two more.

Not bad. I've nicked the right side of the target's bullseye and then landed a few shots farther to the right. If that were a person, it'd be just about at the left side of the heart. Enough to get the job done, for sure. Glancing over, I can see more of him from behind his partition. He's stepped back and out of his ready stance. I have his attention. Now, I need to impress the hell out of him.

It's odd. On the one hand, my anxious gut that's been on edge since I arrived in Hoppa a few days ago is calming down, like a dose of his masculine, protective energy is wafting over to comfort me, but at the same time, my heart's racing.

And the truth is, I don't need—and sure as hell don't want—some neanderthal to come charging into my life and pissing all over my property claiming me as his. I need backup. Just in case.

What I didn't plan was my next step after he saw me shoot…

I strike again. Better. Even closer to the center of the chest.

And again.

I can feel him behind me, hovering in the hallway—checking out my ass. Well, I guess whatever works. But one thing's for certain, as much as I want into the Knights, I sure as shit won't be somebody's old lady, and I'm not joining Steel Knights to be one of the WAGs hanging off someone's arm and acting like a brainless bimbo. I want in on my merit. Just like Tess before me.

With my gun facing the target, I pivot around and snap at him. "Don't be a perv." Turning back, I unload the rest of my magazine.

He disappears into his lane.

Bang!

Sure, it's his turn to show me up, but…holy crap. Squinting, I stare down his lane and at his target. He missed. Not massively, but the bullet hole is not where the others were before it. What happened to the man who could shoot a bullet through the eye of a needle?

I turn away, making myself look busy with some stuff in my bag. The last thing I want to do is to embarrass the guy.

I hear the sound of another bullet hitting the target.

Peeking over my shoulder and down his lane, it's like I'm watching a horror movie from behind my hands. I don't want to look. But I have to.

Jeez, this one's worse. Well, one thing's for sure, he won't want to keep me around as his good luck charm, that's for damned sure.

"Well, well, well…"

Looking around and toward the door, I catch some scummy-looking guy with long, filthy hair, wearing a jacket with an Unchained Dogs insignia, sauntter in. He's howling like a damned wolf.

"Nice shot, Bullseye!"

Glancing at Avery, I notice he's holding himself tighter and stiffer. He's expecting a confrontation. This isn't going to be good.

My gut's churning with unease again. Watching them, I can tell the damned Dog won't make a move on Avery. He's too small and too weak. But their conversation is growing more and more intense, and Bullseye is pushing the punk for whatever message he brings. Then, the damned Dog turns to me.

"…I think I'm going to take in the scenery first."

Knitting my eyebrows and dropping my chin, I prepare myself for war. *Forget you, asshole.*

My hands ball into fists as my body relaxes and readies itself. Right now, I am itching to use every single cross-body punch, elbow strike, eye strike, hook punch, and headbutt I've learned in my years of studying Krav Maga. Come on, asshole. Just try.

"That is one hot piece of ass…"

Piece of ass? His damned smile widens from ear to ear, and he steps even closer to me. My teeth clench and I bear down, ready to spring and fight. It's all I can do not to pick up my gun and take him out, but one murder charge in the family is enough.

"Hey, why don't you come over here and sit on my lap—"

That's it. Before I can react, Bullseye grabs the Dog by the collar of his jacket and lifts him into the air, holding him off the ground. The Dog's feet dangle.

"Storytime is over. Now, you're gonna talk, while I beat the shit out of you."

Part of me is disappointed that I won't get to show Bullseye my hand-to-hand combat skills, but I know better than to interrupt. Letting go of his collar, Bullseye drops the Dog who crumples on impact. Placing one hand on his chest, he tries to straighten himself.

"This isn't going to help you, Bullseye." The Dog snaps. "All the Dogs know. You're low on men. We know your membership is down. Even that sweet piece of ass, Tess, is gone. Heard she was something with those brass knuckles of hers. Wouldn't mind being on the receiving end of that one time."

With a lightning-fast jab, Bullseye lands a punch on the Dog's cheek, and he staggers back.

"Hey!" Shaking his head, he snarls at Avery. "This was supposed to be a friendly meeting."

"Friendly?"

Avery strikes him again, this time in the gut, and the Dog doubles over, clutching his stomach and gasping for air.

"This is friendly. If I were to throw a punch at you with even a fraction of my true strength, you'd be dead."

Watching the Dog writhing on the ground, I believe it.

"You can't kill me, Bullseye. It'll be war. You know the rules. You can't kill me when I come with a message. Or have you forgotten everything since that 'walking rulebook' freak Taylor bit the dust?"

One more quick punch to the stomach drops the Dog onto his seat. With bent knees, he scrambles back against the wall.

"What do you care, man? Taylor was insane!"

"Yes, he was," Avery replies. "But he was also a Knight. And our President's son. Show some respect."

The Dog spits in the Steel Knight's direction, and Avery rushes up to him, hovering above. "What's your damned message?"

The man glares up at him, as Avery kicks him with the heel of his boot. That's got to hurt.

"Tell me."

"The message is…" The Dog gasps for a breath. "We know you're low on men, and the next time we attack, you won't be so lucky."

"Is that a threat?"

"A warning. Now, you don't have that damned fighting machine who ran off with your President's daughter, and your membership is low…maybe the Knights have had their day."

"We'll be at capacity soon enough. And expanding. Don't you worry about us."

"Yeah? And where are your guys coming from?"

Avery uses the toe of his boot to poke the Dog. "Don't worry about us. We're recruiting. Matter of fact, we're hosting an open night for prospects. Tomorrow night at Hoppa's Taphouse. Wanna come?" A broad smile covers Avery's face.

"You know if we were to turn out, it would be war."

"Okay by me."

The Dog looks away, snarling, then spits again.

"We're expecting a shit-ton of men," Avery continues. "More than the Dogs would ever see. You've got no respect in the community. Only people who want to pledge with the Dogs are losers, like, well, you." Standing up straight, he crosses his arms and looks down, towering over the Dog.

With my bag held tightly to me, I sneak out of my lane that thankfully, is closest to the door. Hurrying past Jackson, I rush through the lobby and throwing myself against the cold brass of the door handle, I practically fall out into the cool night air.

I don't need to stick around for whatever comes next. I've gotten what I wanted. And then some. I was hoping Bullseye would notice me. Now, I have the opportunity to flat-out make him pay attention.

All I have to do is get a member to nominate me, so I can pledge for the Steel Knights.

With my heart racing, I glide my leg over my bike, and straddling it, throw it in neutral, depress the clutch, and shift into gear. With a short burnout, I take off, leaving the range behind me in a cloud of Arizona's fine reddish dirt.

Chapter Three

Bullseye

"Which one is Clyde?" Harry asks, spinning an empty bottle of beer between his huge palms while standing behind the bar at Hoppa's Taphouse. Maybe it's just me, but the energy in here is different tonight. It feels electric, like little zaps of electricity are shooting across the room. It's almost like the walls and floor know something's about to happen. Or maybe I'm just projecting.

"Clyde? Late forties. Skinny. Long hair." It's damn hard to sit still, so I sway back and forth on my stool on the opposite side of the bar. Around us, there's a commotion as some of the guys prep for our scouting event tonight. I'm toying with the corner of a bar napkin, anxious.

"Yeah." Tossing the bottle into the recycle bin in the far corner of the bar, Harry sighs. "I know him." He leans forward, resting his elbows on the bar. He looks at me, setting his eyes in that intense way he does.

Crumpling and then smoothing the napkin, I fidget. "What?"

He nods to my hands. "Bullseye. I have known you since college. I know everything there is to know about you."

I always wince internally when he says that, but I also know it's for his own good. Harry "Bullet" Booth does not need to know that I was mixed up with the Bordono Crime Family that year he thinks I was MIA playing house with some girl, and he sure as hell doesn't need to know I did time, was sprung early, and now, may very well have two thugs looking to kill me.

"You're weird tonight."

"Nah, I've just got to grab the monthlies for you. It's on my mind." I decide to change the subject. "Did you tell Nick about Clyde yet?"

Harry shakes his head and stands up straight. "Nah. And I've been with the man pretty much all damn day. And by all damn day, I mean since this morning. Not noon, the start of your day."

My eyebrows knit together as I try to figure it out. "Something up with the books, Mr. Bookkeeper?"

"No." He shakes his head. "Ever since this kid Seth has come on as a kind of honorary bookkeeper, things are easier. Kid's a whiz with numbers. Like, a real genius."

"Impressive," I say.

"Yeah…"

"What?" Peeling my napkin into shreds, I nod to Harry.

"He's just…a bit of a wildcard. And I'm never sure when he's going to blow, or what makes him blow."

"Well, shit, man. They call him 'Dynamite' for a reason," I point out.

"Yeah, I just don't think I want to find out the reason."

Chuckling, I look at the back room. "So, if Seth's good and you've got backup, why've you been here all day? The books?"

Shrugging, Harry looks at the counter and back up to me. "Nick and I, we've been working through some business. Tess had this model for expansion, she had some good ideas. Talked about twice as many officers for the club, new revenue streams, even ways for marketing, and eventually, higher salaries."

"Not bad for a woman, huh?" I tease.

Harry glares at me. "We'll talk about that later. Right now, we've got to get ready for tonight. Opening is soon. We're going to be exposing ourselves quite a bit with this open call we're hosting. Any one of those damned Dogs could infiltrate."

"Even if they do, what will they find out?" I shrug. "We vet all the candidates. And with the exception of CJ, everyone is a prospect for a least a year before they become a member. And it takes even longer to become an officer."

"Do me a favor." Harry levels his eyes on me again. "Don't mention CJ to Nick when we go talk to him about Clyde."

"You don't have to tell me twice. I know the man still feels sick he trusted him like he did. And I'm not talking to Nick, you are."

I grin, but Bullet doesn't take the bait. He's stoic.

"It's interesting who Nick decides to trust and who he doesn't."

I know what he's saying. Despite the fact that I'm an officer, Nick doesn't seem to trust me all that much. But the truth is, he shouldn't. Yes, I love the Knights and would kill for my brothers if I had to, but I'd really rather not. My killing days are behind me. And my plan is to never take another man's life, ever again.

Aside from that, I lied my way into the Steel Knights. Thanks to my connections with Don Bordono, my criminal record was expunged after my early release, and I never told the Knights, or Harry, that I was on the inside. A record is no big deal for the Steel Knights. Seth has done time, but the fact that I was—and my father is—connected to the Bordonos is trouble.

Don Bordono moves product through a couple of the motorcycle clubs back in the Tristate area of New York, and their leader, an asshole named Ironclad, would make trouble if he knew I was with the Knights. Even though we're two-thousand miles away.

Better just to stay clean. Especially now that Mikey and Tony are out and maybe looking for me.

"Bullet, you need to tell Nick about Clyde, while I go grab the monthlies."

"Shit." Bullet lifts his large frame up and begins ambling toward the back room. "I guess there's no time like the present."

"I know you hate social interaction," I tease as he makes his way into the back room, "but try not to hang out in there all night!"

He's gone.

Sighing, I let my heavy shoulders slump forward onto the bar and a searing pain shoots from my upper arm to the base of my skull when I do. But pain is okay. It helps me keep my mind from worrying about old business dealings, and new female possibilities.

Damn, who was that girl at the range last night? I've tried to stay busy all day today to keep my mind off of her, but it keeps making its way back. No, I can't blame her for taking off the way she did when the fight, or more accurately, the beating broke out, but I would have liked a chance to talk to her. Although… thinking about it, it's better I don't.

Lifting one arm and rotating in a circle, I try to work out the kinks from yesterday's shooting—and punching—sessions. My jacket bunches around me when I do, reminding me that Harry, and the rest of these guys, have my back.

As long as I stay in Hoppa and the hell away from New York, everything should be just fine.

Plopping the monthlies on the desk in front of Harry in the back room of Hoppa's Taphouse, I grin at him. "Even Nick's out front. What the hell are you still doing back here?"

After some obligatory chitchat where he grumbles about the noise and "all the commotion" like some grumpy grandfather, he finally stops what he's doing and looks up at me.

"Wait, what's going on?"

"*All* that commotion," I explain, "is hopefuls."

"What?"

Shoving his papers into a locked drawer, he follows me out to the bar area that must have at least dozens of hopefuls. Each of them seems happy and generally in good spirits. Don't seem like any punk-ass losers to worry about. The tight muscles in my neck relax. This is good. A good way to keep my mind off of my problems and onto club business.

The night passes fairly quickly. Yeah, this social crap is hard for Harry who kept disappearing into the back, but for me, it's a breeze. Despite the fact that I was raised by a hitman for the Bordonos, I actually *like* people. I find them interesting and enjoy hearing their stories.

I talked to person after person, sometimes with our Road Captain, Bucky, by my side, and sometimes alone. Bucky is like me. He enjoys getting to know people without divulging all that much about himself.

Spying this incredibly tall guy with slicked-back hair and a Mr. Monopoly type mustache hanging in the corner and nursing a beer by himself, I go over to talk to him. And damn, I'm glad I do. With a hearty handshake and a smile that lifts his cheeks and spreads from ear to ear, he introduces himself as Joey. As he starts blabbing away, I realize we have a shitload in common. Not the least of which is his taste in music, and that's when I know I've got to go tell Harry about him.

I stay for one more fairly well-delivered joke, and he has me laughing as Bucky and Vil, two of the Steel Knights members, join us. For a moment, I'm sidetracked. Vil's a cool guy, but with his face piercings, shredded black jeans, and mohawk hair, he looks like a punk rocker. Which, of course, makes me think of her. That hot girl from the range last night.

Would she be there again if I went back tonight? She definitely noticed me. She told me off, after all.

"Bullseye." Bucky's nodding to me. "Where'd you go?"

"Right here, sorry."

"Okay, but I think you missed that joke and it was freaking hilarious," he laughs.

"Going to check up on Harry, I'll be back in a second."

Excusing myself, I find Harry talking to some guy who briefly introduces himself as Mario. The guy looks like he's as uncomfortable as Harry is, and is grateful when he has the opportunity to make it back to the bar. The bar is packed now, with people buying drinks and standing in the parking lot to drink them. I knew our rep was good, I didn't know it was this good.

"Come on," I tell Harry, "you've got to come meet this guy, Joey. He's funny, and he's a huge Age of Logic fan."

"Seriously?"

"Yeah. Someone who loves the same music you do? You've got to meet him."

"Okay, let me just—"

"Bullet?" Turning back, I see what has his attention. Celia. The woman he likes, but who ghosted him.

"I'll be over with Joey," I tell Harry.

Getting away as fast as possible, I choose to hang again with Bucky, Vil, and Joey. Eyeing Harry, I can tell by his clenched jaw that he's seething. He's skirting Celia, who's making it her job to flirt with every man in the room. Okay, back to Joey. He'd make a good prospect. Nah, his jokes aren't all that funny, and I think he even screws up a punchline or two, but he's got genuinely good energy. And I'm pretty insightful about things like this. The guys tease me about it pretty regularly. Tell me I should have been a therapist. What none of them, except Harry knows, is that I wanted to be a high school science teacher. But that was a lifetime ago.

Forcing myself to concentrate on Joey, I glimpse Harry approaching with a scowl on his face.

"Bullet!" I clamp a hand on his shoulder. He looks like he needs a boost. Women. They are absolute trouble. "Oh, this is the guy I was telling you about, Bullet." I look at Harry. "Joey's a huge Age of Logic fan!"

"No kidding?"

Age of Logic plays at MiD, Music in the Desert, the fundraiser the Steel Knights and our allied clubs host in the desert every year. It's a cool coincidence and one that'll make Harry happy. And he deserves to be happy. Especially since he thought this girl Celia may be the one.

Harry excuses himself to the back room, and I spy Seth on his heels. Seems the expression, "God makes them and matches them," applies to work situations as well. Neither one of those men are all that into social situations. But it's nothing for me. Considering some of the situations I've been in, this one is rather enjoyable.

We finish our small talk with Joey, and I'm pretty sure he's getting a nomination. Another hour or so passes easily, but the masses are restless. Derek "Small Fry" Myers, one of the Steel Knights' non-officered members, shouts out, "Let's get to nominatin'!"

People clap and cheer and Nick holds out his hands and whistles to get everyone's attention. The crowd quiets down and gives Nick their attention. Again, that feeling of electricity hangs in the air.

"All right," Nick says. "Can I have all the *members* of the Steel Knights come stand behind the bar please?"

Moving forward, I join Nick, Harry, and Seth already behind the bar, and the rest of the guys pack in with us—Jonathan "Jonesie" Jones, Bucky, Texas, Small Fry, and Vil. In our heavy leather jackets in that confined space, we must look like one menacing and impenetrable wall.

I chuckle as Nick reminds us that a prospect needs a nomination and then a second to qualify. He announces the start of the nominations.

Surprising everyone, quiet, no-personality Seth, is the first to nominate.

"I nominate Colt Hardy."

"Colt?" Nick calls out, and Colt makes his way up front.

Although he isn't as tall as Seth and looks younger, they can be twins.

"Uh, there's gotta be a relation here, right?" Nick asks.

Okay, so I'm not the only one who notices it.

"Yes," Seth answers. "Colt's my brother."

Here we go. The energy shifts as everyone behind the bar swallows what he wants to say. Considering the disaster we just lived through with Tess, CJ, and Taylor, are we really going to welcome Seth's brother?

And Seth… Yeah, he's okay and great with numbers. Harry even mentioned that he's got connections back at his old job as a manager of a construction company, and he can get us a deal if our dream of a new, private clubhouse becomes a reality… But can we trust him? We don't know anything about him.

A searing pain rushes across my gut.

Maybe the man has secrets. I can respect that. It's not like I've been forthright.

Glancing at Seth, I decide. If Nick asks me, I'll second the nomination. I'm all about giving someone a chance.

And a second chance.

Nick mumbles uncomfortably, but Bucky steps up and vouches for Seth and Colt. Okay, that smooths it over.

The rest of the nominations are no surprise, but I'm done. I'm standing here behind the counter, sweating my balls off, and itching to get to the range. I "second" those I know, and nod along with those I don't.

Growing more and more restless, all I can think about is that woman. Who is she? And will she be there now? At the range?

Why do I care?

Thankfully, Nick begins wrapping things up, and there's a final call for any last nominations. An uncomfortable-looking Texas steps forward and immediately, my senses go on high alert. Why? I was the one who told the Dogs what we were doing here tonight. Are we about to be ambushed?

Without drawing any attention to myself, I reach for my piece that I keep stashed in the back waistband of my jeans.

Texas clears his throat and speaks. "I'd like to nominate Seneca Villetrio."

It's like the freaking Red Sea parts as the crowd moves aside to let a woman, dressed in a deep purple tank top and tight black pants with a belt slung low around her hips, short black hair, tan skin, and giant gray eyes step forward. She makes eye contact with me and then turns away, exposing a shaved side of her head.

"Whoa." Not my most eloquent moment, but still. I whisper to Harry. "She's been here all night?"

While I try to figure out if this is the same woman who was at the shooting range, Seth seconds the nomination.

"I talked to Seneca for a bit." Seth offers. "She's never even driven a car before, just bikes. That's…" He chuckles. "That's pretty cool."

Something about the way he says this makes the hairs on my arms bristle. Does he like her?

Some of the other guys continue on with a "third" and "fourth" of her nomination, but I'm too caught up to say anything. It should be that easy, but it never is. Harry has serious trust issues with women, and Nick's leaving it up to him.

Despite it all, Harry's a good guy and puts his own feelings aside to let Seneca in.

Watching her smile as she's congratulated by the guys over her nomination, I can't help but smile with her.

Shoot. I don't need to be grinning along with her. I shouldn't want her in this club. I shouldn't want her, period.

Yet… I do.

Glancing down at the bar to collect my thoughts, I keep my eyes focused on the intricate patterns made by the wood grain finish. If she becomes a member, how the hell am I going to stay clear of her?

Letting my gaze lift, I find her again, taking in her tough-but-vulnerable biker image, and sexy-as-hell body. Despite my insane attraction, I'll just have to force myself to stay away, because there's no way I can bring her into my world. I can't risk her safety now that Mikey and Tony are free.

A dull ache forms in my gut, and I rub at it with the side of my fist. Yeah, it sucks, but there's no way in hell I can ever be with Seneca Villetrio.

Chapter Four

Wildfire

Here I go again. Stalking.

Tucked into a corner of Hoppa's Taphouse with a domestic beer in one hand and a group of Steel Knights members forming a barrier around me, I don't really have to worry about Avery spotting me. No one could see me hidden behind this wall of leather. Besides, he's busy talking to some freakishly tall guy with a handlebar mustache and laughing, anyway.

Yes, I want Avery to notice me, but not until it's the right time, and I have the upper hand. Like everything else I do in life, I'm going to go about this on my terms.

Besides, I've got an extra shot at getting nominated that I wasn't expecting. These guys are pretty damn cool, and they're asking real questions, wanting to learn more about me. Maybe one of them will nominate me.

Making a mental note, I commit their names to memory: Vil—easy. Punk rocker style, like me. Bucky, their road captain, older than the rest of the guys, with long hair that looks like it's been windblown for so many years and just naturally flows down his back. Road Captain is someone I definitely want on my side. Not only does he do all the research for the trips, but he's in charge when we're on the road. He can decide who takes the trip, and who doesn't… and who's strong enough, or, in my case, expendable enough, to ride ahead into danger. Texas. The guy with the oversized cowboy hat. He's quiet, and maybe not all that confident compared to the rest of these braggarts, but he comes across as really nice and supportive. And then, there's Small Fry. Judging from the fact that he's not much taller than I am, I'll bet the guys gave him his nickname. I'd also put money on the fact that he spends a lot of time proving to the ladies that his height is the only reason they call him, "Small Fry." Poor guy. And finally, there's the young one, Seth, with the light brown, thick top-style hair and odd energy. He's stoic and quiet but strikes me as a dormant volcano. I sure as hell wouldn't want to be around him when too much pressure forms.

But he's nice enough and seems really interested in finding out more about me. They all do. Too bad I can only tell them a version of my truth.

"Okay, Seneca," Seth addresses me with a smile, exposing teeth almost as nice and straight as mine. Seems someone else grew up with some money. "Let's say you could never ride a bike again…"

"What? No!" With a mocking gasp, I grab my chest and pretend to stumble backward. The guys chuckle.

Grinning, Seth continues. "What kind of car would you drive? Think carefully. Your future is riding on this answer. A lot of these guys have strong opinions on this."

"Well..." I chew the corner of my lip like I'm really pondering the question. Like the subject matter is insightful, or that it means something. *Anything.* Like it's the decision as to whether or not Matt gets out on parole. The decision that comes tomorrow.

Pushing away my sarcasm that's going to take me down a rabbit-hole of anger and resentment, I force a smile. I have to stay connected to the moment. I can't help Matt if Mikey and Tony decide I should be dead. And to stay alive, I may need protection.

"What kind of car?" Shrugging, I hold my hands up and then let them drop. "I'd have to say I can't answer that one."

The guys look at each other. Disappointment clouds their hopeful expressions, and Seth's brow furrows.

"Come on. You've got to have one car you can tell us." It's Texas. He nods his encouragement. Realizing that like Bucky, he's a bit older than these twenty and thirty-something guys, I understand his place here. He's not the "Dad" of the group, that's Nick, but he's certainly an older, wiser "uncle".

I smile at him.

"Yeah," Small Fry raises his bottle in encouragement.

He's holding the same beer as I am. Glancing at each one of them, I realize they're all drinking an American-made domestic beer.

"Sorry guys," I say. "I can't tell you what car I'd drive because I've never driven one. Only bikes."

"What the...?" Bucky slaps his leg in astonishment.

The guys murmur and laugh.

"I knew I liked her," Vil adds.

Seth gives him a dark, sideways glance. "You're telling me..." He stares hard into my eyes. "That you've never driven a car?"

Holding up my three middle fingers and latching my thumb and pinky together, I offer a "Scout's Honor."

"Well, damn." Small Fry tucks his beer bottle under his arm and puts his fingers to his mouth, whistling. Thankfully, it's so packed and so loud in here, no one looks our way. "That is some hot shit right there!"

Smiling, it feels good to finally tell the truth about something. It's not a lie. I have never driven a car. The part I omit is the reason I've never driven. I grew up an American princess on Long Island with so much money, I had my own chauffeur. It wasn't until I began rebelling and breaking away from my parents, that I learned to ride.

"But..." Holding up my free hand, I get their attention again. Remembering that we're all drinking domestic beer, I add, "If I could never ride my bike again and *had* to choose a car, I'd choose classic American muscle all the way. Give me a sixty-six Barracuda or a sixty-eight

Mustang any day." Thank you, Matt, for the pictures of cars you had taped up all over your bedroom walls.

"Classic American muscle," Bucky assents with a tip of his bottle.

All the guys raise their bottles and toast my exemplary answer. With a racing heart, I glance over in Avery's direction. Thankfully, he hasn't noticed our mini-celebration. Grinning, I toast them back. I didn't end up with a four-point-oh GPA at Columbia University by being stupid.

"How is it you're no one's WAG?" Seth asks.

Damn it. Anger replaces the excitement I felt only moments before. Feeling my eyes narrow, I push myself to smile again.

"Well…"

"Seneca's her own woman. She's here to pledge. Right, Seneca?" Texas comes to my rescue and lifts his eyebrows, encouraging me.

Damn, this guy must have daughters. He reminds me of Johnny, the one man I trust from my past life. My surrogate father, the man who taught me to ride and fix bikes. Smiling at Texas, I try to calm myself. Nerves are making my hands tremble slightly.

Taking a deep breath, I close my eyes for a moment. *Come on, Seneca. Hold it together. Mikey and Tony are out. You need this. You need these guys.* Opening my eyes, I stand taller and look at them directly.

"I am absolutely here to pledge. If you'll have me. And I think you'll find that I can ride as well as any man and fix anything on two wheels. I'm good with a hog…" Thumbing the parking lot, I explain, "I saw quite a few Harleys out there…" I joke. The guys elbow each other.

"And I can even fix that old Indian I saw. I've got a connection who can manufacture parts."

Bucky steps forward. "You can fix an Indian?"

I knew it'd be his. "Yes. The man who taught me had a classic." Thank you, Johnny.

"Well, all right then."

Bucky extends his hand, and we shake. I'd love to tell them I can shoot, and I've studied Krav Maga for the past four years, but I have to be careful not to be too pushy.

Then, Small Fry cups his hand to his mouth and shouts out, "Let's get to nominatin'!"

Oh shit. I spent so much time with these guys, I never even got to Avery. Chewing the corner of my lip, I brace myself for whatever is about to come. He was the one I was counting on.

The guys rush up to stand behind the bar with all the other members, and there's a cold void around me now. What if these guys aren't sold on me?

Holding my breath, Nick gets right to the nominating process. No surprise, it's all guys. No one even mentions my name. Shit. The final call for any last nominations means Nick is wrapping things up.

Damn. Crickets. I can hear freaking crickets. I blew it. Dropping my head, I swallow back my tears and frustration. *It's okay,* I tell myself. *You will find a way to stay alive and save Matt.*

Murmuring makes me pull my head up as I see Texas, front and center. He toys with his hat and clears his throat. "I'd like to nominate Seneca Villetrio."

The relief rushes through me as the guys start cheering, and I make my way through the sea of men who step back to let me pass. More damned imaginary crickets decide to taunt my brain as I wait for someone, anyone, to second the nomination. Well, I know it won't be Bullet over there with Bullseye, but maybe one of the guys…?

"I second!" It's Seth.

Whew.

There's a third, fourth, and fifth to my nomination, and as I walk closer to the members, I can't help the giant smile I'm wearing. It feels good to have something go right. Stepping up to the bar, I make eye contact with Avery. His eyebrows are raised, and his mouth hangs open. He's shocked. Hopefully, he's shocked because I'm here, and not because I was nominated. Well, no matter the reason, I am here. And I got my nomination.

Grinning, I take my place alongside the other prospects.

"Wildfire, huh?"

I fight my smile as Avery comes up and stands next to me while I'm throwing darts. Glancing at him, I now get the answer to my question from last night. Blue. His eyes are blue. In fact, they match the T-shirt he's wearing. And now that his jacket is off, I can see not only his T-shirt but his muscles bulging out from the armbands. Oh hell, he's even better looking than I thought.

"If I were you, I would give me some space. I've got a lethal weapon in my hand," I warn playfully. No, I can't have a relationship, but a little innocent flirting never hurt anyone. I'm riding high on my nomination and the possibility of Matt's parole tomorrow.

Throwing the next dart, it sticks just outside the bullseye.

"Not bad. May I?" He nods to the last dart in my hand.

Handing it to him, I hope he doesn't notice that it's sweaty from my palms. With his cropped hair, light eyes, and wide shoulders, this guy is way too good-looking to be real.

He throws and… bullseye. Of course. Thing is, he makes it so I don't mind losing to him. But if I lose, I'll only do it as a worthy competitor. There's no vapid little damsel in distress here, and the sooner he knows it, the better.

"So…" He smiles after he comes back from retrieving the darts. "You didn't tell me. Why do they call you Wildfire?"

"Why do you think?" Taking a dart from him, I throw, and this time, I hit the bullseye.

"Nice shot." He's genuinely happy for me. Crap. He *is* a nice guy like everyone says he is. "Tell you what. Why don't we make this game interesting?"

"How's that?" Throwing again, this shot's almost as good as the first. "Money? I don't have any extra to spare."

He crosses his strong arms. "Nope. More like secrets."

No. That's the last thing I'm going to give up.

Walking toward me like a freaking wild animal marking his territory, he steps around and stands just behind me. We're not touching, but he's so tall, strong, and wide, it's like he's created a masculine, protective bubble around me. And it feels way too good.

Leaning in close, he whispers in my ear. "Ever since I saw you shoot last night, I've wanted to know everything there is to know about you."

My heart is racing and a trickle of sweat drips down my spine. Not moving from my position and staring at the dartboard, I mumble, "You knew that was me?"

Chuckling, he adds, "Not a lot of women in Hoppa who look like you."

He's so close and the moment's so intimate, I don't want to move a muscle. Chills of excitement that outdo the anticipation of the coldest Christmas morning rush up and down my body. His warm breath caresses my neck, and my nipples harden from excitement.

"Why do you think I have secrets?"

"I can see them. Buried deep in those beautiful, dark gray eyes." Damn, if this guy's a player, he's a pro. "So..." He stands up straight. I miss the warmth of his body so very close to mine... "Every point I win, you tell me something I want to know. And every point you win..." He grins. "I tell you something."

"All right."

"Hey." Whipping around, I see Seth standing there. Talk about lousy timing.

"Hi, Seth." Trying to pull myself from the intimate moment I just shared with Avery, I focus on Seth. "Um, thank you so much for seconding my nomination." I've already thanked Texas and the rest of the guys, but Seth hasn't been out here, mingling.

"You deserved it." The words are meant for me, but he's looking at Avery.

Oh. Now, there's going to be a pissing fight? I don't need this. No one needs this. Just because I'm the only female here...

"So, uh..." He pulls his gaze off of Avery and speaks directly to me. "Are we playing darts?" He raises his eyebrows in anticipation.

My stomach turns to stone as disappointment settles in my belly. I don't want to turn this kid down, but there's no way I'll owe him just because he nominated me. Seneca Villetrio owes no one. And that's the way it will always be. Besides, I was rather enjoying the sexy game I was playing with Bullseye... And I don't necessarily mean darts...

"Sorry, Seth," Avery answers. "Seneca and I have just laid down a wager. It's a two-person game. We'll be playing for a while. We'll let you know when the board is free."

Scowling at Avery, Seth mumbles, "See you around, Seneca." Standing up tall and nodding, he walks away.

Shit. I'm not even in yet, and already I'm causing trouble.

I glance at Avery, and it's like he can read my mind.

"Don't worry about him. He's fine. I promise."

Nodding, a flush of warmth covers me, rushing up my spine and stinging my cheeks. He must have seen me blush because he's smiling, and in this instant, I realize that I was just claimed by Avery "Bullseye" Pairings.

The thing is, after everything I've been through, and all the trouble that lies ahead, I can't let it happen. I cannot get involved. And I certainly cannot allow this nice guy to get dragged into my world of drugs, and jail… and murderers.

Then, it's like all the noise of the bar falls away as Avery comes up to me and stops much closer to me than he should. As he stands here, his wide chest rising and falling with his labored breath, my heart does this funny little skip-a-beat thing. Oh no.

I cannot, under any circumstances, fall for this man.

"So, shall we play?" he asks. The sparkle in his eyes… the smoothness of his voice…

Crap. Yes, a million times, ye—

A vibration in my back pocket pulls my attention. "Excuse me, one sec." Pulling my phone from my pocket, I read a long text from Johnny.

"Sen. I'm sorry, hun. They moved his probation hearing up to this afternoon. No one knew. I think it was because of our "friend"."

Fucking Ironclad. He buried Matt even further as a fuck-you from Mikey and Tony, now that they're out. Fuck you, fuck you, fuck you too.

"I'm sorry to say it was denied. But we'll keep fighting. In the meantime, you lie low and stay safe until we know what those two shits are doing. Don't tell me where you are or what you're doing. Just stay safe. Love you, kid."

Even Johnny had to get dragged into this. I'm poison. Just being near me, he'll get burned to the ground. No wonder people call me, "Wildfire."

"Seneca?" Avery asks me. "Everything okay?"

"Yeah, yeah." Burying my feelings along with my phone, I walk back over toward the dartboard. No, there's no way I can have any kind of relationship with Avery, but it doesn't mean I can't have tonight. There's no way I can go home alone right now. "Secrets and darts sound perfect." He grins. "But we're going to need some alcohol to go along with it." A freaking boatload of alcohol.

"I'm on it."

As he dashes back to the bar, I watch his strong muscles flex under his T-shirt as he leans across and orders. Turning back to me, he's balancing two shots and two beers in his large hands. He smiles.

Damn. To forget about Matt tonight, I am going to need a hell of a lot of alcohol, and that's perfectly convenient because to turn down Avery, I'm going to need the kind of strength I can only find in the bottom of a bottle of bourbon. Thing is, I'm also going to have to stay lucid enough to be careful of what I say.

Taking the shot from Avery, I shoot it back with him, and we both pound our glasses on a nearby high-top table. Glancing at his rugged good looks and charming smile, my stomach bottoms out, feeling like it's dropped to my feet. I'm doomed.

Yeah, I've got to be careful of what I say…

But I've got to be even more careful of what I do.

Chapter Five

Bullseye

Damn, she smells way too good. Not flowery or prissy—but more tangy, like faint cinnamon and exotic spices. And it's an incredibly subtle scent. Which means to smell it, I have to lean in really close to her. Which I've been doing, all damn night…

"So? Really no crazy initiation for Steel Knights?" she asks.

"Really not."

"Whoa. That's a relief. Some of the stuff these clubs make the women do…"

Grinding my teeth, I nod. "Yeah, I know." I hate how so many clubs consider women second-class citizens, or worse, disposable property.

She lets her hand holding the dart rest at her side, while she looks me dead in the eyes. "And for the record, I wouldn't do those things. I've been invited to pledge for other clubs, and I've always said no."

"I'm glad you did." And I'm freaking glad she's here, but I can't admit that to either of us.

"Me too."

While she lines up her shot and shoots, I walk away a couple of yards, taking another glug from my bottle, trying to cool off. Being too close to her is like touching the sun, but I don't dare step away more than a few feet. If I do, Seth, or someone else, will come swooping in.

No, I can't have her. But I'm going to make damn sure no one else can have her, either.

Shit. I am acting like one spoiled bastard. But, looking at those strong, toned arms, flat belly, and high, tight butt… I can't help myself.

"All right, Bullseye, beat that one."

Spinning away from the board, she faces me. Staring into those hypnotic eyes, all I want is to run her out of here, put her on the back of my bike, and rush her home. But I can't. This "relationship" has to stay in Hoppa's Taphouse.

"What?" She tilts her head.

"Nothing." Shit. Caught in the middle of a fantasy.

She holds out the dart to me, but rather than taking it, I place my hand on hers, covering her hand completely. With the tiniest guttural gasp, she looks up into my eyes. I can tell by her wide eyes she's shocked. But she doesn't move. Allowing myself just a glimpse downward, I can see her nipples harden underneath that sexy purple tank top.

Damn.

Ever so slowly, I slide my hand down hers, until, grasping the dart and spinning my hand, I pluck it away from her. She doesn't break eye contact or flinch. I was right. This woman is hot shit.

Clearing my throat, I walk over and ready myself in front of the board. I talk as I throw. "The only thing we ask of our prospects is the grunt work. Cleaning, inventory, stockroom, and for the guys who can do it, fixing and maintaining the bikes."

Clamping her hands on her hips, she grins at me. "I think you'll find I can fix a bike as well as any guy here." Releasing her hips, she holds her hands out to the sides, showcasing the clubhouse like she's a game show hostess. "Probably better."

"Really?" Raising an eyebrow and cocking my head, I question her. "Where'd you learn how?"

Shaking her head, she chuckles. "Nope. Not your turn for a question."

"Got it. But still, that's freaking impressive." This girl is just one hot surprise after another. "Damned straight."

"Well then, wait here." Dashing to the bar and back, I approach her with another two rounds. "I think that deserves a toast."

Taking a shot glass from me, she holds hers up, and we clink glasses. Out of the corner of my eye, I see Harry look over from behind the bar, but then he turns his attention back to his phone.

Okay, time for me to show her what I'm made of. Leaving the shot glasses on our table, I walk back to the board and throw another three darts. Damn. One bullseye after another. My aim just gets better and better, or maybe the tequila is just making it look like it...

Either way, considering Mikey and Tony are on the loose, and I've been stressing over them since yesterday, this is turning out to be a pretty fine evening. Speaking of fine... watching Seneca shimmy away from the table and pull the darts out of the board, I can tell she's also looser than she was before. Her normally sexy-but-calculated walk is now freer and flat-out sexual. Smiling at me on her way to set up for her shot, I can see her eyes are glassy.

We have been drinking for a couple of hours straight, and in that time, we've put back quite a few beers each *and* a bunch of shots. It's certainly not enough to make me drunk, but probably enough to make her start to feel it.

Huh. Just to be safe, maybe I'll take her to the diner for breakfast before she goes home. Not because it's a date or anything, just because I want to make sure she doesn't drive drunk.

Frankly, I could use some black coffee to sober me up as well, but my need for sobering doesn't have anything to do with the booze.

She throws three darts but hits the double ring. Frowning, she turns back to me, and her lush bottom lip juts out. Okay. We've both had enough tequila.

After I'm certain she makes it to the table okay, I hit the mark and take my shot. "Bullseye." Grinning, I turn to her. "We almost lost track, but it's your turn to answer some questions."

"What else do you want to know?" She takes a long swallow from her bottle. "I've told you everything."

"Really?" I raise an eyebrow, skeptically. Somewhere, hidden behind that tough exterior and armor of black leather, multiple ear piercings, and punk hair, are secrets. I can see them.

I know secrets. And the thing I can tell about her secrets is that these particular ones must be so painful, she's buried them in the deepest regions of her soul. And I'm desperate to find out what they are. *Hypocrite*. It's not like I'll be sharing mine any time soon.

"I don't think you've told me anything," I tease. My voice is low, and I stand close to her. It's almost like we're talking while we're basking in the afterglow. "If I recall, your answer to, 'Where and when were you born?' was, 'Long, long ago in a town far, far away'." Nodding at her, I smile. "It's okay. We all have our secrets."

Her eyes flash then. She's interested. And I can tell by the slight sway in her stance that she may be drunk enough to reveal more.

"Come on, at least tell me your age."

"I'm twenty-four." She sighs. "You?"

"Twenty-six. And that was my turn, not yours. So, just remember I gave you a freebie, and what a great guy I am."

"That may be hard to forget," she mumbles.

For some reason, her kind words and unfounded trust in me—when I'm completely undeserving of it—sit in the pit of my stomach. I wait for that dull ache that feels like I've just been punched, but it doesn't come. Instead, the feeling radiates downward... making my night-long hard-on even stiffer.

"I'm not such a good guy, Seneca."

"I'll bet that's not true," she says, offering me another dart.

Clearing my throat and taking the dart from her, I come up right next to her again. "Okay, we said secrets, not facts. So, whoever wins this shot has to answer something real. 'If I had anything I wanted, I would have a man—or woman—who...' and we fill in the blank."

"Okay," she agrees. Hopping up onto one of the barstools next to our table, she leans back, resting against the high top. Fuck, she's beautiful.

Throwing the dart, I hit the bullseye.

"I'm not even going to try," she jokes, yawning.

Glancing at my watch, I see it's three-thirty in the morning. Most of the other prospects have gone home, which means she's staying for me. There's no doubt about it.

The bar's mostly empty now except for a few stragglers, Seth and Bucky, and Harry, but frankly, right now, I don't care who sees me do what. I have that driving force of a man who may have nothing left to lose.

Walking to her chair, I place my hands on the table, one on each side of her, trapping her between my arms. When she looks up at me, her eyes are suddenly full of fire, and very awake.

"So? Your turn to answer, and then I'm dropping you off at your house." The diner will have to be some other time.

"My bike."

"No one would dare touch it here." I can't help the smirk that crawls across my face.

"I guess that's true."

"So? Answer. 'If I had anything I wanted, I would have a man who…'"

"Who liked to hold me, protectively, in his arms." Her eyes are half-closed when she speaks, and it's like the little area I've created between us suddenly becomes charged. "Your turn. 'If you could have anything you wanted, you'd have a woman who…?'"

"Liked when I held her." I move closer, closing the gap between us.

"And?"

Shaking my head, I look into her eyes. "Nope. Your turn." My leg accidentally bumps hers and voltage shoots up my body like that time I touched an electric fence. "And?"

"I'd want a man who liked to kiss… slowly."

"Definitely a woman who liked to kiss slowly." Bumping her knee on purpose this time, I prod her for more. "What else?"

Staring up at me, her eyes are as vulnerable as a lost deer's. "If I could have anything, I would have a man who takes me as I am. Just now. Today. The complex mess of a person that stands before him. Not a man who tries to change me to fit his ideal. Not someone who wants only one part of me and not another. Not someone who expects the woman I was or desires the woman I might have been." Taking a deep breath, she lets it out slowly. "If I could have anything, I would have a man who loves me for me. That's it."

Christ. It's like every freeform idea that's ever run through my brain, was just formulated into one concise thought. Yes, I would love to have a woman who could love me for who I am right now.

And yet, there's nothing I can do about that. I want to be with this woman more than I've ever wanted to be with anyone, but that's all the more reason I can't drag her down with me. No, even Wildfire isn't safe with me.

"Come on, Seneca, I'm going to give you a ride home."

It's odd. We're closer than I've been with a woman in a long time, but I can't shake this looming feeling that she's going to bolt at any moment. And for some reason, although it makes no sense, dropping her off at her house will make me feel better. Like she's anchored there, at least for some period of time. No matter how short.

Sure, I'd love to invite myself in and stay the night, but I'm sure as hell not going to crap where I eat. Pulling a one-night stand with a prospect—no matter how gorgeous and sexy—will just get messy and ugly. And one-night stands are all I can offer right now.

Nodding, she slips her hand in mine, and I help her down off of the stool. Once she's on her feet, she takes her hand from mine, and latching her thumbs in the waistband of her sexy leather pants, lets her hands dangle.

It's a definite statement, telling each and every man who may be left here that she is her own woman. She's not in this club, Steel Knights, or in Hoppa's Taphouse, because she's with me. She's here because she is hot shit. All on her own. Well, no shit, Seneca. No shit.

Together, side by side, we walk out the door, under the watchful eye of Seth.

I sure as hell wish that blue balls only came around "once in a blue moon." But for me, they have been a twenty-four-seven occurrence for the past month ever since Seneca Villetrio pledged for the club. No, it hasn't helped that I've tried to be around her whenever possible, but I have this need and it's damned near impossible to stay away.

But I have to. Stay away.

Her relationship with Harry is helping. She's been spending a good deal of time with him, talking about women, and I think she's even starting to win him over. The more time she spends with him, the more I can keep track of her while keeping my distance. Honestly, she handles his gruffness like a champ and really doesn't seem to give a crap that he doesn't like, or trust, women.

Funny. For me, it's just the opposite. I've always found men are the ones who are willing to lie, cheat, steal, and kill to get what they want. I should know. I'm one of them.

"Avery?" She narrows her eyes. "You okay?" She leans across our table at the bar and taps the back of my hand gently with her fingertip.

I like that her nails are short, and I even like the chipping black polish.

"Yeah." Shifting in my seat, I mentally kick myself for not being cooler. "Why?"

"You seem a million miles away."

About two thousand miles away, but who's counting? "Nah." Just freaking melancholy.

"Well, I'm off work tonight, but I'm still coming by around six in the morning to work on Texas' bike."

I purposely push the thought of her alone in her apartment all night out of my brain. It's easier when I think she's working. But to imagine her in her pajamas—what would they be? Boxer shorts and a purple tank top?—alone, in the dark, pleasuring herself before sleep overtakes her… it's more than I can stand. Draining my bottle, I shake it, looking for any last drops.

"You sure you're okay?"

"Yeah, yeah. So, uh…" I shift uncomfortably in my seat. "The bike, it's the one he's restoring for Glinda, his wife?"

"Yeah. He says it's no rush, but he's been so nice to me, I feel like it's the least I can do." She spins her bottle between her delicate hands and then glances up at me. "I'm not much of a sleeper, anyway."

This admission pulls me out of my own thoughts. "Why not?"

Shrugging, she tries to laugh it off, but I see the sadness in her eyes. "Sometimes, it's hard to fall asleep. And then sometimes, when sleep comes, the nightmares come with it. Do you have any idea what I mean?"

Closing my eyes, it replays in my mind.

"Move!"

"No way, man! No freaking way!"

"No!"

Mikey and Tony and that stupid, unlucky kid.

Opening my eyes, I stare into hers. "Yeah. I know what you mean."

"So, we'll be non-sleepers together."

Jeez, how I wish that meant something else.

"You'll be here again at six tomorrow morning? I'll bring you coffee," she adds.

"Yeah, sounds great. I've got some work to do. Really great. Six AM."

Fuck. Freaking Harry's been razzing me about suddenly becoming an early bird. Since Sen works the night shift at the gourmet grocery outside town, she comes to the Taphouse early most mornings to pay her dues by working on the bikes. I've changed my work hours to make sure I'm around when she is. That's one of the many nice perks about being Treasurer.

And no, it's not that I'm crossing any lines, it's that I don't trust anyone else around her. Yeah, this is certainly a woman who can take care of herself, but men can be such assholes sometimes. Especially Seth. I just don't want to leave her to have to watch out for herself.

Seeing me around will let them know they have to keep their damned mitts off of her. Maybe that's not fair to the liberated woman she is, but frankly, it's just the way of the club.

Staring down the neck of my empty bottle, I replay the phone call I just took. For the first time in years, I heard from my old man. It was a nothing call, with no real purpose. We chit-chatted about my mother and how long it's been, but he purposely avoided small talk about the weather. That's how I knew Mikey and Tony were there. My weather is different than his, and any mention of our ninety-degree days to his cold rain would at least narrow down, if not pinpoint, where I am.

Mikey and Tony must have paid him a visit, and just to fuck around, told him to give me a call. They just aren't smart enough to realize by omitting the weather talk, he just tipped me off. My father almost never says what he means. He speaks in code. The rest is left for me to figure out. The guys in the Knights think I'm a whiz at reading people, but the truth is, it's only because I've spent almost all of my twenty-six years deciphering code.

Unease is a feeling I'm used to, but not being able to do anything about it really fucks with me. That's the reason I'm drawn to Seneca like a moth to a flame, and the reason I should stay the hell away from her.

But I've promised myself, if Mikey and Tony get anywhere near Hoppa, I'll make sure Seneca is safe, guarded by the guys, and I'll be gone before anyone realizes what's happened. And they'll be hot on my trail.

I hope.

"Icy." Harry approaches, and I'm glad for the reprieve from my thoughts. "We're heading to the diner for some good old-fashioned greasy food. You guys in?"

"Not sure about tonight, Bullet."

"Well, I'm in." Seneca smiles, brightening with his offer. "I've got the night off, and it's loud in here tonight. Thanks for the offer, Harry."

"Okay." Harry stiffens, but giving the devil his due, he's really trying. "Let me just grab Seth and we'll head—"

"Yeah. Cool." Like hell, Seth's going to be anywhere near her without me. Not if I can help it. "On second thought, I'm hungry. I'll ride over with Sen if that's cool with you, Seneca?"

"Yeah, I'd like that."

Looking down his nose at me, Harry smirks. "See you guys there in ten."

"Cool." Draining her last drops of beer, Seneca stands, and then, walking back to the bar, she hops up, leans against it, and reaching across, tosses the bottle into the recycling, giving me the perfect view of her ass.

That was intentional. Dropping back down onto her feet and glancing over her shoulder, she winks at me.

So was that. So, after this month of playing games and dodging around each other, she's giving me the go-ahead. But why now? Or... maybe she's been green-lighting me all along, but tonight is the first night I'm actually considering it.

And why am I considering it?

Because although the idea of leaving Harry, Nick, and the rest of the guys absolutely kills me, I may have no choice. If Mikey and Tony are looking for me, it'll only be a matter of time until they—or someone smarter, like Ironclad—figures out where I am.

And then, I'll have to leave her. And leaving her will be the hardest thing I've ever done, but I'll do it, to keep her safe.

Yeah, tonight may be my only chance to be with Seneca Villetrio. So, I say, the hell with caution.

Carpe. Freaking. Diem.

Chapter Six

Wildfire

"It was very nice of you to ride home with me."

We're parked a few spots away from each other in the lot next to my apartment building. Pulling off my black and purple skull cap helmet, I run my fingers through my short hair as Avery approaches. Swinging my leg back and over the seat, I hop off of my bike.

Even though the highway is right behind the building and there's always the incessant roar of traffic passing by on their way to or from Phoenix, at this hour, it's quieter. Cutting the engines of the bikes makes it downright peaceful.

Nodding, he walks toward me with a swagger I've never before seen from him. Unfastening his gloves, he puts a fingertip between his teeth, pulls, rips off his gloves, and then tosses them. They land on the ground right next to his bike.

Hanging my helmet off of my handlebars, I turn to catch Avery moving even closer to me—and his walk is all animal. It's like his shoulders are just too heavy to keep balanced over his hips, and he's about to burst out of his jeans…

"I wasn't being nice." His voice is gruffer than the usual slick Avery I know. "I did it for me."

"Oh?" Yeah, I am definitely a woman who can take care of herself, but that doesn't mean I don't have needs. And the stronger I am, the more masculine I need my man to be.

And looking at him walking to me right now, his leather jacket with the Steel Knights emblem open, exposing a tight black T-shirt that hangs just right over his jeans… Avery "Bullseye" Pairings is the definition of masculinity.

My heart races, and I swallow as he steps up to me. Before I even know what's happening, he's standing directly before me and reaching out, placing a hand on my cheek. His hand is warm and strong, and feels so damned right…

Tilting his chin downward with the tips of my fingers, I look up into his eyes. Even in the dim light of the parking lot, I can see them blaze with hunger and passion. And I want more…

But what am I doing? How can I do this when Matt's parole has been denied, and he's sitting in jail on a bogus charge?

Nuzzling against Avery's hand and feeling the calluses graze against my skin, some long-denied hunger comes raging forth. Clamping my hand onto his, I press his hand harder against my face, worrying that if he were to let go, everything in the universe would just float away.

There is nothing I can do for Matt right now, and this night will pass whether I'm with Bullseye or not.

"Why are you here?" I ask. I know the answer, but it feels too good to let go of the moment.

"I was worried about Seth causing you trouble. He was staring at you the whole damn night, and I don't like the way he looks at you."

"Well, no matter how he looks at me, I don't look at him in any way at all. I would have thought you knew that by now."

Closing my eyes, I let myself get caught up in his scent and the energy bouncing between us. Feeling protected by his uber-masculine aura, the feeling radiates downward, causing a moistness in my panties...

Even though tonight will have to be make-believe, like the rest of my life, it's nice not to have to be alone for a while.

Opening my eyes, he looks hungry. Leaning down, his strong, full lips graze against mine... He hovers just above me, inhaling my exhales, drinking me in. He presses his lips harder and—

"What was that?" Pulling away and standing up tall, he reaches out with his hand and grabs me, pushing me back behind him. "I heard something in the bushes on the side of the building."

My breath is racing even more, and I'm caught in this whirlwind of excitement and terror as he backs us up, onto the cement walkway leading to the building.

"What was it?" I whisper. Something in my gut stirs and closing my eyes, I fear the worst.

Mikey and Tony.

No, I can't drag him into my world, but if it is those two thugs, and they've finally found me... Selfishly, right now I am so very grateful I'm being sheltered by Bullseye.

"I don't know," he whispers. "Don't move."

His left hand is still cradling me and holding me behind his back, and with his right, he reaches into the waistband of his jeans and puts his hand on his piece.

Considering everything I've been through and known in my life, this should terrify me. But it doesn't. Avery isn't Ironclad or his punk-ass minions who framed Matt. Bullseye knows how to handle a gun. He isn't going to shoot if he doesn't have to, and he sure as hell isn't going to miss when he does.

"Who is it?" Avery snarls. It's like he morphs into some taller, stronger, even more sexual creature.

Squeezing my eyes shut, I will the sound to be a stray dog, going through the garbage cans looking for food.

Suddenly, a flash of a figure runs from the bushes and into the parking lot. I can feel the energy from Avery's body. He pounces away from me, and breaking out into a full run, chases the figure into the parking lot with his piece drawn. He jumps into ready-position, with his feet wide and knees bent. He's going to shoot.

Damn.

I know I should turn and run into the house, but I don't want to leave Avery out here alone, and I'm so relieved that it is one person and not two... I squat down, catching my breath, very nearly crumpling to the ground.

The roar of a motorcycle engine starts, and a motorcycle spins around the parking lot, then drives off. Watching it go, I note its direction—it's heading back into town. Into Hoppa.

"Are you okay?" Tucking his piece into the back of his jeans as he moves, Avery comes rushing up to me.

Holding out his hand for me to take, I slip mine into his, and he pulls me to my feet.

"Thank you." I'm reluctant to ask, but I have to. "Do you know who it was?"

Nodding seriously and looking me dead in the eyes, he answers. "Seth."

"Seth?" Relief washes over me and putting a hand to my mouth, I fight back a giggle. "As in, our Seth?" Oh, good grief. Here I was thinking it was the punk-ass hitmen from a high-level drug dealer who's connected to the New York mob come to kill me, but it was only some guy from the club who thinks he's crushing on me.

"Why are you laughing?"

"Because that's a huge relief." As soon as I say it, I realize what I'm saying.

"What do you mean 'a relief'? Who were you expecting?"

Crap. Looking down at my purple Docs, I kick the path. Little pieces of the broken cement crumble under my boot. I hate lying, and yet it seems to be the thing I consistently do.

"No one. I just meant I'm glad it was only Seth. Not like a mugger or a serial killer or something."

He looks me straight in the eyes. "Do you know what Seth's nickname is?"

"Yeah, Dynamite."

"Exactly. He seems like this really quiet, antisocial guy, who just keeps to himself and works with Harry on the books, but underneath it all, he's a volcano ready to blow. He did time when he was younger—"

"That doesn't mean anything."

He raises an eyebrow quizzically. I'm too quick with my response. I need to be cooler.

I explain. "What I mean is, people deserve a second chance. Don't they?"

Nodding, he steps up to me and closes the void between us again. Stroking my cheek once more, he nods. "Yes, they do. But what I was going to say was that he was in juvie. And he was in on a manslaughter charge. He was fighting, and it got out of control. You're new here. To Hoppa and to the club. I just want to make sure you're safe."

"Why?" Rocking forward onto the balls of my feet, I bump against him playfully. "Why do you care if I'm safe?"

"Because…"

Bumping against him again, I bite the corner of my lip and stare up into his eyes. "Because why?"

"Because I don't want you to be hurt. Or in danger. And frankly, I don't want to have to hurt someone—like Seth—if they touch you." Reaching out, he wraps his hands around my forearms. But his expression changes from pure passion in his eyes to… sadness. "And you also have to be smart. You have to know that a guy like Seth can't be trusted. If ever you need anything, and I'm not around, Harry's your go-to guy."

"Harry hates women."

Nodding, Avery agrees. "Yeah, but he's working on it. No matter what, he would take care of you."

Leaning down, he kisses me gently on the lips, and the feeling of electricity rushes up and down my spine again. But still, the way he said it…

This is what I've been worried about all along. For some reason, in my gut, I feel like Avery could just bolt, and be gone at a moment's notice. Yet… when he wraps his arms around me and pulls me to him, his lips pressed to mine, his kiss tells me he's not going anywhere. At least for tonight.

And honestly, tonight's all I can promise him as well.

With his arms still wrapped around my waist and his mouth devouring mine, he backs me up until we bump against the front door of the apartment building.

"Oh," I yelp as he presses me against the door, his two hands cradling my face possessively. Floating away, I'm nothing but animal instincts as he opens my mouth with his, and his tongue darts in and out with a forceful, steady movement. Pushing his hips against me, the bulge in his pants grows harder and bigger.

Damn, that is one package. Taking my hands from my sides and lifting them, he pins me to the door. If any one of my neighbors were to open the door now, we'd both go tumbling inside, with Avery landing on top of me…

Holding me pinned to the door, he pulls his hips back without breaking contact and then pushes them against me again—creating a slow, sexy, thrusting motion. My eyes roll back into my head as I stand here defenseless, with my arms overhead and my body being devoured by Avery.

Unlatching his lips from mine, he slides his mouth gently past my jaw and finds my neck. The warmth and darkness of the evening cover us like we're wrapped in a thick blanket, and as he leaves little nips up and down my neck, my already-taut nipples tighten into hard nubs. His warm breath brushes my collarbone, and goosebumps pop up all over my body.

Still holding me against the wall, his trail of kisses ends in the hollow of my collarbone, and he licks the hollow, lapping up my sweat and salt. Dropping my arms, which tingle when they fall to my sides, he bends and bites at my nipples that are popping through the thin material of my tank top.

"God, Seneca…" he growls as he slides one hand into my top and frees a breast from my thin bra and tank top.

Grabbing it greedily with his large hand, he latches onto my nipple, licking, biting, and nipping until I don't think I can take any more. Snaking my hands through his hair, I try to pull him tighter to me, but he resists and stands.

"We're going inside," he commands. "Before we go so far, I've got to shoot the security cameras and anyone who sees the footage."

Ecstasy, in the form of sharp, little bolts, shoots upward from between my legs, through my breasts, and out my hands. "The darkness will protect us," I answer, panting. He runs a finger across my lips, and I feel their puffiness.

"Come on." Taking my hand in his, he pulls me off the door. "Key," he demands, holding out his open palm.

"In my jeans pocket." I begin to slip my breast back into my tank top, so I can fish my keys out of my pocket, but he reaches out and stops me. Taking my hand, he places it by my side.

"Leave it," he snarls.

"My breast?"

Looking up into his eyes, I see power coupled with lust. A deep ache forms on top of the dampness between my legs.

"Yes. Now, give me the keys."

Feeling incredibly exposed in the sexiest of ways, I dig into my pocket and, retrieving the keys, I hand them to him. "The larger one is for the front door," I explain, although it's a miracle that I'm forming any coherent thought.

Watching as he slides the key into the lock and pushes the door open quietly, we step inside, and I have to keep myself from jumping on top of him and straddling him here in the hallway. Catching him staring at my exposed breast, my cheeks heat. The lights are harsher here, and a hell of a lot less flattering, and there's no doubt he can see every blue vein leading to my erect nipple.

"You are the sexiest woman I have ever seen," he mumbles, assuaging my fears. Leaning down, he kisses me again. Then, standing straight, he looks at the staircase to our left, and the hallway dead ahead. "Which way?"

"Second floor, apartment 2B. Beautiful view of the parking lot." I don't know why I'm nervous. It's hardly the first time I've been with a man, but it is the first time I've been with a man who's this alpha and possessive, and one I like this much. Wrapping his hands around my waist, he glides me up the stairs. Moving me to the spot beside my door, he pushes it open.

"Careful of the boxes," I warn as he pulls me inside. I've been here for over a month, but I never bothered to unpack. Who knows when I'm going to have to pack up and run?

Closing the door behind us, he slides off his jacket and tosses it onto my kitchen counter, and then places his gun down carefully on top of it, and facing away from us. Then he presses me against the back of the door. This time, when he kisses me, it's slower and deeper.

Reaching up and resting my hands on his shoulders, I pull him closer. Stroking both sides of my face again, he looks at me in a way that's almost heartbreaking. I release my hands, and he takes them, pulling me to the bed, which is really only a mattress piled on top of a box spring in the middle of the floor. With a soft push, I plop down onto the mattress with a small bounce.

"Raise your arms," he commands softly.

I find myself raising both arms overhead. Turning my head slightly, I rub my cheek against my shoulder. Watching me, he places a hand to his chest and takes a deep breath. With a sigh, he releases his hand.

Reaching for the bottom of my tank top, he pulls it overhead and then tosses it aside. Climbing down onto the bed next to me, he balances on his knees. His weight on the mattress makes me move slightly, and reaching behind me, he unclasps my bra and frees my breasts. They spring forward as he lays me back.

Sliding my way up the bed, I place my head on my pillow and roll to my side, tucking a hand under my head. Lying down on the side of me, he mimics my position. Reaching out, he wraps a hand around me and pulls me closer as his lips find mine. The moment is so tender, I feel tears threaten my eyes.

I can't let myself get caught up. This man is a good man, and he deserves way better than what I can give him. I'm being selfish enough just risking having him here. What if this were the moment Mikey and Tony track me down? Yet his hands feel so good, and I feel so protected with him...

The hell with it. Kissing him with so much force, I roll him onto his back, then I climb onto him, straddling him. Leaning over him gives him complete access to my breasts, and as I sit up tall, the seam of my faux-leather pants presses against his hard package. As he squeezes my breasts and pinches my nipples, I rub against him. It feels so good, I swear I might explode just like this. As I drop my head back and roll it forward slowly, he leans upward.

"Oh no. Not without me." Grinning boyishly, he grabs me by the hips, and in one fast move, lays me down next to him.

Resting on my side, he opens the fly of my pants. Sliding down on the bed, he gets to his feet. Reaching for the ankles of my pants, he pulls them off of me. Lying there in my black lace panties while Avery "Bullseye" Pairings stares at me, running his gaze up and down my body like he's drinking me in, is the most erotic moment of my life.

With one quick move, he reaches behind him, and grabbing the back of his T-shirt, yanks it over his head and off.

Staring at his chiseled chest and sculpted abs, I have to keep from swooning. Damn, he is gorgeous. Slipping a finger into his button fly, he yanks downward, popping all of the buttons open. In his boxer briefs, he looks like he belongs on a billboard in Times Square and not in some clubhouse in Hoppa, and for a moment I wonder, *does* he belong here? Or is he just stopping by—like me?

As he pulls down his briefs and exposes his entire impressive length, I forget everything but the moment. Running his hand up and down his shaft, I lick my lips in anticipation. I want to taste every square inch of this man...

Climbing back onto the bed, he kisses me as he hovers above me. Then, moving to the side and using the very tips of his fingers, he traces a line from my abdomen up between my breasts and back down again, hooking his thumb in the low band of my panties. Sliding them down my thighs, past my ankles, and off of my feet, my toes wiggle in anticipation.

"You are so beautiful," he whispers, leaning over me. "But I have to ask..." This time, he runs his fingertips from my chin all the way to my mound. Then moving to the side, he continues his trail down the top of my thigh and up the inside.

"Ohh," I murmur, closing my eyes.

After repeating the movement on the other leg, he stalls on my mound. Letting his fingertips work their way downward, he finds my sensitive nub. Pressing against it, his finger travels farther downward, and dipping into my wetness, slides back up, rubbing with just the right pressure and speed.

"Ahh…" I mumble.

"So…" Leaning out, he kisses me gently on the lips. "How does a woman as fiery and sexy as you not have any tattoos?"

I try to form a thought as he leaves my nub, and running down the length of me, finds my opening. Slowly, he pushes his finger inside, taking his time, and exploring every bit of me.

"So?" he asks again as he pulls his finger out slowly, and this time, as he slides it again, he uses more force, going deeper, bumping against the spot that makes me moan… "How is it you have no tattoos? Not your thing?"

"What about you?"

"We're not talking about me…" He presses harder and his finger goes deeper, bumping against me again.

"Oh, Avery…" Gripping the sheets on the side of me, they ball in my fists.

"No tattoos?"

"Turn me over," I whisper.

With a grunt, he pulls his finger from me, and taking a hand on either hip, he flips me onto my belly. Running his finger from my shoulder blades down my back, he makes little circles around the infinity tattoo just above my tailbone.

"Should I be jealous?" he asks, lowering himself down and nipping at the tattoo.

Moving to the side, he runs his hand across my bare bottom, and I wiggle in anticipation.

"So?" he rubs harder. "Give me a reason not to shine this little bottom right now until it's as red as your nipples…"

"Mm…" I mumble. "What do you want to know?"

He lifts his hand and lets it fall with a sharp smack on my butt. It's so damned erotic, I press against the mattress, nearly exploding.

"Now, before I do that again, and harder…" He rubs the warm tingly spot with his callused palm. "You'd better tell me who you pledged infinity to."

"What if I don't?"

With another sharp smack, he spanks me again.

"Ow! That smarts."

Wiggling my bottom beneath his hand, I can hear his breathing grow heavy and labored.

"The next one will be harder. Who did you pledge infinity to?"

The game is way too much fun to become serious, but the thought of that tattoo drags me back to reality. Hard.

"It sounds stupid, but I pledged to myself."

Rolling me over onto my back, he balances on his elbows as he looks into my eyes. "What do you mean?"

Shrugging, I run my fingertips across the sexy stubble on his chin. "I found that most people let me down. So, I decided I would always take care of myself. I knew that no matter what, I could always be the person I depended on." Glancing into his eyes tentatively, I ask, "Is that stupid?"

Shaking his head, he strokes my cheek with his fingertips. "No. Not stupid. A little sad, but very, very powerful."

"Thanks."

Leaning over me, he kisses me again, and this time, he reaches down and lines himself up. Bumping against me, he takes his member, gliding up and down the length of me until he's beyond rock-hard, and his tip is glistening. Nudging me, he pushes harder and enters me.

"God, Avery." Clenching my teeth, I exhale, trying to relax to take him in as much as I can.

Leaning down more, he wedges his arms beneath me, holding me. "I've got you, baby."

Plunging deeper, he goes as far as I can take him, and with my head rolling back against the pillow, I cry out.

"Damn, Sen, you are so sexy." His rhythm increases as he drives harder into me. Pressing down with his pelvis, he bumps against me in just the right way.

Deep inside, he hits that spot, and a flood of hot, sharp waves releases from my lower back, down through my legs and toes. Grasping at his back, our rhythm increases again, and as he thrusts harder, I match his tempo. My arms are tingling, and wrapping my legs around him, I pull his hips tighter to me.

"Fuck, Sen, baby…" Reaching with one of his hands, he takes my hands from his back and pins them to the bed next to me.

"Oh God…" Pressing against him, I'm completely unable to move. Not that I want to. All those years of Krav Maga, would I stand a chance against a man this strong?

Right now, I don't give a fuck. I just want to be all female to his all male.

Locking his mouth on mine, he grips my wrists harder and pressing down against them, keeps me controlled beneath him. I moan into his mouth and he pulls back, looking into my eyes. Perspiration forms between us, and his face is covered in a slick film.

"Baby, I am so close."

"Oh God, yes. Avery, I need to…"

Latching his mouth back onto mine, he holds me tight as a wash of ecstasy covers me from my tingling scalp to my toes, running down my spine, and morphing into a giant shudder and release from deep inside.

With another thrust, he falls into a heap on top of me.

I float around, basking in the feel of disconnect until my thoughts come crashing in. The thing is, as ugly as the thoughts are—Matt trapped in that hellhole, Sing Sing, Mikey and Tony free and probably on the hunt—lying there, underneath Avery, I feel safe and protected. Like nothing bad can ever touch me while I'm with him.

But the thing is, because of me, he's in danger just by being here. And although it may kill me to do it, tomorrow I have to tell him I'm a lone wolf. This was a one-time thing.

The infinity symbol proves that. As much as that symbol shows that I can always count on me, it also shows that I am bound to myself, and there's no escaping who I am, and what may be coming my way. So, no matter how good he feels, and no matter how much I want to be with him, Avery deserves so much better than me.

Rolling onto his back, he pulls me close, and I rest my head on his chest as he wraps his protective arm around me.

If only *this* was our infinity.

Chapter Seven

Bullseye

Waking up from a short, afterglow doze, holding her soft but toned body tight to my chest, I can't think of a time I've been happier. Sure, there have been other women—lots of other women if I'm being honest—but it's never felt like this with any of them.

Yeah, the sex was scorching hot, but this was more than that. We had a connection.

Just thinking about being with her… She was like this fiery little lamb—letting me take charge completely, keeping herself exposed outside when I commanded her to, nearly exploding when I disciplined her by spanking her sweet ass…

Cripes. Running my free hand through my hair, I suck in some deep breaths, trying to calm the frig down. Damn straight this woman is Wildfire.

And when Wildfire allowed me to dominate her completely… Well, shit, it made my dick harder than it had *ever* been before.

Just thinking of her, so wet and responsive, with her soft breasts, tight ass, and dangerous curves… Oh shit. I'm hard again, already.

Chuckling, I glance down at her to see if there's a chance she's up for round two like I am, but she's asleep. Truthfully, I didn't even have to look. I could tell by the gentle rise and fall of her chest against mine. But I want to look at her again, just to make sure she's real.

That it was all real.

That it *is* all real.

Damn, what's happening to me?

The apartment's dark except for the dim light that sneaks in from the edges of the drawn curtains, but glancing at her, I can see the gentle pink flush of her sculpted cheek. Reaching out with my free hand, I stroke it softly, and she raises her chin and lowers it again, giving a small smile in her sleep.

I like that she trusts me enough to fall asleep with me, but at the same time, it worries me. She shouldn't trust me. No one should.

Suddenly, a flush of anxiety rushes up my spine and I feel so trapped, it's all I can do to lie here, pinned beneath her beautiful body. No, it's not that she's actually keeping me here. Sure, I could jump up and toss her across the room if I needed to. But she looks so peaceful, I don't want to risk disturbing her by sliding out from under her.

Still, I can't calm my racing mind.

With my gaze darting frantically over the few, still-packed boxes she has thrown about the apartment, my mind is reeling with questions. Why hasn't she unpacked? What's going on in her life? Really?

Stop, Bullseye, stop.

Closing my eyes, I take more deep, calming breaths. What I'm feeling isn't real. It's just anxiety. There's no boogeyman who's going to jump out of the closet at any moment. Or is there?

Shit. Have I been careful enough? What was I thinking, dragging her into my life, even for one night?

Come on, Bullseye. Get a grip! Thank God that little voice in my head has some sense since the rest of me sure as hell doesn't right now. The chances of Mikey and Tony finding me on this night, just to follow me to her apartment at this time, are nil. The entire scenario is preposterous.

I don't have the luxury of thinking stupid thoughts. The only thing I can do is to be calm and collected like I always am. That's why they call me "Bullseye". Shooting depends on being calm. If there's one thing I am, it's cool.

So, why am I so damned worried about her?

Scrubbing my face with my free hand, I stare at the white-tile ceiling. I'm worried because the most dangerous thing that ever could have happened did—we made a connection. And if the past teaches me anything, it's that connections are dangerous.

But…

If this moment—holding her tight while she sleeps on my chest—tells me anything, it's that I will do what I have to, to protect her. No matter what that may be. Glancing down at her, I wrap both arms protectively around her and pull her closer—

Smash!

What the hell?

I'm out of bed like a shot, and still naked, rush to the kitchen counter where I left my gun.

Shit! I should have kept it on the nightstand like always. But only in the deepest, darkest areas of my mind did I ever think that they would really find me here. Why the hell did I ever think that I could have any kind of normal life? Even for one night?

"Bullseye?" Rolling over, she leans up. Resting on her elbows, she draws the sheets over her beautiful breasts.

Moving toward the window with my gun drawn, I see the curtains blowing from the newly-welcomed breeze, and a brick, lying on the floor.

Those assholes tossed a brick through her window.

Checking the kitchen and doing a quick once-over of the place, I'm grateful she's living in a studio apartment. Fewer places for anyone to hide.

"I'm here," I snarl. "Don't turn on any lights. Stay low. Slide out of bed, and hide on the side farthest from the window." Damn, how I wish she had a regular bed that she could climb under. "Do not move until I tell you to."

In my peripheral vision, I see her shimmy out of bed, doing exactly what I told her to do. Even though it's the right thing to do, it strikes me as odd. Even the most terrified people ask questions when you don't want them to. What's going on? What's happening?

Because most people don't understand the gravity of the situation… So, why the hell does she? No. There's no time for questions about her right now. I have to be clear-headed.

"Sen, how many closets are in here?"

"Just the two. The linen closet by the bathroom behind me, and the coat closet by the door."

If anyone were in here—which, based on the brick coming through the window, I doubt they are—the likely spot for them to hide is the bathroom. Which means, she is in the most vulnerable spot in the apartment. *Stay cool, Bullseye, stay cool.*

No, I would have known if someone had broken in here. Unless… they did it when I dozed off…

Using breathing control to tame my heartbeat that wants to take off into a wild gallop, I crouch low and bound across the apartment. Thankfully, it's small, and I make it in a few seconds. Checking the bathroom and closet, we're clear. That leaves the window.

With my gun drawn, I walk toward the window, slowly. Stepping to the side, I press my back flat against the wall beside the window, and bending my elbows, I point the gun toward the ceiling so it's not facing her. Closing my eyes and calming my breathing, I count to five.

Then, using my free hand, I pull back the curtain and in one swoop, I step into position, pointing my gun out the hole in the window, ready to fire.

Come on, Mikey and Tony. Show your punk-ass, ugly faces. Give me a reason to shoot.

Looking down, I see nothing. Daring a step closer, I point the gun downward, using extra care as I approach a public area with my finger on the trigger. No, I've never made a rookie mistake, but I've also never before defended someone I cared about.

A woman I cared about.

Checking again from right to left, there's nothing. Pulling my Ruger back through the hole and keeping it steady in one hand, I push the windows open and glance downward. Nothing.

Okay. There's only one more place to check, and it has to be fast. This is easily the deadliest direction.

"Sen?" I whisper.

"I'm here. Behind the bed. I can't get to my gun, it's locked away."

Again, I notice she didn't mention *where* it was. If there were ever a time that someone were listening, or god forbid, hiding inside the apartment, they'd know where the weapon was. These aren't the thoughts of a civilian under stress. Damn, this girl knows a whole hell of a lot more than she lets on. So, who the hell is she?

Shaking my head and exhaling, I clear my brain from the clutter. "How many floors is this building?"

"Five."

"Think hard. Is there a fire escape on this side of the building? Stairs? Platforms?"

"Yes." Her voice is a whisper, but it doesn't waver. She's certain. "Each floor above us has one platform and a set of stairs leading to the next. Looking out the window, the fire escape is on the right side. We only have stairs. There are no apartments to the left of us, so that side is clear."

Well, shit.

It would not surprise me to find out this girl is CIA. But that doesn't matter right now. What matters is if there's anyone outside this window and if there is, *who* it is.

Taking a deep breath, I push my torso through the open window and twisting from the waist with my gun drawn and my finger on the trigger, I cover each of the platforms above us.

Nothing. One final sweep up, down, left, and right again, and I'm certain we're clear.

"All clear," I tell her, pulling the window shut and drawing the curtains for all the good it will do. "I'm checking the hallway and parking lot. You stay put. There's no way someone could get up to this window before I get downstairs, but I want to keep you safe. Understand?"

"Yes."

With my gun still drawn, I move toward the door.

"Avery?" she whispers.

"Yeah?" Turning back, I see she's holding my jeans.

"You're naked. Put these on in case it was just some random kids." Raising one shoulder and letting it drop she adds, "The gun's one thing. Seeing you naked would really intimidate them."

She tosses the jeans to me and grinning, I grab them. She's making a joke to lighten the situation, but even from here, I can see the terror in her eyes.

Putting my piece on the counter for only a second, I pull on my jeans and grab her house keys. Sliding out the door, I turn, and quietly, lock her in. Hugging the walls, I hurry up all three flights above us—taking the stairs two at a time. Certain that the building is clear and locked down tight, I double back, rushing down the stairs. Checking the empty hallway on the ground floor, I feel confident that I can leave her upstairs and go outside.

Shoving my piece into the back of my jeans, I burst through the front door, and run down the cement path toward the lot. The chilly Arizona night has cooled the ground beneath my bare feet, but I press on, slowing only to jump over a hedge of desert holly lining the walkway. Rushing into the quiet lot, there's nothing but a few empty cars and our bikes, which are untouched.

Suddenly, I remember. Seth.

"Oh, shit." Mumbling, I squat down, scrubbing my face with my hand and chuckling. "What an ass I am."

If the brick had happened at my place, that would have been one thing. It could have been Mikey and Tony. But her place? No way. If Mikey and Tony wanted me, they would have tried to get to me at my place, or the clubhouse—if they were stupid enough for that. And knowing them, they might just be stupid enough. But this amateurish brick crap? That's got Seth's name written all over it.

Standing, my adrenaline starts to tank, and it's replaced by a really freaking foul mood. I am sick to death of this middle-school crap. Seneca is mine, for as long as I'm here, and he'd better just back the fuck off.

Staring up at the black and starry Arizona night, I take a deep breath of the cool desert air. Yeah, she's mine for as long as I'm here, but I wonder—while rubbing a burning pain in my stomach with the side of my fist—how long will that be? And would a woman like that go for a punk kid like Seth when I'm gone?

Turning and looking up at her window, a feeling of sadness washes over me. No, I don't want to leave her, but I may not have the choice. Just before, when I was holding her to me, feeling her warm, soft body draped across mine, I swore I would do whatever it took to protect her. Even if that means leaving her.

But I sure as hell will not leave her to *Seth*. And I will take every second with her that I can.

Turning from the lot, I make my way back inside and up the stairs.

"Sen? Baby? It's me. Don't be scared. I'm coming in."

Unlocking her door and pushing it open, I walk in to find her buck naked, standing by the side of the bed. Moving like a stealthy panther toward its injured prey, I hold out my arms to her, and rushing toward me, she jumps into my warm embrace.

"It's okay, baby," I whisper into her ear. "It's okay."

Her soft body trembles against me. I knew it. Despite the jokes, she's scared.

Dropping my head and inhaling the scent of Seneca—spice, now coupled with sex—I can't help but think she's scared for more reasons than just the brick through her window. Releasing her, I put a hand under her chin and tilt her head upward. For a moment, I'm sidetracked by those gorgeous gray eyes.

"It was only Seth," I assure her.

"What?" Shaking her head, she steps back. She must be trying to make sense of it the way I did. "Why would he throw a brick through my window?"

"Because he's jealous."

"Of?" Her eyebrows knit together.

"Us. Being together. In case you didn't notice, he has one hell of a crush brewing."

"But to throw a brick through my window? To scare me like that?" The way her chest is heaving, I can tell she's incensed. "What an asshole."

Damn, I would not want to be Seth tomorrow when she finds him at the club.

Crossing her arms in front of her, she shivers. She must be cold standing there, naked.

Dashing over to the floor near the bed, I grab my T-shirt. Walking back to her, I slip it over her head while I talk. "Yeah. That's what I've been telling you. He's a grade-A asshole. You don't want to be around a jerk like that when he blows." Tilting my head, I take her in. "Jeez. I hate to cover you up, but you look sexy as hell in my shirt."

Fighting with the oversized shirt that looks like it's trying to swallow her, she finally sticks her arms through the sleeves and then crosses them before her. Shaking her head, she continues with her previous thought. "Yeah, but it doesn't make any sense. A brick through a window… that's petty, juvenile stuff. That's not a guy who blows. It's more like a warn—"

She stops short and looks down at the ground.

"It's more like a what?" Bending down, I look into her eyes. "More like a warning?"

"Oh, who knows what I'm saying," she mumbles, dropping her arms and letting them swing freely by her sides. Then, looking up at me, she flashes a big, bright smile. There's no doubt she's trying to distract me. "It's late, and my adrenaline's tanking."

"Yeah, I think we could both use some rest. Let me just get your window boarded up, and we'll hit the sack. Do you have anything we could use?" Looking around the apartment that she hasn't bothered to unpack, I doubt she has a stash of tools and plywood hanging around. "Tools? Even something I can cover the window with?"

"No tools." Shrugging, she chews the corner of her pouty lip. "I use Nick's tools when I work on the bikes. I like to travel light, so I don't really have anything here."

"Yeah." Why the hell does she travel light? "Seneca, where are you from?"

"What?" The look of surprise in her eyes… I've caught her off-guard.

"You heard me."

Shrugging, she swallows hard. "What does it matter?" Deep in her eyes, I see the sincerity.

"Because when you don't tell me, I think there's a reason why. And I'd like to know."

"And do I know everything about you?" she asks.

"No." I see her point. She's right. Actually, she doesn't know shit about me, and neither does anyone else. Including Harry, my best friend.

Sighing, she answers, "Florida."

"You're from Florida?"

Glancing over my right shoulder, she nods.

She's lying. But why?

"Makes sense," I say. "Your tan skin, you seem to like the heat."

"Yeah." She shrugs. "It makes sense. So, how about a sheet? I have an extra sheet and a staple gun."

"That'll do."

Smiling, she turns and walks to the linen closet. Bending down to reach in, she gives me the perfect view of just a sliver of her shapely ass peeking out of the bottom of my shirt. Oh, fuck.

My reaction sits straight in my groin again.

Standing up straight, she yanks down the T-shirt and walks to me with the sheet in her hand. She points to the kitchen. "Staple gun is in the kitchen drawer near the fridge. And I hope you weren't staring at my ass."

"What if I was?"

With a smirk, she turns, and looking over her shoulder, reaches down with one hand and flashes me her bottom. That's it. Dropping the sheet, I rush forward and grab her. She squeals as I spin her around in my arms, and then gently toss her onto the bed.

My raging hard-on wants to take her right here and right now again, but my heart and brain know better. I want to get her someplace completely safe, and then spend the rest of the morning making love to her.

Hopefully, I can persuade her to go to the club later in the day. No one's bike needs that much attention.

"Come on. Grab a bag," I tell her. "We're going to my place. None of the windows are broken there, so we won't wake any of the neighbors when you moan and cry out."

Raising an eyebrow, she tilts her head. "Pretty sure of yourself aren't you, Bullseye?"

"Why, yes, ma'am, I am. Now, go. Before I have to put you over my knee and paddle your ass for making me wait. And then, I won't be able to stand it. I'll have to take you right here on your bed next to the open window. What will your poor neighbors think?"

Smirking again, she turns and grabs a bag, doing as I say.

Hanging with Seneca Villetrio is going to be exhausting.

But the more I watch her perky breasts and tight ass, the more I know I am just the man for the job.

Chapter Eight

Bullseye

Holy shit.

Damn.

Watching them race back from the gas station at speeds that have to top ninety miles per hour, I hold my breath. After the night we had, I'm not sure she's in top form to race. But you'd never know it by watching her corner and handling that bike like she was born on it.

Which, for all I know, she was. The only thing I *do* know is that she wasn't born in Florida. And I only know that because that's where she told me she was born.

"Come on, Sen, baby," I mumble under my breath, purposely slowing my breathing. "You got this." Crossing my arms and tucking my hands into the crooks made by my elbows, I stand tall, taking up as much room as I can. I need some space right now.

As much as I love my brothers in the club, I've got a ton of shit I'm working through. Not the least of which is that hot number racing toward me. Cripes. I've only been with her for one night, and I already have it bad. So bad, in fact, that I haven't even noticed—until right this second—how sexy Harry's girl, Celia, is.

Speaking of Harry, he's gaining on Seneca who, until a few seconds ago, had been in the lead. There's no way she'll stay ahead of him, but if she can just maintain her speed, he'll be the only one who can pass her. I know she'd love to, but she won't beat Harry. She doesn't have to. All she has to do is show Harry, Bucky, and Nick that she can hold her own. And she sure as hell is doing that.

Seems I've underestimated her. Again.

This morning as we got dressed to come to the club, I told her I could talk to Harry and Nick and get her an extension on her race today. I meant well. Since this race is all about checking out the new prospects, she needs to be in top form.

"Babe, there's no need for you to take the new prospects' test today," I told her. "Not after what you went through last night." Reaching out, I tucked a loose piece of hair behind her ear. "Freaking Seth. It's all his fault. We'll get it rescheduled for you."

"Yeah?" Her eyes lit up and then she dropped her chin demurely. "You'll talk to Nick and Harry for me?"

"Of course I will."

"And you'll tell them that because I was kept up by you most of the night—who seems to be insatiable, by the way—I may be too sleepy to drive?" She batted her eyes.

"Uh…"

"That poor little me—the woman, the girl—can't handle her bike because she's *tired*?"

"Well, not just tired…"

"What? Scared, too?"

"Um…"

In her cropped black tank top and a pair of sweatpants that hung low on her hips, showing off her belly button ring, she stormed up to me. I was freaking grateful I had my boots on, otherwise, I think she would have stomped on my toe with one—or both—of her purple Docs.

I tried really hard to only look into her eyes, but, despite the fact that I had talked her into going in late, and I had had her again, and *again*, this morning, I wanted more. She's right, I am insatiable. But only when it comes to her.

But it's not my fault. I couldn't—and can't—stop thinking about that tantalizing little belly button ring she wears…

Poking me in the chest with her finger, she narrowed her eyes. "Well, fuck you, Bullseye. I told you I can handle myself. I told you I refuse to be someone's WAG. I am a prospect. Me. All by myself. Without any help from you. You didn't even nominate me."

"I didn't know you."

"You saw me shoot. You recognized me. The least you could have done was to second the nomination. But you didn't."

She stepped even closer and the energy bouncing between us was tangible. All I wanted was to reach out, hold her head back, and clamp my mouth onto hers, kissing her until she nearly passed out... but, thankfully, I was smart enough to know that would have meant my slow, and painful, death.

"You know who did second my nomination?" She moves in for the kill. "Seth." Fucking Seth. "And I know you think he has some schoolboy crush on me, but maybe it's more than that. Did you ever think that maybe I'm worth more than what I look like? That maybe he respects me?"

"He respects you so much he threw a brick through your window?"

"You don't know that was him."

"Who else could it be?" She knows something, but she won't spill.

"I don't know? Random kids?" Storming around my apartment, she threw yesterday's clothes, a brush, and some random things she brought with her, into her overnight bag. "Harry? He hates women."

"Harry? He's my best friend. He wouldn't do that." She grabbed my remote and shoved it into her bag. "Hey, uh, I think you grabbed my TV remote."

"Yeah? So?"

Standing as tall as she could, she gave me her pissed-off, don't-mess-with me, biker-chick look, but all that did was make me want to mess with her all the more.

"Sen, baby. Please. I do respect you. And I think you're worth a hell of a lot more than your appearance. But look—"

"No, you look. Last night and this morning. We had fun."

"Fun?" Her words felt like a shot in the gut. "Fun?"

"All I'm saying is, do you know what happens if I look weak now? If my guy swoops in and calls in favors for me?" I knew she was pissed, but I enjoyed the moment of being called *her guy*. "Forget it. I'd never pledge. For me to even have a chance to make it as one of the Steel Knights, I have to work twice as hard as any man there, and be twice as good."

She was right. Especially if she was going to win over Harry.

As I stand here now, watching her lead the pack, damn… I have to admit, she is twice as good as any one of us. I knew she could drive, but I had no idea she could drive like *that*. The only one of them who'll be able to catch her is Bullet.

But that man can handle a bike almost as well as I can handle a gun. What about her? Can she continue to handle her bike that way? Moving at those speeds? Closing my eyes, I imagine her hitting a patch of grease, spinning uncontrollably, wiping out, and ramming straight into a tree.

Christ. What an image.

A world without Seneca Villetrio is not a world I want to live in.

"Your girl's something, huh, Bullseye?" Using his beer bottle, Texas tips his hat to me.

My girl. I let those words float down over me. I would like Seneca to be my girl.

But I have no business making her mine.

Yet last night, that's exactly what I did. I claimed her, and she let herself be claimed. That was no one-night stand. No matter what I tried to tell myself.

What have I done? If I've made it so obvious that the usually oblivious guys at the club have picked up on my feelings for her, how will she feel if and *when* I have to take off and leave her behind?

She'll be destroyed.

Running a hand up through my hair, I clamp it onto the back of my neck, letting my head hang low. That's it. I have to cool it. I'm the man here, and I have to set the pace for us. And, unfortunately, the pace for us is no pace at all.

Watching the bikes approach and slow down, it's Harry and Seneca, neck and neck. He glides easily over the finish line, but she is a damned close second. Harry takes one final spin and flips his bike around to impress his girl, while Seneca parks her bike and a thousand pounds of worry fall off of me. Yes, I know she's a big girl and can handle herself, but it still doesn't mean I can't worry. Pulling off her helmet, she's wearing a giant grin. She should.

That was some impressive driving.

Shaking her hair, she runs her hands through it, finger-combing it in that sexy way where it falls over one eye and exposes the whole shaved side of her head.

I stand there like a doofus as the rest of the prospects pull up and park.

Seneca looks at me and nods, and I raise my chin in response. It's like we're total strangers, and it's getting icier between us by the second. And sure as I'm standing here, I know it's not only because of this morning's disagreement. Ever since that brick went through her window, she's been... off.

Even through the lovemaking this morning, she was holding back. Last night she gave herself to me so completely there were moments when I could not tell where I ended and she began, but this morning, even though she was buck naked, it was like she was donning her Seneca armor.

I know why I have to keep my distance, but why the hell does she?

Naturally, fucking Seth is the first one over to congratulate her, giving her a high-five. Smooth. But what, I've got a better move than a high-five? What am I going to do? Dip her backward and plant a wet one on her?

Damn. I was so lost in my thoughts about her, I didn't even notice he was nearby, watching us. I should have known. The man really doesn't engage with anyone except Harry and Nick when they do the books, but he's always here. And I think he sees everything. Harry tells me he's a nice kid, but something about him just irks me.

"Come on, gang!" Nick sounds happy, and it warms my heart. If anyone deserves some happiness, it's him. Since Taylor died and Tess ran off with CJ, he's been completely alone, with the sole exception of the club. Now, more than ever, we're his family. "Beers on the house!"

With lots of whooping, hollering, and patting each other on the back, the prospects make their way inside with the members hot on their tails.

"Bullseye, you comin'?" It's Texas.

"Be there in a sec." Out of the corner of my eye, I spy Harry looking around. Maybe for Celia since I don't see her anywhere. I need to give him some space. Besides, I have enough woman problems of my own.

Walking into Hoppa's Taphouse, I can feel the scowl on my face. Something's wrong tonight. The energy is off. It's nothing anyone else would notice, but I can feel it. Yeah, so, maybe I'm a little psychic. The guys tease me all the time about being sensitive and tuned in, but I can't help it.

After all the years of growing up under my father's watch, and my year spent with the Bordono family, my senses are razor-sharp. It's like how some people can smell spring in the air... I can sense trouble.

No, it's not going to be an attack by the Dogs, but standing here, looking at the four walls of the bar that are covered in Steel Knights emblems, helmets, darts, and pool cues—the same walls that I've stared at a million times before—I know something is different.

There's going to be a seismic shift in the world tonight, and when the sun rises tomorrow, *if* the sun rises tomorrow, it'll all be different. But no one else seems to notice. And that's why sometimes, being me can be exceptionally lonely.

Damn, listen to me. If anyone ever heard my thoughts...

My gaze finds its way to Sen, who's sitting at the bar. She clinks her bottle with every person here—prospect and member—toasting her victory. Good for her. She's getting herself at least a taste of the respect she wanted. And she did it all on her own.

Just behind the bar is Nick, who's over there beaming, acting like a proud poppa, handing beers all around, toasting with his surrogate family. Seneca glances at me, and the hairs on my arms stand on end.

Something's not right. She's as disconnected as I am. It's like we're two stickers stuck to a painting—easily peeled off and removed.

God, all I want to do is to rush to her, swoop her into my arms, throw her on the back of my bike, and take her home… but something in the way she looks at me—the way she sits stiffly and the way she holds her chin high—I know that's not going to happen.

Frankly, it may not ever happen again. And that makes me very, very sad.

Seth, who's standing a few men down from her, leans over and whispers something into her ear. She smiles and nods, but she tightens and leans away. She's not engaging.

Slumping down into a chair at a table far away from the bar, I nurse my beer that's getting warmer by the second. But right now? I don't give a fuck. Staring at the label, I pick at it with my thumbnail, and little bits coat my palms. It's like I'm sitting alone in a dark kingdom, and there's a real-life moat around me. Screw this. It may be time to cut my losses and go.

No sooner do I put my bottle down than Seneca jumps down from her spot at the bar. Saying goodbye to all the guys, she walks past me on her way toward the door. Stalling and turning her beautiful head toward me, she gives me a small, sad smile before she hurries out. A noise at the bar grabs my attention, and I turn back to see Seth, polishing off his drink. He slams his empty glass onto the bar and wiping his mouth with the back of his hand, he hurries out, following Seneca.

Oh, hell, no.

Standing up and sliding into my jacket, I walk out as casually as I can. Yeah, I have to let her fight her own battles, but sometimes a man will only listen to another man. Hanging off to the side of the parking lot near my bike, cloaked in the darkness of a thick shadow, I watch as he approaches her.

From my hidden place on the opposite side of the door, I can't exactly hear what they're saying, but I can see him move in on her. He's way too close.

He's not touching her, but from her body language, the way she's leaning back and holding up her hand, it's obvious she doesn't want him to come any closer. And yet, he does. Bastard.

Standing straight, I ready myself to pounce. Balling my hands into fists, I slow my breathing and heart rate, just so I'm on top form if I should need to fight.

"Hey." She's much louder now as she ducks out from under the arm he tries to put around her shoulder. "I said no way. Don't make me hurt you."

Damn, she's one tough woman. Putting his hands up like the chicken shit he is, he steps closer still. Placing her hands on his chest, she pushes him back, and giving the devil her due, she moves him. Staggering back, he rights himself and then moves toward her again.

"Listen…" he seethes.

He's loud, and as I approach, I can hear every disgusting word he says:

"I'm a full-blown member of the Steel Knights, and you're damned lucky we're even considering you. And that we haven't asked anything of you. Other clubs, they pass their women prospects around for their initiations. I know you brought fucking Bullseye home last night, so maybe it's my turn now. What do you say? Or are you just all show, Seneca Villetrio? Is that it, are you a tease?"

Reaching out, he clamps one of his sweaty, oversized mitts on her forearm, holding her there.

"Hey!" Coming out of the shadows, I rush up to him. "Leave her alone." Fuming, my chest moves up and down with my racing breath.

Moving fast, Seneca uses her other hand to grab his thumb, and bending his thumb backward, she twists his arm off of her. She finally releases, and he bends forward, holding his hand to his body like she damn near crippled him. Righting himself and shaking out his hand, he takes a step closer to me.

"Well, Bullseye, how'd I know you would make an appearance? I thought after that little cold-shoulder routine she gave you, you'd given up. But always the gentleman, aren't you?"

Moving away, she distances herself from us. "Guys, stop it. This is ridiculous."

"What's ridiculous," Seth snaps, "is Bullseye over here swooping in and claiming you before the rest of us even had a chance."

"Excuse me, claiming me?" She's incensed.

If the moment wasn't so charged and tense, I'd probably enjoy the beating he's about to get.

"No one *claimed* me. I'm not some freaking piece of property. I'm a human being, and I don't have time for your stupid little pissing games. I have real problems to worry about."

I knew it. What the hell does she have going on?

"Sen," I nod to her. "Come on."

"So, what?" Seth rages. "You're going to swoop in again, Bullseye? With your muscles and your movie-star face…? Well, fuck you."

He lands his grubby paws on my chest and pushes me backward. Losing my balance, I stumble, but righting myself, I charge at him, taking him down by the waist. A cloud of Arizona dust forms around us on impact. Lifting up onto my knees, I straddle him, and with one good punch, I clock him on the jaw. His head rolls to the side.

That should be enough to teach him a lesson.

Balancing on my knees, I wipe my hands down my jacket and then jump to my feet. Yeah, Nick's going to be pissed. We don't need this shit at Steel Knights—we're supposed to have each other's backs and form a brotherhood—but sometimes, this shit has to go down. Nick will understand.

Putting my hand out toward Seneca, I beckon her. "C'mon. Your window still isn't fixed from this damned punk. You're staying at my place." I'm loud enough that I'm certain he's heard me.

"Shit, Bullseye." She marches up to me.

Despite how pissed she looks, it feels good to be this close to her again.

"I had this under control," she insists.

"Maybe. But he's a wildcard, Sen—"

Suddenly, her face morphs from pissed to scared. Her eyes widen. "Bullseye, look out!"

As I turn around, Seth swipes at me with a switchblade.

"Damn it, Seth!" I duck back just before he slices me on the arm. "What the hell are you doing?"

Standing there, with his eyes fixed on me, hunched over—with his chin down and the corners of his mouth turned up into a sneer—he no longer looks human. His chest heaves up and down with his racing breath. Fucking Dynamite.

"I don't know what you think you're doing, Seth."

I walk in a circle around him with my hands up in front of me, and he moves along with me. In my peripheral vision, I glimpse Seneca making a run for the bar. Good girl. Stay the hell away from this mess.

My gaze drops to his feet as a trickle of sweat drips down my back. The asshole's going to lunge, and I'm going to know, by the way he distributes his weight, when it's going to happen. There's no way I'm dying out here tonight. Not at the hands of this punk, and not after everything I've been through in my life.

And I sure as hell won't let him hurt Seneca.

"Seth!"

Daring a glance upward, I see Harry rushing out of the clubhouse with Nick and Sen on his heels. Shit.

"Drop the knife, Seth," Harry commands.

Of course, Seth doesn't. I can feel the energy of the guys filling in behind me, and Seth seems to be getting bigger, feeding off of it.

"Seth..." Nick admonishes.

Still nothing.

"No, no, please, no. No one die here tonight..." Seneca's mumbling some mantra about no one dying, and I close my eyes for the briefest second...

"Move!"

"No way, man! No freaking way!"

"No!"

Opening my eyes, I look into Seth's. She's right. No more killing.

"Seth, please, let's just call this—"

Suddenly, he's leaning forward. Looking down, I see his weight has rolled forward onto the balls of his feet as he draws his arm back. The bastard's going for a jab. Moving fast, I come up on his right, grab his arm with the knife, and snap it down, trying to force the knife out of his hand. But he holds tight.

"Give it... up... Seth." My words are coming in spurts as I keep him in a chokehold with my left arm, and holding his right wrist, I snap his hand downward, trying to break the knife free. "No one needs to die tonight."

The bastard's strong; way stronger than I'd thought, and at that one moment when I lessen my hold on his wrist, he lifts it across his body to stab at me.

I drop him and duck out of the way just in time, but the momentum of his arm can't be stopped, and with a gruesome "popping" sound, the knife lodges deep into his shoulder.

"Ugh!" Seth drops to his knees, clutching the knife that's stuck in his shoulder.

I can barely process what I'm seeing—it looks more like a bad Halloween costume than it does something that's happening in real life. The knife went clear through the thin T-shirt he's wearing, creating a hole so perfect, it looks like part of the T-shirt design. A ring of red is forming around the entry point of the knife, and blood rushes down his arm and chest. The damned blade has almost completely disappeared in his bulk of muscle, and only the wooden handle is visible.

"Seth."

Dropping down on the ground next to him, he nods to me, but I can see terror in his eyes. His teeth begin chattering as additional streams of blood rush from the injury, and his body starts trembling. With his rapid breathing and the color rushing from his face, I'm worried he's going into shock. I know from my years of training with my father that thanks to the major arteries, a shot to the shoulder is almost always deadly. I really hope it's not the same for a knife wound. Taking Seth's wrist, I feel for his pulse—it's weak. Fuck.

"Someone get some towels," I instruct, and a couple of the guys rush into the Taphouse. Looking at Seth's shoulder—the way the knife pierced him, the damned force he used, and the momentum he had—I know better than to try to yank it out.

Harry tosses towels at my feet, and I wrap up his shoulder as best I can.

"We need to call an ambulance," Seneca yells.

"No," Nick instructs. "Ambulance takes too long. We'll get him to the hospital. My truck's around back. Here." He tosses his keys to Harry who takes off.

Seth's face contorts with pain, and he draws his legs up beneath him. Looking up at me, he shakes his head. "W-why?"

"Why the hell don't I kill you or just leave you here to die?"

"Y-yes." His teeth are chattering so bad, he can barely form words.

"Because we're a brotherhood. And the Steel Knights stick together."

"B-but I'm an a-asshole, m-man."

"Yeah, you are."

I don't freaking know why, but I smile at the little shit, and he smiles back.

Harry comes peeling up in the truck and with the engine still running, he hops out to help us carry Seth, and lifts him into the flatbed.

"I'll ride with him here," Harry says.

Still no sign of Celia, so they must be on the outs, too. It's going around.

I glance at Seneca's gorgeous face clouded with worry. She gives me a small smile.

"Nick and I will take Seth in. Bucky and Tex, you watch the Taphouse, and Bullseye, take Seneca home," Harry instructs.

"No." Shaking my head, I turn to her. "We're coming. We'll meet you there."

She nods.

Nick revs the engine, ready to go.

Harry yells over the engine. "Bullseye—"

"—I need this, Harry. Selfishly, I need to see that he doesn't die."

"You didn't do it."

"Doesn't matter."

Suddenly, I feel a warm, slender hand in mine. Looking down at my hand, I see Seneca has interwoven her fingers with mine.

"Go, Harry. We'll be right behind you."

Nick peels off, and I turn to Seneca.

"Something tells me you also need to know he doesn't die."

"Yeah."

"Yeah."

Reluctantly, I drop her hand so we can rush to our bikes and take off, chasing Nick's truck to the hospital.

Chapter Nine

Bullseye

"Harry." I rush up to him and take his hand. We shake. "What's happening? How is he?"

"They aren't sure yet. It seems the shoulder is a bad place to get stabbed."

"I would think there's really no good place to be stabbed." I knew it. The shoulder is freaking dangerous. That's why the weak pulse, paleness, and shallow breath—with that much blood loss, even Dynamite is at risk of going into shock.

Harry stands stiffly and eyes Seneca.

"Harry." She nods to him.

"Hi, Seneca. Thanks for coming."

"We're a brotherhood, right?" She shrugs.

"Yeah, we are. That's right. A brotherhood."

The way he says it.

Glancing over, I see Nick sitting on a chair in the waiting area, with his arm draped across the back of another plastic chair. His face is drawn and for once, he looks his age. We make eye contact, and then shaking his head and sighing, he leans forward and rests his forearms on his thighs.

Oh crap. Glancing down at Seneca, I see her soft face contort with worry. She knows there's something going on.

"Um." She smiles up at me and then Harry. "I saw a coffee place across the street. I'm going to grab some. You guys?"

"Yeah, that'd be great, thanks."

"Black coffees all around?"

"In honor of Seth," Harry jokes.

"Seth's a big coffee drinker?" I ask.

"No, he hates it," Harry chuckles.

"Okay, well..." She eyes him quizzically. "I'll get coffees for us and Nick. I'll be back in a few."

I allow myself the few moments of watching Seneca walk off in her tight jeans and oversized purple top that hangs off one shoulder, exposing her tank top beneath.

"He's a good kid, you know."

Harry's words pull my attention off of Seneca's fine ass and back to his ugly face.

"Seth?"

"Yeah."

"Is he?" Standing taller, I look Harry in the eye. "'Cause there's nothing I've seen that would make me think that."

"I think he is."

"Well, you sure as hell spend a lot more time with him than I do, doing the books and shit. All I see is him chasing after Sen, and the thing is, I don't even think he likes her all that much."

"Why would you say that?"

"First, because he threw a brick through her window," I say.

"He did what?"

"Yup. And then you should have heard the things he was saying to her outside—about passing her around to the guys and being next." Anger courses through me and my hands ball into fists. Maybe I should have left him to die.

"I'm sorry to hear that. That isn't the Seth I know."

"Yeah, well, that's why they call him Dynamite, right?" Nodding in Nick's direction, I turn back to Harry. "What's *his* deal?"

"He's worried. You know infighting in the Knights is against the rules for him. He doesn't need dissension in the ranks. What if we have another surprise attack by the Dogs, and you and Seth choose that time to settle your differences?"

I glare at him. "I can't believe you're saying this to me. Do you really think I'd choose my own agenda over the brotherhood?"

"I think you'd defend your woman."

"Wouldn't you?"

Harry shakes his head. "I don't have…"

"Oh bullshit, Harry. Come on. I don't know what kind of game you and Celia are playing, but it affects you just as much as Sen affects me."

"But Celia's on the outside. She's not part of the club. I can keep her separate. Nick was just saying that fighting over a woman is trouble. And I'm afraid it's become pretty clear that the last time we had infighting was when Tess was here, and now, it's because of Seneca."

"He's blaming her?" I'm incensed, but I need to pull my shit together. Walking away from Harry a few feet, I take a deep breath before looping back up to him. I get in his face. "And do you agree?"

"Well…" Harry sighs as his wide shoulders rise up and down. "I don't know what to think."

Nodding, I back down from him.

"All I know," he explains, "is that we're planning an expansion. And we need Seth. His connections with the construction company get us materials at cost. And he knows what he's doing with the books *and* the build. Nick's worried about a delay in expansion."

"Because Seth acts like an asshole around Seneca." I can barely believe what I'm hearing. I've always known that Harry had a problem with women, even that he hated them, but I never expected him to act like such a douche. "So, she's to blame because he wants to get into her pants and she said no."

"No one's blaming her—"

"—No one's blaming who?"

The look in Sen's eyes right now nearly breaks my heart in two. I was so caught up in my conversation with Harry, I didn't know she had come back in and was standing near us. I should have realized it just by the feeling of excitement running through me.

"Bullseye? Bullet?" Standing there holding a tray with four coffees, she looks from me to Harry and back again. "Me, right? No one's blaming me for what?"

Neither of us says a word.

"Oh my gosh." She takes a step back. "I really thought you guys were different. I thought the Steel Knights was a club that took people at face value. That you were judging me on how well I ride and fix bikes, not based on the fact that I'm a woman who some guys might find attractive. I mean, what is this, the nineteen-fifties? Here." She hands us each a coffee, and balancing the remaining two, she looks back up at us. "I am so disappointed in you and your club."

Turning, she walks away and hands a coffee to Nick. He takes it and smiles at her. She walks several seats away from him and plops down. Crossing her legs, she sits back, and her raised foot bounces nervously, making it look like her boot is dancing. Opening the top of her coffee, she blows on it to cool it off and takes a sip.

Damn it. She's right. This is completely unfair.

Leaving Bullet standing by the door, I begin walking over to her.

"Mr. Nicholas?" Just then, a gorgeous African-American woman with long black hair pulled into a ponytail and wearing a white coat hurries up to Nick.

He stands, and they shake hands. Sen jumps up to join the group, and Bullet and I gather around.

She speaks as Nick continues to shake her hand.

"I'm Dr. Boling. Dr. Holly Boling. I'm the ER doc on call tonight, and I'm the one taking care of Mr. Hardy."

"Yes, yes." Nick shakes her hand several more times.

Finally, smiling politely, she pulls her hand away.

"Do you have good news, doc?" he asks.

"Actually, yes. Mr. Hardy—"

"Seth."

"Okay, Seth got lucky."

"Thank the Lord!" Nick offers up, a little too loud. "Oh, and you too, doc."

She smiles. "The shoulder can be a tricky injury. Along with bone, nerves, and major blood vessels, there are three major arteries running through the shoulder. It's an extremely vulnerable area, and if he had caught an artery, this could have been very, very bad. Thankfully, the knife went in in such a way that I was able to remove it cleanly, without risk of further injury."

"Wait, you removed the knife?" Nick asks.

"Of course. I'm his doctor."

I know what Nick sees—this gorgeous, educated, elegant, tall but slim woman who just yanked a knife out of a biker's shoulder. Damn. Go her.

Seneca grins at her.

"You can see him now if you'd like."

"Yeah," Nick says. We all nod in agreement.

"Fine, follow me, please."

Tossing our empty coffee cups in a nearby garbage can, we follow as she leads us through a set of double doors and into a busy ICU unit. Located somewhere between Phoenix and Hoppa, this is a major hospital, and it's packed. As soon as we step through the doors, I'm immediately hit by the stench of medicine and bedpans that need emptying. As we walk across the newly polished floor, Nick puts a hand to his nose. Glancing down at Seneca who's at my side, I see her nose is wrinkled. But Dr. Boling doesn't appear the slightest bit affected. Walking past room after room of people talking, or yelling, and being treated for all sorts of various injuries, she points to an area farther down the hallway.

"He's down here. I have his shoulder set in a sling," she explains, "but he refused painkillers. And with no history of drug dependency..." Her voice trails off. "He's, uh, an interesting man, Mr. Hardy."

"Dr. Boling?" We stop short as another doctor rushes out of a room. "We've got a problem in here."

"Excuse me. Go ahead, right in there." She points to Seth's room as she follows the shorter doctor into another.

Seth's sitting up on his bed with no shirt on, and his left arm in a sling. He's bandaged around his shoulder.

"Hey guys," he says as we walk in. "I wasn't sure you'd still be here."

"Where else would we go?" Nick's first to shake Seth's good hand and bro-hug him.

Bullet steps up next to do the same, and that leaves an awkwardness around me and Seneca. She steps closer to him. "Hello, Seth. You look well. The doctor said there was good news. I'm really glad you weren't hurt any worse."

"Thank you, Seneca." He takes a deep breath and then exhales through his clenched teeth. "Sorry, just a wave of pain." Giving her his full attention, he continues. "And, uh, Seneca. I am really sorry about what I said. There's no excuse, and sometimes I say and do really dumb things, but I would never have hurt you. I hope you know that."

Nodding, she smiles. "I do know that, Seth. Because as you might have guessed when I twisted your arm back there, I'm a black belt in Krav Maga. If you had gotten any closer to me, I would have kicked your ass."

"Ha!" Nick slaps her on the back, and she jolts forward slightly. "Sounds just like Tess, doesn't she? Except with my Tess, it would have been brass knuckles." We all share a chuckle, but Seth looks unhappy.

"Seth." She sits next to him and takes his good hand. "I'm not here to make enemies. And I've been told that my presence is a distraction for some of the Knights..."

"Well, I don't feel that way." Seth looks at Harry and glares.

"I'm glad. And I wish that I could have told you this privately, but after what just happened, I'm just going to say it. I like you, a lot. But I was never into you… like that. And I don't really think you're into me, either. I think I just happened to be there, and female. Seth, I've seen the way you look at some of the women who come into the Taphouse—the ones who get your attention aren't dressed like me. You like the classically beautiful type. There just aren't that many of those types of women who frequent Hoppa's Taphouse. But there is one particularly beautiful doctor who matches that description."

She raises her eyebrows, and he grins in response. I'll be damned. He likes Dr. Boling. Well, good luck there, Seth. Good luck.

"Seth, this was more about your relationship with Harry and the fact that he's Avery's best friend. I think sometimes we feel threatened by people we want to be in with and do stupid things because of it."

And the guys think I'm intuitive? Holy crap.

Seth cocks his head. "And you're willing to just forgive my stupidity?"

"I've had to forgive a lot worse than this."

What does she mean? Moving closer to her, I wait for her to say something more… anything more.

"I…" She pauses and sighs deeply before looking up at Seth. "This may not be what you want to hear, but I have a kid brother, and you remind me of him. He's made some stupid decisions in his life, but I love him anyway. I am the last person who's here to judge anyone."

"Thanks, Sen."

He balls his good hand into a fist and they bump. Standing, she gets up and walks over to a wall opposite the bed and leans against it. So, she has a kid brother. There's something I learned about her today.

Seth glances at me.

"Hey, Seth," I offer, nodding.

"I'm not sure what to say, Bullseye."

"You can start with a sorry."

"I am sorry."

"So am I, but that still doesn't excuse you pulling a knife on me."

Dragging his good hand through his hair, he nods. "I know."

"You and I, we're gonna have some real trust issues for a while."

"No doubt." Seth nods.

"But Bullet trusts you. And he's my best friend. So, that gives you some points in my book."

"Thanks."

"But it's going to take some time until we're square."

"I get that."

Quiet falls over the room.

"So," I say to Seth, "no painkillers, huh?"

"I did this to myself. Now, I've got to feel the pain to remind myself never to do it again."

"Knock, knock?" Dr. Boling pulls back the curtain on the room.

"All clear, doc," Nick tells her.

"Thank you, Mr. Nicholas."

"Please." He smiles. "Call me Nick."

Raising her eyebrows, she asks, "You're Nick Nicholas?"

"Yup. My parents had some sense of humor, didn't they?"

"I guess."

"You can call me Squared if you like, all the guys do. Not that you're a guy."

I want to palm my forehead for Nick. He's so nervous, he's running off his mouth.

She turns to Seth. "How about you? Do you have a nickname?"

"We call him Dynamite," Harry says.

"Does that have anything to do with your temper?"

"No." He's fast with his answer. "Well, maybe. But I don't go around hurting people."

"Only stabbing yourself in the shoulder?" She smirks.

"Yeah." Nodding, his eyes lock on hers.

There's definitely something going on here.

"But I have never, and would never, hurt a woman."

"Good to know," she replies softly, scribbling something in his chart.

"Holly?" A tall, handsome, but generic-looking man with dark hair brushed to the side and wearing a white coat pops his head in. "Excuse me, guys, and ladies. Holly, I'm grabbing Indian food. Want anything?"

Shaking her head, she answers him, "No thanks."

"You're on until midnight, right?"

"Yes."

"Okay. I'm off, I'll see you at home later."

She locks her eyes on Seth. "No. Not tonight."

"Oh, okay." Glancing at Seth again, the man disappears.

"Sorry for the interruption."

"Your boyfriend? Husband?" Seth levels his eyes on her.

"Boyfriend once. And would like to be again."

"I can't blame him."

Clearing her throat, she flips through his chart. She's moving so quickly, I'm sure she's not actually reading a single word.

"Well, it's time we take off," I say. "I'm going to make sure Seneca gets home okay."

"Yeah, and Nick and I will be in the waiting room," Harry adds.

"Well, uh, thanks, guys. Bye. And Seneca, thanks again for, uh, understanding."

"Yeah. It's okay. Just, as soon as you're out of here, you're going to fix my window."

"What window?"

"Dr. Boling?" The man from across the hall pops in again.

"Excuse me one moment. I'll be right back," she says directly to Seth. Then, she turns to us. "It was a pleasure meeting all of you."

With that, she disappears out of the room, and I turn to Seth.

"What do you mean, what window?"

Seneca steps closer. "The brick through my window…?"

"Brick? I wouldn't throw a brick through your window. I have no idea what you're talking about."

"But I saw you," I tell him. "Behind the bushes at Seneca's building. And then a brick came through the window."

"That was me in the bushes, yeah. I'm sorry. But I swear on the brotherhood, I didn't throw a brick."

Unease sits in my gut. Was I right to be worried all along? If it wasn't Seth, then was it Mikey and Tony? Had they followed me?

Glancing at Seneca, I see her face blanch.

Slowly, she backs away, and then in an instant, she turns and races out of the room.

Chapter Ten

Wildfire

"Seneca, wait!"

Rushing away from Avery, I know there's no chance I'll be able to outrun him. But I need to find a way if I'm going to keep him safe. Bursting through the sliding doors of the hospital, the cool nighttime Arizona air smacks me in the face, hard.

Good, maybe this is the wake-up call I needed. How could I be so stupid? Why did I think I could be safe here? Just because I'm two thousand miles away…? I'll never be safe. No matter where I go. Because in trying to clear Matt, I pissed off Mikey and Tony, and their asshole boss, Ironclad.

Damn it, Matt!

Breaking out into a full-blown run when I hit the parking lot, I can hear Avery's labored breathing behind me. He's gaining on me.

"Seneca, wait, please."

It breaks my heart, but I keep pushing. I know it's stupid, I have to at least slow down to get onto my bike, and he'll catch me then, but all that makes sense to me right now is to keep moving. My bike's only a few yards away and reaching out, I can almost touch it…

"Seneca."

His strong hand takes my arm, and together we slow down.

"What's wrong? Why are you running?" Panting, and trying hard to catch my breath, I look up into his smart blue eyes. "Sen? What's going on? What are you so worried about?" I want to tell him everything, but I can't. "You can trust me. Please." His eyes harden when he says it. He's hiding something, just like I am.

"I, just… I need to go home. I think I may know who threw the brick."

"Who?" His brows knit together.

Shaking my head, I step back. "I-I can't tell you."

"Does it have something to do with your brother?"

"Yes, actually."

"Well, that's all the more reason you need to come with me. If that was some kind of warning…?"

I shrug.

"Seneca. Come with me. Let me keep you safe."

"You can't." Sighing, I fish my keys from my pocket, and taking my helmet from my handlebars, I plop it on my head, tightening the strap beneath my chin. Hoisting a leg over the seat, I straddle my bike and turn the key, the bike purrs beneath me.

"Seneca. I don't understand."

"You don't need to. It was fun, Avery. Really."

"So, what, you're taking off? Leaving the Knights? Hoppa?"

"I don't know." That was the truth. Where can I go where I'll be safe? I have one life, and I'm not keen on giving it up so easily.

But more than anything, I don't want Avery to lose his over me.

Anger boils up inside of me, and jolts of adrenaline shoot down my hands, prickling my fingertips. I'm sick to death of living like this. This constant fear and worry. Mikey and Tony need to be stopped. One way or the other.

But one thing is certain, I cannot drag Avery into this.

"You can't go home, Seneca. It's not safe."

"You can't tell me what I can and can't do, Avery."

"I'll come with you. I'll stop by the club and grab my piece. I can protect you."

Gosh, how I want that to be true.

"I don't need your protection," I hiss. "Don't you get it? I'm every bit as capable as you are. I don't need some big strong man to rush in and save me. Listen," I yell over the roar of the bike, "we've had our fun, but it's over now."

"I can't let you go alone."

Forcing back the tears, I look him in the eye.

"You have no choice. If you come, I will call the police and tell them you're harassing me. Then, I'll tell them that I was at the clubhouse and I saw a fight. Someone drew a knife. Last I checked, the Steel Knights really didn't want the cops snooping around their businesses."

"Seneca."

"Bye, Avery." Backing out of my spot, I pull away.

With one quick glance over my shoulder, I see Avery standing there, watching me speed away. I had to do it. But who knew it would hurt this bad.

Damn it, Sen!

Maxing my bike, I tear away from the hospital. Risking a ticket, or worse, I drive at dangerous speeds, even over the winding back roads with no streetlights. One wrong move, one stray stone… Forcing that thought out of my mind, I push on.

If I have any chance of getting away and leaving him behind and forgetting everyone here that I've come to care about, then I have to move. I have to go somewhere where Mikey and Tony will never find me.

Like I thought would happen in Hoppa, Arizona.

My only real chance is to make it home to grab my stash of money, my ID, passport, and those few things I absolutely need, and then to take off again. If what I think happened did, and that brick came as a warning from Mikey and Tony, then there's nothing stopping them.

They're playing with me. Taunting me. And when they're ready, they'll find me, and all the people that I care about. That means Avery isn't safe anywhere near me.

That's why, no matter how cruel leaving him in that way was, it was the only thing I could do. And it was all because I thought I'd be safe. If I dared to take a hand from my bike at these speeds, I'd slap myself in the head.

Damn it, Sen! What were you thinking?

Why would I believe it was Seth who threw the brick? Because I wanted to. I wanted to think that my biggest problem was two men at the club fighting over me. I didn't want to realize that the brick was meant as a warning. Those sadistic assholes, Mikey and Tony, had to scare me. They're too pissed about all the fuss I made trying to free Matt.

The lights from my building are just ahead, and thankfully, the road leading to it is quiet, as usual. Rolling my bike into my parking spot, I feel incredibly exposed—not the fun type of exposed with the games I played with Avery. This time, I feel like my soul is exposed.

I've never before felt "off" on my bike, but tonight, I do. Tonight, I wish I had thousands of pounds of metal around me, sheltering me from the world. Ah, who am I kidding, it's not a car I wish were protecting me—it's Avery.

Parking my bike and darting through the parking lot like an alley cat chasing a mouse, I feel like a kid who's sure that monsters are chasing her. And maybe they are.

Tripping over my own feet in these clumpy boots, I can't run fast enough.

Stalling at my front door, I struggle with the keys in my shaking hands.

"Damn it!" The key slips out of my grasp, bounces off the welcome mat, and falls into the grass just to the side of the door. Glancing over my shoulders to make sure I'm alone, I get down on all fours and feel around for the key.

Whew. Finally.

Holding it so tightly I think I may bend it, I shove it into the lock and turn. Rushing inside, I slam the door shut and stand with my back against the door, panting, willing my breathing to slow, and trying to catch my breath.

The warning just came last night. So, the chances of them being here…

I've got fifty-fifty. At best.

Mustering up my courage, my feet feel like they weigh a ton each as I push myself to move faster and faster up the stairs. Finally, I jam my hand into my pocket and pull out my door key. My palms are sweaty, but I manage to keep a hold of the key while I force it into the lock, turn, and push the door open.

Stepping inside quietly, stress rushes through my body, and it feels like needles are pricking me all over. Glancing first around the kitchen, and then over at the bed, my entire being is alive with fear. There's no way I can stay here tonight. But where else can I go?

Feeling my phone in my pocket, I consider calling Avery and apologizing. If he would just sit here, on my bed, and listen, I could tell him everything. Then, I'd sit with him, and draping my legs over his, I'd beg him to forgive me.

If he would, if he'd care enough to protect me, then I'd have someone to be with me when the wolves come knocking on my door…

But all that would do is to get Avery killed, too.

No. I have to do this on my own. All I have to do is to gather the courage to do one quick sweep of the apartment like Avery did last night, and then I know I'll be safe, at least for a moment. Then, I'll stuff a bag with essentials, and get the hell out of here.

I hear Canada is nice this time of year…

Come on, Sen. Forcing myself off of the door, I move into the apartment, and walk automatically to the bathroom. Standing outside and holding my breath, I count silently…

One, two, three…

Pushing the door in, I exhale. It's empty. It's all empty. I check the closet next, but it's clear, too. Okay, so if those assholes are coming to fuck with me, they haven't arrived yet.

Moving faster than I knew I could move, I rush through the apartment, stuffing the one bag that will fit on my bike with only those things that are absolutely necessary.

Shit. A ride from Arizona north is going to kill my kidneys. Bikes just aren't made for cross country—or intercountry—rides. Tossing the bag and my phone onto my bed, I take a run to the bath—

Ring!

Damn. Placing a hand to my racing heart, I glance at the phone on my bed. With my sheet-covered window, I am so incredibly exposed here… anyone could see me. Anyone could know that I'm home. Alone.

Ring!

Feeling like the girl in the horror movie who knows she shouldn't answer the phone but is going to anyway, I walk toward my bed. Reaching out, I flip the phone face up so I can see the caller ID. It's not Avery, it's… Crap.

Grabbing the phone, I answer. "Hello? Johnny? Are you okay?"

"I'm okay, Seneca, sweetheart. But you're not. I just had a visit."

"No." I drop down onto my bed and rest my head in my hand. "Did they hurt you?"

"No. They simply wanted me to call you and to tell you that the brick was a warning. That they know you've been trying to set them up as the murderers."

"They *are* the murderers. Was it the two of them?"

"Yes."

Whew. I'm safe for a day, anyway. "Then, who threw the brick?"

"Some local punks they hired who were up for making a quick buck. Someone from a motorcycle gang—"

"The Unchained Dogs?"

"Possibly. Sounds right. Seneca, listen. Our friends. They're pissed. They just got out, but they've already seen Ironclad and have his protection. They want you to stay put and let your brother be."

"Let him rot in jail on a bogus murder charge? No way."

"You held on for him to be up for probation and that was denied. You've appealed. What more can you do?"

"I don't know. Hire more lawyers, I guess."

"Seneca. You've run through your entire life savings."

"I'll ask my mother for money."

"Will she give it to you?" he asks.

"Can she abandon her son?"

"She did once. Listen to me. They've already chased you from Long Island."

"I left because they were getting out. You and I thought it was the right thing to do. Matt agreed."

"It was."

"Then, why do I feel sick every moment of every day?"

"Because you're a good person." He sighs heavily. "Why not stay where you are? That's what they want. You'll be safer."

"Will I? Or will they hire a Dog to kill me, just to be safe?" Shaking my head, I stare at the ceiling. "I have to run, Johnny, because I'll never stop fighting for my brother. He doesn't deserve to spend his life like this."

"No, he doesn't."

Right now, I know what I have to do.

"Thank you, Johnny. And remember, no matter what else happens, thank you for everything you've done for me all these years…"

"Sen? Sen, wait."

I hang up.

Sitting on my make-believe bed in my pretend apartment, I sigh. This is no life. Living so that I can take off at a moment's notice, never making connections so that I can cut and run, pretending I don't care so I can keep those I love alive…

Mikey and Tony have stolen two lives—Matt's and mine. And frankly, it's time it ends.

Looking around my apartment, I catch a glimpse of myself in the mirror hanging inside the open coat closet. Standing, I look myself over, from head to toe.

"Time to be a big girl, Sen," I mumble. I wanted to be independent, so here's my chance. I'm through running.

"You want me to stay here and let my brother rot away, so you can run free to torture and murder more people?" I ask an imaginary Mikey and Tony.

"Well, fuck you, boys. I'm not staying put. And I'm not going to quit until he's free. I know you're guilty, and he's not. And one way or another, I'm going to prove it."

Nodding at my reflection, I understand what I'm up against. It will be me, alone, fighting off two low-level punks and their drug-dealing boss.

Three against one.

Staring at my reflection, I see the woman I have become—punk hair, too many earrings, a kick-ass body trained to be a lethal weapon, and a heart that will *never* quit. Hell yeah, three against one sounds like just about the right odds.

It's almost as if the dimly-lit apartment is bathed in some magical white light, making everything finally clear. The hell with running and waiting around. That's gotten me nowhere.

I'm going back to New York to hunt down Matt's attorney, give her whatever money I've managed to save, and stir up some trouble. That'll draw them out. Like rats off a sinking ship.

Then, I'll take those two thugs and beat the answers out of them.

And that's why they call me Wildfire.

Chapter Eleven

Bullseye

Standing in the parking lot of the hospital and staring at her fender and taillight as her bike speeds away, a sharp pain shoots across my chest. Reaching up, I rub it away.

Why the hell is she acting like this? Even though I have no business making it so, last night was way more than a one-night stand. She even called me, "her guy" today. And damn, I liked it.

The way her beautiful gray eyes filled with desire when she looked into mine, the way she held onto me, passionately—with her arms around my shoulders and legs around my hips—clinging to me like she was taking her very last breath…

Hell yeah. She felt it as much as I did. So what the hell is going on?

Glancing at the main entrance of the hospital, the doors open and close with annoying regularity. People go in broken and come out fixed. Why the hell can't I do that for Seneca? Why can't I help her through whatever this is she's going through? Why?

Because just by being with her, you put her life in danger, you stupid, selfish dick.

Lifting a hand and scrubbing my face, I try to wash away my damned thoughts. Yeah, it's true, I shouldn't be with her. And just by being with her, I can put her life in danger, but why is it all I want to do is to rush to her, pull her into my arms, and protect her?

Yet the one she needs protecting from is *me*.

Spinning in a circle, I take a breath and then squat down, next to my bike.

"Think, think, think…" I mumble as I beat my head with the side of my fist. Talking out loud to no one as I always do when I'm working through something, I take a deep breath and go over what I know, counting out the facts on my outstretched fingers.

"One, it's highly unlikely that Mikey and Tony would send the brick through *her* window. Even if they wanted me to know they could find me anywhere. Just hunting me down in Hoppa is proof of that, so chances are, they would have thrown it through mine. Two, that means, the warning was for her, from her world. And whoever sent her that warning is someone she's running from."

Standing as I mumble to myself, I catch a glimpse of an older woman and man, stalled in the middle of the parking lot, staring at me as I talk to no one.

Oh shit, I can only imagine what I must look like standing here in my Knights' jacket and colors, next to my Harley, talking to myself. Fuck. I hope I don't give these poor old people a heart attack on the way into the hospital. Trying to make myself look less intimidating, I offer a small wave and follow it with, "Hi, hello. Nice evening."

The man wraps his arm around the woman protectively, and they hurry past. That's all right. He's doing what he thinks is best for her. He's a good man. And that's what good men do. They protect their women. This poor older woman is probably scared. Just like Seneca.

"Damn it, Sen!"

No. No way, I don't care what the risk to me is—or the way it may jeopardize the club— I'm not going to leave her alone. I'll just have to apologize to Nick and Harry and the rest of the guys, but I know that if they were in my situation, they'd do the exact same thing.

And no, I can't have anything long-term with her, because it would be just too damned dangerous to drag her into my world. But the truth is, she needs me right now. It's like saving her from a hurricane when there's a tsunami threatening. But the hurricane can be just as damaging… and deadly.

I don't care what she says, I'm going to help her now, and then when she's safe, I'm going to get the hell out of Hoppa—making sure she stays that way. Sighing heavily, I know it's right. The last thing I want to do is to leave Seneca Villetrio, but I'll have to, to make sure she's protected forever.

Even though I may be risking the club to save her, they'll take care of her for me. I know they will. That's the brotherhood of the Steel Knights.

Hopping on my bike, I rev the engine and—

"What the…?" Feeling the inner pocket of my Knights' jacket, there's a vibration. My phone.

Moving so fast I nearly drop it, I yank it out of my pocket and put it to my ear.

"Sen?"

"Avery? It's Dad."

Cutting the engine and standing, balancing the bike between my legs, I can actually feel the blood rush from my face. I might as well have seen a damned ghost. And frankly, that's what he's been to me for these past three years.

"What do you want?" My voice is gruffer than I mean it to be.

"I know we haven't really talked in a while…"

"A while? How about years? That last call we had was bullshit."

"Glad you have the same number."

"I'm loyal."

"So am I. Just maybe not to those things I should have been loyal to."

"What were you loyal to, Dad? The Bordonos? Gambling? Sure as hell not to me and Mom." Sure, saying the Bordono name on a cell phone is risky, but I did time for Don Bordono, and he rewarded me. We're on good terms—as much as is possible with him, anyway. Mentioning his name on a cell won't mean a thing.

"Aren't you a grown man by now? You're still sore over your childhood that happened decades ago?"

"Yeah, I'm sore that the only thing you ever taught me was how to kill. Never how to love."

"Aren't you the romantic."

"What do you want, Dad?"

"I wish you were happier to hear from me."

Nodding, I keep my anger in check. "You and your choices stole my life from me." Rather than having been in the Bordono family, working as a trained killer to pay off my father's debt, I could have gotten my teaching certification. I'd be in a high school science room right now, explaining atoms and balancing chemical equations, and who knows… maybe even going home to Seneca after…

"I'm sorry to hear you say that." I imagine him dropping his chin and rubbing his eyes. Those eyes that are so damned important in his line of work. "Listen, Avery, I'm in a bit of a mess."

The hairs on the back of my neck stand up straight. There it is. The reason he called.

Dropping the tone of my voice, I speak slowly and clearly. "There is no way in hell I'm going back in for you…"

"I just need to see you, son. Please. I'm your father."

His words form a lump in my throat, but I push it down, swallowing hard. My father? Yeah, he's my father, and no matter what, I don't want him to die this way.

"I just need you to come home. Just for a bit."

Closing my eyes, I will my anger down. I've got to keep it under control. *Okay, think clearly, Bullseye, if he wants you there, it means they're not here.*

That means they're nowhere near Seneca and the Steel Knights. That's good. But why are they being lazy? Yeah, sure, maybe Mikey and Tony don't want to worry about taking me out when I have the protection of the Knights, and I can't blame them, but there's got to be more.

For some reason I can't quite put my finger on, I know Don Bordono wants me back in New York and this is the way he's letting me know. But if he wanted me to work for him, he would have just summoned me.

So, why?

The searing pain in my gut tells me that it has something to do with Ironclad. If Mikey and Tony have been given cred for doing time and taking the heat for an Ironclad deal gone bad, maybe they're being rewarded. By him. Maybe Ironclad is a hell of a lot more powerful than he was when I left over two years ago.

But Don Bordono would never willingly let that happen. That means there will be war between the Bordonos and Ironclad's gang in the clubs and drug rings of Manhattan. And just for fun, as a show of appreciation for Mikey and Tony, they'll bring me in for a sacrifice. Just like Don Bordono's show of appreciation toward me was to get me out of a three-year sentence after only six months.

"Why, Dad? Why do you need me to come home?"

"Because I've been taken prisoner." His voice is strained now. Like he's in pain. They must have given him a warning punch.

Christ, Dad.

"Avery, you're the only one who can help me. Come to New York. See Don Bordono. He wants to talk to you."

"Okay, Dad. Okay. I'll come."

"That's my boy, and Avery?"

"Yeah?"

"I've been thinking about you a lot lately. Remember when we used to shoot together when you were a kid? Remember what I always told you?"

"Sure, Dad."

"Never step out of the lane with your finger on the trigger, Avery. Remember that—"

Never step out of the lane with your finger on the trigger is code for "stay put". They want me in New York. They're trying to kill me, and he's willing to sacrifice his life for mine.

Fuck. Who knew he could be this selfless? Now, I feel *obligated* to help him. No, he wasn't a great father, but he's the only one I have.

"Hey, Bullseye?" A thin, raspy, ugly voice cuts in on the line.

"Who's this?" I know damned well who it is, it's one of the three voices I constantly hear in my head.

"Move!"

"No way, man! No freaking way!"

Followed by the voice of that poor, dumb kid crouching in the corner.

"No!"

"Aw, don't you recognize me?" that voice asks.

"What do you want, Mikey?"

"Just wondering how the weather is there in Hoppa?"

Gripping my phone, I snarl. "Fuck do you want, Mikey?"

"Just some friendly chit chat. Shit, man. Haven't seen you in years, but I'll bet time has been good to you. Your skin's probably nice and tan by now, seeing as you've been in the beautiful Arizona sun for the past couple of years while Tony and I have been rotting away in a six-by-six cell."

"It wasn't my fault. I didn't choose to get out, and I didn't ask for you to stay in."

"Oh, I know. You were just Don Bordono's favorite. Always were. But guess what? I don't give a fuck anymore. We're gone."

"Not with the Bordonos anymore?" I press him for all the info that I can.

"Oh, we're still with them. But let's just say we're playing the field. There's gonna be a new boss in town."

"Ironclad?"

"Hey, Bullseye, if I were you, I'd watch my back."

"Yeah?"

"Oh yeah."

"Well, you'd better watch your back too, Mikey."

"Me? Nah. I'd much rather watch the ass of that fine girlfriend you have. What's her name?

Seneca?"

Fuck, they know. Clicking off my phone and shoving it into my pocket, I clamp on my helmet, jump on my bike, and take off. Taking such a sharp turn by the entrance that I have to put my foot down to steady myself, and spinning my wheels, I burn rubber, leaving the parking lot. As soon as I hit the open road, I let my bike out to its max.

"Come on, Sen, be there. Be there," I mumble as I race down the deserted streets.

Maybe if I call her…? No, I'm not stopping now, and she probably wouldn't answer, anyway.

Pushing my bike to its limit, I race down dark streets way faster than I should. But since Mikey and Tony know about her, that brick could have come from them…

"Come on, come on…" Shifting down and leaning forward, I push as fast as I can. There's no way I'd ever be able to stop at these speeds…

But I can't stop. They know I'm here. They know about her.

In his warning, my father told me to stay away from New York. So why wouldn't they just kill me here? This whole scenario has to be bigger than me. That's it. It's like a real freaking lightbulb goes off over my head. Don Bordono trusts me. They're going to use me to take him down, leaving Ironclad in charge. Then, Ironclad will promote those punk-asses Mikey and Tony and let them kill me for fun. It only makes sense.

And they'll use Seneca as the bargaining chip every step of the way.

Damn it. I never should have gotten involved with her, but the truth is, from the moment I saw her at the range, there was no choice for me. I had to have her, and now, she's going to pay the price because of it.

"Come on, baby…"

My racing breath calms slightly as I see the lights of her apartment building dead ahead. And squinting, I can just make out… Is it…? Yes, thank god. Her bike. She's here. Now, I just have to make sure she's safe.

Flying into the lot faster than I should, I stop my bike with a jolt and hop off. Taking off my helmet and glancing up at her broken window, I spy the figure of someone moving behind the stapled curtain.

Okay, good. I release a deep breath, trying to figure out the best way to get to her. I can't get in the front door without a key.

"Seneca!" I whisper loudly, but there's no way she'll hear me.

Her shadow appears to be looking down, staring at something—her phone. Maybe she'll answer it if I type nine-one-one…

"*Sen, it's me. It's an emergency. 911. I'm okay. You may be in danger. Please call me.*" Send.

I don't want to terrify her, but she needs to understand.

"Sen, baby, answer your text. Call me…" I hiss in frustration.

Staring up at her window, I see her figure glance at her phone; she must have received the text.

Waiting for my phone to ring, I stare at her silhouette, feeling freaking useless and defenseless.

"Come on, Sen. Call me."
Stepping away from the window, she turns, just as another figure walks up to her. And she backs away...

Chapter Twelve

Bullseye

"Seneca!" Yelling to her from the street outside her apartment building does no good. She either doesn't hear me, or someone's keeping her from answering. My heart races, pounding in my chest, and sweat drips down my back. How am I going to get inside?

Running through the lot and jumping the bushes, I rush up to the door, throwing myself against it. Fuck. I don't even have my piece to shoot the lock or the glass. I left it back at the club, figuring they wouldn't let me into the hospital with a gun shoved into the back of my jeans.

"Hello?" Banging on the door with the side of my fist, I yell, "Hello? Is anyone there? It's an emergency!"

Nothing. Shit.

Rushing back to the side of her building, I stare up, but the light's out now, and I can't make out anything. Not a single shadow or movement.

Well, one thing is for sure, she's worth more alive than dead to Mikey and Tony, and there's only one way out to the parking lot. That's the front door. And even if they went out the back door, they'd still have to pass by me to get to the lot.

With sweat dripping into my eyes and stinging them, I run to the front of the building and throw myself against the door again, banging and pulling at the handle. There's only one way in—and that's to break the glass. Stepping back, I spy a garbage can off the side of the path. Grabbing it, I hold it up over my head as wrappers from candy bars and empty drink cups fall down around me.

Taking a deep breath, I rush toward the door. I need to catch the thick glass with the bottom edge of the garbage can—that's my only way of breaking it. Damn, how I wish I had my Ruger right now. With a deep growl, I lift the can higher and turning it in just the right way, I—

—catch a glimpse of someone in the doorway. Tossing the can to the side, I rush up to the door, trying to grab it before it closes.

"Avery?"

"Seneca?"

Her gorgeous eyes search mine, and then her gaze runs up and down me. Panting, I try to calm my racing breath.

"What are you doing here?"

"I saw someone in your window with you."

"You were watching me?" Her eyes widen in disbelief.

"I texted you. You're in danger."

Her eyes narrow, and her voice drops. "What? What do you mean, I'm in danger?"

Shit, just hearing it out loud sounds ridiculous. How do I explain this one?

"Are you okay?" I ask. "Who was that in your apartment?"

"I'm fine." Pushing her way past me, she leaves the building, shifting a large bag up higher onto her shoulder.

In her jeans and sexy lace-up-the-back black leather chaps, a long tank top, and with a jacket tossed over her bag, she's obviously prepared to ride. A long ride.

She keeps talking as she walks down the path. "You're not still jealous, are you? You couldn't possibly think it's Seth. Last I checked, he was at the hospital."

"No, I don't think it was Seth."

She's trying not to be obvious, but she's hurrying. She's trying to act like she didn't just run from Seth's hospital room and threaten me with the cops.

Reaching out, I take her arm, stopping her. Dropping her head back, she looks up at the sky. Righting it, she looks into my eyes, blinking away tears.

"Sen, baby." Stepping toward her, I reach out and stroke her cheek gently. "What's going on?" The panic I felt the entire ride here is subsiding now that I see her here, and she's okay.

"Bullseye, I have to go."

"Where?"

"Away."

"Who was that in your apartment just now? Is he the reason you have to go?"

Tilting her head and narrowing her eyes, it's like she's trying to read into my question. "It was my landlord. I rent from month to month. No lease. I explained about the window and said I'd pay for it, but I wanted my security deposit back."

My twisted gut starts to relax, and then, realizing what she's saying, it ties itself in knots again. "Security deposit? So what? You're moving? Where are you going?"

"Away. I told you."

Panic rushes up and down my spine, and all I want to do is to reach out, grab her, and whisk her away somewhere safe. Damn, I haven't really thought this through. Where could we go to be safe? Some quiet island somewhere?

No. For right now, the best I've got is Hoppa's Taphouse. No matter what, she'll be safe there. I can leave her to be looked after by Harry and the guys. No, it won't be the most comfortable thing ever, but she can sleep in the back room and there's plenty of food and even company.

She'll be fine while I get the hell out of here and disappear somewhere.

Then, even if Mikey and Tony want to come after her to get to me, they'll have to get past the Steel Knights. And considering how that went for the Unchained Dogs who outnumbered us… Mikey and Tony do not have a prayer. But what? She's going to live in the Taphouse forever?

No, just until I can figure out a way to stop Mikey and Tony without having to set foot in New York. Because if I do, I'll be dead. No questions asked.

Putting this out of my mind, I allow my heart to slow with the promise of this little plan.

"Seneca, you can't leave."

But I can't say much more. I have to be cool.

Control your breathing, Bullseye. You have one bullet here. Everything is riding on this. If you miss this bullseye, she's gone. Opening my eyes, I know this is the highest stakes "shot" I've ever taken.

Turning her hot little body toward me, she plants one hand on her hip and drops her chin. "Excuse me? What do you mean I can't leave?"

"It's not safe for you to be on your own. I won't let you go. Seneca, I... I forbid it."

"What the hell did you just say to me?" Her eyes are narrowed, and her voice sounds like a demon has just possessed her.

Oh, shit. I didn't just miss the bullseye, I've missed the whole damned target. But I don't have time for games. I need to get her somewhere safe.

Planting her hands on her hips, she stares into my eyes. "I don't know who the hell you think you are, but we had one night together. *One night*." She holds up her index finger for emphasis, and I know she's purposely omitting the morning we shared—and it's probably better if I don't correct her. "That's nothing." Her words are bitter, but her tone is soft. She's hurting. "And in case you didn't notice then, let me explain it to you now. I am a grown-ass woman and you cannot *forbid* me to do anything."

Sure, she's pissed, but that fire in her eyes is more than anger. It's passion and desire...

"I'm sorry, I'm just concerned."

"Well, don't be. I think I've proven I can handle myself and anything that gets thrown at me. I've always been on my own." Turning herself around with a huff, she starts storming down the path and toward her bike.

"Seneca? Please. Baby, please." Being on her own now that Mikey and Tony know who she is... "I can't let you go."

Glancing over her shoulder, she adds, "Just try to stop me."

Well, that's a dare I can't pass up... Walking up behind her and grabbing her by the waist, I swing her around and toward me. Momentum makes her body fall against mine...

Bending her arms upward, the bottoms of her forearms land against my chest, and she stays, wedged there, held in my arms.

"I won't let you go, Seneca. Stay with me, I can protect you."

"You can't keep me against my will."

"You're right. I would never do anything against your will."

Her soft, warm body relaxes in my arms, and she begins to give in slightly. She's still resisting, although I know she really doesn't want to.

"I'm sorry. I'm just worried about you."

"Because of the brick?"

"Partly."

She looks up into my eyes, and I get lost in hers. She presses against me harder, and then, freeing her arms, she snakes them around me. As she pulls me closer, I lean down, and brushing my lips against hers, ever so gently… I drink her in. All of her—her softness, her strength, her intelligence.

Letting my lips brush against hers for the briefest second, I pull back a fraction of an inch, just gliding my lips over her soft, pouty mouth, marking her one last time. Then, using my bottom lip, I open her mouth with mine, and finally, allowing my tongue to claim her, I thrust in and out, hungrily, exploring her mouth with my tongue, devouring her with my kiss.

I pull her closer still, and it's almost painful to be standing here, dissolved in this one last embrace. Stopping for a breath, I pull back, resting my forehead against hers. Our racing breaths crash and mingle, and God, what I wouldn't give to carry her back into that building and up the stairs to her bed. But I can't. I have to keep her safe.

Reaching out, I take her hand. Even just being out here is risking exposure.

"Come on. Follow me to the Taphouse. I can't explain everything now, but you'll be safe there until I can figure this whole thing out."

"Okay."

"Okay?"

Bending slightly to look into her eyes, I can't believe it was that easy.

But I'm sure as hell not going to look a gift horse in the mouth. Hand in hand, quietly, we walk to our bikes.

I'm thrilled she rode right alongside me on the way to the Taphouse. I don't know why, but some part of me was worried that she was just going to veer off and go at any moment, and then I'd have to chase her down. Which I would have.

But after that kiss we just shared, I can feel that she wants to run as much as I want her to. Which is not at all.

"Bullseye? Seneca?" Nick looks up from fidgeting with something behind the bar.

Since it's after hours, there's only Nick, Harry, and Seth hanging around. Harry and Seth are at a table, and Seth is wearing a now one-sleeved T-shirt with a big white taped-up bandage and sling on his left shoulder.

"Great look for you, Seth," I tease. "Is that how we wear our shirts now?"

"Only since Dr. Holly made the shirt for him so he'd have something to wear home," Harry tells me.

"Dr. Holly, huh?"

Seth glares at me good-naturedly. It's a relief to have Seneca safely in the hands of the Knights' clubhouse, and I can relax for the first time in I don't know how long.

"More importantly, you guys okay?" Nick nods to us.

"Yeah, thanks, Nick."

"Sen, darlin', the way you ran back there…"

Nodding, she smiles. "I know. Sorry. I just had some things to work out."

"Well, maybe we can help. Take a load off." Harry pulls two more chairs up to the table.

Whoa. That's some gesture coming from Harry. Maybe all those conversations he's had with Seneca over the past month are paying off. He seems almost… human toward her.

Thanking him, we plop down into the chairs. Pulling her oversized bag onto her lap, she sits stiffly, and her eyes shift from person to person. This is not the Sen I know. Something's really bothering her.

"Sen, baby." Leaning forward, I take her hand and rub the back of it, gently. Hell, who cares if the guys see? This will just prove that she's mine, and when I'm gone, which will be as soon as she's settled, she'll be taken care of.

Maybe if I can get rid of Mikey and Tony and handle Ironclad without too much drama, I'll be able to come back here, to Hoppa, pull her into my arms, and make little hot-headed, punk-rock babies with Sen. Shit. Just the thought of it makes me grin.

"All right, beers all around because you two definitely look like you need it." Nick slams bottles of our house beers on the table.

"Thanks, Nick." Placing a bottle in front of Sen, I take a long drink from the other. Yeah, the damned Arizona nights are cold, but the cold beer still hits the spot. Especially after the stress we've been under today.

"You drinking, Dynamite?" I ask him with my eyebrows raised.

Elbowing his good arm, Harry jokes, "He's trying to get sick enough to go back to the hospital and see Dr. Holly again."

"We can stab you in your other arm, no problem," Nick offers, laughing.

Seth glares at him but holds his temper. Who knows? Maybe Dr. Holly will make the difference. Yeah, right. As if he has a chance with a woman like that. But who knows? Maybe they'll find something in each other they both need. It's amazing what the love of a good woman will do.

I'm living proof of that.

Shit! What am I thinking?

Glancing at Seneca, I noticed she hasn't touched her beer, and she's chewing the corner of her lip. And the way she's going at it, it looks like she won't quit until she draws blood.

"Sen? Baby?"

Turning to me, her eyes flash with something I just can't read…

"Well, speak of the devil," Nick whispers, nodding toward the front entrance.

Turning to the door, we all murmur and shift in our seats.

There she is, an apparition of a woman—beautiful, with her hair pulled back, large diamond earrings flashing, and a floor-length camel-colored coat.

"I'm sorry," she says, thumbing the door behind her. "Are you closed?"

"Never for you, Doc." Nick's out of his seat and to her side in no time. "Can I take your coat?"

"Thank you." Unbuttoning her coat, she slides out of it. Beneath, she's wearing a simple

V-neck sweater that hangs over a pair of black dress pants.

She's absolute class.

Taking her coat, Nick walks to the bar and lays it gingerly over a couple of the stools. Putting a fist to my mouth, I hold back a chuckle. I have to admit, Nick sure knows how to be a gentleman when he wants to be.

Looking back at Dr. Holly, I'm floored. She's gorgeous, but oh-so-out-of-place here. Why the hell is she here? Even Sen takes notice and sits up taller.

"I hope it's okay I just popped in like this. When I was working on Mr. Hardy, I noticed you all had jackets with Steel Knights emblems. Anyway, we got to talking about the club and it sounded fascinating."

Really? To this extremely educated goddess?

"So, I just stopped by to check on Mr. Hardy."

"Seth, please." He smiles.

"Okay, Seth."

Standing there in awkward silence, she clasps her hands before her.

"Gentlemen," says Nick from behind the bar. He clears his throat and motions to us.

"Oh, yeah." Harry gets to his feet, but not before Seth takes the hint, and jumps up to get her a chair.

As Dr. Holly settles in her seat, Seneca leans over and whispers in my ear, "I'm going to run to the ladies' room."

Nodding, I smile at her and then let myself be distracted by Seth and his girl. Damn, if there was ever a real-life beauty and the beast…

Holding her bag tightly to her, Seneca stands and then slips into the back to go to the bathroom. Shit. Sen's so quiet. Way too quiet. She's not at all her usual exciting and charismatic self. As soon as she comes back, I'm going to whisk her into a corner and talk this thing through. Okay, I can't tell her my troubles, but I sure as hell can support her through hers.

Nick brings Dr. Holly a beer, placing it on a bar napkin like a coaster, and Dr. Holly drinks hers straight from the bottle.

Damn, this woman is going to keep Seth guessing. But it's good that way. I know this from experience because I have a woman like that.

Glancing at Sen's empty seat, I feel the void even though she's only been gone a few minutes. What's going to happen when I have to leave her for good? Or at least for a while?

Furrowing her brow, Dr. Holly gestures to Seth's reddening bandage. "Your wound is seeping through your dressing." She scowls. "Something tells me you haven't been resting it the way you're supposed to."

"You're supposed to be resting it?" Nick uses his fatherly voice when he asks.

"I haven't done anything but sit here all night."

"Well…" She's on her feet. "I have some bandages in my car. It's right out front. Would you mind if I redressed this?"

"No. Thanks. I'd appreciate it." Seth nods at her, and they share a smile.

Damn.

"Let me just grab my kit," she says.

"I'll walk you."

Following Dr. Holly to the door, Seth pulls it open for her and they disappear outside.

While Sen's in the bathroom, this is as good a time as any to corner Harry. No, I can't tell him what's going on, but I can tell him that I need some help keeping an eye on her.

"Hey, Bullseye?"

Before I can even open my mouth to talk to Harry, Seth comes rushing back in.

"I don't want to alarm you, but Seneca's bike is gone."

"What?" I'm on my feet. "Are you sure?"

"Before we grabbed the supplies from Holly's car, I walked her over to show her my bike. There were only three others."

"Mine, Harry's, and Nick's. But how?"

"She must have gone through the bathroom window," Nick replies.

"I'll check if she's in there." Dr. Holly runs to the back and comes back out, moments later, shaking her head. "No, she's not there. Sorry. And the bathroom window is open."

"Damn it, Sen!" Picking up a barstool, I'm dying to throw it across the room, but I don't want to scare Dr. Holly. Instead, I force my anger down, and rushing to the back room to grab my piece from the safe where we keep the weapons when we don't need them, I stuff my Ruger into the back of my jeans.

"She must have walked her bike pretty far if we didn't hear the ignition turn over!" Nick calls after me.

He's right. That's the only shining spot in all of this. She could not have gotten that far on foot pushing a bike.

But now, I've got to figure out where the hell she went, and how the hell to find her.

Chapter Thirteen

Bullseye

"Seneca? Seneca!" Rushing around the parking lot and checking the perimeters of the building, my heart is pounding. This is useless. She's gone.

But where the hell would she go, and why?

One thing's for sure, running around like a freaking chicken with its head cut off in the dark Arizona night isn't going to get me anywhere. She could be gone in any direction by now. That means I need to go home and call in some favors…

"Bullseye?" Harry's calling to me from the door of the Taphouse, but I can't stop now. "Where should we look?"

Lifting my arm in a gesture of thanks, I hope he understands I appreciate it, but I just can't stop to explain. I'm sure he does. No matter what he knows or doesn't know about my life, he's still my best friend.

Jumping onto my bike, I spin out of the parking lot and speed back to my apartment building. I damned near throw my bike into its parking spot. Hopping off, I rush around the courtyard of my building, past the pool, and up to the front door. Slipping my key into the lock, I glimpse the elevator to the right, but deciding the stairs will be faster, I rush to the back of the building and slip into the stairway. Taking the stairs two at a time, I nearly burst out onto the fifth floor and stumbling from momentum, I catch myself before sprinting down the hallway and to my apartment door.

Quieting my racing breath, I slip the key in the lock and push open the door. Tossing my keys onto the kitchen counter, I rush for my computer. After flicking on my small desk lamp, I light up my computer.

"Come on, come on…"

All right. A quick Google search turns up the usual—pictures of women who aren't her, profiles on social media that also aren't her, and Whitepages results that promise her arrest records. Nothing different than the first time I Googled her—that night she was nominated into the Steel Knights. Nothing strange.

In fact, there's nothing about her at all. And that's what's strange…

I didn't think about this the last time I checked. I just figured she wasn't a woman who liked people to know a lot about her. And that may very well be true, but shit, even my dad turns up on social now and again, and there's no one more careful than the Bordono family.

As I sit hunched over my desk, I rub my burning eyes and force my shoulders down from my ears.

"Come on, Bullseye," I mumble. "Come on. Where do I look?" It's obvious that regular methods aren't going to get this done, so, hurrying to my kitchen, I yank open the drawer nearest the fridge. Pulling the drawer all the way out, I turn it over to find my burner phone taped to the bottom. The one I use for absolute emergencies. Like this.

Peeling off the tape, I know the phone's got to be dead. Plugging it in, I wait for the lightning bolt. As soon as it shows, I text my connection in New York.

"*Need info on Seneca Villetrio. Female. Age: 24. By any means necessary.*" Without pausing, I hit the send button. Yeah, this particular connection of mine flies under the radar, but I need his help to get this done.

Then, fishing my regular cell out of my pocket, I text Seth. I hate to interrupt his "date", with Dr. Holly at the bar, but these are desperate times. Yeah, Seth is a numbers guy, but he's more than that. Like me, he has some "abilities" and connections that he doesn't talk about from his time managing a construction company. And from knowing what I do about the Bordono family, I know they are nose-deep in the construction business. Since I can't call in any of those favors right now, I need to see if Seth can.

"*Need help tracing a phone.*" Send.

Crap. I would have hated it if someone interrupted Sen and me.

"*Sorry to interrupt.*" Send.

If I believed in luck or were superstitious at all, I'd be crossing my fingers and toes right about now. Before I can even contemplate how I'd do that, my phone vibrates in my hand.

"*All cool. Just walked her to the car. Be there in 10.*"

I was right. He's connected one way or another. Damn, after very nearly killing each other a couple of hours ago, he's now running to my rescue, and it's like we're starring in some freaking bromance together.

"Come on, come on…" While I wait for my connection to get back to me, I run through my apartment, grabbing whatever I may need for a couple of days' travels—toothbrush, phone charger, an extra pair of jeans, a sweatshirt, and a couple of clean T-shirts and underwear. Then, from a box under the bed, I grab my passport, extra ammo, and five grand.

The vibration from my burner cell on the counter is so jarring, I nearly jump out of my skin. Great. Way to stay cool, Bullseye.

Rushing to it and grabbing it, I read the text.

"*Possible hit. Check email.*"

My otherwise steady hands are shaking as I open the laptop I also store under the bed. Giving it a minute to load, I click onto my heavily encrypted email account—although, what part of my life isn't heavily encrypted?

Holy fuck. What the hell…? Staring at the screen, I squint to get a better look. No way. No. It can't be.

There, staring back at me is my gray-eyed goddess, only this girl—dressed in a fitted, white ribbed-knit sweater with matching pearl earrings and long hair that falls around her shoulders in loose, flowing waves—looks like freaking Miss America.

Scanning down the file, I find the text:

"*No match: Seneca Villetrio. Age: 24.*"

"*Match: Sloane Villetrio. Age: 24. Born: Sag Harbor, New York to New York hedge fund manager, Donald Villetrio, and socialite, Patricia Villetrio. HNWIs—high-net-worth individuals. $600+ million annual yearly salary, plus assets in the Caribbean and other offshore accounts.*"

"Holy shit, they're loaded. Seneca grew up filthy rich..." My brain can barely process what my eyes are absorbing.

"*Sloane Villetrio attended Johnson Academy Prep School before graduating early, summa cum laude, from Columbia University with a degree in Women's Studies.*"

"And brilliant."

Raking my hand through the front of my hair, a strange tingling covers me from head to foot, and I've got to sit down. Flopping onto my couch, I lean forward, placing my fingertips to my temples, and rub, fighting back a headache.

"But she's also a liar." Sitting back and closing my eyes, I let my restless thoughts roam freely for a few moments. Have I been duped all this time?

Or am I the one doing the duping? Fuck it. She may be a liar, but I'm one too. Something else we have in common.

And frankly, that might be a harsh way to describe us both. Like me, it's not that she *lied*—well, except the bold-ass Florida remark—it's more that she *omitted* things. Like, where she grew up, what her life was like before moving to Hoppa, and who she actually is... Still, I've never been completely sold on that whole idea of a "lie by omission", anyway. Omission is simply being smart and choosing what you might want to share.

What I need now is some freaking coffee and a plan.

A cold chill washes through me, and I feel like I've been dipped into ice water from the inside out.

New York. She went to New York. I know it. She has a brother she loves. She said it to Seth. And she was born on Long Island, like me. Only hers was a very different part of the island.

I know it in my very soul—the woman is on her way to New York. The one place I should not and cannot go.

One wrong step in New York means Mikey and Tony would trap me, Ironclad would use me to kill Don Bordono, and then, with Ironclad running the drug scene, they'd kill my father, and then they'd have fun killing me.

But that's not the worst part. The worst part is what they'll do to Seneca when they catch her in New York. And they will catch her.

Fuck. Who knew fate would be this cruel?

I can't sit here and wait for Seth any longer, I'll have to meet him downstairs. Tossing my laptop and burner into my bag with the extra ammo and sliding the strap over my head and one shoulder, I let it hang across my body and close to my chest. Then, throwing on my Knights' jacket, and grabbing my keys for the truck I haven't used since I met Sen, and my bike, I rush out of my apartment and hustle down the stairs.

In the parking lot, moving as fast as I can, I drop my bag stuffed with every important document I own, plus the ammo, laptop, and burner phone, onto the seat along with my Knights' jacket. Then, I tie down my bike in the flatbed of my truck. My truck's a sweet little number, black with an extended cab and a flatbed customized for my bike. I've missed driving it, and I would have loved to park somewhere quiet with Sen and climb into the back of the cab… but we never got the chance.

"Damn it, Sen," I mumble. "There's so many things we never got the chance to do."

Of all of the things I would have liked to do with her, the truck was low on the priority list. But still… She loved the bikes so much, we just rode. And that was fine by me. Besides, I knew in my gut that we may never get a chance for more.

Suddenly, headlights flash in my eyes. Holding up my hand to block the light, Harry's truck pulls up.

"Hey!" Seth calls from the passenger's seat.

"Hey. Thanks for coming." Walking to them quickly, I furrow my brow, trying to figure out why Harry is here. He's too good of a guy to get mixed up in this. Besides, with the life he's had, he deserves a break from this kind of shit.

Did Seth tell him?

Seth's sitting there with some kind of old-fashioned spy contraption that looks more like an old metal suitcase than it does anything high tech. On closer inspection, I can tell it's a computer, but one I've never seen before.

Harry jumps out of the driver's seat and rushes around to my side. Walking at me with his shoulders broad, I have to take a step back to maintain some distance. Christ, will this be the second fight I get in today with one of my brothers from the Steel Knights? And this time with my best friend?

But I don't have time for this.

"Why the hell didn't you tell me what was going on?" Harry's pissed.

"There's nothing to tell."

"I don't believe you."

He stands to his full height, and I have to turn my chin up slightly to look him in the eye.

Clamping my hand on his shoulder, I move him backward. "Bullet, you know I love you like a brother, but there are some things that even brothers can't share."

"Bullshit."

"And even if I could, I don't have time right now."

"Make time," he demands.

"I can't."

Ignoring Harry, I jog up to Seth. Pushing the door open, he moves his body so he's facing outward, toward me.

"How does the shoulder feel?" I ask.

"Hurts like a mother."

I'd nearly forgotten about his bandaged shoulder and his arm in a sling. I can't believe all that happened only a few hours ago.

"It's freaking hard to type one-handed," he mumbles. Glancing up at me, he asks, "Do you have the number?"

Holding up my phone, I show him Seneca's number. He starts typing furiously.

Harry comes up behind me. "What are you doing?"

"I've got a hit." Seth turns the computer to show me a screen with a red blip. "She's on Interstate ten. Heading east."

"Toward fucking New York," I mumble. Looking at him, we make eye contact. "I may need to be gone for a while. Will you keep tabs on her for me? I'll make sure to check in."

"Yeah. Of course."

"And Harry says you're really good with the books. Can you pick up some of my weight as Treasurer? Just so he's not stuck doing it all?"

Seth glances at Harry and then looks at me. "Yeah. You got it." He holds up his good hand, and we lock hands in the air, nodding to one another.

Turning and passing by Bullet, I rush over to my truck. He beats me back, blocking my way. He's fuming.

"What's going on?"

"I have to find Seneca."

"Maybe she wants some space."

"It's not that simple." Stepping around him, I make my way to my truck and yank my door open.

"What does that mean?"

"Nothing. Harry, I have to go."

Climbing up into the cab, I try to close my door, but he grabs it, and holding it, keeps me from slamming it shut.

"Harry, you're being a freaking child. I need to go."

"Why?"

"Because I think Seneca needs help."

"She seems like she can take care of herself," he says.

"Yes. She can. I just need to go, okay?"

Damn, I don't want to get into this with Harry. He doesn't know about my connection to the Bordonos, and if he finds out what really happened to me that year after college, he'll never forgive me. He thinks we have a relationship based on trust, and if he were ever to find out where I was, who I was, and the things I did, he'd never forgive me.

I've kept that part of me a secret for too long. If he found out now, he'd think it was a betrayal. Turning the key in the ignition while he's still holding the door, I keep the truck in park but rev the engine.

"I need to go, Bullet."

"Why? What was Seth doing for you?"

"Tracing her. I thought he might have the connections to do that, and I was right."

"Why are you in such a damned hurry?"

"Fuck, Harry!" I slap my hands against the steering wheel. "Enough! I have to go."

Without batting an eye, Harry reaches across me and grabs my bag. Before I know what's happening, he pulls it open. His eyes widen as he stares inside.

"Damn, Avery, what is this?"

"Just things I need."

"Fuck man, who are you?" He stares into my eyes. The question is legit.

"The same guy I always was."

"Then what the hell do you need all that ammo for? And all that cash? Are you skipping town? Are you in trouble?"

"It's nothing I can explain, Harry. I've told you."

"Why, Avery? Who are you mixed up with? Did she drag you into something?"

"No. I'm trying to keep her out of it and safe."

"I know everything there is to know about you, and there is no reason that you would need extra ammo and a wad of cash in your day-to-day life. For God's sake, you were a science major in college!"

"Harry. Listen to me. I will explain everything when I can. Right now, every moment I sit here is a moment she gets farther away and closer to danger."

"What kind of danger?"

"Harry—"

"Damn it, Avery! What kind of danger?"

"I have some guys looking for me, okay? And they know about her. But she doesn't know about them. And now she's gone…" Fear settles on me, spiking my adrenaline.

"Guys? What guys? From where or when? From that year after college you spent in Europe with that girl you liked so much?"

"Harry, there was never any girl."

"Of course there was. You were gone…" A flicker of understanding lights up his eyes. "Where were you?"

"I have to go."

"Avery? Where. Were. You. That year after college?"

"I was in trouble, Harry. Real trouble. And now I may be in even worse trouble. And she'll be the one to pay if I can't get to her in time."

"In jail?"

Sighing, I nod.

"What the fuck, Avery!" Harry steps away and then back to me. "You know what? Now, it all makes sense. Why I never got one phone call. One lousy text. But why wouldn't you tell me?"

"Because it was ugly. And there's so much about my life you don't need to know."

"You know everything there is to know about me. My damned alcoholic, abusive mother. The cop and attorney who fucked me over. The reason I can't trust women. You know it all. We trusted each other. And now, I find out my best friend since college did time for… How long?"

"Six months."

"Six months and I didn't know? What the hell, Avery?"

"I was protecting you, Harry."

"I don't need your protection! Save it for your girl. Damn it! This is not how a brotherhood is built, Avery."

"I know."

"Do you? You know what? I don't think you know the first thing about brotherhood." He points to my jacket on the seat next to me. "Give me your jacket."

"What? Why?"

"Because you don't know what brotherhood means, and you don't deserve to be a Knight. Give me the fucking jacket."

"We pledged together. You can't do this. I'm an officer."

"Give me the jacket before I beat the crap out of you for it."

Reaching over, I grab the jacket off of the seat next to me and hand it to him through the open window.

"Harry, man. Don't do this."

"I'm not doing anything, Avery. You are."

"At least let me keep the fucking thing for warmth. I'm heading northeast. It'll be cold. I'll send it back to you once I get a new jacket."

"Don't think so. Maybe this way you'll get an idea of what it's like to be left out in the cold."

"Harry…"

Mumbling, he walks off and climbs into his truck. Revving the engine, he peels out and they're gone.

So, I'm no longer a Knight. And Seneca is gone. At least two men are trying to kill me, and I'm heading back to the one place my father warned me not to go.

Fuck. Sounds like another typical chapter in the life story of Avery "Bullseye" Pairings.

Chapter Fourteen

Wildfire

Uh-oh…

Oh crap. Bouncing on my toes to try to stay warm as I stand here, gassing up my bike, I throw my nose into the air and sniff. The weather is changing. I can tell by the air. Yeah, I've been riding as many hours a day as I can, clocking about three-hundred-and-fifty miles per day—which is a crazy number, and is absolutely killing my kidneys—but I'm probably as far as Ohio by now.

Thank heavens for these little gas stations and minimarts in the middle of nowhere.

Even without looking at a GPS or a single street sign, I can feel that I'm closing in on the east coast. Settling on me now is that certain type of cold air that seems to be exclusive to New York and New England. It's a bone-chilling, wet cold, and when the air is like this—cutting right through my jacket, jeans, and leather chaps like it's nothing—crap. That means some serious freaking snow is on the way.

Damn, these thin leather gloves I use for riding never keep my hands warm. Blowing air into my free hand to give it some heat, I glance around and at the store behind me. The big sign in the window lists rules about cigarettes and Ohio State Law. Maybe a pack of cigarettes would work to keep me warm? I don't actually have to inhale the damned things, just let them work as my own miniature heaters?

Chuckling, I turn my attention back to my bike that's nearly filled. Yeah, cigarettes are a great plan. Flicking away little bits of burning embers that fly into my eyes, that is, if the cigarette would last more than a second as I whiz down the highways at eighty—or ninety—miles an hour.

Sighing, my mind wanders to Avery, and I wonder what he's doing now. Has he forgotten me like he should? Closing my eyes for a moment, I imagine him shirtless in the warm Arizona sun, walking toward me…

That's an image that's warming me from the inside… *No. Focus, Sen. You needed to leave him behind. It's the only way to keep him safe.*

Stopping is always hard because it's the only time my mind is free enough to think about Avery. It's only been a couple of days since I've seen him, but God, do I miss him. I used to bump into him at the Taphouse every day, and even though we were only together that one night and morning—we had something real. I know we did.

And that's why, every time sadness feels like a real, tangible thing that's choking me—threatening to tighten its grip and suffocate me—I remind myself that it's because I do care about him so much that I have to run. Now that I'm certain Mikey and Tony know where I am, it will only be a matter of time before they come after me. Then they'll go after the people I care about—and that means Avery.

Replacing the nozzle in the pump and screwing on my gas cap, I shake my head when I think about my plan for coming to Hoppa. It was such a short time ago, and yet, I had such a different perspective. I was going to find Bullseye, the one guy in the club who had a rep for liking women and believing in equal rights in the club, make him like me, and then pledge for the Steel Knights so I would have protection if Mikey and Tony decided to pay me a visit. It all seemed so logical. And it was; until I did the most illogical thing of all.

I fell for Bullseye. And now, I can't let anything bad happen to him, no matter what I have to do. Even if that means never seeing him again.

Securing my bike, I decide to give my kidneys a much-deserved break and hit the restroom and grab some snacks. Pulling open the door of the minimart, I'm immediately welcomed by warm air. I don't even care that it smells like burnt hot dogs and orange bathroom cleaner. Compared to some of the places I've had to stop on the way…? I'm grateful this place bothers to clean its bathrooms at all.

Removing my helmet and finger-brushing my hair, I nod to the man behind the counter. He looks up from eating his package of crumb donuts and nods back, as he yanks up the waistband of his pants. Then he looks me up and down.

With my training in Krav Maga, I'm not the slightest bit worried about him accosting me. One try, and I could knock him on his out-of-shape ass, killing him.

A shudder washes over me and I close my eyes, willing the man to stay put… I don't want to kill anyone. Ever. Not only would I never want to take someone's life—even someone who was attacking me—I'd never want to suffer the consequences. I've seen the inside of a jail too many times when I visited my brother.

I take a deep breath, trying not to worry about Matt.

After rushing to the women's room to do my business, I slow down when I wash my hands. Staring into the foggy and cracked bathroom mirror, I see a woman I don't know. Sure, I changed my look from the Long Island princess that I was all those years ago, but it's more than that. I look tired. And hardened. And… discouraged.

But I will not give up. Matt needs me.

Drying my hands in the air dryer, I sigh. It's been so long since I've seen Matt, and I miss him, but he was right. I had to run. The irony is, by telling me to run, he thought he was protecting me, but I only agreed to it so I could stay alive to come back and fight his case. And now that Mikey and Tony are out, there's going to be hell to pay. For them. I will make sure those scumbag lowlifes fess up to the murder and get my brother acquitted if it's the last thing I do.

One thing's for sure, this would be so much easier if there were another witness. Someone who could step forward and say that Matt didn't pull the trigger. Yeah, Matt was there on a drug deal gone bad, and he's not innocent, but he did not do this.

However, it's not like that person's going to come riding up on a shining Harley—like a knight on a stallion—and offer himself up. So, as usual, it's up to me, and me alone.

Yanking open the bathroom door, I march out into the minimart and grab some granola bars, healthy chips, and I splurge on a fruit cup that looks like it was made within this century, at least. Walking over to the counter, I lay my things down and turning my head, I look outside. The sky is gray. Dark gray. Shit.

Glancing up at the man behind the counter, I nod. "Bad weather expected?"

"Oh, yeah." He takes my items and drags them across a scanner. "Storm. Nor'easter. We're going to get zonked. It's all anyone's been talking about. You haven't been watching the weather?"

Shaking my head, I glance outside again. The snow has started falling, and it's that fast-falling sideways snow.

"Well, you got a friend who can trailer your bike? Sweet ride by the way."

"Thanks. And no."

"Then, you'd better get yourself to a motel for the night. And fast. We're expecting over two feet. Blizzard conditions. Whiteout." He starts putting my things into a bag as he nods to the outside.

"No bag, thanks."

"Suit yourself." Turning the bag upside down, it all falls onto the counter. "I'm leaving here in ten minutes myself. If I were you, I'd get going."

Careful of my cell phone screen, I shove the goods into my bag. "How close is the nearest hotel?"

"Forty minutes back that way." He points in the direction I just came from.

Damn.

"How much do I owe you?"

Holding up his hand, he shakes his head. "It's on the house."

"Thank you."

"You're welcome. Grab yourself a hot coffee, too. Gonna keep your belly warm for a bit."

"Thanks." Hurrying to the coffee machine, I pull the lever and fill a cup. Walking back to the door, I hold up the coffee. "Really, thanks again."

"Ain't nothing. Now go. I've got to close down and get out of here myself."

Taking a few sips of coffee, and basking in one more moment of warmth, I gather my courage and step outside. Instantly, the wind and snow smack me, and it's already miserable.

Tossing my coffee cup in a nearby trash can, I hunch my shoulders up and trudging forward against the wind, I try to stay upright. Thankfully, there's nothing sticking to the roads yet, but it'll probably be just a couple of minutes until that happens.

Pushing myself forward, I make my way to my bike. Placing a hand to my face, my cheek stings and burns in response. I'm already windburned. Damn, that short stay in the hot Arizona sun has thinned my blood and turned me into one hell of a wuss. Okay, I have two options: I can double back and find that hotel forty minutes in the wrong direction and lose ground, or I can push forward. But as the wind smacks against me, I wonder if that's even possible.

One thing is for sure, standing here won't do anything. Straddling my bike, I turn the key and roll forward, moving my bike to face the street.

Ahead, there's a set of headlights bobbing in time with a car that's rising and falling in and out of potholes. Another poor soul caught in this. The headlights grow brighter as the car comes nearer and nearer.

"Wait a sec," I mumble. "That's not a car, it's a truck. And it… it looks a lot like Avery's truck…"

Shaking my head, I know my mind is playing tricks on me. Yes, I would fall to my knees and kiss the snow in gratitude if that were truly Avery, but… it makes no sense. He has no way of knowing where I am, and considering the way I left things between us, even if he did know where I was, he probably wouldn't care.

"Seneca!"

It's him. His window is open, and he's waving frantically as he calls my name.

Standing here, straddling my bike, shivering—freezing from the cold and drenched from the snow—I'm warm for the first time in days.

"Seneca."

Parking the truck, he hops out and comes running toward me. Leaning over my bike, he pulls me into his embrace.

"Thank god. I didn't know if I would find you."

As he holds me tighter, I give myself over, pushing myself against him, breathing him in.

Pulling back, he looks me up and down. "Thank god you're safe."

"How?" I stare into his eyes. "How did you find me?"

"Seth has a way of tracking your cell phone. It wasn't easy—but we did it."

Shivering, I nod to him, noticing his bare arms. "Your coat. You're in a T-shirt. Aren't you freezing?"

"Yes. Come on." He points behind him. "Get into the truck. I'm going to trailer your bike and fill up the truck." Tilting his head upward, he looks at the sky and then lowers it, looking at me. "The weather's getting really bad. Go ahead. Get in and get warm."

For about a billion reasons, I shouldn't let this happen. However, as the snow begins to stick, I take it as an omen.

Opening the passenger's door, I consider hopping into the driver's seat and taking off, but I would never leave him behind in the snow. Yes, I would do anything I had to, to keep him safe—including "borrowing" his truck—but the snow now poses a more imminent threat than Mikey and Tony.

Climbing up into the cab of the truck, I'm immediately warmed. "Oh, ow." Pulling off my gloves, I hold my hands out to the heater that's blasting warm air. "Oh, that feels good." Rubbing my red hands together, trying to let them defrost, they're sore from the cold. But that's not nearly as bad as my damp clothes that now feel heavy and wet.

The driver's side door opens, and he climbs in and shakes off the snow that's collected in his hair. Looking at him—his short hair speckled with snow and ice, the slight scruff that's growing on his chin, the way his T-shirt pulls across his wide shoulders—he looks like he's posing for a women's, "Hot Motorcycle Guys" calendar.

"What?" His brow wrinkles.

"Nothing. I was just thinking you look good."

"You do too."

Shaking my head, I turn to look out the window. "Nah, but thanks. I've been on the bike for days." Right now, I'm grateful for the short nights I've spent in the motels, and the quick showers I've taken every morning. I'd hate to be sitting here, stinking up his cab.

The snow comes down faster now.

"It's really coming down." Turning back to him, I ask, "Are we safe to drive?"

"Safer than you were on your bike. I have chains on the tires. There's a motel about forty-five minutes back. We'll head that way."

Reaching out, I place my hand on his, stopping him. "I'm not going back."

"Where are you going?"

"It's complicated."

"Is it?" His eyebrows raise, and I see the concern etched on his face. "What were you thinking, Seneca?" Shaking my head, I stare at the rubber mats on the floor. "I mean, you could have been killed out here in this storm. You could have frozen to death or hit a patch of black ice and wiped out. It's so incredibly dangerous."

"I know that," I mumble, still looking at the floor.

"Seneca, why did you run? We were going to work things out, and—" he slams his hand against the steering wheel. "I thought we had something special. A connection. Or was that connection I had with Sloane, not Seneca?"

"What?" Whipping around, I face him. "How did you—"

"I have connections. Why didn't you tell me?"

"Because that's part of my past and this..." Pointing out the windshield, I explain, "Is my future. What does it matter?"

"It matters because I thought you were one person and it turns out, you're a very different one."

"No, I'm not. I'm exactly the person you knew in Hoppa."

"You're an Ivy League grad."

"I never said I wasn't. What? Just because I look a certain way means I couldn't go to an Ivy League school?"

"That's not what I mean. You're also loaded."

"My parents are. I own my bike and the clothes on my back. That's it. I left as soon as I graduated high school. I went to Columbia and paid my own way."

"Still, you have people to support you. I thought you were on your own. You could always run back to Mommy and Daddy if you needed something. I'm sure they'll throw you the millions you need."

I can't help it. Pressure builds in my eyes, and they ache and burn. No matter how hard I fight them back, tears begin dripping from the corners of my eyes. It has been years since I've cried.

"Sen?" His eyes widen, and his harsh expression softens. "I'm sorry—"

Taking a deep breath, I nod. "My parents are assholes. Well, not so much my mother, but my father. Once he realized I wasn't going to marry one of his friend's sons and give him hedge fund grandchildren, he lost interest in me. Then I learned to ride a bike, and fix one, and then when I changed my look, he disowned me. I was an embarrassment to him."

"Sen, I'm so sorry…"

My tears are flowing freely, and I realize they've been pent up for years now. It's a release to let them go.

"Then my kid brother started hanging with the wrong crew, and now he's in jail on a bogus charge relating to drugs." I omit the part about Mikey and Tony who sent the brick and are now looking for me. I don't want Avery getting any deeper than he already is. "My parents won't have anything to do with him, so that leaves me. I have spent every dollar I can possibly make on his attorneys and trying to get him freed."

"Seneca, I am really sorry. I had no idea."

"No, you didn't. But you were so willing to forget the Seneca you knew, and judge me on what, a picture you saw and some info about my past? Without knowing anything about me."

"You're right. And I was wrong." He looks down at the seat between us and then up into my eyes.

Reaching out, he touches my cheek. His hand is so warm and strong and makes me feel protected.

Pulling myself together and wiping my tears, I glance at the windshield. "The windshield is covered in that wet, packing snow." I nod to it. "Look."

He gives his attention to the windshield and tries the wipers, but even on the highest setting, the snow falls faster than the wipers can clean.

"We can't drive in this," he says. "I'm going to pull the truck around to the side of the building where we'll be protected on one side, at least."

I take deep breaths as my heart races faster and faster. The severity of the situation is finally hitting me. What chance does one woman on a bike have against *all* these odds?

"Are you okay?" he asks, cocking his head.

We stay still as he stares at me. His brow is furrowed, and it's obvious he's concerned.

"It's just, if you hadn't come…" My voice is a squeak as I hold up my hand, pointing at the snow. "I would have died out here."

"Hey." Reaching out, he puts an arm around my shoulder and pulls me to his chest. "There was no way I wouldn't come. No matter where you go, I will find you. And protect you. Okay?"

Although it's so wrong, it feels so good.

Nodding, I smile.

"Good. So I'm going to drive us over there." He points to a spot by the minimart, and then we're going to get you out of your wet clothes and wrapped up into some nice warm blankets I have in the back."

"Really?" I ask, smirking.

"Absolutely. I told you I would do whatever it takes to keep you safe. Even if it means something as horrible as undressing you, wrapping my arms around you, and keeping you warm against my naked body."

"Even something that awful?"

He puts the truck into gear. "Why, ma'am, I'd even make love to you if it meant keeping you safe."

"Well, aren't you the gentleman."

Winking, he smiles. "Absolutely, little lady. You can just think of me as your own personal knight in shining armor."

As the truck rolls forward, and Avery keeps me safe and literally sheltered from the storm, I wonder if he isn't exactly that.

My own personal *Steel Knight* in shining armor.

Chapter Fifteen

Bullseye

The blizzard conditions make it challenging just pulling around to the side of the building—I can't imagine what it would have been like for her, all alone on her bike out here... No. I push that out of my mind and concentrate on the fact that she's here, safe and warm, in my truck.

"We won't be able to keep the engine running all night," I explain as I yank off my gloves. "It's dangerous. And as much as we're not going to want to, we'll have to crack the windows to reduce the risk of carbon monoxide poisoning."

"Yes." Her eyes blink lazily. She's not paying any attention to what I'm saying—but she is watching my lips move... and damn, how I want them moving on her now...

My attraction to her is so great, right now I don't even give a damn about finding out why she ran. We have all night for that. And hopefully, the entire ride back to Hoppa.

"C'mere," I murmur, taking her by her jacket and pulling her closer to me. "Damn, right now, even though I've got to climb over it every time I need to get to the back area, I am so glad this old truck has a bench seat."

"Me too."

"Let's get you out of those wet clothes."

"Yes," she mumbles.

As I draw her nearer, she gives herself to me, like putty in my hands. She wants this, maybe even as much as I do. But as much as I want to make love to her, she scared me when she left, and because of it, I've got this *need* to control her and bend her into submission...

Aw, hell. Truth is, around Seneca, I always have that desire. She makes me feel so damned masculine.

Reaching out, I find the top of the zipper of her jacket and unzip it. Pushing it off of her shoulders, it stalls, stuck around her arms. She reaches out to pull it off of her arms and over her wrists.

"No," I snap without meaning to.

Looking up at me, her eyes are wide and filled with passion. Shaking my head, I reach out and pull her jacket gently off of one arm and then the other, and then lay it out on the dashboard to dry.

Sitting there in her long-sleeved, lilac-colored shirt, she looks young and beautiful. When she looks up into my eyes, for a moment I see the girl in the picture on my computer screen… the Long Island princess. I imagine her in her parents' mansion, sitting on her king-sized bed in her room with purple-painted walls, with a fleet of cars and butlers and maids at her disposal—and I can't help but wonder, what happened to make her the kick-ass woman she is today? Whatever it was, as long as it didn't hurt her, I'm grateful for it.

Taking the hem of her shirt, I pull it up, over her head and off of her, and then lay it on the dashboard, next to her jacket. She shakes her head to let her hair fall gracefully into position, and I smile at the black tank top she's wearing.

"It's like one of those Christmas presents people wrap up in a box inside of a box…"

Slipping my fingers under the bottom of her tank top, she shivers.

"Sorry." Pulling my hands back, I blow warm breath into my cupped hands and rub them together. "They're cold."

"No." She shakes her head. "It's okay. They don't bother me."

"And finally, the last box." Slipping my fingers under the hem of her tank top again, I slide it up over her head. Then, reaching around behind her with one hand, I unhook her bra and slide it off of her.

Her gorgeous, full breasts spring forward, and she shivers again.

"Cold?" I ask.

"No." Shaking her head, she bites the bottom of her lip and it nearly sends me over the edge. "Just excited."

All I want to do is to reach out, grab her, tear off her jeans and chaps, pull her onto my lap, and make love to her, but there's a long, cold night ahead of us, and so I'm going to take my time. My gaze falls to her nipples… Damn. They're already tight and erect, and I need them. But first…

Stroking her cheek gently, she nuzzles against my palm. Placing both of my hands on the sides of her face, I tilt her head backward and moving closer, I kiss her gently on the lips. Without letting go, I pull back and look into her eyes. Her pupils are dilated, and she wants more…

Taking my hand from her cheek, I move it slowly toward her mouth. As I run my thumb across her pouty bottom lip, she parts her lips. Damn, this woman is sexy.

Pushing down on her bottom lip, I open her mouth and slide my thumb in.

"Mm…" she moans, as her tongue teases the tip of my finger. Dropping her jaw open more, I push my thumb in farther… She runs her tongue from the base of my thumb to the tip, before settling into a pattern and rhythm of licking and sucking.

"Fuck!" Moving in my seat, I've got to calm myself, before I burst through my jeans.

Pulling my hand from her mouth, I reach out and cup her breasts, as she drops her head back.

"Avery, you feel so good."

Good God, this is going to be fun, and we've just barely started.

Leaning forward, I take one of her nipples into my mouth, biting and nipping at it. When her bud is so hard and tight it feels brittle, I ease off and begin licking. Finally, I clamp my mouth onto it completely. I take as much of her breast into my mouth as I can, and wrapping my arms around her back, I draw her closer. Unlatching from one hard, pointy nipple, I move to the other. Damn. I don't just want to make love to this woman. I want her body and soul, and in every way possible.

Releasing her breasts, I take a breath, staring at her beauty, and she seizes the moment and reaches out for my T-shirt.

"No." Shaking my head, I stop her. "Not yet. My clothes are staying on right now. I want you completely naked in my truck, wrapped up and warm in a blanket before a speck of my clothing comes off. Understand?"

"Yes." Somehow, her already erect nipples grow harder. "Why?" she whispers.

"To keep you warm, and because I want you… completely exposed to me."

"Ohh…"

She moans again, as I pull off her chaps and then unzip her jeans and slide them off of her. I place them on the dash with the rest of her clothes.

"Damn, Sen," I growl at her, sitting there in her black silk panties before I reach around and pull a blanket from the back of the cab. Shaking it out, I drape it across her shoulders, and then, looking into her eyes, I slip my fingers in the sides of her panties and pull them off. She tucks the blanket under her naked bottom as I lay the panties on her jeans.

"Well, this would be tough to explain to an officer passing by," I chuckle.

She nods, and I can tell she's barely able to form words.

"Lucky for us, that won't happen. No one can drive tonight. So, you're all mine."

"Yes." Her voice is deep and throaty.

"Lie back," I command her.

Her eyes light up, and then she does as I say. Because there's not enough length on the seat for her entire body, her head rests near the passenger's door, and her legs are off to the side, with her feet on the floor.

"Raise your legs," I tell her, "and bend your knees, put your feet flat on the seat."

"Avery…"

She's hesitant for a moment, but then gives in, and her compliance is almost as sexy as she is, lying there. With her knees bent and tight together, and her feet flat on the seat, she is completely mine…

Climbing onto my knees, I reach out and drawing her legs apart gently, I slide upward, over her delectable body, looking at her beautiful face.

"I missed you, Sen."

"I missed you too."

Leaning down, I press my lips to hers. Wrapping her arms around my neck and pulling me to her, she responds with so much passion, her head and torso lift from the seat. Taking my tongue into her mouth, she becomes the very willing recipient of my thrusting and prodding…

As we lie here, moaning and clawing at one another, I grow even frigging harder. How is that possible?

Unlatching myself from her, I hover above her. "Now, you are going to stay right here…"

When I kiss her neck, she shivers from my touch. Running my tongue up and down her torso, I stop on her stomach and flick her belly-button ring with my tongue, and she moans. Damn, this is going to be too much fun. Moving farther down, I take her thighs in my hands and settling myself on the seat between them, I plant tiny kisses on her tanned, strong, inner thighs.

She shudders in response. "Oh God, Avery…"

Finally, resting on my elbows, I roll her thighs further apart… and Seneca is completely mine…

"Damn, Sen…"

I move in for just the tiniest taste, and she raises her hips in response.

"God… Like I said, you are going to stay right there, as I…" With my tongue, I gently flick the small bundle of nerves between her legs.

"*Avery…*" she moans.

"…Make you…"

Pressing against her nub with my tongue, she squirms beneath me. As I settle into a smooth rhythm of licking her, with tiny nips when she least expects it, she opens her knees wider, and slides her bottom closer to me, giving me even more access.

"…Crazy…"

Balancing on one arm, with the fingers of my other hand, I explore her delicious folds, while she wriggles beneath me, moaning incoherent words. Letting my finger run up and down her, I find her tiny opening and push just the tip of my finger inside, teasing her.

"Avery, more, please…" she cries.

Damn, she is already so wet and her suction is so strong… all I want is to dive into her. And I will, but first…

Pushing my finger deep inside her, she gasps.

"I've got you, baby." Sliding my finger in and out slowly, bumping against the spot deep inside that makes her back arch and lift off of the seat, I move back in for her nub. Settling down with my finger thrusting, I let my tongue work her, licking and teasing… When she reaches out with both hands and clamps them onto the back of my head, I know she's close.

Keeping my pressure steady with my tongue, I press against her harder and bury my face against her, as I twist my finger and put direct pressure on her spot deep inside.

"Oh God, Avery!" Arching up off of the seat, she cries out as her body quivers beneath me. "Don't stop."

Pushing against her with more pressure as I force my hand even deeper inside her, her muscles tighten around my finger as she rolls her head back and moans. Finally, she drops back into a heap on the seat.

Looking at her lying there with her face relaxed, and her breasts rising and falling with her racing breath… I need more.

"I want more of you. Now."

"You can have all of me, Avery. Every bit."

Her words make my already throbbing cock threaten to explode.

"I will take every bit of you. I can promise you that." Climbing up and over her, I rest at her side, stroking her beautiful cheek with my finger. Fuck, how I never want to let her go. "But I'm not ready to give up this power play that's working to my advantage just yet. I like you naked and submissive. Once my clothes come off, and I'm buried deep inside you…" Shaking my head, I think about it. "Then, I lose control, too. And since you've run away from me once already, I think I need to stay in control… maybe all night." I grin at her, as her eyes widen.

"You're going to keep me naked all night?"

"I'm thinking so." Leaning over, I trace her pouty mouth with my fingers. "And maybe all day tomorrow, too. Thinking about it, I've decided that clothes are highly overrated. I like blankets much better on you. So, maybe when I get you home with me, I'll just keep you this way. Naked—always…"

"Ah, but I may get some second glances at the club."

"True." Nodding, I play along, knowing she's into this little fantasy as much as I am. "So, I'll let you wear clothes in public, but as soon as you cross the threshold of our apartment, you are required to strip, so I can have full access to all of this…"

Leaning down, I find her mouth with mine while I run my hands up and down her body. Pulling back, she smiles at me.

"Well, if you insist on staying dressed tonight, it's going to make it difficult for you to have any fun."

"Not the way I see it," I reply.

"Oh?" Cocking her eyebrow, I can see the gears turning. "Well, why don't you have a seat then, and let me see if I can guess what you're thinking…?"

Wrapping the blanket around herself, she pushes herself up. I sit up next to her, leaning my head against the back of the bench seat. With her eyes locked on me, she reaches out and pulls open all the buttons of my button fly, and then reaching her hands into my boxer-briefs, grabs my member. It's rock-hard and ready for her, and her warm touch feels too good…

"I know you're staying dressed," she purrs into my ear, "but would you consider sliding your jeans down just enough to give me full access?"

Sitting up, she looks at me and licks her lips. Reaching forward, I cup her chin with my hand and shove my thumb into her mouth again. This time, she closes her teeth around my thumb—so very gently—before sucking me, and it nearly sets me over the edge.

"All right." Pulling my thumb from her mouth, I lift my T-shirt out of the way, and I slip my hands into the sides of my jeans and briefs, pulling them down so that they're just low enough to expose the full length of my long member.

"Avery…" She exhales deeply and wraps a hand around my shaft. Leaning forward, she kisses me gently on the tip. Licking it like I'm her favorite flavor of lollipop, she laps up the juice that leaks out…

"Damn, Sen…" Sitting back, I let my knees fall open, and my arms rest on the back of the seat, feeling big, powerful, and so-frigging-male right now. There will be time to grab her head and coach her to my rhythm, but first, I'm just going to sit back, enjoy, and see what surprises Seneca Villetrio has in store for me…

Opening her mouth wide, she takes my tip in, licking, and then pulls back. Then, sliding down on me again, this time, she uses her teeth lightly—scraping me ever-so-gently—and it damn near sends me over the edge. Toying with my tip, she licks it again, teasingly.

"Wanna know something?" she asks as she takes one more long lick of my rod from the base, up the shaft, ending with a circle at the tip.

"Yeah?" Right now, she could tell me the damned truck is flying to the moon, and I wouldn't have the wits about me to argue.

"I've never done this before…" Looking up at me from her position over my rod, she smiles.

"Shut the fuck up."

"It's true." Grasping my full width with one hand, she flattens her other hand, so the base of my rod sits between her thumb and forefinger, and then she presses down.

"Shit!" Sitting up, I nearly explode from the force of her hand wedged against my balls as her mouth and tongue work me up and down.

"Oh, damn, Sen…"

My eyes are rolling back, and I start thrusting against her mouth as I grab the back of her head. She moans in response.

"No. No way." It would be way too easy to finish like this—so, reaching down, I slip my hands under her arms and raise her up.

Smiling, she licks her swollen lips. "Not bad for a first-timer, huh?"

Shit. Sliding my pants all the way down so we have full access, I reach for her and taking her by her small waist, I drop her onto my lap, lining her up with me. Still holding her by the waist, I bring her down on top of me, filling her with as much of me as she can take. Her eyes close as her head rolls back.

"Oh, Avery…"

I'm damned close, so I move faster than I want to, but she's right here with me, matching my rhythm. Her hips thrust in time with mine, and as I reach up for her breasts, she puts her warm hands on my shoulders.

"Avery… I'm so close…"

Her muscles tighten and clench as she releases, and I clamp my hands on her hot little ass.

"God, Sen, baby…" Grunting, I let go with a final thrust. "Damn."

She falls in a heap on top of me and wrapping my arms around her, I hold her close. We don't speak for whole minutes… just holding each other…

Then, her body shakes and she draws in short, jagged breaths like she's gasping for air. Holding her away from me, I see the tears streaming down her cheeks.

"Baby, are you okay?"

Nodding, she lets go of a sob, and her body convulses on top of me. Wrapping her up tight in the blanket and laying her down on the seat, I yank my pants back up and lie next to her, holding her close to me.

"Whatever it is, baby, we'll handle it. Together," I tell her solemnly. "You don't have to face this alone. Whatever it is."

But somehow, from her silence and the tears soaking my T-shirt, I can feel that that is exactly what's going to happen. She believes she has to face this—whatever *this* is—alone.

And sure as I'm lying here, I know the snow is the reason I found her tonight, and if I don't hold on tight, with the first rays of sunshine, she'll just disappear again. No one ever said loving Wildfire would be easy, but damn…

I never thought I'd need an act of God or a force of nature to help me do it.

Chapter Sixteen

Bullseye

"Hey…"

After I shake her gently, she begins to rouse.

"What's going on?"

Turning the heater up full blast, I'm able to get the defroster to begin clearing the windows. The sound of plows going by makes her sit up.

"It's morning, and the plows have been clearing the roads for a couple of hours. They're okay to drive on. We'll be able to move soon."

"Oh." She looks down. "That's good news."

"Sen, baby."

"No." Reaching out, she places her hand on mine. "Please. Thank you for holding me through my mini-meltdown last night."

"It's okay. We all have them."

She eyes me quizzically. "You have meltdowns?"

"Of course. But when I do, I pump a bunch of holes in a target."

She barely smiles.

"So, as fun as this has been, how about we get you dressed? Your clothes are at least drier than they were last night. They should be okay for the ride home."

"Home?"

"To Hoppa."

"Yeah, of course." She smiles. "To Hoppa."

Do you have any other clothes?" I point to her oversized bag on the floor.

"No, no. Just money and my keys and such." Grabbing her clothes off the dash, she pulls on her bra and panties quickly. Then, she slides into her jeans, tank top, shirt, and jacket. She goes for her chaps.

"As sexy as those are on you, you don't need them to ride home in the truck. They'll probably get uncomfortable."

"Yeah, of course." She folds them up and puts them on the seat between us.

"How about I go grab us some coffee? I need the restroom, anyway. And the lights just flicked on in the store." Looking around the parking lot as a few cars and two semis come pulling in, I shift in my seat. This place is obviously busy since it's the only gas station for miles, and we're too close to New York for comfort.

"Sounds good." I want to tell her to be quick, but I don't want to worry her. "I'll clean the snow off the truck."

"Great."

She goes for her door, but reaching out, I place my hand on her arm, and she freezes. She's incredibly tense and jumpy this morning. Well, we have a long ride back to Hoppa to talk through all of this and to get to the bottom of whatever is torturing her. And I'd really like to find out why she bolted from the hospital when Seth said he hadn't tossed the brick.

"Hey, Sen, I had a great time last night. I mean, aside from the you-almost-freezing-to-death incident."

Nodding, she looks out the windshield and back to me. "Me too. Thank you, Avery."

"I think it's thank *you*..."

"No, I mean, for coming to find me. I don't know what would have happened to me if you didn't come for me." Her eyes grow glassy.

"Well you don't have to worry about that, okay? I promise I will always take care of you."

"Yeah." Moving away from me, she pushes open the door and jumps down out of the truck.

Watching her disappear into the minimart, I rub at the pain in my gut while my brain wrestles with this feeling of unease. There it is again—that damned feeling that Seneca Villetrio is going to vanish out of my life as quickly as she came in.

"Get a grip, Bullseye," I mumble. Hopping out of the truck, it's freaking freezing out here in my T-shirt. It dawns on me that I have a zip-front and hoodie with me, I'd just forgotten because I was in such a rush to get to Sen.

Rummaging through my bag in the back area, I grab the zip-front and throw it on. Then, tossing the hoodie on the seat for her, I store her chaps and climb back out with a scraper. One good thing about wet, packing snow, although it's heavy, it cleans off the truck fairly easily.

By the time I've finished removing snow from the roof, and even cleared out the flatbed and bikes so we're not carrying extra weight from the snow, she comes out of the minimart with two cups of steaming coffee.

Rushing to the door to meet her, I take a cup from her and wrap my hands around it. "Damn, you are a sight for sore eyes."

Smiling, she nods to the truck and then looks at me. "Why don't you take a run to the restroom, too? I can watch the stuff."

It's a good idea. It makes sense... but something in the back of my brain is screaming at me not to leave her. But my bladder is screaming something else.

Come on, relationships are built on trust, right?

"Cool. Thanks. I'll just be a sec."

"Take your time." She holds out her hand. "I'll take your coffee into the truck with me."

"Yeah, thanks." I don't know why, but the knot in my stomach relaxes when she takes the coffee. Maybe because it all seems so normal.

Walking to the door of the minimart, I glance back to see her sitting in the cab, sipping her coffee. Reaching forward, she disappears out of sight for a moment, and my stomach flips, but then she pops back up. She must be playing with the radio or digging in her bag for something. Okay. A smile sweeps across my face. She's there. And she'll be there, so I can get her home and safe with the Steel Knights before I have to handle Mikey and Tony. Pulling open the door, I hurry into the minimart.

"Damn, the truckers made the wait for the men's room forever…" I mumble as I walk to the truck carrying two bagels slathered in cream cheese. I'm sure she hasn't eaten in forever, and since we're closer to New York, there's a chance the bagels will be decent. Even from a gas station. She probably can't hear me, but I'll explain when I hop in. Nearing the truck, I look for her through the windshield, but… I don't see her.

"Sen?" My heart is racing as I rush toward the truck. "Sen?" Yanking open the door to the cab, I pray she's there—she's just hidden from view because she's messing with the radio.

But there's nothing.

"Sen?"

Rushing around to the back of the truck… It's gone. Her bike is gone.

"Goddamnit!" Throwing the bagels onto the ground, I pound my fists against the sides of the truck. "Seneca, why?" Taking a deep breath, I rush to the driver's side, pull the door open, and hop in. She couldn't have gotten that far, so I'll just have Seth put another trace on her phone…

Thankfully, the keys are in the ignition, I knew she wouldn't leave me stuck, but why would she run…? Again?

Glancing at the floor, I see her bag is gone and then, looking at the seat, I notice my hoodie is gone, too… but her cell is here. Next to my friggin' TV remote.

If the moment wasn't so dire, it would almost be funny.

"What?" Picking up her phone, I tighten my fist around it. Now, there's no way for me to trace her. "Why, Sen? Why would you do this?" I resist the urge to crush it in my hand. What an asshole I am. Why would I trust her again? She ran from the clubhouse—actually went out the damned bathroom window—why would I think that she's changed?

Some force is driving her to take these crazy chances. All the more reason I have to find her. I can't let her drive straight into danger. I just can't.

I would never want to put anyone in that kind of danger—but especially not the woman I lo… care about so very much.

Dragging my hand down my face, scrubbing it, I try to clear my mind so I can think.

"Damn it, Sen!"

Revving the engine of the truck, I know I've got only one shot. She grew up on Long Island, and I know her disappearance and running has to do with her brother.

That means, just as I'd thought, she's heading for New York. The one place I shouldn't go. The one place my father told me to stay away from.

Peeling out of the parking lot, I click on my turn signal and jump on the road leading to the highway, heading east. This is the one place that, if I'm not incredibly careful, will bring me right to Mikey and Tony. But more importantly, will deliver her to them.

I am driving myself straight to my death. And probably my father to his as well.

Once Mikey and Tony find Seneca, and they will, they'll use her as bait. Then, they'll use my relationship with Don Bordono to get me close enough to him to kill him. Then they'll get promoted in Ironclad's organization, and then, that's where the real horror begins.

Because they won't just slaughter me for fun, they'll make me watch all the horrendous things they'll do to her, before killing us both.

"Damn it, Sen!" Slamming my fist on the wheel, I push the truck faster. It's about eight hours from Ohio to the city, but she's going to be moving a hell of a lot faster on her bike. I've seen the woman ride. She'll be able to dodge traffic and take shortcuts and—forget it. When she gets to the city, she'll weave her way through the tie-ups, hitting the Midtown Tunnel heading for the island before I barely make it to Eighth Avenue. I'm going to have to ditch the truck.

Shit. But… thinking it through as I hit a speed of eighty on the empty highway heading toward Pennsylvania, right now, I have the upper hand. It's harder to go longer distances on a bike. And it's freaking freezing out. She'll need to make more stops. Good, that's good. So, I'm going to ride straight to Staten Island—so I can bypass the city—and then store my truck on Long Island. The one place I should never, ever be.

"Holy crap!"

Checking my phone again for the address Seth sent, I shake my head. This is it.

Staring at the mansion ahead of me, I can't believe *this* is where my Seneca grew up. It's a stone house with smaller buildings set off to the back of the main house. A circular driveway wraps around the front, with a damned fountain in the middle of the circle. A massive porch, complete with columns, surrounds the front door.

The only place I've ever seen that compares to this in real life is Don Bordono's home. And even his house isn't as impressive as this. But I'm sure as hell not going to tell him that.

Sitting at the end of the driveway with my bike balanced between my legs, I take a deep breath. This is my only shot. I stored my truck back in a hidden alley next to a nightclub where I used to hang and rode my bike here to get to her faster. If fate were on my side, she'd be sitting in there. With her mother. But since she hates her parents, or at least her father, the chances of that are low.

So… hopping off of my bike and walking it up to the front of the house so as not to disturb them with the noise from my pipes, I park it out front and then, jogging to the door, I ring the doorbell.

An older woman with her hair in a bun and an actual gray, maid's uniform with a white apron, opens the door. She smiles. "Can I help you?"

"Yes, please." Looking past her, I take in the marble flooring, massive chandelier, and double wrap staircase. "Is Mrs. Villetrio available?" It's such a long shot, but the only one I have.

"May I ask who's inquiring—"

"Meredith? Who is it?"

A gorgeous woman in her mid-fifties with tanned skin like Seneca's, and shoulder-length black hair that hangs loosely at her shoulders, steps up next to Meredith. She's dressed in wool slacks and a V-neck sweater with an impressive diamond around her neck that's only dwarfed by the one on her finger. Cripes.

She opens the door wider and looks me up and down. For the first time since I left New York for Arizona a couple of years ago, I feel underdressed.

"Can I help you?" She's pleasant enough.

"I'm Avery Pairings. I'm a friend of your daughter's. I'm here to see if Seneca—sorry, Sloane, is here. Or, if you know where she could possibly be. I think she's in trouble."

"Please..." Without a frown or any crack in her perfect exterior, she moves back and beckons for me to come inside. "Won't you come in?"

Stepping inside, I glance around at the cavernous space and the art hanging on the walls. It's like stepping into a museum.

"Your home is exquisite." It just slips out.

Raising an eyebrow like Sen does, she smiles. "Thank you." Holding out her hand for me to follow her, she adds, "Won't you please come through?"

Following her into a huge front parlor with white tufted couches and a baby grand, I stall by the couch, suddenly feeling self-conscious about sitting on her pristine furniture in the clothes I've been in for days. Besides that, I really want to move this conversation along. Every second I'm here, Seneca gets farther away.

"Please, have a seat." She nods to me as she sits, smoothing her pants as she does. Lifting a leg, she crosses her knees, and I glimpse the red bottoms of her shoes. I don't know exactly what that means, but I know it means they're expensive.

"I think I'd better stand. I've been on my bike for days. Probably a greasy mess."

"Suit yourself," she says with a smile. "But I sit on them all the time after riding. I'm covered in dirt and horsehair."

"Thank you."

Daring to sit on the very edge of the couch, I smile at Mrs. Villetrio. I see where Sen gets her coolness from.

"You said she could be in danger?" Thankfully, she gets right to it.

"Yes, I'm afraid so. Have you seen her?"

"Not for years. What has her brother dragged her into now?" Her beautiful face is strained with worry.

"Her brother?"

"Matt. I assumed this was about him?"

"No… but what can you tell me about him?"

Sighing, she uncrosses her legs. "What's to tell? It was a typical story at the beginning. Boy with too much money grows up and gets his hands on drugs at his prep school that costs more than most people make in a year. And he likes the drugs way too much."

Standing, she walks to a window, and pulling the curtain back, gazes out. "My husband insisted we cut him off. Without money, he can't buy drugs, right?" She turns to me. "Well, he was wrong—my husband—like he is about just about everything. Being broke just sent Matt to work with the dealers."

"I don't want to overstep, but why didn't you pay for him to get treatment and away from the dealers?"

"I wanted to. But do you know what I came into this marriage with?" She draws a circle around her face. "This face. Thirty years ago. Oh sure, he's found many more faces he's liked just as much through the years, but I'm still Mrs. Villetrio. For whatever that's worth. But without it, thanks to our prenup, there's nothing." Taking a deep breath, she sighs it out. "And then, when the tragedy struck, we were already so distanced…"

"I'm sorry, tragedy?"

"Yes. When those dealers framed him for the murder of some junkie. I never believed that Matt could have killed anyone, but my husband wouldn't do anything. But Sloane, she never stopped fighting for him. Visited him in that godforsaken place weekly. Until…"

"Until what…?" My heart is pounding so fast and so loud, I strain to hear her words above it.

"She just up and left for some reason. Told me some of the men he was involved with got short sentences, but Matt was in for life. And because she had tried to free her brother by putting the blame on them, they were pissed, and she was afraid they may be coming after her." Tears fill her eyes. "I can't imagine all of this is happening. If I could do it all over again, I'd pack up my babies and run. We might have been poor, but we might have been happy."

Christ. Flopping back against the couch, I rub my temples. There is no way that fate could be this cruel. Not only did we grow up in the same backyard, just to find ourselves hiding out two thousand miles away in Hoppa, Arizona with the Steel Knights, but… is it possible?

Is her brother the poor kid that got framed during my visit to the junkie that turned into a mob hit gone bad? Closing my eyes, I see it all again.

"Move!"

"No way, man! No freaking way!"

"No!"

That was him. I know it. I can feel it in my gut. And if that's so, then *I* am the reason for all of Seneca's misery. *I* am the reason Matt is in jail and has been this long. If I had told the truth in court—that I was there to give the junkie a message from Don Bordono, and then ratted out Mikey and Tony as the killers—then Don Bordono would have been pissed, yeah, but he wouldn't have killed me for it. I would have done my three years, but Mikey and Tony would be in for murder, and the kid might have walked.

No, I wasn't at the kid's hearing. Maybe if I were, I would have stepped up and done the right thing, but I don't know.

I wanted out of the Bordono family, and I wanted out of jail. The cold, hard truth is that I chose myself over everyone else, and because of it, Seneca's brother is rotting in jail.

Can Seneca ever understand? And can she even begin to forgive me?

Fuck Mikey and Tony. Fuck my father for bringing me in. Fuck Ironclad and Don Bordono. Fuck this whole damned world.

And fuck me for what I did.

"Mrs. Villetrio, did Sloane ever mention the names of the men she was scared of?"

"No. I'm sorry. She was very secretive."

Nodding, energy courses through me like floodgates just opened in my veins. "I understand. No doubt it was to keep you safe." Standing, I try to calm my racing heart and shaking hands.

Closing my eyes, I take a breath. *Come on, Bullseye, get it together.* I imagine squeezing the trigger—only this time, I'm not shooting at a target, I'm taking down Mikey…

Tony…

Ironclad…

And even Don Bordono…

Slowly. Methodically. One at a time.

When I open my eyes, I'm calm. But I've got to go.

"Thank you, Mrs. Villetrio."

As I rush for the front door, I see Meredith. "Do you have paper and a pen?"

Luckily, she carries them in her apron and hands them to me. Jotting down my number, I hand the paper to Mrs. Villetrio who has followed me to the door.

"If you see Sen—uh, Sloane—or hear anything, please let me know."

"Yes." Holding up the paper, she smiles at me. "Avery. If you can keep my baby girl safe, do it."

"I plan to, Mrs. Villetrio. I plan to."

If only she'll let me.

Hopping onto my bike, I rev the engine with no time to worry about my pipes or the neighbors.

Rushing out of the circular driveway, it's like my bike knows the way without my mind telling it to. There's no way I can find her "somewhere" on Long Island or in Manhattan.

But every second she's away from me, she's in danger. So, I need to find Mikey and Tony before they find her. And the last contact I had with them was through my father. And if he's being held, no doubt it's at… Shit.

Hanging a sharp turn west, I hop onto the Long Island Expressway and head straight for Don Bordono's house.

The one place I swore I'd never return to.

Chapter Seventeen

Wildfire

"Oh, come on," I mumble to myself. "Damn it." Crouching down in the thick bush outside Johnny's garage on the south shore of Long Island, I fight back against the damn sharp twigs and thorns that prick me. The snow falls from the branches and slips into the back of my hoodie. Thankfully, I have Bullseye's sweatshirt to keep me warm and give me at least one layer of protection from the sharp little bastards... but they're still scratching my hands and cheeks. Another clump of snow falls from the bush and drops onto my neck, trickling down my back...

"Shit," I curse, wiggling around. Tears threaten again as I think about being in my warm bed in Hoppa with Avery's arms wrapped around me.

"Oh, come on, Sen," I growl, "get a grip. Enough with the drama. So, it's cold. So? Matt's dealing with a hell of a lot worse. Every moment of his life."

Good. Thinking about Matt in that hellhole sobers me up. Ever since that meltdown in Avery's truck, I have been a prissy, emotional wreck. And if there's ever been a time to be strong, this is it.

Taking a deep breath, I watch person after person ride in on their bike—and the occasional car—paying Johnny to work his miracles. And damn, he does. He is a master mechanic.

My stomach feels hollow. I just hope he's also a master at keeping himself safe.

I shouldn't be here. Sinking back farther into the shrub to stay invisible, I palm my forehead. What was I thinking? Johnny has done so much for me already—teaching me to ride, to fix bikes, being there for me when Matt went away...

Is this really how I repay him? Hanging outside his shop waiting for two punks to find me at his door? Yes, he probably has info for me. Johnny has lain low for all these years, but he always has intel. Since he fixes the bikes for pretty much all the clubs' members in the Tri-state—including Ironclad—he hears it all. And he's trusted.

That's how he found out that Mikey and Tony were looking for me, and that they had someone throw the brick as a warning. A warning to stay put. In Arizona.

And yet, here I am on Long Island—near Ironclad's turf. And what I'm doing here is putting myself, and more importantly, Johnny, in danger.

I've got to start thinking clearly and get better at keeping those people I love, safe. Not just Matt, but Johnny...

And Avery. Damn. Why the hell did I have to fall for him?

Looking over my shoulder at my bike, I plan my exit strategy. I don't know where the hell I'm going to go, but it has to be away from here. This isn't safe for Johnny. Hopping on, firing up the engine, and taking off is sure to attract attention—so I'll have to wait it out a while longer and then sneak off during his next lull in business. Which is probably lunchtime.

Damn. Considering I raced in here before sunup, lunchtime is a long time away—

"Seneca? Kiddo, is that you?" Johnny comes over to my bush, unrolling a hose as he walks. Standing over my bush, he turns the water on and it sprinkles down over me.

"Johnny? What the fuck, man?" Holding my hands over my head, I try to keep the water from soaking me as I whisper as loud as I can. "You trying to drown me? It just snowed! It's freaking cold out here."

Chuckling, he moves the hose to the opposite side of the bush. "I thought that was you. Didn't I tell you to stay put? It's bad news for you here."

"It's bad news everywhere. And I can't just sit there any longer and leave Matt here."

"This wouldn't have anything to do with a tall, dark member of the Steel Knights, would it?"

"How do you know?"

"Seneca." He sounds like a parent. Or, like a parent should sound if they gave a damn.

"He's not safe with me, Johnny. And what was I supposed to do? Sit and wait for Mikey and Tony to show up and kill everyone I care about?" I wince when I realize what I've said. "I mean, you know how much I care about you…"

"Yes, Sen, I understand what you're saying. Just like I understand that waiting around has never been your strong suit. So? What's your plan?"

"To find out if you know anything more. Since Mikey and Tony are out, they must be talking."

Sighing, he puts down the hose and smacks snow off the branches.

"Seriously?" I ask.

"If anyone sees me, it has to look like I have a reason to be here."

"As long as you don't take a leak on me."

Stifling another chuckle, he works on his story. "I'm cleaning the bush of snow because… Oh, who the hell knows. I'll think of something. Now, shut up and listen."

I do.

"There's been talk that Mikey and Tony were acting on their own. That Don Bordono didn't send them. Seems the hit that Matt was framed for wasn't just some lowlife junkie. He was a significant dealer, and he was starting to import his goods from another family."

"So, Tony and Mikey were trying to impress Ironclad?"

"Correct."

"But this doesn't make any sense. Don Bordono would never let someone go. Especially a dealer. He must have been planning his own hit."

"That's what I thought. And it seems we're correct. Don Bordono knew the junkie dealer was good. Had strong connections. He could be groomed to be the next Ironclad."

My legs are cramping from holding the position, so I shift down onto my knees. The snow and water soak through the denim, and immediately, I regret it. Squatting again, I concentrate. "So, Ironclad sent Mikey and Tony."

"Yes. And rumor is, they interrupted what was supposed to be a warning from Don Bordono."

"Wait." Staying crouched in the bush, I lift myself higher, until I'm nearly standing. "But if Don Bordono didn't send them…"

"That means he sent someone else."

"So, there was someone else there?" Adrenaline mixed with hope courses through my veins and it's all I can do to stay here and stay hidden. "If there was someone else, was he the shooter?"

"Nah. It's pretty solid that Mikey and Tony both pulled their triggers and shot the bastard. But along with poor Matt, someone else was there, Sen."

"Someone who could ID Mikey and Tony as the killers. And his testimony could free Matt." Anger starts churning in my gut. Why didn't he speak up when he had the chance?

"Maybe. But Sen, they say this guy who works for Don Bordono, he comes from a family of sharpshooters. You've got to be careful. They say he's a real Bullseye."

"He's a…?"

The words won't even form in my mouth. It could never be. It would all be way too coincidental.

With my heart thumping, my brain keeps racing with thoughts. Why did Avery want me back in Hoppa so badly? Why was there talk of keeping me safe in the club? Who the hell is Avery "Bullseye" Pairings, anyway?

"Seneca, no. I can see the gears turning. I told you about this guy to scare you and get you to stay clear."

Peering through a break in the branches, I look Johnny in the eye. "Really? Did you really think that would make me back off? Matt is rotting away in *jail*."

Sighing, he starts coiling up his hose. Thank God. I couldn't take being any wetter or colder.

"Seneca, you know you're like a daughter to me. So I'm going to say this only one time. Keep your nose the hell out of it."

"Johnny."

As he slings the hose over his shoulder, he holds up his hand to quiet me. "But as a surrogate father who knows his child well, I know you won't. So all I'm going to say is that you don't have to do it alone. From what I've heard about the Steel Knights, they're fair guys but tough guys. If one of them likes you enough to risk his life to help you, let him."

Nodding, I swallow hard. That's the one thing I don't want to happen. Avery has unknowingly risked enough by just being with me. Now, there's only one thing I can do. And that's find Mikey and Tony and beat them into submission.

"I miss you, Sen. Be careful."

Coiling the last bit of hose around his arm, Johnny turns and heads back to his garage—and I sneak out the back of the bush, balance my bike, and walk it as far down the road as I can, before I hop on and take off for Manhattan.

Shifting my bike into low gear as I glide through Alphabet City—which has been gentrified almost past the point of recognition—I think about how alike this area and I really are.

Like this area of the Lower East Side, my life has changed dramatically. When I was in high school, I used to come into the city by limo with my mother, father, and Matt, to go to an event at the Met or a gallery. Most weekends, I'd spend strolling up and down the streets of the East or West Villages, shopping with my friends, and grabbing lunch. I never really enjoyed it, but damn…

The Sloane of then could never imagine the life of the Seneca of now. Here I am, chasing down low-level drug dealers to try to force them to come clean about my brother while avoiding getting killed—and more importantly—getting my bad-ass, biker boyfriend killed.

I lull my bike to a hum while I downshift again, skirting past my target—the entrance to a trendy noodle shop. College students and brave tourists flock to this shop that has some of the best dumplings in Manhattan, but they've got no freaking clue what's located below ground…

The heart of Ironclad's operation. The place he calls "Mammon". It's named Mammon after the god of wealth and profit. And to Ironclad, wealth and profit come by any means necessary.

No, I can't go waltzing into Mammon alone and unarmed, demanding Mikey and Tony's heads on platters, but I can do some snooping around… just to see where they are and more importantly, find out who this mystery shooter on the Bordono payroll was.

Taking a deep breath, I slide the bike into a parking garage on the corner, and hopping off, and clutching my bag tight to my chest, I muster up all the courage I can. I've got close to ten grand in this bag. I'm just praying I won't need to use it, but if I do, that it's enough to get someone to tell me who the other shooter was, without getting me killed. Above all, I really need to save it for another round of attorney's fees for Matt.

Crossing the street and walking past the entrance of the noodle shop, I check over my shoulder before I disappear down into a staircase that leads to Mammon. My clumpy boots make a dull thud with every step I take closer to uncertainty.

I've only been here once before, when Matt first went inside, and I tried to get help from Ironclad by pledging with one of his motorcycle clubs, like Lucifer's Riders. Thing is, the initiation for women in his clubs requires taking a beating to prove your strength, and then sex with a member, or members, to prove your femininity. Ironclad and his whole enterprise sucks.

Just thinking about it makes my hands ball into fists and my breathing grow deeper and slower… He's going to need a hell of a lot more than the fear of an initiation to stop me this time.

Because this time, I have nothing left to lose.

Raising my hand, I pound on the door with the side of my fist. There's a whole world down here—a wild party of drugs and sex and orgies—but all I need is to get past the front guards, find Mikey and Tony, and toss them a beating. No one will bother me once I start. In Ironclad's world, if a woman is pounding the shit out of you, you deserve it.

Once I've beaten them into submission, they're going to tell the truth about Matt—I don't care who else they decide to blame, it's not my problem—and then they're going to tell me who the other shooter was. As long as I can handle both guys at once, and Ironclad doesn't see me and decide I'm too much trouble, I should be okay.

Despite the below-freezing temperatures, a bead of sweat trickles from my temple to my jaw. I'm too focused to wipe it away. Once that door opens, I need to fight my way inside.

Pounding on the door again, my heart accelerates when it opens slowly.

"Yeah?" A man in his late thirties with a bald head and an earring pops his head out. That earring has to be what I go for… before he can think to go for any of mine.

"Ironclad here?"

"Who the fuck wants to know?"

Shaking my head, I jump up and with a growl, I land an ax kick to his thigh. He's heavy enough that he stumbles backward and his momentum plasters him against the hallway door. Praying there's no one else his size here, I follow with an elbow strike to the nose and circle out and away from him before he can grab my arm or my leg.

Holding his nose while blood gushes from it, he looks at me with his chin dropped and his eyes filled with fury. Fuck. I just poked a bear.

There's no time to think, only act. Charging at him with my head down, I rush to his left side, and as he moves his sizable body in that direction, I dart back the opposite way following an inside chop with an eye strike. Then, I grab the earring and tug. Hard.

"Oh!" he yelps, dropping to his knees.

Not daring to get too close, I stand by the door. "Who wants to know if Ironclad's here? Wildfire. That's who. Now, I'm going to repeat my question. Is Ironclad here?"

"Fuck. No." This entire attack has been filmed, and thanks to one of Ironclad's messed-up rules, he can't retaliate. Because he lost to a woman.

Not that he'd dare.

"Mikey and Tony?" I ask

"Ain't seen them around."

"Why not?"

On his knees, holding his bleeding nose, damaged eye, and torn earlobe, he looks up at me. "They out looking for someone."

"Me?"

"Naw. Ain't no woman they looking for. If that's what the hell you are. More like some demon."

Daring a step closer, I press on. "Who then?"

"Some sharpshooter guy. Works for Bordono."

"You all work for Bordono," I hiss. "That punk Ironclad works for him. And everyone knows it."

Turning to the corner of the hallway, I look up and face the camera, flipping Ironclad the bird with one hand, and waving with the other.

Turning back to the mountain I dropped, I speak quickly. "This is what's going to happen. You are going to let me in there—" I nod to the steel door dead ahead. "—to find out what I need to know. And you're never going to tell anyone that you saw me or that I was here. Understood?" Of course, Ironclad may see the tape. But I don't need any extra trouble tonight.

Still holding his ear, he stands and limps to the door. With a knock, he pushes it open, and there ahead of me, are flashing lights, pounding music, mostly naked women—and men—dancing, packed bars, and drugs everywhere.

Fuck. Welcome to Mammon.

Taking a deep breath, I walk in and immediately get groped on the ass by the first hopped-up asshole who comes my way. Turning toward him, I grab his head in my hands and land a headbutt. He staggers off, and I turn and push my way past the dance floor, and over to the entrance of the VIP room.

A man sits alone at the bar, drinking something clear. Behind the bar, a bartender cuts limes into wedges using a small paring knife. Plopping up on the stool next to the man, I grab his drink from him and take a sniff. Water.

"Hey!" he protests, looking me up and down and taking his drink back. "I'm not into that rough biker-chick costume. Like my women to look like women."

"It's not a costume, asshole, and I don't care what you like and don't like. You're drinking water, and that means you're working. So, you're going to answer some questions for me. Where are Mikey and Tony?"

"Mikey and Tony who?"

In one fast movement, I grab the paring knife from the bartender and shove it into the guy's leg just above his knee. I keep my hand on it, applying pressure.

"Okay, so now that I have your attention, I want some answers. Where are Mikey and Tony?"

Grimacing, he speaks through his pain. "Last I heard, they were at the Don's house."

"What do you know about that hit gone bad? About some sharpshooter?" Wrapping my fingers around the handle tighter, I press harder against the knife, and he crumples over. "Last chance." He paws at the knife. "Make a move, and I will yank this out and move it a foot higher. It's a small target, but I'm a really good shot. I promise I will impale you." Sweat drips off of me as I lean closer. "So, was someone else there?"

"Yeah, yeah. I heard there was a guy. Worked for Don Bordono."

"Worked?"

"He's out."

"How'd that happen?" I ask. "Nobody's ever out."

"Don Bordono liked him."

"Who else knows that Mikey and Tony pulled the trigger and not my brother?"

"Your brother? Shit! You're Seneca? What, you got a death wish being here?"

Pressing against the knife harder and forcing it deeper into his leg, the color drains from his face.

"Who else knows?"

"Just the guy. Some sharpshooter," the man groans.

"Where do I find him?

"He ran." His cheeks are puffed, and he's blowing air through his clenched teeth. "Years ago. Don Bordono got him sprung early, and he ran. Nobody seen him since. Rumor is he's somewhere in the Southwest."

It's like a punch to my gut. I know it's all a coincidence, but damn...

Nodding, I hop off the stool. There's no way anyone's going to talk. Mikey and Tony won't ever come clean, and this sharpshooter's missing.

It's hopeless. To free Matt, someone would have to squeal on Mikey and Tony, or magically announce they are the shooter, and who the hell would be stupid enough to do that?

And finding the sharpshooter who's not afraid of Don Bordono? After all this time and all this fighting, it's freaking hopeless.

Rushing through the crowd, pushing them aside and parting them as I go, I make my way to the back door I remember from the last time I was here. I've made enough of a mess tonight. What I need is to regroup and figure out what the hell to do next. Slipping out the door and up the stairs, I stumble out onto the sidewalk and run to the parking garage, sucking in the cold Manhattan air until my lungs may very well burst.

Hopping on my bike, I rush up to the Midtown Tunnel, and out onto the island. Once I'm clear of Queens and farther out on the island, which means I'm out of Ironclad's turf, I pull into the first seedy motel I can find. Stopping next door at the gas station to fill my tank in case I need a quick escape, I look at the minimart attached, and immediately think of Avery and the night we spent in his truck. Despite the freezing New York night, a flush of warmth envelopes me.

Fuck. No. I have to forget him to keep him safe.

Buying some dry-looking slices of pizza, a box of chocolate-covered raisins, and a couple of mini bottles of wine, I run back to the motel, park my bike in the most hidden spot I can find, drape its cover over it, and go in to get a room.

Nearly falling into my room from exhaustion, I pull off the orange-colored spread that's probably been here for decades and is covered in god-knows-what. Collapsing fully dressed on the bed, I cross my feet at the ankles. Propping my head up with extra pillows, I open the screw cap on the wine and flip on the old TV set. Taking a long swallow, I change from channel to channel. There's nothing on except sappy romances, which make me think of Avery even more.

Crap.

Channel surfing, I land on a commercial of a daughter bringing her mother a box of chocolates. Sitting up fast in bed, I suddenly have such a strong desire to talk to my mother, it hurts.

But why? It's been years... The woman abandoned me when my father decided I wasn't good enough, and she left her son to rot in jail. But still...

When the mother embraces the daughter, my eyes begin to prickle. Damn. It's just exhaustion. I need sleep. Finishing off the first bottle of wine, I crack open the second and change the channel.

What the fuck? Moving closer to the TV, there it is again. The same damned commercial. Looking over at the nightstand, I spy the old-fashioned hotel phone. My cell's gone. I left it in Avery's truck, but... Does she still have the same number? Is it possible after all these years?

Without thinking, I dial the number, and she answers on the second ring.

"Mom?"

"Sloane?" I hear her gasp. "Sloane, honey is that you?"

Shit. Why did I do this? "I-I shouldn't have called. I'm sorry—"

"Wait! Sloane, your boy, Avery was here. Looking for you. He's a nice man, Sloane."

Despite it all, her approval makes me smile.

"Yeah." It dawns on me. "Wait, what? He was there?"

"He's looking for you. He's worried. He thinks you may be in danger. But, Sloane, here's the strange part. I don't know why, but the way he asked questions, the look on his face when he asked the names of the men who may be after you. Those two dealers who—"

"Yeah. I know, Mom. What did he say?"

"Nothing really. And I don't know why... Call it mother's intuition. Even after all this time. But, Sloane, I think Avery knows something about Matt."

No...

Shaking my head, the phone slips in my grasp. As my mother rambles on, my mind races.

No. There's just no way. There's no way *my* Bullseye could be the man who made the conscious decision to let my brother rot in jail for a crime he didn't commit, just so *he* could be free. That would never happen. Bullseye's a good guy.

A good guy who I know nothing about. And who's on the run from...

...somebody.

Slamming the phone down, I slump on the side of the bed and stare at the filthy carpet.

There's just no way that Avery "Bullseye" Pairings could have fucked me over like this...

Chapter Eighteen

Bullseye

"Jesus," I mutter to myself while turning off my bike. Staring at the giant white house with covered archways lining a mammoth porch and the long path leading to the front door, I cannot believe I'm at the home of Don Bordono. Again. The one place I swore I would never return to.

But I have to see where they have my father. I owe him that much at least, and I have to find out what Mikey and Tony know about Seneca. Underneath all of that... I have to find out the truth. Is Seneca's brother the kid at the hit that went bad?

And the most important part of all of it—I have to keep Seneca safe. Damn it, Sen. Where are you?

Dropping my kickstand and swinging my leg up and over my bike, I draw in a deep breath as I take off my helmet. I'm still a good distance from the mansion and the guardhouses that flank the house, sitting on both sides of the driveway. No doubt I'll be visited by guards soon enough. Obviously, they don't think I'm a threat; otherwise, I'd be dead already.

Even though there are several secret entrances and exits to the house and I know where they are, there's no sense in trying to sneak up or come in quietly from a back road. Don has cameras set up for miles down all the roads leading to his house, so he can catch anyone who dares come to his family home.

Regardless of the cameras, "sneaking up" is not a good game plan when dealing with Don Bordono.

Standing up tall, I don't make any sudden moves. No doubt I'll be paid a visit from the guards watching from the guardhouses.

Looking up at the second-floor balconies that may be the size of my entire apartment building back home, and then down at the walkway made of flagstone and slate with patches of real, one-hundred-percent, freaking *gold* overlay, I chuckle.

No, the situation isn't funny, but considering the amount of time I've been spending in Hoppa's Taphouse and my tiny apartment in Arizona, it's absurd that I've been to two sprawling mansions in the past couple of hours.

The floodlights kick on and shielding my eyes, I turn my chin away from the glare.

"Who the hell are you?" A guard with a thick body and carrying a shotgun materializes out of one of the guardhouses. His long hair is dark black and greased back.

For a moment—although he doesn't look anything like him—he makes me think of Bucky, and a feeling of melancholy for the club and all the guys—Bucky, Vil, Jonesie, Small Fry, Texas, Nick, and especially Bullet—washes down over me, threatening to render me useless. Man. What I wouldn't give to have the guys back me up right now. But are they still my guys? And would they still have my back?

But I was right to leave. Although it felt like I was peeling off a layer of skin when I handed my Steel Knights jacket to Harry, I had to, and *have* to, do everything I can to keep them—and Seneca—safe.

"I said, who the fuck are you?"

He lifts his shotgun, pointing it at me, and I raise my hands in response.

"Avery Pairings. Friends call me 'Bullseye.'"

"We ain't your friends."

"I know that. But Don Bordono is. Call him." Nodding to the guardhouse, I point to the guard's phone. "He'll want to see me."

"You got a set..." the guard mumbles, keeping his gun on me.

"Joe, wait." Another guard—this one thinner and taller—materializes. Even though my father is in deep with the Bordonos, and I was with them for a year, I don't know either of these men. "The boss called. He knows this punk. Wants to see him."

Without a word, the second guard walks up to me and pats me down. Thankfully, I knew enough to store my piece in my tail bag, and I'm not carrying.

"He's clean." The way his voice trails off and his pitch drops, the second guard sounds disappointed I'm not packing. Must not be a lot to do around here lately. Just wait, boys. Just wait.

Using the barrel of his gun to point the way, the first guard motions to the house. "Come on, cumwad, you're not gonna keep the boss waiting."

Exhaling, I walk ahead of the two men, and it's like I can actually feel the guns pointed at my back. In another place and time, I would have spun around, grabbed both guns, and shot the assholes—dead.

A cold chill passes over me, and I close my eyes and collect my thoughts. But it's not then, it's now. And enough with the killing.

Standing at the front door, the taller guard presses the doorbell and it opens quickly. A man in his mid-sixties and dressed in an expensive suit—Benny Bordono, consigliere of the Bordono family and Don Bordono's younger brother—answers. The fact that he answered the door shows that they'd never suspect I would hurt them. Ironclad's plan is foolproof.

"Bullseye."

"Benny."

Benny pulls me into his warm, sweaty embrace, then, wrapping an arm around my shoulder, walks me through the main hallway and toward the don's business office. We pass a sitting room stuffed with oil paintings, leather couches, opulent lamps, and walls covered in heavy, red-textured wallpaper.

"I gotta tell you, Bullseye, this is a surprise." His breath reeks of expensive brandy. "Life not treating you well in Arizona?"

Another chill washes over me. Obviously, they knew where I was, but hearing him say it…

"No, it's great. Really." Or at least it was until freaking Mikey and Tony got out.

"Knock, knock?" Benny stops at the don's office door, which is cracked open. He's expecting us. Benny knocks on the frame for emphasis.

"Come in, come in." Don's voice is cordial and enthusiastic.

As I walk into his office, I'm overwhelmed by the smell of brandy and cigars and the feel of the warmth from the modern fireplace that's built into the floor-to-ceiling stone wall.

Don Bordono lays his cigar in his silver ashtray on his mammoth wood and marble desk and gets up from his leather desk chair, fanning the air as he does. "You know Mimi won't let me smoke anywhere but here." He shrugs happily. He loves Mimi. "But if Mama ain't happy—"

"—no one's happy."

I finish his statement for him as he comes to a full stop before me.

"Avery, Avery, Avery…" He repeats my name like he's making sure that I'm real. Like a grandparent seeing a grandchild for the first time in a year.

He opens his arms, and I step into his embrace. I'm taller than he is, so I squat down. Pressed against his suit; what must be thousands of dollars of the finest Italian merino wool, I'm being held too tight, but I don't dare move. Holding my breath, I wait. Don Bordono has his ways, and anyone who's been with him long enough knows them. There are no bro-hugs in this world.

If he trusts you, you are embraced with both of his stocky arms wrapped around you—like I am now. That's good. But it's where it goes from here that matters.

Pulling back, he clamps one of his chubby, smallish hands on the back of my neck and holds my cheek, slapping it slightly as I smile. That's a sign of love.

Still not daring to breathe, I wait for the next moment that will tell all.

A kiss on either cheek by Don Bordono is a death sentence.

"Avery Pairings," he chuckles as he speaks, dropping me from his embrace.

Exhaling slowly, it's all I can do to stay upright and not collapse from exhaustion and relief. But I need to stay strong and focused on one thing only: keeping Seneca safe.

"What could have possibly brought you out of the sunshine and back to the cold?" He raises his eyebrows as he speaks. He's not really asking me that. Nothing is ever literal with him. Everything is a matter of deciphering his code. Thanks to my father, I'm a master at that.

What he's asking me is, "Are you a fucking fool? I gave you an out, so why are you back? And are you going to make me look like a fool too?" Because no matter how much he likes me, making him look like an idiot will not be tolerated.

I choose my words carefully. "I so appreciate being in the warmth, Don. But there's something I need to discuss with you. It's a matter that could only be spoken about in person."

"Please." He holds out his hand to the chair opposite his desk. "Sit."

Glancing up at Benny, the Don nods, and Benny leaves. This would all be so easy. When

Ironclad tries to use me to kill Don Bordono, which he will, it could go off without a hitch. Even if I didn't kill him—if, out of loyalty, I let him go with just a warning—it would still be a suicide mission for me. But the thing is, none of them would give a shit. Glancing at the Don's smiling face and ruddy cheeks, I smile back. Not even him.

I may be like a son to him, but business is business.

"So, what's the real reason you're here, Bullseye?" He steeples his fingers, leaning forward against his desk.

"I got a call from my father."

"Dominic called you?"

"Yes. And an… acquaintance of ours said that you wanted to see me."

"You know if I'd wanted to see you, Avery. I would have had you summoned."

"Yes, I know that. But I wanted you to know your name is being used to further other people's agendas."

"I appreciate the information."

Nodding, I go on. "I believe Dominic is being held against his will, and that Mikey and Tony have him."

Sitting back, he sighs, rocking back and forth in his desk chair. "That's a mighty big accusation, Bullseye."

"I know it is. But Dominic called me for the first time since I left New York. I know he's in trouble." I leave it at that.

"He is." Don nods, sitting forward again. "He got a bit, well, let's just say, out of control lately. Gambling. His debt is high, and he's been working it off for me—but…" Shaking his head, he puts both hands on the desk. "You know I love you like a son, Bullseye. That's why you've been working on your tan for the past two years and not rotting in a jail cell."

"I know that. And I appreciate it. I've told you that."

"Yes, yes." Holding up his hand, he spins away and then back again. "I'm not looking for thanks."

Swallowing hard, I force the words past my tightening throat. "What are you looking for, then?"

Locking his eyes on mine, he smiles. "Well, it seems that maybe we can help each other out."

"What's it going to cost me?"

"A job."

"Why not my father? He loves this shit."

"Well…" Smiling, he sits back and claps his hands together. "Your father is getting older and shaky." He holds out his hand, wobbling it for emphasis. "He's not the sharpshooter he was. Not the sharpshooter you are." He nods to me. "One job, Avery. If you'd like to pay down Dominic's debt, you can work it off. Like old times."

"What would you have done if I were still in Arizona?"

"What does it matter? You're here. And I'm making you an offer." His eyes twinkle.

No one ever says no to Don Bordono when he's made them an offer.

"I appreciate it, Don. But I think you would understand that I have some reservations."

Chuckling, the Don lays his round forearms on the desk. He's gained a significant amount of weight since I've seen him last, and it's like his forearms are straining against the wool of his charcoal-colored suit as they try to burst free.

"Listen, Bullseye. Mikey and Tony weren't supposed to be at that hit. It was a solo job. Your solo job. They're wildcards."

"The kid there. The one doing time for Mikey and Tony. I think I know who he is."

"Oh?" He raises his eyebrows. He's intrigued. This is a turn he wasn't expecting.

"I think he's Matt Villetrio. The brother of—"

"—the lovely Seneca Villetrio."

"Yes." My voice is weak, so I clear my throat and repeat myself. "Yes."

Fuck. Just saying it makes a chill rush up and down my spine. If it's true, she'll never forgive me. How did fate bring us together like this, only to mess with us in the end? Oh, screw it. It's not fate's fault. It's mine.

"Don Bordono, I love you like a father, but there's someone I love even more."

"Seneca."

Nodding, I go on. "So, I have to insist that my price has gone up. I will do this job for you…" My stomach ties into knots just saying it. "But in return, I ask three things. First, that my father is let go. He'll have to pay down his debt to you, but that's on you two. Second, that Matt Villetrio is freed. And lastly, that Seneca is kept safe and allowed to go back to Hoppa."

No, it won't be with me, but at least she'll be safe and the guys will look out for her. Maybe her brother can join her—Nick's a good guy, he'll set Matt up with a job. And maybe even Harry will forgive me enough to take care of them.

"That's a lot of demands."

"Don Bordono." I sit forward in my chair. "I would never make demands of you. They are simply the cost of my skills."

"I see." As he leans forward, we're so close, I can feel the warmth of his breath. "And what happens to you?"

Pushing aside my angst, I sit up taller. "I replace my father, of course."

No, it's not the life I want, but it gets Matt freed and keeps Seneca safe. And it beats the hell out of jail. His eyes light up. He wants this.

"Can Matt be freed?" I ask.

"If I say that Mikey and Tony are the real murderers, then yes."

"What will it take for that?"

Smiling, he pushes his chair back from his desk and stands up. Walking to an old-fashioned wood filing cabinet, he takes a key from the chain around his neck, and bending down, he slips it into a lock and opens a drawer. Rifling through a few files, he chooses a manila envelope and pulls it out. Then, locking up the cabinet and tucking away his key, he turns back to me.

He tosses the envelope onto the desk and nods to it. Staring at that damned file, a strange sensation courses through me. It's like there's a poisonous snake inside that's ready to strike. Steadying my hand and my breath, I open the envelope. Shit. It is a snake.

Ironclad.

This is exactly what I thought would happen, only in reverse. My shoulders relax, and I take a deep breath. No, I don't want to kill anyone. But if I have to, then yes, I'd sure as hell rather it was Ironclad than Don Bordono.

"He's getting too powerful. Those two buffoons, Mikey and Tony, were at that job because Ironclad is sticking his nose where it doesn't belong. He's supposed to move product for me through Lucifer's Riders, but lately, he's dabbling in other areas. Getting his own shipment. It's one thing to let him think he controls a few clubs, it's another to let him gain any real power."

"Will that get Matt freed?"

"Get rid of Ironclad, and Mikey and Tony will go down for murder."

Anger, resentment, fear—it's all swirling in my gut and making me want to jump up out of my chair, but I have to stay here and stay cool.

Lifting a leg, he hoists himself up to sit on the edge of his desk closest to me. "Love, Avery, is a bitch." Nodding, I have to agree. I'd do anything to keep Seneca safe. Even to go back into this world. "How far will you go?"

Looking up, I make steady eye contact. "All the way. I will go all the way in to keep her safe."

"Glad to hear it."

"Knock, knock?" Benny sticks his head in the door. "Boss? Okay to come in?"

"What do you have, Benny?"

"That question you had. I have the answer."

"Ah, very good." Don Bordono walks back to his chair and sits down. He motions to Benny. "Go ahead. Tell us what you know."

Turning to me, Benny explains. "The boss. He asked me to check on your girl. Our guys tell me that you can find Seneca right now, hanging out with Ironclad."

"What?" I'm on my feet before I realize it. "Is she okay?"

"Apparently, they're getting along real well."

All I want to do is take everything in the room and rip it to shreds.

Don Bordono stands as well. "My guess is she's getting chummy with Ironclad, so he'll help her free her brother. Tough girl. Makes sense."

"And you're just telling me now?"

"I just found out," Benny explains.

This is all too weird. If Don Bordono really didn't expect me and wasn't sure what I wanted, then why did he have Benny hunt down Seneca moments after I arrived? But there's no time to worry about any of this now. Now, it's about getting to her and keeping her safe.

"Where are they?" I ask Benny.

"At Mammon, of course."

Fuck it. Mammon is Ironclad's underground world and the clubhouse for Lucifer's Riders. Seneca's not just up against Ironclad there, she's up against everyone who works for him. Fuck.

"Don Bordono, I humbly ask your permission to leave." It's killing me to stand here, but there's protocol to follow.

"Go, go," he tells me. "Seems this is an advantageous time to do what needs to be done." He crosses his arms before his chest and raises his eyebrows.

"I understand. Don, Benny." I nod to each man before I turn and, doubling back through the house, rush out the door.

Hurrying toward my bike, I know that I can make it to the city in less than half an hour, then Mammon is all the way downtown...

Jumping down the front stairs off the porch, I run—

"Avery Fucking Pairings."

Shit. Turning around, I catch Mikey and Tony walking toward me.

"Mikey. Tony." I nod to them. Both of them seem leaner since jail, and both a hell of a lot angrier. "Where's my father?"

"What?" Mikey grins. "No hug for your old friends who did time for you?"

Turning my back on them isn't my greatest plan, but I know my father is at least alive, and I need to get to my bike and get to Sen—

Suddenly, a heavy metal chain clocks me on the side of the head, clipping my ear. Holding my hand to my ear, I pull it away. Blood is streaming down my arm.

"What the fuck is your problem?" Backing away, I ready myself for the fight, but my mind's not here, it's with Seneca and Ironclad. Swallowing the bile in my mouth, I take a few steps away from them, just making it to my bike.

With one fast swoop, Tony wraps the damn chain around my torso and yanks me off my bike, somehow, keeping me balanced on my feet while pinning my arms behind my back. Somewhere, in my deepest subconscious, it's like I've decided to take the damned beating. At least, when it's over, I can go.

Mikey walks closer to me, flashing his slimy grin, and lands a hard sucker punch to my gut. Bending forward, I try to protect my abdomen, but Tony pulls the chain hard and forces me upward again. The large metal links cut into my arms and hold me upright.

"What the hell do you want, Mikey?"

"Revenge. For the two years and six months we did inside that you didn't."

He lands another punch and another—and yet I know that the less I fight, the faster it will be over.

"What, not fighting back?"

I see the disappointment in his small, dull eyes.

"It had nothing to do with me. It was Don Bordono. He sent me that day. It wasn't supposed to be a hit. You weren't supposed to be there. He got me out. Maybe if he'd sent you..." At least I still have the wits to try to make sense of the situation.

"Don Bordono's done," Mikey hisses.

"What do you mean, done?" I know Don Bordono must be watching this on at least one of his cameras. And I also know he's going to let it play out to see what info he can gain from these two assholes.

"We've been working with Ironclad ever since we went down and did time. Our loyalty lies there."

"You're making the wrong choice."

With another blow, he lands one more punch to my gut.

"Think of this as your warning, Bullseye. If we catch you working with Don Bordono again, we'll kill you, your father, and Seneca—that hot piece of ass you screw."

Watching Mikey's slimy lips move as he speaks, I wonder why they haven't killed any of us yet. It dawns on me. It can only be because there is someone bigger than them forcing them to keep me alive.

Ironclad. I was right. Ironclad wants me to kill Don Bordono. It only makes sense.

Hawking a disgusting loogie, Mikey spits in my face, and then Tony drops the chain, letting me fall to my knees. Bracing myself on all fours, I take some deep breaths, trying to stop the humming in my ear. Collecting myself, I glimpse Mikey and Tony rushing off, disappearing into the shadows. Wiping my face in my sweatshirt sleeve, I glance up just as Mikey stops and turns. He's pointing at me.

"Stay the hell away from Don Bordono."

So, they're trying to scare me into working for Ironclad.

Dragging myself to my feet, I stumble to my bike and throwing my leg over, I rev the engine. My ear is ringing and my gut aches from the beating, but I can't care. All I need to do is to stay balanced on the damn bike and ride straight into Mammon to kill Ironclad and free Seneca. Then, once she's safe—I'll explain everything and beg for her forgiveness.

And then, I'll pray she doesn't finish the job Mikey and Tony started here.

Peeling out and racing down the driveway and onto the side streets, I push the bike to its limits. But what does it matter if I'm safe? Once Seneca finds out that I'm the reason her brother is in jail—

Crap.

Dead Man Riding.

Chapter Nineteen

Bullseye

Blood drips down from my ear, but before it makes it to my cheek, the force of the wind against my face blows it back, and it pools into one big sticky mess on the back of my neck and in my hair. Thankfully, my hair's dark, so it shouldn't be noticeable.

"Come on, Sen," I murmur, "hold on. Be safe." Bending into my right side to try to relieve the pain, I'm rewarded with a stabbing sensation. "Damn. If those little shits broke my rib…"

Revving the bike, I swerve in and out of traffic on the Long Island Expressway, praying there are no cops around that I'll have to outrun. Luckily, just ahead, I spy the Midtown Tunnel. Once I'm through the tunnel, all I need to do is hang a left onto Second Avenue and it should be smooth sailing all the way down to Alphabet City.

Traffic slows at the entrance, and I glimpse the police and guards monitoring the tunnel. This is not the time or the place to speed through—no matter what horrible, graphic images my mind is conjuring about what may be happening to Seneca, and what she's dealing with.

"Come on, come on…" I mumble. I'm in the cash lane, and some asshole three cars ahead is arguing over change. It's all I can do not to rev my bike, swerve around them, ditch the payment, and rush through the tunnel. As time seems to stand still, I seriously contemplate getting off my bike and paying this dude's fare. Before clocking him on the side of the head.

Instead of just sitting here and letting fear control me, I take the time to clean myself up by wiping the blood on my face onto the sleeves of my sweatshirt. Then, quickly, I unzip my sweatshirt and turning it inside out, I slide it back on again. Reaching inside, I pull up the zipper and force the hood out. I'm so damned exposed on this bike, I want to do anything I can to make sure I'm not noticed and singled out.

I cannot afford to waste one more second.

Finally, the cars ahead of me move, and I glide up on my bike. Without making eye contact, I pay my toll. In my peripheral vision, I catch one of the police officers—holding a rifle—and staring at me. Shit.

That's all I need. Nodding to the cop, I wait patiently as he lowers his rifle and walks toward me. Here goes. I have to sit here and listen to what he says. It's not like I have any choice. I could take off and probably even outrun him, but he'll just get on the radio and call me in on the other side of the tunnel.

"Officer," I say, nodding. He looks behind me to check out the traffic. "Everything okay?"

The officer points to my tail bag. Christ. That's where my piece is stored.

"That tail bag…"

Swallowing hard, I take a deep breath. *This is okay, it's all okay. I will get to Seneca. I will get her to safety.*

"How'd you get one that slim that fits that well on a Harley? Mine is too bulky. I mean, what are we carrying in there, right?"

Holy Mother of God, he smiles. Whew.

"Right." I laugh it off, praying he doesn't ask what in fact, I *am* carrying, or ask to see the inside. "It's retro. Bought it off a guy on the island years ago. He's a master at bikes and sells vintage parts."

"Johnny?"

"Sounds right. Don't really remember. Just stopped by once."

"I'll give him a try."

Nodding, I look ahead. I'm desperate to get moving.

"Well, all right. Have a good day."

"You too, officer."

Holy crap. Pulling away as nonchalantly as I can, I don't pick up speed until I can no longer see the entrance to the tunnel in my rearview. Fuck. That was way too close.

Speeding through the tunnel, it's like I'm trapped in a video game. Thanks to the damn barriers, I can't really zigzag in and out of my lane, but moving quickly and handling my bike expertly, I pass the cars ahead of me. The lights overhead blur into long yellow streaks as I speed through an open section.

Finally, I see the lights of the city ahead. The sun has gone down on a freaking cold, New York night, and damn, I wish I had the warmth of the Steel Knights jacket around me. Who am I kidding? It's not the jacket I miss, it's the feeling that someone has my back. Especially when I'm about to face Ironclad and his asshole minions.

Downshifting, I exit the tunnel toward downtown and pull a sharp turn left, deciding last minute to merge onto the FDR Drive—it'll be faster. Speeding down the drive at a higher speed than I ever could have cruised down Second Avenue, I take the exit way too fast and have to catch my balance as I right myself and rush into Alphabet City. Purposely passing the entrance to Mammon, I make a lap around the block. Pulling off to a dark, hidden spot next to an old tenement, I reach behind me and grab my Ruger from my tail bag. Stuffing it into the back of my jeans, I ride on to a busy street a couple of blocks away and park my bike.

Hopping off, I pull my sweatshirt up from the collar, covering my neck, and round my shoulders forward—staying as warm as possible, while I draw as little attention to myself as I can. Glancing around, I don't see anyone on Mammon's block, so I hustle back, and passing the main entrance, I rush to a side door of Mammon. The one that Don Bordono uses.

Using the side of my fist, I pound on the door. No answer. Crap. I really hope I don't have to pull out my piece and shoot at the damned door, but that's what I'll do if I have to. Pounding on the door again, I hear movement on the other side.

Stepping back, I draw my weapon and point at the door as it's pushed open.

"Yeah—" The man on the other side of the door takes one look at me and steps back, dropping the arm that's holding his weapon. His chin is low and his jaw hangs slack. The color drains from his already pale skin. He looks like he's seen a ghost, and around here, that may be exactly what I'm considered. "B-Bullseye."

Grabbing the door and propping it open with my foot, I keep my piece on the guy.

"I'm here to see Ironclad."

The man reaches for something—probably a radio—but I step closer and press my gun to his skull. Lifting my arm hurts my side, but it's not the shooting pain of a broken rib. Thankfully.

"Don't even think about it," I warn. "I'm here on official business for Don Bordono. You are to turn around, not make a sound or a motion, and take me to Ironclad immediately."

"Y-yes."

He's stuttering, which means he's terrified. That's good. God knows what they've said about me here.

Stepping back, I distance myself but keep my gun drawn on the man. "If you signal anyone on the way to Ironclad, I will pump a bullet into your skull. Understand?"

"Yes."

"Now, walk."

Following the man down a long, dingy, empty hallway, I hear the booming bass and pulsating rhythm of Mammon ahead. Drawing a deep breath, the odor of stale beer and old piss collects in the back of my throat, making me gag. Damn, this place is disgusting. Thankfully, we don't have to walk through the actual club, and we hang a left at the end of the hallway. Walking down another narrow hallway, this one lined with filthy, ripped, brown carpet, I wonder why, with all the money Ironclad has, he doesn't make his work environment a little less... putrid. If you never knew the club part of Mammon was here, and you only saw these hallways, you might think they belong in a building slated for demolition.

Keeping my heart rate under control, we walk up to another door at the end of the hallway. Taking another breath to calm myself, I prepare for what's on the other side. Closing my eyes for a moment, I visualize what's ahead. A large room with a couple of couches, and a door leading to Ironclad's office. But what matters is that there will be several men on the other side of this door—and they'll all be happy to kill me. Really happy to kill me.

However, I'm betting on the fact that they won't. Because if I'm right, Ironclad needs me to do a job for him that only I can do.

Opening my eyes, I know that he has been watching me through his cameras ever since I was outside the club, so there's no element of surprise here. I tap the end of my Ruger on the man's head. He opens the door, and we step in.

Sure enough, three more of Ironclad's men—each bigger than the next—are standing there, waiting for me. And fuck, these guys don't seem the slightest bit intimidated by me or my rep. One with a bald head and a bandaged ear steps forward. "Bullseye." He clasps his hands in front of him.

"I'm here to see Ironclad. It's official business from Don Bordono." I stand taller, showing

I'm not intimidated by these punks.

"We were expecting you." He walks to Ironclad's office door. "Come on."

This is it. The only way I'll live through this is if I was right, and Ironclad needs me.

He puts a hand on the door and a strange sensation—like a chill from the inside—passes up and down my body. It's an eerie, finite feeling, and behind my closed lids, my brain is flooded with memories.

It's not that my whole life flashes before my eyes, but my life with Seneca does. I see her—at the range that first night, flirting with me as we play darts at Hoppa's Taphouse, fisting the sheets in her hands as I make love to her… and I bask in the feeling of being lost as I look into those big, beautiful gray eyes.

My every memory is Seneca. So, maybe my entire life *has* flashed before my eyes—because my whole life is her.

Without her, there is no reason to live.

Oh, Sen, baby. Be in there. Be okay.

The lug with the bandaged ear pushes open the door to Ironclad's office, and I move to step inside, but he puts out his hand, and it lands against my chest with a thud.

"Your piece."

Handing him my gun, I stand still as he pats me down. Thankfully, I'm smart enough to know not to bring more than the one piece to Mammon.

"He's clear," the mountain of a man calls out. He pushes me through the door to Ironclad's office, and it closes behind me.

Shit. I haven't been here in a while, but it hasn't changed much. Looking around, I take in the large semicircular office desk in the middle of the floor with at least a half-dozen leather chairs on my side and one large leather office chair on the other, the array of computers on the desk, the wall of technology and screens showing all parts of the club, and tall armoires lining the opposite wall with Asian-influenced screens dividing the back parts of the oversized office. A door to a private bathroom is hidden behind one of those screens. Every time I step in here, I would swear I was standing in the office of some mega-rich asshole in Silicon Valley, and not Ironclad's office where he runs his illegitimate businesses and meets with Lucifer's Riders.

With its cleanliness and spaciousness, it's a complete contrast to the rest of the club. It's exactly as I remember it—but it's also empty. Which means, there's no Seneca.

Shit. Was I duped? Or just plain wrong?

It's only another second before one of the back doors to the office opens and out comes Ironclad dressed in his signature tight-fitted charcoal suit and thousand-dollar shoes. He's always impeccably dressed and groomed, and today is no exception. His goatee is short and his hair slicked back into a tiny ponytail.

Like the gentleman he loves to pretend to be, he steps into the room, and turning, he offers his hand to the woman behind him.

Seneca.

She steps in, and her eyes lock on mine.

Doing my best to communicate without speaking, I widen my eyes and shake my head.

Ironclad isn't stupid. He knows who she is to me, but he doesn't know how much she means to me. She drops her chin and looks at the ground. Good job, Sen. Good job.

Ironclad looks from me to Seneca and back again. "Oh, come on now, man. You two are not really trying to pretend you don't know each other."

Lifting her head, she looks at Ironclad. "I know him. So? That has nothing to do with us."

"Us?" The word is out before I realize I'm saying it.

"Yes, us." She steps closer to me. "I'm here because Ironclad and I are working a deal."

The way he looks at her... his gaze running up and down her body... it's all I can do to stand here and not reach out and rip his small slimy head clean off of his shoulders.

"I was here earlier, too," she explains. "I beat the crap out of that mountain in the other room. That's why his ear is bandaged. Now, Ironclad and I have some business."

What the hell is she up to?

"Seneca, Ironclad isn't your business partner." My chest is rising and falling with my rushing breath, but I draw another deep breath, calming myself, and forcing my feet to stay still.

"Who are you to say who is and isn't anything in my life?"

The way she glares at me... Is she acting? Or does she know...?

"What is it you want, Bullseye?" Ironclad steps up and slips his hand around Seneca's, holding her hand.

She freezes, and her shoulders stiffen as her body tenses. Yanking her hand away, she whips around and faces him.

"You saw the ripped earlobe on one of your guys and the knife in the knee of the other. Want to experience some of my other moves?"

Hiding my grin behind my fist, I chuckle quietly.

"You are one feisty woman, Wildfire," he says, licking his lips, and backing off.

I don't know why I'm surprised she can handle Ironclad just like she handles everyone else.

"She is that," I agree. "And that's part of the reason I'm here for her. Come on, Seneca." I beckon her with my hand. "We've got some things we need to discuss."

Chewing the corner of her lip, she pauses for a moment—no doubt thinking this through—and then steps toward me. Ironclad holds out his hand, preventing her from moving forward. Shit. What I wouldn't give for my Ruger and Ironclad's head on a target.

Stay calm, Bullseye. Stay calm.

"What's going on, Ironclad?" Her voice is strong and frankly, it's the same question I was going to ask him. "I came here of my own free will. We have things we're discussing. Now, it seems like you're saying I can't leave."

"It's just..." Lifting a hand, he runs his fingers down the sides of his goatee. "When you came here, I thought you just wanted something from *me*. Now that I see how useful you really are... it doesn't make sense for me to just let you walk out of here..."

"What's it going to cost, Ironclad?" My voice is deep, and my heart is thumping in my chest.

"Don Bordono. It's going to cost Don Bordono."

I knew it. But now I'm caught between the two of them—each wanting the other dead.

"And what do you want with Don Bordono?"

"Come on, Bullseye." Ironclad walks to his desk and plops down onto his oversized leather chair. He leans back, rocking from side to side. "You know what I want. Do I have to spell it out for you?"

"I think you do."

Stopping, he sits up and stares me in the eye. "Don Bordono is getting old. He's caught in the world of the past. It's time some new, younger blood began running the show."

"Like you?"

"Like me."

"Seneca comes with me."

"No." Standing, Ironclad places both hands on his desk and leans forward. "We know how you got your nickname, Bullseye. You could be blindfolded and still shoot an apple off a man's head from a mile away. And this one…" He thumbs Seneca and smiles. "It's obvious why she's called Wildfire. But do you know why they call me Ironclad?"

"Why?"

"Because no matter what goes down in my world, I have an alibi. And not just any alibi—an ironclad one. She will be much more useful to me here as an alibi, then she would be there with you, getting in the way." Standing up taller, he looks me in the eye. "Bullseye. Make Don Bordono disappear in a way that cannot and will not be linked to me. And then, you can have Seneca."

She moves like she's about to say something but doesn't. She must realize this is the best deal she's going to get. And once I get back, the two of us will have a chance to finally get out. For good. What he says is exactly what I expected, but it's still unsettling.

"If you touch her, Ironclad, I will make you suffer in ways you never knew possible…"

"I understand."

Moving to the door he came in from, Ironclad smiles and salutes me before disappearing and leaving Seneca and me alone in his office.

"Sen."

"Avery." Rushing forward, she jumps into my arms and throws her arms around my neck. "Oh… what?" Pulling away, she fingers the pool of dried blood on the back of my neck.

"It's nothing."

"How did you know where I was? I ditched my phone. Bought a burner."

"I just got lucky."

The hell with my ribs and the beating I just took. Pulling Seneca tightly to me again, the pain magically falls away now that I have her in my arms. Leaning down, I find her pouty lips and kissing her over and over, I wrap my arms tighter around her as I lock my mouth onto hers. Opening her mouth with mine, I devour her hungrily as one of my hands travels up to the back of her head, holding her and keeping her hostage in my strong arms, while my other hand travels down to her fine ass.

Pulling her even tighter to me, our bodies press together, and I grunt as she moans. Finally, she pulls back, and dropping her head, she shakes it. I wrap my hands around her arms, holding her.

"Avery... I'm so sorry you've been dragged into this. I wanted to leave you in Hoppa. I tried to leave you in the truck that morning. You shouldn't follow me. I'm bad news. You don't know what I'm dealing with—and you shouldn't have to."

"Sen, baby. Look at me."

Raising her eyes to mine, I swallow hard. Hell, there's no time like the present.

"You don't need to apologize to me. I should be the one apologizing to you."

"Why?" Her eyes narrow, but she doesn't look surprised.

"Your brother is Matt Villetrio. He was framed for a murder he didn't commit. He was in a drug den in St. Mark's Place, buying, when a hit came in on the dealer. The dealer was killed and your brother took the rap."

"Yes."

"Sen, I need you to concentrate. Did Matt ever mention the names of the guys at the hit with him?"

"Two of Ironclad's thugs were there. They're the ones who killed that guy. I know it."

"Were their names..." Taking a deep breath, I squeeze her arms. "Were their names Mikey and Tony?"

"Yes." Her eyes narrow more. "No." She steps away, distancing herself. "No. How? I've been putting together the pieces, but it was just all too coincidental. How could we both end up in Hoppa, Arizona and in the Steel Knights? It doesn't make sense."

"Fate can be a bitch."

"So, you were there?"

"Yes. I was only supposed to warn the dealer. He wasn't supposed to be killed. Don Bordono needed him. But fucking Ironclad sent Mikey and Tony and they panicked."

She takes a step back, shaking her head.

"You have to know, what happened to your brother—I never knew who he was. It haunts me daily."

"It *haunts you daily*?" Stepping closer to me, her face becomes redder as she uses a finger to poke me in the chest. "It *haunts you daily*?" Storming away to the opposite side of the room, she turns and rushes back. "What the fuck, Avery? My brother is sitting in jail—rotting away—God knows what is happening to him, and you... you could have saved him?"

"It's not like anyone asked or gave me the opportunity, Sen. I was working for Don Bordono."

"Fuck this! When will you ever take responsibility, Avery? You fucking child! You could have made all the difference."

Before I realize what's happening, she comes at me and swipes my feet out from under me, dropping me onto my back. Jumping on top of me, she straddles me and pummels me with her fists against my chest.

Over and over she beats me. It hurts, but I know she doesn't mean to do any serious damage or she would go after my eyes or groin... she's just venting. Keeping my elbows bent and my arms parallel to my body to protect myself, I let her beat me until she's exhausted.

Falling off of me and onto her hip, she lands on the side of me. Daring to lift my hand, I reach out to brush a hair back from her cheek, but she yanks her head away.

"Seneca."

Climbing up to my feet, I put a hand out to her to help her up, but she stays still, just looking away.

"Sen, baby. I know you hate me right now, and I know you don't want to hear this, but all I want is for you to be safe, and you're as safe here—with Ironclad—as possible. He won't do anything to you while I'm doing a job for him."

She doesn't answer, she only stares at the ground. Her silence and disappointment are so much worse than when she was beating me.

"I know you're pissed."

She glares at me.

"Okay, you're more than pissed, and you have a right to be. But we have one goal here. Let's stay alive so I can get you back to Hoppa where you will be safe. You can be pissed there. And we'll figure something out with your brother."

Looking away again, her chest heaves with anger.

"I'm going to go, Seneca." Backing away from her like she's a hungry lioness, I make my way to the door. Reaching out behind me and putting my hand on the door handle, I open the door. "I will be back for you. I promise."

Glancing up at me one more time, she snarls, and I catch her finger twitching. She's coming for me.

"Seneca."

"Fuck you, Avery!"

With a growl, she charges at me just as I step into the hallway and slam the door shut behind me. Like a wild animal trapped in a cage, she lands hard against the door.

Slamming her hand against it, I know that serves as her solemn pledge to get even for everything I've done. And that means, while I spend the next couple of hours figuring out how to fool Ironclad into thinking Don Bordono is dead even when he's not…

Seneca Villetrio, the woman I've risked everything to save, will be planning my brutal demise.

Chapter Twenty

Wildfire

"Fucking Avery Pairings…" I'm like a bull seeing red. "Who the hell does he think he is?"

Mumbling like a madwoman, I peel myself off of the door and storm around Ironclad's office. My boots clump against the uncarpeted floor, creating a noise that sounds like it's made by a much bigger, taller me. And that bigger, taller me—she's as pissed as I am. Back and forth, with no particular destination in mind, I move in a circle from Ironclad's desk to his door.

"How could I have been so stupid?" I mumble, trying to work this out. Slowing, I begin to rationalize. "But how could I have known?" I went after Avery. He didn't even nominate me for the Steel Knights and truthfully, I do believe that he had no idea of who I was and what was happening in my life until he spoke with my mother.

But, that doesn't matter. You don't help people just because you know them. You don't do what's right just because you're going to get caught. He should have stepped up for Matt all of those years ago.

Fuck you, Avery.

And why has he been chasing me? All the way from Arizona to New York? He must have been trying to keep me safe from Mikey and Tony, just like I was trying to keep him safe from the very same people.

How freaking ironic.

So, the two assholes—who between them don't have a sixth-grade education and don't know all the letters of the alphabet—outsmarted us. Me with my Ivy League education. Fuck.

Yeah, okay, Avery was trying to protect me, but that doesn't change the fact that *he was there*. He was there when that drug dealer was shot, and he was there when those assholes, Mikey and Tony, framed Matt.

He was there when Matt went down. He was there and…

Nothing.

He did nothing.

He let Matt, a kid with his whole life ahead of him, go to jail for *life* when he could have prevented it.

"Fuck you, Avery. Fuck you."

There's no doubt that Avery has to suffer. So, the only question is, how?

I'm getting dizzy from the walking, so stopping, I lean against one of Ironclad's office armoires that's probably crammed with guns and ammunition. To think that I gave my body to Avery… that I willingly played along, and was happily submissive to his alpha… that I let myself feel good and feel loved… that I wanted to protect him from all of this chaos…

…and to think that he was as much to blame for it as anyone.

Okay, not as much to blame, but still.

"Fuck you, Avery. Fuck you."

Pushing myself off of the armoire, I start moving again. Each time I make a circle around this glorified holding pen I'm in, I think I have the answer to "what happens next". But then, each time I think I may have a plan, it's like a freaking train comes crashing through my skull, scattering all of my ideas into a heap, and I have to stop, and start planning all over again.

"Who the hell does he think he is?"

Forcing myself to close my eyes and to take a deep breath, I go over what I know for sure. As usual, with the exception of Johnny, there's no one I can trust but me. Avery isn't who he said he is, and he's left me here, with Ironclad, while he goes to do a hit on Don Bordono, the most notorious and feared mob boss in the Tri-state. And finally, Matt is rotting in jail, and I have to get him out. That means I'll have to get it done. And I've never been closer to an answer than I am right now, in Ironclad's office in the middle of Mammon.

"So, how can I use this to my advantage?" I mutter as I move to the wall of screens that are linked to cameras in all parts of the club. Of course, I don't see Ironclad—and Avery is gone, but I do see guards who are now stationed outside my door. And not just one or two, but three large men, all visibly packing.

"Shit."

So, Ironclad decided to keep me here, and they know what I'm capable of, physically anyway. Three men who are that large and are carrying guns will be hard to stop. Not impossible, but difficult. All they'll have to do is grab me from behind and lock my arms, stepping just outside of the reach of my legs, and I'm rendered useless.

Staring at the screens until my eyes begin to blur, it hits me.

"That's it. When you can't beat 'em," I mumble.

I have to join Ironclad and trick him into admitting that he sent Mikey and Tony to the hit that went bad. And then, I've got to get him to say that Mikey and Tony were the ones who pulled the triggers—and then finally, Matt can be acquitted.

Closing my eyes and taking a deep breath, I calm my racing heart. No, this won't be easy, I'll have to pledge with Lucifer's Riders and that means…

"Shit."

A chill runs up and down my spine, and my entire body begins to ache as I remember the warm Arizona sun on my back as I downshifted my bike, racing against Harry, Bucky, and the new prospects… I can taste the cool microbrew beer sliding down my throat after a long, hot day of fixing bikes… and most of all, I remember how on any given night, my heart would race as I watched Avery "Bullseye" Pairings walk across the crowded bar with his eyes locked on me…

But that was forever ago now. And none of it was real. It was only a short dream, and I've woken up smack in the middle of my nightmare. There is only one way out of this horror story. And that's through Ironclad.

Thank God I tried to pledge with Lucifer's Riders years ago, so this won't seem like a total setup. Plus, the fact that I just had that fight with Avery—and no doubt Ironclad saw it on one of his cameras—makes it all even more believable.

And if Avery goes down because of my connection with Ironclad and Lucifer's Riders, well, hell, that's just the cherry on top.

As I turn away from the screens, I notice one screen that's blank. It must be the room where Ironclad is now. Catching my reflection on the blank screen, I see that woman again—that strong, capable woman.

I can do this.

Glancing at the front door of the office, I know what's waiting outside. Three goons. But the other door—the one that Ironclad uses—I don't know what's on the other side.

My mother used to have an expression she spouted often; "The devil that you know is better than the devil that you don't know." I think that was her reasoning for staying with my father for all those years, but I don't agree with her. I remember in one of my world religion classes, I learned that in medieval times, some thought devils were matched to different sins—like Mammon for extreme greed. If that's the case, then, "Sloth" could be waiting on the other side of this door.

And I'd sure as shit rather fight Sloth than those three armed mountains standing outside the main entrance. Especially since I've already maimed one of them, and there's no doubt he's looking for revenge.

I need to get to Ironclad.

Damn, what I wouldn't give for my bag right now that's holding my piece—but I know if I had brought it here, they never would have let me keep it. They'd never give me access to my gun. I was smart to keep it locked in that motel's safe, even though my new burner phone is buried in the back of my jeans. I'm surprised they've let me keep that. But truthfully, except that one time at the door, they haven't patted me down. It was easy to get past that guard. All I had to tell him was that I was a WAG of one of the guys in Lucifer's Riders, and he let me in.

I *hated* having to say that. I am no one's old lady. Taking a deep breath and pushing aside my annoyance, I gather my courage and pound on the back door of Ironclad's office. Nothing.

"Ironclad," I yell through the door, pounding again, but still there's no response.

I'm not surprised. I don't know why I thought he'd be waiting for me to call for him. Shit. So I'm stuck in here. Damn it.

"Ironclad!" I try again, pounding louder, but still nothing. If I had my piece, then I could shoot at the lock—

Wait. Reaching out for the door handle, I press down on the lever and… it opens…

Makes sense. Ironclad would never create an office where he could be trapped. Taking another deep breath, I push the door wider and step all the way through. The door clicks shut behind me. Crap. Ahead is only a long, dimly lit hallway…

I really hope I'm not locked in here and left to die.

There's a single lightbulb overhead, and moving quickly, I hug the wall, hoping I get… somewhere. As I move, I'm certain the heavy bass—the heartbeat of Mammon—grows louder.

"I'm moving toward the club," I mumble.

Knowing that I can get into Mammon, some of the billion pounds of stress I'm feeling falls away. In the club itself, I'll at least get a chance to find Ironclad. If he's still here. If not… I'll have to move on to drastic measures.

And damn, I really don't want to have to do that.

Finding another door, I squat down low and ease the door open slowly. This is freaking Mammon. For all I know, this door could open into an arena with gladiators and tigers. Peeking through the door that's only open a crack, I see that I'm behind one of the large bars on the main floor of Mammon. Okay. I can work with this.

Closing the door again, I stay crouched low in the hallway and text Harry. Thankfully, I remember his number, and I'm even more thankful that I created that social account from this burner… in case I ever needed it. Exhaling deeply, I type.

"*Avery and I in a shitload of trouble. Can't explain. Get Seth. Contact NYPD to watch livestream from my social media.*" Send.

Please, God, I know Harry's pissed, but please let him help.

The phone vibrates in my hand.

"*Ok.*"

That's succinct. Well, what did I expect?

Pushing the door all the way open, I slide through and eyeing the underbar passage, I squat-walk my way toward it. Ducking lower, I slide under—

"Hey!" A bartender grabs the hood of my—or Avery's—sweatshirt. "Who the hell are you and what did you steal?"

Standing to my full height, I spin around and glare at him.

Letting go, he backs off.

"I'm Seneca Villetrio. I'm here to pledge for Lucifer's Riders."

Grinning, he flashes a gold tooth as he looks me up and down. He lifts his hand and runs it through his long, filthy black hair and settles his gaze on me. His beady little eyes flicker. Fuck, no.

"You have no fucking clue who you're up against," I snarl, stepping deeper into the shadows and closer to the wall in case I need to use it.

He follows me. Stupid, stupid man.

"We've never had a girl pledge," he tells me. "You know what the initiation is like for bitches?"

Taking a deep breath and relaxing my tense shoulders, I cross my arms in front of my chest. If I kill him now, it'll delay my plan.

"Do ya?" He licks his lips, and his gaze drops to my breasts.

Aw, fuck it. I can't help myself. Reaching out, I grab his tiny member in my hand and squeeze.

"I imagine that it must feel something like this. That is, when you pass the woman from biker to biker."

"Oh, ow!"

Even in the shadow, I can see his face turn a dark red as his knees buckle, and he begins to sink down. My grip on his tiny dick holds him upright.

"Huh. Never thought something this small could cause so much pain."

He beats on my hand, trying to make me release, but it just makes me squeeze harder. Taking my other hand and shaping it like a claw, I swoop upward under his neck and pin him to the wall in a front chokehold. With my index finger, I press against his jugular. This is almost too easy. As he sputters and chokes, I glance around. No one notices what's happening here; everyone at the bar is too wrapped up in their own worlds. That's the good part about Mammon.

"Okay, dickwad. Here's the thing. I am here because of Ironclad. I'm looking for him. Do you know where he is?"

He tries to shake his head as sweat drips down from his forehead, making my hand slick. Cripes. I don't need to worry about killing someone. Even if this is Mammon, and it goes unnoticed.

Letting go with both of my hands, the slimy bartender falls into a heap on the ground, but I've got no time to lose. Ironclad's probably seen this anyway, and he doesn't want me to leave. I'm his collateral. Using a wooden box for a step, I climb up onto the bar and stomp my way to the center. Standing in the middle of the bar, I look out at the crowd that is just barely beginning to notice me.

"Hey!"

A couple of Mammon's patrons look up at me. Two guys in Lucifer's Riders jackets raise their shot glasses in a toast. A topless woman walking through the crowd claps for me, although I'm not sure why.

"I am Seneca Villetrio, and I am here to pledge for Lucifer's Riders."

The two guys in the jackets leer at me. Shit.

"But I am also here because of Ironclad. And I will not pledge for anyone but him. Bring me Ironclad." I'm vaguely aware that I sound like a peasant demanding to see the king.

Silence falls over the crowd. Aw, fuck. Maybe I should have thought this over… Why would I imagine that I wield enough power that—

"Very, very nice." It's Ironclad, making his way through the parting crowd. "Wildfire. You didn't have to make this spectacle. I was coming back for you."

"I want to pledge, Ironclad. With Lucifer's Riders."

"Why would you want to do that?" He stops and looks up at me.

"Because I need protection. Avery turned out to be a disappointment. And you know I need help with Matt. The kind of help only you can give me."

Turning to his bodyguards, he nods to them and they walk to me. Without asking, they reach up and take me by the arms. Lifting me, and floating me off of the bar, they place me down in front of Ironclad.

"Shall we go?" he asks, offering his arm.

Sliding my arm in his, he nods to the bar and the passage is opened. As we pass behind the bar, I glimpse the bartender who's still sitting against the wall, nursing his wounds. He flips me off as I walk by.

Ironclad leads me through the door behind the bar. Exhaling, I'm relieved to find that he's taking me back to his office. That eliminates the scary aspect of surprise. As we walk down the hallway toward Ironclad's office, I know I've got to come up with a way to get this stream started without him knowing.

He pushes me into his office ahead of him. The two goons stand just inside the door.

Crap. My heart rate increases as I look at these guys and wonder what they are planning to do to me.

Thinking fast, I turn to Ironclad. "I want to initiate with you. Only you. You know if you pass me off to anyone else, Bullseye will torture you and kill you. No matter how pissed I am at him, he loves me, and he will hunt you down like an animal."

"Oh, I know that. I have no intentions of sharing the goods of Seneca Villetrio with any of my coworkers."

Exhaling audibly, my shoulders drop.

"But…"

"But?" Fear climbs up my spine, and my heartbeat thumps in my brain.

"But you know very well there are two parts of the initiation. First, you prove your strength, and then, your femininity." He steps toward me and gently runs a hand down my cheek. Freezing, I wait for the slap.

Removing his hand, he smiles. "And since I would never hit a woman unless she deserved it, they're here for the first part."

Nodding, I swallow hard. How did this happen? Being with Ironclad in his disgusting world is a place I never thought I would be. I'm going to have to take a beating, and I won't be allowed to fight back.

Looking at the two men by the door, I wonder which one of them will hit first, and how I'll take it. I can't dodge or step away.

Standing here with sweat trickling down my spine, I wait. Even if I could somehow manage to start the stream now, the police might come too early—to stop the beating. What I need is to get Ironclad literally with his pants down, and admitting to what happened with Mikey, Tony, and Matt. Then, I'd really appreciate it if the police—or anyone—came barging in.

Still, the mountain men don't move.

Oh shit. This can't be good. Or maybe, is it only about intimidation with a woman?

Just when this little glimmer of hope passes over me, there's a knock on the door. The mountain men open the door, and I brace myself for what's to come—nunchucks, throwing stars, ball with spikes…

Instead, it's even worse. It's the mountain of a man I maimed, and he's still wearing a bandage on the lobe I tore.

"Fuck…" I whisper.

The three other men chuckle.

"Well, Seneca, this is your one and only chance. Once he starts, no matter how you beg for mercy, he will not stop until I tell him to."

Oh fuck. What am I going to do? I can't kill all three of these men. And if I did, Ironclad surely wouldn't help me with Matt.

It's only pain, I tell myself. *And it's my only chance to free Matt.*

"Seneca?" Ironclad lifts his eyebrows.

"No. Let's do this."

"Very well." He seems almost sorry as he nods to the mountain with the bandaged ear.

"Wait." Putting up my hand, I stop them. "He's got to be three times my weight. He could kill me with one punch. There has to be rules."

"Okay," Ironclad agrees. "No killing her."

"Ironclad…"

"Well, Seneca, what do you have in mind?"

"No closed fists. No chokeholds. No choking. No breaking limbs. No losing an eye. No tearing."

As I speak, I remove my earrings and put them into my back pocket. Discreetly, I feel for my phone that's wedged in the back of my pants. I have to be careful not to fall in a way that cracks the phone or this will all be for nothing. The man glares at me, but I continue, undaunted.

"No permanent damage. No ripping off fingernails or toenails. No lifting me. No dropping me over something to crack my spine. No weapons. And my clothes stay on. Period."

"Teeth, boss?" The bandaged mountain of a man looks at Ironclad.

"You have to give him something, Seneca."

Nodding, I swallow hard. Losing a tooth is painful, but it's not life-threatening. And at least I know he's going to go for the face first. But the hardest part of all of this will be stopping my impulse to fight back.

Taking a deep breath, I consciously relax all the muscles in my body. Taking a hit on tense muscles is way more damaging than on relaxed ones. That's why so many drunk drivers walk away from car wrecks.

Shaking out my hands, I stay still as the man approaches and lifts his hand. With an open palm, he strikes me across the face. My head ricochets to the side and my cheek burns, but I can survive this. Righting my head, he barely gives me time to prepare before he slaps me in the other direction. It feels like my eye is going to pop, but again, I bring my head up.

This time, I see it like it's happening in slow motion; he lifts his hand but to the opposite side—he's going to backhand me. Fuck.

The glimmer of his ring with the signet of Lucifer's Riders flashes in the harsh office light, and then he lets his hand come down hard across my cheek.

My skin feels like it's tearing open, and I put my fingers to it. Pulling them away, I see they're slick with blood. Looking up at the asshole, I glower as he pulls his hand back and punches me hard in the gut.

Putting out my hands to steady myself, I drop to my knees, but he follows me, and with another hard strike, backhands me again—across the same cheek. Blood gushes down, and I hold my sweatshirt sleeve against it, trying to stop the bleeding as my abdomen aches.

This is nothing, I tell myself. *I've had so much worse when I was training for Krav Maga.*

On my knees with my stomach flipping and my face aching, I watch helplessly as he lifts his boot.

Oh fuck, I should have stipulated no kicking.

Thankfully, he's slower than I am, and as he raises his boot behind him, I know he's going to kick me in the teeth. Turning away just in time, he lands his kick right between my shoulder blades. Something pointy wedges itself into my back.

"Oh fuck!" Falling forward onto my chest, there's a danger that my phone is exposed. Scrambling, I right myself and back myself against the wall. A stupid move, but at this point, I'm just trying to survive…

He lifts his foot again and—

"Hold it."

He drops his foot as Ironclad steps forward.

"You've had your revenge. She's proven her strength. You can all go now. Leave us to the next part of her initiation."

The way Ironclad smiles… I realize he *likes* watching women be beaten. It's his foreplay and obviously the reason he set up the rules of his club the way he did.

"Seneca."

He holds out his hand to me, and although it hurts to move, I slip mine in his. He helps me to my feet.

"Not hurting too badly, I hope? Not so much that you won't be able to enjoy our fun?"

Blood trickles from above my eye and runs down my cheek. I need to stop it.

"Let me go to the bathroom first, Ironclad. I need to stop the bleeding."

"Of course." He holds out his hand and points me to another door hidden behind a screen.

Stepping into the bathroom, I wonder if he has cameras in here as well. Hovering at the sink, I look at my reflection. My wounds hurt like hell, especially the one between my shoulder blades, but nothing is life-threatening. And nothing will cause permanent damage. At worst, I'll get a scar.

Cleaning my wound, I apply paper towels, trying to stop the bleeding. Then, taking off my sweatshirt and lifting my jacket and T-shirt, I check my ribs which look red and are sore, but I don't think any are broken. Removing the phone from my jeans as discreetly as I can and making sure it's silenced, I start the live feed, and tuck it into my front pocket. Then, I pull the sweatshirt back on and head out to Ironclad.

I've got one chance.

"You look better," he tells me.

"Thank you." Walking to him, I know I need to keep control here. "But I'm still in pain."

His eyes flash. So, I was right. This asshole loves it when a woman is hurt.

"What kind of pain?"

So, this is his foreplay. Okay.

"I'll tell you," I counter, stepping in front of him and dropping to my knees, "but you have to answer my questions, too."

Waiting for the perfect moment, I reach up and begin unbuckling his pants. He drops his head back and bam, I slip my hand into my front pocket and lay the phone on the floor. Now, I've got to make sure he doesn't see it.

"I know you get excited when you see a woman is injured."

"It's that obvious?" he jokes. He must be referring to his tiny hard-on.

Swallowing the bile in my mouth, I press on. "But I like it when a man tells me how he outsmarts someone else."

"You would like that."

He reaches for the back of my head, but I pull away.

"Not yet. First, tell me you sent Mikey and Tony to that hit that went wrong on September twelfth, three years ago."

"I think, Seneca, first we play my game, and then we'll play yours."

"Fine." Thinking fast, I try to calm my shaking hands. "But I work better with motivation."

"How much better?"

He makes eye contact, and although I want to barf all over his thousand-dollar shoes, I keep it together and force a smile.

"Wouldn't you like to find out? Tell me, Ironclad. Tell me what happened that day that Matt Villetrio was framed for murder…"

"Okay, Seneca. We'll play your game. But you give me something, too. Take off your sweatshirt."

Leaning back from Ironclad, I peel off Avery's sweatshirt and toss it carefully on top of the phone. This way, the police will still be able to hear the confession, but the phone will be hidden. Maybe I just caught a break.

Looking up at Ironclad from my position on my knees before him, I shiver in my fitted jacket. No, there's no catching a break here. That sweatshirt was the last connection I had to Avery, and the last layer of protection I felt. And now, it's gone. And I'm alone. As always.

But that's okay because I've always relied on myself.

Maybe Avery will come back, and maybe he won't. I may not know much about what's going to happen here, but I do know one thing for sure, if we get out of this alive…

I'm going to kill Avery "Bullseye" Pairings.

Chapter Twenty-One

Bullseye

"What the fuck?" Balancing my bike between my thighs, I yell at Harry over the phone. Looking up, I catch the cross street—Twenty-Eighth. Thank God. It won't take that long to get back downtown. "She did what?"

"She'll be live-streaming on her social media. Nothing yet, but Seth is standing by and we've called NYPD."

"She's trying to trap Ironclad all on her own." I'm barely able to contain my anger and disbelief.

"Who?"

"Harry, I'm sorry. I'll explain when I can. You need to tell Seth something for me."

"He's here."

"Harry? Wait. Uh, thank you, man. Really, thank you."

Will Harry and I ever be able to repair the bond I've broken? Who the hell knows? But I sure as hell don't have the time to think about it now.

"Bullseye?"

"Seth. I need a hand. I need the security cameras jammed at a place in Alphabet City. What can you do?"

"Nothing from this far. But I've got a guy in the city who can help."

"You do?" Despite everything, I hear the awe in my voice.

"We were in juvie together. I got this. Give me the address and go."

After spitting out the address of Mammon, I click off the phone, rev my bike, and whip it around, facing the cross street. Reaching into my tail bag, I grab my Ruger that I was able to snatch on my way out of Mammon, stuffing it into the back of my pants, and then another two pieces. Each of these I slip inside the holster straps in my boots. I strap more rounds of ammo to my waist.

Taking off down the avenue, I dodge traffic and pull up to Mammon in record time. This time, I don't worry about being discreet. Racing around from the front entrance to the side, I drop my bike and, rushing to the door, I lift my Ruger. With one single shot, I pop the lock, bursting inside.

"What the fuck, man?" A surprised guard reaches for his gun, but he's too slow. Without a thought, I take down both guards at the door—not killing them but injuring them enough that I'm sure they'll stay down. There's no way Seth's guy could have taken down the security yet, so there's every chance that Ironclad is watching all of this. Unless Seneca has him otherwise occupied.

Fuck.

Either way, I have to move fast.

Stepping over the two moaning men who smell like blood and fear, I pat them down and take their weapons, and then I make my way down the hallways of Mammon and toward Ironclad's door. And this time, hell yeah, I'm packing heat. And a whole hell of a lot of it.

Barely stopping at the outer door to Ironclad's office, I repeat my move on the front door and shoot—popping the lock. Rushing to the side of the door, I wait for the first guard with my back flat against the wall. As a giant man steps into the hallway wielding a gun, I shut the door with my foot, come up behind, and land the butt of my gun on his skull. He drops like a demolished house.

No doubt the next one will look in my direction, so before he can come through the door, I have my piece drawn and aimed through the crack at the hinges of the door. One shot in the knee drops him down, and another in the shoulder maims him. He falls facedown as well. Finally, crouching low, I sneak to the other side of the door, and as that last guard rushes out, I kick my leg, tripping him. As he goes down headfirst, breaking his fall with his wrist, I hear the snap.

Damn. A clean break to the wrist has to hurt.

Screaming, he holds his hand beneath his mammoth body as I come up behind him and clock him on the back of his head with the butt of my gun. Rushing through the now-empty outer office, I stall just before I burst down the door to Ironclad's office.

Slow down, Bullseye, I tell myself. *She's in there. You can't go in shooting.* Pausing, I listen, but I can't hear anything. Of course not. Ironclad's office is soundproof.

Fuck. I can't take this any longer.

Drawing my gun and stepping back from the door, I kick it down and barge in, wielding my gun.

"Ironclad! Get on your feet. Let's move."

There she is, Seneca… on her knees before Ironclad. Sizing her up quickly, I see her face is badly bruised. Oh, those assholes are going to rue the day…

Our words overlap one another while Seneca jumps to her feet and moves for her sweatshirt.

"What the fuck did you do to her, Ironclad—?"

"—Not me, Bullseye—"

"—What the fuck, man?—" Grabbing a phone from beneath the sweatshirt on the ground, she hurls it at me and it bounces off my chest. "—You ruin everything! I don't have his confession yet!"

"—What confession? Seneca?—" Ironclad takes a step closer to her.

"—Avery, you asshole! This was my only chance! How could you do this?"

She's still screaming at me as I grab her by the arm and pull her to me. Fighting me, she starts punching me in the chest. She looks like she's been dragged through the mud and then beaten, but she keeps fighting. Damn, no wonder they call her Wildfire.

Out of the corner of my eye, I see the monitors with the feed from the cameras all go down. Ironclad doesn't seem to notice. Instead, he stares at me—his jaw is clenched, and his eyes are narrowed. He's pissed.

"That was your plan, Seneca? To trap me into saying what? That I sent Mikey and Tony to that drug dealer's crack den and ordered a hit?" He laughs. "You think if I had that much power, I'd have told Bullseye to kill Don Bordono?"

"What?" Some of what he says makes sense… but he's such a slimy snake, it's near impossible to know what's true and what's not.

Still holding her, I can tell that even Seneca is tiring—I can feel her energy drain as her fight weakens. Eyeing the bathroom door at the back of the office, I know there's no choice. Dragging a fighting Seneca to the door, I force it open as I keep my gun on Ironclad. Pushing Seneca inside, I yank the door closed and, still with Ironclad in my sights, I jam his desk against her door. She's trapped.

She doesn't need to see this.

Walking up to Ironclad to the sound of Seneca beating against the door, I stop just before him.

"So, Avery, what is it you want?" His voice is cool, but I can see the fear in his eyes.

"What I wanted was for none of this to happen, Ironclad. But it seems we have a problem. Two of your goons killed that damned dealer, and her brother was framed for it."

"So what?" A bead of sweat drips from his temple and drops onto his expensive suit. "What do you want? You want me to say Mikey and Tony did it?"

"Well, I'm afraid it's too late for that now. Besides, it would be your word against theirs. One low-level drug dealer against another."

He stands up taller, adjusting his jacket. "That's not true. I'm way more connected than those punk-ass pussies. Ask Don Bordono."

As he speaks, he moves his hand ever so slowly into his suit jacket. He's going for his gun.

"I did ask Don Bordono. And it seems he doesn't trust you either."

"So?"

"So, my only option is to shoot you dead, and then to have him finger Mikey and Tony."

"Well, shit. No wonder," Ironclad laughs.

"No wonder what?"

"No wonder Don Bordono likes you so much. You really are as stupid as he says you are."

A chill rushes up my spine. "I hate killing anyone, Ironclad, but considering what you've done, and what you did to her, this time it will be my pleasure."

With a slimy grin, he pulls his gun from his pocket and aims—

With a quick pop to the head, he's down.

Shit. I do hate killing, and I despise this world. But this time, there was no choice.

Doubling back, I push the desk away and open Seneca's door. She's standing there, staring at me.

"Let's go."

She shakes her head.

"Seneca, I don't have time for these games. Let's go!"

Again, she shakes her head and then crosses her arms in front of her chest. Fuck.

Rushing to her, I take one of her arms and forcing it to her side, I bend down low and toss her over my shoulder. Then, running out the door, I see the three bodyguards lying there, moaning. Ironclad is dead, but the cameras are down and none of these goons saw me, so they can live. Thankfully.

However, they did see Seneca.

Doubling back in with Seneca bouncing over my shoulder, I go to Ironclad's desk and shoot out all the links to the feeds, destroying any proof of me—and more importantly, Seneca—being here. That'll also keep anyone from connecting the outage to Seth's connection.

Then, with Seneca still over my shoulder, I rush out the doors past the injured guards. Even if they can ID me, they won't. These guys are pros, and they know better than to mess with Don Bordono's Bullseye.

"Thank God," I mutter as I spot my bike waiting there like a lifeboat in a raging sea. A couple of blocks away, I spy a police car, but since she cut the feed before anything happened, there's nothing they can do. Dropping Seneca on the bike, I peel out before she can get away—probably taking her against her will.

Fuck. After years of keeping my nose clean, in just one night, I can add murder and kidnapping to my resume. But the only person who can link me to any of it is Seneca—the sister of the man who's doing time because of me.

The woman I love but who'll *never* forgive me.

But she has to. Without Sen… There's no reason for any of it.

Downshifting, we speed out toward Don Bordono's house. The only person who can free Matt.

Because if he doesn't, then the only way to get Matt out is if I go down. I only served a short sentence before Don Bordono "convinced" the right people that I wasn't in the room at the time of the murder. If I were to admit who the killers were, then I'd have to admit I was there. And I'd have to take the rap—not for murder, but for everything else.

I could be looking at *years*.

Fuck.

"What is this place?"

After the harrowing ride back out to the island, during which she clawed at my back and even covered my eyes one time—until I swerved and nearly killed us both—we're in front of Don Bordono's mansion.

I wait for her to hop off the bike before I swing my leg over and dismount.

"Looks like home sweet home, doesn't it?"

Raising an eyebrow, she glares at me. "It's a little small for me."

Sighing, my tense shoulders slump forward. I'm sick of this. All of it; the pettiness, the secrets, and the anger around each other. All I want to do is to pull her into my arms and take her to bed, but that doesn't seem to be an option any longer.

Stalling by the bike, I realize that strangely, this time, I'm not met by Don Bordono's security.

What the hell is going on?

Taking her hand, I turn to her. "Sen. This is probably my only chance to say this. My one shot. So, listen, please. We're here for a couple of reasons. Don Bordono is our only hope. He's also holding my father somewhere because of some inflated gambling debts, so once we tell him that Ironclad's been handled, he'll release my father, turn in Mikey and Tony, and Matt will finally be free."

Her eyes light up, but then she tilts her head sideways. "What's the catch?"

"It was only to hold up my end of the bargain. To… take care of Ironclad."

"Really?"

"Yes." And then to send her away while I work for Don Bordono, but she doesn't need to know that yet.

Yanking her hand away, she scowls. "It still doesn't make up for what you did."

"Seneca. I'm going to tell you something, and whether you believe it or not, it's the truth. I never knew who your brother was. He never came up. He wasn't connected to Don Bordono in any way."

"You could have—"

"What, Seneca? What could I have done? Asked for ID and a history of every person when I walked into that room? Yes, I noticed him. And he was young, yes. But I went in there to do a job, and Matt happened to be there. I know you'll hate me for this, but Sen, he's not innocent."

She moves to speak, but I put up my hand.

"No, he didn't deserve what happened to him, but he wasn't just innocently walking down the street at the time. He was there. And he was high, in a drug den, in St. Mark's Place. He knew the dealer, and he knew Mikey and Tony. I thought he was in with them. When the hit went bad, I was worried about myself—yes. I was worried that I had been framed. I was worried that my father was in too deep. That I'd never be able to work off his debt. And after, I was pissed that those two assholes, Mikey and Tony, were the reason I went to jail." Taking a deep breath, I continue. "I think about your brother every day of my life. But at that moment, when my world was blowing up, I'm sorry, but I wasn't worried about him. To me, he was nothing more than some other random drug addict who was in with Mikey and Tony. I took care of myself. And you can't tell me you wouldn't have done the same thing."

"I wouldn't have."

"Oh, really? And how many men did you maim today? Tear an earlobe? Stab with a knife? How many have you? How many *would* you?"

"That's different."

"Why?" I ask.

"Because…"

"Because they were men who chose to be in this life? So, it was an occupational hazard?"

"Yes."

"Don't you see how it was the same for me?"

"He's not a random drug addict who was working with Mikey and Tony."

"Not to you, no. And not to me any longer, either. But at that moment, that's all he was. Seneca, how could I have known anything else?"

"I…" Glancing down at the driveway, she shakes her head.

"Come on, let's see what Don Bordono can do for us."

Nodding, she follows me as I lead the way down the long path to Don Bordono's front door.

The door opens as soon as we step up onto the porch.

"Bullseye." This time, Don Bordono himself meets me at the door. "Twice in one day. To what do I owe the pleasure?" He eyes Seneca. "And I'm assuming this is the lovely Seneca Villetrio?"

"Yes." Sucking a breath through my clenched teeth, I force myself to stay calm. What I need is to free my father, and to get Don Bordono to turn in Mikey and Tony. Then, to get her out of here as fast as possible. "The job, Don. It's done."

He raises his eyebrows and glances at Seneca before putting his focus then back on me. "So soon?"

Since Seneca is with me, no doubt he thinks I'm being sloppy. And I probably am.

"Yes." The cold, wet air sits heavily on us, and I glimpse Seneca who shivers. Turning back to the Don, I lower the pitch of my voice. "Now, I'm going to ask that you hold up your end of the deal."

"Oh? And what's that?"

Glancing around him, I see two of his security close behind him, waiting in the front lobby. So, not exactly a warm welcome.

"Let my father go. Turn in Mikey and Tony. Get Matt Villetrio freed."

"Bullseye." Sighing, he gives me a fatherly smile. "I've always liked you. Do you know why?"

"Because I'm a good shot?"

"Of course. Yes. But so was your father. But I like you for other reasons, too. You have something your father doesn't have. You see the good in people. You want to see the good in people. You want to believe in happy endings. It makes you both very likable, and very easy to convince."

"You saying I'm stupid?"

"No, no. You're anything but. But your belief in the good in humanity and the way you trust others…" Sucking his teeth, he shakes his head. "Bullseye. If I name Mikey and Tony, then this will be linked to me."

"They were working for Ironclad."

"Who worked for me." Sighing, Don Bordono explains. "Bullseye. The dealer they took care of, he was getting too big, and too connected. Ironclad was just a low-level thug—although an ambitious and hungry one. But he wasn't smart enough to know what was going on. I needed the dealer gone, but I needed it to look like it was Ironclad's fault. So, I let Ironclad think that he was controlling Mikey and Tony—and those two boys—shit, one is dumber than the next. Ironclad was just a convenient scapegoat."

"So, you're the reason my brother is in jail?" Seneca steps closer to Don Bordono. "It was you behind this all along?"

"I'm afraid so, dear. But in my defense, your brother wasn't supposed to be there."

"So, what happens now?" she asks.

"I would think that's up to Bullseye."

She looks up at me, and it's like daggers are lodged into my soul… not because she looks angry, but because she is devastated.

"The one chance I had, Bullseye. The *one chance*, after all this time, was Ironclad. And now, my brother will rot in jail forever."

Swallowing my agony, I turn to Don Bordono. "I want my father. I did the job. I want him."

"Your father is at home, Bullseye. He knows the whole story, and he's also sorry it's going down like this, but sometimes…" He holds his hands up in the air and then lets them drop. "That's the way this world works. Call him yourself if you don't believe me. You did the job. That was the deal. And now, because I couldn't do more, I'm going to throw you a bone. The next part of the deal is for you two to run. You're not working for me, Bullseye. Go back to Arizona. This way, there will be no connection between Ironclad's… demise… and me. You'll be safe there. No more looking over your shoulder. I'll see to it."

That means Mikey and Tony are as good as dead.

"And… Bullseye, Seneca…" He looks from me to Seneca and back again. "I suggest you run while you have the chance." Pushing his front door open all the way, he reveals not just his two immediate bodyguards, but an army of armed men standing in his foyer.

Nodding, I take Seneca by the hand, and this time, she walks to the bike willingly.

Although it makes it a hell of a lot easier to get her on the bike and drive her back to my truck, I hate that she's compliant. That her spirit has been broken. That *she's* broken.

Thanks to me, my Wildfire has been extinguished. And it's a damned tragedy.

Chapter Twenty-Two

Bullseye

Dear Sen…

I'm sorry.

Shit. Just scrawling the note is hard enough. How am I going to face the next years knowing that she hates me? The ride back to Hoppa was horrendous. It would have been one thing if she sat there and screamed the whole ride back, but she didn't. Instead, she just stared out the window and didn't speak a word. The only stops we made were for gas and to pee, and even then, I followed her into the women's room and waited outside the stall for her just to make sure she didn't try to run again.

And I'm not sure she isn't trying to run now. The only way I'll ever be sure that she's safe, is, ironically, when I'm away from her and on the inside. Then, when I'm in and her brother's out, they can make a life here in Hoppa with the Steel Knights, and she can finally stop fighting.

I'll do it for her. I'll take the rap and let her brother go free, but it would all be so much easier if I knew that she'd be here, waiting for me, when I got out. But that's the crap that happens in fairy tales, not in the lives of bikers who work for mobsters. Shit.

Crumpling up the paper, I try again.

Dear Sen…

I hope you know how sorry I am that this happened to you and Matt, and I hope you know what you mean to me.

After taking care of some unfinished business here in Hoppa, I'm heading back to NY. I'm going to take the rap for the dealer and get Matt freed. I've already told Don Bordono, so it's a done deal.

Stay here with Harry and the Steel Knights. Give them a chance. Your brother will join you here. Soon. Please tell Nick, the guys, and especially Harry, that I'm sorry.

And most of all, Sen, I'm sorry for everything I've ever done that's upset you.

I love you, baby.

Avery

Grabbing a bag, I stuff it with those few things I need to go cross country again, and my Ruger. Yeah, I need to go, but I need to clear my mind first.

And the range is the only place for that.

Bang! Bang!

Bullseye after bullseye. Why can't I handle the rest of my life as well as I handle a gun?

Taking my stance, I lift the gun again and aim at the target. I'm going to get as many shots in as I can. This may be the last time I shoot for a very long time.

Looking down the sight of my Ruger, I see the bullseye, and closing my eyes—

"Those are quite the shots. How come you don't lean in like I taught you?"

"Dad?" Dropping my arm, I pull off my goggles and ear protection and turn to face my father. He's wearing a cashmere coat that's opened, exposing a three-piece-suit beneath and an old-fashioned wool cap. The way he dresses always made me look like a schlub in my T-shirts, jeans, and boots.

As he reaches into his pocket, I tense, and ready my finger on the trigger of the gun still in my hand. When he pulls out a white handkerchief and dabs the sweat on his forehead, my senses kick into overdrive.

"How do you ever get used to this Arizona heat? And in the middle of winter?"

"It's cold at night."

Neither one of us breaks eye contact.

"What the hell are you doing here, Dominic? How did you find me?"

"A father has his ways."

"Don Bordono sent you."

Sighing, my father takes a step closer.

"And what? I've become too much of a problem?"

"Something like that. Avery, it's nothing personal on my end. It's the only way for me to pay off my debt. You know too much. Damn it, haven't I always told you not to get involved?"

"Why here?"

"It's less messy out here in Arizona. It will look like biker violence and not a Bordono hit. And, of course, no one would ever suspect me." Dropping his head, he removes his hat and runs a hand across his thick gray hair.

"Of course not. Because no father would kill his son…"

"What?" It's Seneca's voice.

Whipping around, I see her walking up to me, flanked by Harry and Seth.

Moving to them, I shake my head. "Why are you here? You shouldn't be here."

In the intensity of the past couple of moments, I never heard the front door, or any of them enter the range.

"We came to find you," Harry explains.

"How did you know…?"

Harry cocks his head. "You said in your note, 'unfinished business'. If you weren't at the Taphouse, then you had to be at the range."

"I should have come to talk to you, Harry." Dropping my gaze, I look at the cement ground and then lifting it again, I look into his eyes. Considering I'll be looking down the barrel of my father's gun soon, it's an odd time to come clean with everything, but my father is old-school. He'll wait for me to make my peace.

"I need to talk to you, too," Harry adds.

"You were right to kick me out of the Knights…"

"No." Shaking his head, he steps closer. "I wasn't. And thankfully, someone very wise came to tell me I was wrong."

"Who was that?"

Harry nods to Seneca.

"I just explained that I'm pissed too. But we all have our secrets and regrets. All of us." She looks at Seth and then Harry before turning to me. "I reminded Harry of how he pretty much ran Tess out of the Steel Knights because he hated women so much. And now, he's changing, thanks to Celia. I explained that you have a right to change, too."

"Do you believe that?"

"I do."

"These your friends?" My father interrupts. That means my time is dwindling.

"Yes. Absolutely." Nodding to each of them, I turn back to Dominic.

"And your girl?" he asks.

"Yes." Standing stiffly, I communicate silently to my father by dropping my chin and clenching my jaw. "But none of them have anything to do with this. Understand?"

"She does," he says, nodding to her.

Fire rushes up my spine as I take a step closer to Dominic. "She has nothing to do with this, do you understand? Nothing."

Quickly, I turn to Seneca. "Your brother will be out soon. I told the police what happened. How Mikey and Tony were the dealers. I said that Don Bordono ordered the hit. I said I did it. Now, you have to go with Harry and Seth, and I have to finish some business with my father."

"No, Avery. No." She steps closer to me, and it's like I can feel her, although we're not touching. "I was wrong. I understand that you didn't know who he was."

"But I can make things right now."

"Yes, I want Matt free, but I don't want to lose you. Not again. Not now that everything is finally out in the open."

Reaching out with my free hand, I stroke her cheek. "We can't, Sen. There's no way. It just isn't meant to be for us. But I love you."

"I love you, too, Avery."

Dropping my hand and wrapping it around her waist, I pull her close to me. Leaning down, I caress her lips with mine—kissing her, feeling her, holding her… one last time.

"Now, go." Fighting my every desire, I put my hand on the small of her back, turn her, and push her toward Harry hard as I pull my gun on my father.

And he pulls his gun on me.

Out of the corner of my eye, I see that she stumbles but lands next to Harry. He helps steady her and stepping in front of her, he moves her farther behind him, protecting her. Good job, Harry, good job. I knew I could trust you.

Sweat gathers on my lower back as I nod to Dominic. "Let them walk out of here and then you and I will settle this."

"It's not that simple."

"I told you she knows nothing."

"No, listen, Avery. Listen to your father one last time. I went to Don Bordono and told him everything. That I ratted on him. I went to the police, Avery, once I got wind of what you were trying to do. I told them that I was at that hit and that I did the job. I said you would try to take the rap, but I did it. I also said I was to blame for Ironclad. Just in case. But that's moot, because not only do the police not care what happens in Mammon, it seems the cameras were out that night. It makes sense that I'm responsible since I've been doing this most of my life. With my connections, I was able to jump bail and come out here one time. I'm on the run, Avery—from Don Bordono and the police." Taking a deep breath, he turns to Seneca. "Matt will be released soon. It's already being processed."

"What?" Seneca rushes out from behind Harry. "Thank you, Mr. Pairings. Thank you for doing this."

"Don't thank me yet, my dear."

Fear swirls in my gut. There's more. There has to be more.

Dominic turns back to me. "Bordono still wants you dead. You threatened him when you said you would take the rap for Matt. But lucky for you, it all happened so fast, the only ones who know this are Bordono and me."

"So, you're going to kill me?"

"No. And the good news is, I think Don Bordono will leave you alone out of respect after."

"After what?"

"Threatening Don Bordono is a death sentence. But so is what he's asking of me. No one, not even me, can kill their own child."

"What are you saying?" I force my breathing under my control, so I can slow my heartbeat and focus.

"I can't kill my own child, Avery, but I *can* kill. So, the thing is, you need to kill me before I kill her." Looking at Seneca, he adds, "I'm sorry, my dear."

"No!"

Turning sharply, he aims the gun at Seneca and moves to pull the trigger, but before he can fire the shot, I've landed one bullet to his temple.

Wearing an odd smile on his face, my father falls dead at my feet as my arm holding the gun lowers slowly.

"Avery!" Seneca runs to me and jumps into my arms.

Holding her tight, we sob together, falling into a heap, as around us, Harry and Seth pick up my father's body and carry him away.

Epilogue

Bullseye

"Nice jacket," I tease.

Standing outside the main gate of Sing Sing, Seneca and I are wearing matching Steel Knights jackets.

"I think so, thank you." Bouncing on her toes on the cement ground, she looks like a kid on Christmas morning. "But mine is shiny and new. That was really nice of Nick to have mine waiting for me before we left for New York."

"You sure as shit earned it, Sen. No one knows that better than I do."

"Yeah." She nods. "I did. And that's true. You do understand. And always have. You always got that I wanted to be a member and not just your old lady."

"Seems to me a women's studies major from Columbia needs to be an equal in a relationship."

Taking her hand and pulling her to me, she comes willingly and falls against my chest. Her soft breasts press against me, making me ready for her, again. Right now. "And you are an equal, in everything except… Just remember, I'm the one in charge of making you moan every night…"

"Mmm…" she purrs, "always…"

"So…" Holding her by her upper arms, I distance us and look into her eyes. "What are we going to do now?"

"Well, we're waiting for Matt to come walking out of here a free man."

"After."

Tilting her head, she says, "Just like we planned. Since Don Bordono doesn't want you in New York, we're all heading back to Hoppa. Nick said he'd give Matt a job…"

Leaning down, I place my forehead against hers and slide my hands down her arms. Wrapping them around her waist, I pull her closer.

"I mean, what do we do when we get to Hoppa?"

"I would think the same thing we've done every night since that night at the range." Lifting her head, her eyes glass over. She's sad for me. "I'm sorry, Avery."

"It's okay, Sen. He chose his life. Yeah, I'm sorry it went down the way it did, but it was the way he chose. And for a man like him, it was maybe the best ending he could get. So much better than the options he could have faced."

"Yeah." She smiles.

"So..." I rock her in my arms, playfully. "By doing what we've done every single night since that night at the range, do you mean climbing into bed together? Naked...? And as I pull your tight, little body against mine, I kiss you from head to toe...?"

"Something like that, yeah..."

Closing her eyes, she gives in even more to my embrace, and my heart swells.

"Well, I think, if it's okay by you, I'd like to make it a more permanent situation."

Narrowing her eyes, she looks deeply into mine. "What do you mean?"

"I mean, Sen, that I don't want to be away from you—ever again."

"We don't have to be. Except maybe if I ever take that trip to see my mom, and you don't come to the island. But I don't know about that..."

"No." Chuckling, I drop to one knee. "I mean..."

"Avery...?" Her gorgeous gray eyes widen. "What are you doing?"

Reaching into the pocket of my jacket, I explain. "You didn't seem like the diamond type of girl to me. So, I went with amethyst—your signature color—on platinum. I've been waiting for the right moment, and I don't know why, but here, with the sky-high barbed wire fence, and the armed guards only a few yards away, it may not be the right place, but I just can't wait any longer."

I pull out the ring I bought weeks ago. The one that made me think of Seneca.

"Avery, it's perfect." Tears fill her eyes as she looks into mine. "Is this?"

"An engagement ring?"

"Is it?" Her eyes dance back and forth.

"It is if you say yes, you'll marry me."

"Yes, Avery. Yes. I will absolutely marry you."

Standing, I lift her into my arms and spin her around just as Matt, giving us a big wave, comes running out.

Placing Sen down on her feet, tears streak her cheeks as she turns to her brother and opens her arms. Rushing to Seneca, he falls into her embrace.

This is good. And right. And exactly as it should be.

Wrapping my arms around them both, I move us forward and toward our truck—walking them away from our awful past...

And into a new, wonderful beginning for all of us.

BOOK 4

HUGE DYNAMITE

Chapter One

Dynamite

Blink!

Ignoring the fifth text that's come in since I stepped into the shower, I let the hot water beat against my tense neck muscles. I know the text isn't from Colt, my kid brother, because he has a different text tone, and I doubt it's Bullet, our club VP, or Bullseye, our treasurer, or Nick, our president, because I've just left them at Hoppa's Taphouse, the current meeting place for the Steel Knights. That means it's got to be someone from the construction company with questions about the build of the new clubhouse. Our proposal is due on Monday, but their texts can wait.

Bending my neck forward, it feels good to let the hot water work its magic against my tight muscles, but it doesn't offer any reprieve from all the freaking stress. Lifting my head and then letting it drop back, I turn into the water stream, and the water bounces off my naked chest.

Between trying to make things right with my kid brother and my constant obsession with the memory of *that* night and Dr. Holly Boling—Christ. It's a miracle I'm functioning at all.

I met this woman just over a month ago when I went to the ER at her hospital with a freaking knife stuck in my shoulder. But it wasn't just any knife—it was my own knife, and it was put there by me when I was fighting Avery. In the heat of the moment, when he grabbed me from behind, I swung my knife up and over my shoulder to stab him. He ducked, but my shoulder didn't. She fixed me up, and since that moment, I haven't been able to think of anyone but her.

"*Seth!*"

"What is that?" Turning my head in the direction of the bathroom door, I'm certain I heard my name. Whoever's yelling is so loud I can hear them over the sound of the shower. Reaching out, I quickly turn off the water, grab a towel, and tie it around my waist.

"Seth!" It's my name, and someone's yelling it as they pound their fists against my apartment door.

"What the hell?" With my heart thumping, I jump out of the shower and—careful not to slip on the tile floor of the bathroom—I rush to my front door. "Who is it?"

"It's Harry and Avery. Let us in."

"What the hell is going on?" Yanking the door open, I take in the stern looks on their faces. "Guys?" It feels like all the blood drains from my face. "Is it Colt?"

"No. Colt's fine." Harry shakes his head as he quickly moves inside, followed by Avery.

"Seth, listen." Harry's speaking quickly, and I can hear the urgency in his voice. "There's a fight going down right now. We just got word that the Unchained Dogs attacked the Raging Vipers at their clubhouse."

"They also attacked a Viper-run business," Avery tells me.

"Fuck. Do you think they're coming for us next? Or the Blazing Rebels? They need backup?"

"No, we think they're isolated fights. They say the Vipers infringed on their turf. That they started running product through a business in Dog territory." Harry sighs heavily.

"That business…" Avery shakes his head. "There are civilians involved. That's why it was so important that the land we got for the new build wasn't on anyone's turf."

"So, what's our move?" Suddenly, it's like the room begins spinning and I'm caught up in it. Dropping the pitch of my voice, I make eye contact with one man and then the other. "Why are you here?"

"The Vipers' clubhouse is farther west than ours," Harry explains.

"Closer to Phoenix." As my heart rate takes off again, I begin to put the pieces together.

"The business they attacked," Avery says, "it's in what the Dogs call their turf. Just outside of—"

"Phoenix." My heartbeat is so loud, I swear it's beating in my brain. "Are there a lot of injuries?" Injuries need doctors and ER rooms…

"A lot so far." Harry nods solemnly. "And the fight is still going."

"But there have to be a ton of hospitals in a city as large as Phoenix, right?" Trying to calm my racing thoughts with logic isn't helping, so I take deep breaths.

"Yeah, but no Dog would go to a hospital unless the injury was life-threatening. They wouldn't risk someone contacting the police. Like us, they have doctors who are connected to the club who can handle smaller wounds. If they have something so bad it needs medical attention—like a knife or gunshot wound—they won't risk driving all the way into Phoenix. Like us, they'll find the closest hospital."

"The closest and the largest," Avery adds. "The busier it is, the less risk of being called out on anything—like weapons charges. Too much going on."

"The largest hospital between us and Phoenix," I mumble. "Dr. Holly's hospital." Just saying it out loud—the words hit me like a ton of bricks.

"That's what we're worried about, yeah." Harry scrubs his face.

Turning away from the men, I rush back to my bedroom and jump into the jeans that I wore earlier today. There's no time to rifle around looking for clean clothes. The men are on my heels.

"Seth, you've got to cool down," Harry tells me. "Checking on her is one thing. But you can't go barging in and risk a fight with the Dogs to save a woman you've only just met."

Turning to him, I ask, "Can't I?"

"Fine. Then we'll ride with you." Harry sighs deeply.

"I'll get the Knights." Avery picks up his phone to text. "We'll make a united front. The damned Dogs won't make a move on her if we're there in colors. They won't admit it, but they're still scared after the beating they took from us when they tried to ambush us at Hoppa's Taphouse."

"No." Pulling open a drawer in my dresser, I grab a clean T-shirt. Tossing it on, I turn to Harry and Avery as I try to push away the thought of beautiful Holly caught in the middle of a biker fight. "No, not the Knights. That's the last thing we need. If the damned Dogs catch a glimpse of us there in our colors…" Shaking my head, I let a shiver of fear pass through me. "Then, we've brought all-out war to Holly's doorstep."

Harry steps closer to me. "You can't do this alone. Think this through."

"I don't have time to think. I know what you're worried about, that I'll do something impulsive—"

"We do call you Dynamite for a reason," Harry mumbles.

Looking him square in the eye, I ask, "What would you do to save Celia, huh? I'll bet you'd face an entire army of Dogs if you had to." Turning to Avery, I nod. "You, Bullseye, you left all of us behind to save Seneca. So, don't tell me you wouldn't do the exact same thing. You already have."

"But, Seth, Celia and Seneca are our girlfriends," Harry counters.

Ignoring Harry and rushing into the living area of my apartment, I grab my wallet and keys. Picking up my Knights jacket, I hold it in my hand and stall. I can't wear this. Everything I do tonight has to be on the down-low, and I need to go. Now.

Sprinting past the men, I make it to the front door. My heart is thumping too fast; I take deep breaths to control it. If I go now and push hard, I may make it there before any of the Dogs or Vipers make it to the hospital. Then, who the hell knows?

"Seth?" It's Avery, standing behind me. "What are you going to do when you get there?"

Wheeling around, I look from man to man. "Protect her. What else?" Turning back, I hustle down the stairs of the apartment building two at a time.

"Seth!" Harry calls after me. "We're begging you. Stay out of sight. If the Dogs see you, they'll think you're a spy. For the sake of the Knights, be cool about this…"

Harry's words fade away as I push through the front door and catch myself just before I stumble onto the street. Running up to my bike, I toss my leg over and mount it, revving the engine like a rocket between my legs. There is no way in hell I am going to let those bastard Dogs anywhere near her. I know what they think of women—how they pass their WAGs around from member to member like they're nothing more than club property. The whole idea makes me sick. Forcing down the bile, I turn and spit on the gravel next to my bike, trying to get rid of the bitter taste in my mouth.

When the damned Dogs get to the hospital and see a female doctor… Christ. How will they react to that? They'll try to destroy her, for sure. Maybe, if they can't do it physically—although some of them may try—they'll harass her and taunt her, try to break her. A female doctor is a direct threat to their manhood, the bunch of assholes. But no, they won't do anything to her, because I will be there to stop them. If it's the last thing I do, I will protect her from those damned Dogs.

Peeling out, I balance my weight expertly, so I don't wipe out on the hairpin turn. Racing down the road from my apartment building, I turn onto the side street that runs parallel to the expressway. I'm forced to slow as I near the entrance to the expressway, and looking around, I notice how run-down my neighborhood is. The street is lined with old, faded billboards and chain-link fences. There's trash tossed everywhere, littering the small patches of burnt grass that pop up along the sides of the broken asphalt. Slowing my bike even more, my mind starts racing.

What am I doing? How could I possibly think this beautiful, classy woman would ever want anything to do with me? Pulling over and gliding to a stop along the side of the road, I breathe heavily. The cars stacking up along the entrance to the on-ramp honk at me.

What can I offer a woman like her? Closing my eyes, I see her standing before me the night that we met in the ER. In her white coat, she had to be five-seven or five-eight and thin. With gorgeous dark brown skin and deep brown eyes, she was absolutely stunning. This is a woman who probably has her entire life worked out and her whole world running exactly as she wants it. So, what *can* a man like me offer her? Then, I see it in my imagination: the Dogs riding up to the hospital with colors raised, demanding medical treatment when they're greeted by Dr. Holly Boling.

Fuck.

What can a man like me offer her? Protection. Which means I need to get to the hospital. Fast.

Shaking my head, I calm my racing mind and pull myself together. Leaning forward, I rev my bike. Glancing over my shoulder and finding my opening, I race forward, dodging the traffic as I merge onto the expressway heading toward Phoenix. Once I'm free of the merging traffic, I let my bike out to its full capability. I must be running eighty or ninety miles an hour, but I don't dare take my eyes off of the road to check the speedometer.

"Come on, come on," I mumble to the traffic that's backing up just ahead. Damn, this area between Hoppa and Phoenix is getting busier by the day. Slowing to veer around a large truck that's spewing black soot and doesn't belong on the damned expressway, I get clear of him and open up my bike again. No, I don't want to drive so fast and so erratically that I get nabbed by a cop, but this area outside Hoppa is rarely patrolled. If I do get caught, I will learn from my mistakes and play nice.

The last time a cop tried to arrest me, I fought back, and it cost me an extra two years in juvie and my relationship with Colt. I can't make the same mistake again. If I get pulled over for driving like a madman, I'll have to hold my temper and do better this time.

Except Holly's life may be at stake. Which means I'm sorry in advance to any cop who tries to catch me—but I won't stop, and I won't get caught. Because when it comes to keeping a woman like Dr. Holly Boling safe, anything goes. Anything.

Accelerating, I blow past some expensive model sports car. Suppressing a chuckle, I know this guy's car cost a hundred grand, and he probably bought it to race down open highways just like this one, blowing past every other car out here. Thing is, it can't outrun my bike. Holding the clutch and giving it full-throttle, I rev my engine just to let the sports car guy know I'm here and I'm passing. I can't help it. As I catch a glimpse of the car in my rearview and the scowl on the dude's face, a little thrill rips up through me from my head to my toes and, despite everything, a grin spreads across my face. As much of a loner as I am, I do get a high off of fucking with certain people. I guess that's all part of my impulsive "Dynamite" behavior. But a car like that and its douchebag driver are good news—it means I've come so far that I've left the small-town rural areas and am getting closer to the city.

Leaving the sports car in my dust, I open up and race down the highway. Finally, I see the exit for Holly's hospital, and I slow enough to take the exit without killing myself.

Downshifting, I glide through the off-ramp. Thankfully, there's no traffic at this hour. Pulling out onto a side street, I'm caught by how different this road is from the one near my apartment. This street is clean, and the only things littering it are expensive office buildings and high-end grocery stores. It's too dark to really see, but I'm confident the grass lining the sidewalk is green.

Leaning forward on my bike, I calm my racing thoughts. *It doesn't matter, Dynamite. It doesn't matter that you're from two different worlds. She's not into you anyway. She never even responded to the damned flowers you sent. That was a clear message. You're not here to propose, only to keep her safe.*

That thought doesn't thrill me—but it calms me. There's no way a woman like Dr. Holly Boling could ever want me. But I *can* protect her. Holding my breath, I see the hospital just ahead. Squinting, I spy bikes in the parking lot.

"Shit," I mumble under my breath. Daring to ride up a bit closer, I see the outlines of a large emblem on the bikes—a Dog in broken chains. Fuck. The Dogs are here. I can practically smell them.

There's no way I can park in the lot next to them, so I double-back to an overflow lot I noticed on my way here. Pulling into the almost-empty lot, I park and jump off my bike. I don't have any weapons with me—not even my knife—but it wouldn't matter anyway, because I have to pass a metal detector to go inside. Metal detectors are good. Knowing that there's not a chance a Dog, or anyone else, could pull a weapon on her calms my racing heart a bit.

Staying in the shadows, I debate how I'm going to rush in through emergency. Spying a doctor on the street corner near the side of the building, I hustle over and see a side entrance. Pushing through a large revolving door, I enter a hallway that opens to the side of the lobby. This is perfect. From here, I can see what's happening in the lobby without being spotted. Although, it's obvious that I can't see everything. Daring a few steps closer, I walk to the end of the hallway and peer into the lobby.

Shit. It's busier than I anticipated—with Dogs and their families everywhere. It's like they've exploded in size. How many friggin' Dogs are there now? They must have come in by truck, not just bikes. The good part of all of this frenzied chaos is that I blend in, and none of the staff will know I don't belong here. With my tats, short hair, wide, muscled shoulders, and rough skin that appears permanently dirty, I look like any one of the bikers here. Unless you're on the inside, you'd never know one club from the next. All you can be sure of is that with our collection of nicknames, tattoos, colors, and jackets, we're not hospital staff.

Craning my neck, I look for Luther, their president, but I don't see him anywhere.

Suddenly, the sound of the opening and closing of the front emergency door grabs my attention, and I turn to see more Dogs rushing in.

One Dog in a leather coat has an arm draped around another, who's doubled over and barely able to walk.

"Can I get some help here?" he yells. "My friend's been shot."

Fuck. The fight must have broken into gunfire. I wouldn't expect anything less from the Dogs. Stepping into the lobby and sliding along the wall, I find a place behind an arrangement of potted trees where I can see and hear everything that's happening, but I won't be spotted. Yeah, maybe if these were normal conditions a Dog would sniff his way over to me, but considering the chaos in here, I doubt it will happen.

Glancing back and forth from one end of the lobby to the other, I keep looking for Dr. Holly, but I don't see her anywhere. Forcing deep breaths, I try to think logically. Maybe she has a day off? The woman can't work every day. As more Dogs come in and fill up the waiting room, and one doctor after another walks up to the intake station, I grow calmer. Maybe she's not here and won't get caught in this disaster. Unless she's so swamped in the back she's not able to come out here...

A tall, well-groomed male doctor hurries into the lobby from the ER.

"Dr. Covens?" A nurse from triage rushes forward to him. "Gunshot to the abdomen."

Stiffening, I stand up taller. I know Covens. I know who he was to Holly and who he'd like to be again. But I can't worry about that now. Now, my only focus is making sure she's safe.

Running to the patient while he pulls on rubber gloves, he quickly sizes up the situation as the damned Dog is laid out on a gurney. Covens barks a few orders and then, grabbing one side of the gurney, he rushes into the back with the Dog. Covens is probably about to save that man's life. He has the skill and the knowledge to do that—and here I am, with barely a high school diploma, hiding behind a freaking dusty potted tree.

Screw this. Who do I think I am? What makes me think she needs me—

"It's a fucking Knight. And he's hiding behind a plant!"

Whipping around, I catch one of the Dogs standing to one side of me, licking his lips. He's so freaking happy, he's salivating.

"What are you doing here, Knight? Did you come to water the plants?" Laughing, he looks me in the eyes. "Or are you just hiding?"

The idea of him thinking I'm hiding doesn't sit well with me, but I push aside my anger because he's right. I *am* hiding.

"What do you care?" I ask him. "The hospital isn't on Dog turf." Standing taller, I study him. His shifty eyes are glassy, and his face is beet-red. He looks like he's been fighting all night, and he's probably high on adrenaline. A man high on adrenaline can be a dangerous thing—he can have superhuman strength and heightened senses, but he's still not as dangerous as a man who's fighting to protect a woman.

The only way to handle this situation is to show immediate dominance, but I'm wedged into a corner—caught between the wall, the plants, and the damned Dog.

Turning, I step closer to him, but he doesn't budge. "Listen, Dog, I'm not here for trouble.

So, unless you want to start a war with the Knights—considering how well that went for you last time—I'd shut the fuck up and leave."

"We were undermanned then, and you had that freaking fighting machine."

He means CJ, and he's right. We can all fight, but CJ's a damned warrior.

"We won't lose again," the Dog hisses.

"You sure of that?" I inch my way a bit closer, and because I've got a good five inches on him, I look down at him.

"Yeah, I'm sure."

He talks an okay game, but my presence has gotten him to back off a bit, which means I'm almost free of the trees. But this asshole is pulling my focus. I should be watching out for Holly, but now I've got to be doubly careful—the last thing I want is for this asshole to know who I'm here for and why.

Suddenly, I hear sirens. The red flashing lights of an ambulance flood the lobby, and just as the front door opens and one of the Vipers is rushed in on a gurney, Dr. Holly Boling runs in from the back. Her white jacket is stained with red, and she's wearing blue scrubs beneath. Her face is hardened into a look of determination. Covens is on her heels.

Pushing my way past the damned Dog next to me, I step out into clear view to see better. The Dog is so focused on his biker brother who came in with a gunshot wound, he steps back and lets me pass without mention. Right now, he doesn't seem to give a crap about me being here. I know that will change and this will come back to bite me—hard—when things calm and he tells the other Dogs there's a Knight in the same hospital…

But I can't worry about that right now. Right now, all I can focus on is Holly.

"Why the hell didn't you come through the ambulance bay?" Holly yells across the lobby to the EMS workers.

"No time, doc. There's a wait back there. He's crashing."

"Holly?" Covens catches up to her, and the way he holds his arm out around her back as they move forward—not touching her, but still protecting her—I know, despite all his education and sophistication, he's claiming her in front of all these punks. Myself included.

"I've got this, Robert. Go. They just said the ambulance bay is backed up."

"Holly." He tilts his head in a way that's meant for only her to understand.

Making eye contact with him, she repeats, "Go, Robert. Go."

Nodding, Covens listens to her and disappears into the back as fast as he came out.

Rushing, Holly pushes a few Dogs out of the way as she catches up to the EMS workers and the gurney. "What do you have?"

The EMS worker rattles on, "Presenting with gunshot wound. Femoral artery. He's crashing."

"Let's go," she barks. In the next second, she steps onto the side of the gurney and then, in a move like she's getting onto a bike, she throws her leg up and over the top of the gurney, climbing on. Straddling the man's waist, she's careful of his hips and legs as she leans forward and begins chest compressions. Her lips move like she's counting. Repeating her actions over and over, she breaks to reach up and feels for something in his neck. "We've got a pulse. Let's go. Surgery. Now!" she commands.

A couple of the other Vipers file in from outside as the EMS workers spin the gurney so that Holly, still on her knees on top of her patient, is riding backward. Hospital security comes rushing in from another back area, wearing black, shiny jackets and carrying handguns and tasers.

"Doc?" one of them asks.

"We're good. Stay out here—"

Just then, as Holly—straddling her patient—is being wheeled away, she raises her gaze and looks me square in the eyes. Her eyes widen and her mouth drops open. "Seth?"

She sees me.

Nodding, I step farther into the room. With my gaze locked on hers, I back out of the front hospital sliding doors, praying the Dog next to me didn't see that moment I had with Dr. Holly, because if he did, if he figures out that she means something to me—

Damn. Then I've put her in serious danger.

The best thing that I can do now is leave. I'm no good to her here. She's okay. Hospital security is armed, and they'll protect her. Taking a deep breath, I let it go through my clenched teeth. Yeah, hospital security will protect her, and so will Covens. I saw his protective move in there. I've seen the way he looks at her. Who could blame him?

I'm no good to her now. I've been made by a Dog, and there is absolute chaos. The last thing we need is for the Dogs to start something because I'm here.

Shit. I did it again. When I raced here to make sure she was safe, I probably did more harm than good. Once again, I let my passion win over logic, and I acted before thinking.

As the clear glass doors close before me, I catch her still staring at me. She raises her hand that's encased in a bloody glove just as they wheel her into the back.

Sighing, I turn and rush back to my bike, knowing in my soul that may have been the last time I will ever see Dr. Holly Boling.

Rubbing an ache in my gut, I jump onto my bike, and after one last glimpse at the hospital, I ride away.

Chapter Two

Holly

Holy crap. What a night! Leaning against the nurses' station, I'm scrolling through texts when I hear my name.

"Dr. Boling? Hello? Holly?"

It's like my heart jumps into my throat when I think it might be Seth who's come back to see me. But I recognize this voice—it's Robert. Frankly, his is a voice I hear way too often.

Sighing, I force myself to put Seth Hardy out of my mind. *Come on, Holly*, I remind myself. *He was only here tonight because his motorcycle buddies were hurt. It had nothing to do with you.*

Collecting myself, I take a deep breath. "Yes?" The hell with it. Clicking off my phone, I shove it into my jacket pocket. I'll return the text to my mother later tonight. Or maybe tomorrow. Or maybe, with the way I'm feeling tonight, never. Does she really need to know what I'm wearing to dinner at the country club this weekend? No doubt it's some version of the same damned dress I wear every weekend. After the night we've just had—saving the lives of *fourteen* different bikers—dinner at the country club sounds fairly inane.

Turning away from the nurses' station, I catch Robert standing there, grinning at me. I can practically feel the nurses swooning behind me, and why not? Dr. Robert Covens is a catch. He's around six feet tall and keeps himself in great shape. He likes to say he's naturally in good shape, but I know his body comes from three sweat sessions a week on his Peloton.

Personally, I think working for something is more admirable than just having it handed to you, but he doesn't agree. That's why he also won't admit the caramel-colored highlights in his side-swept, perfectly mussy hair aren't put there by the sun. Good grief. The sun? I have to stop myself from rolling my eyes. Please. We're ER doctors who work the nightshift. We *never* see the sun. But his bright blue eyes are natural, and putting the whole package together, he is handsome. And smart.

And considering the night he's just had, I'd expect him to show some kind of wear and tear. But after his shower and break, he looks even more perfect than he did before his shift started. Crap. Doesn't it just figure. I can't help myself. I go ahead and roll my eyes just this once.

Yes, Dr. Robert Covens would make any sane woman's heart race and toes curl. So, what—exactly—is my problem?

"You okay, kid?"

Kid? I'm twenty-eight to his thirty-three. I'm hardly a kid. But he means it as a term of endearment. So, what does he want?

"Mm." Holding up my tablet with the list of my patients and their conditions, I force a smile. "Just busy." Gripping the tablet until my knuckles whiten, my breathing becomes shallow. Truthfully, I'm not okay. In fact, I'm so fed up with everything, I just want to tear off my white coat and run screaming through the lobby and out onto the street—letting the cool Arizona night calm me. It's really all I can do to stand here acting civilized, so I bite the inside of my cheek, hoping it will ground me and slow my racing heart. As soon as I can break free from Robert, I'm going to rush into the women's locker room and gnaw at my almost-nonexistent fingernails.

Sighing, I glance at my destroyed nails. They, like everything else I do, are an embarrassment to the great Dr. Elijah Boling and his wife, Monica Boling—my parents. No matter how much my heart longs for a change, everything I want, everything I *need to experience*—from getting a tattoo, to opening my clinic, to hooking up with a really hot biker—would be sacrilege to them. No, there's no time for me to live my life; I'm too busy perfecting it.

Robert furrows his brow and scoffs. "Busy? Now? This is nothing to you. Look at what you did earlier tonight. With all the other cases we had, you single-handedly saved that biker hemorrhaging from his femoral artery."

Glaring, I correct him. "Chris."

"Excuse me?"

"The biker I was working on. His name was Chris."

"Okay. Who cares? They all sound alike, look alike, and act alike, anyway. The point is you saved him, and with that amount of blood loss, most doctors would have called it. You're a rock star, Holl."

Ah, flattery. Nodding, I place my tablet on the station and cross my arms. Whenever Robert kisses up to me, it means he wants to get laid. But the thing is, I don't. Not by him, anyway, and that's a real serious problem.

I don't want Robert, because I have my sights set on a certain biker who was my patient about a month ago and whom I haven't been able to stop thinking about since.

Then, when he showed up here tonight, it was like my body began having all these primal responses I didn't even know I was capable of having.

"Holly? How about breakfast later? I know how much you love French toast."

"Breakfast?" Here I am fantasizing about being *had* by Seth Hardy—and I'm pretty sure just thinking about him the way I do crosses all kinds of ethical lines—and Dr. Robert comes at me offering French toast. But it's not like he's actually offering to make *me* breakfast. French toast is the breakfast I always end up cooking for him whenever we hook up. Robert's not so big on doing for others. "Um, I don't think so, thanks."

Discreetly, I glance at my smart watch. 11:15 PM. It's like time is standing still. Suddenly, the area around the nurses' station grows so warm, my cheeks flood with heat and perspiration forms under my armpits. I can't stand here anymore. I need to move.

Glancing back at the nurses who are practically mooning over Robert, I shake my head. *He's all yours, ladies*, I want to scream, but of course, I don't. Instead, I leave word that I'm taking a half-hour break and to text me if there's an emergency. Rushing away and stopping in the locker room just to grab my wallet, I take off toward the side of the hospital and the large, shiny, silver revolving doors with Robert on my heels.

"Holly?" Touching my arm, he slides in next to me in the revolving door.

Crap.

"What's going on with you tonight?"

He speaks over my shoulder, and his warm breath sits heavily on me. Closing my eyes to keep from freaking completely, I take a deep breath. What *is* wrong with me tonight?

"Holl? We've been together for almost two years. You can tell me—"

"We are not together," I snap. Mercifully, the door deposits me on the sidewalk by the side entrance of the hospital. "We haven't been together for a long time now."

"I know." His expression hardens. "It's been six weeks, and I'm getting tired of waiting, Holl."

"What?" Incensed, I storm away and then turning, I march back up to him again. "If you're tired of waiting, then don't." Throwing up my hands in exasperation, I shake my head at him. "I don't want you to wait for me. There's nothing to wait for. Yes, we dated once upon a time. But that was a year ago."

"We did more than date. We were a couple. We were planning a future together—"

Staring up into his eyes, I speak as forcefully as I can. "You were planning a future for us."

"Not just me. Your parents, too."

"My *parents*?" Shaking my head, I look deep into his eyes. "My parents. Do you hear yourself? I'm a grown woman. A smart, successful grown woman. My parents don't decide who I marry."

"They were upset when you called off the engagement."

"I didn't call off anything because we were never engaged. Yes, my parents were devastated when we broke up—they love you. You're everything they want in a son-in-law." My words are coming so fast I'm not sure I'm making any sense. "You're clean-cut, smart, they can show you off at the country club, and to top it all off, you're a cardiothoracic surgeon—like my father. *They* would marry you if they could."

"Well, then, don't you think that the people who know you best in the world would make the right decision for you?"

"Make the right decision *for me*?" Worried I might slug him, I take a few steps away and then, turning back, I rush up to him. Before I speak, I force myself to take deep breaths to calm my racing heart. "This isn't the Middle Ages, Robert. I'm not going to be 'given away' by my father. You think you know me best? None of you—not *one* of you—knows one damned thing about me."

"I know that you're a cardiothoracic surgeon, too, and you could be in practice with your dad, making seven figures like he does. But instead, you work as an ER doctor on the nightshift."

"So do you."

"I work as the surgeon on call, and you know it. But you, you'll take any case. Hell, you even pulled a knife out of some asshole's shoulder, and no one knows why you did it."

"He wasn't an asshole, and I know why—you don't have to. Don't you get it? Or are you just too damned arrogant to see that?"

"Oh, crap, here we go with the arrogant speech again. How many times did I hear that while we were dating? You think I'm arrogant? Well, you're naïve. When are you going to get over your childish dream of being something you're not?"

"What?" Narrowing my eyes, my heart thumps so loudly I can hear it. "What did you just say?"

"Come on, Holly. I know you have some secret dream to 'help people out.'" He makes air quotes as he talks. "That's fine. Really. Noble, even. But why not go to work for your dad, make a shitload of money, and donate to the less fortunate like the rest of us plan to?"

"I…" Staring up at this man, I have a hard time imagining that I ever saw anything good in him. A couple of weeks ago, when he sent those flowers, I was really touched and almost folded. Maybe, if I hadn't been thinking about Seth nonstop, I might have. Robert never does anything spontaneous or romantic like sending me flowers at work, and I thought maybe he was turning a corner. Maybe he was thinking of someone other than himself.

"Come on, Holl." Leaning forward, he nudges me with his shoulder. "We're both tired. What do you say we go back in, finish our shifts, and I come by later? I'll bring coffee. Good coffee. Not from the place across the street, but how about from that little place in Hoppa you like so much?"

"Hoppa?" My heart starts racing even faster just at the mention of the town. It's been a month now, but he was here tonight. The way he was staring at me… was that all a coincidence? Or is there a chance that Seth Hardy remembers me?

"Yeah?"

"I live in Phoenix. What makes you think there's anything in Hoppa I want?" My voice is low and breathy. I couldn't have been that obvious, could I?

"Okay, there's the Holly I always knew you could be." He grins. "A little shithole like Hoppa couldn't possibly have anything for you. Cool. I'll stop at that place on High Street in Phoenix you like."

"No." I force back the bitter taste in my mouth. "It's not Hoppa. And Hoppa's not a shithole. I don't want any coffee, Robert. We're not getting together."

"Why not?" He takes a step closer and my stomach aches. "Come on, Holl." He reaches out and tries to stroke my cheek, but I pull away.

"No?" He raises his eyebrows. "Wow. I thought we'd decided this friends-with-benefits deal was good for both of us. We're both incredibly busy, both have high-stress, demanding jobs, we work the same shifts…"

"No more, Robert. I'm done." Turning away, I walk around to the front of the hospital. Coffee. I need coffee. I'm going to drown myself in an extra-large black coffee. Robert walks up next to me just as I make it to the door of the coffee shop. I wait as a man with a full-sleeve tattoo popping out of his T-shirt comes waltzing out.

"Hey." He nods to me and raises his cup.

"Hey." Instead of entering the shop, I turn back and call to the man who's walking away. "Excuse me, can I ask you something?"

The man turns around. "Me?"

I nod.

"Yeah. Sure." Shrugging, the man walks up to me and eyeballs Robert. "This guy bothering you?"

"No." Shaking my head, I smile for the first time all night. "Well, yes, actually, but I can handle it, thanks."

"Holly," Robert snaps.

The crisp night air energizes me, and as I focus on the man, I tune out Robert. "I want to ask you about your tattoos. How did you decide what to get tattooed on you? How did you know you wouldn't get tired of it?"

"Didn't." Taking a long sip of coffee, he lowers his hand and rests it by his side.

"What do you mean?" Out of the corner of my eye, I catch Robert rolling his eyes, but I don't give a fuck. I walk up closer to the man. "What do you mean?" I repeat my question. "You didn't know if you'd get tired of it?"

"No, I didn't choose it. A tattoo chooses you."

"Really?"

"Holly," Robert barks. "You're a surgeon. You going to buy into this crap?"

Turning to Robert, I glare at him. "Last I checked, this conversation didn't include you."

"Holly, you're embarrassing yourself."

"Hey." My new tattooed friend walks up to Robert. He's considerably shorter than Robert, but he doesn't seem the least bit intimidated. They stand toe-to-toe. "The lady and I are having a conversation. Last I checked, this is a free country, and she's free to talk to whoever she wants."

"It's 'whomever' she wants. But why would I think you would know that?"

"Robert." Shaking my head, my cheeks flood with color. I feel awful for dragging the poor man into this. Turning to the man, I apologize. "I'm sorry. He doesn't get out much."

Using his thumb, he points at Robert. "This guy your man?"

"No." Shaking my head, I smile and cock an eyebrow at Robert. "Actually, he was just leaving. Weren't you, Robert?"

"No, actually, Holly, I thought we were heading in for coffee."

"I think I'm going to stay here and talk to…" Leaning toward my tattooed friend, I nod to prompt him.

"Paul."

Turning to Robert, I smile. "I'm staying here and talking to my new friend, Paul."

"What about the coffee?" Robert sounds dejected.

"You can have the rest of this if you want." Paul holds out his cup to me. Without thinking, I grab the cup and take a long sip. The coffee is milky and sweet and freaking delicious.

"Hol-ly," Robert barks. "I don't think I have ever been so disgusted—"

"Oh, cram it, Robert." Holding the cup back out to Paul, I smile at him. "Thanks. It's really good. I always drink black coffee. I think I may be ordering this from now on." What the hell am I doing? I have never shared a drink with anyone before, let alone a complete stranger. Is this what the beginning of a nervous breakdown feels like?

"Just tell them you want a 'New York Coffee Regular'," Paul explains. "They'll know what you want. Glad you like it. Keep it."

Nodding my thanks, I turn away from the two men and start walking out toward the parking lot. I've got my phone and wallet on me, and the valet guys will have my keys…

"Holly?" Robert calls after me. "Holly? Where are you going? Your shift's not over!"

"Seeing if there's a tattoo that calls to me!"

"What?"

Giggling, I yell to Robert without turning back, "I'm taking a personal day!" Giving him a tiny wave over my shoulder, I have to force myself to slow down so I don't full-out sprint to my car. On second thought, why the hell shouldn't I run? My walk turns into a slow jog, and then suddenly, I'm racing toward the valet booth. Not waiting for the guys to get them for me, I step up into the booth and grab my keys.

"Dr. Boling?" One of the valets comes running toward me from the other end of the parking lot, but I can't stop. "Is everything okay?" he asks as he nears.

"Yes, thanks!" Racing to my car, I jump in, and faster than I mean to, I pull out of the parking lot. I don't even have to think about it. I know where I'm going—straight to Hoppa. Yeah, so maybe I am having a breakdown, but yet—for the first time all night, I feel good. In fact, I feel almost giddy.

But this isn't me—I have responsibilities.

"Wait a second." Easing my foot off of the gas and slowing down, I pull to the side and pause for a moment. Ahead of me lies a world I don't know at all, and behind me, a world I know all too well.

But I'm desperate for a change. And he was there tonight. I saw him. That *has* to mean something, right?

My gaze drops to my dash, and I look over all the knobs and buttons I almost never use. Then, my attention falls to my keys on the seat next to me and the one button on my fob that I *never* press. A thrill rushes up my spine as I take the fob into my hand and press the button for the very first time, and… the roof of my car opens.

"Holy crap," I mutter to myself. "I drive a convertible."

Giddiness fills me from head to toe. Slamming my foot against the gas, I pull out, heading toward Hoppa. The wind blowing against my face feels exhilarating, and for the first time—maybe ever—I feel alive. With every mile I push, I feel freer and lighter. There was no way I could go back into that building with its shiny floors and sanitized counters and everything sterile… God knows I need a little fun.

As I pass the sign that reads, "Hoppa 12 miles," my heart pounds, my palms grow sweaty, and a full grin takes over my face. Yes, a little fun is what I need. And yes, I know *exactly* who I want to have that fun with.

Chapter Three

Dynamite

"Earth to Seth?" It's Bullet. He's walked up from behind the bar and is standing next to me.

I'm frozen, standing just by the bar door. Sure, I'm looking around at the busy bar, but I'm not really seeing anything. Or anyone. What I just witnessed at the hospital… damn. It's going to keep replaying in my mind over and over again, like it did on the ride here.

"Seth?" He waves his hand in front of my face.

"Yeah?" Shaking my head, I snap out of it. I was caught in a fantasy again.

I can't help it. Every freaking time I step into Hoppa's Taphouse now, it's no longer just the current clubhouse of the Steel Knights for me—it's the place that Dr. Holly came to check on me after my injury and we had our first almost-date.

Standing here, exactly where I am right now—with her hair pulled back, her large diamond earrings flashing, and a floor-length camel-colored coat… damn. She was stunning.

Drawing in a deep breath, the smell of testosterone-laced sweat and beer fills my nose, and it helps calm my desire. As I exhale, I make my decision. I need to move on, and that means it's time to hook up with the next woman I see at the bar tonight. It doesn't matter who she is as long as she's willing. I need some kind of release, and one thing is for sure: I cannot waste one more second thinking about Dr. Holly Boling. She didn't need me tonight, and probably never will. Hell, until tonight, when we made eye contact for that flash of time, she probably hasn't thought of me once.

Our connection that night was a one-time thing. She liked my tattoo. She was intrigued by the novelty of a man like me. Maybe she went slumming for the night. That's all it was.

"Seth?" Bullet furrows his brow when he speaks. "Not one single text? You couldn't shoot me one quick text to let me know what was happening?"

"What are you, my wife?" I have to be careful here. Harry's been my only friend for a while now. He was the one who vouched for me to pledge for the Steel Knights, and he was the one who took me under his wing and gave me a job as his right-hand dealing with the accounting and the books. Even when things got really bad between Bullseye, who is Harry's best friend, and me, Harry still stuck by my side. That's saying something. "Sorry."

Narrowing his eyes, Harry sighs. "We've had enough drama for one night, so instead of kicking your ass for the smartass remark, I'm going to let it go. Come on."

"Where?"

"The back room. Nick has some new ideas he wants to run by you."

"Now?" I question. "We had a meeting this afternoon. I go to the construction company with our proposal in two days."

Bullet shrugs. "I think your actions tonight inspired him."

"Fuck, man, you told him?"

"Come on." Harry motions to the back room.

Shoving my hands into my pockets, I follow Harry past the busy bar area and nod to some of the guys: Bucky, our Road Captain, Texas sitting next to him, and Small Fry and Jonesie, who are sitting on the opposite side of Bucky. Vil's hanging down at the other end of the bar, talking to some woman I can't see from here, and Travis is playing darts alone. None of them give me a second glance. Thank god. That means Nick didn't tell them that I may have just put the club at risk so I could go rushing in to save a woman who didn't need saving.

Hustling past them, I don't feel bad about not stopping to talk; they all know I'm the kind of guy that keeps to himself. No, it doesn't win me a lot of friends, but they have my back. That's all I need, and it's just fine by me.

I don't need relationships. Never have. That's why if I never see Dr. Holly again, it won't change things for me one bit.

The only one I'm worried about having a relationship with is Colt, my kid brother. After the rocky start we had, I'm still floored that he hunted me down here in Hoppa, Arizona and decided to pledge for the Steel Knights.

Walking into the back room, the tension is so thick, it's like I'm walking into a bowl of jelly. Bullseye is sitting in a chair with his torso sprawled across the table littered with blueprints I created for the clubhouse and papers about the plans for expansion. Nick's sitting near the window, puffing on a cigar. He's got the window cracked, and when the breeze blows in just a certain way, the cool evening desert air feels great against my burning skin.

"Jesus, guys." Waving my hand through the air, I make my way to the table, pull out a chair, and spin it. Plopping down, I rest my elbows on the back of the chair. "No one else left to grab a shower? It smells like a freaking locker room in here." I don't know what else to say to break the ice.

Lifting himself off of the table, Avery raises his bottle in a toast. "Some of us had reasons to come right back to the clubhouse."

"Your reason's gonna run when she smells you," I joke, trying anything to ease the stress that's downright tangible. "Where is Seneca, anyway? Working around back?"

"Damn straight, and I want to finish this up so I can go help her."

"You mean slow her down," Harry adds. "I've never seen anyone who can fix a bike like Seneca."

"True." Avery grins.

Damn, he's got it bad.

"All right." Stamping out his cigar, Nick stands and waves his hand through the air to clear it of his smoke. "Enough with the chitchat." He turns to me. "Son, I need to find out if we have a problem on our hands."

"What are you talking about?" My voice is low and breathy.

"I'm just going to ask point-blank. What were you thinking, going to that hospital alone tonight when you knew the Dogs were there?"

Dropping my head, I stare at the table before me. The truth is I wasn't thinking. And everyone knows it. Raising my gaze, I look Nick in the eye. "It's over. I can promise you that."

"Seth, I don't want it to be over for you. I want you to find love like the rest of us. I hope it's with Dr. Holly if—"

"It won't be." I cut him off, and he raises his eyebrows at me. "Sorry," I mutter. "Finish, please."

"I was going to say that I hope it's with Dr. Holly if that's what you both want. She's an amazing woman."

"Yeah. But there's nothing between us."

"Getting shot down once doesn't mean crap," Harry adds.

My face warms as the blood rushes to my cheeks. "What are you talking about?"

"I know you sent her flowers."

"Sent who flowers?" I say through clenched teeth, and my tight jaw makes the muscles in my shoulder ache.

Harry tips his head. "Dr. Holly. Who else?"

"How did you—?"

"I heard you on the phone ordering them. I waited in the other room. I didn't want to barge in on you."

"So you eavesdropped?"

"Seth." Nick raises his eyebrows.

Sighing, I scrub my face with my hand. "It was only as a thank-you for helping me out."

"It was the right thing to do," Nick adds.

"She never got back to you?" Avery asks.

Shaking my head, I toy with an empty bottle on the table. "No. That's one of the reasons I know it's over before it even began. She's just not into me. And why would she be? It took seeing her in action tonight, but I've finally woken up and realized that nothing can happen between us. She's a brilliant, gorgeous doctor and I'm, well, *me*."

"Cut the freaking pity party," Avery snaps. "I read people, Seth. That's what I do. You know that. I grew up under the thumb of the Bordono crime family, and I learned. That's part of the reason why I'm an expert marksman—I can read people and anticipate their moves. That night, when she was here and you two were at a table by yourselves, I called you 'Dynamite', and there was a definite reaction from her. She raised an eyebrow and sat closer to you, not farther back. She may be all class and brains, but that doesn't mean she doesn't want and *need* an alpha in her life."

"Come on," Nick reprimands. Whenever the teasing touches on anything real, Nick steps in. "Give the kid a break. He's handling it his way."

"His way is bottling everything inside until he explodes. That's why we call him

'Dynamite'," Bullet offers. There's real concern in his voice.

"Speaking of." Nick walks over to the table and plops down in an open chair. His gun hangs over his belt, and he adjusts his posture, leaning back on the cushioned office chair. "What happened at the hospital tonight?"

"Dogs everywhere. Vipers, too. It was chaos."

"Did you see Holly?" It's Harry. Damn, for a man who hated women for all those years, who wouldn't and couldn't trust them, not until Celia walked in, he sure cares a lot about love now.

"Yeah. From a distance."

"Was she okay?" Avery leans forward.

"She was…" Shaking my head, I remember her there on the gurney. "She was amazing. I watched as she saved a Viper's life. She…" Sighing, I look away and then back again. "She doesn't need me. She's got everything under control."

"And you?" Nick tilts his head. "Did you have everything under control? Were you spotted by any Dogs?"

Nodding, I swallow hard. "One. Yeah."

"Fuck!" Harry's on his feet. "At best, they're going to think we went to spy on them—to see how many men they're down. They're probably waiting for an ambush right now."

"And at worst?" Raising my gaze, I ask Nick.

"At worst, son, they've figured out what Dr. Holly means to you and then…" He shakes his head. "If we have a war on our hands, she'll be caught in the middle."

"No." Shaking my head, I look from man to man. "I won't let that happen. Besides, Holly and I weren't together. There's no Dog that could know why I was there."

"All right." Nick nods. "Let's just keep our eyes and ears peeled. If the Dogs have had as many serious injuries as you say, then they're not going to come knocking any time soon. The best we can do is move on with the build of the new clubhouse and with our lives. Agreed?"

As we mumble our agreement, Nick eyes me.

"You know, Seth, it might help you find some peace if you let Colt be more involved around here. Sen's kid brother, Matt, is out there right now helping her with the bikes. One thing about kid brothers…" He pauses and looks me straight in the eye. "They seem to learn pretty damned quick."

I know what Nick's saying—I need to open up to Colt. Yeah, I nominated him, but since that night, I haven't done much for him. And lately—shit. I have been so preoccupied with Dr. Holly, I haven't been much good to anyone. Well, that all changes tonight. Because tonight is the night I move on.

"I am working on spending some time with Colt," I tell Nick.

The guys nod.

"Your kid brother is cool," Harry adds.

"He's been learning a lot about the bikes," Bullseye throws in.

"You know…" Nick has to get the last word.

Despite everything, it makes me chuckle.

"I knew he was a good kid, I hope you know that. When you nominated him, I was hesitant, yes. But it wasn't about you or him. I just wasn't sure I should support any kind of family connection in the club. Not after…"

"Tess and CJ." Nodding, I look at Nick. "I know. But thanks to your daughter, we've got some kickass plans for the club. I also, uh…" I'm not really a man of many words, and I hate anything mushy but here goes. "I appreciate you guys showing Colt the ropes. He's never really had a man in his life, you know?"

They all nod in agreement. They know the deal—yeah, our dad split when we were kids—so? Lots of people's dads split. But Colt never had anyone. He should have had me but he didn't, because I let my stupid temperament get in the way. I was sent to juvie for freaking armed robbery—and served a longer sentence because I lashed out at the cop who tried to arrest me.

They call me "Dynamite" for a reason. Yeah, a lot of people earn their nicknames, but mine is one I wish I could live down.

Glimpsing Avery, I notice he sits up taller as he stares down at his empty bottle and spins it on the table. Talk of Matt always makes him melancholy like this, and I don't blame him. I know what it's like to live with guilt. I can't even imagine the guilt he must be carrying for indirectly being the one who kept Sen's brother in jail for years.

"So? What's the new idea, Nick?" Harry starts pacing by the door. Thank god he's changing the subject. "Some of us have places we want to go with people who look a lot better than you." He grins. "We've gone through every bit of Tess's plan, and her ideas are solid."

Nodding to Harry, who's still hovering by the door that's the entrance to the bar, I point to it. "Wanna crack the door? Get some air in here?"

"I got it." Avery stands. "I'm gonna get some beers, anyway."

As he walks out of the back room and into the bar area, he leaves the door open for me, giving me a direct view of the front windows and the darkness of the night sky. Little jolts of energy rush up my spine. Nighttime always gives me hope—maybe she'll decide to drop by for a drink.

Fuck, Dynamite. Let. It. Go.

Glancing at the door, I try to will Avery to hurry up with the damned beer.

Looking out at the bar area, I scan the small section of the bar I can see from back here. Tonight is about one random woman. Someone to take home who can help me forget Holly, but so far, there seem to be slim pickings—a woman with long, wavy blonde hair who's already drunk and hitting on poor Travis, who's now joined the other guys at the bar, and a woman with shoulder-length dark brown hair in a too-tight shirt. I guess, if she's interested, she'll have to do.

Avery finally comes back with another round of domestic beers. Thank god. Grabbing a beer, I nod my thanks. Taking a long drag from the cold bottle, it does little to quench my thirst and nothing to quell my desire, but I'll take it. Like that brunette in the skin-tight Harley shirt.

She turns just then and glances back at me and we lock eyes. Raising one shoulder and then dropping it, she gives me a tiny wave. She's cute. Yeah, she'll be fine. Christ. It has been a freaking long month.

"So, Nick. What's your idea?" I ask.

"You know how Tess had quotes for several locations and we picked the best for us?"

"The one farthest from Dogs' turf," Harry adds, glancing at me.

I shift in my seat.

"Right. Well, her plans, as we know, have an office for each of the officers, a club room, some secret rooms…" He taps on the new blueprints I've drawn up as he speaks. "And our favorite part was the bar for 'Regulars and Friendlies only.'"

"Yeah?" He's got my interest now.

"Well, all of it is great. But I'd like to propose more. This piece of land will allow us to build a bunker. Underneath."

"What do you mean, Nick?" Furrowing my brows, I lean closer.

"A bunker. Like a safe house. It'll be a secret room in addition to the private rooms. But this would be underground…"

"A place to hide?" I can hear the disdain in Harry's voice. "Nick. We can't give the impression that we're scared. I know the fight with the Dogs on our turf cost you your only son, and indirectly, your daughter, too, when she left. But this will make us look weak."

"Only if people know about it," Nick adds. "The point is to have a place to house our weapons and ammo. A bunker where we can collect and regroup if we need."

"Nick." Avery shakes his head. "I'm not sure on this one. It sounds a little risky."

"What if any one of you needed to protect the woman you love? Avery? You know about this more than any of us. I'm sure your connections in New York have a safe house. Most people who run with fringe organizations do. It doesn't make us weak, it makes us stronger."

Sighing, I glance at Bullet and Bullseye. It's clear that Nick is finally on track to be happy again, and he's going to do anything he can to protect it, which includes all of us. Then, tonight, I might have let my damned impulsivity ruin that for all of us.

"But, Nick," I add. "There's no way we can keep this build secret. The Dogs will find out, and we will risk looking weak."

Nodding, Nick stands. "All I ask is that you consider it. Especially now."

Ouch.

With that, the meeting is over. That's good, because the damn tension was getting so high, I didn't know how much more I could stand. Harry and Avery stay at the table, muttering as Nick slides out the backdoor. Probably to cool off, which is exactly what I need to do.

Reaching my hands above my head and taking one long stretch, I leave the back room and head to the now-crowded bar area. Damn, when the Knights leave Hoppa's Taphouse, business is gonna take some hit.

There are people everywhere now, three-deep at the bar and still filing in from the parking lot, but Harley girl finds me. She bounces up to me and, taking me by the hand, she leads me to the bar and plops herself down on a stool she had reserved. Looking at her—with her full lips and bright blue eyes in a heart-shaped face—she's even cuter than she looked from a distance.

"Hi." She taps the now-empty stool next to her.

Damn, I really don't want this, but I need something. I just can't bring myself to sit, so instead, I lean against the bar next to her with my back to the meeting room and my torso toward the front door. Just in case I need to run.

"You're Seth, right?"

She holds out her hand and we shake. Her hand is tiny and warm, and it just doesn't feel right. Nothing about this feels right.

"I'm Tracy." She moves in her seat. Glancing down, I catch her hard nipples poking through the T-shirt. "How about a drink?" Batting her lashes, she smiles at me.

Caught in my thoughts, I don't move.

"Seth? You okay?"

Glancing at the door, I know I have to give up on the fantasy of Dr. Holly. Yeah, we had a connection. But the fact that she didn't even send a thank-you for the flowers should have been my wake-up call. Dr. Holly, in all her perfection, is not the type of woman for me. Tracy is.

"Seth?"

"Yeah, sorry. Fine. You want a beer?"

"Yes." She smiles so wide it looks like her cheeks might break.

Ducking behind the bar, I reach into a cooler and I grab two beers. Popping the top off of both with my hands, I give her one.

"With your hands!" She playfully fans herself with her own. "So strong…" she mumbles, reaching out and squeezing my arm. "All these muscles."

Reaching her hand up higher, she lays it behind my neck, and before I realize what's happening, she lifts herself up, balancing on the rung of the stool, and plants a kiss on my lips. Pulling back, I resist the urge to wipe my mouth with my hand. She tastes like fruity gum and cigarettes.

"So, you wanna go somewhere?" Staring up at me, her small blue eyes grow wider.

Damn. Picking up my beer, I lean back and take a long pull from the bottle. Anything would be better than all this noise and all these people. Placing the bottle down, I let my gaze run over the crowd, wondering where to take this girl because I don't want her knowing where I live… and my focus goes to the front door where—

Fuck.

Fuck!

Fuck!

There, by the front door of Hoppa's Taphouse, wearing a white doctor's coat hanging open over a blue V-neck shirt and a pair of dark gray dress pants, is Dr. Holly Boling.

"Holly?" Pushing my way through the crowd, I fight to get to her, but I'm too late.

Shaking her head at me, she turns and disappears out the door.

Chapter Four

Dynamite

"Holly!" Yelling her name, I rush out to her.

Catching up to her at her car door, I resist the urge to reach out and touch her. My breathing is almost as fast as hers, and it's like I can feel the energy rushing back and forth between us.

"What do you want, Seth?" She presses the key fob on her fancy car and the doors unlock.

"You. I mean, I wanted to see you." Coward. "You surprised me."

Looking up at me, I can see the hurt written all over her face. "Yeah? Well, you surprised me, too." Dropping her gaze to her door handle, she mutters, "I mean, by coming to the hospital tonight." Taking a deep breath and letting it go, she looks up at me. "Why were you there? Did you know those men? They weren't part of your club, were they?"

Shaking my head, I look into her eyes and refuse to look away. It's like I'm holding her here with me. "They're not part of the Steel Knights, no. One club there tonight, the Raging Vipers, they're our allies. The man you saved in the lobby… when you climbed onto his gurney?"

She nods.

"He's a Viper. They're a good group of guys."

"You said, 'one club.' What about the other club?"

"The Unchained Dogs. They're a rival club—and an outlaw gang."

Her eyes widen.

"Those guys are bad news and real… jerks." For some reason, I don't want to curse around this woman.

"Okay, but you haven't answered my question. Why were you there? Was it to help your ally club?"

Still staring into her eyes, I take a step closer.

"Seth? Why were you there?"

No matter how stupid I sound, she deserves the truth. "Because of you. I was there to make sure you were okay. I know how awful the Dogs can be and that they treat women like garbage. I wanted to make sure you were okay and no one was messing with you."

"Oh. I…" Glancing up at me, her face softens and the side of her mouth twitches like she might break out into a smile.

"But I was wrong," I explain. "You can take care of yourself. You also had hospital security and…" Swallowing hard, I force myself to say it. "Your friend Covens was there. He'd protect you if you needed it."

"Robert?" Rolling her eyes, she glances at the ground and then looks back up at me. "The only thing Robert is interested in protecting is himself." Tilting her head, she smiles. "And maybe his tan. And his Alfa Romeo."

She smirks, and I can't help but smile along with her.

Looking down and then back up at me, she asks, "So, you really came tonight just to check on me?"

"Yes. I know it was stupid—"

Reaching out, she takes my hand and gives it a small squeeze, and it's like a bolt of lightning shoots up my arm. Never, in my thirty years of life, has anything ever felt like that before.

"Not stupid, Seth." She shakes her head. "It was very, very kind. And…"

"And?" I dare a step closer until we're nearly touching.

"It's nice to feel like someone's looking out for me." Her voice is low and breathy, and she stares at the ground as she speaks.

It takes all of my will not to reach out, place a finger under her beautiful chin, and turn her face upward to look into her eyes—

"Seth?"

Whipping around, I glimpse the brunette from the bar standing there. She looks from Holly to me and then back again.

"My kiss make you so dizzy you need medical attention?" Walking up, she shoves her hands into her front pockets and raises her shoulders. Letting them drop, she looks Holly up and down, and then nods to her.

"I forgot I was wearing my lab coat," Holly mumbles and then smiles at the girl. Reaching out, she takes the girl's hand and they shake.

Standing here like a numbskull, I can't even do the polite thing and introduce them, because I have no friggin' clue what this girl's name is. I know she told me inside and I think I knew it once, but right now… Fuck. This is not how I want this to go down.

"I'm Holly." Dr. Holly smiles at the girl.

"Tracy."

Yes. Tracy. That's it.

Releasing the girl's hand, Holly smiles. "I just stopped by to check on Seth. He was my patient in the ER about a month ago." Turning to me, she adds, "I was just wondering how you're feeling?"

"Wow." Tracy claps her hands together and her long nails make a clicking sound. "That's nice of you to drive all the way out here to check on him. We really appreciate it." Moving closer to me, she grabs my arm and hangs on it, leaning her weight against me. Looking up, she smiles at me. "Wasn't that nice, babe?"

Glancing at Holly, I catch her mouthing the word "babe."

"Well." Holly clears her throat. "I'm glad everything seems to be in working order."

She eyeballs me, and I know she's not referring to my shoulder.

"I'm going to head back to Phoenix." Grabbing the driver's door handle, she opens her car door. "So you two can get back to your night."

"Nice meeting you!" Tracy offers. Still hanging on me, she gives Holly the same cutesy wave she gave me before.

"Hold on." Breaking free of Tracy, I turn to face her. "Can you go get a beer? I need to speak to Dr. Boling alone. It'll only take a moment."

"I get it. Doctor-patient confidence, huh?" Tracy asks, looking Holly up and down once more.

Cringing at her misused word, I glance at Holly, who doesn't so much as flinch. She is a class act.

"Um, something like that, yes," I mumble.

Shoving her hands back into her front pockets again, Tracy nods to Holly. "Well, uh, bye, Holls. It was nice meeting you."

Holly smiles. "It was nice meeting you as well, Tracy."

Holding my breath, I watch Tracy walk back to the clubhouse. She stops at the door and gives a wave before disappearing inside. Turning back to Holly, I'm desperate to explain.

"Holly—"

Cutting me off, Holly stands by her still-open door while she speaks. "Your girlfriend seems nice."

"She's not my girlfriend," I clarify. "Just met her tonight—a couple of minutes before you came into the bar."

"Well, your friend, then."

"She's not my friend."

Holly looks up at me. "The way she was holding onto you and calling you 'babe', I don't think she knows that."

"She doesn't seem to know a lot," I add. "Doctor-patient confidence?"

I'm hoping for a chuckle out of Holly. Instead, she narrows her eyes.

"So? She misspoke. At least she tried. I don't think she went to medical school. You can't go around judging people, Seth. Who knows what opportunities she's had for education versus what I had—private schools all the way to an Ivy League college and one of the top medical schools in the country. I'm sure that if I looked at your motorcycle and tried to rebuild the engine, I'd sound just as uninformed." Her breath is racing and her chest heaving. "I…"

Her eyes dance across mine. Leaning her arm on the inside armrest of her opened door and dropping her head, she shakes it. "I'm sorry, Seth. You didn't deserve that." Raising her head, she looks me in the eye again. "I-I was raised by—and am surrounded by—incredibly arrogant and elitist people. I just wanted to believe you were different. It's not fair of me to expect you to be one way or another. For god's sake, you let the woman kiss you. You must have seen something in her. Unless…" Tilting her head, her beautiful brow furrows again. "Were you just using her for the night?"

Was I? No. "I wasn't doing anything with her. I didn't want to be there. She kissed me, you're right. But it was a surprise, and that's as far as it ever would have gone." In my heart, I know that's the truth. "And I'm sorry. I shouldn't have judged her like that. Truth is…" Taking a deep breath, I let it go in a sigh. "The truth is I'm incredibly glad to see you, and…" I take a step closer to Holly. "I really don't want you to go."

Looking up at me, her eyes bounce back and forth, reading me.

Walking around so we're on the same side of the opened door, I look at her. "Holly? Please don't go. Do you want to come in for a drink?"

"I don't think that would be fair to Tracy. What do you think?"

"How about we go somewhere else?"

Standing up tall, she whips around to face me and raises an eyebrow.

"There's another bar not too far from here." I make sure I'm perfectly clear.

Shaking her head, she stares at the ground and then looks me in the eye. "I did come here for a reason tonight, and it was to see you."

"I'm glad."

Nodding, she continues. "Do you remember that night we met in the ER?" She looks me in the eyes.

Jesus, do I remember? That night plays over and over in my mind constantly. "Of course, I remember."

"Well, do you remember that I noticed your tattoo?" She points to my arm with the tattoo. "I mentioned how nice it was, and you said that if I ever wanted one, you could get me in contact with a really great tattoo artist?"

"You want a tattoo?" I thought it was impossible for this woman to be any sexier. But I was wrong.

"I think I do." Nodding faster and faster until I worry she might shake her brilliant brain loose, she stops abruptly. "Yes, yes. I do want a tattoo. I've wanted one for as long as I can remember. But no one in my life has been exactly supportive of it. Until you."

"Hell, yeah, I'll support your decision to get a tattoo. Getting a tat can be one of the most liberating and freeing things you ever do."

"Yes." Her eyes are smoldering as she stares up into mine. "I need that. I need something liberating and freeing."

Smiling at her, I can tell it's true. "But you have to be sure this isn't an impulse thing. A tattoo is forever."

"I know that." She takes a deep breath. "I have thought about it nearly every day of my life for the past twelve years—since I was sixteen."

"Why have you waited?"

"Because I wait for everything. That's what I do. I think it over until I talk myself out of it."

Nodding, I pull my cell out of my jeans' pocket and shoot a quick text.

"Come on. Let's go."

I hold out my hand. She looks at it and then up to me. "What? Where?"

"To get you a tattoo."

"Now?" Her eyes light up. "We're going now? Don't we need an appointment or something?"

"Got one." Smiling at her, I explain, "I told you, I know a guy."

"I…" Looking at the ground and then back up to me, the expression on her face changes from unsure to resolute. It's the same expression she had when she jumped on that gurney and saved that Viper's life. "I'm game."

Dropping her keys into my palm, she smiles. Holding my arm out for her to walk around the back of the car before me, I open the passenger door for her and she climbs in.

Hustling around to the driver's side, I jump in. Running my hands up and down the expensive leather of her steering wheel, I breathe in the new car smell. "Beautiful car." Feeling the knobs and buttons and the expensive leather interior, I mumble, "Nothing like German engineering."

"So I've heard."

"Is this new?"

"The car?" She shakes her head. "No. It was a med school graduation present from my parents."

"Nice present."

"Yeah, I guess." Leaning back, she rests her head against the seat.

"You guess? With these features and this finish, this is around an eighty-five-thousand-dollar nice gift."

Rolling her head so she faces me, she asks, "Do you measure the quality of a gift by its price?"

"No." Shaking my head, I understand what she's asking. "No, I don't. And I'm guessing neither do you?"

Sitting up straight, she turns to me. "It was incredibly generous of them. Anyone would be thrilled to receive a car like this for a gift."

"But?"

"But it's not the car I wanted. I know I sound crazy and spoiled… but it's the car they wanted me to drive. Not the car I wanted."

"What car do you want?" This woman gets more and more fascinating by the moment.

"You'll laugh."

"Well, now I've got to know. I won't laugh. Promise."

Shaking her head, she presses her lips together. "Don't make promises you can't keep."

"Never do."

"Okay, then, let's make a bet."

"A woman who bets? This gets better and better. What's the wager?"

"Don't know yet. How about a prize—agreed upon by both parties—but to be named at a later date?"

"I like it. Okay. I'll take your blind bet. So? What kind of car?"

"I probably sound like a walking quarter-life crisis, but I want a Jeep. A hot pink Jeep."

Stifling a chuckle, I turn and look out the driver's side window.

"Seth?"

Leaning forward, she tries to look at me, but I stay facing away from her. I'm fighting hard not to laugh, but I keep picturing this gorgeous, classy woman pulling up to the hospital with her hot pink Jeep covered in mud.

"Seth?" Her voice is flirtatious. "Are you trying not to laugh?"

"No, no." Clearing my throat, I fight back a chuckle. "Nope."

"Well, if that doesn't make you laugh, how about the image of me in that car with a lucky rabbit's foot hanging from the rearview?"

"Rabbit's foot?" My chest is rising and falling with a chuckle that's building in my gut and wants to burst free, but I refuse to let it out. Lifting my hand, I cover my grin and keep my head turned, looking out of the driver's window.

"Yup. A big, neon-green lucky rabbit's foot, one that's so big that every time I go off-roading and over a bump, it bounces back and forth."

She leans even closer and rests her hands on the console between the front bucket seats. If I were to turn now, she'd be inches from me, and I could just reach out, stroke her beautiful cheek, and kiss her so very gently.

"I want one so big it looks like it came off of Bugs himself." Miming, she pretends she's holding a carrot like a cigar. "What's up, Doc?"

"Ha!" A huge, rolling laugh pours out of me. There's nothing I can do. The moment isn't all that funny, but it's like all the millions of pounds of stress pour out of me, and I feel happy. For the first time in a long time.

"Ah-ha!" Pointing her finger at me, she smiles. "You are laughing."

"That wasn't fair," I protest. "That was an awful impression. It was more like Groucho Marx than Bugs."

"Yup. I'm the worst at impressions, but that doesn't stop me. I do them all the time."

"I look forward to hearing more, maybe."

"The important part is that you're laughing." She grins at me. "That means I win."

"But you're laughing, too." Catching my breath, I'm once again caught by how beautiful this woman is. "So, doesn't that mean we both win?"

Shaking her head, she smiles. "Nope. There can't be two winners. It doesn't work like that. Besides, I'm not laughing. Just chuckling. There's a difference."

"Yeah? Not laughing, huh? Well, how about now?" Reaching out, I tickle her waist.

"Oh!" Laughing, she squirms up and down in her seat.

Reaching around, I tickle both sides of her waist at once. "How about now?"

She's laughing so hard her eyes close and her mouth opens. Laughing along with her, I get caught up in the moment.

"All right… Seth… I-I give—" she mutters between breaths.

Immediately, I release her.

"Oh, my goodness." Sitting back in her seat, she's wearing a huge smile and it makes me grin along with her. "I never knew I was ticklish."

"Excuse me? You didn't know if you were ticklish? How is that possible? You've never been tickled?"

"No." She knits her brows together. "Thinking of it now, I've never had anyone tickle me. Huh. That's kind of sad." Her face becomes determined again. "Well, I guess it's just a night of firsts."

"I guess. So, ready for your tattoo?"

"Yes."

"Okay. Give me five minutes to go tell the guys I'm taking off, and then I have to let Tracy know I'm not coming back."

Nodding, she glances out the front window and then points with her finger. "I don't think you'll have to. I think she just got the message."

Looking at where Holly is pointing, I see Tracy standing in front of the Taphouse scowling at me.

"Oh, crap. This isn't what I wanted right now. Or ever."

"You owe her an explanation, Seth."

"Yeah. Just give me a sec." Climbing out of the car, I begin walking toward Tracy, who's standing at the front door of the Taphouse. Glancing back, I catch Holly fixing her hair and checking her appearance in the rearview—which is completely unnecessary, because she's the kind of woman who could wear one of my old concert shirts and still look stunning.

Thinking about Holly in one of my concert tees with nothing but a pair of panties underneath... Crap. Now I have to fight back the growing hard-on that I've had since I first laid eyes on Holly tonight.

Facing the door again, I step closer to Tracy. "Tracy, I'm sorry. She's—"

Before I can finish my thought, Colt, my kid brother, walks out of the bar grinning. He links his arm around Tracy's waist and they kiss.

Turning toward me, she makes eye contact. "Seth, this is Colt. But since you two could be twins, my guess is that you already know each other."

"Colt?" I step closer. "I thought you'd gone home for the night."

"I did." Nodding, his grin grows even wider. "But then I came back."

"How'd I miss you coming in?"

"You were having your checkup with Dr. Holly in the car," Tracy adds, smirking. "That's when Colt drove up, and the moment he walked into the bar, I knew he was the one for me."

"And damn." Pulling Tracy tighter to his side, Colt says, "I am so glad I did."

Smiling at Colt and Tracy, I nod. "Okay, you guys have fun."

"We will." Tracy links both her arms around Colt's waist.

"Cool. Colt?"

I nod to my brother meaningfully. He untangles himself from Tracy and walks up to stand next to me.

"Just be careful. Please. You've, uh, you've got protection?" This big brother stuff is still new to me, but I think that's something I should double-check.

"Yeah, Seth, of course, I have protection."

"Good. Then use it."

Shaking his head, Colt runs from me and over to Tracy. Putting his arm around her shoulder, he rushes her over to his bike. I can't help but smile as he gives her a helmet and the two of them hop on Colt's bike and speed off together.

"Use it!" I call after him. "The hell with it." Deciding to text the guys later, I hustle back to the car and to Holly.

"Everything okay?" Tilting her head, she looks concerned.

Climbing into the driver's seat, I answer, "Yeah. Fine. Tracy seems to have found love with my kid brother—Colt."

"Well, let's be happy for them." Turning to me, she smiles.

"Okay." One look at her, and I forget everything else. "So, Dr. Boling." I press the button to start the car and listen to the quiet hum of the engine. "Are you ready to continue your night of firsts?"

"Why, yes, Mr. Hardy. I think I am."

Putting the car in reverse, I begin to back up but she reaches out and puts her hand on my arm.

"Hold on."

"Everything okay?"

She picks up the key fob resting on the console between us and shakes it in her hand. "Look at what I just found out this car can do." Pressing a button on the fob, the top of the car opens.

"You have a convertible."

"Why, yes, I do."

Smiling, she plops back against the seat. Turning her gorgeous face up into the cool air and bright moonlight, she whispers, "Let's go, Seth. Let's go."

Revving the engine, I pull out of the parking lot, and with the cool Arizona air brushing against our faces, we rush off into this night of firsts.

For both of us.

Chapter Five

Holly

"This is a tattoo parlor?"

Holding open the door of the shop for me, Seth grins as I step inside. Looking around, I'm surprised by what I see. Okay, yes, it's dark and kind of "vintage-looking" like I anticipated, but everything is so clean and sterile.

"What were you expecting?" He lets the door close behind us.

"Honestly? The inside of Hoppa's Taphouse—a place filled with bikers and beer and maybe even with wood shavings on the floor. But this…" Walking in a circle, I take in a cute, small room that could just as easily double as a coffee shop—and smells like one as well. The wood floor is worn in a cool, trendy way that looks like someone paid a bunch of money for reclaimed wood to create their perfect floor. In the middle of the floor is one large reclining chair with black cushions. That must be where I'll sit. Or, uh, lie. On one side of the room, long, purple velvet curtains cover the windows that look out onto the street, and on the other, a brick wall showcases about a million framed photos of tattoos on various body parts. Walking closer, I study the pictures showing tattoos on arm after arm, leg after leg, lower back after lower back. Each is more beautiful than the next.

Damn, it's getting warm in here. Pulling my shirt away from my chest, I blow down into my stretched collar, hoping to cool myself off. Reaching around, I loosen the shirt from my lower back, but the sweat building there, along with the slight tremor in my normally steady hands, confirms what I worried about on the whole ride here: I'm about to chicken out. Like I always do.

"See anything you like?"

Seth's voice is a deep purr, and it sends shivers up and down my body—and the combination is now causing cold sweats. Walking over to me, he's standing so near I can feel the energy coming off of him. Closing my eyes for a moment, all I want is to get even closer.

"I like them all," I whisper. "Each one is so beautiful. It's hard to choose." In my mind, I recall some of the tattoos I've just looked at. "The butterfly, the crescent moon, the dandelion, the star—how do you choose?" Opening my eyes and reaching out, I run my finger over the glass covering the picture of a tattoo of birds flying across a girl's wrist.

Letting my hand glide down to my side, Seth moves even closer now. Shifting my weight to the foot closest to him, our bodies are nearly touching, and a light prickling feeling rushes up and down my extremities.

Reaching out, he clamps a strong hand high on my hip—and I close my eyes, nearly swooning. Leaning back, he pulls me to him, so my back is against his wide chest, and his arm slides forward and wraps around my waist. With his other hand, he runs a finger down my arm, and it's like he's opening a floodgate of electricity.

I try to breathe deeply, but my chest begins heaving, and I can feel him behind me, his wide chest moving in sync with mine.

With the same hand that's been running up and down my arm, he reaches out and takes my hand. With the slightest amount of pressure, he spins me so we're facing each other. Looking up tentatively, I stare into his gorgeous eyes. Wrapping two powerful arms around me, he pulls me closer.

Suddenly, I freeze and look away.

"Holly?" He doesn't let go as he bends lower, trying to make eye contact.

Shaking my head, I reach up, place my hands on his chest, and gently push him away. "I-I'm sorry," I mutter.

"You don't have to be sorry, Holly. What's wrong?"

Looking around, the walls feel like they're closing in on me. Suddenly, the small, cute room seems dark, dingy, and oppressive. "I can't breathe."

"Are you having an allergic reaction to something?"

As my forehead grows slick with perspiration, I shake my head, and my gaze darts back and forth, looking for the exit.

"No allergy. Just… hot."

Taking a deep, trembling breath, I spy the exit. Holding my small purse tight to my chest, I run for the door just as a short man with curly black hair and a wide smile materializes from the back room. I'm out the door and down the front steps before I hear the man calling.

"Seth?"

"Just a minute!" Seth answers the man. "Holly?" He jumps down the front steps and hurries up to me. "Are you okay?"

Fanning my face with my hands, I breathe in and out through pursed lips, trying to calm my breathing, but it's not doing any good. The cool fresh air should feel great, but sometimes the darkest nights can feel so claustrophobic—like the black sky is a weighted blanket pressing down on top of me, and all I can do is squeeze my eyes shut and hold on until morning.

"What can I do?" Seth's brows are knitted together and he looks concerned. No. More than concerned, he looks worried.

Doubling over at the waist, I clamp my hands on my hips and suck in deep, cleansing breaths. Shaking my head, I look up at him. His brow is furrowed, and creases line his forehead. He's worried about me. Squeezing my eyes shut again, I mentally beat myself up. Like I always do. *Way to be smooth, Holly. Way to be smooth.*

"If it's what I did in there…" His eyes flash with concern. "I'm sorry. I pushed too far. I can do that—"

"It wasn't that." A warm feeling I don't recognize overtakes me, and I have this sudden urge to run my hands through his hair and comfort him. "I'm okay, Seth. Really." Standing up straight, I look into his eyes. "It has nothing to do with you, and there's nothing anyone can do about it. I have panic attacks sometimes. Thankfully, they don't happen in the emergency room or in surgery—they only happen when I have to make a decision about my life. Even minor decisions, like what kind of juice to buy, can keep me in the grocery store for hours."

"You don't have to get a tattoo."

"But I want to." Searching his eyes, I realize he's the first person I've ever talked to about this who cares enough to listen. "I want a tattoo—and so much more."

"Like what?"

"Oh." Chuckling, I look away. "I have plans, you know? Things I want to do that aren't scheduled and approved by my parents and…" Sighing, I just blurt it out. "Seth, I can't even buy kitchen towels at Target without being worried that I'm making the wrong decision." Raising my fingers to my mouth, I gnaw on the corner of a nail.

"Hey." Taking my hand from my mouth, he holds it at my side. "Don't do that."

"Attractive, huh?" I can hear the desperation in my voice.

"Holly, you're gorgeous. The most beautiful woman I've ever seen—including all of the women I've ever seen in movies. There is nothing you can do that would be unattractive. I just don't want you to hurt yourself. Come here."

He holds out his arm and I walk up next to him. We're not touching, but it's like he has this protective aura that surrounds me.

"I think, Holly, what you need is a break. A moment to just live without judging or feeling judged."

"I go to yoga, but it's not helping."

Smiling, tiny creases form in the corners of Seth's eyes. He chuckles. "I think we may need more than yoga to get through this."

"Therapy?" I stare up into his handsome face. His cheekbones are so strong they look chiseled, and his nose is slightly wide but straight and strong.

"In a sense. Yeah." Raising his hand, he points to something across the street. "See that?"

"The liquor store?"

"That's your therapy."

"I don't know, Seth."

Smiling, he nods. "Do you have work tomorrow?"

"No, I'm off for the next two days."

"Good." Reaching out, he taps me on the nose. "Holly. No one is saying you should make it a habit, but there's a reason tequila exists—for times just like these. It's worked for centuries. What do you say?"

"I say…" Glancing at the store across the street, I take a deep breath. "I say that flashing 'welcome' sign on the door is an omen."

He grins at me.

What the hell—everything I have done and accomplished up until this time in my life has made me miserable. Why the hell shouldn't I take a chance? Glancing up, I look at Seth's strong jaw and steal a quick peek at his broad shoulders and—hell, yeah.

With Seth Hardy as my guide, why wouldn't I take a chance for once in my life?

"No, no, no." Sitting in the back seat of my car that's still parked in the lot of the tattoo parlor, I hold the bottle of tequila in my hand. Squinting really hard, I try to wiggle my nose. "Seriously. There was a television show once—way back in the 1960s—and there was a woman who was a genie and when she wiggled her nose, she could make things happen." Sighing, I look at Seth. "I wish I could do that. I wish I could just wiggle my nose and things just magically manifested."

"What would you manifest? Just before, when we were talking about getting tequila—"

"—which was an excellent idea, by the way," I interrupt, smiling.

"Agreed. You said you wanted to do more. To do something that wasn't scheduled and approved by your parents. What is that?"

"Oh." Releasing a pent-up breath, I drop my head back against the seat and look up at the night sky. "It is beautiful out tonight." Turning in my seat, I draw a leg up between us and face him. "Do you know that before driving out here tonight, I had no idea that this car was a convertible? I mean, I must have known but I really never thought about it."

"That's kind of funny."

He turns to me, and just looking at him—his gorgeous face, his strong body, the way I feel safe and protected around him—an ache forms between my legs. Whoa. I have never had a reaction like this in all of my life.

"Why is it funny?"

Shaking his head, he puts his arm up across the top of the back seat in an uber-masculine move that just about makes me melt.

"I don't mean funny," he corrects. "Just that it's an odd thing that you've never done anything spontaneous—like open a convertible. Sometimes I think that's all I do—act without planning ahead. That's why the guys call me 'Dynamite'."

My brow furrows as I look into his face. "I don't think that's true. The impulsive part, that is."

"You haven't known me that long. And how can you of all people say that? When you met me, it's because I had just stabbed myself with a knife I pulled on my friend. Remember the night we met?"

"How could I forget? From what I gathered, you were fighting and passion got the best of you, Seth." Leaning forward, I make steady eye contact. "It's not that you're impulsive. It's that you're passionate. There's a difference. In the ER, I see all kinds of different people every day. Most of the time, people with impulse control issues have a mental disorder—something like kleptomania or pyromania. People with impulse control issues often think about what they're going to do and then go through some form of anxiety attack—like I just did."

Smiling at him, he smiles back and nods.

"Most often, people with impulse control issues don't have the ability to resist urges. You're not that person. If you were, frankly, I couldn't trust you the way I do."

"You trust me?" His eyes light up.

"Seth, I'm a woman who plans what color underwear I'm going to wear tomorrow—*and writes it in my agenda book.*"

"I think I'd like to see that agenda book," he jokes, smirking.

Tilting my head, I chuckle. Damn, it feels *so good* to laugh and be this carefree. "Yes, Seth, I trust you. Yes, you're passionate, and it's true, I don't know you well enough to know if you should make different decisions at times. But your impulses—from what I've seen—have been completely under your control and based on passion."

His face relaxes and the tight muscles in his jaw release. Nodding, he looks away. I touched on something—and he's relieved.

"Tequila?" Holding out the bottle, I offer him some.

"Nah, thanks. I need to stay sober. One of us has to drive." Sighing, he chuckles and runs both hands down the legs of his jeans.

From the tension I'm feeling coming off of him, I can tell he wants to keep his hands to himself about as much as I want him to.

"So…" Staring at the back of the driver's seat, he doesn't make eye contact with me. "Speaking of, what do you say I drive you home?"

"Home?" It's like a brick has just formed in my belly. "I don't want to go home."

He glances at me, raising an eyebrow.

"I want my tattoo. We came here for a reason, and I'm not chickening out on something else I want in my life because my parents wouldn't approve. For god's sake, I'm twenty-eight years old. I literally have people's lives in my hands all night—just about every night—and I care what Mommy and Daddy think? Pathetic, right?"

"No, it's not pathetic." He smiles. "It's just learned behavior. Once you stand up to them and survive, you'll realize it's okay to be you." Smiling, he turns away and then looks back at me. "Actually, you're better than okay. You're amazing."

My cheeks heat as I smile at him.

"You really want that tattoo?"

"Yes."

"Do you know what you want?"

"No. That's the problem. I've been back and forth—hey!" It dawns on me. "You know that bet you lost? When you laughed because I want to drive a hot pink Jeep?"

"I chuckled, I didn't laugh. And yeah, I know."

"Well, when I won, we decided that the prize would be named at a later time."

"And?" His eyebrow lifts skeptically.

"I've decided on the prize. We are each going to get tattoos—and we're going to pick the tattoo for the other person."

"What?" Leaning forward, he rests his forearms on his thighs and turns his head to look at me.

The way he sits is so damned masculine, I can feel the pull between my legs. His presence is so powerful and strong, it's like he takes up all the room in the back of my car, and I swear, he must have a thousand times the testosterone level that Robert has.

"You heard me." Raising my chin, I dare him. "You don't want another tattoo?"

"I do, actually. I just wasn't planning to get it just yet."

"So, why don't I start tonight? You pick for me—just something small, please—something that will fit right…" I point to the upper outside of my right hip. "Just no words, please. No sayings or anything like that. Then, we'll come back and I'll choose for you."

Sitting back, he sighs. "Holly, as much as I love this idea, I can't help but wonder if this is the tequila talking."

"Maybe. But it's just the right amount of tequila."

"But I don't want you to make a decision while you're impaired. You might wake up tomorrow and regret this."

"Like I regret every day of my life?" I stare into his eyes. "I'm buzzed, yes. But I'm not drunk."

"I don't know."

Holding out my hand, I nod to him. "Let me have your hand. Please."

"Okay."

Taking his strong hand in mine, I draw in a deep breath and focus. "There are twenty-seven bones in your hand." As I trace his fingers, I name the medical term for each. "Finger metacarpals. Proximal phalanges. Middle phalanges. Distal phalanges. Thumb metacarpal. Thumb sesamoids. Thumb proximal phalanx. Thumb distal phalanx." Looking up into his eyes, I smile. "Should I keep going?"

"N-no. That was quite impressive." He doesn't pull his hand away.

"Thanks. My point is if I'm sober enough to name every bone in your hand, I'm lucid enough to make this decision." Pausing, I look into his eyes. "I want this, Seth. But it seems I can't do it without you. Please."

Spinning his hand over, he holds mine in his. "Come on. It's time for you to get a tattoo."

Getting out of the car, he pulls me gently, and I climb out next to him. Standing on the sidewalk, I take deep breaths, trying to slow my racing heart and calm myself. But this time it's not because I'm having an anxiety attack—this time it's because I'm standing so near Seth Hardy.

Looking into my eyes, he takes a deep breath, too. "Do you know where, um, on your body you want the tattoo?"

Nodding, I glance at the ground and then up into his eyes. "I've thought about it a lot. The spot I mentioned on my hip."

He draws in another deep breath, and his grip on my hand grows tighter.

"My right hip. I think it's the perfect spot," I explain. "I don't want it somewhere that's visible if I wear a formal dress, but I'm okay with it showing in a bikini. Does that make sense?"

Nodding, he swallows hard. "Yeah. Um, you don't happen to have sweats in the car, do you? It'll make it easier for Marco to work rather than you having to, uh… slide those pants down." His cheeks redden.

"No sweats, but, oh! I have clean scrubs in the car."

"Great. Grab those, and let's go in and get you changed. Come on. I think I know exactly what you need."

Glancing up at him, I bite the corner of my lip and then smile. "Yes, Seth, I think you do."

Squeezing my eyes shut, I hold on tighter to Seth's hand. It's not that I'm afraid of the needle or the pain—truthfully, nothing like that affects me much. Never has. That's why becoming a surgeon was a natural fit for me.

What I am afraid of is who I'm becoming. Afraid and thrilled.

Lying on my side, I'm amazed at how comfortable this chair really is. The chair reclines all the way back and it's shaped to fit my body, so my left hip is tucked snuggly into the soft leather of the chair and my right hip—the one getting the tattoo—is easily accessible to Marco, my tattoo artist. My scrubs are pulled down just enough for Marco to access my hip, and my sweater is tucked up just under my breasts. Sitting on a rolling stool next to me, I catch Seth's glance at my tummy. Raising my eyebrow, I smirk at him, but he pinches his lips together and turns away like it never happened.

But it did, and when he glanced at my naked tummy and hip, a shiver shot up and down my body, settling as a warm feeling deep in my gut.

Marco, my tattoo artist, speaks calmly in his deep, melodic voice. "Okay, Holly. We printed out and tried a couple of different sizes of your design, and we're confident we have the right size and shape for your tattoo. Seth did a good job choosing."

Making eye contact, Seth nods.

"You may feel some sharp pricks and even some localized pain," Marco explains. "It's a small tattoo so it will be quick, but there will still be pain. If it becomes too much—"

Looking into Seth's eyes, I think of him lying on the table in the ER with a knife impaled in his shoulder. I can do this. "It's fine. Really."

"Holly." Seth slides closer and wraps my hand tightly in his. "This can hurt. You don't have to be a hero. If you need a break, we take one."

Nodding, I smile at him and he smiles back. Without another word, Marco begins.

"You'll feel something wet and a little sticky," Marco tells me. "It's the stencil. I create all my designs freehand and then run them through the computer and create a stencil. Just to make sure my proportions and placement remain accurate."

As soon as he puts the needle to my skin, it feels like a small but sharp bee sting. "Oh, ow. That is prickly." Closing my eyes, I take deep breaths and soon, the pain normalizes.

"You're doing great, Holly."

Seth's deep voice makes me open my eyes, and I see he's smiling at me. We stay like this—looking into each other's eyes—for the next half hour or so.

"This next part can be a bit more painful," Marco explains. "It's the very top, and your hip bone is so pronounced you may feel this a bit more. Best thing to do is to keep taking slow, smooth breaths."

"Got it." Deepening my breathing, the pain suddenly becomes sharper and more severe. "Oh, ow, that does hurt more."

"I'm almost through. If you need to, take short breaths in and out—like Lamaze breathing."

Closing my eyes, I clench my jaw and take little breaths in and out of my mouth. Opening them and glancing at Seth with his brow furrowed and the worried look on his face, I have to suppress a giggle. Anyone walking by would think I'm in labor. He squeezes my hand so tight, it begins to hurt more than the needle.

"I'm okay, Seth." I squeeze his hand back. "The only thing I need is for you to lighten up your grip a bit."

"Oh, sorry."

When he releases my hand, a cold shiver runs up my spine.

Biting the corner of my lip, I close my eyes in a moment of pain and then open them and smile at Seth. "I didn't want you to let go."

Taking my hand again, he smiles at me and all I want to do is to climb off of this table and onto his lap. My mind is racing in a million different directions, but it finally settles on one semi-cohesive thought: *Dr. Holly Boling with a tattoo—who the hell are you? And where have you been all these years?* Sighing, I relax. In another couple minutes, it's done.

Standing, Seth releases me to go see Marco's work, and I miss the feeling of him holding my hand so much, I suddenly wish I were getting a full-body tattoo.

"Wow. It's beautiful." Seth nods to Marco.

With Seth standing there beside me, staring at my naked hip… it's maybe the sexiest thing I've ever experienced, and I squeeze my legs together in response.

As Marco explains my aftercare and tells me that he's going to wrap my hip in plastic wrap, Seth grabs a hand mirror hanging on a hook on a nearby wall and comes back to my chair.

"Ready?" he asks, standing next to me.

Nodding, I take a deep breath. "I think so."

As Seth positions the mirror so I can stay lying down and still see the tattoo, a million more thoughts race through my brain. *What was I thinking? How could I trust a man I don't know at all to pick something that will be burned into my flesh for the rest of my life?*

But looking into his eyes, once again my fear falls away and a sense of calm overtakes me.

"Yeah." Gathering my courage, I prop myself up on my elbow. "I'm ready." Glancing down at my hip, I see the simplest, most beautiful bird with her wings spread wide. Reaching down, I move to run my fingers over it.

"Not yet." Seth grabs my hand before I can touch it. "It needs to be covered for twenty-four hours."

Nodding, I'm so mesmerized I can't make a cohesive thought. Finally, I mumble, "A bird."

"A bird soaring with her wings spread wide," he adds. "She's free."

Nodding, I try to process this, but for the first time maybe ever, my brain fails me and instead, my emotions come pouring forth and tears spring into my eyes. As I look at Seth, a giant tear rolls down my cheek.

"Holly?" Leaving the mirror on the table next to my chair, he rushes up to me and takes my hand. "I'm sorry. You don't like it?"

Shaking my head, I fight back a sob. All of these pent-up emotions, everything I've been feeling for the past twenty-eight years, come pouring out of me in a flood of tears. "I couldn't have picked anything more perfect. Thank you, Seth."

"Holly, I don't want you to cry." The way he looks at me, his brows knit together—he wants to comfort me.

Nodding, I hold out one arm, and he moves forward and wraps his strong, protective arms around me, holding me tight in his embrace.

"Thank you, Seth," I mumble into his shoulder. "I love it."

He holds me even tighter as I take a deep breath, and on my exhale, I let about a billion pounds of stress go.

No, I don't know who this newly-tattooed woman is who drives a convertible and cries in the arms of Seth Hardy, the world's sexiest biker, but one thing is for sure—now that I've found her, I never want to let her go.

Burying my face in Seth's shoulder, I close my eyes tight and pray that he never wants to let me go either.

Chapter Six

Dynamite

Damn. Even the tequila didn't help drown my thoughts of her. Not that I had all that much to drink—I wanted to stay lucid for her tattoo—but still. It would be nice if the tequila could have taken off just the tiniest edge. Dropping my head, I let the warm water from the shower beat down on my still-tight neck muscles, and then I right my head. Glancing down, I catch a view of my raging hard-on. Fuck. It's not like I didn't know it was there—it's just, I don't know. I had expected it to calm down some as the days went by, but whenever I think of her—damn, there it is. Then tonight, seeing her lying on that chair with her scrubs tugged down low on her hips, getting a tattoo while I held her small but capable hand in mine… aw, fuck. Now my damned dick is standing out in front of me like a rock-hard divining rod that leads me in only one direction—her.

The thing is I haven't allowed myself even one moment of release, because every time I start handling myself and I think of her, it all seems kind of crass. It's just too tacky to think of a woman like her in this way.

But, damn. Tonight, after spending all that time with her, I may need to. Tonight, I just need a release.

Sighing, I take matters into my own hand, so to speak, and while I place one hand on the shower wall, I wrap the other around my thick shaft—just holding it for a moment as I close my eyes and allow my thoughts to be flooded with the memory of not just tonight, but that first night we met just about a month ago…

"Dr. Boling?" A short doctor in a white coat who was nervous as hell called to her as I laid on the exam table in the ER with a freaking knife stuck in my shoulder after my fight with Avery. Thankfully, after the fight, he and his girl, Seneca, raced to the hospital with me, and we've been square ever since. At least I hope we are.

Opening my eyes, I realize my rock-hard erection softens slightly when I'm thinking about anyone but her. Thank god. Maybe now it will just go away, because otherwise I may need some serious medical attention.

"Aw, fuck," I mumble through clenched teeth. *Medical* attention? Did I really have to think that?"

There it is again, harder and thicker than ever. Well, it leaves me no option. This time I have got to get a release. It's getting ridiculous.

Moving my hand slowly up and down my rod, I close my eyes again and think back to that first night we met. A lot of things were said around me that night—things like "vitals" and "shock" and "impaled." Impaled was the word that seemed to make the short male doctor pretty damned nervous.

At least I think it was the fact that I had a knife stuck in my shoulder, but to a guy as soft as that, everything about me—my cropped hair, my muscled body, my skin that is scarred, tough, and always looks dirty, even straight out of the shower, not to mention my tattoo—is probably damned intimidating.

"Dr. Boling?" he called to her again as he backed away from me lying on my table.

I was in so much freaking pain, I really would have rather he just yanked the damn thing out and got on with stitching me up. Of course, then I didn't know that Dr. Boling was a "she," and that she was a freaking gorgeous one, too.

"Yes?" She came as far as the door, and then she stalled to look over my intake papers that were on a clipboard and placed in the vertical wall rack near the door. Christ. I'd never seen a woman as beautiful and confident, and she appeared so smart. She placed the clipboard back, moved to a computer, and looked over my chart. Then, she turned to me and crossed her arms over her chest. Just from the way she cocked her eyebrow when she looked at me, I knew this was a woman who wouldn't put up with any bullshit.

Walking farther into the room, she stopped next to my bed, where I was lying back at a forty-five-degree reclining position. Even though she was working and probably had been all day, when she came up near me, I was overcome by the faint scent of flowers.

"Huh." She stood there, scowling at my shoulder with the knife sticking out, but if she was grossed out, she sure didn't show it.

Who knows, a knife in my shoulder may have been a big deal to me, but to her, maybe it was nothing.

Going to a mounted box on the wall, she pulled out a pair of white gloves and slipped them on. Then, walking up and stopping close to me, she inspected the injury. With a light but firm touch, she pressed the area around the knife wound. It didn't hurt any more than the wound already did—it was kind of like she was relieving the pressure.

"All right." With a serious tone, she looked me straight in the eye. "I'm Dr. Holly Boling. Can you tell me your name?"

"Seth. Hardy." It hurt like a mother to even speak, but I did what she asked.

"Good. Do you know the day of the week?"

"Friday."

"Okay." Pulling something that looked like a pen from her breast pocket, she used it to flash a light in my eyes like I'd seen done on television. Then she paused, and looking down at my tattoo on my outer left arm, took a deep breath. "What does it mean?" she asked quietly.

"The tattoo?"

"Yes."

"It's the Chinese character for strength." The way my jaw was clamped tight from pain made me speak through gritted teeth, but I really, really wanted to answer her.

Nodding, she cleared her throat and stiffened. "Mr. Hardy, I'm going to give you a course of antibiotics through an IV."

Out of nowhere, a young nurse with pink hair materialized and set to work on my right arm. She cleaned the inner elbow and then she tried poking a good-sized IV needle into my arm, but my skin wouldn't give. Screwing up her face, she tried again, but still nothing.

"Doctor?" the nurse spoke quietly. "His skin is tough. I can't pierce it."

Turning my head back to Dr. Boling, she made eye contact again before looking away, and then she walked to my right side and stood next to the nurse. Pressing against my veins with a gloved finger, Dr. Boling glanced up at me. "Tough skin. Why am I not surprised?" Giving me a small smile, she took the needle from the nurse and then spoke directly to me. "This is called an IV cannula. It's a small, flexible tube made of plastic that I'm going to insert into your vein so you can get an antibiotic."

Looking at her just in time, I caught her expression as she leaned down closer to my arm. After the nurse cleaned the area again, Dr. Holly's face tightened, and she grimaced slightly as a look of determination flooded her soft features. With a strong push, she managed to get the needle—or the IV cannula, or whatever the hell it was—into my arm.

"There." She stood up and patted my uninjured shoulder. "This will start making you feel better. Any idea when your last tetanus shot was?"

"Never had one."

Nodding, she instructed the nurse to get the shot. "I didn't see it on the chart, but my colleague already administered a painkiller?"

"He said no." Dr. Morton, the short doctor, finally chimed in.

"No. No painkillers," I reiterated.

Dr. Holly took the shot from the nurse and turned to the short doctor. "Give me a moment with Mr. Hardy, please. Just wait outside; I'll need you both in a minute."

The short doctor pushed his way past the tiny nurse to be the first out the door. Creep. I don't care who you are or where you are in the world—a woman always goes first. Call me old-fashioned, but a woman is made to be protected and respected.

If I hadn't been in so much freaking pain, I would have explained that to him.

"Mr. Hardy." Still holding the shot, Dr. Holly stepped up closer to my bed.

"Seth, please."

"All right, Seth. I can tell by the sweat on your forehead and the way you clench your teeth when you speak that you're in considerable pain. But when I looked over your intake papers, there was no record of habitual alcohol or drug use. No addictions. This is not the time to lie, Seth."

"I'm not a liar," I snapped at her, louder than I meant.

Her eyes widened, but she didn't back away. "I wasn't calling you a liar. I said this is not the time to lie. There's a difference."

Nodding, I agreed. It was true. I'd just never come across anyone else who thought the way I did.

Tilting her head, she smiled. "When my mother asks me if I've stopped biting my nails, I tell her I have. Even though…" She held up her gloved hand. "Well, you can't see them through the glove, but trust me, I haven't. I've stopped for the moment. It's not a lie. So, I need to know why you're not taking painkillers, as I'm about to pull an impaled knife out of your shoulder."

"Fine." Staring up at the ceiling, I answered her. "I did this to myself. I need to feel the pain so I don't do it again."

"Okay."

Rolling my head toward her, I furrowed my brow. "That's it?"

"If you tell me that's how it is, that's how it is. I don't lie either, and I recognize the trait in you. But I'm required to ask, was this some kind of illegal activity? Gang violence?"

Shaking my head, I sigh. "No gang. I'm part of the Steel Knights motorcycle club. But we're not a gang, and we're not an outlaw club. I fought with one of my brothers. I can act… impulsively sometimes. I pulled a knife, and thank god I was the only one who was hurt."

Standing there, she took a deep breath and then shook her head. "No, you weren't."

Fighting against my tight neck muscles, I craned my head to look her in the eye. "What do you mean?"

Cleaning my upper right arm with an alcohol pad, she prepped me for the tetanus shot by squeezing my skin between her fingers. I could tell she had a hard time grabbing anything but muscle.

"You may be the only one who has a physical injury, but the people who love you also suffer when you're hurt." Her words were soft, and I knew they were laden with something, but what? Stabbing me with the needle, she injected my tetanus shot.

"All right." Walking to the door, she let in the other doctor and the nurse as she tossed the syringe. "The first thing we're going to do is clean the wound, and then we'll remove the object. Mr. Hardy, we're going to sit you up now."

So, we were back to Mr. Hardy. Guess it made sense when the other doctor and nurse are around. Besides, I kind of liked how she called me Seth in private.

She and the short doctor each reached behind me and lifted gently to help me to a sitting position. Hell no. I'm not one to physically rely on a woman, but it wasn't time for me to argue, and I could barely think straight. Between the freaking knife lodged in my shoulder and being this close to Dr. Holly…

The short doctor held a tan, U-shaped bin under my shoulder as Dr. Boling poured some warm liquid around the wound. She spoke as she worked.

"My guess is that you have gotten very lucky and this knife has missed the major arteries in the shoulder. However, we can't take a chance. I'm going to prep you for surgery just in case."

Suddenly, she started barking orders as the short doctor and nurse buzzed around the room. New IV bags were added and hung, and all kinds of sterilized instruments were placed out on a table next to me. "Normally, surgery would mean moving you—but we have an unusually busy night tonight. So…" Examining my shoulder, she had a very serious look on her face. "In evaluating the direction and track of the object to see how best to remove it, it looks like a clean wound and the placement—although deep and impaled with a great deal of force—" She glanced at me and then back to my wound. "It looks like it may have missed the major arteries."

"That's good, right?" I chuckle.

"That's exceptionally good, Mr. Hardy. If this had impaled an artery, the amount of blood loss would be life-threatening. In addition, we could be talking about loss of range of motion and even paralysis." Placing her hand on my arm, she moved a finger high onto my shoulder. "This is one of the three major arteries, the 'subclavian artery'. Thankfully, we're nowhere near that. We're also clear of the 'brachial artery' that's located lower down. Here."

She placed a finger on an area low in my shoulder, and her touch sent a shiver through me.

"The only major artery of concern is the 'axillary artery'." She nodded for the short doctor to come closer. "I think we're clear with this, too, but we need to pull it directly out because there is concern that we could nick the thoracoacromial artery when the knife is removed." Turning to the short doctor, she added, "Be ready for me to suture immediately."

Swallowing hard, she placed both hands on the knife. Turning to the short doctor, she nodded to the wound. "I want constant pressure around the area as I remove the knife, and then immediate pressure on the wound to control the bleeding."

When she glanced up at me, I noticed a fine layer of perspiration over her top lip.

"Do you want something to bite down on, Mr. Hardy? It sounds primitive, but it helps."

"No. Thanks." Taking a deep breath, I looked at the black dots on the white ceiling tiles.

"Okay," she told me. "Keep looking at the ceiling, and under no circumstance are you to look at the knife removal. Understood?"

"Yeah." Swallowing hard, I ready myself. No worries about me watching; it wasn't like I wanted to see the freaking thing getting pulled from my body.

"I know this is counterintuitive, but do your best to keep your muscles relaxed as I remove the object." As she spoke, she injected the area around the wound with something. "No painkiller is one thing, but I need to numb the area. Everything now hinges on how cleanly I can remove this. The stiller you remain, the cleaner my removal. The numbing will keep you from making a jerking movement when I pull."

Almost immediately, the tight muscles on the left side of my neck relaxed and my shoulder slumped.

Without another word, the short doctor pushed back against the skin around the wound, which didn't feel half as good as when she did it, and Dr. Holly, with that incredibly serious look on her face, started to pull. Within a few seconds, the knife was clear out of my shoulder, and she dropped it into that tan basin. It landed with a dull plink.

Pressing a piece of gauze hard against the area, her stern expression relaxed. "Good news, Mr. Hardy. As I had hoped and expected, the knife missed the major arteries. Once I close you up, you'll be good as new."

Stepping closer to me, she began to stitch me up. "You do have tough skin." She glanced at me, and then looked back at the wound. "Sometimes, I wish my skin were a little tougher," she mumbled so quietly I think it was meant for only me to hear.

Damn, how I wanted to know what she meant by that, but it wasn't the time or place. That was a question for when the two of us were alone. But when would that ever be?

How could that ever be?

"So, did they have trouble tattooing you?" Her bottom lip wavered as she spoke.

"Nah. I've got a guy. He's good."

Nodding, she finished stitching me and began wrapping long strips of gauze around my shoulder. "That is really nice. The tattoo. The symbol itself is beautifully done, but the circle it sits in—the detail, all those patterns—it's exquisite."

"Well, if you're ever looking for a tattoo, let me know. I can hook you up."

Hook you up? Fuck.

Her eyes flashed with something when she looked at me. A hunger I couldn't place. It didn't belong in the eyes of a woman like her—a woman so perfect.

And it was a look that stirred something deep inside of me…

"I'll keep that in mind. Thank you."

We made eye contact again, and she held my gaze longer than she should have. Clearing her throat, she turned to the short doctor and nurse. "Dr. Morton, we're all set."

"Thank you, Dr. Boling. I, uh… wasn't sure. Well, thank you."

"It's okay." She nodded to him. "Would you please take the next case? I'm going to go speak to the group Mr. Hardy brought in with him." She smiled at me. "There's an older man. Before I came in here, I was told he keeps asking about you at the front desk. Is he your dad?"

"Nah. I don't have a dad."

"I'm sorry." The way her eyebrows squeezed together, she looked genuinely saddened.

"That guy you're talking about—Nick—he's the president of the club. He's like a dad to all of us."

Nodding, she turned to the nurse and added, "Please get Mr. Hardy fitted with a sling."

"Wait, wait. A sling?" I had to ask.

"You've got to keep the area immobilized for a day or two until the swelling goes down, and then it's important to move it. But you've got to take it easy for a while. I'm also going to prescribe a course of antibiotics, so no drinking for ten days. Is your job physical?"

"No, I'm a numbers guy. I run the books for the Steel Knights."

"Huh."

That was all she said, making me wonder, still now, what that "Huh" meant.

"We're working on a new construction project," I added. "A new clubhouse." God knows why I kept blabbing around this woman, but one thing was for sure, it didn't hurt to speak nearly as much now that the knife was out and the area was numbed.

"Where's the current clubhouse?"

"Hoppa's Taphouse. You ever been?" I still cringe at the stupidity of that question. Why would a woman like Dr. Holly Boling hang in a place like Hoppa's Taphouse? She's not exactly the type to play darts or shoot pool while she chugs domestic beer and hangs with a bunch of bikers. This is a chardonnay-at-the-country-club type of woman.

For some reason I couldn't and *can't* explain, that realization makes me… unhappy.

"No." Shaking her head, she smiled sweetly. "I've never been. I don't get out much."

"Well, if you ever do get some time off and want a tour, let me know. I'm there most days. And nights."

"Okay, I will. Thanks."

Nodding again, she lowered her chin and glanced up at me with her giant brown eyes before leaving to go get my group.

The way she looked at me—sweetly, innocently, with those beautiful eyes…

That was then, about a month ago, on the night we met. Tonight, my attraction to her went past the physical. Now that I know she's vulnerable and real, I want her even more. Something stirred deep inside me—in a place no one has ever accessed—and it riled my protective instinct. I don't just want her, I want to protect her as well.

She is so beautiful and smart…

I grasp my rod tighter and begin to stroke up and down, jerking in strong, swift motions, but suddenly, I stop.

I can't do this.

Again.

I cannot relieve myself at home in my own damned shower, because *again*, I feel like she's worth so much more than that.

I don't want to taint the memory of this incredible woman with something as base as jerking off.

Christ. What the hell is happening to me? Even though tonight was amazing, we still left it awkwardly. There was no talk of getting together again, and this may have been the last time I'm ever going to see her. So, that means I'm going to have to spend my life drowning my hard-on in a freezing cold shower, because when I tried to replace her with someone else, I couldn't get away fast enough.

Aw, damn it.

Dropping my hold on my rod, I reach out and turn the shower all the way to cold.

"Oh, fuck!" Slamming my fist against the shower wall, I stay as long as I can with the cold water splashing down over my rod, and then I stay longer still as the freezing water cools me off, giving me some reprieve from my aching hard-on…

But it does nothing for my thoughts.

If only there was something—anything—I could do to stop thinking about Dr. Holly Boling, even for one minute.

Turning off the shower, I shake my head to get the water out of my hair, and then grabbing my towel, I wrap it around my waist and step out onto the cold tile floor. After toweling off, I walk to my bed and plop down onto my back, staring at the ceiling fan spinning overhead. I know how that fan feels, going around and around in circles and never getting anywhere.

Enough. Covering my face with my hands, I decide what I'm going to do. I'm going to head to the clubhouse early tomorrow and get to work finalizing the plans for the build—including the new bunker Nick wants included—before Monday and my meeting with the construction company. Then, I'm going to find Colt and take him out for lunch to get some bonding time in. I am going to bury my thoughts in work and bonding with my brother because one thing is for sure: I cannot waste one more second thinking about Dr. Holly Boling.

Because the sad truth is after tonight, her one night of breaking all the rules, she'll go back to her life of saving lives with *Robert* and dinners at the country club with her parents, and she'll probably never think of me again.

Chapter Seven

Holly

"Oh, my gosh." Standing in my bedroom in front of my full-length mirror in a pair of panties and a T-shirt, I stare at my reflection and my new tattoo. I have been waiting all day to see it without the wrap on. To keep my mind off of it and Robert's incessant texts, I volunteered for a double-shift at the soup kitchen where I work every Sunday. Every time I step into that soup kitchen, I'm reminded how desperately these people need healthcare, and how important it is to offer them free, accessible care in the outskirts of Phoenix. That's why I have to get my clinic going.

Looking myself in the eyes, I nod. "Here goes." It's been twenty-four hours, so I peel off the plastic wrap and run a finger over the skin. It's smooth and looks… amazing. It's a solid silhouette of a bird in flight, and it's so elegant but freeing. I need to wash the area with soap and water to keep it clean and healthy, but first, I take a moment to just look at it. I can't believe it. I have wanted a tattoo since I was twelve years old. "I have a tattoo." Covering my mouth with my hand, I stifle a chuckle. "Oh, my gosh, I have a tattoo!"

Grabbing a hairbrush off of my vanity, I turn to my smart speaker. "Play hits from the sixties, please."

As soon as the beat of the first song starts, I begin singing along—loudly—using my hairbrush as a microphone. "Hey, where did we go? Days when the rain came—" Shaking my head and lifting my hands, I do one of my old routines from high school cheer. Amazingly, I remember it. "Woo!" Tossing my hands up in the air when the routine finishes, I shake my brush like it's a pom-pom. "Damn, I used to love cheering."

Dancing around more, I cross to the mirror and shake my hips, watching the bird that looks like it's taking flight whenever I lift my hip. "In the misty morning fog with you—"

Then, Van Morrison blares, "—my brown-eyed girl." My body freezes. How could I forget? My father used to play that for me all the time when I was little, back when George was still alive. George was just an infant, but whenever that song played, my father would pick me up in his arms and as we danced, George would laugh and gurgle.

Plopping down onto the edge of my bed, I slump forward. "What the hell am I doing?" Tossing my hairbrush onto the vanity, it lands with a thud. "I owe them more than this. All three of them."

Staring at my reflection again, my heartbeat starts thumping in my ears. "Oh." Holding my stomach, my world feels like it's turning upside down. "No, no, no…" Glancing at my nightstand and my prescription of benzodiazepine tranquilizers, I take a deep breath. "They're there if you need them," I tell myself, drawing my feet up onto the bed and rocking myself. The thing is, I don't want to take them. All they do is dull everything and make me fall asleep. I don't want to live my life in a fog. Not when I've just finally started living it.

"Stop," I command my smart speaker, and it cuts off, leaving me in suffocating silence.

As I sit here holding myself, the walls begin closing in on me. "Shit." Lifting my head, I squeeze my eyes shut as fear washes over me. It's like a million prickly thorns are attacking me all at once, and it feels like my body is upside down. Holding my head, looking for something to ground me, I go through my mantra that I use whenever the anxiety gets to be too much. "I will not have an aneurysm. I will not have a stroke. I will not die. I can breathe. I am strong and healthy. If I do die, they will be okay. They are not my responsibility. I am okay. I am not alone." It's always this last one that's the hardest to believe.

Taking deep breaths in and out through my nose, I press my thumb and the tip of my middle finger together in a mudra, the way my yoga teacher taught me. Of course, I couldn't tell her that I needed something for anxiety—who wants their doctor, or *surgeon*, to have panic attacks? So, without mentioning why I needed it, she taught me this mudra to bring a feeling of stability. After a few more deep breaths, I'm calmer.

Reaching around, I feel for my tattoo, and although I was raised to believe everything about getting a tattoo is completely wrong, it also calms me. "How can anything that feels so right be bad for me?" I mumble as I sit hunched over into myself.

Lifting my head, I catch my reflection. I look tired, but despite the memory of George and the thoughts of my parents, I look happy. That's because, for the first time in a very long time, I am happy.

Blink! Another text comes in. Crud. It's either my mother asking again why I didn't make it to dinner at the country club last night, or it's Robert again. Standing, I make my way to my vanity and glance at the text. It's Robert. Again.

Hey, kid! You and me. Catalina Island. 52-ft Beneteau sailboat. Next weekend. Bring a bikini.

"Screw you, Robert. I don't even like to sail!" Anger churns up from my core, battling the anxiety, and suddenly, I can't sit still.

"I don't even like sailing, Robert," I mumble, tossing the phone onto the bed. Closing my eyes, I take another deep breath. With every inhale and exhale, I calm my sympathetic nervous system and find a greater feeling of peace.

"Screw this." Standing, I know what I have to do and who I need to see. Stripping out of the remainder of my clothes, I rush to my bathroom and hop into my shower, carefully washing the tattoo. So what if I'm making an appearance at Hoppa's Taphouse two times in two days? The worst he can say is no. Besides, I owe him a thank you for yesterday.

No, asking him, Seth Hardy, out on a date may not be something the old Holly would do, but it is something *new* Holly would. Besides, Seth Hardy is the only person who seems to understand this new version of me—and he likes me for it.

"What the hell?" Driving into the parking lot of Hoppa's Taphouse, I glance at a large group of men, many wearing their Steel Knights jackets, standing outside the bar. Even from here, I can tell from his stance and build that one is definitely Seth. He's standing next to a couple of other men I recognize from the hospital that first night we met. One is sweet, kind Nick. He's just fun to be around, and just looking at him brings a smile to my face. Two of the other men I recognize as well—Bullet and Bullseye, I think they were nicknamed.

Gripping my steering wheel tighter, I freeze for a moment. "If Seth is nicknamed Dynamite because of his outbursts, then why they hell are these guys named Bullet and Bullseye?" I mumble.

I know I should be scared of this world and these men, but I'm not. It's like I have this inner pull bringing me closer to them rather than pushing me away.

Thanks to the packed parking lot, no one has noticed my car yet. Although I've been enjoying the heck out of my convertible, right now I'm happy I decided the night was chilly and it was best to keep the top closed. It offers me some protection. Still with my gaze glued to Seth, my attention is pulled away for a moment by four other men, all wearing jackets with dogs in broken chains on them. I recognize the emblem from that night in the hospital—they're the Unchained Dogs—and from what I understand, they are the rival group of the Steel Knights. I'm too far to see exactly what's happening, but there seems to be animosity between the men. More and more members of the Steel Knights come out of the bar, including one who is tinier than the rest—the woman, Seneca. I remember being here the night she left and how worried Bullseye was. It's good she's back.

After glancing behind him, Seth steps up closer to the Dogs. He hasn't thrown a punch, and I can't hear what he's saying, but damn, he is sexy. The way he carries himself with his broad shoulders and his powerful presence—he is all male.

Sitting here, on the opposite side of the parking lot, tucked in shadows, I let myself get caught up in Seth's strength and masculinity, and I grow warm in my loose jeans and T-shirt.

No, I don't condone violence in any form—most people don't understand the true damage they do to their bodies when they take a punch or a hit—but Seth is not fighting. It seems he's able to settle whatever is happening with these men with his words.

Then, a young man who's the spitting image of Seth, although a little smaller in size, steps up next to him. Squinting, I recognize him. It's Seth's brother, Colt. He was the man I saw last night. The one who left with the woman who had been hanging on Seth—

Suddenly, Colt steps forward and pushes one of the men wearing a Dogs jacket. Before any of the men can retaliate, Seth throws his arm in front of his brother, protecting him.

"Oh." Gasping a little, I'm caught by how protective and paternal Seth appears. No, Colt is not his kid, but what would Seth be like as a father? "Oh, my gosh, Holly!" I snap at myself.

"You pulled a knife out of the man's shoulder and then he took you to get a tattoo—maybe not father material." And besides that, Seth may not even want kids. If he does, he may not want them with me. "Get a grip," I mumble.

In the middle of me beating myself up, a fight breaks out. One of the Dogs punches Colt, and soon it's a mess of men-on-men. Tilting my head back and forth, I strain to keep an eye on Seth, but the rest of the Knights who aren't fighting begin to form a circle around the fight, and it's harder to see. In one corner, I catch Seneca straddling a man—she punches him in the face.

"Oh, ow." Sinking down into my seat, I know I should run. I shouldn't want to be around this—all this violence and mayhem—and yet, I can't pull myself away. Glimpsing Seth again, I exhale when he appears unharmed. Damn, remembering that night in the ER when he refused painkillers—it's like the man is superhuman.

I should be so turned off by this, but instead, it's having the exact opposite effect. Yes, I'm watching for any serious injuries that may need my attention, but in the meantime, my nipples are hardening and poking through my shirt. With every punch Seth throws, I watch his strong legs bear down into the earth while his wide shoulders keep him balanced, and all I can think about is what it felt like when he had his arms wrapped around me.

Watching him defend his turf, I wonder how he would defend me…

Cripes. Why the hell am I thinking like this?

Closing my eyes for a moment, I imagine Seth here, sitting next to me, reaching across my front seat and sliding his powerful hand behind my head as he pulls me closer and his strong lips find mine—

Opening my eyes, I catch a glimpse of Seth just as he rushes forward and knocks a knife out of one of the Dogs' hands. Exhaling with relief, I relax slightly until I see another Dog reach into his jacket and pull out another knife.

"No, no, no!"

Sitting up tall in my seat, all I can do is watch as the man lunges at Colt and slices him on the upper arm across his deltoid. Since Colt's not wearing anything but a T-shirt, he has no protection, and he drops down to his knees and then to a seated position. Even from here, I can see he's hemorrhaging from his injury. Seth is at his side, holding his hand against the cut. He must be trying to contain the bleeding.

"Oh, fuck." Jumping out of my car, I rush to the trunk and grab my doctor's kit and a blanket. Running, I slide on gloves as I cross the parking lot and come up onto the group of men who are all standing around, staring.

"Holly?" Seth looks up at me with disbelief in his eyes.

"What the hell is it with you Hardy men and knives?" Kneeling down next to Seth, I give him a small smile.

"You shouldn't be here."

"I'll be fine," I say, as I wrap the thin blanket around Colt's arm to try to contain the bleeding.

"These guys mean business, Holly."

Looking him in the eye, I explain. "I took an oath, Seth. I can't just witness someone get injured and not help." In my gut, I know I'm fine. There's no way that Seth or any of the other Knights will let anything happen to me. Especially not while I'm fixing one of their own.

"Okay." Standing, Seth goes toe-to-toe with the four men in Dogs jackets. "It's time for you to go. You heard our answer. This is through." He punctuates his last word with a growl that makes them back away, while my insides turn to jelly.

"Doc." It's Nick. "Boy, are you in the right place at the right time."

Glancing up, I see the Dogs staring hard at me—like they're memorizing my face. It's completely unnerving, but I can't pay attention; I have a job to focus on. Suddenly, one Dog slaps another on the shoulder and nods toward Seth. Turning quickly, they take off. I don't know what any of that meant, but—did Seth scare them off?

As the Dogs leave, I compose myself and, taking a deep breath, I glance up at Nick and smile. "I hope so, Nick."

Directing my attention to Colt, I nod. "I'm Dr. Holly Boling. I'm a cardiothoracic surgeon and an ER doctor. I'm a friend of your brother's. I treated him when he was injured about a month ago. You're lucid, so you need to give me a verbal okay to treat you outside of a sterile environment."

"Do it, Colt." Seth prods his brother.

"Listen to the doc," Nick adds. "She knows stuff."

Colt nods.

"If you can speak, Colt," I explain, "I need you to say yes to my question. Do you want me to treat you?"

"Y-yes."

Snapping my head around, I look at one of the men in a Knights jacket who's wearing a cowboy hat. "Go get towels," I command.

He scurries off as I remove the blanket from Colt's arm.

"What you have is a laceration." I smile at Colt. "You're lucky. Your brother had a puncture—those are riskier."

"Yeah, he always one-ups me," Colt murmurs.

Furrowing my brow, I look at Seth to see if he caught that and wonder what it could possibly mean. It didn't sound like Colt was teasing. Maybe there's some animosity between the brothers?

The man with the cowboy hat comes back and hands me a stack of clean towels. "Here ya go, doc."

Nick takes them from the man and holds them for me.

Thanking them both, I turn my attention back to the injury and explain my process as I work, pressing towels against the cut. The way I'm situated, wedged next to his injured arm, his blood seeps onto my shirt and jeans. "Again, luckily, the laceration isn't deeper than a half inch and—" Removing a towel, I look at the wound. "—the bleeding seems to be lessening with pressure, so I think I'll be able to take care of you here." Nodding to my bag, I turn to Seth. "Can you please grab the large brown bottle?"

He hands it to me, and I flip open the top. "This is sterile water," I tell Colt as I begin cleaning his wound. Nodding to Seth again, I point to the bag. "Now, the antiseptic. It's in a long white tube."

Our hands touch briefly as Seth hands me the tube, and I look up at him, making eye contact.

Clearing my throat, I continue. "Colt, the laceration is mostly cleaned, so now I'm applying antiseptic ointment. Then, since the bleeding has slowed enough, I'm going to wipe down the immediate cut and use something that's like a medical-grade skin glue to suture it closed." Leaning closer to Colt's arm, I feel all eyes on me as I wipe down the wound and then suture it closed. Applying butterfly bandages, I explain, "These will keep the pressure off of the wound." Grabbing gauze from the bag, I apply it over the laceration and tape it in place with medical tape.

The whole time, I feel Seth's gaze on me, and I grow warm in my belly.

"Without a puncture, you won't need a tetanus shot, but you will need to follow up with your own doctor next week."

"Okay. Thank you, doctor."

Sitting back on my heels, I exhale. "You're probably cold." Turning to Nick, I give directions. "We need to get him wrapped up and keep him warm."

"Aye, aye, doc." Nick salutes me.

Smiling, I turn to Colt. "You need to keep an eye on this. I think the ointment will take care of any possibility of infection, but if it feels warm to the touch or sore, or if redness develops around the wound, it means there's an infection and you need antibiotics right away."

"Thank you, doctor."

Smiling at Colt, I get caught up in how much he looks like Seth. He's younger and sweeter looking, but they have the same eyes and strong chin. "Call me Holly, please."

As he nods, Nick claps his hands together. "How about we buy the good doctor a beer?"

As I stand, I get a round of applause from the men, who cheer for me. Laughing, I get caught up in the moment. I save lives nearly every night of my life, and no one so much as says, "Good job." These men are ready to throw me a parade for fixing little more than a scratch. A warm feeling builds inside me.

Turning around, I look for Seth. I glimpse him standing just outside the group of men with his chin dropped down and his hands tense at his sides.

"Seth?" The warm feeling in my tummy turns to lead. "What's wrong? Seth?"

Glancing over at Bullet, I see him motion to Seth and raise his eyebrows. Avery nods in response. Then, the two men walk by Nick and slap him on the shoulder.

"Come on," Avery says.

"Well, uh, doc." Nick smiles at me as the Knights begin to walk off. "Thanks again. I hope you'll come by soon for that thank-you beer. Come on, boys."

Nick leads the entire club inside the bar, leaving me alone with Seth. It's like they all speak this secret "man language" that I don't understand. What is happening here?

"Seth?" My heart is thumping so hard I can feel it in my head. "What's the matter? You seem—"

Before I can finish my sentence, Seth steps up to me, and lifting one strong, powerful hand, he reaches out and slips it behind my neck, weaving his fingers into my hair. With the gentlest tug, he holds my head still and looks deep into my eyes.

My knees grow weak and my eyelids become heavy. Looking deep into his eyes, I realize what's happened here tonight.

I have just been claimed by Seth Hardy.

Chapter Eight

Dynamite

It's time.

Walking to Holly, I take her hand in mine. She's wearing only a V-neck T-shirt that's covered in Colt's blood—she must be cold. The tiny hairs on her arms bristle, and goosebumps cover her exposed flesh. Sliding out of my jacket, I drape it around her shoulders. Although she's tall, the jacket hangs down low in the back, coming almost halfway down the backs of her thighs.

"Seth, I don't want to get blood on it."

"No." Shaking my head, I whisper, "Wear it. It'll keep you warm."

Nodding, she holds the jacket closed at her neck as I pick up her doctor bag and, slipping the strap over my shoulder, I walk her to her car. Glimpsing me out of the corner of her eye, I can tell she's wondering what I'm doing, but the energy that's passing between us is tangible.

She knows as well as I do. It's time.

Tonight, all of the doubts and worries that normally hold me hostage in the darkest of times—the feelings of insignificance, my concerns about being impulsive and letting down those I love the most—just fade away. No, I'm not good enough for her, and no, there can't be anything long term between this country club goddess and me—but we can have tonight. Turning to her, she gives me a tentative smile. Nodding, I walk her to the passenger's side of the car.

Stalling by the door, I whisper, "Let me have your keys."

Nodding, she digs into the pocket of her jeans and pulls out the fob, handing it to me. I unlock the car and open her door. Climbing in, she glances up at me as I close the door behind her. It feels so right to have her tucked inside a car... heading to my place.

Walking around the back of the car, I drop her bag into the trunk and then, coming to the driver's door, I climb in. Without a word, I start the engine and pull out of the parking lot of Hoppa's Taphouse. Yeah, tomorrow will be a busy day squaring away the build of the new clubhouse, but we're ready. Okay, the recent alterations by Nick might throw a monkey wrench into everything, but I'll worry about that then.

Tonight is only about Holly.

We drive for about fifteen minutes in complete silence, and the only sounds we hear are the humming of the car's engine and our breathing. As we come up to the outskirts of Hoppa, she glances out of her window and leans forward, looking at the sign that points to Phoenix in the opposite direction. Turning to me, her eyes flash with hunger.

"If you'd rather go home, just tell me."

Shaking her head, she bites the corner of her lip. "No. I don't want to go home." Settling back into the seat, she sighs, and I know she's made her decision. "I don't think I want to go home—ever." Her words are just a mumble, but she's said them.

Driving down the highway in silence, I can hear her breathing growing faster. Glancing at her, her chest rises and falls with her hurried breath. Letting my gaze drop just for a moment, I glimpse her hard nipples poking through her shirt. Damn.

Quickly, I force my eyes back on the road.

Not slowing until we near my building, I catch her looking around the neighborhood—will this be the thing that makes her see how different we really are? Will she decide that this is all too much—or too little—for her? She doesn't say a word as we turn into the lot and glide into a spot.

Turning off the engine, I sit for a moment, staring out the window. Yeah, it may only be for one night, but I will do everything in my power to make it one night she won't soon forget.

Hurrying to her door, I open it. Taking her by the hand, I lead her across the lot, down my path, and to the front door of my apartment building. Unlocking the door, I wait as she waltzes past me. Despite being drenched in my brother's blood, she still smells like flowers.

Stepping inside after her, I take her hand and lead her up the stairway. By the time we reach my apartment door, our breathing is audible.

Sliding the key into my lock, she watches as I unlock the door and push it open. Stepping into the dim light of the apartment, she squeezes my hand.

Closing the door behind her, I turn and back her against the door, cocooning her in the space before me. Stepping even closer to her, I gaze into her beautiful eyes.

"Are you hungry?"

"No." She shakes her head.

"How about a drink?"

"What do you have?"

"Only beer. If I had known you'd be here tonight, I would have picked up wine."

"Beer is perfect, thank you." She smiles.

"Yeah?"

"Yes." Glancing down at the ground between us, she raises her eyes back up to meet mine. "Um, would you mind if I took a shower?"

"Mind? Of course not. I'm sorry I didn't think of it." Of course, I thought of it. Holly, naked in my shower is *all* I've been thinking about. God knows I don't need any more of a nudge around her. "Come on."

Taking her by the hand, I lead her from my minimalist kitchen, through my sparse living room, down the hallway, and to the master bedroom.

Holding out my hand, she walks before me and then turns back and raises an eyebrow as she stalls outside my bedroom. Right now, I'm incredibly happy that I'm pretty clean by nature and that my bed is made up with a decent cover and there are fresh sheets on the bed.

"I, uh, the bathroom is bigger and nicer in the master bedroom," I explain.

Nodding, she walks into my bedroom. When I see her standing there, it's all I can do not to pick her up, toss her onto the bed, and claim her once and for all.

"I'll get you towels—" Doubling back to the linen closet in the hallway, I grab a couple of my softest towels and bring them to her.

"Thanks." Taking them from me, she smiles. "Um, you wouldn't happen to have anything I could wear, would you? An old T-shirt? Sweats?"

"Yeah, of course." Damn. The thought of her wearing one of my shirts and nothing underneath is giving me a raging hard-on. I am so freaking grateful that my dresser is on the opposite side of the room to give me some space. Turning my back to her as I rummage through my drawers, I do a quick adjustment, but nothing helps. Shit. Thankfully, the light in here is dim, so when I turn back toward her, I have some kind of camouflage. Walking past her, I place the clothes on the counter near the sink in the bathroom. Turning back, I find her standing close to me. Really, really close.

"I, uh…" Putting a fist to my mouth, I clear my throat. "It's all yours."

"Thank you." As she passes by me, she reaches out with her finger and runs it from my wrist to my fingertip. Her touch is light and it happens so quickly it would be almost imperceptible if it wasn't for the shiver it gives me running straight up my spine.

"I'm sorry about what happened to your clothes." I have to say something to break the tension.

"It's okay." Smiling, she shrugs. "An occupational hazard, right?"

"Right."

Stalling, neither of us moves.

"Well, uh, I'll just be a second."

"Sure, right. Please, take your time. The shower has good water pressure."

"Okay. Thanks."

Good water pressure? As soon as she goes into the bathroom and turns on the shower, I rush to the kitchen to get as much space and distance between us as possible. Doing anything I can to keep my mind off of the naked goddess in the room next to me, I busy myself by answering emails and returning texts, but nothing helps. Tonight, like every night of my life since I've met her, I can't help but think about Dr. Holly Boling.

And right now, I'm thinking about her in my shower…

Damn. I was not anticipating this surprise visit, and I am freaking grateful that I cleaned the place this morning before grabbing lunch with Colt.

Colt. What was up with him tonight? When Holly told him about my injury, he murmured something about me one-upping him. But the weird part is he didn't sound like he was kidding. What the fuck is going on there? We had an okay lunch today—I took him to that place outside of Hoppa with the really good barbeque and he seemed happy, so what was all that about?

Turning so I'm leaning against the counter, I cross my arms, replaying our lunchtime conversation. Sure, we talked about our aunt who raised Colt when I went away for those years, but he didn't seem to hold a grudge against me for abandoning him when I went to juvie. No, I can't go back and change what happened then, but I can try my best now.

Standing up straight, I'm certain I heard the water turn off. Shit. How the hell am I going to keep it together?

Beer. We need beer. That'll cool me down. Opening the fridge, I grab two bottles of beer, glad that I have a backup sixpack.

Rummaging through the drawers of my refrigerator, I look for anything I can offer her, but all I turn up are some old carrots and leftover Chinese food. Crap. I haven't been food shopping in forever, and if I knew she was going to be here tonight—well, hell, I would have had the night catered. Fuck. Abandoning the fridge, I plow through my cabinets, but the best I can come up with are a couple of boxes of cheap chocolate cakes. One box falls from the cabinet, but I catch it just before it lands.

"Are those Ring Dings?"

Whipping around, I nearly drop the box, but juggling it, I grab it and hold on. "Uh, yeah. I was seeing what I had for snacks, but it seems this is it. Sorry." Shaking the pitiful box, my gaze runs up and down her body. She's wearing my oversized T-shirt but didn't bother to put on the sweats. Christ. "Holly, you look beautiful."

Smiling, she chuckles. "Yeah? An old Van Halen T-shirt is your thing?"

"Um, yeah, actually. You look stunning."

She places her hands on the counter behind her and pushes forward, leaning her torso toward me. Her breasts are so noticeable that I can see the outline of her already-taut nipples, and it's obvious she's not wearing a bra.

"You sure you don't want dinner?" I force myself to look her in the eyes.

"No, thanks. But maybe I can grab a Ring Ding or two?"

"Seriously?" Dropping my chin, I try to figure if this woman is for real or not.

"Yes. Those were my guilty pleasure in med school. Haven't had one in years."

"Sure, have a box if you'd like."

Standing on opposite sides of the galley area of my kitchen, we both lean back against the cabinets. Holding out the opened box, I smile as she reaches in, takes one, and then unwraps the plastic covering. I do the same. Collecting our plastic wrappers, I toss them before turning to her and raising the Ring Ding.

"Here's to memories of Ring Dings in college."

"And here's to new memories with Ring Dings," she counters.

Raising an eyebrow, she "clinks" her Ring Ding against mine.

Taking a good-sized bite, she covers her mouth with her hand as she chews. Closing her eyes, she moans, and it sends a very direct current to my groin.

"Oh, my gosh." While she speaks, she fans herself with her hand. "I haven't tasted one of these in years."

"As good as you remember?" I finish mine off in three bites and wipe my hands on my jeans.

She watches me with heavy eyelids. I don't know if it's me or the chocolate, but something is turning her on.

"It's better," she answers. "Nothing else can compare to the taste of artificial chocolate stuffed with sugary cream."

Holding out the box, I offer her another.

She shakes her head. "No, thanks. Maybe later." Taking her last bite, she licks her lips, and a little smear of chocolate sticks to her pouty bottom lip.

Fuck.

Pushing off the counter, I walk up to her, closing the gap between us. "You have chocolate…"

Licking her lips slowly, she stares up into my eyes. "Did I get it?"

"No."

Reaching out, I rest my fingers beneath her chin and use my thumb to rub away the chocolate smear as we look into each other's eyes.

Even though the chocolate is long gone, I glide my thumb back and forth across her lip once more. Closing her eyes, she sighs.

Fuck. Dropping my hand, I exhale out through clenched teeth and move back to my side of the galley kitchen where it's safer for both of us. My erection is so full and hard now it's beginning to hurt, so I shove my hand into my pocket and grab a cold beer off of the counter.

"Beer?"

She takes the beer I'm offering, and I grab another. After one more toast, I down a long pull from my bottle, trying anything to cool off.

Taking a swallow, she turns and looks out my picture window. "Do you have a balcony?"

"Yeah. Not much of a view, though."

"Can I?"

As she crosses the room, I watch her long, toned legs peeking out of the bottom of my T-shirt as she walks away.

"Let me get that."

Unlocking the patio door, I open it for her, and leaving our beers on my table by the balcony door, we both step outside.

"Gosh, what a beautiful night," she whispers.

From my balcony, we can see the dirty street and the busy entranceway to the highway.

"I love the city," she murmurs as she rests her hands on the railing. "I love the feel of it, the electricity, the heartbeat, the realness of it—I don't think I really care which city, but I would never live anywhere else by choice." Shivering, she runs her hands up and down her arms. "It's chilly tonight."

Walking up behind her, I open my arms wide and reaching around her, I hold the balcony rail on either side of her. She leans back against my chest and rests her head on my shoulder.

"Are you cold?" I whisper into her ear.

"Not anymore."

Letting go of the balcony, I wrap my arms around her body, pulling her even closer.

"Seth…" Purring my name, she snuggles tighter against me.

Taking her hand, I spin her around so we're facing one another, and my arms are wrapped around her small waist. The red light from the flashing sign across the street reflects off of her gorgeous face.

"You are so beautiful," I whisper. Reaching out, I slip one hand behind her neck and slide my fingers through her soft hair.

"Seth…" She takes a deep breath and lets it out in a sigh.

Holding her, I move in closer, and finally… after all this waiting and wondering… I lean closer still. As her breath races, meshing with mine, my lips find hers.

Pressing her mouth against mine, she snakes her arms up around my shoulders and rests them on the back of my neck, sending little shivers down my spine.

"God, Holly…"

Kissing her with more force now, she lets me open her mouth, and my tongue makes its way in—darting in and out, thrusting hard and strong as my hands grip her hips and my fingers grab at the sides of her T-shirt greedily. My mind races with images of her slim hip with the tattoo of the bird in flight.

Backing us up against the patio door, we hit with more force than I intend. She lands with a gasp but pushes against me harder still.

Leaning my hips against her, the freaking bulge in my jeans is now rock-hard—there's no way she's missing this. Bending my knees and stooping down, I line up the top of my member with her soft silk panties. Because of my damned jeans, I can't feel the silk, but I glide against her easily.

Moving against me in response, she whispers, "That feels so good."

That's it. Reaching down and grabbing her by the waist, I hoist her up onto my hips. Straddling me, she murmurs as my hands cup her round, tight ass, and I carry her inside and to the bedroom. Gently laying her down on the bed, I pause to yank my shirt over my head, and her gaze runs up and down my body. It's like she's taking inventory as she looks from one of my strong arms to the other. Then, her gaze lingers on my abs and the strip of hair I have cascading upward from my jeans.

I need to be closer to her. Climbing onto the bed, I crawl my way to her. Stopping when I'm above her, I hover there, leaning down over her, kissing her gently on the lips. Arching her back, she meets my kiss with so much passion, I have to force myself to slow down.

Dropping down and resting on one side, I reach out with my free hand, and taking her chin lightly, I turn her to face me.

"Is this okay?" I whisper as I trace her cheek.

"It's better than okay," she whispers back.

Nodding, my hand cups her chin, and my thumb slides back and forth across the adorable dimple between her chin and lower lip. Sliding my thumb higher, I trace the outline of her lips like I did just before.

This time she opens her mouth, and her warm, soft tongue teases my thumb. Working my thumb through her parted lips, she licks and nips gently.

"Damn, Holly."

Pushing my thumb in further, she takes the length of it, sucking and licking as she closes her eyes.

"Holly, baby…"

Her eyes open and flash with hunger. Freeing my thumb, I place my hand on her cheek, and holding her softly, I kiss her again and again, each time getting closer and closer as the kiss grows deeper and deeper.

Grabbing at my jeans, she pulls me, and I roll on top of her. Latching my mouth to hers, we kiss in time with the quickening thrusting of our hips. Reaching down, she grabs at my button fly and pops the top button. Immediately, some of the pressure releases, but now I've got nothing but a pair of briefs containing me.

Dropping my weight down, I use my legs to widen hers so I can rest between them. Then, balancing on my knees, I lift her T-shirt, and moving closer, I kiss her toned tummy over and over again…

Giggling, she turns her head and covers her mouth with her hand. Undaunted, I run my kisses up one side of her beautiful belly and down the other. Reaching up, I slide her T-shirt farther upward. Looking at me, she stares into my eyes as I lift the T-shirt up and over her beautiful breasts. Taking her hand, I pull her up to a seated position and then lift the T-shirt over her head. She shivers, and her already-hard nipples tighten into buds.

"Good god, Holly."

Sliding her onto her back, I immediately take one tight, full breast into my hand and set to work on her nipple—nipping and licking while she arches her back off of the bed and moans beneath me.

"You are so damned responsive…" I mumble. Reaching around, I hold her back with one hand and cup her breast with the other.

Then, laying her down again, I slide onto my side and pop the rest of my button fly open. My throbbing member springs forward, straining to be free. Climbing on top of her, I reach out and slide her panties down around her ankles and off. She rubs her legs together and drops her chin to her shoulder. Moving next to her hip, I settle in and kiss her tattoo gently.

"Does it hurt?"

"No," she whispers. "It's tender, but not sore."

"Well, we'll be careful, okay?"

"Yes." Reaching out with her hand, she wraps it around my forearm. "Seth. Just so you know. I, um, I'm a little out of practice."

Her words sit straight in my dick. I love that she hasn't been with anyone in a long time, and I love that she trusts me enough for it to be me.

"Baby," I murmur. "I promise we'll go slow, and I will never let anything hurt you."

Her eyes light up at my promise, and it's one I make to her and to me. As soon as I say it, I know it's true. I would never let anything hurt her. Nodding, she smiles, and I know she believes me.

Jumping off of the bed, I slide out of my briefs and watch as her gaze drops to my member that's rock hard and so ready for her.

There are so many things I want to do to her, but right now, more than anything, I want to make her mine. Climbing back onto the bed, I place one hand on the mattress on either side of her shoulders and settle between her legs. Balancing on my knees, I run my hands down her body, stopping at her hips. Careful of the sore tattoo, I roll her onto her side and kiss the tattoo gently.

"Seth..." she mumbles.

Dropping down onto the side of her, I spoon her, holding her close. Taking my hand from her hip, I rest it between her legs. Then, moving slightly, I roll her onto her back and gently, watching and reading her reactions as I go, I move my finger toward her opening and slide it inside.

"Holly, baby, you're so tight and so ready."

"Yes." Rolling her head back, she moans. "God, that feels so good."

Pushing farther, I increase my rhythm as she begins to move in time with me. Rolling her head to one side, she grips the sheets. Removing my finger slowly, I bring it to rest on the nub of nerves between her legs, pressing and rubbing as I watch her head move from side to side, and then, slowly, I slide back inside. I follow this pattern—moving from her nub to her opening—back and forth, just to drive her wild. Every time she settles in and her hips raise, and her breath quickens—I change my pattern to keep her enjoying it as long as possible... until that moment she can't take anymore, and I bring her over the edge.

"Seth, I want you. Please."

I don't need to be asked twice. Removing my finger from inside her, I reach around and grab a condom from the nightstand. I tear it open with my teeth and then roll it on. Then, placing one hand on the mattress on either side of her head and lining myself up, with just the tip of my erection, I bump against her gently.

"Mmm," she moans.

Using more force, I'm able to push my tip in, and slowly, I begin to bury myself inside.

"God, Holly, you feel so good." Careful not to hurt her, I slide in as slowly as I can. "I don't think I've ever felt anything this good... ever." Hovering over her, I drop my head back and clench my teeth to hold on. It's like being dipped into warm honey, and I want to make it last.

Finding a nice, steady rhythm, I let her take me in as far as she can. Looking down at her expression, her face contorts and releases with my thrusts, and reaching out, she clamps her hands onto my hips. Leaning down, I press my weight against her nub, and she moves against me. Her fingers dig in at my waist, and she pulls me closer. Thrusting harder, I know she's on the edge.

"Holly, baby, just let go."

"Mmm..." she mumbles, turning her head to the side.

With my next thrust, her back arches off of the bed, and she cries out as I press against her in just the right way. Pulling back just a tiny bit, I thrust again, bumping against that spot deep inside that makes her crazy, just as I take her to her peak.

"Oh god, Seth!"

With her gorgeous body trembling beneath me, she falls back against the mattress, and with a few more deep, final thrusts, I bury myself deep inside and let go.

Falling into a heap around her, I cradle her in my arms as our sweat mingles and our breaths slow together.

Somehow, this brilliant country club goddess and guy from the streets have come together for this one night, and nothing has ever felt better.

Lifting my head, I roll onto my side and pull her toward me. As she lays her head on my chest, she looks up at me. Gazing down into her beautiful, relaxed face, I know I'm fucked.

We had a connection I've never had with anyone else, and I'm destined to keep that promise I made a little while ago. I will protect her, no matter what. That means, even if we're never together again, I will make sure that no one ever hurts her.

Because the guys may call me Dynamite for one reason—but none of them bothered to learn the characteristics of dynamite. Yeah, it's explosive, but its primary asset is that it's incredibly loyal.

Dynamite is loyal to whoever lights its fuse.

Pulling Holly closer, I kiss her on the top of her head.

And there's no doubt who lights mine.

Chapter Nine

Dynamite

Rolling over, I smile when I see Holly on the opposite side of the bed from me. She's still out cold. Frankly, after the third round last night, I was also out, but this morning, I'm feeling pretty great. Looking at Holly's gorgeous face and beautiful naked body tangled up in my sheets, I know exactly why. Smiling, she murmurs as she sleeps. Does she know she does that?

Suddenly, my good mood darkens as I realize that for her to know she talks in her sleep, someone would have to tell her. Unfortunately, I know exactly who that someone is—Dr. Robert Covens. Reaching up with one hand, I scrub my face, trying to wash away the thought of Robert's manicured hands all over her beautiful body. Yeah, he's rich and a doctor and probably smart, but what does a spoiled man like that know about taking care of a woman? What can he offer her?

The light coming through my bedroom window catches my attention, and I turn toward it. Looking out, I see morning dawn and the sun rise on my neighborhood—a neighborhood filled with poverty and filth and decay. Sorrow swallows me like I'm being sucked into a blackhole.

What can a man like Robert offer her? Everything I can't.

Careful not to wake her, I roll onto my side and place my feet onto the cold wood floor. I stand, stretching my arms overhead.

Stealing one more peek at Holly lying there, now with a gentle sunray falling across her face, I'm overwhelmed. Putting a hand to my chest, I take a deep breath.

So what if this was only one night? At least I had the one night with her.

On that thought, I make my way to the kitchen to scrounge together some breakfast.

Carrying a tray into the bedroom, I'm pretty proud of the fact that I've managed to pull together a breakfast of eggs, toast, and fruit—even if it is canned fruit—and make it look presentable. On the tray, I've also added a Ring Ding with a candle to make up for not having flowers. Yeah, I could have run to the florist up the street, but I really didn't want to leave her. Besides, after the last flower debacle, it's probably better not to mess with them.

"Seth?" Waking up, she slides into a seated position, leaning back against the wall behind the bed. Right now, I wish I had a headboard. And a way to keep this moment preserved forever.

"Morning."

Pointing to the tray, she smiles. "Is that for me?"

"Yeah." Nodding, I lay it on her lap.

Rubbing her hands together, she looks over the tray. "Eggs and toast. This looks delicious, thank you."

"You're welcome." Staring at her, I am absolutely floored by her beauty. And even more by the person that she is. Standing up taller, I take a deep breath.

"The Ring Ding with the candle is a really nice touch. Is it my birthday?"

"Is it?" She catches me off-guard.

"Nah, July 15th. I'll be twenty-nine. Yours?"

"August 30th. I'll be thirty-one. I didn't have anything nicer to put on the tray, so the Ring Ding is supposed to take the place of flow—"

Fuck. Why did I have to bring it up?

"Take the place of flowers?"

I don't answer her.

"Seth? Why don't you want to mention flowers?"

"Just because, you know. Our history with flowers."

"I'm sorry." Sliding up further in the bed, she tilts her head. "We have a history with flowers?" She wiggles her finger back and forth between us.

"Just that I sent you those flowers, and I never heard from you."

"Wait. What? You sent me flowers? When? Where?"

"At the hospital. After the night of my injury. I put my cell number on the card. The flowers were a thank-you for what you did, and an apology for acting so stupid."

"Seth, I never received any flowers. If I had, I definitely would have thanked y—" Her mouth drops open, and then she slams it shut, hard. Nodding, she looks out the window and back. "Well, no wonder."

"No wonder what?"

"Seth, were the flowers you sent a large bunch of purple and blue wildflowers?"

"Yeah?"

"I'm sorry. I did get them. But there wasn't a card."

"So you assumed they were from someone else?"

Her expression hardens. "No. Someone else *told* me they were from him."

"Robert."

"Who else?" Shaking her head, she looks down at the sheets and then back to me. "I'm so sorry, Seth. They were such beautiful flowers, and the whole time we were dating, Robert never sent me flowers. Not once. I should have known better. I can't believe that son of a bitch did that. But I'm not surprised."

"It's not your fault." Although the conversation has turned to the topic of Robert, an overall sense of peace falls over me.

"Come on." Her eyes light up. Patting the bed next to her, she nods to me. "Enough time spent on that idiot. Come, sit." Picking up the Ring Ding from the tray, she smiles. "Besides, as much as I love flowers, I like this even more." Pulling out the candle, she picks off tiny pieces of the chocolate shell and eats them. "Do you mind if I start with dessert? I do love these things."

As she snuggles down into my bed and picks at the Ring Ding, I chuckle.

"What are you laughing about?"

"Nothing, really. It's just that you are a woman of many surprises."

"Yeah?" Sitting back up, she moves on to the eggs.

Shoveling in a bite of eggs, her eyes widen. "Oh, my gosh, Seth, these are delicious. You can cook?"

Scooping up another bite of eggs, she offers it to me, holding her other hand beneath to catch anything that might fall. It's all so normal and feels so nice.

Taking the bite, I chew and swallow. "I cook a little."

"Where'd you learn? Your mom?"

"Some." Looking into Holly's brilliant eyes, I suddenly feel like talking. "My mom died when I was a teen. Colt was just a kid. That's when we were split up—he went to live with our aunt."

"I'm sorry." Her brow furrows. "But if you were just a teen, who did you live with?"

Nodding, I swallow what feels like a lump the size of Montana in my throat. "I was sent to juvie."

Sitting forward, she puts the tray down. "As in juvenile detention?"

"Yeah."

Looking away, I stare at the blanket between us, waiting for her to jump up and run. Instead, she reaches out and takes my hand. Turning it, she strokes my palm with her thumb. It's the most calming thing I've ever felt, and it's like a million pounds of stress fall off of me. Taking a deep breath, I exhale.

"I'm so sorry you went through that."

Looking up into her eyes, I wait for more—the questions, the judgment, the abandonment. But there isn't any of that. Instead, she leans toward me, and laying a hand behind my neck, she moves closer and kisses me so very softly.

If only kisses could cure.

Pulling away, she moves toward her side of the bed. Reaching out, I grab her hand and hold on. She looks startled, but not the least bit scared.

"I want you to know." I hold her hand tight. "I was stupid then. And I guess I'm still stupid now—like that night I fought with Avery."

"You're not stupid, Seth. You're passionate."

Giving her a small smile, I explain. "We were living in Ohio then, and I was a bad kid. I was always in trouble—nothing all that bad at the beginning—petty theft and eventually stealing cars, but when I was fourteen and my mother died…" Shaking my head, I fight to keep my voice even. "I just freaked, you know? Instead of comforting Colt—who was just a friggin' baby—I bought a shotgun and went to the local liquor store. I was arrested for armed robbery."

"Seth…"

With her free hand, she strokes my cheek. Closing my eyes for a moment, I take a deep breath. Letting my breath go, I open my eyes and look at her.

"When they arrested me, I just lost it. Dynamite, you know? I lashed out at the cop. Got an extra two years for that. The judge was lenient on me because I was considered a kid from a troubled environment, although I don't know why. Yeah, my dad had split, but my mother was an accountant. Maybe the judge felt bad because she had just died. I got one year for the botched armed robbery since I didn't actually steal anything or hurt anyone, but I got an additional two for my behavior. I learned to cook there." Looking into her eyes, I feel myself pleading. "I heard you last night, when you told me the difference between impulse control and passion. But what does it matter when the end result means hurting someone I love?"

"Colt?"

"Yeah." Sighing, I try to push the sadness away. "That's why this new clubhouse is so important to me. I feel like it's a way I can contribute to the Knights, who've welcomed me with open arms, and bond with my brother at the same time."

Nodding, she smiles. "I get it."

Exhaling loudly, I shrug. "Sorry. What a way to bring us down."

"No, I'm glad you told me. And you're not bad, Seth. You just done some stupid things. Haven't we all?"

Looking at her out of the corner of my eye, I tease, "I'll bet you have never done one stupid thing in your life."

"Ooh." She rubs her hands together. "Another bet. I love betting with you because I win."

"Is winning everything?"

"Hell, yes." She smiles playfully. "You're in bed with the captain of the cheer team, president of the debate club—with an undefeated record that still holds today—valedictorian, and then the top one percent of my Ivy League med school's graduating class. Hell, yeah, winning is everything." She takes a bite of the eggs with a triumphant smile on her face.

"All right, Dr. Wins-at-Everything. Spill. Name one thing you have done in your life that was stupid."

Holding my breath, I hope she's not counting the tattoo or me.

Nodding, she counts things out on her fingers as she goes. "Let's see: I was captain of the cheer team, president of the debate club—with an undefeated record that still holds today—valedictorian, and then the top one percent of my Ivy League med school's graduating class."

"Ha."

Chuckling, I pick a piece of chocolate off of her Ring Ding and she smacks my hand away playfully.

"Do not mess with my chocolate." Her face changes then and she looks at her nails, picking at them. "Seth? Why did you laugh?"

"Because you just named a bunch of accomplishments that would make anyone proud. Heck, I'm proud of you."

"Thank you. But I didn't laugh at your list of stupid things. Why are you laughing at mine?" She's serious.

"Holly, I'm sorry, I don't understand what you could possibly mean."

Turning in bed, she tucks the sheet around her breasts. "With all that, Seth, everything I've done, I forgot to live."

"What do you want to do?"

Her face lights up. "The same thing I have wanted to do since I was six years old, playing with my dolls and pretending they were sick. I want to open a clinic and help people. With the healthcare system in this country, so many people come to the ER for every little thing, and I can't blame them. It's the only way they can get medical treatment. At my clinic, I'll offer low-cost or no-cost healthcare. The same as you would get in the ER, but in a nicer, smaller environment with excellent doctors. I even know the place I want it. There's a little town just between Hoppa and Phoenix…"

My stomach flips over as I wonder where exactly she means and whose turf it is on. Pushing my concerns away, I smile at her. "Holly, that's an amazing goal. Why not do it?"

Sighing, she flops back and crosses her arms before her. "Because I've let too many people run my life for me. That's why my greatest accomplishments are also my greatest regrets. I'll be thirty years old soon, and I know that's not old, but I've never really lived a day in my life." Smiling, she adds, "Well, until these past couple of nights."

There's something in the way she says it… "Is that why you're here? With me?"

"Excuse me?" She stiffens.

"Are you here because I'm an experience? You want to try something out? See what it's like to go slumming?"

"*Slumming*?" The corners of her mouth dip down into a scowl. "I'm sorry, Seth, I can't imagine what made you say something like that. I have never alluded that you and I were different in any way. I wouldn't be here if I thought we were incompatible, or if I didn't really like you." Reaching down to the floor next to the bed, she grabs my Van Halen T-shirt and slides it on.

Damn, she's pissed, and it's making me feel so bad I barely notice how great she looks in my shirt.

"All I meant is that a woman like you—"

"A woman like me?" Jumping out of my bed, she grabs her panties off of the floor and slides them on. "What is that, huh, Seth? A woman like me? Snobby, spoiled, rich—a Daddy's Girl?" Storming to the bathroom, she comes back with her bra, the sweats I lent her, and her dirty clothes. Lifting my T-shirt just over her belly, she slides on her bra and with some magic-like move, she gets both arms through and fastens it. Standing there, the way her forehead is creased and the corners of her mouth turn down, she looks genuinely sad. "What if I said that I never expected breakfast in bed from a 'man like you'?"

"Is that true?"

Tilting her head, she sighs and her shoulders slump. "You know, I thought you were different, Seth. I really did."

"I am different." Holding my hands out to either side, I motion to my apartment. "Just look at this place."

She takes a step toward me. "Don't you get it? That's exactly what Robert would have said. And no, it's not fair to compare you to that jerk, and I'm sorry for saying that, but my point is that Robert judges everyone by their image and their surroundings, and you just did the same. Did I want to be with you because you were different? Yes, absolutely. But was it because you're a Steel Knight, or a biker, or not a doctor, or rugged? No. It's because I thought we had a connection, and you never judged me. *That's* how you were different. From that first night in the hospital, you just talked and listened. But now I see I was wrong. You're as quick to give us labels and fit us both into neat little categories as anyone else."

Clutching her dirty clothes to her chest, she turns and leaves my room. I follow on her heels.

Stopping in the living room, she turns to me. "I came to Hoppa's Taphouse twice, Seth. Two times." She holds up her fingers. "You don't do that if you're looking to go slumming for one night." Shaking her head, her eyes become glassy.

She's really hurt. Shit.

"Holly, listen."

"No." Putting up her hand, she stops me. "I think we've both said plenty. Thank you for breakfast and… last night. Bye, Seth." Turning, she grabs her keys off of the kitchen counter and rushes out my door.

Standing here like an asshole, I let her go. It's better this way.

After all, what could a woman like that possibly see in a man like me?

Chapter Ten

Dynamite

"So, you just let her leave?"

Colt and I sit on a rock wall looking out over a canyon just outside Hoppa. It's on the way to the high school we're heading to. We're going to work with some kids who need extra help with math. I go once a week or so, and today I decided to recruit Colt to go with me. It's no secret I'm not so great at relationships, and maybe Nick is right, maybe I need to put in some extra effort. We're in full gear—leather jackets, colors, chaps, and riding boots. The kids I coach get a kick out of the gear, and it makes them listen to me more. I found this school because it's on the way to the area where we hold Music in the Desert, a huge live music event where all the ally clubs gather every year.

"It's not like I had a choice," I explain, looking at Colt. I should be on a high: I just had a great meeting with the construction company yesterday, and they're supplying us materials at cost, so we're about to break ground on the new clubhouse, but instead, all I can think about is Holly and how badly it ended with her.

"You could have stopped her." Colt takes a bite out of one of the sandwiches we picked up on the ride out here.

"You do mean with my words, right?" Glancing at my sandwich, I let it lie next to me. I haven't been very hungry since I said goodbye to Holly two nights ago.

"What else?" Colt turns to me with wide eyes. "Christ, Seth, this big brother stuff is getting old. I've made it to twenty-four on my own. I think I know a thing or two about how to treat a woman."

Good. At least one of us does.

"I know, Colt. I'm just sorry I missed all those times you needed a big brother. I'm sorry I missed all those years with you, you know?"

"Well, what could you do? Not punch the cop who was arresting you? That's not you, right, Dynamite?"

Picking up my sandwich, I stare at it and then put it back down. "All right, Colt. That's twice now. Two days ago, when you were cut in that fight, you said I one-up you in everything."

"That was a joke." He stares out at the canyon.

"I don't think it was. And now the cop remark? I get that you're pissed and you hated living with our aunt and that your life sucked. But mine wasn't any better. I'm sorry for everything I did to make it happen. But I didn't kill Mom."

"But you left."

"I'm here now, and I've changed. I'm not letting my outbursts rule me. I'm in control. I don't plan on missing one more moment of life because I'm Dynamite."

"Really? Seems to me you just did."

"What?"

"Why did you let Holly leave?"

"I-uh…" Why *did* I let Holly leave?

"I'll tell you why." Colt turns to me. "Because you're reactive. Being around you is like being around a walking time-bomb. Because of it, I lost my big brother, and you lost her."

I don't have to sit here and listen to this crap. Standing, I take my sandwich and, wrapping it up, I walk over to my bike and stuff it into one of the saddlebags on the sides of my Harley. There will be someone we pass on the way to the school who will need it. Maybe even one of my kids.

Throwing my leg over, I mount my bike and turn the key. Revving the engine, I yell to Colt, "You coming?"

"Yeah." Standing, he tosses his empty wrapper in a nearby garbage can and hops on his bike.

Thankfully, bikes make it impossible to talk, so we ride in silence. It's only a few more miles to our destination, and we fall into line the last mile as he follows me to the school. In the parking lot, we glide into spots next to each other, turn off the bikes, and hop off. Gathering my things, I turn and spot a man sitting by the road with a sign that reads, "Homeless and hungry." Shit, that didn't take long.

"Give me a sec," I mumble to Colt.

Walking up to the man who's wrapped in a blanket, I notice he's sleeping, so I leave the sandwich by his side and sneak back to Colt, who's watching my every move. He furrows his brow.

"What?" I ask as I make sure my helmet is stored safely.

"Nothing." He shakes his head but looks at me quizzically again.

"Okay. Come on." Nodding to the school, I lead him to the entrance that goes directly to the cafetorium.

Opening the door, I'm immediately hit by the smell of tempera paint I remember from when I was a kid. This isn't what this place usually smells like—it usually reeks of sloppy joe meat and teenage sweat. When we step inside, a hush falls over the room. A bunch of kids I don't know are standing around on the opposite side of the room with paint brushes in their hands, painting a big green building made of cardboard. Rather than the cafeteria tables and chairs that are always cluttering the room, today there is a yellow brick road on the floor.

"Excuse me?" A young woman dressed in jeans with a tie-dye T-shirt and long, loosely curled blonde hair emerges from behind the green building and walks up to us. She has a pin in her mouth and others are stuck into a pin cushion shaped like a tomato velcroed to her wrist.

She glances at Colt and then pulls the pin from her mouth, sticks it into the tomato, and hides the wrist with the tomato behind her back. "Can I help you?"

"I'm Seth Hardy," I tell her. "I tutor the kids in math once a week."

She looks me up and down, and I can't help but narrow my eyes at her. This is exactly what Holly was talking about. Being judged on appearance. It's the same damned thing I did to Holly, and she's right, it sucks. Crossing my arms in front of my puffed-up chest, I narrow my eyes at the little blonde girl, and she glares at me. Huh. Feisty, and not the least bit intimidated. Good for her.

"How about you?" She has a surprisingly deep, raspy voice for such a small thing. She nods to Colt.

"Colt. Hardy. I'm with him."

Colt smiles, and she smiles back. Smirking, I turn away and when I turn back, she's glaring at me again. Guess I'm not exactly popular with women right now, although I haven't done a damned thing to this one.

"Erica Peters. Nice to meet you both."

When she puts out her hand, I give her mine and she shakes it and then let's go quickly. Then she takes Colt's hand and shakes it, holding on just a little too long.

"Well." Slipping her thumbs through the belt loops of her jeans, she sways back and forth. "I'm sorry to tell you, but there's no tutoring this week. We have the cafetorium for rehearsals. We open with *the Wizard of Oz* this weekend." Looking directly at Colt, she rocks forward on her toes and smiles. "Do you know the show?"

"Sure."

"Maybe you'd like to come see it?" Raising one shoulder, she smiles at Colt. When she does, her blue eyes sparkle and dimples form in her cheeks. She is cute.

"I'm not much of a musical kind of guy."

Clearing my throat, I elbow Colt.

Rubbing his side, he blurts, "But, uh, the set looks so good, maybe I will stop by. That is if you're in it?"

Laughing, she reaches out and touches his arm. Bingo. "I'm the director, silly. The drama teacher." Glancing at the emblem on the front of my jacket, she squints and drops her hands. "Sorry, are you guys Steel Knights?" Just like that, her demeanor changes from flirtatious and happy to serious.

"Yes, actually." Colt's not a full-fledged member yet, but he has the jacket and wears our colors. "You know the Knights?"

Nodding, she frowns. "I'm originally from Hoppa. Moved out here for this glamorous job." Holding out her hands, she spins in a circle. "I knew CJ. He was in my sister's grade. I knew Tess, too. Has anyone seen her?"

Shaking my head, I push away the feeling I'm getting from this girl. How well did she know Tess and CJ?

"I'm guessing Nick is still in charge?" She scowls when she mentions him, and I can't help but wonder why. What's going on here, and what does this woman know?

"He is," I add. "The Knights are a good group of guys—and girl now," I throw in, just in case it's the idea of a motorcycle club that's scaring her off.

Nodding, she looks me in the eye. "Oh, I know. That's why you're named the 'Steel *Knights*' instead of the Hellhounds or whatever that other group near Hoppa is called."

"The Unchained Dogs," I tell her. She does know a lot more than the average person who lives in Hoppa. Just saying their name causes agitation in my gut that momentarily distracts me. Today, I found out from my connections that the Dogs know about our build and they're not too happy about it. I don't blame them. When we were just set up in Hoppa's Taphouse, it was one thing, but now that we're expanding, it means we'll have more opportunities to build the organization so we're not only stronger in numbers, but we can also stick our fingers into more business dealings. That's what pisses Luther and the damned Dogs off more than anything.

And right now, since I'm heading the build, I'm Number One on their Shit List.

"Anyway." Just like that, she's back to smiles and sunshine. "Thanks to having no school funding—" She points to the set made of cardboard to show what she means. "—there's only one performance, and we were lucky to get that. The set is all made of cardboard I collected from recycling bins, and I sewed each of the costumes by hand."

"That's impressive," I comment.

Frowning at me, she turns to Colt. "The show starts at seven on Friday, and it'll be over by nine. There's a cast party after. Maybe you want to come?"

"Sounds great." He nods and smiles.

Holding up her hands, she laughs. "I'm afraid this is also where we have the after party. The catering will also be done by yours truly." She bows. "But we'll have boxed cookies, and I make a mean fruit punch." Stepping toward him, she grabs the lapel of his jacket and leans forward. "Of course, Colt, if you want to spike the punch in our paper cups, I won't tell." Winking at him, she lets go of his jacket. Looking at us both, she adds, "I'm sorry the tutoring was canceled and no one told you. It's time for me to go back to work. Now, if you'll excuse me, I have to carry some heavy paint cans up from storage." She turns to walk away and then looking back over her shoulder, she adds, "It was nice to meet you both."

"Uh, wait." Yanking off his jacket, Colt tosses it on a chair. "I can help you with that. The heavy paint cans, I mean."

"Wow." She stares at him wide-eyed.

Looking at Colt, I try to see what she sees—he has arm muscles bulging out of his T-shirt sleeves for sure, but he's scrawny compared to me. Walking up next to her, however, he looks like a friggin' bodybuilder.

Blink! Glancing at my cell, I read a text from Bullet.

The guys at the construction company say they can't break ground. Materials issue.

What the fuck?

"You sure you have time to help?" Erica smiles at Colt as they walk away.

"Colt?" I call after him.

"Yeah?" Turning back to face me, I can hear the annoyance in his voice.

"I need to head back to Hoppa. You all set?"

Putting up his hand and waving me off, he rushes up to Erica. Walking off together, she looks up at him and smiles. Good. I'm happy for him… I think. She's cute and seems sweet and determined, but I can't help but feel something is off about her. Nah. Shaking my head, I let that go. I've been thinking that of everything and everyone since Holly and I split. But there is one thing that is off for sure—there is no fucking "materials issue" on my watch. No way. I handled that negotiation and ran all the numbers myself. Everyone was happy.

Quickly, as I walk out the cafetorium door, I type back, *WTF? We're set to go. What materials?*

The text comes back: *Concrete.*

Concrete. That has "Dog" written all over it. I can smell them from here. Shit. This is going to be bad. The tension has been heightened between us ever since that surprise attack on our turf—when they came crashing in, colors blazing, to pick a fight. Even though they outnumbered us, they lost, mostly because we had Tess and that fighting machine, CJ, on our side. That night, the Dogs learned that even though we're not an outlaw group like they are, we're not to be fucked with.

Then, just a few months back, when Clyde brought that warning to Bullseye, we knew we had to be on alert, but now, things are really bad. Since Colt was slashed with a knife by one of them on our turf, they know we have to retaliate—and we will—but on our terms and in our way. That's what they're afraid of. But, by forcing our hand by stopping our build, they think they have control. We have to confront them *and* walk into their trap. That's a win-win for them. Thing is, they can't force us out of the new property because it's not Dog turf. Which means there has to be a fight.

Shit. All of this makes me think of Holly that night at the hospital and the poor business owners who were brought in—nearly beaten to death—by the Dogs who attacked their businesses because they were unknowingly running product for the Vipers on Dog turf. Yeah, a couple of them were in with the Vipers, but a bunch of the people who were hurt that night were civilians. The freaking Dogs don't care. They have no moral code or laws they follow—if you're in their way, they do whatever the hell they want with you. Christ, I feel bad for anyone who lives or works on Dog turf.

Making my way to my bike, I focus on the text Bullet sent. Concrete. Concrete is a union job—and this particular union is connected, which means…

Fuck. Are the Dogs playing in the big leagues now?

It was one thing when they were only connected on their own turf and in Rumble, their town. Yeah, Rumble is bigger than Hoppa, and the Dogs do work with some organized crime members to control the builds in Rumble, where they pretty much own everyone and everything. But if those damned Dogs think they can put their filthy paws on areas outside Rumble—whether it's our territory or an unclaimed zone—well, shit—there'll be no stopping them. They will just grow and grow, feeding off of everyone in their way. With organized crime backing them, nothing will be able to stop the Dogs from claiming all the open territories between here and Phoenix and beyond—and taking anything they want that's there when they arrive.

Like Holly.

Mounting my bike, I rub away the uneasy feeling in my gut. Holly's hospital is in unclaimed territory between here and Phoenix, and the damned Dogs have already seen me with her.

Christ. Just by knowing me, I have put her into serious danger when all I wanted to do was protect her. Fucking Dynamite. Why do I always act before I think?

No, Holly is safe at the hospital. Hospitals are always autonomous, and there's no way the Dogs would be able to claim a hospital. Good. She'll be safe at the hospital and in her apartment in Phoenix. One small, crap bunch of bikers wouldn't be able to rule Phoenix, not without serious backup and support from connections way bigger than they have access to.

Bullseye, on the other hand, may be able to get those connections—so Phoenix is clear.

That's something. But it doesn't stop the Dogs from expanding onto other turfs. Only we can do that. Now, thanks at least in part to my impulsivity—being spotted by a Dog at the hospital and then fighting with the Dogs outside our clubhouse and buying cement from a connection they've been working—the only way to protect Holly and stop the damned Dogs is going to be all out war.

Chapter Eleven

Holly

"Hey, baby!"

Catcalls and whistles become my theme music as I walk down the old street in Greenville, just outside of Hoppa. How ironic that it's named "Greenville" when there's not a patch of grass anywhere. Looking around, I feel like I'm trapped on the set of an old musical where all the buildings are red and yellow and clotheslines hang from building to building. There's a convenience store on one side of the street and a fruit stand on the other. The street is clean, and I smile at the few row houses that have potted plants and flowers before them.

A little thrill of energy shoots up my spine, and I break out into a smile. As an orange and white cat darts across the sidewalk just before me, I decide there isn't anywhere that could be more perfect.

"I said, 'hey, baby.'"

"Oh!" Stopping short, I catch myself before I bump into a man who just popped out of a building and is now standing before me. Shit. I really hope he's not about to ruin this. Taking a deep breath, I glance down at his hands to make sure he's not carrying a weapon—because if he is, the can of mace I'm carrying in my oversized bag won't do a damned thing. There's no weapon. Whew. Relaxing, I shake my head. There I am, judging someone—and what's worse, judging them on their appearance and location. Just like Robert and, I guess, Seth would do.

Not me. I'm giving this man a chance. Besides, I was told this area was "emerging", and it's a family neighborhood. There are no gangs, and the crime rate is low. I run my gaze up and down the man who's still blocking my way, and I notice he's wearing jeans, no-name sneakers, and a clean white tank top. He's just a kid. Looking back up into his eyes, I smile and adjust my bag strap. "Hello," I answer.

"You lost?" He nods to me. "Fine lady like you out here. Don't make sense."

"No, actually." Standing up taller, I take a deep breath. "I'm going to look at a building."

"Why?"

"Because I might buy it."

"Why?"

"Because I'm thinking about—" I catch myself. Breathing deeply, I remind myself of my yoga teacher's mantra: *Positive thoughts yield positive results.*

Just then, an azure bluebird flies by and lands on the top of a bus stop sign. Looking at the kiosk next to the stop, I notice it's clean and there's no graffiti scrawled on it, but there is a homeless woman sitting on the bench inside.

Looking down, I exhale deeply. "No. I'm not thinking about it. I'm buying that building over there." Nodding toward the end of the street, I point at a run-down building next to a chain-link fence. Honestly, it's the ugliest building in this quaint neighborhood, and it could use some TLC. In my gut, I know that building is meant to be mine.

"What'd you buying dat for?" He tilts his chin higher to look me in the eye.

"I'm opening a clinic. For anyone who needs it."

"Here? In effing Greenville?"

"Yes." Smiling, I nod. "In effing Greenville."

"What, you like a doctor or something?"

"Yes, I am. Not like one, I am. A surgeon and an ER doctor."

"Damn. Well, welcome, doc. You need anything, Julius is your man." He bangs his chest and then puts out his hand.

Suppressing a chuckle, I smile. "Thank you, Julius."

"See you around, doc." He disappears as fast as he popped up, and the catcalls disappear with him.

Doc. When Julius calls me doc, it reminds me of Nick and the Steel Knights and, of course, my mind floods with thoughts of Seth. How he clamped his strong hands on my waist, how when we kissed, his mouth opened mine as he pulled me closer and held me in his strong arms—

Crap. I have been trying to push him from my mind, but it's not working. *Everything* seems to remind me of Seth. Damn it. Why did it have to end like it did? Taking a deep breath, I look up at the sky. The view is only partially blocked by power lines, but the sky is a bright blue—the same color as that bluebird's wings. It's a gorgeous day. I just wish Seth were here to enjoy it with me.

Breathing deeply, I push away my sadness. No way. I will not let my life's dream be affected by a fight with a man I barely know. No matter how much he rocked my world.

A car drives by and pulls up alongside my building. My heart races and my palms begin to sweat—is someone else looking at my building? There's no way. Clutching my bag tight to my chest, I begin moving faster down the sidewalk, dodging a man walking three dogs and a woman who's hand-in-hand with her daughter. With my eyes glued to my building, I watch as a woman with curly hair gets out of the car. She clamps her hands onto her hips and looks up at the building.

Shit.

"Excuse me!" Passing by a man walking his dog, I run faster. The smell of freshly-baked bread fills my nose and burns my lungs as sweat trickles down my spine. Moving quickly, I come up on the chain-link fence. There's no way I'm going to lose this building to some gentrifying—

"Holly?"

The woman turns and smiles as I approach.

"Yes?"

"I'm Clea. Your agent."

"Right." Trying to calm my breathing, I shake her hand.

Releasing my hand, she glances at me sideways. "You okay?

"Yes, uh, yes." Catching my breath, I smile. "Fine. Thank you."

"Where's your car?"

A logical question. "I parked down the street." I point behind me. "I wanted to walk around the neighborhood."

Nodding, she raises her eyebrows. "Be careful. Well, it's nice to finally meet you in person."

"You as well."

"I've known your parents for a long time." She nods. "They're wonderful people. They've done so much for the community."

"Have they?" I ask, tilting my head.

"Well, yes." She furrows her brow. "The donations they made last year to the Fourth Street Collective—"

"They bought laptops for a small group of kids going to college."

"Yes." She raises an eyebrow.

"And made a tax-deductible donation."

"I suppose."

"And let me guess, you're on the board of the Fourth Street Collective."

"I am." She nods.

This was the reason I didn't want to work with Clea Saunders—because of her connection to my parents. I'd never met her before, and when I scheduled the appointment, I didn't know who she was. It wasn't until I gave her my name that the connection was made. By then, I was already in love with the building and it's her exclusive listing.

Besides, there's no way she'll rat me out to my parents and risk them talking me out of it. She's not going to want to give up this commission.

Looking up at the building, Clea uses her hand to shield her eyes from the sun. "You sure about this one, huh?" Turning to me, she shrugs. "I have some great listings in the suburbs if you'd like to see something there. Most people, when they hear Greenville, think it's different from this—"

"No." Cutting her off, I'm louder than I mean to be. "No suburbs." The thought of the suburbs covers me in a blanket of depression, but I refuse to get caught up. I grew up in the suburbs, in a five-thousand-square-foot house with a pool and everything I could ever want—and I never want to go back.

Clea nods. "I get it. Just thought you were making a move from the big city. Anyway, you're thinking about a clinic here?"

Looking up at the three-story brick building with plywood covering the windows, I focus on the stone arch above the front door. Closing my eyes, I imagine the words "All Are Welcome Here" painted above that door.

"Yes," I answer. "I'm opening a clinic here." My words are a whisper as I soak in the moment. This is the fulfillment of my lifelong dream.

"Well." She climbs up the stone steps and slips a key into the lock that turns. Then she does the same with two more locks. "Let's see if you like it first."

Pushing open the door, she motions for me to step in before her. As I do, I'm immediately struck by the cold air that smells like dust and mildew. My heart feels like it drops out of my body.

"Were there mold tests run?"

"Yes, absolutely." Letting the door close behind us, Clea fishes through her bag and pulls out a flashlight.

She clicks it on and shines it above us. Preparing to crouch and run from bats flying at us, I chuckle when I realize the only things greeting me are cobwebs and dust.

"The place has good bones," Clea tells me as she steps into the space. She knocks against a column in the middle of the floor.

Reaching into my bag, I grab my phone. "Flashlight on," I command. Leaving Clea in the middle of the room, I start snooping around. The ground floor has a solid wood floor, high ceilings, and large picture windows on one side. It's so perfect, I have to slow my racing heart.

"What was here before?" I ask Clea.

She looks up from scrolling through her phone. "It was a manufacturing plant of some kind. I think they made gloves. Like, dress gloves women used to wear once upon a time." When she chuckles, her curls bounce along with her.

Moving past her, I make my way to the opposite end of the building. "The bottom floor is empty except for a couple of large machines back here."

"Yes." Tucking her phone into her bag, Clea looks at me. "The second and third floors are mostly empty as well. There is working plumbing, so that's a nice break. There are two half bathrooms on the main floor, and one full bathroom on the second floor and two on the third floor. The third floor has the kitchen, of course."

"I'm sorry, kitchen?" The word makes my heart thump even louder. But why?

"Yes. The people who owned it lived here."

"They lived in the building?" My mind races. If I could give up my exorbitant rent, I'd have even more money to use here, and the commute to the hospital wouldn't be that much longer. Plus, it's a bit of a hike, but it's still walking distance to the city of Phoenix. The location is perfect.

"Yes, but, Holly, I don't think that's something you want to consider. This isn't a neighborhood for a single woman."

"Why not? There seem to be plenty of single women out there." I point to the front door.

"Yes, but you know what I mean."

Plopping my hands on my hips, I shake my head stubbornly. "I'm sorry, I don't."

"Holly."

Clea walks up and stands so close to me I can see her in the dim light even without a flashlight.

"You need to be smart here."

"I assure you, Clea, I *am* smart."

"Oh, I know you're a surgeon and run an emergency room, but I'm talking about being smart with your investments. With your money and connections, why not hire a financial advisor?"

"I have a financial advisor."

Nodding, she smiles. "And did they tell you this was a good idea?"

"I didn't ask. I'm not buying this for an investment, Clea. I'm opening a clinic. In an area that needs it."

"Holly." Reaching out, she places a hand on my arm. "This town is static. There's no room for growth. Between us and off-the-record, because I could lose my license for this, the area is dead." Pursing her lips together, she nods solemnly. "Hell knows I need this commission: it's a seven-figure deal. My lease is up soon, and I'd like to trade up from a sedan to a crossover, but, as a friend of your parents, I feel I should warn you. This area is not emerging, it's just dead. No one is buying here."

"Which is exactly why I should. Clea, these people don't need gentrification. They don't need a yoga studio and a coffee shop. If it changed like that, they'd never survive the rent hikes, and they'd be kicked out. What the people here need is opportunity, education, and, most immediately, healthcare."

Sighing, Clea steps away. "You're so young, Holly." Shrugging, she throws up her hands like she's conceding. "It's your money."

"Yes, it is." Walking downstairs, I head to the staircase and up to the second floor. It's a completely empty open space that would work for storage or could be opened up to the third floor, making a great two-story permanent living area. Climbing up to the third floor, I find a door at the top of the stairs. Reaching out, I put my hand on the doorknob and turn. Thankfully, it's unlocked. For some reason, I really want to see this by myself, without Clea at my heels. Pushing the door open, I find the relics of a family's life.

"Oh, my goodness." Putting a hand to my mouth, I'm completely overcome as I step inside. Dead ahead is a living area with two tall windows that are covered with some type of black material. Sunlight pours through the cracks in the coverings, illuminating a corner that houses an old black, dust-covered sewing machine that's built into a table. Farther into the room, an old couch leans up against a wall. To the right is a table and a couple of chairs. Just past that is a large, square kitchen with black and white tiles on the floor. There's even an antique gas stove. The living space is large and welcoming. Moving to the back of the room, I push open a door that leads to a long hallway.

Looking down the hallway, I suddenly have the strangest vision of Seth laughing as he chases a squealing little girl down this hallway. He's carrying another little girl—tucked under his strong arm—who's also laughing. Everyone is having so much fun, and the image is so real it takes my breath away. Could Seth and I really have a future together? Regardless, I have such a strong pull and connection to this place, I can feel it in my very soul. Not even bothering to look into the bedrooms, I turn around and march down the stairs.

"I'll take it, Clea."

"Really?" She raises her eyebrows in response. "You're sure?"

"I've never been more sure of anything in my life." Standing here, I can't help but notice the calm and peace I feel. I don't feel the need to bite my nails, and my anxiety is at bay. "Please tell the seller I'll take it at asking price."

"You don't want to think about it or make an offer?"

"No." Grabbing my phone, I send a quick text. "I'll have the inspector here later today. All I'm worried about is the gas coming into the building. But I don't think it will be an issue. The title search is done, I've been preapproved for the mortgage, and I'm putting twenty-percent down. I want to close as soon as possible—tomorrow, if you can. I'm taking some time off from work this week, and I'd like to get as much done here as possible."

"Okay."

Clea shakes my hand. Turning away from her, I nearly glide down the front steps and onto the street in front of *my building*. Just as I turn around to look at it, a group of small children comes running up. Circling around me, they hurry down the street, probably on their way to school. If I wasn't a doctor and didn't know better, I would swear my racing heart is swelling. Healthcare. For this community. What could be better? From there, who knows? Maybe I can open clinics in all different emerging areas around Arizona, and then the country, and then maybe Doctors Without Borders and…

A grin spreads across my face. Never, in my entire life, have I ever felt so free. Sure, I'm emptying my entire life savings into this, and no, I don't have a fallback plan if it doesn't work out but I'll make it work. There's never been anything I've ever wanted more. Closing my eyes for a moment, I place my hand on my hip and think of my bird tattoo, imagining it taking flight.

This is it. For the first time ever, I'm free.

Warmth churns in my belly and I'm so damned giddy, I just wish I had someone to share it with. Picking up my phone, I stare at the screen. After the way we left things, would Seth even take my call?

Sighing, I push Seth from my mind and call the hospital to confirm that I won't be in this week, and maybe next week as well. Since I've never so much as taken a vacation week, they're surprised but fine with it. No sooner than I hang up, it rings.

My heart does a little flip-flop. When Seth and I exchanged numbers the other night, I never thought it would cause this much angst. Maybe he's thinking of me like I'm thinking of him?

Looking at the number—damn. It's Robert. What a way to bring down a day. Nope. Not answering it. I don't owe him or anyone else an explanation of what I'm doing with my life. Tucking the phone back into my bag, I look back up at my building, imagining everything it can be—

The loud rev of a motorcycle engine grabs my attention.

"Seth?"

Whipping around, I see two men on motorcycles riding by slowly.

Crap. Disappointment churns in my gut, replacing the warmth that had just been there. No, it isn't logical to think Seth knows I'm here, and even if he did, would he care? But still. Taking a deep breath, I focus on the two men driving by. As they pass, I read the backs of their jackets: Unchained Dogs. The rival motorcycle club of the Steel Knights.

Shit. A chill shoots down my spine and I shiver. Watching the men on their bikes practically crawling down the street, my hands grow cold and my breathing becomes shallow.

Maybe it's because of the other night, when some of the Unchained Dogs were fighting with Seth and the other Knights, but I know in my gut that these guys are bad news.

At the end of the street, they circle back and slowly come toward me again.

Tensing, my knees lock and I swallow a gulp of air. What the hell do they want with me? The most I ever did to them was fix them up when they came to me in a million pieces. Fight or flight is kicking in, and part of me wants to run, but no. Standing tall, I take a deep breath. There's no way I'm going to be intimidated. This is my building, and maybe even my home, and no one is going to ruin it for me.

As they pass by so slowly, I wonder how they can stay balanced on those machines, one man raises his hand and salutes me. The other points at me and nods. They are definitely sending me a message. But what is it?

A cold breeze passes over me, and looking up to the sky, I see a dark cloud blocking the sun. Shit. Something is wrong. I can feel it. Nodding to the men in response, I swallow hard.

After the second pass, they pick up speed and race away. Whew. With a shaking hand, I lift my phone. Seth should know. It's not that they did anything, but something in my soul tells me he should know the Dogs were here and—

Feeling something off, I glance up from my phone, and looking across the now-grayish dark street, I spot someone standing there. Squinting for a better view, I see it's a tall, thin man in a leather jacket next to a bike with an Unchained Dogs emblem on it. Leaning back against a building, his arms are crossed before his chest.

Noticing me, he stands up tall, uncrosses his arms, and places his hands on hips. When he does, his jacket opens at the waist, exposing a shiny gun.

Lifting what I think is a phone, he snaps a picture of me just as a seven- or eight-year-old boy runs up to me. He's breathing heavily and gasping for air.

Squatting down, I look him in the eye. "Are you okay?" Keeping an eye on the man, I make sure he doesn't pull the gun while there's a child around.

Nodding, the boy takes one more deep breath. I can hear the rattle of asthma in his chest.

"Just my rattlesnake breath," he answers.

"Rattlesnake breath? Is that when it feels like your lungs are shaking and it's hard to breathe? I get it." Nodding, I force a smile. "Where's your mommy? Or daddy?"

Pointing in the opposite direction, the boy smiles. Turning, I see a heavyset, middle-aged woman carrying grocery bags hurrying up to us.

"Jonny!" she snaps when she approaches. I can hear from her voice that she's relieved he's there and okay. "Leave the lady alone."

"It's okay." I stand to talk to her. Putting out my hand to shake hers, I realize she has groceries in both arms. "Can I take one?"

Smiling, she hands me the bag.

"My name is Holly," I tell her, balancing the groceries in one arm and shaking her hand with the other. "I'm moving in here. I'm a doctor."

"Oh! A doctor. You must be rich."

"No," I tell her, laughing. "Especially not once I sign those papers."

"Excuse me?" She tilts her head. Of course, she doesn't understand my lame joke.

"I'm going to be opening a clinic here. I'd like you to bring Jonny by to get checked. I think he has asthma. Do you know what asthma is?"

Nodding, she sighs. "His rattlesnake breath."

"Yes."

"But I can't afford the medications," she tells me. The corners of her mouth droop and her eyes glass over.

"My clinic will be low-cost or free," I explain. For the first time, this is all becoming real. Suddenly, I understand that I'm not going to be able to keep this clinic afloat all on my own. I'll need financial—and physical—support.

Looking into Jonny's smart brown eyes, I smile. The hell with it. One way or another, even if I'm in debt up to my eyeballs for the rest of my life, I will make this happen.

"Free?" his mother asks, shaking her head skeptically.

"Yes. But it will take a couple of weeks to get up and running. When you bring him in, he'll need a lung function test and maybe some x-rays. In the meantime, if he gets to a point where he can't breathe, I want you to take Jonny to the hospital that's between here and Phoenix. The large one. Do you know it?"

She nods, so I go on.

"Good. Stop by tomorrow, maybe around noon. I'm going to get you a free appointment with my friend in Phoenix."

As we talk, Jonny runs off a few feet, then slows his pace and leans forward to catch his breath. Damn it. No child should ever be sick.

"Thank you, thank you. I've got to go." Taking the groceries from me, Jonny's mother walks off after him.

"Wait!" Hurrying up to her, I catch her and give her my business card. "I had one in my pocket." I smile at her. "Please take it. It has my cell number. If you need anything, please call."

The woman nods as she rushes off, thanking me again as she goes.

Glancing across the street, I see the Unchained Dog is still there, staring at me. He raises his phone again and snaps another picture.

I don't give a crap.

Turning, I make my way up the stairs and open the still-unlocked door of my decrepit building. Stalling at the door, I turn. Glaring at the Dog, I flip him the bird.

I can't help myself, and damn, it feels good. Chuckling, I realize I'm sounding a little like Seth—and I kind of like it.

Nodding, the Dog hops onto his bike, and with an ear-shattering rev of his engine, he peels out, taking off.

Good riddance. No, I probably shouldn't have done that, but I don't care. It's true that the Unchained Dogs in my neighborhood, driving by my building and snapping pictures of me, isn't good but I refuse to be scared.

It's clear they're sending me a message, but so what?

Biting my bottom lip, I take a deep breath. Who cares why they're trying to intimidate me? I've never let anyone scare me off before, and I'm not about to start now. No way. There's nothing, not even a pack of wild Unchained Dogs, that is going to keep me from helping Jonny and the other children of this neighborhood.

Chapter Twelve

Dynamite

"You tending bar?" I nod to Seneca's kid brother, Matt, who's standing behind the bar at Hoppa's Taphouse.

Grinning, he grabs a beer from the cooler, pops the top, and hands it to me.

"Yup, and anything else I can do. Just glad to be alive, you know?"

"I do."

Holding up my bottle in a toast, we smile at one another. The kid's been through way worse than me. He was in Sing Sing for three years, but I'm the only other person here who knows what it's like to have been on the inside—and how fucking good it feels to be out. Shit, even the crap jobs, like cleaning the bar, are a downright pleasure when you know you're doing it by choice.

Looking around, I only see a handful of the guys. "Where is everyone?"

Matt dries a glass as we talk. "Don't know about the rest, but Seneca and Bullseye are home, and Bullet and Nick are in the back."

"Thanks." I make my way to the back room of Hoppa's Taphouse. Bullet's there, pouring over some books.

Nick looks up from his stack when I walk in. "Where you been all day?"

"The construction company. Since they agreed to our deal, I knew they'd be on our side. I figured I'd spend some time nosing around to see what they know about the cement mess." Truth is I haven't stopped thinking about Holly for a moment since she left my place last week, and I'm doing anything possible to keep my mind off of her. Grabbing a chair, I hop up and sit on a nearby counter, sliding the chair under my feet.

"You find out anything?" Nick looks concerned.

"Nothing we didn't already know. My guys at the company have no idea how the cement got blocked." Taking another long pull from my bottle, I place it down next to me and then turn to Bullet. He hasn't so much as glanced up from the stack of papers he's plowing through. "What are you looking for?"

Grumbling, he looks up. "Money in the budget, what else?"

"We're short?" Hopping off the counter, I walk up to him. "Impossible. I've been through the numbers about a billion times."

"No, we're fine for the time span we'd planned," Nick explains. "But with my proposed extension and the concrete holdup, we're starting later, which means guys are on retainer—"

"I'm sorry about that," I interrupt Nick. "I had no idea the Dogs had their hand in the unions now."

"None of us did."

Blink! A text comes in, and my heart nearly jumps into my throat. Closing my eyes just for a second, I silently will it to be Holly texting. I feel like shit about the way I left things with her the other day, and all I want is an opportunity to make it right. But considering the way she left me, after what I said… damn. I haven't bothered reaching out to her because she probably never wants to speak to me again.

Still, I have to look. Glancing at it, I see the text came from a cell number I don't recognize but with our area code.

Normally, I'd just delete the damned thing, but something in my gut is telling me to look at it.

Scrolling down, there's a picture. It's grainy and hard to see, but—is that Holly? It's pixelated, but squinting and focusing hard, I can just make out the silhouette of Holly standing next to a child in front of an old building. Two more texts come in, and then two more. Each has a picture of Holly coming and going from that same building. The last picture is of her hugging a little boy. Blowing up the picture, I see the address on the building identifies this as Main Street in Greenville.

Greenville is Dog turf.

From what I can tell from the time and date stamps, Holly has been in a building on Dog turf for the past week, and they've been snapping pictures of her every damned day.

One more text comes in, but this time, it's only a short message: *To really be a saint, you have to be dead.*

"What the fuck?"

Jumping to my feet, Nick and Bullet look at me.

"What's going on?" Nick asks.

"It must be the Dogs. Someone just texted me a week's worth of pictures of Holly, and the last text is a death threat. She's standing in front of a building in Greenville."

"That's Dog turf," Bullet says, standing tall.

"I've gotta go."

Hurrying to the door, I hear Bullet and Nick call after me.

"Dynamite! Make sure she's safe, but don't do anything crazy." It's Nick's voice.

Yeah. Sure. Don't do anything crazy. You might as well tell a freaking wolf not to howl at the moon.

My heart is pounding so loud, it's making almost as much noise as I am as I bang on the door of the old building in Greenville. I drove so fast to get here, what should have been a forty-five-minute ride took me just under twenty minutes.

"Holly? Holly!"

Where the hell is she? Glancing around the neighborhood, I don't see any Dogs, so I let go of the breath I've been holding. It's evening, but the street is pretty well lit so I can see just about everyone and everything that's happening.

"Come on, Holly," I mutter to myself.

Pounding on the door again, there's still no reply. Planning to try the side windows, I jump down the few front steps and come toe-to-toe with some kid in a tank top and jeans. He doesn't look much more than fourteen or fifteen.

"You the one who's been shoutin' for Ms. Holls?" The kid walks closer and looks me in the eyes.

"Ms. Holls? You mean Dr. Boling?" I don't have time for this little punk and his questions.

"That's right."

He raises his chin, and when I move right, he steps to his left, blocking me.

"Listen, punk, I don't have time for this shit."

"I ain't no punk." He slaps himself on the chest.

"No?"

"No, man. I'm Dr. Holly's assistant. I handle whatever she needs—and I do mean *whatever*." He looks me up and down.

That's it. Grabbing the kid by his tank top, I lift him and push him back against the building. He lands with a thud. "Don't you ever," I snarl at the stupid kid, "ever say something like that about her ever again. Do you understand me, you little punk ass—"

"Seth?"

Whipping my head around, I see Holly standing there. She looks like a vision in an army green jacket and old jeans, holding a bag of groceries in one hand and a half-eaten apple in the other.

"What the hell are you doing with Julius?" Tossing the apple into her bag, she steps closer to us.

Not letting go of the punk, I keep looking at her over my shoulder. "Teaching him some manners. Little punk seems to think he can say things about you that he shouldn't."

She cocks her head and frowns. "Good grief, Seth, let him go. He's just a kid."

Turning back to face Julius, I lock eyes with him, and with a quick jerking motion, I push him back against the wall one more time just so he remembers who's boss around here. She may think he's all innocent, but I remember all too well what fifteen-year-old boys are capable of. Dropping the kid, I turn around and face Holly. I know she's going to be pissed that I just roughed up some kid, but she's already mad at me, so all I can do is to face it like a man. Standing up tall, I make eye contact with her.

She glares at me, and then turns to the damned punk. "Julius? You okay?" She uses a younger, sweeter voice with him—the same voice I heard at the hospital.

"Yeah." Standing up straight, he fixes his stretched-out tank top. "He didn't do nothin' to me."

Nodding, she smiles. "All right. I'll see you tomorrow? I have some boxes that need to be moved."

"Boxes?" Stepping up to her, I look her in the eyes. "What do you mean boxes?"

"One second, Seth."

Turning to the kid, she says bye and he walks off, glaring at me as he goes. Once he's down the street, she faces me. Her eyes light up for a moment and then dull again. She sighs.

"What are you doing here, Seth?"

"I need to talk to you."

"The way you just talked to Julius?"

"Holly." I cock my head at her. "Be serious. You know I would never touch you in that way. The kid was saying things he shouldn't."

"He's fifteen, Seth. What's your excuse?" She lifts an eyebrow.

"Okay, yes, I deserve that, but please, Holly. It's important. Really important."

"Fine."

She pushes her grocery bag at me and then fishes in her bag, pulling out a giant set of keys. Keeping my eyes peeled, focused on the street, I still don't see a single stray Dog. Walking up the steps of the decrepit building behind her, I wait while she puts the keys in the locks. Stepping back, I put my hand out, but there's no railing. Crap. I catch my balance no problem, but she could easily fall any day if she's not extra-careful.

Her phone rings. Pulling it out of her jacket pocket, she glances at the number. "Shit." Mumbling under her breath, she switches off her phone and then buries it in her pocket again.

Pushing open the front door, she nods for me to follow her. Walking in, I realize that the railing is the least of her problems. Turning in a circle, I look around and—damn. Is she joking with this place? What is she doing here? Why would she rent some shithole like this? It's pretty dark, but I can make out a few things. My gaze jumps from boarded-up windows to filthy floors and crumbling walls to spiderwebs everywhere.

Eyeing me, she locks the door behind us. Then, she walks to a wall and clicks on a switch.

"Ta-da!" Light comes from the overhead fixtures. "I have electricity. And plumbing. All in less than a week." Taking the bag of groceries from me, she plops them onto a tiny nearby table. "Isn't that amazing?" Pointing to the light, she smiles. "Now I can start cleaning and scrubbing I have to do as much as I can myself, and then I'll call in a service. This is going to cost me even more than I anticipated, and since I can't work at the hospital around the clock to cover expenses *and* be here at the same time…" She takes a deep breath. "Well, I'll be busy." She covers her smile with her hand and shakes her head. "I'm sorry. You came here to say something, and here I am rambling on about the place."

Smiling at me, I see she's absolutely glowing. This is the happiest I've ever seen her, but that doesn't change anything. She can't be here. I hate to be the one to crush her dreams, but it's better to live with a broken dream than to die.

"No, it can wait." It *can* wait. As long as I'm here, she's safe.

"Well? Isn't it great?" She nods to me.

"Um." Is she serious?

Tilting her head, her bottom lip pouts just the slightest bit, and all I want to do is pull her into my arms, keep her safe, and kiss her—over and over again. Her gorgeous face clouds over. She's looking for more of a reaction from me, but what can I say?

"Well." She pulls herself together. "Maybe it doesn't look all that great yet, but you have to use some vision and imagination. Look." She gives me a tour as she talks.

Conceding, I stay put and listen. Yeah, I'm desperate to tell her why I came and to get her the hell out of here, but with the door locked and me here, she's about as safe as she can get.

"The bottom floor is obviously for the main clinic." Holding out her hands, she twirls around in a circle. Moving closer toward me and the front door, she explains, "I'll have a big front desk for check-in as well as a large waiting area over here." She motions with her hands. "Then I'll have private rooms back here, separated by curtains like they have in the ER." She walks backward as she narrates. "Then, on the second floor—"

"How many floors are there?"

"Three. Come on."

Gesturing for me to follow, she leads me up a staircase to the second floor. As we step out into a big, open loft area, she seems even more excited to tell me her plans.

"This will be storage for now. But maybe—come on. Let's see the third floor."

Following her up another flight of stairs, I'm selfishly glad this one is also missing its handrail. Focusing on not missing a step and plummeting to my death keeps my eyes off of her incredibly fine ass.

Pushing open an old door with chipping paint, she reveals the third floor. Smiling, she has an incredibly proud look on her face. "The third floor."

Walking in, I spy an old, dusty couch and some other random furniture. Huh. Whoever rented it before her lived here. Poor bastards.

"So, my big plan for this is that someday I'll open up this floor, and over here, I'll put an inside stairwell between the two floors. I'll have a two-floor living space."

"W-wait a second. Living space?"

"Yeah." Moving over to the area that was probably the dining room, she explains, "The kitchen is so big, there's no way anyone needs a separate dining area. So, my idea is to knock out the dining area and the floor here and put in a staircase to the downstairs." Sticking her hands into her jeans' pockets, she smiles. "And you know what else? There are three bedrooms." She holds up her fingers to emphasize the point. "And there are—"

Holding up my hand, I cut her off. "Holly, you can't live here."

Crossing her arms before her chest, she scowls. "Excuse me?"

"You heard me. You can't live here. You can't even work here."

"Why the hell not?"

"Because it's way too dangerous."

"Too dangerous?" Throwing her hands up in exasperation, she sighs. "Oh, my gosh. Seth Hardy, I don't think I have ever been more wrong about a human being than I was about you. We spent one night together when I thought you were this cool, accepting guy. Then, the next morning, when you had the audacity to tell me what 'my kind of woman' would do—" She uses air quotes. "—I left. I would have expected you to get the message. But here you are again, judging the people in my neighborhood. I'm perfectly safe here. I've already made friends. You know how many people I'm friends with in my luxury apartment in Phoenix?" She forms her hand into the shape of a zero. "Zip. None. Not one holiday card, and barely a 'hello' in the elevators. Here, I already have dinner invitations."

"From Julius?" I scoff.

"Really, Seth?" Sighing, she looks me up and down before staring into my eyes. "For your information, Julius is a nice kid, and he's helping me out."

"He's crushing on you."

"So what? What does that matter? Maybe hanging around me, he'll learn a thing or two about how to treat a woman with respect. And no, he's not who I have dinner plans with. It's Mrs. Drakos down the street. I'm treating her son for asthma."

Pushing past me, she hustles down the stairs and I hurry to keep up.

"Holly, I'm sorry. I know I sound like a jealous asshole—"

"—Yeah, you do."

Ouch. "But you have to hear me out."

Making it to the bottom floor, she whips around and faces me. "I do not *have* to do anything, Seth." Holding her hands up by her ears, she shakes her head in frustration. "All of my life, I have done exactly what people told me to do. I'm done with it. This isn't some rebellion against my parents, and I'm not moving from one set of people who boss me around to another who does exactly the same." She gestures to me. "No. No more. I do not need to do anything anyone tells me anymore. I am a grown woman. I'm building a clinic for people in need and, hell, I even own a building."

"Wait. You own this place?"

"Closed on it last week."

"Holly, you have to sell and get out."

"I most certainly will not." Her voice is louder now. "Didn't you hear what I said to you? You can't tell me what to do."

"You're in danger here."

"Ugh!" she yells in frustration. "Will everyone please stop treating me like I'm a fragile princess?" She moves closer to me. "I pulled a friggin' knife out of your shoulder. I fish bullets out of people's bodies. I save lives. Stop treating me like I'm a damned—"

"Holly, be quiet and listen to me!" I snap at her. Lowering my voice, I explain, "Your life is in danger here."

"What?" Shaking her head, she steps back. "What are you talking about?"

"The Dogs. They made a threat against you." Pulling out my phone, I scroll through the texts and bring up the pictures of her.

Taking another small step back, her voice is quieter. "I did see someone taking a photo of me. Why would they do that?"

"They did it to antagonize me."

"Why? Who would connect us?"

"The Dogs."

Her eyes light up in recognition. "They were here. The first day I came to see the place. They drove by slowly, and then I saw one of the guys take a picture of me and I-I sort of flipped him off."

"What?"

"Never mind about that now. Why would they think I'm the link to you?"

"They saw me that night in the hospital when there was a Dog and Viper fight. One of the Dogs spotted me, and he must have realized why I was there. Then again, the night at Hoppa's Taphouse—when you took care of Colt—maybe someone saw us leave together. I'm so sorry, Holly. I dragged you into this."

"You didn't drag me. I went willingly. But I still don't understand: why me?"

"They want to take the Knights down, but we're too strong as a group. So, they're dividing us—starting with me. The other guys who have girls, their women live with them. They're safer. But you and I…" Shaking my head, I wish this would all just go away. "I'm heading the build of the new clubhouse. The connections are mine, and so is the plan. The clubhouse is being built on unclaimed turf. The Dogs wanted it, but now that we've already broken ground, it will clearly be ours. They're pissed and they're blaming me. They know I have feelings for you, and they know that I'm impulsive. They're counting on it. It's a perfect situation for them."

"Wait. You have feelings for me?" The way she drops her chin and her chest rises and falls with her quickening breaths…

"Yes." I dare a step closer. "That's why I need you to leave. Right now. You're not safe here."

"I get it. Thank you. I'll be careful, but I'm not leaving. These people in this neighborhood need me. They're counting on me. I'm not going to run just because some bullies are trying to scare me off. Who's going to take care of those kids out there? Believe me, I've dealt with intimidation before. I'll figure something out."

"There's nothing to figure out, Holly. Not only are they using you to get to me, but this building is on Dog turf."

"Excuse me?" A look of disbelief washes over her face. "Dog turf? This is not their building. It's mine. I bought this place. It's in my name. I'm the one carrying a seven-figure mortgage and who plopped down my life savings for repairs."

"Holly—"

Her phone rings again. Shaking her head, she glances at it.

"Shit. It's my mother again. She's called a hundred times. I have to take this." Walking to the opposite side of the space, she answers the phone. "Yes, Mom. What is it? What? What kind of emergency? Oh." She relaxes. "You shouldn't say things are an emergency if they're not. Fine. Urgent, then. What is it you have to talk to me about so desperately? No, Mom, I really don't want dinner at the club." Her gaze flashes to me. "Okay, you know what? Fine. Yes. Dinner at Southward Pines Country Club, tonight at eight. Fine."

Clicking the phone off, she shakes her head. "That is about the last thing I want to do right now—go back to my apartment, dig out a dress, go to dinner, and make small talk."

"Then don't go. But, Holly, you can't stay here. You need to come with me now. We'll figure out a way to sell this place and recoup as much of your investment as we can—"

Putting up her hand, she glowers at me. "Seth. Enough. I am not selling this place, and I am not going to be afraid anymore. The people in this neighborhood need me, and I will be damned if I let my parents, you, or a group of men who call themselves the Unchained Dogs stop me from helping these people and fulfilling my life's purpose."

"Holly—"

"Goodbye, Seth."

Walking to the front door, she opens it and nods for me to leave.

Walking past her, I take a deep breath. Even after everything, she still smells like flowers. "Be careful, Holly. Please."

Crap. I have to fix this and keep her safe. Hustling down the stairs, I know there is only one way to do that. There's only one thing I can do, and one place I can go. The last place I ever want to be seen.

In enemy territory.

And I have to go alone. Bringing the Knights with me would be seen as a threat, but walking in by myself won't, although—damn, it might be certain death. Thing is, I'll have to risk it if it means keeping her safe.

But going to the Dogs' clubhouse means leaving her unguarded from anyone who stops by. Glancing over my shoulder, I spot Julius hanging in a doorway a few buildings down.

"Hey!" I shout to him.

He stands up straight, glaring at me.

Walking toward him, I see him tense as I approach. His jaw clenches and his hands ball into fists. Shit. I don't have time for this crap.

"Stand down, kid." Stepping up to him, I hold my hands up to show him I'm not here to beat the crap out of him. "I want a favor from you."

Raising his chin, he glares at me. "Yeah? Why should I do anything for you?"

"You shouldn't. You should do it for Holly."

His expression softens and he turns his head, looking at me out of the corner of his eye. "What is it?"

"You ever see guys around here with biker jackets on? Not like this one." I slap my chest. "Big pictures of dogs in broken chains—"

"The Unchained Dogs. Yeah, I ain't stupid. I know who they are."

"They around here a lot?"

Lifting his shoulders, he shrugs. "Some."

Swallowing back my anger, I take a deep breath. "You got a phone?"

"Yeah. What's it to you?"

"Let me have it." Holding out my hand, I beckon for him to hand me the phone.

"Aw, shit, man. I just got this. You robbin' me?"

"No, I'm not robbing you. Now unlock the damned thing so I can give you my number."

"You giving me your digits?" He unlocks his phone and hands it to me.

"Yeah." I input my number quickly, and then the number for Hoppa's Taphouse. Holding his phone out toward him, I show him the new entries. "Anything goes down with the Dogs, or if Holly is in any kind of trouble, you call me first. If, uh…" Clearing my throat, I don't even want to think of this as a possibility. "If you can't get me, call the Taphouse. It's the clubhouse for the Steel Knights. Tell them who you are and that I said to call. They'll know what to do."

His eyes light up. "Okay."

"Now give me your number in case I need you."

"You gonna need me?" He eyes me skeptically.

"I might. You're my man on the inside now. You've gotta look out for Holly when I can't be here. All right?"

"A-right."

After inputting his number, we shake hands and then I rush back to my bike. Hopping on, I glance at Holly's building. She's there, peeking through one of the front windows. Looking over, I catch Julius parking himself on her front steps. Revving my engine, I nod to both of them as, all alone, I rush toward enemy territory—the Unchained Dogs' clubhouse.

Chapter Thirteen

Dynamite

What the hell am I doing? Cutting my engine, I stay back a good distance from the Dogs' clubhouse, hiding my bike in the bushes. It's not easy to hide anywhere in Rumble. The town is so old and sunbaked that pretty much any tree or bush you could use for cover has died off. I did find one bush across from the clubhouse, and I'm able to store my bike in the alley behind it. Crouching down, I use the bush for camouflage, but the damned thing has thorns that scratch my face and neck. Using my arms, which have a thick layer of leather from my jacket to protect them, I push my way through the branches to get a closer look. There it is—the Unchained Dogs' clubhouse. Shit, I swear I can smell the nasty scent of wet dog all the way over here.

The clubhouse itself looks like the first stop you'd make on a tour of Hell. Its faded red façade is crumbling around the edges of its one picture window that's half-boarded with plywood and half-covered with a large, black plastic garbage bag. Sure, there are run-down buildings in Holly's neighborhood as well but at least it looks like someone is trying to keep it from becoming decrepit. This just looks like crap, and I've got to be crazy to go walking in there alone and unarmed. But if I were packing, it would be an invitation to kill me. Sure, one guy can approach another in neutral territory, like the range or something, but not on another club's home turf. Taking a deep breath, I have to accept the fact that just for walking in there, I may not walk out again.

Some guy with long hair wearing a Dog jacket comes out of the clubhouse and looks around. Glancing up at the night sky, he swings his arms back and forth. Another guy walks out and bums a cigarette. Shit. I got here during freaking teatime. Ducking down and back into the shadows, I slow my breathing. The only thing I have going for me is the element of surprise. I don't want to be spotted and blow my chance.

Finally, after chatting it up like two old ladies, the guys hop onto their bikes and speed off. So, this is it. My chance. Standing up, I stay in the shadows as much as possible as I approach the building. No doubt they have cameras everywhere, and I don't want to be spotted until the last possible second.

Taking a deep breath, I feel a little like a man without a parachute about to jump from a plane. But what choice do I have? They threatened her life, and she doesn't fully understand the danger she's in. They have to be stopped, and someone has to pay.

As I approach the last few yards of the road before their sidewalk, I stand to my full height, letting my presence be known. Fuck yeah. Now it's time to let them see who they're dealing with.

The door swings open just as I approach. The stench of cigarettes, stale beer, and old piss is suffocating.

"Dynamite." Some clod I don't recognize in a Dog jacket steps outside. He meets me on the street in front of the clubhouse. Damn, if I'm over six feet and thick, this guy must be the size of a freaking mountain. He clasps his hands before him, and his oversized shoulders roll forward. One thing about guys like this is when they fall, they fall hard.

"Do I know you?" Raising my eyebrow, I stand tall before him.

"Guys call me Two-Ton."

"Don't need to explain that one, huh?" Looking him up and down, I search for the perfect place to strike, and my hands ball into fists at my sides. A kick to the kneecap will bring him down. "I need to see Luther."

"Luther ain't got no dealings with a damned Knight. He's got better things to do with his time."

"Tell him I'm here."

Cracking his knuckles, he steps forward. "I said—"

"I heard what you said. Now you need to hear me. I want to see Luther." Taking a deep breath, I try to picture how many more of these punks I'll have to fight off. How many will come out to keep me from Luther? How many of us would head off a Dog outside of Hoppa's Taphouse before we'd let anyone close to Nick? All of us. Shit. But then again, these guys are a different breed.

"I don't think you understand," Two-Ton repeats. "Luther ain't coming out, and you sure as hell ain't going in."

"I was afraid you might say that."

Chuckling, he looks away and then back to me. "Yeah? Why the hell is that?"

"Because now I have to do this."

Before Two-Ton can think, I land a low roundhouse kick to his knee. He buckles, but he doesn't collapse like a regular-sized guy would. Crap. He's stunned enough for me to keep going, so, lifting my foot, I kick him directly against the front of his knee. Because of his enormous size, his knee buckles backward. Fuck.

"Aw, shit!" Collapsing like two tons of bricks on the sidewalk, he moans in agony.

Rushing up to him, I pat down his legs and ankles—which are nearly as thick as my arms—finding two guns. Two, but he probably still has one at his waist. Crap. Straddling his enormous girth with my feet, it takes nearly all my strength to roll him onto his side and—nothing. No weapon.

"Fuck!" Sweat drips down from my brow, stinging my eyes. Repeating my movement on the opposite side, I discover the gun hidden under his massive gut. Pulling it out, it's wet from Two-Ton's sweat.

The Dogs inside must have seen what's happening by now, so darting around Two-Ton before he can grab my ankle, I burst through the clubhouse door with three guns stuffed into my jeans.

Blinking to see clearly in the dim light of the clubhouse, I catch a topless woman sitting on a stool at their makeshift piece-of-shit bar next to an oversized man with a long gray beard. His hand is on her ass, resting on the stool. She looks over her shoulder at me and then turns back to her drink. The man she's with glares at me and, with a good deal of effort, brings himself to a standing position. Placing his hands on his hips, he opens his jacket to show me a gun stuffed into his waistband. Behind the bar, a tall, pimply-skinned guy with a long nose stops wiping a glass and watches. Scanning the rest of the empty bar, my gaze falls on Luther, who is sitting at a small card table off to the side of their bar. On the opposite side of the table sits a man in a turtleneck sweater—his mouth is covered in duct tape and his hands are tied flat to the table with his fingers splayed. He's whimpering, and I can see the sweat pouring down his cheeks.

Shit.

"Hello, Dynamite." Luther smiles. The bar is freaking hot, but Luther looks cool, calm, and collected—even in his colors. "I thought we might be seeing you. I just didn't expect you tonight. If I had, well…" Holding up his hands, he motions to his empty bar. "I wouldn't have sent my boys off for some fun."

My heart feels like it jumps into my throat, and I swallow it down, hard. "Where are they?"

"Oh, don't be alarmed. They're not in Hoppa." Smiling, he leans closer. "Or in Greenville if that's what you're worried about."

"I'm not worried about anything." I take a mental note of the feeling of my phone in my pocket. If the damned Dogs show up at Holly's, Julius will let me know. "But you should be."

The man at the bar moves toward me, but Luther holds up his hand, motioning for him to stand down.

Luther cocks his head. "Is that a threat? Is there a Knight on Dog territory making a threat? Because if so, you know, Dynamite, that means war."

"You lost the last battle, Luther. Why the hell would you want to go to war with us?"

As we talk, the man in the chair opposite Luther tries pulling one of his hands from the table, but it's tied tight. Reaching out, Luther slaps the man's hand still.

"I'll deal with you later," Luther growls. Turning back to me, he says, "We only lost because of that damned machine you had fighting with you—CJ. Everyone knows that. Now that he's gone, well…" Reaching out, he grabs a beer off the floor next to his table and takes a long drag.

"Forget CJ," I snap. "We could beat you anytime and anywhere. What the fuck, Luther?" Sweating and pissed off, I'm getting tired of this little game. Moving my hands to my waist, I wrap them around two of my pieces like it's a showdown in the Old West. So much for appearing unarmed. "Why are your men in Greenville? I want an answer now."

"Tsk, tsk, tsk. So demanding," Luther purrs. He is such a slimy little prick. "Greenville is the territory of the Unchained Dogs. You know that."

"It's time to give it up."

"What do we get in return?"

Swallowing hard, I choke it out. "Land. Where we're building the clubhouse."

Raising his eyebrows, Luther sits back. "Isn't the fundamental rule of any club brotherhood before all else?"

"It is."

"And you're willing to turn on your brothers for a woman?"

Taking a deep breath, I sigh it out through my clenched teeth. "I'm not turning on anyone. This has nothing to do with my brothers or a woman." Forcing the tone of my voice lower, I try to mask my urgency. "I'm making a deal. We'll give you the land outside of Hoppa in exchange for Greenville."

"Sorry. Hoppa and its surrounding areas are nothing. Greenville has businesses. I need those people."

"The people who live there aren't your property."

"They'll learn."

Looking at the man sitting opposite him, Luther reaches under the table, and as he does, I drop to one knee and pull a gun, pointing it at Luther. Graybeard pulls a gun on me, but he's way too slow to match my speed. The woman jumps down and crawls behind her stool. The bartender disappears into the back, and a door slams shut. Good. That must mean there's a back door. As sweat rolls down my face, I am acutely aware that I hear motorcycles in the distance.

Fuck. The Dogs are coming home.

"You don't want to do that, Dynamite," Luther warns, nodding to my gun.

"You're wrong, Luther. *You* don't want to mess with me. Leave Greenville alone. Am I clear?" I need to end this before a dozen or more Dogs come barging in and attack me.

"Why should I?"

Staying low, I swing my leg around and sweep the legs out from under the asshole at the bar. Jumping up, I rush behind him, and with a swift move, I knock him down with an elbow blow between the shoulder blades. Standing over him, I lift his head from the floor. Raising my hand with the gun high, I bring it down hard, clocking him with the butt of my gun. With Luther's bodyguard, Two-Ton, crippled outside and this asshole down, I've got a clean shot at Luther. But killing Luther could bring certain and almost instant death to my brothers and sister of the club.

Still, for the moment, I have Luther—unprotected. He's wielding a knife, which is nothing against my three guns.

"Say you'll leave Greenville alone, Luther. Pull your men out."

"I'm not sure I can do that."

As the roar of Dog bikes grows louder, all of my protective instincts kick in, and like a wild animal, I lunge at Luther. Coming up from behind him, I grab his head and bend it back. The man sitting opposite Luther yelps and screams through his tape.

"Shut up," I snap. With my arm wrapped around Luther's neck, choking him, I'm suddenly aware that I have no idea what I'm doing. If I kill him now, in essence, I kill us all. "Listen to me, Luther. I got to you once, I can get to you again. Pull out of Greenville now, and you'll get something in return. If you don't pull out, we'll take it, and you and your men—those who survive—will be left with nothing. Think of this as your one offer."

The roar of the bikes is louder—they're almost outside.

Letting go of Luther, he falls to the floor, gasping for air. Reaching out, I grab his knife, and quickly, I cut through the man's binds. The man wastes time trying to remove his mouth tape, but I have no time to warn him to go. I've got to get out. Backing up, I exit behind the bar the same way the bartender did, and I move toward the back room just as the shadows of wild Dogs fill the doorway.

With my heart thumping, I rush into the back room—but nothing. There's nothing but folding tables and chairs stacked against the walls and no friggin' door.

"What the fuck?"

"Boss?" One of the Dogs is inside talking to Luther.

Bang! Bang! No doubt Luther's prisoner is dead. That means I'm next. Spying a large sack of potatoes that's down a short, empty hallway off of this room, I rush toward it. Looking left and right, there's no door but there's sunlight falling on the sack—sunlight that is coming from somewhere. Turning my head upward, I see it: a window.

Stepping onto the sack, it crumbles under my feet. Shit. I must weigh more than that skinny bartender.

"Hey!"

There's a voice behind me, but I don't dare turn. Instead, in an act of blind faith, I leap up and grab the windowsill. Holding on and hanging off the ground with one hand, I slap at the window with the other. Sure enough, it opens. That must have been the door I heard open and shut.

"There's a fucking Knight in here!"

Footsteps grow closer. With every ounce of strength and adrenaline I have, I pull myself up, using the toes of my boots as traction to climb the wall. Pressing myself fully up, I dangle headfirst out the window. "Shit!" It's a freaking long drop down, but it's better than the alternative.

Somebody grabs at my feet, so I kick and flail, hoping I get at least one Dog square in the teeth. Bending farther forward, I "walk" my hands down the side of the building. Falling from about five feet, I land on my injured shoulder.

"Fuck!" I mumble through clenched teeth. I can't care about pain. I can't stop. Rushing out toward the street behind the alleyway, I pray I can outrun this group and then double back for my bike. Glancing over my shoulder, I see three guys running toward me. None have weapons drawn, so Luther must want me alive.

Oh, crap, that's even worse.

Plowing forward, I cut through an alleyway and scale a chain-link fence that reminds me of the one next to Holly's building. It hurts like a mother to use my shoulder, but it's pain or death. As I throw myself over, the men catch up to me but stall on their side of the fence. Two snarl at me as they try to climb it, but thank god, none of them are in good enough shape to jump it. Good. Running as fast as I can, I cut through a few more alleys and then, doubling back, I come up on the back entrance of the alley where my bike is.

Sneaking up slowly, I crouch down beside my bike. There are no Dogs outside, which means they're all inside or chasing me down the back alleys. But all they need is one sound from my bike, and they'll hop on theirs and chase me down.

Out of the corner of my eye, I catch a gang of about six thugs in colors wearing trucker hats and bandanas that cover the bottom halves of their faces. They're coming this way. Throwing their hands up, they yell and laugh. They're just what I needed. Hopping onto my bike, I balance it between my legs.

One of the gang members takes a gun and aims it toward the sky.

"Not yet, you stupid punk. Not yet." Turning the engine over, I idle quietly.

Holding my breath, I wait for the thugs to get just the right distance from the clubhouse. As soon as the first one comes up hollering and dancing his way to the Dogs' bikes, I rev my engine and take off, driving by the bikes and shooting out their tires. Taking off in the opposite direction, I look into my rearview. Dogs run from the clubhouse, yelling at the thugs. One throws a punch and then another.

It's going to be a nasty fight.

Swallowing hard, I focus on the road before me. Shit. Yeah, I feel a little bad about causing a fight, but what the hell could I do? Besides, this gang is bad news and they fight with the Dogs all the time.

Slowing my pace, I sigh, replaying what just happened in my mind. Did I actually accomplish anything? Will Luther pull his men out of Greenville because I said so?

It hurts like hell to downshift the clutch but I do, and I take off in the direction of Greenville. No, she may not want to see me, but I need to know she's okay.

I'll fucking park myself in front of her building night and day if I have to.

Sighing into the wind, I know that I shouldn't have done what I just did. I put us all in danger, and it was stupid and impulsive.

I've got to do better. Imagining Holly in her new building, unpacking and building her clinic—something stirs deep inside of me. I want to protect her, yes, but there's more. I also don't want to blow it again. I blew my chance to be a big brother to Colt when we were just kids, and it's been freaking difficult to win back his trust. I don't want that to happen again. Maybe it's time for a change—Dr. Holly Boling deserves better than this. She deserves a better man. Someone who does better than throwing lighter fluid onto a burning fire.

Shaking my head, I mumble to myself as I push my bike to its limits. "Fucking Dynamite."

Chapter Fourteen

Holly

Glancing around the country club, I'm not only uncomfortable in my clothes—my skirt and tank top feel tight and restricting after being in jeans and T-shirts all week—but I'm also uncomfortable in my skin. Yes, I always knew there was a discrepancy between the "haves" and the "have-nots", but until these past couple of weeks, I had never lived it.

Sitting back in my chair, I lift the glass of water to my lips and scowl. My mother is conducting her usual harassment of our waiter, James, as she tells him exactly how to instruct the chef to cook the grilled fish that she eats here every single week. Poor James must have done something really bad in a past life to have to wait on Monica Boling in this one.

"Blackened tonight, please, James." She smiles as she orders.

God love him, James just stands there and listens intently, not rushing her or screaming, "I fucking know what you want! You order the same damned, privileged food every single week! Some weeks, twice!" But he doesn't.

I, on the other hand, make no promises.

"For you, Dr. Boling?" James turns to my father, Elijah.

"He'll have the same," Monica interjects, like she always does.

Rolling my eyes, I take a deep breath and swirl the water in my glass.

Poor James turns to me. "And you, Dr. Boling the Second?" He means it kindly, and it's become something of the "thing" to say around here, but tonight it may very well be the straw that breaks *this* camel's back.

"Side salad, raspberry vinaigrette, please and thank you, James. I know I tell you every week, but you can call me Holly. I'd prefer it."

"Very well, Dr. Holly."

Disapproving, my mother clicks her tongue against her teeth. Closing my eyes, I take a deep, cleansing breath. When I open them, I glance at my smart watch. Eight-fifteen. At this rate, I may not make it until eight-thirty.

"What would you like for a main course?" James waits patiently.

"That is my main course, James. Thank you."

As soon as James walks away, my mother shakes her head at me.

"All right, Mom." Sitting upright, I place my water glass down and lean forward. "What was it that was so urgent you had to see me tonight?"

Looking at my father, my mother shifts uncomfortably in her seat.

"Oh no." Shaking my head at my mother, I can feel the anger building in my belly. "Don't do that."

"Don't do what, dear?" She tilts her head condescendingly.

"You know what. You call me fifty-five times today, and then, when you are finally faced with confrontation, you hide behind him." I nod to my father.

"Holly, I just don't know what's going on with you lately." Glancing at our neighboring tables, she takes a sip of her Pinot Grigio.

"How so?"

"Holly." My father clears his throat like he always does before he makes some kind of declaration. "We're worried about you."

"Worried about me?" Smiling, I cover my mouth with my hand. "I'm happier than I've ever been in my life."

"With that… building in… *that* neighborhood?" my mother whispers.

"Mom. You don't have to whisper. Yes, I bought a building in Greenville. I'm opening a clinic." Sitting forward, I rest both elbows on the table and look from parent to parent. "You know, I would have thought that you would be incredibly proud of that. I worked hard and had the down payment. I secured a mortgage on my own, all so I can do some good in the world."

"But, Holly," my mother reprimands, "you're so smart and so beautiful. Let someone else do good."

"Do you seriously hear yourself right now?"

"All I'm saying—" My mother reaches out and pats my arm with her warm hand. Her perfectly manicured nails shine. "—is that you need to get married and have a family. You're almost thirty years old." She whispers my age in case the Lowneys at the next table hear.

"What is this? The eighteen-hundreds? I will get married, Mom, if and when I want to. Not because I'm almost thirty."

"You're awfully snippy tonight," she counters.

"No, I'm standing up for myself. Isn't it about time?"

My father gives me his displeased look that used to floor me when I was a kid. But tonight—nothing.

"Sorry, Dad, that you're displeased but this is ridiculous."

Picking up my water glass, I take a large gulp. In my peripheral vision, I see someone moving toward us quickly. Oh no.

"Hello!" Dr. Robert Covens comes rushing up.

Oh, cripes. Could this night get any worse?

Holding his tie against his chest, he bends down to kiss my mother on the cheek, and she pats his hand. Then, standing, he shakes my father's hand. "May I?" He points to the empty chair.

There's always an empty chair next to me that seems to eventually be filled by Robert. Cripes. Spotting him, James comes rushing up and pours him a glass of wine.

"He'll have the blackened fish, too," my mother tells James.

"Very good, ma'am, sir." With a small bow, James backs away.

Turning to Robert, I furrow my brow. "What are you doing here?"

Sitting up tall, he smiles. Damn. Have his teeth always been that white?

"What am I doing here? Having dinner with you. Like always."

"It's not like always, and you shouldn't be here. We are not a couple, and we haven't been for a very long time."

"I invited him, Holly." My mother nods encouragingly.

"Why?"

"Holly, don't be rude," my mother whispers.

Turning to Robert, I ask him directly, "Why did my mother invite you?"

"Because." My father clears his throat again. "Because we're worried about you."

"Worried about me? Why would you be worried about me? I've just told you that I'm happy for the first time in my life. For the first time, I am using my gifts for good and helping people. Or at least I will be once the clinic is up and running. I feel fulfilled and actually look forward to waking up in the morning. Can any of you say that?"

Of course, the little ache in my tummy tells me that's not entirely true. I was at my happiest during those few moments with Seth, and there's a part of me that's really sad he's gone.

"I can."

Oh, screw you, Robert. "Really?"

"Yes." Nodding, he smiles at my parents. "And I'm looking forward to next month even more."

My mother winks in response.

"What? Why?"

Robert lifts his glass in a toast.

"What's going on here?" Turning my head sideways, I feel like I'm caught in some abstract play where I'm the lead character but also the only one who doesn't know what the hell is going on. "What's next month?"

"Well." Robert places his glass on the table, and then lifts it up and places it down again, moving it back and forth like he's playing checkers. Rings form on the white tablecloth. "I've just given notice at the hospital."

"What?" Leaning forward, I'm finally interested in something he has to say. "You're quitting?"

"Yes."

Suddenly, this has all become very real. No, I don't want to be with Robert, but I will miss working alongside him. He's an excellent doctor and could always carry half the workload.

"Wow, Robert, I don't know what to say. I'll miss working with you, of course—"

"You don't have to miss me."

"No, you cut me off. I didn't say I was going to miss *you*, I said I was going to miss working alongside you."

Not one of them is listening as they toast each other. I don't even get the chance to ask where he's going.

"Come on, Holly." My mother raises her glass. "Let's toast to the newest—"

"—and only," Robert interjects.

"—partner in the practice of Boling Cardiothoracic Surgery!" Monica lifts her glass high. "Salut!"

"Salut," Robert answers.

"What?" Gripping the table hard, I nearly knock over the water goblets. "What did you say?"

Robert grins. "You are looking at your father's new partner, Holl. Boling and Covens Cardiothoracic Surgery."

"You're changing the name?" Looking at my father, I see he's not smiling quite as much as Monica and Robert. "Dad?"

"He's going to be a partner, Holly," my father explains. "God knows I've asked you enough times. Then, when we heard that you bought that building... Why did we have to find out from Clea?"

He sounds hurt. Shit.

Tilting his head, he smiles. "You could have told me, you know."

Nodding, I swallow hard.

Reaching across the table, my dad takes my hand and covers it with his. His hand has always been so large and powerful. "I knew you were never going to join me at the practice. It's not your world, Holly. It never has been." Sitting back, he takes a deep breath. "But your mother and I were talking, and we decided that it was time for me to slow down a bit."

"Slow down? Dad, you're one of the best cardiothoracic surgeons in the southwest. You're still young—you love working. Why?"

"Because he works too much," Monica butts in. "Like someone else I know." She raises a single eyebrow at me. I could never understand how she did that. "It's time for us to travel and see the world. We need to get out of Phoenix for a while."

My dad stares at the table, and as James arrives with our food, my stomach flips over. Three forty-dollar fish and a twenty-five-dollar salad are placed before us, and all I can think about is my neighborhood, where people have to choose between rent and healthcare. Well, not anymore. I'm going to make sure of that. Staring at my salad, I lift my fork and pick at the lettuce. Stabbing a cherry tomato, I twirl my fork around.

Glancing up, I see my father is looking at me. Swallowing hard, I smile at him. Placing my fork down by my untouched salad, I sit up tall and put both hands in my lap.

"Well." Clearing my throat, I bend my fingers and start picking at my nails. "Congratulations, Dad and Robert. And thank you all for inviting me tonight, but if you'll excuse me, I have a ton of work waiting for me."

Pushing the chair back from the table, I begin to stand, but my mother motions to Robert to stop me. Reaching out, he grabs my wrist with his hand. Looking down at his hand on me, I feel nothing. The man is touching me, and there's nothing—no spark, no excitement—and I don't think there ever was.

"Holly," my mother says, looking up from her fish. "We're not through yet. Sit, sit."

"Not through with what?" I ask as I comply.

My mother places her fork down and nods to my father to do the same. With a sigh, he obliges.

"Holly." She leans closer. "We told you before. We're worried about you. All of us."

She looks at Robert, and he nods in agreement, wearing a serious look on his face. Rolling my eyes, I scowl at him. *Come off it, Robert. That's the same damn look you use when you're debating which side to part your hair in the morning.*

"I've already told you, Mom, I'm happy. Why can't we all just accept that changes are happening and be happy for one another?"

"Because you're being crazy," my mother whispers.

"Excuse me?"

"You bought a building in *Greenville*." She hisses the word. "You spent your life savings, and Clea tells us the mortgage is seven figures."

Thanks, Clea. "It is."

"What?" Robert decides to chime in. "Holly, you'll be tied to that forever. You'll never make your money back at the clinic."

"I don't need to. It's not about making money, Robert. Don't you get that? Besides, I can afford the building."

"What about the equipment, and medical supplies, and everything else you'll need?"

"I know. I've thought of that. I'll need some investors. There are grants. And I'll find staff who are willing to donate their time."

Robert chuckles, and I swear it's like nails on a chalkboard.

"Donate their time?" he counters. "Who is going to donate their time to a place like that?"

Nodding, I try to unclench my jaw. "There will be doctors who want to. Doctors who want to help in a community that needs them. Do you know why I chose Greenville?"

Looking around the table, I make eye contact with each of them. My father holds my gaze.

"Where my building is—on Main Street, the city area—is only part of the town. Greenville is a large community, and nearly everyone lives below the poverty level. They're poor, but it's a family neighborhood. They want more for themselves and their families." Taking a deep breath, I go on. "There's a little boy who has asthma. Poor kid can barely walk down the street without wheezing, but he's a little boy, so he wants to run and play with his friends. Once the clinic is up and running, I can treat him for his asthma and give him his inhaler and meds for free. That will change his life."

Leaning forward, I look for a spark of anything in any of them. My father is still looking at me steadily.

"Who knows?" I continue. "After Greenville, maybe more clinics in more places. Maybe, eventually, Doctors Without Borders."

"Hol-ly." My mother reprimands me with her tone. "You cannot be serious. Didn't we get you over that little fantasy when you wanted to join the Peace Corps right out of college? Please. After all the time and money we spent making you a cardiothoracic surgeon. Do you know how much med school costs?"

"Yes, and I was on scholarship."

"We paid for room and board."

Cocking my head, I look her in the eyes. "Would you like it back? I'll write you a check."

"After everything we've done for you, Holly, how can you abandon us like this?"

"I'm not abandoning you, Mother. I'm changing. I'm finding out who I am."

"I'll tell you who you are," she says. "Dr. Holly Boling, cardiothoracic surgeon and our daughter. You are not changing. You are the same girl you've always been—quiet, loyal, dependable—and it's high time you start acting like her."

"Really?" My breath is rushing too fast now. I know I shouldn't do this, but I can't help myself. "Does the old Dr. Holly Boling do this?" Getting up and hovering just over my chair, I lift my tank top on the right side and pull down my skirt slightly, exposing my tattoo.

"What the hell is that?" My mother looks like she's seen a ghost.

"A tattoo. A bird in flight, actually." Sitting down, I smooth my skirt as I pull my chair closer. "I have wanted a tattoo my entire life, and I finally have one."

"How did you even know where to get something like that?" She glares at me.

"A friend took me."

"Was that friend a biker?" Robert raises his eyebrows condescendingly.

"Yes, he is, as a matter of fact."

Nodding, Robert glares at me.

"My god, Holly!" My mother grabs at her chest. "What were you thinking? How could you do this to us? *All* of us?"

She points to the ceiling, and I know exactly what she means—George. Monica believes that I have to be perfect to make up for George passing. If he had lived his life, maybe he could have been the flawless child they deserved.

"Don't you dare bring George into this." I'm seething. "My tattoo has nothing to do with you. Can't you see that?"

My voice is louder than I intend, and the Lowneys look up from their entrees.

"But you've ruined yourself!"

"Good lord, Mother, it's a tattoo. On my hip. It's no big deal. I like it."

"You had no right to do that." My mother's face turns red.

"I had every right. It's my body—"

"Ladies."

Robert butts in, and it makes my skin crawl.

Dropping my chin, I snarl at him. "Stay out of this, Robert."

"Please. Can't we all just get along?" He reaches out and takes my hand.

Yanking my hand away and whipping around, I face him. "Can't you just butt out? This has nothing to do with you."

"Actually, it has everything to do with me."

"Why?"

Glancing at my mother, I see her compose herself and nod to Robert. Reaching into his breast pocket, he pulls out a black velvet box.

"What the hell is that?" I move back away from the box like it's made of toxic waste.

"Holly." Sliding out of his chair, Robert gets down on one knee and opens the box. There, staring at me, is what must be a three-carat diamond with large diamonds surrounding the main stone and more diamonds making up the band.

"What the hell is that?" I repeat. "Jesus." I've never seen a ring that large—or that showy. If I wore the damn thing swimming, I'd drown.

"I think you know what it is. Dr. Holly Boling, will you marry me?"

Looking over at my parents, I catch the smile on my mother's face but my father looks almost as surprised as I am.

"What?" Grabbing him by the arm, I pull him up to his seat.

My mother glances around at the neighboring tables nervously.

"Is that what this is?" I look around the table. "You brought me here so Robert could propose?"

"He's willing to marry you even after your recent outbursts and that disgusting thing on your hip," my mother whispers.

Sighing, I turn away from her and look him in the eyes. "No, Robert. I won't marry you. I said no the last time you asked also. Can you please stop asking?"

"But this is a bigger ring," he protests.

"I can see that. That's what you think will change my mind? A larger engagement ring?" My stomach aches as I look from person to person. "Don't you people know me at all? Haven't you been listening?" Turning to Robert, I sigh. "You don't want to marry me. You want to marry who you think I should be. That is not me."

"You're wrong, Holly." Robert takes my hand again. "We were good once. I know who you are. You just need to get over this." He waves his hands up and down in front of me. "This—whatever you're going through—and start acting like you again. Then, once you give up this silly dream of a clinic, we can buy a house near your parents—"

"In suburbia?"

"Yes. Then we can have a couple of kids."

"And your father and I will be available to babysit when you're ready to go back to work," my mother adds.

Suddenly, the temperature in the room skyrockets. Looking at my plate, I swear the untouched tomatoes begin moving in circles. Sweat drenches my silk tank top, and all I want to do is pull it off and run screaming. Grabbing my water goblet, I try to lift it to my lips, but my hands are shaking and the water spills all over my hand. My lips begin to tremble, and I can feel my breathing becoming shallow. Closing my eyes, I try to stop myself from hyperventilating.

My parents and Robert are all talking, but no one is looking at me. Gripping the ends of the tablecloth, I ball it into my sweaty palms. My head feels prickly, and suddenly, I can't make sense of anything. Squinting, I stare at my mother's moving lips—she's saying words like "June" and "roses" and "country club wedding." Robert seems to be answering "yes" to everything she says, and adding words like "tattoo removal." Glancing at my father, I see his brows are knitted together. I think he's saying, "Holly, are you all right?"

Shaking my head, I focus on my father.

"Holly? Are you okay?"

No. I'm not okay.

Standing and leaving the engagement ring on the table, I place my napkin on the chair and look at my father. "Yes, thanks. I need to get going. I'll talk to you tomorrow." Grabbing my bag from the floor next to me, I smile at him.

Then, holding my breath and focusing on one spot on the front door before me, I hurry through the restaurant and toward the door. Bursting through, I just about fall into the parking lot, letting go of my breath. Standing up straight, my nostrils flatten as I draw air in and out through my nose, trying to calm my heartbeat. Seeing my car ahead, I nod to the valet, who comes rushing up to me.

"Keys, please. Boling—the blue one."

"Of course, Dr. Boling the Second. Don't you want me to pull the car out for you?"

"No need. Thank you." As I swallow my anxiety and wait for the valet, I look at my nails. Choosing one, I lift one trembling hand to my teeth and set to work, biting the nail down to a nub. Finally, the valet materializes with my key fob. Thanking him, I take another deep breath and rush toward my car.

It's okay, I tell myself. *I'm okay*.

"Holly?"

"Fuck." Stopping short and turning around, I see Robert. "I can't, Robert. Just, please, give me some space."

"I will." He holds up his hands. "All I ask is that you think about what I said."

"There's nothing to think about."

Sighing, he grins in the most patronizing way. "Your parents are a different generation, kid. But I understand you and your need to express yourself. I can even accept the tattoo."

"Robert…" Turning my back on him and clutching my bag tight to my side, I walk toward my car that I don't particularly like. Opening the top of my bag, I feel around for my anti-anxiety meds. I don't want to take them; it just feels good to know they're there. Leaving the meds in my bag, I press the fob to unlock the door. Putting my hand on the handle, I'm just about free when I feel Robert behind me. Crap. "What, Robert?"

Whipping around to face him, he greets me with open arms. Stepping closer to me, he pulls me into a hug. What a crazy, uncharacteristic public display of affection from Robert. He hugs me tight, but my arms stay stiff—one clutching my open bag to make sure nothing falls out, and the other tight by my side.

When he finally releases me, I shake my head. "The whole time we were dating, you never hugged me in public. Not once."

"Like you said—" He grins. "People change."

"Yeah, okay." Jumping into my car, I pull out from my spot as fast as I can. Moving through the lot carefully, I finally make it to the exit, and as I turn onto the street, a sense of calm settles over me, battling my anxiety. Taking a deep, normal breath, I turn in the direction of Greenville. Glancing in my rearview, I see that Robert has walked out onto the sidewalk and is watching me drive away.

Pushing the speed limit, my tight neck muscles loosen and my breathing calms. The faster and farther I go, the smaller and more insignificant Robert—and all of my past—becomes.

With my past behind me, all I have to think about is my future—and whether or not Seth Hardy will be in it.

Chapter Fifteen

Dynamite

What the fuck have I just done? Sitting on my bike in front of Holly's clinic, I glance at the time on my phone—4:30 AM. Where the hell is she? I've been up and down the street a bunch of times, but I don't see her car—or her—anywhere. Maybe she's working or staying in her apartment in Phoenix tonight? Crap—the image of Dr. Robert Covens pops into my brain, but I can't let myself think she may be with him. There's nothing between them, I'm sure of that, because if there was, we couldn't have had *that* night together.

Rolling my shoulders back, I notice I'm almost pain-free. Thankfully, I didn't dislocate my shoulder. What a stupid-ass move, but shit, if I hadn't made it out that window…

Shaking my head, I focus on this moment. None of that matters. All that matters is that I stay put right here in front of her clinic. Not only did I piss on Dog home turf, but by threatening Luther over the town of Greenville, I just gave them the ammunition they need to bring me to my knees.

It all hinges on Holl—

Lights from a car pulling up to her building catch my attention. Putting up my arm, I shield my eyes from the headlights, squinting to see who it is. The tension in my gut releases as soon as I recognize the car and see Holly at the wheel.

Hopping off my bike, I walk up to her as she gets out of the car and moves around to her trunk.

"Holly."

"Oh!" Slamming her trunk closed, she holds a box in one arm and puts her free hand to her chest. "You scared me. Seth? What are you doing here?"

"Checking on you."

Nodding, she sighs. "You're not here to tell me to move, are you? Because I don't think I can take one more person in my life telling me they know what's best for me."

"No. I'm sorry about before. I was worried about you, and I overreacted."

"Thank you."

We stand, staring at one another.

"Can I?" I motion to the box in her arms.

"Yeah, thanks." Handing me the box, she turns and walks up to the door, unlocking it. "I know why *I'm* up at this hour—I couldn't sleep, so I've been packing all night."

Taking a deep breath, I try to calm my racing heart. Fine. If she moves in here permanently, I'll just have to give up my apartment and live on my bike outside.

"But why are *you* awake?" Pushing the door open with her shoulder, she motions for me to follow her in.

"Couldn't sleep. A lot on my mind."

Nodding, she takes a deep breath and lets it go in a sigh. Reaching up, she puts her hands on her neck and starts massaging her neck muscles. Her movements are so damned erotic, I have to take a deep breath myself.

"Let me do that for you." Motioning to her neck, I walk up behind her and clamp my hands on her thin shoulders.

"Mmm." Allowing her body to be moved by my massage, she leans back against me.

"You're so tight," I whisper into her ear.

"Yes," she moans.

Reaching up, she places her hands on mine and runs her fingertips down them. It's so freaking sexy, I know she caught the double entendre as soon as I said it.

"I've had a hell of a night," she explains.

Staying where I am, I keep rubbing as I speak softly into her ear. "What happened?"

"What else? That emergency my mother had and dinner at the club turned out to be an intervention. Obviously, I have to be insane to buy this place and want to live here."

"You're not insane. You're idealistic."

"Naïve?" Turning, she releases herself from my grasp and looks up into my eyes.

"No." Dropping my hands to my sides, I shake my head. "Not at all. You're just a good person. With bigger dreams than most of us understand."

"Thank you." I can tell by the way she holds my gaze she means it. "But why do I get stuck holding onto all this crap that everyone dumps on me? Tonight at the restaurant, I had another anxiety attack. All I want to do is strip out of these damned clothes and go running naked through the woods somewhere, feeling the wind brush against me."

Nodding, I smile. "Grab your jacket."

"What? Why?"

"Because I know exactly what you need. Do you trust me?"

"Yes. I do."

"Then, grab a jacket and let's go."

Taking her by the hand, I lead her out her front door, locking up behind us. Pulling her gently, I take her to my bike. She stalls as we approach.

"Seth, I don't know. Do you know how many motorcycle accidents I see in the ER every week? I've seen injuries, broken bones, amputations, deaths."

As she speaks, I take my helmet and place it on her head, fastening it under her chin.

"Where's your helmet?" She furrows her brow.

Reaching up, I knock on the side of my head. "Hard as a rock. I'm fine."

Sighing, she starts unfastening her helmet.

"Wait, what are you doing?"

"I pulled a knife out of your shoulder. I am not going to follow that up by picking your brain up off of a road and trying to shove it back in through your ear."

"Fine. Let's stop by my place. I have another helmet. An old one, but it'll work. I'll grab that—it's on the way, anyway."

"On the way where?"

Shaking my head, I smile. "Nu-uh. That's a surprise. Damn, you look gorgeous in that helmet, by the way. Come on." Mounting my bike, I pat the small passenger's seat. "Yes, motorcycle accidents happen, but so do car accidents."

"Yes, but cars have metal around them."

"Yeah, an accident can happen. Just like you can slip in the shower. But most motorcycle accidents happen to less experienced drivers. Holly." Reaching out, I slip my hand around hers. "I promised you once before, but maybe you need to hear it again. I promise I will never let anything bad happen to you."

The stirring in my gut tells me it's true. I would do anything to protect her—and the thing is, I may just have to.

"Okay."

Nodding, she looks at me. Deep in her beautiful, dark eyes, I can see that she trusts me.

"Come on, my brown-eyed girl." Turning over the key, I start the bike.

"My father used to sing me that song." With that look of determination she gets, she smiles and hops on the back of my bike, wrapping her arms around my waist.

"Hold on tight." I pat her hand encouragingly. "I'm going to take you on the ride of your life."

Squeezing me, she speaks directly into my ear. "Yes, Seth Hardy, I believe that you will."

Slowing the bike, we pull onto a side road that leads to an open highway.

"We're in the desert?" she says into my ear.

"On the outskirts." Pointing, I nod straight ahead. "We're clear out of the city and on the way to where we hold a music festival every year—called Music in the Desert. There's a spot I sometimes stop on the way. The ride out is spectacular, especially at sunrise. I thought you would like it."

"Thank you, Seth." Her breathy voice sends chills down my spine.

It feels so damned good to have her body leaning against mine, her long legs pressed up hard against my legs, her arms wrapped tight around my abdomen. Damn, I could just stay out here all day—and why the hell not? She's out of Dog turf and safe on the back of my bike. Frankly, I'd love to get her away for a couple of days—or, considering the way things are now, forever. We could go to the empty building up in Mid grounds. That area is in ally territory, and the building is vacant most of the year. Yeah, it can be a place for couples to hook up, but everyone knows if there are bikes out front, you don't go walking in.

Taking a deep breath, I sigh it out. Nah, as much as I want to, running is not going to do us any good. I've got to confront the mess I left back in Rumble. As much as I want to take her away and make love to her again, that's not what this morning is about. This morning is for her to experience what it feels like to be free.

Craning my neck around, I ask her, "You okay? You did great on the highway the whole way here. Your first time on the back of a bike can be a lot."

"Yes." She's breathless in my ear. "I'm better than okay." She squeezes me tight and lays her cheek against my back.

"It gets better," I tell her. "The whole ride before us is open desert, and there's a perfect spot to stop to see the sun rise."

"Sounds like you know your way around."

"I drive this route whenever I can't sleep. I jump on my bike and head out here. I've just never experienced it with anyone else before."

Holding me even tighter, she whispers, "I'm glad your first time is with me."

Patting her hand, I grin. "I'm glad *your* first time is with me, too." Leaning forward, I rev the engine. "Ready?"

"I'm ready."

"Good. Hold on tight, and if you need me to slow down, tell me."

"Yes."

"Okay!"

Revving the bike again, I take off from our spot on the side road. Soon, we're on the open stretch, rolling through the desert, chasing the sunrise. Along the sides of the road are patches of green and brown bushes. Ahead lies far-off mountains. As we coast down the open stretch, she loosens her hold on my chest but tightens the grip of her legs. It's like I can feel her desire to be even freer, so I slow to a comfortable speed. As soon as I do, she pulls away from my chest. Glimpsing her in my side mirror, I catch her sitting up with one hand in the air and a gorgeous smile on her face. She's free.

Leaning forward again, she puts her mouth near my ear.

"Faster," she whispers.

Downshifting, I open the bike up, and we fly forward.

"Faster," she says, louder and stronger as her body pushes harder against me.

Ahead are miles of straight, open road, so I push the bike more. I can feel her daring to lift her head, and she looks straight ahead over my shoulder. As fast as we're going, I would never push the bike to its limits with her on the back. Yeah, the road is open and straight, but that doesn't mean there isn't going to be a snake or a stone in the road.

The open stretch of road morphs into a twisty turn up a small mountain, so I slow the bike. I shift my weight for the corner, and she lets her body move with mine.

As we move, I imagine Holly underneath me—her eyes closed as her body responds to each of my thrusts—Damn. It's too much. Clearing my throat, I push that image out of my mind and concentrate on the road ahead so we can make it to the top in one piece.

Finally, after the last turn, we reach the hidden plateau at the top of the small mountain. Slowing the bike, I cut the engine and drop my custom center stand. As I reach up to take off my helmet, I feel her dismount behind me. Turning to her, I watch as she steps away from the bike and lifts and lowers her legs a few times. They must be stiff from the ride. Then, walking closer to the edge of the cliff, she reaches up and removes her helmet. Her hair moves freely across her shoulders as she tucks the helmet under her arm. The light from the sunrise is just breaking in the distance, framing her. Damn, she is gorgeous.

My jeans grow tight in response. Taking a deep breath, I look away and try to calm myself. Running the numbers of the club build usually helps to cool me down, but right now, the build reminds me of the Dogs. And thinking of the Dogs makes me think of protecting Holly. It seems like all my thoughts come down to Holly nowadays. Throwing my leg over and dismounting, I decide I'm as "together" as I'm ever going to be around this woman. Walking up to her, I stand as close as I dare. Leaning her weight toward me, she presses her shoulder against mine. That's all the invitation I need. Slipping my arm around her waist, I hold her tight.

"This is stunning," she whispers.

Nuzzling against her ear, I answer, "Yes, it is." Tucking my arm under hers, I wrap my hand around her wrist and lift her arm so we're both pointing ahead of us. "That's east, of course, where we can see dawn breaking. Down there—" I move her arm so we point to a flat, open area at the base of this mountain. "—is where we hold Music in the Desert. That's a blast. The music, the vendors, all the ally clubs. It's really an experience. I'd love for you to come with me this year."

"I'd like that." She nods, nuzzling her cheek against my arm.

Bringing our arms down to our sides, I hold her tight. "What I like about it up here," I explain, "even despite the view, is that we're alone on this little plateau tucked behind a mountain. I've never seen anyone here, and I've never heard anyone mention it. It's my private oasis."

"We're all alone..." Her words float off on the wind. "Seth, I have never felt so free in my life as I did on that bike and as I do right now." Her voice is breathy. "It's like I've had this barrier—this, this *armor* around me. For twenty-eight years, nothing has ever penetrated it. I've never felt anything before you." Turning to me, she slips her arms up around my neck. "But now, I finally know what it feels like to be alive, and I never want to let that feeling go."

"Then don't."

Nodding, she looks into my eyes and raises her chin. Leaning down, I plant a kiss gently on her forehead, and she shivers in my embrace. Looking deep into her dark eyes, I suddenly want even more than a kiss. I want a connection.

Reaching out, I place my large hand on the back of her head and pull her into my embrace. When her body falls against mine, I wrap my arm around her, holding her tight. Dropping my head, I whisper into her ear, "I'm sorry about the way we left things. I never meant for any of it to go that way."

Nodding, she lifts her head. "I'm sorry, too."

Reaching out with both hands, I cup her cheeks and run my thumbs up and down her soft skin. Then, pulling her to me, I place my lips on hers. I move slowly, brushing against her softly. I want to take my time and explore every inch of her gorgeous mouth.

She moans softly as she pushes herself closer to me. The way our arms are wrapped around one another, our jackets fall open so that our chests are pressed against one another—T-shirt to T-shirt. Through the soft material of her shirt, I can feel her nipples harden as she presses them against me. Lifting her leg, she wraps it around my waist and I grab it, cupping her thigh and drawing her tighter against me. The force of my pull brings her even closer to me, and she releases a sexy gasp into my mouth.

"Shit, Holly."

"Seth."

As she moans into my mouth, we devour each other in our kiss. Standing near the edge of the cliff with the soft, cool breeze blowing against us and our bodies intertwined, it's all I can do not to tear off our clothes and take her right here on the red stones beneath us.

Placing both hands on her hips, I lift her. She wraps her legs around me tight, and her fingers toy with my hair. My freaking member is bulging, and she moves herself in just a way that the seam of her jeans bumps against my tip. Carrying her, I walk us toward my bike.

"Aw, shit," I mumble through clenched teeth. "Right now, I wish I had a blanket with me."

"No blanket. Your bike."

"My bike?" Fuck, yeah. My cock grows harder just thinking about it. I've never been with a woman on my bike, and I'm not entirely sure of the mechanics of it all, but, hell, I'm willing to try.

Swinging her around, I land her on the passenger's seat. She gasps, and I notice her lips are swollen from kissing. Dropping her chin, she looks up through her thick, black lashes. She's ready.

"I've never been with a woman on my bike."

Her eyes light up. "No?"

"No. I don't even know how, but you can be damned sure that I'll figure it out."

Smiling, she places her hands on the seat and leans forward. The pressure of her arms pins her breasts together and they bulge forward. Her hard nipples poke through her T-shirt.

"Shit." Throwing my leg over, I mount my bike—backward—so we're face to face, and she's higher than me on the small passenger's seat. Leaning forward, she wraps her arms around me and slides closer. I open her mouth with mine, and she takes my tongue, licking and sucking. It's obvious what she wants and how much she wants it.

Catching my breath, I pull back slightly. "Holly, baby, if we go down this road…" Tilting my head, I try to read her eyes. "It's going to be hard to stop. Are you sure? Out here?"

"You said we're alone."

"There's no one for miles. But we're on my bike. It's not going to be sweet or loving. I want to make love to you—but the whole situation—"

"I don't want sweet and loving right now." She lifts her body and moves so the inseam of her jeans is pressing against my rock-hard cock. "I just want you, Seth. I want to forget everything but you and this moment. Please. You can make love to me later—at home."

The words "at home" strike me, but it's not the time for that conversation. Fuck it, right now it's not the time for any conversation.

Clamping my hands on her hips, I lift her and then bring her down on top of my throbbing cock. Thrusting against her, she kisses me back with so much passion, I can feel the warmth and dampness coming through her jeans. As she rubs against me, she drops her head back, and then lifting one hand, she clamps it to her neck. Her fingers dig into the sides of her neck as she rubs harder against me.

Oh, shit! I just realized something. "Holly, baby, I don't have a condom."

Shaking her head, she whispers, "I'm on the pill."

"That's it." She is so damn beautiful and so fucking hot.

Reaching between us, I grab my jeans and rip my fly open. Taking her hips, I move her forward, even closer to me. Looking straight into her eyes, I pop her button and unzip her jeans. Greedily, I shove my hand into her lace panties and slide my fingers down.

"God, Holly, baby, you are so wet."

"Yes." She drops her head back and then, raising it again, she looks me in the eyes.

Pressing against her tiny nub of nerves, she moans as I work her with my finger. As she slides closer and presses harder, I dip my finger further down. My hand gets caught between the seat and her, so I push with more force and slide my finger deep inside of her.

"Oh, God, Seth!"

"I've got you, baby."

Gasping, she leans farther back, taking more of my finger. She moves in time with me as I press harder and move with shorter, quicker jabs.

"God, yes!" she cries.

"Fuck, Holly."

Even though the morning air is chilly, as I watch her growing closer to climax, sweat drips from my brow and collects on my back. This freaking Knights jacket is making me even hotter, but I'm not stopping to tear it off. She moves faster against my hand and her muscles clench. No way. I'm not going to send her over the edge like this.

Pulling my finger out faster than I mean to, I lean her even farther back.

"Hold the back of the seat with your hands and raise your hips," I command as she does what I say.

Yanking her jeans down below her hips and bottom, I stall. The way she's positioned—with one long leg on each side of the machine—her jeans can't go down any further. Hopping off the bike, I collect both her legs to one side and pull her jeans and panties off of her.

Fuck. Thank god for that center stand. It is the only thing keeping us from falling. Throwing my leg over, I straddle the bike again, and this time, I stand with the bike between my legs. Dropping my jeans and briefs, I pull them down just enough that my entire member is exposed.

Reaching out, she grabs me with her warm, small hand and strokes me up and down.

"Fuck, that feels way too good."

While she works me, I reach around and find her exposed bottom. Taking my time, I explore every inch of her naked skin and what it feels like against the leather of my bike seat. Then, moving my hands to her hips, I lift her. My cock protests as soon as she lets go but, lining us up, I ease her down gently on top of me. My tip bursts in and her muscles clench.

"Damn, Holly. I'm going to have to use some force, okay? You are so tight."

"Yes. You're so—"

She gasps as I push on her hips, bringing her down harder on top of me.

"Seth!"

"That's it, baby, we'll go easy."

Pulling herself tight against me, she wraps her arms around my shoulders as I thrust up into her. Our breathing grows deeper and our mouths lock. She moans into my mouth as I grunt into hers. Keeping one hand wrapped around her waist, I put the other on my bike's gas tank to steady us. Breaking free to catch her breath, she shivers as she pants in my ear.

Keeping her balanced on top of me, I slip out of my jacket and wrap it around her back, covering her bare ass. Reaching around her but inside my jacket, my hands find her bottom and my fingers dig into her flesh.

As exposed as we are out here, nothing has ever felt so private and intimate.

"Seth," she whispers. "I can't hold on anymore."

Wrapping both arms around her, I feel her muscles clench and tighten around my rod.

Pressing my mouth to her ear, I mumble, "Let go, baby. Let go."

Dropping her head back, she releases with such a strong shiver, I can't hold off anymore either. My muscles tighten and my jaw clenches as I plant my feet on the dirt and rock ground. Lifting us both up, I give a few final thrusts, burying myself deep inside her.

"Fuck, Holly!"

Finally, with one last grunt, we release together.

Letting go fully, she falls forward against me and hangs on me like a piece of limp spaghetti. Shit. Did I push too far? Sitting back down, I take her by her shoulders and look into her eyes.

"Holly, baby, you okay?"

A beautiful smile sweeps across her face. "Yes, Seth. I have never felt better in my life."

Chapter Sixteen

Holly

"How about coffee and bagels?" I smile at Seth as he unlocks the door to my clinic. He seemed relaxed and at peace on our ride back, but as soon as we crossed the border into Greenville, I could actually feel the change in his body. He became stiffer, and it's like every muscle in his body is on alert. Now, he's downright sullen. "Seth? You okay?"

"Yeah, sorry. Just… just give me a second." Doubling back to his bike, he grabs something out of what looks like a small storage compartment. Turning back to me, he fiddles with the waistband of his jeans as he walks forward.

Pushing my front door open, he nods for me to go first. As soon as I step inside, he moves ahead of me and starts canvassing the main floor.

"What are you doing?"

"Holly." Sighing, he looks deep into my eyes. "I told you those Dogs are bad news. I want to make sure no one broke in while we were away."

"Oh." I can feel my brows furrowing as I think about someone breaking in here and walking around like they own the place. Because they don't own it. I do.

Although he's a big guy, Seth moves lightly on his feet. He climbs to the second floor, and looking up, I can tell where he is by the sounds of closet doors opening and closing. Then I hear him rush up the stairs to the third floor and then nothing. It's quiet as he moves around the upper area. I hate that he feels he has to do this, but I refuse to let this ruin my mood. My stomach grumbles its approval.

"Bagels," I mutter, looking over the mass of boxes and cleaning I need to tackle today. "Bagels and lots of coffee."

For a moment, I consider dashing up the street to the bodega to surprise Seth with breakfast, but at the thought of leaving, an uneasiness swirls in my belly. Maybe there's something to what he's saying.

Damn it. Taking a deep breath, I exhale. Now those damned Unchained Dogs are starting to bug me. I shouldn't be uncomfortable in my own home—if that's what this is eventually going to be—and they have no right to take over an area that isn't theirs. I should get coffee—but no. It'll worry Seth. Damn. There goes my good mood. Now I'm getting downright grumpy. Hopefully, the coffee will fix that.

While I wait for Seth, I pick up my phone and call the bodega on the corner that has the fabulous, strong coffee.

"Hi, Roman? It's Holly. Could I please get a delivery this morning? Two plain bagels with cream cheese and four coffees."

"A long day?" he asks. As he speaks, I can picture his white smock and smile to myself. Glancing up, I hear Seth moving around the second floor again. "I think so, Roman. I think so."

"Well, don't work too hard, Dr. Holly. And you remember I am always available to help you move boxes later."

"Thank you, Roman."

"I'll have the delivery sent as soon as I make a fresh pot."

Smiling, I hang up the phone and my mood is restored. There are good people in this neighborhood, and I am lucky to live here. Digging into my clutch, I still haven't unpacked from last night and I look for some cash to tip Roman when—

"What?" I pull a black velvet box from my purse. "What the hell?" Opening it, I see Robert's ring staring up at me. "That son of a bitch," I mumble under my breath. He must have slipped it into my bag when he hugged me in the parking lot. *That's* why the sudden change of heart and uncharacteristic public display of affection. He set me up. Now I'll have to call him to give it back. No. On second thought, I'll give it to his best friend, my mother, and she can give it back to him. "Screw you, Robert."

"All's clear," Seth utters as he approaches. "Holly? What the hell is that?"

"I—" Standing here with the damned ring in my hand, my mouth drops open. "It's a ring."

"I see that. It's a giant ring. Is it yours?"

"It was given to me." This entire situation is too awkward.

"Is it an engagement ring?"

"Yes." I'm not going to lie to the man. "But I didn't accept his proposal."

"Whose proposal?" Seth's eyes narrow.

Hunching my shoulders forward, I look up into Seth's eyes. "Robert. But, Seth, he's proposed before, too. Every time he asks, I say no. I don't know why he asked last night. He was at dinner and announced he's going to be my father's new partner—"

"What?" He looks as surprised as I was.

"I left the ring on the table, but Robert followed me to my car. He must have slipped the ring into my bag when he hugged me goodbye."

A vein bulges on Seth's forehead. His jaw clenches, and he crosses his arms before his chest.

"Seth? You can't be jealous over this. If I were interested in Robert, you have to know I wouldn't have done what I just did with you. Umm…" Biting the corner of my lip, I smile. "On your bike."

"But Robert is perfect. It makes sense that you're together."

"He's far from perfect, Seth, and why does it make sense that we'd be together? Because we're both doctors? I already told you I don't want him or the life he's offering. Why can't you believe me?"

"Because I find it a little hard to believe that a woman like you—"

"Ugh!" I run my hands through my hair. "Here we go again. 'A woman like me'? Really, Seth? Didn't we just have this exact argument?"

"I just mean that you deserve better than what I have to offer."

"Why do you get to decide that?"

"Fine."

He moves closer to me and I soften slightly.

"You want to be with me?" he asks. "Then, let's make it official. Move out of here and come live with me. That way I can keep you safe from the Dogs."

"What the hell?" Storming away, I walk into the main room and then turn back to face him. "Haven't you heard a damned thing that I've said? That is completely unreasonable and you know it. You know why I don't want to be with Robert? Aside from the fact that I'm not attracted to him, I also hate that he thinks he can plan out my life for me, and here you are, doing the exact same thing!"

"Holly, please. All I'm trying to do is keep you safe. You need to understand. I wasn't there for Colt when he was growing up, and I'm damned afraid of repeating my mistakes. I want to be here for you."

"Then be here for me. But that doesn't mean telling me what to do. Don't you get that? For once in my life, I don't want to plan something out, and I'm sure as hell not going to let you, or anyone else, plan it out for me. Can't you understand that?"

"Yeah." He steps back and drops his head.

"Seth? Are you okay?"

Raising his head, he looks me in the eyes. "I think—"

Suddenly, there's a noise outside, and we both turn toward my front door.

"What the hell was that?" Seth's voice is low and his breathing is shallow.

"I ordered us coffee and bagels. Maybe Roman left them at the door and a stray cat came by and knocked them over?"

Shaking his head, he puts up his arm in a protective move, keeping me blocked behind his body. "That was no cat."

Reaching into the back of his jeans, he pulls a gun from his waistband.

"Seth? What is that?" I whisper.

Turning his head, he glances at me and puts a finger to his lips, telling me to be quiet. I nod my response.

"Stay here," he mouths. "Away from the windows." He walks me to the back of the room and hides me behind a wall.

Looking at my windows, I'm glad that so many of them are still boarded up. Holding my breath, I peek out from behind my wall and watch as Seth moves toward the door. The way he walks, he's so strong and so powerful… I sigh. Flattening his back to the wall next to the door, he looks at me and shakes his head. I duck back farther behind my wall. Then, grabbing the door handle, he yanks the door open and jumps in front of it with his gun pulled.

Squeezing my eyes shut, I silently pray that it's not Julius coming to help me or Roman delivering the bagels. I wouldn't want either of them to be staring down the barrel of Seth's gun.

Opening my eyes, I see there's no one at the door. Moving like a cat, Seth sneaks out the front door.

"Shit!" I hear him curse from in here.

I have to know. "Seth?"

Running across the floor, I rush outside and see him staring at the front of my building. Joining him, I stand beside him and look—Damn. The word "bitch" is spray-painted across the entire front of my building.

"Who would do something like this?" Turning to Seth, I stare at him. My voice is weak, so I clear my throat.

"The Unchained Dogs," he answers quietly. "To a Dog, calling a woman a 'bitch' means they've claimed her."

"What? That's—"

"Go inside, Holly." He nods to the front door. "Now. If you've ever trusted me or ever believed in me—go inside now. Lock the doors. Make sure your cell is charged, stay hidden. I'm going to call Julius to keep an eye on you while I'm gone, and maybe…" Taking deep breaths, he lifts a hand and runs it up through his cropped hair. "Maybe you should call Robert and ask him to come wait with you."

"No." That's where I draw the line. "No way. I do not want or need Robert."

Nodding, Seth turns to me. "Go inside, Holly."

"Where are you going? What are you going to do?"

"Go inside. I've already checked around—they're gone. I saw the bikes taking off out of here, the bunch of assholes. This is what Dogs do—it's their strategy. They mark and run. Now, I'm going to find them."

Nodding, I turn away from him and hurry up my front steps. Stepping inside, I close my door and lock it. Glancing at him out of the front window, I watch as he shoves his gun into the back of his jeans and revs his bike. He takes off down the street.

"Shit." Mumbling, I fall against my door. Is he going to hurt someone? Will he honestly choose to injure another human being? I just don't believe that's the man I know. Yes, I met him because he was injured in a fight—but this? Leaning my head back against my door, I sigh.

Knock, knock!

"Seth?" My heart races as I turn around to face the door. "Seth?" There's no answer. Maybe it's Roman, who's left my delivery at the door, or maybe Julius has just seen my building. "Hello?"

"Dr. Holls? It's Julius. C-can I come in?"

"Julius?" He sounds off. He must have seen the building. Shoot. "Yeah, come in. You shouldn't be out there right now."

I yank my door open. "Julius—"

Standing there with Julius are three large men, all wearing black leather jackets with the emblem of the Unchained Dogs. One is holding Julius with his arms pinned behind his back.

"I'm sorry, Dr. Holls." Julius sounds panicked. "They asked me if I knew you. I didn't know what was happening!"

The man tightens his hold on Julius and Julius grimaces in response. My stomach flips.

"Let him go!" I demand.

The men laugh, and Julius looks up at me. His eyes are wide and his lip is trembling. He's terrified.

"It's okay, Julius." Turning back to the men, I look them in the eyes. "He's just a kid. Let him go. There's nothing for you here." My voice is weak, so I clear my throat and stand up taller.

"Bitch, you've just been claimed by the Unchained Dogs," the shortest one snaps at me.

"What the hell?"

Before I can think, they toss Julius off the porch. He lands with a thud on the dirt patch out front.

"Julius!"

I dash forward to get to Julius, and two of the men grab me and hold me under my arms. As I flail and kick, a third grabs my feet.

"Let me go!" I scream. "This is kidnapping. Let me go! Julius!" Keeping my gaze glued to Julius, I see him stir. Thank god.

The harder I fight against them, the stronger their grip on me grows. One man, who's tall with a long, gray beard, laughs while I struggle. It's everything I can do not to spit on him.

Carrying me down the front steps of my building, I twist and turn, trying to break free from their grasp.

"Make noise out here, and you'll regret it," the tall one snaps at me.

Flailing my head back and forth, I see something in my peripheral vision. Out of the corner of my eye, I realize it's Julius getting to his feet.

"Run, Julius!" I shout. "Get out of here and find Seth!"

Julius staggers, and then takes off in the opposite direction just as one of the men covers my mouth with his oversized hand. It's sweaty and filthy and smells like chicken fat and motor oil, but I know better than to bite. If I do, if I fight back—they'll hurt me. It means nothing to these men to hurt another human being. In fact, they'll probably enjoy it.

"Shut up, bitch!" the man holding my feet yells. He looks over his shoulder at Julius running away. "He gonna be a problem?" He nods to one of the other men.

"Nah, stupid thug is no trouble for us. Let him call Dynamite. That's what we want."

No—they want Seth. They want him to overreact. Damn. Trying to clear my brain, I gather as many details as I can—truck make and model, color, description of the men. Fighting my imagination, I don't even want to speculate where they're taking me—or what they'll do to me when they get me there.

Without a moment to catch my breath, the men push me into the backseat of a black pickup truck. Damn, kidnapped in broad daylight.

Seth was right, and I should have listened to him. These guys are bad news.

Chapter Seventeen

Dynamite

Where the hell are those bastards who spray-painted Holly's building? Gritting my teeth, I growl into the wind as I race out of Greenville toward Rumble. Whichever of those damned Dogs did this—whoever thinks they can claim Holly—Fuck. I would not want to be the man responsible when I find him.

What? What is that? Taking a corner that would have dropped a less-experienced rider on his ass, I'm pretty damned sure I feel the vibration of the phone in my front pocket. With a move that spins my bike around under me, I drop my leg to balance myself as I grab my phone from my pocket.

"Holly?" I don't bother looking at the number.

"Seth, it's Julius. They took her!"

"Julius? Who took her? What are you talking about?"

"A couple of minutes after you left. Three guys in Dog jackets. They grabbed her, man. I wanted to fight them, but she screamed for me to run and find you—" He's out of breath and obviously panicked.

"You did the right thing. Were they on bikes?" I grip my clutch hard as I speak.

"Nah. A big black truck." The tone of his voice rises. "She was fighting them, but there were three of them. They tossed her into the back of their truck."

"Which way did they go?"

"West, out of Greenville."

West out of Greenville is Rumble. The same place I'm headed. I left before them, which means Holly is on the road somewhere behind me. Spinning my bike around in that direction, I rev the engine and pull off to the side of the road. Dust and dirt kick up at me, and little pieces of broken asphalt scatter behind me as I take off, racing directly for their truck.

If I keep at this pace, I'll run into them within maybe ten minutes and then—

Then what? Slowing my bike, I begin to see clearly. What will happen? There are three of them and one of me. The best that can happen is that I get a clear shot at one, maybe two—and then I'm dead, leaving Holly in danger.

"Fuck!" I scream through my locked jaw.

I can't do this. For once in my life, I can't act like a stick of dynamite, ready to explode. I have to own up to my mistakes and do what I never do—ask for help.

"I'm sorry, Holly. Hang in there. I'll get to you, I promise."

Spinning the bike, I cut off into a side road, heading for Hoppa.

"Thank god." Taking the turn into the parking lot of Hoppa's Taphouse way too fast, my tires make a screeching sound. The knot in my freaking stomach that I've been carrying for the past five miles relaxes when I see all the Knights' bikes. Then, at the same time, my stomach flips over. It's time for me to fess up and come clean.

Pulling into a spot near the front door of the Taphouse, I barely take the time to turn off my bike before I jump off and rush inside. Bursting through the door, I stand perfectly still—sweating and panting as I take in my surroundings. The guys are sitting at the bar, most wearing their colors, and Nick is behind the bar opening a beer. He sees me first. Standing up tall, he looks me up and down and then nods to me to follow him to the back room.

No doubt he can read the fear and worry on my face.

As I hustle to the back, I glance around, seeing a good number of civilians. They're people who don't know a damn thing about the Unchained Dogs or what turf they run. They're just hard-working people who come here to grab a beer after a long day behind a desk, or teaching school, or collecting trash. Shit. By being here at Hoppa's Taphouse, all of these people may be in danger—just because I can't control my temper.

Hurrying into the back room, I can feel the guys—Bullet, Bullseye, Bucky, Texas, Small Fry, and Vil—follow. As soon as we get inside, they form a semi-circle around me. Nick moves to speak, but he's interrupted by the back door opening.

Grabbing for my piece in my waistband, I ready myself for what's coming through that door. In my peripheral vision, I catch the other guys who are carrying doing the same. They may not know why, but they'll follow my lead.

"What's going on?" It's Colt.

Exhaling, I release my grip on my gun as he comes in from the back.

"Guys? Dynamite?" Colt looks me in the eye. "What's going on?"

"That's what we're waiting to find out," Nick explains. "Dynamite?"

Looking at Colt, my body stiffens. I want to protest him being here and send him home, but I can't. He's a man now, and he deserves the respect of one. His brow furrows as he looks at me, but I can barely look him in the eye.

The hell with it. I have no time to be a wimp. My knees bounce from adrenaline, and I take a deep breath, trying to still them, but it doesn't work.

"Dynamite." Nick nods to me. "What is it you need to say?"

I don't have time to take a breath. "I fucked up. Really fucked up." The words pour out of me. Looking from man to man, I finally settle my gaze on Bullet. "And because of it, Holly's been marked and kidnapped by the Dogs."

"What?" I can hear the concern in Nick's voice.

"You heard me. You know they'd been snapping pictures of her—and sent them to me with a death threat. I-I ran to their clubhouse and held Luther in a chokehold."

"You did *what?*" Bullet steps toward me. "Fuck, Seth! What were you thinking?"

"I wasn't thinking, okay?"

"That could mean war for us. Why haven't they attacked?" Bullet can't let it go. I don't blame him.

"I think they're waiting. They're trying to divide us up and then attack. They know we're stronger as a group—so they're letting me self-destruct and take all of you down with me. They think I can implode the Knights."

"It ain't gonna happen." It's Bucky, our Road Captain.

"Damn straight." Texas agrees.

"Thanks, guys." Swallowing hard, I go on. "I was inside her house, and then I heard a noise outside. I came out and saw they had spray-painted 'bitch' on the side of her building."

"Doesn't that mean the Dogs claimed her?" Colt asks.

"Yeah." I'm surprised by how he's taken to our culture and how much he understands already. "So, I went chasing after whoever did that—but on the way, I got a message that she was kidnapped."

"Could this be a ploy?" Vil asks. He fiddles with the rings in his ears as he speaks. "Something to draw us out?"

"No." Shaking my head, I look at all of them. "I've got a reliable source. Some kid that hangs out in the neighborhood. He's my eyes on the inside."

I can feel Colt staring at me, but when I turn to him, he looks away.

"That's not everything." Taking a deep breath, I go on. "You deserve to know it all. The Dogs have taken Greenville as their turf, and I don't know—I wasn't thinking."

"That's nothing new." It's Colt.

Nodding to him, I take a deep breath, sucking in my cheeks as I do. "When I went to see Luther, I tried to bargain with him. I told them we'd give up our land for the build in exchange for Greenville. Make a switch."

"What?" This time it's Bullseye.

The guys mumble.

"Guys, listen, they didn't accept anyway."

"The thing is," Nick explains, "it wasn't yours to give."

"I know that. I just panicked. I wasn't thinking—I did my usual Dynamite. But listen, for the first time ever, tonight, I stopped myself and came back to the club begging for your help. I didn't charge forward like I always do, trying to stop three guys alone." Throwing my hands up, I look from man to man. "Yes, I fucked up. But I'm asking for your help, as brothers. If you don't do it for me, then please. Please help Holly, who would help any of you." My gaze lands on Colt.

"He's right," Nick says. "It takes a big man to admit when he's wrong and ask for help."

The tense muscles in my shoulders relax the slightest bit.

"So?" I look around again.

"We ride," Nick announces. Going to the storage in the back of the room, he unlocks the safes and we grab our guns and ammo. I also pick up a pack of zip ties that work better than handcuffs, and a couple of the guys grab brass knuckles and Colt takes a set of nunchucks.

"You know how to use those things?" I ask him.

"That's why I took them." Looking me in the eye, he nods.

"All right," Nick says. "It's a long ride from here to Rumble. May pass the law on the way. No shotguns. Bullet, as VP, your job is to get the word to all the Knights. Let them know we may be preparing for war."

"Aye, aye, Nick."

Turning to me, Nick adds, "I've got to tell the Vipers and the Rebels. They deserve to know what may be going down here tonight. They'll catch word of it soon enough, and it should be from me."

"Nick." Reaching out, I grab his arm as he passes by, stopping him. "I'm sorry."

Nick just nods. "You'd do the same for any of us."

"And have," Bullseye adds.

Damn. A feeling of pride swells up from deep inside me. I'm lucky to have these men for my brothers.

As Nick texts the presidents of the Raging Vipers and the Blazing Rebels, the Knights step forward, grabbing weapons and ammo. I hold my breath when Colt takes a piece. As he shoves it into the back of his jeans, I motion for him to come to me.

"Colt, listen, I know you think I sucked as a big brother and still do. But if this goes bad, you could end up in jail or dead."

His icy green eyes soften when he looks at me. "So could you."

"But it's different—"

He stares hard at me. "As long as you think I'm different, we're never going to be able to move forward. They're not your real brothers, Seth. I am."

Nodding, I sigh. "So, then, let's keep each other alive, okay?"

Holding out my hand, I wait for him to shake. Instead, he looks into my eyes and then walks off. Shit. We are far from okay. But there's nothing I can do about that now.

Turning, I see Bullseye caught it all. Thankfully, Seneca walks in then, and Bullseye's attention is pulled off of me.

"You were fast."

Nodding, she smiles at him. "Hadn't gotten very far when I got your text."

Leaning up onto her tiptoes, she kisses him, and despite *everything*, the smallest smile passes across my lips.

"Colors, Knights," Bullet announces, "and full throttle when we approach Dog territory. We want them to know we're coming."

Most of us are wearing our colors anyway, but those who are just joining us, like Jonesie and Seneca, slide into their jackets.

"What about me, Nick?" It's Matt, Seneca's kid brother.

"No way." Seneca leaves Bullseye to stand by her brother's side.

"Sen, come on." Matt's cheeks turn red.

Nick shakes his head. "She's right. Sorry, Matt. I need someone here on defense."

Seneca smiles in relief.

"Nick." I can hear the agitation in Matt's voice.

Nicks sets his mouth firm. "Sorry, kid. You got a record, and you just got out. You get nabbed—you go down for a hell of a lot longer than any of us. You want that?"

"No."

"Didn't think you did."

Looking at the clock on the wall, I see it's been over half an hour that Holly's been with the Dogs.

"I see you, Dynamite." Nick nods, solemnly. "It's time to go." Turning to the men, he says, "We all know the Dogs are unpredictable. But no matter what happens out there, we get her out alive. She has helped our brothers and our allies without judgment, and she would help any one of us."

"Yes, Nick," the Knights answer in unison.

"Let's ride," Nick repeats.

With that, the Knights hustle out the door, mount our bikes, and head for the clubhouse of the Unchained Dogs.

We ride in a circle with Nick at the front. I'm just behind on his right with Bullet on his left. As we approach the street of the Dogs' clubhouse, Nick puts up his arm and signals for me to ride ahead. Bearing down on the throttle, I rev the engine. As we pull up and make a cacophony of sound, two Dogs come to the front door. Looking back at my club, I nod to them. With our colors, bikes, and the size of us, we do make an intimidating presence. Parking my bike, I climb off and the other Knights follow.

Walking to the door, I'm blocked by the two Dogs wearing their colors, snarling and snapping at me.

"Sorry, boys," I growl. "I haven't had my rabies shot. Now let me the hell by."

"Don't think so." One of the men crosses his arms before him and the other moves forward toward me.

That's it. I don't have time for this shit. Throwing an elbow, I hit one man clear in the nose, and as he stumbles back, I reach out and grab the other's head. Bringing it down against my knee, I snap his nose. He staggers away as blood gushes down his face and he drops to a knee on the street corner. Turning back to the first Dog, I reach around, grabbing the back of his jacket, and toss him onto the street next to his brother.

Nick, Bullet, and Bullseye walk into the club as I finish taking care of these two assholes.

"Fucking Dogs," I growl as I rush up behind the Dog I just tossed. I grab his arms, pull his wrists together behind his back, and zip-tie his hands together. Leaving him face-first on the street, I get up for the second.

"I got this," Colt offers.

Nodding to him, I back away from the men as Colt zip-ties the second Dog's wrists. Turning, I rush into the clubhouse. Barging through the door, I see Nick, Bullet, and Bullseye all standing in the middle of a semicircle of Dogs holding shotguns. The shotguns are still slung over their shoulders, pointing toward the ceiling, but they're there to make a point.

If we were to even reach for our guns, we'd be dead in a second. Scanning the crowd, I find Luther front and center. His greasy hair is slicked back, and he has a new red scar on his cheek.

Locking my eyes on his, I take a deep breath. "Where the hell is she?"

"Who?"

"I'm gonna tear your slimy head clear off of your body."

As I step toward Luther, Nick puts out his hand to stop me. He's right.

"So, Nick." Luther smiles. "It seems we have something you want, and you have something we want."

"What's that?" Nick is always cool and calm.

"It's come to my attention that we do, in fact, want your land outside of Hoppa."

"Why did you say no when I offered?"

Again, I move forward, but Nick holds me back.

Luther looks me up and down. "You wanted an exchange—your land for Greenville. In my plan, we get it all."

"But we get the girl." Nick looks directly at Luther.

"That would seem fair, yes."

Luther wears a smug grin, and I can't be the only one who wants to knock it off his face.

"Why do you want the land?" Bullet steps forward.

"We don't want you to expand," Luther explains. He sounds like he's in a boardroom, negotiating his company's stock. "Although you could never be us, there's a slim chance you could steal some of our businesses away. We don't just want the land, we want you to stop your build on this clubhouse—"

"—which you've already tried to do and didn't succeed." Nick stares Luther square in the eye.

"We have succeeded. I don't see your building."

"Because you froze the cement," I hiss.

Luther's gaze flashes to me and then he looks at Nick again.

"You didn't stop anything. We're negotiating with a new company," Bullet explains calmly. "I'm sure this won't come as a surprise to you, but the Dogs aren't liked. People are happy to jump ship."

Luther narrows his eyes. "You want the girl, you stop the build."

Nodding, Nick sighs. "There's a problem with that, Luther. If we stop, that will mean you win. And there has never been a time when a Knight has lost to a Dog."

Luther holds his hands out to his sides. "There's a first time for everything, right?"

"Not this, Luther."

Nick is doing what he has to do, but I am painfully aware that with every passing moment, Holly is being kept against her will. Sweat builds on my lower back and my heart is racing. I need this to move forward—we need to get Holly. Standing as still as I can, I take a mental count. There are fourteen Dogs staring at me and probably another half dozen keeping Holly and standing watch. Counting our men outside, we max at fourteen—and that's only if any of the new prospects got the call and are waiting outside. Otherwise, we're not even a dozen with Colt. Plus, we have our hand pieces, but they have shotguns and probably an automatic weapon or two.

Shit.

Shifting my weight from foot to foot, I'm getting downright antsy.

"Well." Nick cracks his knuckles and then swings his arms at his sides. "Seems we're at a standoff. Since we're on your turf, I mean no disrespect, but I want the girl."

"But we can't give her to you." Luther is still calm. "She's been claimed by the Dogs."

Fuck. Glaring at Luther, my stomach tightens into knots. "The girl, Luther," I snap.

"Let us know she's okay. Let us see her." Nick is emphatic.

As the seconds pass, my heart rate is pounding in my ears and sweat is dripping down my cheeks. My skin is so damned hot I swear it's starting to crackle. Looking at Luther, I wonder if he knows there's a type of dynamite that can spontaneously erupt—and if he wants to learn.

"You'll have to settle for hearing from her." Luther turns toward the back room. "Clyde!"

At the mention of Clyde's name, I catch Bullseye tense.

"They want to hear from the girl," Luther hollers.

The unmistakable sound of duct tape being ripped from a mouth is followed by a gasp. It's her.

"Nick wants to know you're okay."

"Nick?" Her voice is high. "Nick! I'm here. In a closet in the—"

Slap!

A Dog just slapped her.

Hell. No.

"Fuck you!" I scream as I grab my piece from the back of my jeans. Pointing it at the ceiling, I shoot.

Dogs and Knights duck as pieces of brown, water-stained plaster and ceiling tiles rain down on us, but it doesn't stop me. My adrenaline is so pumped and my heart rate is so fast, I think that not even a freaking bullet could bring me down now. Pushing my way through the mass of bodies throwing punches, I walk up to the first Dog I see, and in a surprise move, clock him on the side of the head with the butt of my gun. He doubles over and falls, and I step over him.

Everything goes quiet as I charge forward. Around me, the men scuffle, but I see only dead ahead—straight into that back room where they're holding Holly. Another Dog blocks my way, so I grab him by the lapel of his ugly jacket and toss him against a wall. He lands with a thud, and his head bounces off the wall.

"Holly?" I yell, walking back. "Holl—"

The end of a shotgun is wedged into my back. Fuck.

"Forget it, Dynamite." It's Luther. "You should have killed me when you had the chance. So now, I'm going to kill you. Arms up and keep the gun where I can see it."

"Fine." As I raise my arms, I force my teeth to unclench. "You want to kill me, then do it. But let her go free. She's never done anything except try to help people."

Luther wedges the gun deeper into my back. "Oh, I plan to kill you. But I'm not letting her go. We can use her around here. We've been short a doctor and with her, we have the added enjoyment of pleasuring ourselves with her whenever we—"

Whipping around, I bring my hands down on the shotgun so fast I can see the look of fear and surprise in Luther's eyes. With my fists and forearms, I knock the shotgun out of Luther's hands. Then, picking him up by his jacket collar, I shove him against the nearest door.

"You son of a bitch!" I scream, banging his head repeatedly against the wall.

"Seth?" It's Holly's voice. "These men want you to stop. Please, Seth."

"Dynamite!" Colt screams. "We need help!"

I'm trapped. I'm needed out front, but I have to get to Holly. I got us in to this—all of it—and there's no way out. As much as it kills me to do it, I know Holly is as okay as she can be for the moment, so dropping Luther to the ground, I rush from the back room into the front. Fuck. The smell of fresh blood chokes me and I cough, covering my mouth with my arm to block some of the scent. Climbing over the bodies of men beating one another, I start swinging at any Dogs I can get. My foot slips in a pool of blood, but I catch myself. Looking to my right, I see Nick on his knees on the floor, holding a gash on his head. The wall behind him is splattered with blood. I look around frantically, but except for me shooting at the ceiling, no one else has drawn a gun. That's because guns mean death—on both sides—and neither the Knights nor the Dogs are ready to let their brothers die.

To my left, I see Bullet and Bullseye pummeling a mountain-sized man. Past him, Colt fights off a Dog with a pair of nunchucks. Damn, he handles those things like he's in a freaking martial arts movie.

As another Dog comes at me, I swing hard but he ducks and charges at my abdomen, knocking me down onto my back. From this supine position, I kick and punch, but the Dog has me trapped. Fuck. Glancing to the side, I see that nearly all the Knights are on the defensive, like me. We're putting up a good fight, but the Knights are outnumbered. That means we're going to lose this fight, some men, our clubhouse, and maybe even Holly.

"No."

Pushing the Dog off of me and onto his back, I spring to my feet but there's another Dog waiting for me. As strong as we are, this fight is almost impossible, because we're outnumbered. Looking at this man, I see he's tall but he uses a crutch—there's no way he can fight me.

"Shit." I recognize him.

He was the mountain of a man I crippled the last time I was here. But as angry as he must be, I'm faster. Dodging him, I rush past him, but the Dog I just knocked down is up again. Grabbing me, he throws me at the giant-sized man. Laughing, the man takes my hands and links them behind my back. He holds me as the other man ties my hands with rope and moves down to my legs to tie my ankles together. *Shit, shit, shit!* No matter how much I fight, I can't break free. The more I struggle, the tighter the binds become, and now they're cutting deep into my wrists. The only positive I can see right now is that the giant man was too careless to check me for a weapon.

I don't care what happens to me—but what are they doing to Holly? Fuck! Sure, I'm caught, but there's no way I'm going to let this hap—

Bracing myself, it feels like the earth moves below us. What the hell? Looking up, I see the ceiling tiles tremble and the walls of the clubhouse shake at the thunderous sound of dozens of bikes approaching.

"What the fuck?"

The Dog who tied me gets to his feet, ignoring me. But the mountain-sized man still stands behind me, and I'm trapped.

It's like time freezes as everyone in the clubhouse halts their fighting and turns to the doorway. Suddenly, the door flies open and there stand the presidents of the Raging Vipers and the Blazing Rebels. Both are wearing their colors—the Vipers a red insignia, and the Rebels orange.

Nick gets to his feet, although he's wobbly when he stands. He's the first to speak. "Venom." He nods to the president of the Raging Vipers. "You're a long way from Collinstown." Then, he turns to the other man. "And you, Bear, you're just as far from Mascid."

Ducking to step inside the clubhouse without hitting his head, Bear steps forward. Crap, I haven't seen him in a while, and I'd forgotten his size. It's easy to see how the man got his name. He must be seven-feet tall, with long dreads down his back and muscles bulging out of the sawed-off arms of his vest. "We could say the same thing to you, Squared."

Nick nods and smiles at the mention of his nickname. "We've got business here. That's why I sent you the text. Thought you should know."

"Seems we got business here, too," Bear answers.

"Really?" Nick raises an eyebrow. "You know this was our aggression. We didn't call for you."

Fighting against my binds, all I want to do is to get back to Holly, grab her, and run, but I'm trapped.

"No, you didn't. We came of our own free will," Bear explains.

Making eye contact with me, Venom steps up. "We hear this gang of Dogs has Dr. Holly Boling hostage."

"What's it to you?" Luther stumbles out of the back room. Shit, I should have hit his head harder.

Venom's chest starts heaving when he sees Luther. "You piece of shit. You had no business attacking us."

"It was just business."

"Business that cost me men!"

Venom lunges for Luther, but Bear stops him. The whole room is on edge. Men stand around with their hands balled into fists as sweat and blood drip from their faces. Everyone is ready to attack.

"That's the price of membership," Luther scoffs, rubbing the back of his head.

"Dr. Boling saved my men," Venom says.

Luther shrugs. "She saved some of mine, too." Grinning, he looks at his men. "Bet she's sorry about that right now."

Laughter erupts, and I fight fiercely against my bonds but nothing. They don't budge.

Venom crosses the clubhouse and stands toe-to-toe with Luther. They are similar heights, but Venom has wide shoulders and thick legs and appears to be so much stronger.

"You're going down here. We are taking Dr. Holly one way or another—you're either dead or alive," Venom snaps.

"What makes you think you can stop us?" Luther hisses, and spit splatters from his lips when he does.

"We've got close to fifty men outside." Venom stands up tall and crosses his arms before his chest. "And more to call in if we need." Turning to Bear, he nods.

Bear crosses to the door and makes a swirling motion in the air with his hand. At his command, what must be fifty bikes rev, and the sound is deafening.

Turning to Luther, Venom smiles. "Every one of my men are packing, Luther. You can't win. Give us Holly, and stay the hell out of Knights' territory."

Sighing, Luther looks over his men. "I don't think I can."

At the nod of his head, the fighting resumes, but now we have backup. With a head thrust backward, I'm able to knock the mountain man back a few feet, and with my feet and arms bound, I jump toward Bullseye like I'm in a freaking sack race.

"Bullseye!" I yell. Motioning to my jacket, I yell to be heard over the noise. "Grab my knife in my jacket and cut me loose."

Reaching into my pocket, Bullseye gives me a look out of the corner of his eye. No doubt he remembers the last time he and I were in a fight with a knife. Doing what I ask, he saws through the thick rope and I feel the binds on my arms fall away. Dropping down, I cut through the bind on my legs.

Jumping to my feet, I rush to the back room again with Bullet and Bullseye on my heels. With the backup we now have, I'm able to push past the Dogs blocking my way as Bullet and Bullseye fight my fights for me.

Finally, I make it to the closet where they're holding Holly. Ripping open the door, I pull it clear off its hinges and toss it aside.

Holly looks up at me. Her beautiful face is stained with tears, but she gives me a small nod. Tears fall from her eyes when she sees me, and my heart aches for her. How could anyone do this? Reaching in, I remove her tape gag and then, reaching around her, I untie her binds.

As soon as I do, she leans forward and throws her arms around my neck, holding on tight.

"Dynamite," she whispers. "Thank you."

Her words sit heavy in my gut. Reaching forward, I move to scoop her up when suddenly, her eyes grow wide.

"Seth! Look out!"

Confused, I lean back from her just as a piece of metal clocks me on the back of my head and everything goes dark.

Chapter Eighteen

Holly

"Seth!" Now free of my binds, I crawl out of the closet and over to where Seth is lying. Kneeling in the dimly lit hallway, I assess his injuries. "Come on, Seth. Come on. You need to wake up."

Checking for a pulse, my tight neck muscles loosen when I hear that his heartbeat is strong and steady. I know the reason he's out—he was struck on the back of the head—but I take all necessary precautions anyway. Putting my head to his chest, I check his breathing. Sitting up on my knees and leaving his arms at his sides, I then lift his fingers to assess circulation. Thankfully, all is fine. His vitals are strong, so I climb around to his head and stabilize his head and neck with my hands. The longer he's out, the higher the risk of serious injury.

"Come on, Seth," I whisper into his ear. "Come on. You came to get me, but now we need to go. Okay? Together. If you wake up, I promise we can put all this ridiculous fighting behind us and just be together. Come on, Seth!"

Looking down at his tanned skin and strong cheekbones, I think of his bright green eyes staring into mine.

"Seth, come on. Wake up!" I hate feeling helpless. I can always fix any situation, *always*. If I just work hard enough and really apply myself, there's nothing I can't solve. Glancing down the hallway, I check to see if anyone is coming. Looking behind me, I search for another door—an escape route of some kind, but there isn't one. Truthfully, even if there were, it's too dangerous to move him, and I don't have the strength to drag him.

Seth doesn't stir, and my stomach clenches. I need an ambulance, but from the sounds of fighting I'm hearing from the other room and the fact that my phone is gone—I know there's no way I can call for one. Or can I? Quickly, keeping his head and neck as still as possible, I move to Seth's side. I feel the pockets of his jeans, where I find his phone. Sliding it from his pocket, I swipe to the emergency screen. Pressing the button, I hold my breath as I keep my eyes glued to the hallway, watching for anyone coming.

"Yes? Hello? I need an ambulance, please—"

"Hey!" Just then, two men in Dogs jackets see me and come rushing toward us.

"I don't know the address," I yell into the phone. "I was taken prisoner—the Unchained Dogs' clubhouse in Rumb—"

One of the Dogs knocks the phone out of my hand and steps on it to break it while the other picks me up by the hair.

"Ow. Ow," I whimper as I get to my feet.

"You little bitch!" he yells. "You called the cops!"

"No," I mumble, trying to keep up with him as we move forward so he doesn't pull my hair clean out of my head. "I called an ambulance. There are so many injuries."

"Who do you think the ambulance is going to call?"

Walking me into the main room, he tosses me onto the floor. Breaking my fall with my hands, I land on my hip. Daring a glimpse up, I see Nick and the other Knights glaring.

"I've had enough!" the Dog yells. Pulling a switchblade from the back of his pants, he flips it open. Walking to me, he grabs me by the hair again and drags me to my feet.

"No, no, no," I mumble.

"Damian, no!" Nick yells. "She's done nothing to you. She helped your brothers. Let her go! Let us settle this by the code of the bikers—not by hurting a civilian."

Still holding me by the hair, he circles around behind me and wraps his arm around my chest, pinning my arms to my sides. It's almost a relief when he's let go of my hair.

Then he puts the sharp knife to my throat. In the same breath, all the Unchained Dogs draw their shotguns and point them at the Knights, Vipers, and Rebels. Closing my eyes, I take deep, calming breaths.

"You think I give a damn that she's helped us?" Damian asks, pushing the knife harder against my throat. "It's time these fucking Knights, and Vipers, *and* Rebels learn what it means to deal with the Dogs. If they're willing to risk their lives for her… Damn, she must be worth a whole hell of a lot to them."

"We'll give you whatever you want, Damian." Nick raises his hands into the air but uses a strong, serious voice. He looks from the man holding me back over to the head of the Unchained Dogs, Luther. "Let her go, Luther. She's innocent. You want our clubhouse—you want our territory—take it. Just let her go. She's young and has a whole hell of a lot to live for."

"But once I let her go—" Damian tightens his grip around my neck. "—then you'll all renege."

"Knights don't go back on our word. Luther—your president—knows that. Tell him, Luther. Tell him we never go back on our word," Nick insists.

Luther stays quiet.

"Vipers don't go back on our word either—"

"Neither do Rebels," adds a giant man with long dreads.

My already-trembling body starts shaking uncontrollably. Damian laughs, and as he does, he moves me.

Damian looks over his shoulder and spits on the floor. "Damn, the fact that you all want her freed so bad makes it all the more fun for me to take this nice, sharp knife and run it across her throat."

Closing my eyes, I stifle a sob.

"Hey, doc, you must know what it feels like to have a whole bunch of nice, warm red blood spill out of someone's body and all over your hands, right?"

"Please, don't." My words are a whisper.

"Oh, come on, doc. All those years of school? You can do better than that. What's it called when someone's blood spills out all over your hands?"

Squeezing my eyes shut, I plead with the man holding me. "Please." Tears stream down my cheeks. "Please."

"Nah, that don't sound right. Try again. The word ain't please—what's it called?"

He tightens the knife against my throat and all of the Dogs raise their guns higher in anticipation of what's to come. Nick keeps his hands up, holding his men at bay. It's obvious that reaching for any weapons—assuming they have them—would mean possible death for them… and certain death for me.

"Doc, you're starting to try my patience." He squeezes his arm tighter around me. "What's the word when someone's blood pours out of them and drips into a big, red pool on the floor?"

He presses the knife so hard I begin to choke.

"I-it's called hemorrhaging."

"Yeah, that's it—"

There's a loud scuffle from behind us, and suddenly, someone screams, "Bullseye!"

Damian turns me in the direction of the voice.

"Seth?" Tears stream down my face as I see Seth come up from behind one of the Dogs, tear the shotgun from his hands, and toss it to Bullseye.

Bullseye stands in front of me now. His feet are hips' width and one eye is closed as the other stares down the sight of a shotgun that's pointing directly at Damian. Bullseye's arms are so sure and so steady, he rivals some of the best surgeons I know.

"Let her go!" Seth commands, rushing up next to Bullseye. "You can't win this, Damian. This is your one chance. Let her go now, otherwise Bullseye will pop you right between the eyes. He's an expert sharpshooter. You know he can—and he will."

Damian shuffles from foot to foot, beads of sweat rolling down his face.

"I'm counting to three." Seth stares me in the eyes as he counts. "One, two, thr—"

"All right!" Raising his arms, the man releases me, and I drop to the ground.

"Holly?" Seth rushes to me and squats down next to me. "Are you okay?" He strokes my hair. "Baby, I'm so sorry."

"Yes, I'm okay." I fight to make sense of the situation as fighting resumes around us.

Moving me back behind a bar, Seth nods to me. "Stay here."

Stroking my cheek, he smiles and then stands and rushes Damian. Jumping him from behind, Seth takes Damian down with a chokehold. Men—and Seneca—are punching and kicking. In the corner, Colt wields a set of nunchucks and cracks a man in his cheekbone. The way the man falls, my guess is he either has a broken cheekbone or a dislocated jaw. Bullet backhands a large man, taking him down. The carnage builds until it looks like I'm sitting in the middle of a slaughterhouse. Men with vipers on their jackets, and another group with an insignia I can't make out from here, are working their way through the clubhouse with the Knights. There are so many of the Unchained Dogs on the ground that the fight has to be letting up. Turning to Seth to see if he's okay, I watch as he pulls a gun from his jeans and points it at

Damian's head.

"You are going to die a long, painful death," Seth warns Damian. "Do you understand?"

"Yes—ow!" The man doubles over as Seth kicks him in the gut. It's probably a bruised liver.

As soon as the man gets to his knees, Seth kicks him again and again. Turning away, I try to hide from the violence.

"Now, it's your time to die." Even above the ruckus, I can hear Seth's voice threatening the man.

Forcing myself to look, I see Seth holding a gun to the man's temple.

"Seth, no!" I'm terrified to even speak, but my voice is strong.

Still pointing the gun at the man's head, Seth looks over at me. "Holly, turn away. Don't look at this."

"Seth, you can't kill him."

"He tried to kill you. He deserves to die."

Braving the chaos, I crawl on my hands and knees toward Seth. "No! Don't you understand? I cannot be the cause of someone's death."

"You won't be," Seth assures me. "I will." He steps even closer to Damian.

"Seth, no, please!"

Damian turns to me with a confused look on his face.

"Seth, please," I plead with him. "Don't you understand what I'm saying to you? If there's any chance—ever—for us to be together, you can't do this. I cannot be with someone who kills—not when I've devoted my life to saving people."

The piercing sound of an ambulance's siren blasts through the noise of the clubhouse.

"If you do this, Seth." My words come faster. "If you kill him, there will never be a chance for us. We can get past anything—but *this*. It's your decision. Only you can make it. Are you going to control your emotions and give us a chance? Or are you going to let your passion overtake you and lose me for good? You don't have to live tethered to that nickname forever."

Still holding the gun on Damian, Seth nods to Nick. "Nick, can you take Colt and get her out of here? Take her wherever she wants to go."

"Seth. Please." Has he heard anything I've said?

"I'm sorry, Holly. But we always knew this wouldn't work. This is who I am." Still pointing the gun at the man, he turns to me. "This is what a 'man like me' would do, right?"

"Seth!" I yell. "You're playing with *lives* here. This isn't you. You're acting like a petulant child."

We make eye contact, and he holds my gaze. Then, turning away, he barks an order at Colt. "Take her and go."

"The ambulance is coming, Seth." Bullet hovers near us. "We all need to go."

"You and Bullseye go and take the guys," Seth instructs. "I'll handle this and catch up with you."

As I watch Seth standing there, threatening another man's life, the tears pour out of my eyes. With Bullet and Bullseye flanking me, Colt takes me by the arm and leads me out of the clubhouse.

Once we're on the sidewalk, the deafening sound of a single gunshot rips through the cool night air, shattering any last glimmer of hope that I had.

It's over.

Even though being with Seth Hardy made me feel alive for the first time ever, there's no way I could ever be with a man who kills.

As the red glow of ambulance lights colors the sky before me, I'm torn between the life I know and the man I left inside. Moving forward, I climb onto the back of Colt's bike, and it feels every bit as foreign to me as the woman I've become.

"You okay?" Colt asks as he revs the bike.

"Sure," I mumble.

But I'm not okay. I was wrong. I'm not supposed to be the woman with a bird on her hip and a clinic in the middle of Greenville. I'm not supposed to be anything more than a rich girl who grew up living a privileged life. No, I can't marry Robert or become my father's partner, but maybe my mother was right about one thing—maybe doing good in the world is for other people.

Leaning back, I hold the grab bars behind the passenger's seat on Colt's bike, and after one final glance at the Unchained Dogs' clubhouse, we're gone.

Chapter Nineteen

Dynamite

Slipping off my boots and socks, I walk back and forth across the foundation of the new club. We're on the opposite side of Hoppa, but exactly where we had planned to be. The cement is warm, and I've got to say, it feels pretty damned good. Actually, it feels better than good. It feels like success.

The Steel Knights are finally getting our new clubhouse.

Shit, with the way I've been feeling lately, it's nice to finally feel good about something.

Looking over to the group of guys standing around Nick, I can't help but smile. None of this would have been possible without the direction of Tess when she was VP. She planned all of this and worked her butt off to build connections with the other clubs. I'm just sorry she can't be here to see it. As Nick points to the far wall where the bar will be, I know that as long as he's in charge of the build, a part of her will always be here.

"What the hell?" Bullseye nods to me as he walks past, carrying a two-by-four. "Break time already?"

Yeah, sure, the guys will razz me for it, but I'm going to take a break, soak up some sun, and enjoy every second of this success because it almost didn't happen. Everyone knows that where we're standing could have ended up becoming Dog turf.

Colt walks up and hands me a beer. We clink bottles and sit on the edge of the platform with our feet dangling in the air.

"It's good that Nick changed his mind about the bunker." Colt leans forward, resting his forearms on his thighs.

"Yeah. I think he's a lot less worried and has a lot more confidence now that the Dogs have been smacked down and put in their place. Still, though." I tilt my bottle and watch the bubbles rush up the sides. "We can never count them out. They may be down right now, but they'll be back—larger and even more pissed off."

"Yeah, I know." Colt shakes his head. "But it's a victory anyway. Greenville is Knights' territory now, so Holly's clinic will be safe no matter what happens. Jesus, so many damned arrests. It's good we got out before the cops hauled all those Dogs away." Looking me in the eye, he adds, "It's good you got out before you got nabbed. Again."

"Yeah, it is." Nodding, my gaze falls on the trees before me. What a backyard this will be.

We can bring in grills and tables, maybe string some outdoor lights. It's a perfect place for a party. The thought makes me smile.

This place will be spectacular when it's finished. I only wish I could take Holly here for an inaugural drink. But, unfortunately, that's not in the cards anymore.

Putting his beer down on the unfinished wood of the doorframe next to him, Colt takes a breath and then turns to me. "That gunshot surprised us all. We all thought it was you."

"I know."

"So? Why not tell her the truth?"

"Geez, you do get right to it, don't you?"

"Seth, it's been almost two weeks. I've been waiting for you to do something and go get her, but you haven't. So, why don't you tell her you didn't kill that Dog?"

Looking into Colt's eyes, I know he deserves the truth. "I don't really know," I explain. "I think it comes down to the idea that if you're with someone—I don't mean for a night or two, but really with them—you want them to get you. If Holly can believe I would kill a man and risk losing what we had—then maybe she's not the woman I thought she was."

"What chance did she have to think anything else? I was there, Seth. She was traumatized and yet she begged you not to kill that man, but you wouldn't budge. You wouldn't even give her a hint that you weren't going to kill him."

"I couldn't very well announce that in a room full of Dogs, could I? They would have killed me on the spot. I had to get out."

"So, you got out, and you should have gone straight to her to tell her. Instead, you've been sulking around like a damned wounded puppy. It's been days and days. You could have told her any time."

"It's not that easy."

"Of course it is." Colt shakes his head and looks me in the eyes again. "Here's the thing, Seth. You want to believe that you two are so different, it makes you the victim. You think because you're not a doctor and don't come from the upper class with an Ivy League diploma that she's not into you. But all that woman did was try to show you how into you she *was*. She was freaking kidnapped by the Dogs and never blamed you. Christ, Seth. She wasn't some rich snob from the other side of the tracks, you know? This woman tried to be with you and your friends. More than anything, she tried to open a clinic to help people in need—and she had no one help *her*."

His words sit heavy in my gut. He's right. About all of it. Why the hell am I being such chicken shit? "What about you?" Taking another long drink from my bottle, I turn to Colt. "Since you seem to know so much about women, anything ever happen with that girl we met? The drama teacher?"

"You mean Erica?" He smiles when he says her name. "Erica Peters. Yeah, we've been hanging out some."

"I didn't know."

"You didn't ask." Sighing, Colt leans back and bends a knee, resting his foot on the edge of the foundation. "She's coming by any minute."

"Here?" Sitting up, I smile at him.

"Yeah. She's good with plants. Going to help us out with some landscaping, and then I'm taking her to dinner."

"Nice." My hat is off to my kid brother. "Well done."

Sitting up again, he stretches his arms overhead and then picks up his bottle and takes another long drink. He looks off at the trees for a moment and then turns back to me. "Do you think you would have killed him? If she hadn't begged you not to?"

Shaking my head, I spin the bottle in my hands. Little bits of the cool, slick label come off in my palms. "I don't know."

Colt stares at the ground. "Want to know what I think?"

"Yeah." I really do. It matters to me what my kid brother thinks.

"I think you use your dynamite personality to keep from getting close to anyone."

It's like a freaking bullet in my gut. "What the hell does that mean?"

"As long as you tell yourself you can't be trusted, you have the excuse you need to never get close to anyone."

A horn beeps and, turning, we see a car pull up. Colt looks up and waves. "That's Erica. We're going to the nursery, and then we'll be back later." Sliding forward on the foundation, he looks at the ground below and then jumps down. Wiping his hands on his jeans, he nods to me. "See you around, Seth."

He rushes up to Erica's little white convertible sports car. When she sees him, a giant smile spreads across her face. Hopping up in the driver's seat, she leans across the car and plants a kiss on Colt's lips. Damn. Scrubbing my face with my hand, I chuckle. Good for them. Glimpsing me, she glares at me before sitting back down. Damn, that girl and I did not get off on the right foot.

"What the hell is your problem with me?" I mutter under my breath.

As she pulls forward, Colt holds up his hand and waves at me. Watching the convertible pull away, all I can think about is Holly and sitting in the back of her convertible on the night she got her tattoo. My skin gets hot as hell and my jeans grow tight in response as I get an overwhelming urge to be with her. Like I do almost every night. And day.

"All right, Seth. What the hell are you doing?" Nick's voice is stern.

"Okay, okay." Jumping to my feet, I turn around and face Nick. "Guess no one gets a break around here."

"I'm not talking about your damned break. I'm talking about what you're doing with your woman, Dr. Holly."

"Shit, you, too? Did you all plan to attack me about this today?"

"Oh, cool it. No one is attacking you. We're all worried about you. And about her. I didn't know what you and Colt were talking about, but I'm just you're getting some bonding time. While we're at it, I'm glad Colt tried to talk some sense into you. So, I'll repeat my question—what are you going to do about your woman?"

"I'm not doing anything about her because she's not mine."

"Bullshit. I saw the way you just looked at your brother with his girl. I know that when you didn't kill that Dog, it went against every one of your dynamite urges, but you did it. And you did it because you knew if you killed Damian, you and Holly could never be together." Nick takes a deep breath and links his hands in through the straps of his workman's coveralls. "You have control, Seth. If that's what you're worried about. You proved it that night at the Dogs' clubhouse."

Looking into Nick's eyes, I ask the question that's been gnawing at my gut all this time. "What if I hurt her?"

"Physically?"

"Of course not. I would never. I mean the way I hurt Colt. Thanks to my damned outburst, I couldn't protect him and stay with him when we were kids, and now we're little more than lukewarm to one another."

"You can't let one action define your life." Nick sighs as he speaks.

"But it wasn't one action. How many times did he need something from me and I just pushed him aside in one of my uncontrolled rages? I wasn't there for him."

"Maybe you weren't there for him then, but you are now. All we have is today, Seth."

"I don't want to do that to her." Looking into Nick's sparkling eyes, I take a deep breath and exhale sharply. "I don't want to make the same mistake twice."

"Then don't." Nick walks up closer to me and puts his hand on my shoulder. "You may be a lot of things, Seth, but I never pegged you as a quitter. It's all so much easier than you think. If you want to be with her, then be a man worthy of being with her."

Nodding, excitement brews deep in my belly for the first time since Holly walked out of the Dogs' clubhouse that night. "You're right, Nick. And I think I know exactly how to start."

"Wow." Smiling at Colt and Erica, I nod to the landscaping outside of Holly's building. "It looks amazing."

Erica raises an eyebrow and plants her shovel into the ground, leaning against the top of it. "Thanks." She's nice enough, but I get a definite chill off of her. Her white tank top is smeared with dirt, and her long blonde hair is pinned up on top of her head. She really is adorable, and a damned hard worker at that. I can see why Colt is into her.

Smiling at Colt, she turns her body toward him while she speaks to both of us. Pointing to the door, she explains, "I am so over all that cactus landscaping they have here in Arizona, so those—" She points to two evergreen bushes lining the newly-refurbished front stairs and their guardrail. "—are Cape honeysuckles. And those orange-red bushes that are framing the new red door? They're called red bird of paradise. When I saw that stained-glass with the single bird, I thought these would be a perfect complement."

The fact that Erica picked up on the idea of the bird in the glass and ran with it hits me hard. I swallow a lump in my throat.

"And this—" Squatting down, she runs her hand over a newly-laid lawn. "—is sod. Also known as grass." She laughs. "Isn't it nice to see some green around here?"

"Yeah, it really is." Stepping forward, I hold out my hand. "Thank you, Erica."

She takes my hand and we shake, but she eyes me in a way that's completely unnerving. What is up with this girl, and why doesn't she like me?

Dropping my hand, she turns to Colt, and she's all happy and smiles again. "Come on, Colt. How about an iced tea? I saw a cute store a couple of doors down."

Wrapping his arm around her, Colt turns back to me and waves, and then walks off with Erica.

Putting the weirdness of Erica's reaction to me out of my mind, I climb the stairs and walk into the clinic.

"I've got to hand it to you." Nick smiles at me when he sees me walk in. He looks around the newly constructed bottom floor of Holly's clinic. "That first day we came riding up to this building, I never thought it could look like this. Hell, I never thought you'd get us in here. We were lucky that it's on the market and the real estate agent—"

"Clea."

"Yes, Clea." The way he says it… does Nick like her?

"Anyway." Clearing my throat, I go on. "We're lucky that Clea likes Holly and gave me a set of keys."

"Yeah—she was quick handing over those keys. I'm sure it had nothing to do with a bunch of bikers showing up on their motorcycles, wearing their colors and asking if we could fix it up."

Chuckling, I smile. "I guess we can be an intimidating bunch. But she cleared it with Holly. Told Holly that she had a construction crew that owed her and was willing to work for free—that way they'd do better on the listing price and Holly could recoup some more money."

"Not to mention a bigger commission for Clea," Nick adds. "We were just lucky Holly didn't stop by."

"I think she's avoiding the place," I add.

"Probably. For now." Nick's dark tone brightens again. "Well, how we got in here doesn't matter. We did. The best part? This place has completely transformed over the past two weeks. It sure looks good."

Glancing around, I have to agree with him. The ground floor is clean and organized, with a custom-built, giant reception desk to the right. We brought in construction guys, and we worked round the clock—with the help of some of the Vipers and Rebels and Julius—but the place has been completely transformed. New windows were hung, the floors repaired and polished, the bathrooms have been gutted, retiled, and made handicap accessible. The sinks have all been replaced and guardrails have been put up everywhere.

"It was expensive, Nick. I can't thank you enough for cutting the clubhouse build to find the money to use here."

"Most of the labor was free. All we paid for were supplies and a couple of professionals. Even they gave us a break when they found out what this building was going to be."

Glancing at the stained-glass window above the front door, I take a deep breath.

"Still not letting anyone help you with the third floor?" Nick raises an eyebrow.

"I had the plumber and electrician up."

"Yeah, but no one else. That's cool, I understand. You're making her a living space."

"I just hope she likes it." My voice trails off.

"She'll love it, Seth. But you have to be ready for her to not want to live here. It has some of her worst memories. Even though this is no longer Dog turf, she may be scared to be here."

"I know." Nodding, I look Nick in the eye. "I just want to give her the option." Taking a deep breath, I continue. "There have been people driving by, you know. Prospective buyers. Some guy in an expensive German car came by a couple of times, scoping it out. The building will sell if she wants it to."

Nick smiles. "Yes. Now we find out if she wants it to. Ready to get this show on the road?"

Swallowing hard, I take a deep breath.

"Got your flowers?"

"They're waiting upstairs."

"Okay." He turns to leave.

"Hey, Nick?"

"Yeah?"

"What if she doesn't want to come?"

He smiles. "The guys have a plan. Don't worry. She'll come."

"What plan?"

He winks. "A good one."

Crap. Still, the nerves in my gut are quelled some by Nick's reassurance, and I rush up the two sets of stairs to the third floor to wait.

Chapter Twenty

Holly

Crap. I need to play back the messages on my home phone. I've been dreading this for weeks, but here goes. The movers will be here in two days, and I need to have all of this cleared up. Plopping down on the hardwood floor next to my rolled-up rug, I prop my hands behind me and drop my head back. I've had the ringer turned off and the volume turned down for almost two weeks now, which means there are probably close to seventy messages from my mother alone. Crap. This is the last thing I want to do, but it's time to put on my big girl panties and just listen to the messages. I've been answering my texts, so everyone knows I'm alive—but that's all I have the energy for. Well, that and packing.

Stretching my legs out, I kick a box labeled "Stuff" and let out a long sigh.

Looking around at all of the packed boxes, I can't help but wonder if this is how it's going to be now—a life of wandering, never really knowing where I belong or who I am.

Here goes. I press the playback button, and the weird-sounding automated voice says, *Message one.*

Followed by, *Holly?* Crap, it's Mom.

Holly, it's your mother again. I have been calling you all day on your cell. You're ignoring me.

Bending my knees, I wrap my arms around them and bury my face in the crook of my elbow. "I've been texting you, Mom," I mumble to the machine.

Texts don't count.

"Mom?" Lifting my head, I look around jokingly. "Are you here?"

Your father took time out of his busy practice to go looking for you. The least you can do is call

"What? I didn't see Dad," I say to the machine, like I'm having a conversation with my mother. Furrowing my brow, I wrack my brain, trying to think of a time when my father could have been here. I've been home for the past two weeks. How could I have missed him? Maybe he stopped by when I was at the gym or grabbing food? Huh.

Message two.

Hello, Holly.

Oh, crap, Robert.

I don't know where you are or what's going on, but the hospital says you gave notice? Why? Does this have something to do with me?

"No, Robert, not everything has to do with you."

Or that little clinic? Holly, it's time to grow up. What's going on? Call me.

Sighing, I roll my eyes at Robert's message. "Grow up? If you only knew what I've been through, you jerk."

Message three.

Holly. Cripes, it's Robert—again.

What is this I hear about you moving back east? What can the east coast possibly have to offer?

"A job, Robert. And a hell of a lot of miles between us."

Message four.

"You know what?" The conversation I've been having with my answering machine seems to be working for me, so I keep it going. "I'm going to finish with you later."

Clicking off the machine, I take a much-deserved break. I just can't listen to any more. I need some space. And wine. It's apparent that the only way I'm going to get through this is with wine.

Looking across the floor, I eye my fridge. It normally houses my yogurt and bottles of water, but right now, it's stuffed with a single bottle of chardonnay and a couple of beers I threw in there in the hope that Seth would someday stop by and I could offer him one.

The thought of Seth sends excitement through my body, but when I realize I'll never see him again… Screw it. There's no time for moping. I'll crack open the bottle of wine and save the beers for the moving guys.

There's only one problem with my plan—wine glasses. Who the hell packs wine glasses two days before her move? Rookie mistake. Wine glasses are the *very last thing* to pack. Every single woman knows the last three things to pack are: toothbrush, cell phone, wine glasses. In that order.

Chuckling to myself, I dig through one of the already well-packed cardboard boxes sitting by my door marked, "Kitchen. Fragile."

"Yes! First try." Pulling out a wine glass, I pump my fist in the air, celebrating my little victory. I've been feeling so down since Seth and I parted—again—I'll take any victory I can get. Now, all I need is to be lucky enough to find the opener.

Digging around some more, I feel something cold and heavy at the bottom of the box.

"A-ha!" Lifting the bottle opener, I hold it in my hands like I'm holding a baby bird. "You are beautiful," I whisper to the opener, "and I was smart enough—no, *brilliant* enough—to pack you along with my wine glasses."

Chuckling to myself, I uncork the wine and pour it into the glass. Lifting the glass to my nose, I swirl the wine around and inhale deeply. "Oh, ew!" Pulling it away from my nose, I stare into the glass. The wine hasn't gone bad; it's just that it smells like the country club, Robert, and my parents all rolled together. Frankly, right now, the aroma is enough to make me want to vomit.

Walking to the kitchen sink, I dump my glass of wine down the sink. I'm done with wine. That was the drink of the old Holly. The one that worried about everything and making everyone happy. New Holly is going to go figure out who the hell *she* is—for better or for worse. Crossing back to the fridge with determination, I yank the door open. Reaching into the otherwise-empty fridge, I grab a beer.

Holding it up, I look at the label. No, I don't know one beer from the next, but this is what we drank that night at Hoppa's Taphouse, so what the hell? Sure, it makes me sad to think of Seth, but it also makes me happy to think of those few fun times we shared and the woman I was with him.

Popping the top, I take a long drink and smile. Damn, that does taste better than wine. As a matter of fact… Grabbing the bottle of wine, I walk to the sink and turn it over, watching as the wine coats the metal basin with a slick shine. If only all changes were this easy to make.

Looking over at my home phone again, I wonder if I owe Seth a call to let him know I'm going. But the thing is it's been nearly a month, and I haven't heard a peep out of him. Maybe he's not interested.

No, shaking my head, I take another long swallow from my beer bottle. It's time to just let bygones be—

My front door buzzes. Turning quickly, it's like my heart jumps into my throat. Closing my eyes, I take a deep breath and think calming thoughts. *No. What happened then was a freak thing. Most of those men are in jail. You will not be kidnapped every time the doorbell rings.*

Still, rushing to my bag, I grab my mace and walk to my door quietly. This time, I'm not opening my door unless I'm certain of who it is.

"Hello? Who's there? You should know I'm not alone in here. I have friends over and the police on speed dial. Who is it?"

"Holly." It's a deep voice I recognize. "It's Bullet and Bullseye, uh, sorry, Harry and Avery from the Steel Knights. Could we speak to you for a moment? We need your help."

Leaning forward, I look out the peephole. Whew. It is Harry and Avery.

"Are you alone?"

"Yes, Holly. We just need you. Nick had an accident. He needs help."

"Why not take him to the hospital?"

"We need someone discreet. Besides, he's asking for you."

My heart rate slows, but my hands are still shaking as I unlock the door. Opening it just a crack, I peek outside, squeezing the can of mace in one hand. "You're really alone?"

"Yes." Avery smiles. "I'm sorry if we scared you."

"Is Nick bleeding or unconscious? Heart attack? Does he need an ambulance?"

"No, no. Nothing like that. Something minor," Avery explains. "He just needs you. Please, Holly."

Nodding, I agree. "Okay, let me just grab my coat and my keys." Sadness washes over me—I can't help it. I'm a little bit disappointed that Seth wasn't the one to come get me.

"Thank you," Harry says.

The two men step inside as I grab my jacket and keys off an empty kitchen counter and leave the can of mace. I'll be perfectly safe with these guys.

"You're packed." The surprise in Harry's voice is evident. "Where are you going?"

"I accepted a job back east with one of my old professors. I'll still work emergency, but it's a teaching hospital. Who knows?" Shrugging, I sigh. "It's near a major urban city with a population that could use affordable healthcare. Maybe I can get my clinic going there. It was such a pipe dream to try to open the clinic here." I'm aware I'm rambling, but I can't stop myself. "I would have needed so much funding and help." Shrugging again, I turn to them. "Ah, well. It's stupid, but I just fell for that building, you know?"

The men exchange glances.

Tilting my head, I look them each in the eye. "What was that about?"

"What?" It's Avery. He's definitely smoother and more outgoing than either Harry or Seth. "I don't know, nothing. So, what happened this time? To Nick?"

"Not sure. But he's asking for you."

Nodding, I pull the door closed behind me and lock my door. "How many injuries do you men get?" I murmur, chuckling to myself. "All right." Turning to them, I smile. "The clubhouse?"

"No, actually," Avery tells me. "Can you just follow us?"

"Okay." Why the hell not? It won't be the first time I've followed a biker blindly. Shaking my head, I suppress another chuckle.

Look how well that worked for me.

"What the heck?" As I follow the bikes ahead of me, we pull up in front of my building—only it's not my building. It's a completely redone version of my building. "What happened here? There's no way Clea did all this," I mumble.

Parking the car in front, I hop out and stare at the front of the building, which has been power-washed and repaired. There's a lawn and beautiful landscaping out front, and looking up, I catch sight of brand-new windows, and above the red front door is a gorgeous stained-glass window. "Is that…?" Putting a hand to my eyes to shield them from the sun, I stare at the stained-glass, making out an image of a bird in flight.

"Holly?" Avery holds his arm out for me to walk up the steps before him.

Grabbing my guardrail, I climb the steps. My heart is racing, and as I put my hand on the doorknob, I feel like a girl in a horror movie about to pull back the curtain to see what's behind it.

"Oh. My. Gosh." Stepping inside, I turn in a circle. This is no horror movie—it's anything but. "This is…" Glancing about, I take in the new floors, scrubbed walls, gorgeous reception desk, and signs for bathrooms. "I cannot believe this." My mouth is open as I gawk at everything.

"Hello, doc."

Whipping around, I see Nick. Tilting my head, I grin. "Well, Nick. You're looking pretty well for a man who needs medical attention." I cross my arms.

"We're sorry about that, Holly." Harry steps up. "We needed to get you here."

"But I don't understand." Shaking my head, I look around again. Every time I do, I see something new—like the hospital lights hanging from the ceiling. "How did you do all this? And why?"

"We had the contractors on retainer for the build of the new clubhouse," Nick explains. "That's the how, and the why is because you deserve this—and," he says, motioning to the group of Steel Knights behind him, "because we think you're awesome."

His words wash over me, warming me from the inside. This may be the first time in my life anyone has ever called me "awesome", and it feels pretty damned great. But as wonderful as all of this is, it's missing one thing—or one person: Seth.

"Thank you, Nick." I smile at him. "I think you're all pretty awesome, too."

"Come on, then." Nick grins. "Let's see the rest of this place."

With its gorgeous flooring, new windows, and scrubbed brick walls, the second floor is as beautifully done as the first. It's just waiting to morph into something—like storage or an extension of the upstairs. Climbing the stairs to the third floor, however, my palms grow sweaty.

Nick nods for me to walk up ahead of him, and I do. I have no idea what to expect when I open this door, and once again, my heart is beating so fast I'm not sure I can slow it.

Taking a deep breath, I push the door open and step inside. Standing there, in the middle of the sparkling-clean, renovated living space and holding the biggest bunch of wildflowers I've ever seen, is Seth.

"Seth?"

Dropping his chin, he makes eye contact. "Before you say anything, I'd like to say a few words if I can."

He takes a step closer, and my body warms. Looking at him in that black T-shirt that pulls across his chest and strains at his biceps, I have to will myself to look up into his eyes.

Clutching the beautiful flowers in his hands, he takes a deep breath. "I've been thinking a lot over these past few weeks, and I realized that the reason you thought we couldn't be together was me."

"Seth—"

"Please." He puts up his hand. "Let me get through this."

"Of course."

"The reason you couldn't be with me was because I wasn't available. Not really. I was caught between the man I was and the man I wanted to be. The man I want to be. The man I *was* would have shot that Dog who held you at knifepoint. I would have walked up to him and plugged a bullet between his eyes—and maybe would have enjoyed doing it. But that was also the man who has lived with regret for all these years. Regret for lashing out at that cop when I was a kid and getting sent to juvie. Regret for not being there for Colt. But as I've watched you grow and change—getting a tattoo, opening your own clinic—into an even more kickass woman than you already were, I realize that it's okay for me to change, too. What you said is right. I don't have to be Dynamite anymore. Instead, I can be a man who's worthy of you."

"I don't want you to stop being who you are, Dynamite. I just want you to be happy."

Reaching up, he runs his hand over his head and then scrubs his face with it. "I didn't kill that Dog, Holly."

Nodding, I draw a deep breath through my nose. "I know."

"Did the guys tell you?"

Taking a step, I'm closer to him. We're so near now it's like I can feel him even though we're not touching. My breathing grows shallow. "They didn't need to tell me. I mean, I didn't know for sure then, when I ran out of the Unchained Dogs' clubhouse, but I've thought about it a lot over these past few weeks, too. I knew in my soul that a man who felt that bad about not being there for his brother when they were growing up, a man who showed me the sunrise, who held my hand through my tattoo, a man who made friends with a kid in my neighborhood who needed a friend, and made love to me in such a sweet and gentle way, wasn't a man who would kill when he had a choice."

"But, Holly, you have to know—if he was going to kill you, I would have killed him first."

Nodding, I swallow hard. "I know that. But that's different, isn't it? Listen, Seth. As an ER doctor, I've had a lot of time to think about these things. Sometimes, someone comes in—maybe a man—and I know he's done something really awful to someone. I know because I've just treated his victim in another room. But it's not my job to judge him, only to fix him. I've taken an oath. That can be really hard. But I've often wondered, if I was that woman who was attacked, or kidnapped, or beaten, would I think differently? Do you know what I discovered? The answer is yes. I am a doctor, but I have a survival instinct. I also would kill someone who was trying to kill me." Sighing, I look into his eyes. "It's not a bad thing to be Dynamite, Seth. Dynamite saved my life—in more ways than you'll ever know. But don't you see? Not killing that Dog means you *can* control your outbursts and your urges."

"Well, most of them." Grinning, he steps closer to me.

"But, Seth." Putting up my hand, I stop him. "We need to do better than petty fighting when we're together. We need to stop assuming the other person is any certain way. No more 'a woman like me' or 'a man like you.' Agreed?"

"Agreed."

"Good." Staring into his eyes, I smile. "Nice flowers, by the way."

"Thought I'd better hand-deliver these this time. Just in case Robert pops in to help out at the clinic."

Suddenly, it's like someone turns off a faucet in my head, and all the happiness I've been feeling just drains out of me. I'm exhausted.

"Holly? What's wrong? I was joking."

"I know, but, Seth… I appreciate all the effort you guys put into this building, and I feel awful about it. I'm sure you saw the 'For Sale' sign out front."

"But I thought that was because you were overwhelmed with the work it took to get the building ready."

"It was. But it's also because I was wrong to think that I could do this alone."

"You don't have to. I'll run the numbers for you. Keep track of the books. I'd love to help out. I know the guys will help in any way they can, as well."

A smile takes over my face. "Seth, thank you. It's so kind of you, but financially, I'm in deeper than I thought. Even though I can carry it—even with the medical equipment—I'll need to make connections. I'll need staff and medical supplies. I did a lot of planning and prepping, but ultimately, I lead with my heart and not my head. I was wrong."

"You're never wrong when you lead with your heart."

"Dad?" Whipping around, I see my father standing in the doorway of the apartment, smiling. In his hands, he also holds a bouquet of wildflowers. Just smaller. "What are you doing here?"

"Hello, Dr. Boling."

"Hello, Seth."

As Seth and my father exchange greetings, my head pops back and forth like a ping-pong ball. "You two know each other?"

"We've met over these past few weeks," Seth explains. "Your father came here looking for you, so we started talking. I explained the situation, and he's been helping us out."

"Is that why the downstairs is laid out so perfectly for a clinic?"

Smiling, my father nods. "Holly, what I told you at dinner was true. I always knew you weren't interested in coming into my practice with me. I've known it since you were a child, and you used to play clinic with your dolls. You're destined for great things, Holly. Trust your heart and do them."

My eyes ache as tears threaten to fall. Lifting a hand, I cover my mouth, fighting back a sob.

My father takes a step closer. "I don't want you to move to the east coast, Holly. Please. Stay here and run your clinic. You know the hospital wants you to stay, and your clinic needs you. I need you." Sighing, he takes a deep breath. "I know you've always thought you had to make up for George passing—that you needed to be twice as good and twice as successful, but I never wanted that. I just wanted you to be happy."

Sighing, I turn to Seth. "George was my brother. He passed when I was very young."

"I know." Seth looks into my eyes. "Your dad and I have caught up on a lot these past couple of weeks."

"For example," my father says, walking across the room and standing next to Seth, "did you know that a motorcycle engine is not so different from a human heart?"

"Really?" Raising an eyebrow, I question my father good-naturedly.

"Really," he answers. "Holly, although you're not coming to work at my practice with me, I do hope I can come work with you. I always knew we would work together. I really want to help, Holly. It would give me great joy and fulfillment. Plus, it will keep me away from Robert and your mother. They're both driving me nuts."

Laughing, I smile at my father. "I'd like that, Dad. Very, very much."

"Good, then it's settled." Turning, he makes his way to the door. "I'm going to catch up with some of the guys downstairs."

I mouth the word "guys" to Seth, and he grins.

"Dad, wait."

He turns back.

"Aren't you forgetting something?" I point to the flowers in his hand. "Are those for me?"

"The flowers?" He chuckles. "No! These are for your mother. She's going to kill me when I tell her we'll be spending our travel time at the clinic, and our travel money on medicine to help people in need." Winking at me, he points to the flowers Seth holds in his hand. "Those are for you." Knocking on the doorframe as he exits, he gives a small wave. "Wish me luck!" With that, my father leaves.

Forgetting everything but the moment, I rush ahead and jump into the safety of Seth's arms. As he spins me around in a circle, I drop my head back, laughing. For the moment, it feels just like I'm flying…

…as free as a bird.

Epilogue

Dynamite

One Year Later

"Dr. Holly!" Julius comes running into the clinic yelling her name.

"What's going on, Julius?" I intercept before he goes barging into one of the clinic rooms.

"We have a line on the street. They're getting restless."

Just then, Holly walks out of a clinic room dressed in boots and dress pants with a white coat over her V-neck sweater. She is even more beautiful today than she was when I met her just over a year ago, and she still takes my breath away.

Catching her eye, my chest heaves with my quickened breath. Her cheeks redden, and she smirks in response. Saturdays are always so busy at the clinic—but Saturday nights, she's all mine.

"Give me a sec, Julius." Smiling, Holly turns to the full-time nurse on staff. "Rebecca, could you please get a bottle of amoxicillin for Peter in Room Two? Then, please call the pharmacy. I'm going to be sending in another prescription."

"Yes, Dr. Holly."

Smiling, Holly turns and gives her attention to Julius, adopting her serious face. "What's wrong, Julius?"

"The people outside. There's a long line. Some of them are coming from as far as Collinstown, man. Maybe we just can't see them?"

"Collinstown?" She looks at me. "Isn't that the home of the Raging Vipers?"

Nodding, I set my gaze heavily on her.

She turns to Julius. "You know our policy is never to turn anyone away. And Collinstown, especially, is dear to me. I have friends there." Then, she turns to me and furrows her brow. "We're getting busy. How are we doing with the grant?"

"We're fine. Go ahead and fill out your prescriptions. Your dad brought in some more investors just this week. Our numbers are good."

"Good." She exhales. "Julius, please tell them to wait. It just may be a long day—"

She wasn't able to finish what she was going to say as three little boys—triplets, of all things—run up and hug her around her waist.

"Hi, guys!"

Damn, she is so good with kids. I get that warm, eager feeling in my gut—the one I've been having lately every time I see her with kids. But I'm sure as hell not going to push her. We'll talk about it when she's ready.

Laughing, she turns back to Julius. "Julius, you can also add that we're working as fast as we can."

"A-right, Dr. Holls. You're the boss."

"Yes, I am."

"Whoa!" Nick comes walking in the front door with a grin on his face. "Those kids out there took all the lollipops. Any more?"

"Sure, I think so," Holly answers. "In storage on the second floor. But, Nick, if they eat any more sugar, I'm going to need to open a dental clinic, and I can't afford that. We're maxed out as is."

"Holly?" Her father walks out of Exam Room Three. "We have another case of strep. Seems to be the thing today."

"We're running low on amoxicillin." She presses her fingers to her temples and rubs. "I'll see what we can get."

Her father nods. "I have another donation coming in later this week. Some golf buddies lost to me and owe me big."

"Thanks, Dad."

"Dr. Boling?" Rebecca looks up. "Your wife is on line two."

"Thank you. I'm going to take this upstairs. Please tell her I'll call her on my cell."

"Doc?" Nick nods to her. "The crowd outside?"

"Um." Thinking, she chews the corner of her bottom lip. "The bikes! Your motorcycles. Can you drive them around front, Nick, and let the kids sit on them? The ones that feel well enough. The ones that don't—please tell them they can have a turn next week. Julius can help you. I know it was the thrill of my life—I'm sure they'll love it, too."

Julius claps his hands together. "Help with the bikes? Hell, yeah."

"Come on, son." Nick smiles. "Let me teach you a thing or two about the bikes. I just have to grab my keys from the back."

Julius waits for Nick, and I smile as the three little boys surrounding Holly pull on her white coat. She doesn't even flinch. As great as she is with all her patients, she's even better with kids. She'd be a great mom. Just the thought of Holly running around with our kids kicks my desire and possessiveness into overdrive. I don't think I can live one more minute without making this woman mine—completely.

"Hey," I say to Trevor, one of the kids who is hanging on Holly. She's perfectly still, reading over a chart. "Trevor. Do me a favor. Would you please tell Dr. Holly that I want a permanent job here?"

"Dr. Holly?" Trevor looks up at Holly and wipes his nose with the back of his hand. "Seth says he wants to work here."

"Well, Trevor, could you please tell Seth that there are no permanent positions here? Everyone is a volunteer." She finishes reading over her chart and tucks it under her arm.

"Ah, she's talking about the job as her accountant. I'm talking about a permanent position as the man in her life."

"Dr. Holly?" Trevor pulls on her coat again.

"I heard, Trevor. Thanks." Holly makes eye contact with me while she speaks to him. "Would you please tell Seth that we both live upstairs together—what could be more permanent?" As she eyes me, her chest races up and down in time with her hurried breath.

Out of the corner of my eye, I catch Nick and Julius huddled in the corner talking. Suddenly, Julius takes off into the back room.

Trevor coughs and then looks up at Holly. "Seth, she says—"

"I heard, buddy, thanks. Would you please tell Dr. Holly that I'm talking about something lasting? Irreversible. Something that's legal and binding."

"What?" Trevor picks his nose, and his eyes grow wide.

But not as wide as hers. As she steps away from the child, Julius comes back with Dr. Boling in tow. They stand next to Nick. Glancing about the waiting room, I see that everyone has gathered around, watching and listening. Dr. Boling holds his cell phone up—I'm assuming so his wife can hear. People come in from the street and crowd into the reception area, leaving the door open so the people on the street can see.

"If you're having a wedding," Nick hollers, "we can have it at the Steel Knights' new clubhouse!"

"Thanks, Nick," I say, while my eyes are locked on Holly.

"No, you don't!" Holly's mom screams through the phone. "We'll have it at the country club!"

"Not a chance, Mom," Holly answers, without looking away from me. Walking to me, she stops when she gets to the opposite side of the desk. "Trevor? Could you please ask Seth to clarify what he's saying?"

Rebecca looks up from her seat behind the desk and listens with her mouth hanging open.

"Trevor." I smile at Holly. "Could you please tell Dr. Holly that I love her and want to marry her? Then, would you please ask her what her answer is?"

"What?" Shaking her head, Holly stares at me in wonder. "What did you just say?"

Dropping down on one knee, I take her hand. "I don't have a ring yet, but I just couldn't wait one more second."

Around us, the clinic grows quiet. "I love you, Holly. I'm honored to be with you. I love what you've created here, and I'd love to create even more with you."

Tilting her head, she asks, "Another clinic?"

Nodding, I smile. "When you're ready. And I was thinking of creating something else, too—how do girls sound? That is, if and when you're ready. I want them to be just like you. No little boys running around here."

"I don't think we get to choose, Seth."

Standing up directly in front of her, I hold her by her arms. "What do you say?"

"I say, the first day I saw that upstairs living area, I pictured you running down the hallway, laughing and playing with two little girls. Our two little girls."

"Then, I think it's settled. But, Holly…" I look deep into her eyes. "I don't want to be impulsive here. I want to do this when you're ready."

"Sometimes impulsive is good, and I am ready, Seth. I've never been more ready for anything in my life."

"Well, then, Dr. Holly Boling, will you marry me?"

"Yes, Seth Hardy, I will."

Nodding to her, I reach out and cup her beautiful cheek. Placing her hand on mine, she smiles as she nuzzles my palm. Looking into her eyes, I know we have just made a silent promise to love one another always. Placing my lips to hers, I draw her toward me as the busy clinic erupts into applause around us.

BOOK 5

RIDING SHOTGUN

Chapter One

Shotgun

There's nothing like a cold beer from the tap on a Friday night after a long slog through a week of work. Though we've got a nice set up at the new Steel Knights Clubhouse, bar included, we still pop into Hoppa's Taphouse to see familiar faces and shoot the shit with the regulars. The bartenders hook us up. The regulars buy us too many drinks, we buy them too many drinks, and we all get shit faced and jolly together and go home happy. My kind of weekend.

I'm sitting next to my brother Seth at the bar, drinking a Coors Lite from a frosted pint. The subpar AC in the bar doesn't keep sweat from trickling down my spine. My T-shirt is glued to my back with the weight of my leather vest, a brand new *member* patch stitched across the back, but I wouldn't take it off. It's my most prized possession, I'd say, and I wear it with pride. Even when it's 110 degrees outside after nightfall in the Arizona desert and I'm sweating like a pig stuck in a pit. The smell of sweat hangs lightly in the air, enough to know that everyone in the place is probably roasting their asses off along with us.

Seth looks cool as a cucumber next to me. He's always had that unnerving ability to be stoic as the grave, no matter the conditions. That is, until his fuse gets lit. Hence the nickname Dynamite. He's always been that way and I suppose it takes some getting used to. As if he knows what I'm thinking, he turns to me.

"So how does it feel to be one of the big kids now?" Seth asks.

I grin at him. "Better than just about anything," I say.

"I thought he would have made you wait much longer," he says. "You got lucky, you little bastard."

"I'm a lucky kind of guy," I say.

"So—"

I didn't register what was happening at first, because I'm focusing on my brother, but he stops abruptly and we both turn at the same time to look at the door. There's a commotion outside and Wildfire erupts through the door, looking every inch as fiery as her nickname suggests. If you're in Wildfire's path when she's lit, it's bad news for you.

She spots us sitting at the bar. "The Dogs followed us here and they're looking for a fight, get your asses outside now."

We're both out of our seats faster than you can saw *brawl*, and behind me I hear the bartender say, "Are you fucking kidding me?"

"Who the fuck do they think they are?" my brother says to no one in particular.

We push through the door and, sure enough, there's a pack of rabid Dogs in the parking lot. One of them is toe to toe with Bullseye and I would bet my last fucking dollar he's shitfaced. Too bad he didn't have the courtesy to wreck his bike on the way over.

This is getting out of control. Ever since we crashed their clubhouse to rescue Holly, they've gone on the offense and they pick a fight whenever and wherever they can.

The Dogs start whooping at us when they spot us crossing the parking lot toward them.

"Come on, you fucking pussies," one of them shouts.

"What are you doing hanging out with these losers, babe?" another one calls out. A couple of them howl and I realize that he's talking to Wildfire. Oh boy, I wouldn't want to be that guy.

At that, Bullseye couldn't help himself, and I guess I don't blame him. He hauls off and slugs the asshole in his face.

It's like someone threw a switch and the chaos begun. I run straight at one of the assholes who howled at Wildfire, hoping I can knock him down with enough inertia. Especially because he's drunk. But he squares off with me, so I take a fighting stance. We begin to circle each other and I can already tell that he's too drunk for this to be much fun. But hey, everyone needs a sweaty, greasy, foul-mouthed punching bag every once in a while. He takes a swing at me, and I duck easily. He nearly falls into me. When he straightens back up, I give him a solid right hook to his stupid face. It nearly takes him sideways, but not quite.

"You little fucking bastard," he says and comes at me with his big, hammy fists. I laugh and skirt around him. I'm not exactly small, but compared to this troll, I guess anyone might be.

Out of the corner of my eye I can see Wildfire putting her boot to the face of the guy who had the audacity to catcall her. You could never accuse her of not being made of solid stuff, our Wildfire.

Bullseye pulls one of the dogs into a headlock and brings his knee up into the guy's face. There's a spurt of blood, almost black in the dark. He broke the bastard's nose. I chuckle.

I hear a shout and look over to see one of the Dogs holding my brother and another one getting ready to kick his ass.

"Hey," I shout. "I don't fucking think s—"

Suddenly, the world is an explosion of stars. It takes me a dizzying minute to realize that I've been punched in the side of the head. I don't have time to make sense of myself or my surroundings before another punch connects, this time in my stomach. I double over. Jesus Christ, I might vomit. Drunk or not, this dickhead can land a punch. I straighten up, deciding it wouldn't be the worst thing if I puked on him. Then I pull my head back and smack him square in the face with my forehead. Which, of course, makes the world explode into a halo of stars again and this time I actually black out for a second. But I succeed in my mission to knock the asshole out and he falls like a putrid sack of potatoes on the ground.

I turn, realizing with a jolt that I was trying to get to Seth. But, of course, no one's holding him now. He's kicking one of the Dogs in the stomach and the other one seems to have run away. Bullseye spits a mouthful of blood and begins to laugh. Wildfire starts to laugh, too, and staggers over wearily to lean against him.

My heart swells with pride. Until I hear the sirens.

"Ah, shit," we say collectively. Before we can even think about whether we'll run or stay and talk to the cops, they're pulling into the gravel parking lot. Four cars, which I think is a bit excessive, but I'm not the one in the uniform pointing guns at people.

"Hands up, all of you. Hands up," one of the cops says into the loudspeaker.

I notice that everyone who was in the bar is standing outside, watching us. I wonder how long they've been out here.

Sighing, I put my hands up. We all do. I'm not trying to cause problems for anyone or for myself. It's one thing to stand your ground when someone else is weaseling onto your territory and looking for a fight. It's another thing to ask for trouble from the cops.

With the number of cars that pull into the parking lot, you'd think there was an all-out war going on instead of a bit of slap and tickle between two unfriendly motorcycle clubs. The cops kick their doors open and every single one has his gun out, trained steadily on us.

"Hands up," one of them repeats. "Where we can see them. Hands up, now."

I'm confused at first, because the Knights are all holding our hands up. Then I realize that one of the Dogs has made his way back to his feet. Just watching him teeter back and forth makes me feel sick, so I look back at the cop cars. The sight of the pistol is only slightly better for my constitution.

"Walk forward with your hands up," the shouting cop instructs us. "If you make any sudden movements, we will open fire."

We all walk forward and a few cops start to come toward us, one for each of us. How nice, we all get a dance partner. Mine keeps his pistol trained on my face as he circles around me. He tells me to put my face on the hood of the car and my hands behind my back. He kicks my feet wide and I really have no choice but to put my full weight onto the car. He slaps cuffs on me so hard that I have to bite the inside of my cheek to keep from squealing like a child. The metal caught me right on the wrist bone, that fucking bastard. I think you must have to be a sadist to become a cop.

He pats my pockets and runs his hands across my chest and around my waist to make sure I'm not armed. I want to make a very inappropriate joke, but I don't think he would appreciate my sense of humor. He yanks me up from the hood by the back of my shirt and walks me to the side of the car.

Shoving my back against the passenger window and he says, "Let's start from the beginning. What happened?"

It's a long and tedious interview. He asks me the same questions over and over again, like he's trying to catch me in a lie. To his credit, people probably lie to him all the time, but I'm over the conversation long before it ends. And even though I tell him the truth from start to finish, he still opens the back door of the car.

"Mr. Hardy, I am placing you under arrest for disturbing the peace. You have the right to remain silent," he says. "Anything you say can and will be used against you in a court of law. Do you understand your rights?"

"Are you shitting me?" I say, because I can't believe that he's actually placing me under arrest.

"No, sir, I am not," he says like the prickly asshole he is. "Do you understand your rights?"

"Yeah, I sure as fuck do," I say. I want to headbutt *him* in the face, but instead I allow him to shove me into the back of the cop car and slam the door almost before I'm in. I only have a minute to stew there before they open the other door and shove Seth in next to me. Suddenly, things don't seem as dour.

"Fancy meeting you here," I say to Seth.

"What a night," he says.

"Yeah, I was just trying to get hungover tomorrow." An ambulance has arrived and they're loading up a couple of the unconscious Dogs onto stretchers. Overkill, if you ask me, but I can't help but chuckle a little bit at the sight.

Seth makes a sound of disgust. "Let 'em sleep it off."

"This is bullshit." I'm starting to feel tired and I am not nearly intoxicated enough to be enjoying any of this.

"Nick is going to fucking flip," Seth says, more to himself than to me.

"They started it," I say. My face is throbbing where that fucking beast monster landed a punch and I'm one hundred and ten percent certain that I'm going to have a shiner the size of the moon by tomorrow.

"Doesn't matter," he says. "I don't really know what the fuck we're going to do about this. They just keep coming at us."

"Fucking filth," My head is aching and it's not making me feel friendly. "I hope they get hit by a bus."

My brother broods for a while before he turns to me with a change of subject that is so left field that it actually makes me laugh.

"What happened to that girl you took out last week?" he asks.

I shrug.

"I thought you liked her," he probes.

"I mean, I did." I look out the window so he can't see my face. Seth and his girl Holly are well on their way to getting married. The plans are in full swing. They've already dragged me to the tux shop and had me poked and prodded and trussed up like a turkey. I don't even want to think about the price tag for the rental, just for the pleasure of rolling around in a monkey suit, and I don't think they've thought about it either. They're way too busy staring into each other's eyes and being madly in love. What is it about people who are living-the-happy-lovebird life that makes them turn into zealots? They're like Holy Rollers, bent on converting everyone in their path to the Church of Love, and they can't rest until they've tormented everyone in their life into settling down into neat little matches.

Well, not this boy. No thank you. I've already had enough of that shit.

Seth moves his head in a *go on* gesture and I roll my eyes at him. I shift a bit because the cuffs are digging into my wrists.

"I mean, it was fine."

"You're being a tight-lipped little shit," he tells me.

"There's just nothing to say," I say. "We went out. It wasn't great, but it wasn't terrible. It was *okay*. I haven't called her for another date. Is that what you're after?"

"Well, yeah," says Seth. "I'm taking an interest. The least you could do is humor me."

I realize he's trying to be funny. It can be hard to tell with him sometimes, which is what's really funny, so I can't help but chuckle.

"And so I am," I say to him. "I am the most humorous man this side of the mighty fucking Mississippi."

Then he says something that snatches the wind right out of my sails.

"Are you still hung up on Erica?" he says. "Is that what this is about?"

I take a deep breath in and let it out slowly. Damn him for being so perceptive. You never really know which gears are turning in Seth's head. It's pretty annoying. Who does he think he is taking so much interest in what's going on in my life? He wasn't there for me when I needed him most and *now*, when I can take care of myself, he's all over me like icing on a cupcake, fussing about my love life and did I change the oil in my bike and Holly says dinner is at seven o'clock on Sunday—don't be late.

On the other hand, I appreciate that he's trying. It's a bitch of a thing to navigate. I don't trust myself to speak, so I take an interest in watching the cops wrestle one of the Dogs to the ground. Stupid mongrels never know when to give up a fight.

Uninvited, Seth takes my silence for a resounding yes.

"Well, why don't you just call her?" he asks.

"I can't call her," I say, automatically. It's the mantra I've been repeating to myself for the past three months and I'm not about to give it up. "And anyway, she's in California now."

"You're too fucking stubborn," he says and I know a lecture is about to begin. "Mom should have named you Donkey instead of Colt. You like her a lot. So what, you guys had a big fight. You're still thinking about her, what, three months later? That's an awfully long time to be hung up on a dame that you're not interested in calling. You said she wasn't going to be in Cali permanently, anyway."

Well, I never quite told him what the fight was about. It still singes me to even think about it. I go back and forth between feeling hurt and ashamed of myself. Any time I approach the subject I start to feel disoriented and I can't get my head around how I feel about any of it. So I just box it back up and shove it into a closet in my brain to deal with later. All I know is that we were both assholes and I haven't called her and she hasn't called me. She made her feelings about me and my lifestyle pretty fucking clear and I know she sure as shit doesn't want to hear from me. I'm not about to go crawling after her like a toothless dog with my tail between my legs after she insulted my brother and all of the people that matter to me.

I can still hear her words ringing in my ears like she just spoke them.

I don't get this—any of it. You're so bent on impressing your big, badass biker brother and you can't even see what a bad influence he is on you. You ride around with these—these people who just get into trouble and make a mess of their lives. Is this really what you want for yourself, Colt? I don't think I can be with someone who wants to throw his fucking life away like this.

Sitting in the back of a cop car with handcuffs on makes thinking about this extra annoying, because it was a fight with the Dogs that catalyzed the whole thing to begin with. My mood has darkened considerably.

"I don't want to talk about it," I say firmly, and I really mean it.

Mercifully, Seth seems to sense that my mood has shifted and he lets it go.

"Holly's going to kill me."

I can't help but laugh and, after a minute, he chuckles a little too.

When they let us out of the clink in the morning, our Road Captain, Bucky, is waiting for us in front of the building, in the SUV that the club has for occasions like this. He does not look like he is in a friendly mood.

"Nick is waiting for you at the Clubhouse," he says.

None of us have to ask if this means that we can't at least go home and brush our teeth first. He takes us back to Hoppa's and drops us off where we parked our bikes.

All of us look grim and none of us speak to each other as we mount our bikes and head out of the parking lot one by one, with Bullet leading the pack. I'm suddenly feeling nervous as I follow Wildfire, bringing up the rear of the pack. Just last night, Seth was telling me that Nick was talking about voting me in. And now we're all in deep shit from what I can tell, and it doesn't look good. Nick is not a morning person as far as I can tell, and this means he's either woken up early or he hasn't gone to sleep at all. Neither of those things seem like a good way to start an emergency meeting at the Clubhouse after five members of the Knights have been arrested.

The Arizona sun is already brutally hot, even this early in the morning, and I'm eager to strip off my helmet. None of us tarry when we get to the Clubhouse. The SUV is already parked around the back, which means Bucky is waiting inside with Nick.

We find Nick at the bar, sipping a Bloody Mary that he presumably made himself. He's wearing his long hair in a braid and a black button down shirt under his heavy, well-loved leather vest that's covered with aged patches. I take a second to feel amused by the added touch of the celery stick in his cocktail before he turns to us, a look on his face that could freeze blood. I realize with a sinking feeling he's watching a newscast on the TV about us. The headline reads "Biker Gang War Erupts at Local Taphouse."

He looks at each and every one of us and I can feel myself withering under his gaze. I don't think I've ever felt more uncomfortable in my entire life.

"Could someone please explain to me why my club is on the 7 o'clock news this morning?" he says in a voice that is a deadly type of calm.

"They followed us to the Taphouse," Bullet says in his ever so reasonable voice.

"That doesn't explain this," Nick says, pointing to the TV. He gets to his feet slowly. He might as well be eight feet tall with the way he seems to tower over us at this moment.

"I know better than any of you that a rabid Dog has to be put down," he says. "But this—" He points at the TV. "—is fucking unacceptable. I haven't spent years of my life building this club to have it publicly put on blast this way. We are not the fucking 1 percent. We toe the fucking line so the fuzz don't come knocking at our door. We don't get lumped in with these low lives on the fucking news. We do not behave like we're in the middle of a fucking trailer park. Jesus fucking Christ." He looks at Bullet. "I would have expected better of you."

"I don't even understand how this ended up on the news," Bullet says, staring at the TV.

"It's a good story," Nick said. "Good for them, bad for us. Thanks to your not-so-discreet bullshit they've taken an interest in us. And let me tell you this: you guys had better keep a low profile until this shit blows over, or there is going to be *hell* to pay. I'm trying to expand this club, not break it down. And I'm also not trying to attract the kind of trash that ends up in clubs like the Dickless Dogs. We have integrity. We have standards. This," he points to the TV again and his voice finally raises a bit, "is fucking humiliating."

Talk about humiliating, I don't think I've ever been more ashamed in my life. Nick isn't even my father, but I can't imagine I'd feel any worse than if I'd let down my real father. I can't bring myself to look at any of the others, because I don't think I can stand to see how ashamed they are of themselves either.

"And what *should* we do about the puppy problem?" Bullet says. "They're at us more and more all the time. We didn't—"

"I don't give a fuck what you do," Nick says, "as long as it does not end up on the news. Stupid is as stupid does. I'll leave it to you to be the judge of what's going to get you into serious fucking trouble. If I see this again, it is going to be judgement day and I am not fucking around."

He looks each of us in the face again and then he goes back to his Bloody Mary. When he picks up the remote control and changes the channel to golf, we know we are dismissed.

I don't move a muscle until Bullseye leaves, Wildfire and Seth follow him. Bullet and I reluctantly bring up the rear.

Bullseye and Wildfire tiredly bid us goodbye and leave to go back to their love nest. Holly is waiting in the lobby for us and the expression on her face is so thunderous that I swear I can feel my big tough-as-nails brother shrink beside me.

"What the hell were you thinking?" she demands. I might as well not exist.

"I'm just going to..." I say.

I started to slip around them, but Holly points at me and says in her most matronly tone, "You stay put."

"Yes, ma'am."

"You both look like shit," she says.

"Come on, now," Dyno says. He's tired and annoyed, and I can see him restraining himself, reminding himself that she's just worried.

"No, you come on," she says. "Up to the clinic, come on."

She follows us upstairs and fusses over both of us, putting ointment on our cuts and bruises while she grumbles under her breath about our injuries.

"You should see the other guy," my brother says, trying to lighten the mood. The look she gives him says quite clearly that it's not going to work.

"I shudder to think," she mumbles.

Dyno clears his throat and then excuses himself to go to the bathroom. Holly leans against the counter behind her, arms crossed while she looks me over. I steel myself for a reprimand but she catches me completely off guard instead.

"I saw Erica at the gas station yesterday," she says and my heart feels like a thunderclap in my chest.

"You did?" Butterflies erupt in my stomach and I feel a bit queasy, not in an entirely unpleasant way.

"She must be back from California." Holly smiles in a knowing way that makes me feel grumpy. "Just thought you might want to know."

My brother comes back from the bathroom and I'm finally excused from Holly's care. I leave them in the examination room together, ignoring the sound of my brother's voice, smooth and low, soothing Holly and apologizing for worrying her. Gross.

I didn't realize how much I wanted to know that Erica was back in town, but Holly's right. I really wanted to know.

I walk out into the sunshine and look up at the pale-blue Arizona sky, aching for a bath and a shave. The day seems brighter already and the shame I feel for pissing Nick off is starting to fall away.

On the ride home, I feel lighter than air.

Chapter Two

Erica

I don't think I'm prepared to be back in Hoppa. In fact, I think that I should have figured out a way to stay in California. Not that I have anything out there anymore, but it would mean that I wasn't back here, a place that manages to fail me more and more as my life goes on.

I stare out the window, my feet up on the dash, while my mother drives us across town to have lunch with one of her high school friends. She's been talking and I realize that I haven't been paying attention at all.

"—shows houses now. Maybe you could get into that once we find some land and get the farm going," my mother is saying.

I make a face at her. "I'm okay, thanks."

"Well, are you going to go back into teaching?" my mother asks, craning her neck to look in the rear view mirror. I hear the tick of the turn signal as she switches lanes.

"I don't know," I say, feeling myself getting tense. What to do with my life next is a topic I've been putting off. I'm twenty-three, so I guess that would make this my quarter-life crisis. I thought my quarter-life crisis would be too many trips to Las Vegas, too many shots of tequila, and too many bad choices in men. But instead I'm having all of the crisis and none of the fun.

My mother shakes her head. "Well, they may have cut the drama program, but maybe you can teach English, or something like that."

"I'll think about it," I say, though I most certainly won't. My mother has always had my back and is always scheming for my best interest, but she usually misses the mark. Even thinking about going back into teaching my heart sinks into my stomach. There's a voice inside me that says if I had been good enough at it, they would have found a way to keep me. I feel embarrassed thinking of myself as a teacher, fresh out of college. All of the mistakes I made, even the ones that I am not aware of.

And beneath that, there's a bigger part of me that wants something more for myself, though I can't quite tell what that might be just yet. I wanted to act more than anything, but I don't think I'm good enough to do it professionally. That's a hard truth to accept, but there's always community theatre. That doesn't quite solve the problem about what I'm going to do with the rest of my life. I suddenly feel so claustrophobic that I roll the window down. A blast of brutally hot air invades the car, breaking up the steady stream of AC that's been circulating.

The open window lets in the roar of a chorus of motorcycles and my heart immediately leaps in my chest. I turn my head slowly as the motorcycles overtake us, I look for an airbrushed knight's helmet and a leather vest with a patch that reads *Prospect*. I'd taken out the clumsy stitches on that patch one by one before I reattached it with neat, uniform stitches. All while trying to keep myself from laughing at the image of Colt bent over his vest and judiciously applying himself to sewing.

It's not his bike gang, motorcycle club, whatever it's called, though. I watch them as they shift into high gear and leap ahead of us on the road. They wear coats with skulls that have a snake protruding from one eye. I can't read the logo stitched onto the leather as they speed off, but I don't really care. None of them are Colt.

I realize that my heart is racing and sit up straight, taking my feet down from the dash. I also realize suddenly that my mother is talking to me.

"—letting all the cold air out, Erica," she complains.

"Sorry," I say and roll the window back up. I watch the motorcycles disappear around a corner and I find myself disappointed that none of them were Colt.

Thinking about Colt doesn't make me feel any better. In fact, I feel immediately like shit, because I've been trying not to think about him since we got into town. Hoppa isn't that big of a place when it comes down to it. I've been dreading running into him, as a matter of fact I've been keeping myself awake at night thinking about running into him. Maybe he's with another woman and maybe he has his arm around her and she's laughing at something he said. Or worse, he's laughing at something *she* said.

It's not like that's any of my business, anyway. I'm technically the one who broke up with him.

We pull up in front of a place that calls itself a gastropub and I climb out of the car, wishing I'd stayed in bed at the Airbnb. Ten seconds in the Arizona sun and I'm already sticky with sweat. I sweep my long hair up into a knot at the nape of my neck and I wonder if this is any better now with the sun biting directly at the flesh I've exposed.

My mom loops her arm around my shoulders as we walk and I'm grateful for the gesture. I take a deep breath and tell myself that everything is going to be better now.

But I stop short, heart pounding in my chest, when I spot three motorcycles parked out front of the restaurant. I scan the windows as if I could possibly see anything through the glass reflecting the brutal Arizona sun.

"What's wrong?" mom asks me and follows my line of sight to the motorcycles. "Ah," she says before taking my arm and pulling me toward the door. "It's perfectly legal to pretend that you don't see him if he's actually here."

"I don't want to have to do that," I say. My mother knows about Colt, sort of. I didn't give her the full details, but she knows enough to be sympathetic. I let out a long breath as she tows me inside behind her.

The kiss of the air conditioner inside the gastropub is a blessed relief from the blistering heat outside. I mean, it's hot in California, but it's nothing like being here in Hoppa. It's already 107 degrees outside and it's not even one o'clock in the afternoon. I think back to my first car when I was in high school, a shitty little beater Honda that I drove around with stubborn pride. It didn't have AC and somehow I managed to get from point A to point B without broiling to death by keeping all of the windows down at all times. Sitting in traffic was a capital punishment for something I must have done in my past life. I would arrive anywhere I was going with a mudslide of makeup and perspiration on my face. I got out of the habit of caking anything on because it turns to clown paint in the heat.

I'm distracting myself with this line of thought while I linger in the doorway. I am afraid that Colt will be there if I turn my head and look, or I'll have to walk past him when I follow my mother down the aisle between booths to where she has spotted the friend we're meeting for lunch. But I am equally afraid that Colt will *not* be here.

I gather the courage and follow my mother, stealing glances a little at a time. I look up at the television as I make my way through the bar area of the restaurant and I stop dead in my tracks. The channel is turned to the news and what do you know, the headline reads, "Biker Gang War Erupts at Local Taphouse." The volume is down, but I don't need to hear it to gather the essentials—the Dogs and the Knights are at it again. I feel nauseous and miserable and also angry. A whole hot mess of things that I don't want to think about or feel, so I shove them aside.

As I pass the bar, I spot three men sitting at the bar top and I am immediately certain that the bikes outside belong to them. I am amused to realize that they're the same bikers that left us in the dirt back on the highway. The big patches with the skulls and the snakes on their backs are actually pretty ghastly in the cool quiet of the bar. The words *Los Brujos* are stitched in beautiful cursive script on a crescent around the skulls. From the Spanish I took in college, I take it to mean something like "The Warlocks" or "The Sorcerers". One of them wears a SGT AT ARMS patch, and the other two wear patches that simply read *Los Brujos*. Goosebumps cover my arms as I pass them, and I don't like the feeling.

I shake it off and hurry along, but not before one of them, bearing one of the regular member patches, catches my eye. He smiles at me in the friendly way that a man smiles with interest at a woman. And goodness he's handsome, but I am not buying what he's selling. In fact, that smile cements the feeling in me that I don't want anything to do with any man right now.

This isn't about Colt, it's about the fact that I'm trying to figure out what to do with my own life.

Okay, maybe it's a little about Colt. Maybe a lot about Colt. Well, fuck Colt, because he's busy getting into bar fights with other motorcycle shitheads.

I avert my eyes and keep walking. I'm relieved when he says nothing, but I still feel immensely awkward when I realize that the booth that my mother and her friend are sitting in is directly behind the bikers seated at the bar. I smile anyway.

"Good to see you," I say to Sharon as I sit next to my mother.

"My god, I haven't seen you in years, girl," she says back. "What the hell are you doing in Arizona? Get back your butt on a plane and get back to California because you are lovely enough to be a movie star!"

I laugh and blush and try not to feel too embarrassed because she's just trying to be friendly. She's always been a sweet lady. There are good reasons why she and my mother have stayed friends all of these years. I don't buy for a moment that I'm movie star quality, but I will appreciate that she would think to say such a thing.

"Tell me all about you," she says. "You married yet? Got any kids?"

"Oh no," I say with a laugh. "Far from it." I suddenly realize that the biker at the bar can probably hear what I'm saying, so I clear my throat and say a little louder. "I'm not interested in dating or anything right now. I'm trying to figure out what to do with my career."

"Smart girl," Sharon says. "Good head on your shoulders, no doubt that you got that from your mother."

"She was thinking about maybe getting into real estate," my mother chimes in. Which is not at all true. I open my mouth to say as much, but the women are already off and running. I let them fall into their conversation and I wander into my own thoughts, nodding and laughing when there's a pause. But really, I have no idea what they're talking about.

I realize after a moment that I am, instead, picking up the conversation that is happening between the men seated in a neat row at the bar to my left. I mean, I can only catch snatches because their voices are so hushed, which only piques my interest more.

"—hope that's a good tip off, because I don't feel like hunting him down like a rat in a sewer."

"*Yo tambien*, I want to get the hell out of this dump."

"The information came from a very reliable source."

"What kind of reliable?"

Their voices drop even further and I find myself leaning toward them ever so slightly.

"—will keep the heat from us, no questions asked. That motherfucker will *vaya con dios*, we'll find what we're looking for, and get the fuck out of dodge."

Vaya con dios. I suddenly feel apprehensive and then almost laugh at myself. There's no way these three men are sitting in the middle of a bar in broad daylight, discussing murder.

I think I hear one of them say, "The fuzz will clean up the mess."

"What if he doesn't cooperate?"

But I lose the thread of their conversation when they hush as the server comes toward us, looking worn out with a pasted-on smile that I feel sympathy for down to the tips of my toes. I definitely did my share of serving tables to get me through college. I am, however, annoyed that she chose the particular moment to show up before I could figure out what those guys were discussing. I know from secondhand experience that bike gangs can get involved in some rough stuff and I am genuinely wondering if I just overheard a murder plot.

I'm no expert in the matters of bike gangs, but it occurs to me that they're not fond of other bike gangs waltzing into their territory. And these guys are definitely on Steel Knights territory. There could be a perfectly reasonable explanation for this. They could have permission or be personal friends with someone in the Knights, but based on their conversation, I have a hard time believing that they're just passing through.

"Earth to Erica," my mother is saying and I realize that the server is waiting for my order.

"Sorry," I say with a smile. "I'll have the succotash."

When lunch is over, I go to use the bathroom and promise to meet my mother at the car. When I come out of the bathroom, though, I'm a bit startled to see one of *Los Brujos* standing by the door. He's looking directly at me and he smiles when I make eye contact with him. His friends are nowhere to be seen and I realize with a very unpleasant feeling that he's about to say something to me.

"Afternoon, miss," he says.

Don't ask me why, but it's a pet peeve of mine to be called *miss*. We're already off to a bad start.

"Hi," I say. Short. Sweet. Not unfriendly. I don't want to engage, but I don't want to be rude. I go to move past him, but he subtly shifts his body weight in a way that would force me to push past him to get out the door. I take a step back from him and try to decide how to handle this. My heart is beating harder now and it's not because I'm excited. I am, in fact, very fucking uncomfortable. I've had men behave like this toward me before and it's never been fun. This man is more intimidating than most and the fact that he seems to be using that to his advantage makes me feel angry.

"Excuse me," I say.

"What's your hurry?" he asks and leans against the door jamb like we have all the time in the world to carry on this conversation. He sure thinks a lot of himself.

"My mother's waiting for me."

"This won't take long," he says. "I want to take you out tonight."

Instead of working up the courage to tell him to fuck off, I do the thing that I hate doing and I fake it instead. I feign a laugh. "Oh, that's really flattering, but I can't tonight."

"What about tomorrow night?" he pushes. His attitude told me that this is all just lip service and that he's certain that he will get what he's after because there is no other possible outcome to this scenario. Arrogance isn't even the word for it. Misogyny is more what I'm thinking. Like it couldn't possibly occur to him that I would do anything other than what he has planned.

"Oh, no," I say. I'm trying to subtly skirt around him and he's not budging. "I can't. I mean, I'm not seeing anyone right now."

"Good news for me," he says, flashing a smile. "I didn't want to have to beat up your boyfriend."

Is this a joke? I'm honestly disgusted right now and he's not taking the hint.

"Well, I don't have one of those," I say, chipper as a bird. "I just am not dating right now. But thank you, it's really, very flattering."

"Well, we won't call it a date," he says and finally moves aside a little to let me by, but my relief lasts exactly half a second before I realize he's holding the door open for me and intends to follow me out into the viciously hot afternoon.

"Really," I say, "I'm really very flattered. But I have to go."

"You're making it a bigger deal than it is," he says and he's starting to sound impatient, which scares the bejeezus out of me. What the hell kind of planet does this guy live on in his megalomaniac mind?

"You know what," I say, because I've reached the limit of my patience, "I do have a boyfriend. I lied. I didn't want to hurt your feelings."

Which makes no sense if you think about it, but I realize I should have led with that because these alpha-dog types only recognize ownership by another male as a good enough reason to be rejected.

"Oh yeah?" he asks. "That's real sudden."

"He's a biker," I say. "Like you. I didn't want to cause any trouble between you all, but he's not going to be too happy if you keep harassing me."

"Harassing," he says and laughs softly. "He one of the Knights? Your white Knight gonna ride in and save you in his whitey tighties?"

"I don't care what he's wearing when he kicks your ass," I say and know I sure as shit am writing a check that isn't mine to cash right now. But if Colt is so hot on duking it out, then what's one more fight for my honor?

"Kicks my ass," he says softly. "All right, I like hard to get." He steps away from me, smiling in a way that tries to play off the fact that his pride is smoldering and that he means to do something about it.

I turn and walk to the car where my mom is leaning forward, watching us out of the window, and I am shaking by the time I climb inside and I lock the doors.

"Go. Go. Go." I say desperately.

"What was—" she starts to say, but I shake my head.

"Can we just please get out of here? *Now?*" I say, because I know they're all three watching me. I can see his companions standing with him out of the corner of my eye and I have the crazy feeling that they're going to follow us out of here. I have a terrible vision of us being run off the road, into a canyon in the desert, and perishing from thirst and the heat.

"What the hell happened?" She quickly whips out of the parking lot, turns right, and blows through a yellow signal.

"He was being real fucking persistent is what happened," I say.

"About what?" she prods, looking in the rearview mirror. I'm also looking in the side view mirror, tense as a coiled spring. But the gastropub falls away in the background and there are no motorcycles ganging up on us.

"He was asking me out," I say. "And he wasn't taking no for an answer. Like a fucking creep."

"Ugh, I hope you gave him the what-for."

"I did," I say, slumping down into my seat. "I sure did."

Chapter Three

Shotgun

I usually hang out at Hoppa's Taphouse if I'm not drinking at the Clubhouse, but my boss, Kyle, talked me into coming down to Mike's Cellar with him tonight. It's not that I have anything against Mike's Cellar. It's a cool place, I've been here a few times, though I can say with absolute certainty that I cannot remember the second half of two of those times. It's a dim little bar that manages to be cozy despite the sticky floors and the terrible paint job. There are Christmas lights everywhere, year round, which manages to make you feel warm and fuzzy while you get shit-faced.

But I'm usually at the Taphouse because they know me there. Once you know a place and they know you, it's just easier to go back. The bartenders only ring up half of what the Knights order. Between that and the beers the other regulars buy for me, I hardly ever end up paying for anything other than buying drinks for other people. It's a nice trade economy we have going on there. And there's something to be said for a neighborhood bar where you walk in and you know that the odds of seeing a face you don't know are awfully slim.

We've just ended a long day at the garage. Kyle owns the garage. It is called Kyle's Garage. The man doesn't get points for creativity, it's true, but he's a good guy to work for. I answered an ad asking for shop help when I moved to town. I know the basics of car work, but most of the job is dealing with customers and cleaning the place up. He's taught me a lot more about car work, though, and I may just end up a full-blown mechanic by the time he's done with me. It wouldn't be a bad gig, you know.

I left my work shirt with my name, stitched on the left breast stuffed in the saddle bag of my bike back at the shop. I'm hoping to get good and drunk tonight, so I left my baby locked up safely in the garage. I'd rather leave her safe at the shop than out front of Mike's Cellar. Mike's is close enough to walk to, which is why this is Kyle's spot—he walks over here straight after work to get started.

"We got a busy week next week," he says as we're walking in. He's talking to himself more than me. Took me a while to figure that out, but now I just nod along until he's worked out whatever he's lingering on.

"I think we're going to have to move some things around," he continues. "Because I think the way we have everything scheduled right now is a bit too tight. My brother is supposed to be bringing his car in this week, but I might be able to push that out."

There aren't very many people in the bar. Just a couple guys at the pool table, a couple guys at the bar near the jukebox, and one guy sitting by himself around the other side of the bar. I make eye contact with him and lift my hand in acknowledgement. He nods to me and smiles, lifting his double shot glass full of neat gin to lips. Just watching him makes me want to gag, but hey, different strokes for different folks.

The bartender, a worn out looking woman in her thirties with a thick ring of black eyeliner, gestures us forward. She looks like she needs a nap, but I keep that observation to myself. I've noticed that women don't take kindly to observations offered without solicitation.

"I'll have a pint of Coors Light," I tell her. "Frosted glass if you have one."

"Jack and Coke for me," says Kyle. He starts to pull out his wallet, but I give him a friendly jab with my elbow.

"Put that shit away," I tell him. "Your money isn't wanted here."

Truth is, I feel like Kyle has done so much for me that the least I can do is buy drinks for him whenever we go out together. I plan on making my way over to the Taphouse later where I'm sure I'll run into some of the Knights, but I'll get a good start here with Kyle. If I can still walk, I will probably wrap the evening up at the Clubhouse. I'm a happy drunk, lucky for me, which means I can go till the end without being ejected from wherever I'm getting my drink from.

"Thanks," says Kyle. "I'll get the next one."

"Like hell you will," I say to him. I hand the bartender my bank card and say, "Leave it open, thanks."

She takes it and scribbles a hasty note of what we've ordered onto a post-it note and then tosses it in a glass behind the bar. A very primitive system in this day and age, but I don't object. She immediately goes back to her phone, and Kyle and I take our drinks around the bar to sit near the old loner.

"Heya, boys," his gravelly voice makes me shudder to think what the inside of this throat looks like. He has the softest touch of a Spanish accent, lending his voice a certain musicality.

"Heya, Johnny," Kyle says back. He gives him a nod and takes a seat at the bar. I sit between him and Johnny. There's one empty chair between Johnny and me.

"Hi." I nod to Johnny.

"How's that garage of yours, kid?" he asks Kyle.

Kyle is in his forties, admittedly with a youthful face, but the salt-and-pepper hair peeking out from the snapback hat on his head betrays his age.

"Busy," he says. "They keep coming back. And then they tell their friends. Can't imagine why."

"Good service," says Johnny. "In my day, kids, everything was good service."

Johnny is probably the oldest biker I've ever met. His hair and beard are like a river of milk over the black leather vest he wears. There are no patches on it and he is not affiliated with any club that I am aware of, but he drives the beautiful Harley chopper that's parked out front. He's always dressed in his black leather vest with a pair of black leather chaps. He wears a black bandana over his white hair and a thick leather cuff on his wrist.

I want to be like him when I grow older.

"What's your story?" I ask. Kyle drinks with Johnny often, and I've met him every time I've come down here. We're on cordial terms, you could say.

Johnny just shakes his head and sips his warm gin. He smiles at me. "Been here, there, everywhere. And now this is where I'm at and I guess I'll probably die here."

"That okay with you?" I ask him.

"Well, sure," says Johnny. "Here's as good a place as any. I wanted to live a quiet life out in the desert."

"You from around here?" Someone puts Lynyrd Skynyrd on the jukebox and I have to raise my voice a bit. I also want to gag. Classic rock is not my scene.

"I'm not from anywhere," Johnny says.

"Is this an interrogation?" Kyle breaks in, causing Johnny and I both to chuckle.

"I guess I'm in the wrong profession, Kyle," I say. "Would you hold it against me if I hung up my shirt to join the honorable sheriff's department?"

It's Kyle's turn to chuckle and Johnny joins him. But he's shaking his head saying, "Those yoyos don't know their asses from their elbows."

We lapse into a comfortable silence, each perhaps reflecting on his own encounter with said yo-yos.

Then Johnny says, "You boys got women at home?"

"No," Kyle and I both say in unison.

Johnny raises his eyebrow and looks between us and says, "Unless ya'll are together?"

"No," Kyle and I say again and we break out into laughter. Johnny laughs too, a wheezing, whooping sound and slaps his hand down on the bar.

"Got nothin' against it," he says. "People ought to be who they are."

"We don't have women at home because we're losers," Kyle says.

"Speak for yourself, boss man"

"Proof is in the pudding," Kyle counters. He flags the bartender down to attend to his empty Bud Light bottle. It's a miracle he even manages to catch her eye with the way her face has been stuck in her phone since we got here.

"I had a girl," I say. "But I sort of fucked it up. She sort of fucked it up. I don't know, we both fucked it up."

Johnny nods knowingly. "I know how that goes," he says. "I sure to God do. If I have any regret in this life it's that I did the wrong thing with the right woman."

I look down at my beer and hope I don't turn into a sad drunk tonight. I'm surprised I even said anything about Erica. I guess she's been on my mind more and more since I learned that she's back in town. Hell, I haven't been able to stop thinking about her. Every time I set foot out of the house, I can't stop thinking that maybe I'll run into her. My mind has been a never ending script of the things that I might say. I've imagined every scenario from me throwing myself at her feet to us having a flat out brawl in the middle of the grocery store with her throwing a jar of salsa in my face. I sigh.

"Well, if you want my opinion, which I'm sure you don't," Johnny says with his gravelly laugh, "because I don't think it's even worth the two pennies anymore—I say, if you still have time, try to do the right thing with the right woman. I got all I could ever want in this world now except for the love of a good woman and it's just too late for that. And I didn't know it until it was too late."

I nod and open my mouth to answer, but the bartender is grudgingly approaching us with a fresh round of beer. She all but drops them on the bar top and scuttles away before we might conceive of something else to inconvenience her with. I shake my head at her retreating back. The bartenders at the Taphouse are a big reason to go back regularly. Maybe I should invite both Kyle and Johnny to join me there. Johnny and the Knights would probably get a nice kick out of each other.

I'm just about to suggest this when the door opens behind me. I start to turn, but I catch sight of Johnny's face first. The heavily lined, sunbaked skin on his face has turned as pale as it possibly can. He looks like he's seen a ghost.

I turn quickly to see who or what could have possibly entered the bar, half expecting to see the walking dead, or something equally as horrifying. Instead, I see three men in leather vests, ornamented with patches, looking around the bar. I have never seen any one of them before. From where I'm sitting, I can see that one of them is the Sergeant at Arms. I can't see the backs of their vests so I'm not sure whose colors they're flying but I'm on high alert. I also am very aware that they're all wearing brilliant yellow one-percent patches. Self-declared outlaws. Based on Johnny's reaction, and the fact that I don't recognize these jokers and I haven't heard a word at all about anyone asking permission to enter our territory, this all smells like serious trouble to me.

The three bikers make their way around the bar in a slow and predatory fashion, like cats who have finally cornered their mouse. Beside me, Johnny is as still as death. Kyle is also surprisingly still, watching and waiting. He's not into biker politics at all, but he's not an idiot. He knows trouble when he sees it. And this definitely looks like trouble.

"*Bueno cabron*," says the man wearing the Sergeant at Arms patch on his vest. He's addressing Johnny as they advance on us. "You look like you've seen a ghost." He laughs and the other two laugh along with him.

"I think I have," says Johnny. Despite his initial shock he seems to be pulling himself together. You'd think by the sound of his voice they were discussing a mildly disappointing outcome to a baseball game. I must say I'm impressed by his composure, but then again, I wouldn't have pegged him for the cowardly type.

"Perhaps the Lord will help you exorcise those ghosts," the Sergeant says. "We'd be happy to arrange a meeting."

"I'm sure you would be," Johnny says. He picks up his gin and sips it slowly. There's a defeated quality to his demeanor now, like a tired man who sits down in the wilderness after days of wandering.

The Sergeant and his members are ignoring us pointedly. "We can discuss it outside."

Johnny doesn't even question this. He gets slowly to his feet and tips back the rest of his gin. He looks at me and Kyle and nods to us.

"Gentlemen," he says to us.

"Hold on," I say. It's probably a bad idea for me to stick my nose where it doesn't belong—I also don't want to make Johnny look bad and undercut him—but this shit isn't sitting right with me. These guys are here to cause trouble and I can't in good conscience just watch it happen.

"You got something to say, *güey*?" the Sergeant asks me. He draws himself up and I see his hands curl into fists. Something tells me he knows how to use them. I can see the muscles working in his jaw as he snaps his head up and down, giving me a sharp assessment. It's an invitation for a problem.

"Who the fuck—" I start to say. But Johnny puts his hand on my shoulder and gives a very subtle shake of his head.

"Don't worry, kid," he says. "I got this." He walks past the Sergeant, who keeps his eyes locked on mine. Out of the corner of my eye I see the two members following him outside while I stare calmly back into the hostile eyes boring holes into me.

"See you around," he says with a sneer and then follows the other three men outside, pausing to give me one more look at the door that promises trouble. On his way out, I can finally see the patches on the back of his vest: *Los Brujos*. The name rings a bell, but I know that they're definitely not local.

"What the fuck just happened?" Kyle says. We both keep watching the door.

"I don't know," I say to Kyle. "But I don't like it." I drain my beer. What the fuck should I do? I mean, Johnny isn't young. He's at least twice as old as these young punks, but Johnny all but told me to stay out of it. Not my clowns, not my rodeo and all that. But I still don't like it. It's still sitting badly with me.

"Something is rotten in Denmark," I say to Kyle. "I don't think those guys should be here."

"What do you mean?" Kyle asks, wiping his forehead with his wrist.

"I mean, they should have asked Nick's permission if they were going to ride into our territory and fly their colors. They're here on official club business as *Los Brujos*." I rub my cheek while I stare at the sticky dried rings on the bar top. "I mean, I'm low on the food chain. Being the new kid, I haven't heard anything about anyone coming through town. Them coming through here without contacting the Knights and acquiring proper permission is kind of a big fuck you."

"So what now?" Kyle says. He's looking a bit nervous, like he's worried he's landed himself in the middle of something he doesn't want to be in.

"Don't worry," I say. "But I think maybe I should go talk to the Knights about what I just saw. I don't have a great feeling about those guys."

"Yeah," says Kyle as I wave my hand at the bartender. Miraculously, I caught her attention.

"So I'll be taking off," I say. "Sorry to cut the night short."

"No worries," Kyle says. "That sounds like a headache and a half."

"I mean, it'll probably be more Nick's headache than mine," I say. "But I am the newest member, and I've got to earn my brownie points where I can." I flash Kyle a grin.

"Tab, please," I say to the bartender when she slouches over. She's been watching us with suspicious owly eyes ever since *Los Brujos* came into the bar, as if we were the ones causing trouble. She brings it to me and I give a good tip even though I don't think she deserves it, but I don't want to make Kyle look bad at his place. A man's drinking spot is a sacred thing and I must respect that.

"See you around."

"See ya," he says.

Really, I'm in a hurry because I want to see what's going on outside with Johnny. For all I know, they've already all left. He basically told me to mind my own business, but I have a conscience about the whole thing. I'm a strapping young buck. He's an old man. While he may still be a majestic, old biker-badass, he's probably beginning to exhibit the frailty that older people get when they reach a certain point. And there are only so many slugs of warm gin you can take and cigarettes you can drink before your body just starts to break down.

I make a mental note of this—maybe I should lay off the drinking a bit.

The door closes behind me and I don't see anyone in the parking lot. However, Johnny's beautiful custom chopper is right where it was when I arrived and I can see three other choppers parked in the parking lot. Presumably belonging to *Los Brujos*.

They must be around here somewhere.

Mike's Cellar stands alone in a gravel parking lot. There's a cinderblock wall that runs along behind it and a cinder black enclosure around the back of the building where I'm sure the dumpster lives. The lighting isn't great around the back of the building because of the few street lights that were burnt out.

I edge my way along the front of the building and peer around the corner. There's no one along the side of the building, but I can hear angry voices. They're hushed, like they're trying to keep things under wraps but that hard when things get heated. I step very carefully over the gravel, wishing that it was paved asphalt because it would be a hell of a lot quieter and I'd be able to move a hell of a lot faster. I realize that the voices are coming from all the way behind the dumpster enclosure. I continue to step carefully, making my way over there. The voices don't pause, which means no one has heard me approaching yet, thank God.

"—for the last time, where the fuck is it." It's the Sergeant asshole talking.

"I don't know what you're talking about," Johnny says in his calm, gravelly voice.

"Don't play games with me, *cabron*," the Sergeant says. I hear a step and a dull thud. Johnny groans and I hear the sound of spitting.

The bastard must have just hit him in the fucking face. I tense and keep myself from springing around the corner because it occurs to me now that these guys mean serious business. And they just might even be armed. I don't have any weapons with me at all except for my fists, and well, I don't think it's well-advised to bring fists to a gunfight.

"Tell us where it is," he repeats, "and I'll send you to *dios* quickly. If you keep quiet, I'll send you slowly. Piece by piece, *vato*, do you hear me?" I hear the sound of a switchblade spring.

"You think you're the worst I've ever met?" Johnny laughs. "You think you're so big and tough, *hijo*? Let me tell you something, there's nothin' you can do to me that I haven't already done to myself in one way or another. Go ahead. I'll never fucking tell you."

The Sergeant makes a sound of frustration, and I hear another blow land. The sound of spitting again. Johnny's breathing is a bit more ragged which makes the Sergeant laugh.

"You like that? Plenty more where that came from."

Then the blows start falling one after another. And I can't stand here and let Johnny get beat to death. I throw myself around the corner and tackle the first asshole I see. It's one of the members. He's holding a pistol in his hand, which he tries to point at my head, but I grab his wrist and twist his arm. I manage to pin him to the ground, but he's strong. I slam his wrist on the ground over again, trying to force him to drop the gun.

I pick it up and jump to my feet, keeping the pistol trained on the man on the ground. I expect to see two other people trained on me and I'm already preparing myself for defeat and chastising myself for being such a stupid asshole, but the other two are only keeping an eye on me out of the corner of their eyes. Johnny has a gun in his hand, a beautiful old revolver with a mother of pearl handle that I can only assume is his.

"You fucking idiots," he says to them in the same calm voice he's been using all along. I am more impressed than ever, considering that one of his eyes is nearly swollen shut and his white beard and hair are positively soaked with the blood oozing from his mouth. I'm willing to bet there are at least a couple of teeth on the ground somewhere.

"What are you gonna do, *abuelo*?" the Sergeant asks. He's clearly still trying to feel like he has control of the situation, but it's obviously not the case anymore.

"You tell Trueno that I say hello," says Johnny. "And you also tell him to go fuck himself." He smiles a grim smile. "And you tell him that he will dig for a hundred years and he'll never fucking find it. My parting gift."

I don't realize what's happening until it's too late. Johnny turns that beautiful revolver on himself and pulls the trigger. He drops like a sack of potatoes and the sound of him choking on blood fills my ears.

The Sergeant grunted and suddenly the world was an explosion of stars. The asshole I took the gun from took my moment of shock to his advantage. But I didn't lose the pistol. He throws himself at me and we both slam into the cinder block enclosure. He grabs my wrist like I did to him and starts slamming it into the concrete, trying to get me to drop the pistol. It hurts so much I think he might break my fucking wrist, but I don't let go. I slam my head into his face and judging by the nasty crunch, I think I've broken his nose. He falls away from me, and I start to bring the gun down.

But it's too late, one of the other assholes opens fire. The shot is loud, a roar that blocks out the whole world for an instant and leaves my ears ringing. My arm is burning suddenly, but it's a sensation I'm only dimly aware of. I return fire, but the assholes are fleeing around the enclosure, their footsteps fading away. I go to Johnny, who's still making gurgling sounds in his throat. He's alive.

I hear the roar of motorcycles starting in the distance as I get to the old man. In the dimness, the blood bubbling from his chest looks black on the hands that he has pressed over his wound.

"Johnny," I say. The adrenaline pouring through me is so strong that I barely know what I'm saying. "Johnny, can you hear me?"

"It's in the… *al dentro del oso…*" he says in a ragged, wet voice. "In the bear, kid."

In the distance, I hear sirens. Johnny tries to speak again, but he can't get the words out.

"Come on, stay with me." But he takes a couple more ragged, gurgling breaths, and then there are no more. His chest stays still. His body goes still in a way that only the dead can. "*Fuck*," I say.

The sirens are getting louder. And it occurs to me that I need to get the fuck out of here. Nick is going to kill me, that's all I can think about. I haven't done anything wrong, but just being here is going to ruin any chance I might have at being patched in. Fuck. Fuck. Fuck.

I put my hand on Johnny's shoulder one last time before I get to my feet. I look around the corner of the enclosure—the cops aren't here yet. I walk to the edge of the parking lot and turn onto the nearest street, trying to look as casual as possible.

As soon as I'm out of sight of the bar, I start running like I've never run in my life.

The sirens are still wailing, but I don't think they're coming after me. I have one thought as I run: *I've got to find Seth.*

But another thought crosses my mind as I draw close to Kyle's Garage to retrieve my bike. *What the fuck is in the bear?* As I reach the door and fumble the keys out of my pocket, I realize with shock that my arm is black with blood. And as soon as I notice, my upper arm starts burning like someone has lit it on fucking fire.

Jesus Christ, those fucking assholes shot me. And I'm losing a lot of blood. I don't know anything about any medical stuff, but I know that it can't be good. Now I need Holly a hell of a lot more than I need Seth. There's never a more convenient time for your brother to be on his way down the aisle with a licensed MD.

I cannot believe they fucking shot me. And that it's taken me this long for me to really notice. I must be in shock. Or maybe it's the adrenaline. Either way, I'm not really interested in bleeding out. I need Holly to put me back together so I can find these assholes and give them a little bite of their own medicine.

I pull my bike out of the shop and get my T-shirt off before I start the engine. I tie it around my arm as tight as I possibly can because I remember hearing somewhere that pressure helps stop the blood.

I start my bike up and kick it into gear. I just hope I can make it to them before I pass out.

Chapter Four

Shotgun

It's not a far ride over to Seth's house, but tonight it feels like it's taking an eternity. I keep thinking I hear sirens, that the cops are coming after me, but I realize it's only my imagination. Or maybe my ears are still ringing from the gunshot. Or maybe I'm losing too much blood. It's hard to tell.

As I drive, I think about what happened over and over again. My mind is still really scattered, but I keep coming back to a few strange points—why the fuck would Johnny kill himself? And what were those dickheads looking for?

I pull up in front of Holly's clinic and park my bike illegally in the loading zone at the front of the building. I don't have the presence of mind to care at this moment. I don't even know if they're home and it occurs to me that I should have called. But I don't even think I could have fucking dialed with the way my hands are shaking. I see a light on in the window where their apartment is. I get to their door feeling awfully shaky and pound, praying to anyone who will listen that they're home and they'll let me in.

It's Holly who answers the door. I feel immediate relief, but I also know right away that I am in for the scolding of my life.

"Holly Berry," I say, trying to give her a charming smile. I realize that I'm drenched in sweat. "You're looking great today."

"Seth!" she all but shouts over her shoulder into the apartment. "Colt," she says, turning back to me, "what in God's name happened?"

I let her help me to a chair in the dining room and I hear my brother's footsteps coming toward me.

"Jesus *Christ*," he says. I look up into his face and his expression is a combination of terror and fury that I think might scare the pants off of anyone. "Who the fuck did this to you?"

I start to speak, but Holly interjects. "That can wait," she says. She peels the blood-soaked T-shirt from my arm and her eyes widen. "You've been shot," she says, sounding vaguely like she can't quite believe what she's seeing.

"Yes, ma'am," I say.

"Seth, my bag," she orders. Her entire demeanor has changed now and I am looking at Dr. Holly, no longer Holly Berry, my brother's fiancée who is loving in a stern kind of way. She's a no nonsense lady to begin with, but seeing her go into doctor mode is like watching a switch flip. I'm tickled.

Seth seems used to it and I realize that he's left. I picture an old fashioned doctor's bag, black leather with a clasp opening at the top, but Seth comes back with an uninspired-looking duffle bag. I would have bet there were dirty socks in there, but Holly grabs it from him and opens it up to rifle through her things. She comes up with a stethoscope and a blood pressure cuff. She dons the stethoscope and puts the end over my heart. Then she moves it lower over my chest, instructs me to breathe in. She moves it to my back and does the same. She's frowning all the while, and has been frowning since I arrived, so I have no idea what she's thinking or if I am about to drop dead.

With a loud belch of velcro, she opens the blood pressure cuff and puts it around my arm. She pumps the thing and lets the air out, the stethoscope pressed to my inner arm. When I start to feel the gross pounding feeling in the vein there, she looks at her watch until she has what she needs.

"Your blood pressure is a bit low," she says. "But not low enough to frighten me. And I would expect that after a shock like yours. You're coming down from quite the adrenaline rush, I'm sure."

"I sure am," I say. And I'm realizing how tired I am. I also realize that I have no idea what time it is. I have no idea how much time has transpired between the scene behind the dumpster at Mike's Cellar and now, with me sitting on a chair at my brother and his fiancée's place.

"I'm going to have a look," she says. "It might hurt a bit."

She rummages around in her bag until she comes up with a pair of gloves, some gauze, and a bottle of something or other. She pulls the gloves on and wiggles her fingers, a practiced motion, before she pours some of what I assume is alcohol over the gauze. She wipes the skin around the bullet hole, leaving a nice, cool feeling and taking the dried blood away. Then she wipes the wound that is now oozing dark, thick blood. I jerk because I'm startled by how much it fucking stings. It wasn't the kind of pain I was expecting.

"Ow," I murmur.

"You're gonna tell me you got shot in the arm and rode all the way over here on your bike without batting an eye and *now* you're going to whine?" Seth says. I look over and see he's leaning against the counter with his arms folded, watching the whole proceeding. He still has a fire burning in his eyes that tells me that if he finds who shot his baby brother, it's TNT time. I feel oddly fuzzy about this. As much as I bitch about him not being there, it's good to know that he has my back. Not that I'm going to fucking tell *him* that.

"It just—it fucking *stings*," I say. "It feels like it's on fire."

"I'm cleaning it," Holly says in her most terrifying mom voice.

"Sure," I say. "Sure, go ahead." What other choice do I have? I'm not about to tell her she *can't*. I want to make sure I'm not going to lose my arm, I'm not trying to also lose my head.

"I'm going to have to get the bullet out," she adds. "You're not going to enjoy that."

"Whatever do you mean?" I say, already feeling tired of being in pain. "That sounds just swell."

"Okay, Mr. Sassy Asshole," Dyno says. He walks over and swings one of the chairs around to face him, then he straddles it with his arms across the back. Oh my god, he's so cool without even trying that it makes me hate him. I open my mouth to make a snarky comment about this, but Holly does something to my arm that makes me grit my teeth. "What happened?" Seth asks. This time, Holly doesn't dissuade him from questioning me. I'm sure she's just as curious as he is now that she knows that I've been shot.

"It wasn't my fight," I say, right off. I don't want him jumping all over me, thinking I'm a dickhead that went out and started causing problems right after Nick tells us to pull our shit together.

"Then?" He gestures toward my arm with his eyebrows raised, looking not at all amused. "What's this about?"

"I went to Mike's Cellar with Kyle," I started. "After work. He likes to go over there to get some beers after he's off the clock. He invited me to walk over with him and I figured, why not. I'll start there and then move onto the Taphouse, see who's there, and then I'll close down the Clubhouse with the rest of the Knights."

"Sure," he says. He's rubbing his bottom lip with his thumb, which is a sure indication in the dictionary of Seth Body Language that he's growing impatient and he's trying to keep it under the hatch.

"Well, there's this guy, Johnny, that hangs out there all the time," I say. Holly chooses this moment to pull the bullet from my arm and I yelp like a Dachshund someone has just stomped on. "*Jesus fucking Christ on the cross!*"

"There, that wasn't so bad."

And the look on her face tells me that she knows exactly how bad it was, that it was just as bad as it sounded and that I *deserve* it. Well, I'm not going to argue with Doctor Holly. She holds the warped little blob of metal out to me and I open my shaking hand. She drops it in there, gooey with my blood. Weird, to think that this thing hitched a ride inside me all the way over here.

"I don't think you'll have any permanent damage," she says. "But, you'll want to see a physical therapist to make sure, and I'll be wanting to check in with you at least once a week after I get you stitched up."

"Do I get the numbing stuff?" I ask her. I look at my brother as if he just called me out for being a wuss, though he said nothing. "*You* try getting shot in the arm."

He holds up his hands while Holly goes to get the local so she can inject a lovely numbness. He watches her go and then looks at me, very anxious to hear the rest of the story.

"Okay, so there's this old guy who hangs out at this bar," Seth says.

"Yeah," I say, "So he's just this old biker dude. Really nice guy, Kyle is friendly with him, I've gotten friendly with him. Don't know a thing about him, seems like a super private guy. Anyway, we're just shooting the shit and these fucking assholes roll in. They're from a one-percent club called *Los Brujos*." My unpracticed tongue stumbles over the words. I haven't spoken Spanish since high school and it shows.

"I've heard of them," my brother cuts in. "I don't remember where they're based."

"Yeah, they're flying their colors high," I say. "And I don't recall hearing anything about anyone asking permission to."

Seth shakes his head. "I haven't heard a goddamn word," he says. "Chances are, they shouldn't be here."

"Like I told Kyle," I say, "That's a big fat fuck you."

"No kidding. Anyway." He gestures for me to continue.

"Anyway," I say, picking up the thread. "So they fucking come in and they take him outside."

"What do you mean they take him outside?" Seth asks, straightening up a bit.

"I mean he goes willingly," I say. I hear Holly's footsteps coming back. "But they've all but got him at gunpoint. They mean bad business."

"I hope you're taking notes, Dyno," Holly says. "Because I'm going to ask you to repeat everything I missed."

"Of course, darling," he says.

I pause in my story until she's poked me a few times with her scary needle. The numbness begins to set in right away and I breathe out a whole chunk of the tension I've been carrying around with me.

"Better?" she says.

"Better," I say. I give her a tired smile, but she's focused on her work. I look back at my brother. "Anyway. They take him outside. And I decide that it's time for me to go too, that I should tell Nick what's happening. But when I go out, their bikes are all still there. And man, it's not my business, but I don't feel right about leaving an old man to get dogged by these three assholes. So I find them behind the dumpster and they're beating the shit out of him."

"Jesus," he says. "You said he's an old man? Like *old* old?"

"I mean, like, he's at least in his seventies old," I say. "Old enough that it's fucked up to be beating the shit out of him. I don't know anything about this guy, he could be a terrible fucking person. But it felt wrong to me, so I fucking did something about it. I jumped into the fray or whatever. And in the commotion, this old guy, Johnny, pulls out his own fucking gun. And he *shoots himself in the fucking chest*."

"What?" Seth says. And he looks genuinely disturbed.

"Yeah," I say. "So these fucking jokers take off, but not before firing off a few rounds. Talk about a parting gift, Jesus."

"So this dude just fucking killed himself?" Seth says.

"Yeah," I say. "Oh, I sort of left out something important. They kept talking about finding *it*, that he was going to tell them where *it* was. And right before he killed himself, he said for them to tell someone 'hello, that he could go fuck himself, and that he could'—let me see if I'm remembering this right—'dig for a hundred years and never find the thing.'"

"Buried treasure," Holly deadpans.

"I wish," Seth says. "Digging up some pirate treasure that was buried in the Arizona desert."

"Wouldn't that be nice," I say. "But I don't know what the fuck he was talking about. But the epilogue goes like this: after those shitheads dipped, I went over to the old man. He was still hanging on by a thread. And he tells me that *it* is in the bear's stomach. The belly of the bear. Whatever."

"What the fuck," Seth says.

"He could have been delirious," Holly says. "In fact, it's likely he was. People can get very confused at the end."

We let this grim sentence hang in the air for a moment. Then I clear my throat. "The cops were coming, so I ran. I mean, Johnny was dead. He died after he said the bit about the bear. So I figured there was no point in sticking around. I don't know, maybe I did the wrong thing. Maybe I should have stayed until they got there. I wasn't scared or anything, but I just kept hearing Nick's voice in my head. I didn't want this to come back to bite me, or any of the Knights, in the ass. That's all I could think about, so I booked it."

"You probably did the right thing," Seth said. Which makes me feel a bit better, because I was starting to feel kind of gross for running from the scene. "Who knows what they could have pinned on you after a scene like that. But," He gets to his feet. "Nick can't find out about this. I know you didn't really do anything and it wasn't your fight and all that, but it would be a bad idea after the scolding we just got. I'm just not sure how he'll react. So just don't say anything."

"What about *Los Brujos*?" I ask. "I'm kind of in a shitty situation. On the one hand, I don't want him to kick me out of the Knights. And on the other, these assholes were out for blood and now they're roaming our territory."

Seth looks a bit uneasy but shrugs. "We'll figure out a way to bring it up—without mentioning that you were at the scene of a crime."

"Technically, I'm the victim of a crime," I say, looking over at Holly's handiwork. I like to think I have tough nerves, but there's something pretty disgusting about watching a needle and thread passing through your own bloody skin.

"Not as much of a victim as the other guy." Seth points out.

"I guess," I say. "Jesus."

I don't think reality has quite set in yet. It all seems like a weird dream. I have to keep reminding myself that I'm actually sitting here with Seth and Holly and that I'm actually holding the bullet, which was just lodged in my arm, in my hand.

"I'll go make up the spare room," Seth says.

"Thanks," Holly says in the distracted way you would expect a person to speak when she's stitching up another human.

"Thanks for doing this," I say to Holly when it occurred to me that I haven't demonstrated an ounce of gratitude yet.

"Yeah, well," she says, "I'm getting awfully tired of stitching up the Hardy boys."

I can't help but laugh and she laughs a little too, then quickly orders me to sit still.

"I'm almost done," she says.

"Thank God."

"You call Erica yet?" she says.

I raise my eyebrows at her, but she can't see me. "No," I say. "Was I supposed to?"

"I just thought that maybe since she's back in town you might consider it," she says. And she's sounding a bit smug about it, if I do say so myself.

"I mean, I don't know what to say to her. She made it clear to me that she finds things that are very important to me to be objectionable." I resist the urge to fidget. "She made it clear she finds my *brother* objectionable. Says he's a bad influence."

"Well, that isn't a lie." she chuckles a little bit. And then added gently, "Maybe you ought to give her another chance. I can see how this world can be hard to get used to if it's not something you're out looking to involve yourself in."

"Oh, like you were?" I say, which makes her laugh again.

"I was an ER surgeon," she says. "What can I say, I'm an adrenaline junkie."

"Well," I say, "I guess she's not."

"I think she's good for you," Holly says. "I think you could use a little bit of her good influence and she could probably use a little bit of your bad one."

"Oh, jeez."

Seth comes back down the hall. "Got the spare bedroom made up for you, bro."

"I don't think that's nece—" I start to say.

But Holly cuts me off. "I'd feel better—and I'm sure Seth would too—if you stay here tonight."

I sigh. "Okay, Mom."

Holly smiles, but more importantly, I see my brother smile out of the corner of my eye and I scowl at him. He turns away quickly.

I realize, sitting here with Holly stitching the bullet hole in my arm closed and my brother leaning against the counter, that I truly feel family right now. I don't even remember the last time this was the case. It's a good feeling. But, in the back of my mind, there's this gnawing feeling that someone is missing and suddenly a mane of blonde hair and a flash of green eyes are all I can think about.

I take my cell phone out of my pocket and stare at it. I'm having a harder and harder time remembering why I'm being so stubborn about Erica.

Maybe by tomorrow, I won't remember at all.

Chapter Five

Erica

His lips are pressed against my ear and his voice is a hot breath against my earlobe. "I want to taste you."

I can't help but squirm with pleasure. One of his large hands holds the side of my face and his lips are trickling down my jaw and onto my neck. They travel to my decolletage and pause there. His tongue sliding along the swell of my breast as his hand glides from the side of my face down to hold my rib cage. His thumb fit just below my breast.

My heart is in my throat and my belly is full of butterflies. His scent is filling up my nose—a faint kiss of soap and the golden, masculine scent of his body. I'm drowning in my senses. My fingers go to his beautiful brown hair and slide through the thick, short locks. His body is claiming mine completely and I want nothing more than to yield to him. His hand comes away from my rib cage and lifts my shirt to caress my stomach. His fingers find the button of my shorts and make quick work of it. He pulls the zipper down and, with his forehead pressed against mine, begins to slip his fingers inside—

I sit up, breathing hard, with my hand pressed against my chest. The clock on the bedside table reads 4 AM. I am alone, in my bed, at the rented Airbnb I've been staying at with my mother and her boyfriend, Ted.

I look around the darkened room, feeling like I've fallen out of time. I've never had such a vivid, sexy dream. I've dreamed about Colt a lot in the last few months, but I've never had a *sex* dream about him. I'm nearly ashamed of how much I enjoyed it. And how disappointed I am that it ended.

I touch my fingers to my lips and expect them to feel swollen from kissing; it felt so real. I can still feel the roughness of his jaw against my fingertips and smell the lingering scent of him. It's almost like I forgot how much of an effect his body had on mine. It was nearly involuntary. Sometimes I wonder if it's strictly pheromones because when I get around that man, I'm like a cat in heat. I can't help it, my body just responds. It's embarrassing to admit, but I guess that's only to be expected of someone so utterly... masculine, for lack of a better word. It's not just his stupid good looks. There's something so animal and male about him.

The heat between my thighs is still there. I'm nearly shaking with my desire for him. I lay back on the bed and slip my fingers between my legs, stroking my slick, velvet folds. I'm back in the dream, imagining his fingers slipping into me, his thumb pressing against my clit and rubbing while he fingers me just right.

I gasp quietly and remember the way his lips felt on mine, the way he was caressing my bottom lip with his tongue. I finish hard with his name on my lips and the smell of him lurking in my memory.

My heart starts to slow as I study the ceiling, thinking of him. A certain sadness swallows me as the magical beauty of my orgasm begins to subside. I rest my hand on my stomach, thinking of him, wondering where he is right now. With someone else? Probably. A man like that doesn't stay alone for long, and who could blame him? Women probably drop like flies at his feet. I know I did.

He told me that he's not usually the relationship type, but that doesn't mean he lacks company. I roll on my side and feel a tear run off my cheek. Have I made a mistake? I've only asked myself this question thirty thousand times. It's been months and I'm still thinking about him. Dreaming about him. Aching for him—if we're telling the truth.

I stare at my phone, sitting on my bedside table and for a moment, I'm having trouble remembering why I didn't pick up the phone and call.

"Yay, we're almost there." My mother is sitting in the passenger seat of Ted's Forerunner and she's bouncing like a little girl. Ted is in the driver's seat, and I see him glance over at her and smile at her from the back. I'm not just happy for her, but happy to be here with her.

On the one hand, I'm really glad my mother found someone who genuinely likes, or really genuinely loves, her.

On the other hand, I make myself a little jealous wondering if I'll ever find that person for myself. I sigh inwardly, thinking about the dream I had last night, the dream of Colt, and I feel the press of his lips on my throat like a ghost. It makes me sigh again, with longing and with a dash of sadness.

The Arizona desert is whipping past outside my window. The sun is directly overhead. We left the limits of town twenty minutes ago and we've only passed a couple of houses since. I like the idea of being out in the country, I can't help but think it's a lot harder to run into people in town if you're out in the sticks. Or, in our case, the sagebrush.

Ted slows the car down as we come to the end of what looks like a long driveway. There's a big, elaborate gate made of beautiful, red sandstone and an arch reaching over it. The words *Escondido Ranch* are welded to the arch in blackened metal. A pair of bison horns attached above the words wrap up the perfectly cliche view.

"*Escondido* means hidden, or secret, something like that," my mother says, sounding for all the world like a third grader presenting for the class. Her enthusiasm is, admittedly, infectious. I sit up straight and crane to look as Ted gets out of the Forerunner and goes to unlatch the gate.

He gets back into the car and pulls through the gate. My mom turns to look at me with a smile bigger than the world, and says, "We're home."

"I can't believe you didn't even look at it before you bought it," I say. It made me uneasy. My mother is so good natured that I always worry that she will be taken advantage of.

"No way," she says, waving her hand. "My girlfriend guaranteed me that this is a steal of a lifetime. We've known each other since we were twelve, I'll take her word on it. She said there were other cash buyers who were also pushing to buy, sight unseen, and I wasn't going to wait around for someone else to snap it up while I hemmed and hawed. Here's as good a place as any."

I wonder why I moved back to the desert as I stare out the window. I fucking hate sagebrush. But, like my mom says, here's as good a place as any. At least, until I figure out what to do next. And I'm pretty excited about helping my mom set up a little permaculture homestead. If there's one thing I know I love aside from show business, it's gardening. And unlike show business, which always carries with it the murky uncertainty of one's true abilities and the inevitable crippling self-doubt, I *know* I'm good at gardening. And I've spent the last several months reading about how to farm most efficiently in the Arizona desert. It's one thing to arrange a landscape design, it's another thing to figure out how to garden year round and work toward the eventual goal of becoming entirely food sovereign.

The property doesn't look like much, to be honest. Just a whole lot of that sagebrush. The driveway is so long we lose sight of the road well before we come into sight of the house.

"Pretty," I say. A modest-looking, single-story adobe comes into view that is painted a beautiful terracotta color.

"Isn't it just dreamy?" my mother asks. We all sit in silence, contemplating our feelings on the initial sight of our new home.

Ted gets out first and he goes around to open my mother's door for her. He's a bit of an old-fashioned fellow, but I appreciate his devotion to my mother. My mother smooths her cotton dress and puts her hat on to protect her fair, freckled face from the Arizona sun.

"You got your father's skin," she always says to me, enviously. And it's true, I did. Sunburn isn't even in my vocabulary.

There's a big, beautiful wrought iron gate inset with mosaic pieces. My mother swings it open and we all follow a mosaic path up to the front door, which is carved with incredible detail. Inside, the floor is all terracotta tile. There are rustic, wood beams running across the ceiling and matching the wooden pillars that, presumably, keep the house from falling down.

"The owner died just recently," my mother says in a hushed voice. "The nearest kin asked that all assets be liquidated immediately."

"That's a shame," Ted says. "But we'll take good care of the place for him. Him?"

"I think so. I'm not clear on the story."

"Did he die *in* the house?" I ask, pausing my enthusiasm pending the receipt of further information.

"No," my mother says. "No one died in the house."

"I wonder if ghosts can haunt a place even if they didn't die there..." I say as I wander down the hall. I'm eager to get a look at the bedrooms, but I'm startled—I think we all are—to hear a knock on the front door.

I come back out into the foyer, curious to know who could possibly be knocking on our door. Maybe the neighbors have come by to introduce themselves.

Ted goes to answer it and opens the door wide so my mother can stand next to him. At first, all I can see are the silhouettes of three people standing in the doorway, but as I step in a little bit closer, my heart sinks.

It's my friend from the restaurant, along with his two biker buddies. This time they're not wearing their leather vests. They've made some attempt to look presentable and are all wearing slacks and some version of button downs.

I fight the impulse to duck into the kitchen and to avoid being seen, but what's the worst that can happen? Ted's here. My mom's here. I'm just feeling nervous, I guess, because I'm confused. Did they follow us here? How did they know how to find us here? Is this a coincidence?

"Good afternoon," the man at the door says. Not the one who was aggressively hitting on me. I think this one was wearing the Sergeant at Arms patch on his heavy leather vest. They admittedly clean up very well. I wouldn't know they're biker thugs if it weren't for the tattoos creeping out of the necks of their nice shirts and over the backs of their hands, or the swirling cloud of darkness that seems to follow them. There's something about them that makes me uneasy, something about their very presence that feels like a threat. I can't help but take half a step back.

"Good afternoon," Ted says, all politeness.

"Good afternoon," my mother murmurs apprehensively.

"Are you the owners of this property?" the man asks.

Over Ted's shoulder, I make eye contact with the aggressive-flirting asshole and he looks surprised for a moment before he flashes me a thousand-watt smile. He seems very pleased to see me again. I can't say I return the feeling, I return his smile with a cool look and finally look away. I can tell he's probably the type who is a sore loser, and I am not about to try to get into a staring contest with him.

"Yes," Ted says. "We just purchased it."

"Well, it's your lucky day. I've come to make you an offer that you can't refuse."

"Is that so?" Ted says, raising his eyebrows.

My mother has come to stand by me. I kind of hate it, the two women huddled together behind the man, but right now is not a time for bravado, in my humble opinion. These guys scare me, and they obviously scare my mother.

"We're prepared to give you cash for this place," he says. "Name your price, no questions asked."

"Oh, it's not for sale." My mother breaks in. "I've only just bought it."

"Yes, I understand," the man says in a tone I suppose is intended to sound soothing. "There are many lovely ranches in this area. And now's the perfect time to sell for a cash, asking price, don't you think? Before you've gotten attached."

Admittedly, he has some powers of persuasion, and I can definitely see him selling timeshares in a shopping mall somewhere.

"It's not for sale," Ted says in a firm voice that suggests that the conversation is done. "We appreciate you stopping by, and we wish you luck finding your own ranch."

Ted begins to close the door, but the man puts his hand up. It's a shockingly aggressive thing to do, and my anxiety about the whole situation jumps from thirty to one hundred.

"I have a hard time taking no for an answer," he says. "Any price you want. Name it."

"We're not interested," Ted says. And bless him, I don't know how he hasn't lost an ounce of composure.

"You're making a mistake," the man at the door says. And there's a definite threat in his voice now. "A very, very big mistake."

"I think we'll be the judge of that."

"The man I work for is not going to be happy to hear that his offer has been turned down," says the man. "And you don't want to make this man unhappy."

"I'm sorry for your friend," Ted says. "But we'll be keeping this property. We wish you the best of luck."

He tries to shut the door again, and the man puts his hand up. He looks angry now, I can feel it coming off him in waves like a heat. His eyes are like burning coals in his face.

"I'm going to ask nicely just once more," the man says. "And after that, we'll do this the hard way."

"Thank you for coming," Ted says.

"Have it your way." He takes his hand from the door, adjusts his shirt, and smooths his hair. Then he smiles very unpleasantly. "We'll be in touch."

He turns away from the door without looking back. The other man follows him, but my little friend from the restaurant makes a point to give me his big ol' smile again and blow me a kiss before Ted shuts the door firmly in his face.

We all stand there for a moment in silence before my mom says, "What the *fuck* was that about?"

Ted shakes his head. "That was really..."

"Awful," I supply

"I mean," my mother starts, and I can see that she's really upset now. "Who *does* that? I mean, they all but threatened us."

"They *did* threaten us," I say.

"I think if we just call and file a report with the Sheriff's department we'll feel a bit better about the situation," Ted says.

"Yeah," my mother says. Ted goes to her and rubs her shoulders.

"Don't let them spoil this for you," Ted says. "Guys like that are bullies, and bullies are all cowards when it comes down to it."

Hollow words, but I appreciate that he's doing best to soothe her.

Somehow, I don't think we'll be rid of them so easily. The very nature of their mission is strange to me. I can't imagine why anyone would want a property so badly—unless there's something valuable about it. And if there's something valuable about it, why the hell would we want to get rid of it?

I turn away from my mother and Ted and restart my mission to check out the bedrooms. This time, the happy balloon in my chest is deflated, and the shine has been taken from the whole experience. Nevertheless, I'm determined to find my excitement again.

I just wish I had someone to soothe me too.

I wander down the hallway with a sigh.

Chapter Six

Shotgun

I open my eyes and immediately groan. My arm is aching like someone drove a nail into it. Oh right, those *Los Brujos* motherfuckers did one better. They put a bullet into it. I sit up in bed and look around. The world swims a bit and the ache in my arm goes up another notch, and I immediately break into a sweat.

"Jesus *Christ*," I say. I climb out of bed and stand, riding the head rush that tries to drag me back down.

Where the fuck am I? Oh right, the spare room at Seth and Holly's house. I raise my hands to rub my eyes and immediately regret moving the left one.

"Ah," I say and look over at the white bandage wrapped neatly around my wounded arm. Then, I glance at the bedside table where a sling is sitting. Holly came in and gave it to me before I went to bed and told me to put it on, I totally forgot. I laughed at her when she told me I had to wear it, but this morning I didn't find it so funny.

I wipe sweat off my upper lip as I reach for the stupid thing. The main problem with wearing the dumb thing, as far as I'm concerned, is that I have to explain what I did to my arm. I was hoping I could just slide right along and keep it covered, pretending like nothing happened. That, obviously, is not going to work with a sling.

I slip my arm into the sling and put the strap over my neck. I feel silly instantly. And it seems pretty dramatic to walk around with my arm in a sling. It's such an obvious indication of injury that anyone and everyone *will* ask me what happened. Not only do I not want to be potentially associated at all with what happened last night, but I also don't want that kind of attention. I feel like a giant baby, like I can't just man up and bear it, and I fucking hate that part the most.

I look at the clock on my phone—it's a bit late. 10 AM. Seth is a late sleeper on the weekends, so I doubt he's awake yet. I'm not sure about Holly. I hope she's up, because I'm going to need something stronger than ibuprofen for the next couple of days at least.

Sure enough, she's sitting at the kitchen table with a cup of coffee when I walk in. She smiles at me.

"How's the arm?" she asks. If I'm not mistaken, there's a slightly sadistic edge to her smile. I narrow my eyes at her.

"Never been better," I say.

"Ah," she says. "Then you won't be needing these." She pulls a bottle out of the pocket of her robe and shakes it like a toy rattle.

"Let's not get too hasty," I say as I step toward her with my hand out.

"I'm a doctor, Colt," she says, suddenly very dignified. "I can't go around handing out drugs for no good reason."

"Gimme da candy," I say. She just smiles at me. I sigh. "It fucking hurts. Like a bitch. I'm already sweating bullets."

"In that case," she says. She pops open the bottle and hands me one of the pills. "Have some tramadol."

"Aren't you supposed to give a prescription before you go around handing out controlled substances?" I say. I don't even bother to get a glass for water. I pop the pill in my mouth and go to the sink to scoop a handful of water and gulp it down.

"There's a lot of things I'm supposed to do," she says. "like reporting a gunshot wound."

"Point taken," I say.

"Coffee?" She gestures to the coffee maker.

"No, thanks," I say. "I need to be going. Can you snag one of Seth's shirts for me?"

"Sure." She disappears down the hallway and comes back with a plain gray T-shirt. "I'll help you get it on."

"No, that's okay," I say, hastily. I draw the line at letting other people help me get dressed. That's just too ridiculous. It's only a bullet wound.

"Suit yourself," she says, and the sadistic gleam in her eye is back.

I manage to get the sling off without much pain, but when I try to raise my arms to get the shirt over my head I have to stop because it hurts so fucking bad. I grit my teeth to prevent a whine from escaping me, and I try again. I'm not just sweating bullets, I'm *shotgunning* bullets now.

"Jesus Christ," she says. "Don't be such a baby, just let me help you."

And I grudgingly allow her, comfortable in the knowledge that I didn't *ask* for help, she *made* me accept it.

We get the T-shirt over my head, and the sling back on, and I'm only slightly worse for wear.

"On that note," I say, "I'm out of here."

"Leave Seth your bike keys," she says.

"Wha—" I stop on my way to the door. Oh my God. I didn't think about the fact that I can't ride my bike with my arm in a sling. This is fucking horrifying. Talk about clipping a man's wings. This is more humiliating than Seth's fiancée having to help me get dressed. This is worse than the actual getting shot part. What the fuck am I going to do? You can't be a self-respected member of a bike club if you can't *ride your goddamn bike*.

"Wear the sling for the rest of the week," Holly says. "After that, we'll see. But you just remember, buddy, if you don't let it rest and heal properly, it's going to take even longer to get you back up on two wheels."

"God*dammit*," I say. I want to kick something, but I don't. That probably wouldn't be polite. "Fucking goddammit." I fish my keys out of my pocket and finagle the bike key off my key ring. I slap it down on the counter, letting out a big sigh. "Thanks for the arm—and the sling and stuff."

"Take these," she says, holding out the bottle of tramadol. I slip them into my pocket.

"Thanks," I say. "Tell Seth I said bye. And tell him the bike is in the loading zone so he's gotta move it soon. And tell him if there's one scratch on my baby, he's going to get it."

"With your one good arm?" she says.

I narrow my eyes at her again and head out the door. I can hear her chuckling behind me. Are all doctors sadists?

I call Kyle on my way over to the Clubhouse.

"They fucking *shot* you?" he says. "What do you mean they *shot* you?"

"I mean I'm carrying the fucking bullet in my pocket that they plugged into my arm," I say. "My arm is in a goddamn sling."

"Jesus *Christ*," he says. "The cops came in and interviewed everyone, and I didn't say shit about you. The bartender told them I had a friend with me who left after the other guys, so I told them you had to get going. I thought you went to the Clubhouse. I didn't think you were outside *getting shot*."

"I was going to go to the Clubhouse," I say. "but I took a detour."

"I can't believe this," he says. "What if they arrest you?"

"I mean, they could," I say. "I might have left DNA at the scene. Probably did. It could be a matter of time before they come looking for me. But then again, I don't think I have DNA in the national database or whatever. I don't know, I'm not an expert in forensics or whatever. I just watch the shows sometimes."

"Okay well, I hope I don't have to hire someone new," Kyle says. "I was just getting you trained up right."

"Don't say was, boss," I say. "I always land on my feet. This will all pan out."

"I sure hope so. You should probably take a few days off while your arm gets better. Lay low for a while."

And then the call ends. Kyle isn't one for basic niceties, and he never says goodbye on the phone.

I feel bad for worrying him. He's a good guy.

Well, since I'm in recovery, and it's not like a I can do fuck all with my arm in a sling, I might as well have a Bloody Mary. I don't think I'm supposed to drink when I've taken tramadol, so I guess I'll just have a virgin one. That's fine with me, because I'm just starting to feel the tramadol. I'm craving the salty, spicy tomato goodness that I associate with breakfast. On my way to the Clubhouse, I plan out my story for my arm injury. I hurt it at work, that sounds like the best solution. I fell and hit my shoulder on a corner. It sounds like stupid shit. But it's such a lame way to injure myself that no one will even question it.

It's the weekend and it's just late enough that I'm sure there's someone at the Clubhouse bar. I let myself in, grateful for the air conditioning. It's amazing how hot it can get by lunch time in Arizona.

Nick is sitting at the bar. His back is to me, but I hesitate. I go over my story one more time in my head. But I have this secret fear that he's telepathic and going to know something. I'm being paranoid, but Nick has always made me nervous under the best of conditions. Now that I have something to hide, it's that feeling on steroids.

"Morning," I say, telling myself, *keep it casual, Colt.*

Nick turns to look at me and raises his eyebrows in a not-unpleasant look of surprise. "Oh, Colt," he says. "I would say good morning, but it doesn't look like it's gone that way for you."

"Oh," I say, looking down at my arm nestled in its sling. "Yeah, it sucks."

"What'd you do?" he asks.

"Tripped at work," I say. And it's even more lame out loud than it was in my head. "All that machinery, you know. Caught it on a sharp corner."

"Talk about bad luck," he says. "Well, I guess you should come have a drink." I can see he's already well into a Bloody Mary himself.

"That sounds like the right idea." I approach the bar and sit one chair over from him, what I consider a respectful distance. No need to crowd people at the bar when there's so much room.

I look up at the man behind the bar and realize with surprise that it's not Matt, Wildfire's younger brother. I've gotten so used to seeing him here. This is a man I've never seen before. He's tall, Hispanic, and I'm comfortable admitting when another man is handsome.

"Colt," Nick says, holding his hand out to indicate the man behind the bar, "this is Constantine. He's hanging out with us for a while."

"Nice to meet you" I'm intrigued, but I don't want to pry. Is Nick going to nominate him? That would surprise me mightily, considering the rumors I've heard about how he nominated the guy they called Phantom against his better judgement, then Phantom stabbed him in the back and ran off with his daughter. They killed Nick's son. I shake my head, wondering how shitty that must feel.

Constantine nods to me.

"Bloody Mary," I say. "Just a whisper of vodka, I'm on painkillers. And it's too early to get *that* fucked up." He doesn't laugh at my joke.

He makes me my drink with a speedy efficiency that says he's very used to this, puts it in front of me on a cocktail napkin, and then goes back to wiping stuff down behind the bar without a word. He doesn't offer any conversation, and he seems like he wants to be left alone, so I don't pester him.

"You seen this?" Nick asks, nodding to the TV. I follow his line of sight, and my heart stops beating for a minute.

The headline reads "Shooting At Local Bar."

"No," I say. "Can't say I have." I'm sweating again, and this time it has absolutely nothing to do with the pain in my arm.

A mugshot of Johnny comes up on the screen. Nick picks up the remote control and turns the volume up.

"—was discovered behind the dumpster last night, brutally beaten and shot to death. The police are looking into it. At this time they suspect robbery may have been the motive—"

"Robbery?" I say out loud. And then immediately wished I hadn't said anything at all. But really, how fucking absurd. They can't honestly think that. Nothing about anything that happened last night would indicate that this was a good, old-fashioned *robbery*. As my grandma used to say, *poppycock*. The sheriff's department can't be that stupid, can they?

"That guy," Nick says, pointing at the TV, "founded a gang out of Tucson called *Los Brujos*."

"He did?" I say. And though now it seems obvious that everything is connected by that fact, I still would have felt equally surprised if Nick told me that Johnny was Jesus Christ.

"Oh yeah," says Nick.

"He's been a fugitive from the law for over ten years," the news anchor is saying. "And was convicted on multiple occasions for trafficking, possession, assault, and was implicated in the 2013 murder of Reynato Hernandez Jr. but was never convicted."

"Jesus," I say. It's hard for me not to laugh just because Johnny seemed like such a chill guy. Turns out he was a pretty busy boy for most of his life.

"Weird they're not mentioning his affiliation with *Los Brujos*," Nick says. He's frowning at the television.

"That *is* weird," I say. And it is. This was so clearly what the media likes to call "gang violence" and they've been really eager to shove the Knights under that umbrella, but when someone is actually murdered in a shootout behind the bar, it's probably a *robbery*? I want to say this to Nick, but that would mean admitting that I was there and that I know what happened. So I just stew on it on my own.

"The thing about this guy," says Nick, "is the word through the grapevine that he robbed *Los Brujos* blind and vanished a little over a year ago. I'm sure they've been looking for him ever since. And it's pretty suspicious to me that he's found shot to death behind a dumpster." Nick snorts.

"What did he steal?" I ask. "Money?"

"Actually, word has it they did this big heist," says Nick. "Gold bricks and kilos of cocaine the FBI confiscated from the cartel in Texas. And after the heist, he took off with the goods and let some of the other guys take the fall for the robbery."

"Jesus Christ," I say. "That sounds like some Hollywood shit."

"Truth is stranger than fiction," says Nick. "That's how the saying goes, anyway. My point is that I think there's more going on here that they're keeping under wraps. There might be too many fingers in this particular pie to make the information public. So they say it's a robbery."

"Hey," says a voice behind us. It's Bullet. I give him a nod, Nick raises his hand in greeting. Bullseye follows him in. They both settle in on the other side of Nick.

"How's it going?" Bullseye nods at Constantine. "Bloody Maria, thanks."

"Make that two," says Bullet. "Thanks."

"What are you guys watching?" Bullseye asks.

"Bullshit news report," Nick grumbles. "They found *El Senor* of *Los Brujos* shot to death behind a dumpster and they're calling it a robbery."

"Huh," says Bullet, frowning.

"Bricks of gold," I say, still stuck on this particular detail. "I forgot that's a real thing."

"Sure is," says Nick. "And I'm sure these guys came looking for more than revenge."

"You think he still has all that gold laying around somewhere?" I ask, eyebrows raised.

"Gold is a pretty hard thing to move when you come down it," Bullet says. "You have to have the right connections. You have to have a buyer. And if you're on the run like this guy, you're going to have to sit on it for some time and move it bit by bit to avoid drawing attention to yourself from either the feds or the guys you fucked over."

"Now the cocaine," says Nick, "that's probably long gone." And he has himself a good little chuckle over his own joke.

I hear boots on the laminated concrete behind us and turn my head, expecting to see Wildfire, or maybe Bucky. The other guys turn with me and we all freeze at once. Out of the corner of my eye, I can see Constantine has stopped polishing a glass mid-wipe.

"Morning, gentlemen," says the sheriff's deputy advancing toward us. She's half the height of any other sheriff's deputy I've ever met, and I realize once I get over the unpleasant shock of the uniform. She's almost pretty under all that police woman veneer. My heart is going full throttle in my chest, and I don't dare myself to move or speak, even to swallow.

"Morning, Officer," Nick says in a carefully pleasant voice. "How can we help you?"

"Are you members of the motorcycle club called the Steel Knights?" she asks, looking from face-to-face. She stands a safe distance from us, hand casually resting on her belt. She's trying not to look ready for a fight, but she is, her gun in easy reach if she needs it.

"Most of us," Nick says, inclining his head. "I'm Nick, I'm the president of the club."

"I'm Deputy Wilson," she says, "I'd like to ask you a few questions."

"Sure," says Nick. I am in awe of his relaxed demeanor. I mean, I've heard rumors of his run-ins with the law, and I have to assume that you can only have so many encounters with the fuzz before it just doesn't faze you anymore. And Deputy Wilson, for her part, I'm also impressed. She came here alone, and she is also unfazed. That super aggressive attitude I've come to associate with female cops and dread when encountering them is nowhere to be found. She's not trying to overcompensate for anything—her gender or her height, and I can respect that.

"I see you're keeping up with the news," she says, glancing at the TV.

"As any concerned citizen does," Nick says. And I have to bite down a laugh.

"You know anything about what happened last night?" she asks.

"Just what the lovely news anchor has told me," Nick says. "Some kind of robbery at Mike's."

"There was another brawl," says Deputy Wilson. "At the Hoppa Taphouse a few days ago.

You gentlemen were involved, along with another motorcycle club in the area."

"Just a little fun after a few too many drinks," Nick says. "No harm, no foul."

"And you wouldn't happen to know anything about the shooting last night," Deputy Wilson asks again. "That involved the founder of another motorcycle club."

"Not a thing," says Nick. "I had no idea he was in town."

"Well," says Deputy Wilson. She pulls a card from the breast pocket of her hideous tan uniform and walks to Nick, holding it out to him. "If you happen to remember something, don't hesitate to call." She nods to us and exits as silently as she came, with long confident strides.

We all sit in silence, staring at the doorway that she just vanished through. My heart is still pounding, and I cannot believe my incredibly good fortune. I really thought for a solid minute that I was going to be walked out of here in handcuffs.

"I'm thinking the good Deputy Wilson doesn't think it's a robbery, either," I say.

"It would appear not," says Nick. He glances at the white card with the sheriff's department logo printed on it and puts it in the pocket of his shirt. "Not every day you get a visit from the sheriff's department. I feel honored." A deep crease has appeared between his eyebrows, and he's frowning now. "Another drink, Constantine?"

Without a word, Constantine glances toward the doorway where Deputy Wilson disappeared, and then he starts on another Bloody Mary.

"Make that two," I say, as I drain my glass. At least I'm not drinking alone.

Chapter Seven

Erica

I have to get out of the sun before I get heatstroke. I stagger to the shade on the side of the house, produced by a beautiful, striped awning that comes in and out at the push of a button.

I am covered in dirt, and I'm still parched even after I drain my water bottle, so I walk to the open French doors and call into the house, "Mom? Could you get me more water?"

My eyes aren't adjusted to the dimness of the house, so my mother seems to appear from nowhere, like a specter in white.

"I'm all dirty," I say, grinning apologetically. "Please?"

"I guess," she says, making a big show of crossing the room to get the bottle of water for me. "How's it going out there?"

"I'm roasting like a turkey." My skin is already darkening to a tawny color, even under the layer of sunscreen I've applied to keep the worst of the sun off. My shirt is sticking to my back with sweat, so I grab the front and pluck at it, generating a swirl of cool air against my damp skin.

"I'll make you something yummy for lunch," she says, walking back to me with the full water bottle.

"Where's Ted?" I ask in between gulps of water. I didn't notice him leave, probably because the driveway is on the other side of the house.

"He went to town for a bit," my mother says. "I hope he brings back ice cream."

"Text him and tell him it's essential that he does," I say. "Pistachio. Or *else*."

My mother laughs. "I'll quote you directly, or *else*."

I turn back to the sunken garden beds I'm digging. The popular choice for growing vegetables is a raised garden bed, but in the desert, it's imperative that the garden beds sit lower, or the plants won't have enough water to thrive in the hottest months. I've done landscaping, ornamentals and that kind of thing, but I've never attempted a vegetable garden this ambitious. I've been staying up late, reading books and blogs, trying to figure out my plan of attack. I only hope it's enough. I definitely don't want to put all of this work into this project, just to have it die off because I made a misstep.

Mother Mary, it's hot. I wipe my forehead with my forearm, but it doesn't do much but spread the sweat around a bit. My mother broke her back in a car accident a few years ago, so she isn't much good for physical labor. She gets to make the sandwiches though. So I'm hoping Ted comes back soon so I can put him to work helping me dig the beds. He's been working on building a chicken coop and, amateur carpenter that he is, it's starting to look like it's going to turn out pretty nice.

As if on cue, I hear the front door open and Ted calls, "Hello," into the house.

"Hiya," I say from outside. "Did you get ice cream?"

"Is the sky blue?" he says and walks to the kitchen with his brown grocery bags. "Might have melted into soup just on the ride over. The AC isn't working in the Forerunner. I'll have to take it in. Hope it just needs a recharge."

"Yikes," I say. I sure as hell wouldn't want to be driving around in this heat without AC. I'm surprised he didn't cook to death in the car on the way there and back. I take off my dirty boots and come into the house. The garden beds can wait until I've had some ice cream.

"Hello," my mother says, looking cool and relaxed in her white linen dress. She gives Ted a kiss on the cheek.

"Got some mail," he says, indicating a little pile on the counter.

My mother shuffles through it, frowning to herself while she tosses out junk mail. But there's one white envelope that makes her pause.

"Who could this be from?" she murmurs.

In my haste to ask about it, I gulp down my mouthful of ice cream and immediately regret it when my head is seized with a brain freeze. I press my palm to the spot between my eyes and say, "What is it?"

"There's no return address," she says. "It's addressed simply to *Peters*."

"What is it?" I moved in closer to look over her shoulder. I've recovered enough from the first bite of ice cream that I take another.

She pulls a piece of white printer paper out of the envelope and opens it. We both stare at the words, printed in a black font.

Reconsider. This is your final warning.

"Why?" my mother almost whines. "Why are they doing this?"

Ted looks over my mother's other shoulder. "Christ," he says. "I guess I'll place another call to the sheriff's department."

I take the piece of paper out of her hand and turn it over, looking for some sort of clue. We know who wrote it, but the mystery of their persistence goes unanswered. Why the hell did they want this place so badly?

"I'm going to shred it," my mother says. "I don't even want to look at this thing anymore. I'm going to have to sage the house again to get rid of this evil—"

"Therese," Ted says in his soothing voice. He puts his hands on her arms. "If we shred it, they can't evaluate it for evidence."

"I just don't understand," my mother says, putting her hands to her cheeks. "Why won't they just leave it be?"

"I'll call the sheriff's department," Ted says. "They'll sort the whole thing out."

I'm trying to decide if I'm going to paint my room. I'm standing in the doorway, trying to figure out how a sandy color would look in the natural light streaming in through the big, beautiful windows. On the one hand, painting is a pain in the ass. On the other hand, the sage green walls are giving me nineties-interior-decor flashback nightmares.

Maybe I'm starting to get cabin fever. I'm not bored, exactly. There's plenty to do. I just haven't been off the property in days. My mother is so busy working on house projects that she hasn't left either and, to tell the truth, I just feel nervous about leaving her here while these creeps are hanging over us like a nasty cloud. I wouldn't want to be left alone.

I've been having a harder time sleeping at night. I wake at every little sound. I think I hear footsteps outside, or even laughter. I see their faces in my dreams and I wake up, sweating and reminding myself that I'm alone in a cool, safe bedroom and that Ted and my mother are just down the hall.

My thoughts drift inevitably to Colt each time. He held me so fiercely while he slept that sometimes I wondered if he thought I would drift away or vanish if he didn't hang onto me. My heart hurts thinking of it, the raw need that would come into his eyes at his most vulnerable moments. It would probably kill him to know how open he becomes at times like that. I look around at the hideous sagebrush green paint, at my bed with the simple, white quilt neatly spread across it, and picture him in the room with me.

I close my eyes and imagine his warm breath against my neck, his body linked with mine after an afternoon of passionate lovemaking. How it would feel to lay with him in the cool silence of this house. How it would feel to sit on the porch with him under the misters and drink ice-cold tea and then walk out and show him the gardens. He'd probably offer to help. He was always offering to help me out with projects here and there.

I look down at my hands and sigh. Why do I keep doing this to myself? I *know* I'm never going to call him. I couldn't stand it, not after the things we said to each other. I have this habit of drifting into these reveries where I can linger for long, beautiful moments in fantasy and forget all about what happened—why we went our separate ways. But inevitably, nasty reality sets back in, and I have to remind myself that it's all torture to want and want and never have. Why couldn't I just get over him? And why does it hurt so much not to have him? We broke up because we just couldn't work out. Our lives are just too different. We're just too different.

I hear the crunch of gravel in the driveway and it snaps me back to the here and now. I startle like someone jumped around the corner and yelled *boo*. It must be Ted. He went to town again today, and this time he was fairly mysterious about his intentions.

I hear the front door open, and he calls into the house, "Come on out for a minute."

"What's going on?" my mother calls back. I turn and head down the hallway until I can see my mom standing in the kitchen, wiping her hands on a dish towel with furrowed brows. Ted has the door open enough to stick his head inside. Wouldn't want to let the precious cool air out.

"Just come on out." He smiles, though I can see he's trying not to. He turns his head and looks at me. "You too, Miss Erica."

"What are you up to?" I ask, though I obediently walk to the shoe stand and slip on my sneakers so I don't burn the bottom of my feet walking on the tiles outside. That had happened the second day we were staying here, and I don't know what on Earth I was thinking. I've only lived in Arizona most of my life.

My mother takes off her apron, and I stand and wait for her to join. Ted gestures to her impatiently. "Come on. Come on."

"You're holding up the train," I tell her. She reluctantly takes Ted's hand, and he leads her out into the bright day. I follow, closing the door firmly behind me to keep the heat from creeping inside. The difference between being in the cool house and the stifling heat outside is shocking, like walking into the jaws of an oven.

"What is it?" Mom asks, blinking in the brightness. My eyes are having trouble adjusting too, and I look around to see what could possibly be so exciting. I can see a dark shape in the passenger side of the truck. It begins to move and I realize—

"A dog?" Mom says, sounding more confused than anything.

"Dogs," Ted says. He opens the door to the truck and we both peer inside. Sure enough, there's a second dog seated on the floor of the passenger side of the truck, below the first dog. They're both handsome beasts and look like they're at least a pit bull mix.

"Dogs?" Mom repeats. She tentatively puts her hand out and I loop my arm through the open window of the open driver's door to do the same. The dogs come toward us, sniffing at our hands with uncertainty.

"Guard dogs," Ted says, sounding as proud of himself as a kid who won the spelling bee.

"Guard dogs," my mother says slowly.

"Are you a parrot now?" I ask her.

"No," she says, "I just didn't—well, they're very cute," she concedes. She seems to be warming to the idea quickly. This probably has something to do with the fact that they've both moved forward and are licking her hand. They look like very cheery doggies.

"Leta and Hector," Ted says, gesturing to each respective dog. "Very good dogs." They both look at him when they hear their names. "They're a bonded pair, I had to take both. I thought they would make you feel better."

"Well," my mother says, smiling with her arm around Leta, the beautiful brindle. "They do."

"You said you wanted to get a dog when we got here," Ted says. "I thought I'd surprise you."

A risky surprise, if you ask me, but one that turned out very well. Anyone can see they're very friendly, well-behaved dogs. "Where'd you find them?" I ask.

"Humane Society," Ted says.

"Well then," my mother says to the dogs, "come on inside. We might as well feed you some lunch if you're going to be staying for a while."

Maybe it's the word "lunch" but they follow her like troops marching after their general into battle. I can hear her chatting to them as they walk, but I can't make out what she's saying. They run circles around her, joyful and energetic, as she leads them into the house and shuts the door behind her.

"Guard dogs?" I say to Ted, who walks around the back of the truck and begins to unload a big bag of food, dog bowls, and a bag of toys from Petco.

"I think we all might feel a little better with a little extra help around the house," he says. "After..."

After the chicken incident, he means. Yesterday, on his way out the door to make a trip into town, Ted tripped over three of our chickens, laid out on the front steps. They were decapitated and their intestines were smeared all over the place. The words "You're next" were written on the tile above the mutilated bodies. Like something from a Stephen King novel.

"Holy shit," was what my mother and I heard from the kitchen, still in our bathrobes, drinking our coffee. We rushed to the door and Ted tried to close it on us, saying, "Don't worry about it. Don't worry about it, it's nothing."

But my mother got a hold of the door and yanked it open and let out a bloodcurdling scream. It took us nearly an hour to calm down. I was so worried about getting her to calm down that I didn't even realize how freaked out I was until later.

Ted picks up the dog food and slings the bag over his shoulder. "I don't know what those idiots at the sheriff's department are doing," he says. He shakes his head. "I don't know what to do if they won't help us."

I think of Colt again, but I push that thought away with a vehement. *I don't think so.*

"What did they say?" I ask. Ted took photos of the chickens before scraping the poor things off of the porch and spraying the whole thing down until the water ran clear. Then he said he would call the sheriff's department a third time. I haven't had a chance to ask him about it.

"Kids, they said," he says, shaking his head again. "Stupid pranks. I mean, really?"

"Unbelievable," I say. I feel cold suddenly, even in the heat, and hug myself. "I don't understand that."

"Neither do I," he says. He lowers his voice as I follow him inside. "I bought a gun too. Don't tell your mother, I don't want to make her feel more worked up than she already is. But I'll take you out and show you how to use it soon. I normally don't give in to this sort of thing, but..." He readjusts the bag of dog food on his shoulder, trying to find his words. "This is getting out of hand and apparently the cavalry is *not* coming."

I swallow hard and turn, feeling my hair stand up as if someone might be right behind me. There's no one, of course, but I sweep the horizon with my eyes, searching for any sign of movement. There's nothing. For now, anyway.

The dogs wake me in the night. I sit up, heart slamming in my chest, and I'm shaking so hard that I have a hard time getting a hold on the comforter. They aren't just barking, they're snarling. They're out front of the house, must have let themselves out with the new doggie door.

I can hear my mother's voice down the hall, high and frightened; and Ted's voice, trying to be soothing. But I can hear a note of... not panic, but definitely concern.

I untangle myself from my bed and go to my window, reluctantly peering out into the night. I'm frightened of what I might see, but I see nothing. The moon is high and bright, but nothing stirs on this side of the house. I stumble to my door and open it. Ted is in the hallway with my mother behind him and he's holding a pistol in his hand, pointing down and away from my mother, who has him by the other arm.

The barking is getting farther away. I realize, with a yank in my stomach, that I can only hear one of them.

"Don't go out there, please," she begs him. "Please, just call the Sheriff."

But Ted managed to pry her off him with a gentle firmness that impresses me, considering how stressful the situation is. He goes to the front window and carefully peers through the curtains.

"Do you see anything?" she asks impatiently. I go to her and put my arm around her shoulders. She's shaking inside her bathrobe.

"No," Ted says in a hoarse voice. "I can't see Leta or Hector either."

"Oh no." Mom covers her mouth with a hand.

Ted goes to the front door.

"Oh don't," She says.

But Ted opens the door anyway, the pistol held carefully at his side. He moves out of my line of sight, but I can see his shadow on the floor of the foyer, cast by the bright light of the moon. I can see him bring the pistol up.

My mother and I stand there, clutching at each other while we wait a minute that seems to last an eternity.

Then we hear Ted say, "Oh God. Oh Jesus."

We both creep toward the door.

"What happened?" I say. We stop a couple of paces away from the door.

"Bring me some towels," Ted says. "And the truck keys, hurry."

My mother hurries off to get the towels and I close the gap between myself and the door. I step cautiously outside on the tile and look around. I can see Ted crouched on the ground, nearly around the corner of the house. He's talking in a soft voice. And as I move toward him, I can hear a soft whining.

My stomach clenches. I move faster until I can see Leta. She's laid out on the ground and I can see a black pool beneath her.

"Oh my god," I say. "What happened? Where's Hector?" I turn in circles, searching the moonlit grounds, but I see nothing. I hear nothing.

"I don't know," Ted says as my mother comes out of the house with the towels, the keys, and a pair of Ted's sneakers, "but I need to get her to the emergency vet."

"I'll call the sheriff," I say. And I stumble back to my room. It takes me an eternity to rifle through my bedspread and find my cell phone. I somehow manage to dial 911.

"Nine-one-one, what is your emergency?" says the operator.

"Someone attacked one of our dogs," I say. "It's—this isn't the first time—someone's been making threats against us." I realize I'm probably not making sense. So I try a bit harder to collect my thoughts. "We've filed a few reports. These people have been threatening us, and now they've attacked one of our dogs."

"Okay," the woman said calmly, "tell me what happened."

"They woke us up barking," I say. "And they were snarling. One of them is gone, the other one is hurt. I don't know what they did, I don't know if they stabbed her, or what, but she's bleeding out."

"Are there any signs of intruders on your property?" the woman asks.

"I don't know," I say. "We just woke up when we heard the dogs and went out there and she's hurt. We don't know what happened."

"Is there any sign it could have been an animal attack?" the woman asks.

"I don't—" I hadn't considered this. But I lick my lips and say, "I don't know. It could have been, but we've been having these problems with threatening letters, they've killed some of our chickens. Please, can you just send somebody?"

"I understand, ma'am," the operator says. "One of our deputies will be out there as soon as they're able."

"Thank you," I say.

"In the meantime," the operator says, "I want you to be sure that all of your doors and windows are locked. Do you have someone there with you?"

"My mom and her boyfriend," I say. "Well, her boyfriend is taking the dog to the emergency vet. My mom is here."

"Please lock your doors," the operator says. "They'll be there shortly. Would you like me to stay on the line with you until they arrive?"

"No," I say. "No, that won't be necessary."

"Okay," says the operator. "Call us back if anything else occurs."

"Okay, thank you." I hang up and go back out to the living room. The door is still ajar. I can see my mother outside helping Ted load Leta into the truck. The white towels are black with her blood and I realize that, in my shock, it still hasn't occurred to me that she might die. The thought moves through my mind like a thunderclap and my throat suddenly feels very tight.

Those fucking *assholes*. Why the dogs? What kind of fucking monsters hurts dogs?

Chapter Eight

Erica

"Walk me through this again," Deputy Round says. He's a round-faced, jolly-looking man who by all rights looks like he should be selling crescent rolls or old-fashioned candies. But instead, here he is, being a fucking dick to me and my mother. He has a drawl that sounds like he might hail from Texas and a lazy, condescending way of talking that makes me want to smack him over his stupid head.

"The dogs started barking," I say. "They went outside through the doggie door, I assume, because the doors were all closed and locked. They were snarling and it sounded like there was a scuffle of some kind. Ted went outside and found Leta on the ground, bleeding all over the place. He took her to the vet, we still don't know what happened to her. Hector was gone. I don't know if he ran away or if they chased him—or took him, or what."

"You keep saying 'they'," says Deputy Round with a frown.

"I'm assuming it's those guys," I say. "The biker guys, *Los Brujos*, the ones who have been threatening us."

"And you said you've filed reports about that," says Deputy Round. "But fill me in. The quick version," he adds, like he already thinks it's a waste of his time.

"These three guys showed up here after we bought the house and asked us to name a price, they wanted to buy it on the spot in cash," I say. "We said no and they got very pushy. They said we'd hear from them. And then we started getting these anonymous letters. Last week, they mutilated our chickens and left them all over our porch."

Deputy Round laughed. It was a mean laugh, and it made me cold with anger. "Okay," he says. "I'm hearing two different things. Threatening letters is a whole different world than mutilating chickens and dogs. Now, it sounds to *me* like you want animal control out here. I'm happy to help you call them. But I just don't see the connection between letters and your animals being allowed to roam at night and being attacked. What it sounds to me is like you got a coyote problem, Miss, and that ain't our department."

"What do you mean it's two different things?" Mom says. "How can you possibly dismiss that as not being connected?"

"Ma'am," he says, "I realize you just moved to these parts, but this is just how it is out here. You gotta keep your animals locked up, or the coyotes'll get them."

"I didn't *just move here*," my mother says. "I'm *from* here. I moved to California while my mother was in hospice and I just moved back."

"Well, then," the Deputy says, "it seems like you ought to have known better."

"Wha—" my mother starts to say.

But she's cut off by the other deputy, Deputy Wilson. She's small, shorter than me, and she's been almost silent since they showed up. I have a feeling it's less because she's deferring to her partner than it is that she's just listening and putting things together.

"Were the chickens locked up?" she asks calmly.

"Yes," my mother says. "Of course they were. I *do* know the dangers of coyotes." She gives Deputy Round a nasty look.

"Do you think it's possible this could have been coyotes?" asks Deputy Wilson. There's nothing accusing or condescending in her tone. She sounds genuinely curious.

"Of course it could be," my mother says. "I'm not dismissing that as a possibility. But I think with everything else going on, it's worth looking at this from *that* angle."

"Do you know who these people are?" asks Deputy Wilson. "Did they give you any names?"

"No," I say. "But I saw them in a pub before they came here to the property. I think it was honestly a coincidence. But they were wearing their motorcycle club vests. They ride with a gang called *Los Brujos*."

I could swear I saw a look of surprise flash across Deputy Wilson's face. But it's gone so fast I could have dreamed it. "Los Brujos," repeats Deputy Wilson. But I can't tell at all what she's thinking. She probably should have gone into professional poker.

"Now," says Deputy Round. "I would suggest you keep your animals locked up at night. I am happy to send animal control out here, but other than that, I can't do much to help you. If you think of anything *else*, don't hesitate to call." He doesn't sound like he means it. He tips his hat to us. "Ladies." And then he turns and walks back toward their patrol car.

Deputy Wilson makes as if to follow him, but she stops and looks from me to my mother. "Be careful," she says. She pulls a card out of her pocket and hands it to my mother. "If you need anything, call *me*." I feel like she's trying to tell us something, but before I can open my mouth and ask about that, she turns and walks quickly to the patrol car.

Deputy Round reverses and peels out like the hounds of hell are on his heels. My mother and I are left shivering in the hot night.

"No one is going to help us," my mother says, sort of like she's in shock.

I realize with a jolt in my stomach that there's only one person left to turn to. I stare at the black stain on the ground that is Leta's blood.

The Steel Knights are literally our last hope.

I don't know if I have ever had a worse night of sleep. I'm awake every five minutes it seems, jumping at every small noise. I'm in bed with my mother, who I'm sure is just as sleepless as I am. When I give up and get out of bed at 6 AM, Ted still hasn't returned with Leta. But my mother gets up too, and reads me his text messages with bleary eyes.

"The vet says she thinks Leta was stabbed. But the surgery went okay and she'll live," she says in a hoarse voice.

We both look at each other and the silence is thick. I hug myself and feel frozen on the inside while I think about how much worse things could have been last night. But Hector...

I walk to the front door and open it slowly, afraid of what I might find. But there's nothing, just the cool, dawn light, the terracotta tiles, and the empty spot in the driveway where Ted's truck is normally parked.

"Hector," I call. "Come here, boy." I whistle and call and cajole for a good ten minutes, but he doesn't come. I go back inside, pulling my robe around me, feeling cold despite the warmth of the early morning.

"No sign of him?" Mom asks. She's making coffee, but her hands are shaking so badly that she spills grounds on the counter.

"No," I say.

"I don't know what to do," she says. "I don't want to be bullied into giving up my house, but this is getting out of hand. What the *hell* do they want with it so bad?"

I shake my head and pull my phone out of my pocket, as if I'm expecting a call. I'm not, of course, but I have been fighting with myself about what I've known I needed to do since last night. I was so upset that I almost called him after the deputies left. But I stopped myself. What if he didn't pick up? What if he did? I've gone back and forth about it, and while I stand here and watch my mother try to hold herself together, I know that this is bigger than me and my feelings about Colt. I need to suck it up, be brave, and ask for the help we need. But I still can't make myself pick up the phone and call. It's too personal. Too many things that can be said, or go unsaid.

No, I'm going to do the only thing crazier than calling him. I'm going to go to the Clubhouse. I don't know why, but this is the less scary version of settling this matter.

So I drink coffee with my mother and scrub the kitchen floor to keep myself busy, then I shower and work on looking like I'm not *trying* to look cute, while definitely trying to look cute. It's a very tricky thing to get right, as any woman knows, but I've spent a good hour and a half on my effortless look by the time I hear the crunch of Ted's tires in the driveway. This is by far the most time I have spent on getting ready in my living memory and I'm still feeling anxious about the way I look as I head toward the door. My phone tells me it's nearly 1 PM, which works out nicely. I've been sickeningly impatient all morning, pacing around the house and re-braiding my hair for the ten thousandth time, while we waited for Ted to come home. To see how Leta is doing, of course, but also because I really want to get on the road before I lose my nerve. But I didn't dare leave my mother in the house alone now.

We both meet Ted at the door and stand back while he brings Leta into the house, holding her as tenderly as a baby. She's limp in his arms, unconscious and snoring.

"Doc says she needs to rest for a few days," Ted says, his voice trailing off. My mother follows him to their bedroom and I can't hear what they're saying, but I'll ask for the updates later. With shaking hands, I pull on my sandals and grab my keys and purse.

"I'm going into town for a bit," I call to the back of the house. "Let me know if you need anything while I'm there."

I make sure to lock the door behind me.

The road to town has never seemed so long. I have the radio on, Goo Goo Dolls are playing in the background, and I can't stop drumming my fingers on the steering wheel. There's a jerking feeling in my stomach like I'm falling every time I think about exactly what it is that I'm doing.

I keep glancing in the rearview mirror, half expecting to see bikes on the long stretch of highway behind me, but there's nothing but the reflection of light off a truck's windshield many yards back.

When I get to the Clubhouse, I slow my car to a crawl, grateful there's no one behind me so I can take a minute to totally flip out about what's happening. I can see a number of bikes parked out front, but I'm not sure if any of them are Colt's. I steer my car into a parking spot and just sit there for a moment, air conditioning running, heart racing.

I stare at the plants that I carefully selected and planted. My heart warms for a moment, and I feel a sort of relief that they're still here, that the Knights didn't go and rip them all out after me and Colt broke up. I can see him in my mind, in the sunlight without his shirt on. Sweating, laughing, and wiping his forehead with his wrist. He never looked more beautiful. My heart hurts, and I squeeze my eyes shut. I cover my face with my hands, reminding myself that it's best to stop thinking about any of that while I do what I came to do.

I think of my mother's white face, Leta limp in Ted's arms, and then the silence across the empty land after I called Hector's name. I turn the car off and get out.

I immediately start sweating, and I'm not sure if it's the heat or my nerves. Probably both.

I don't think anymore, I just walk. It's technically private unless they invite people in, but they leave the door unlocked. I open it with a shaking hand and step inside, at once grateful to be in the air conditioning again and also totally mortified. There's no one in the little foyer area. It's just the way I remember, very masculine and spare. Glossed dark gray concrete and chrome. The furniture is black leather, go figure.

I realize I didn't really think past this point. I guess I just sort of thought I'd walk in and there would be someone here.

Then, as if someone read my thoughts, I hear the fall of heavy boots on the ground on the open second level and it echoes through the whole foyer. Impossibly loud to my keyed up nerves. I look up at the railing, feeling my blood pressure rise and my heart pound. I'm pretty sure I might faint. But the face that appears above the rails is not who I had hoped. Instead, it's his brother.

"Erica," he says. He looks slightly surprised, but not put out by the fact that I'm standing in the Clubhouse.

"Hi," I say—more like croak.

"How's it going?" he asks as he walks along the railing to the stairs and begins to descend with slow, careful movements.

"It's going fine," I say. My eyes keep darting up to the railing where Seth first appeared. I can't stop thinking Colt will show up any second, too. "I mean—I mean, it's not. That's why I'm here."

Seth cocks his head to the side and gives me a quizzical look. "You all right? What's going on?"

I just blabber the whole thing in the most jumbled, crazy mess of information. I'm sure he can hardly keep the story straight.

"And last night they tried to kill the dogs," I say. "I don't know, we can't find Hector, maybe they *did* kill him. They stabbed Leta, she had to go to the vet—" I stop for a breath and realize he's actually a very good listener, that he's been watching me with grave attention. I exhale, long and slow. "The point is, the sheriff's department isn't doing anything. And they probably *won't* do anything until—until it's too late."

Seth doesn't ask what "too late" means.

"We can pay you," I say. "We just don't know who else to turn to."

He just nods slowly and says, "Well, this isn't my decision to make. It's Nick's decision. But I'll put it to him and see what he says."

I nod, though I can't help but feel disappointed. What was I expecting? For them to leap to my aid? What Seth is saying makes sense, but it's hard to hear that there's protocol and stuff to be followed. Hoops to jump through, which means there's potential for things not to go in our favor.

"Is there anything else?" he asks. And I can't help but feel that there's a definite meaning to his words. I blush and shake my head. Seth hasn't offered to alert Colt to the fact that I'm here, and I cannot possibly bring myself to ask him. It's actually a pretty mortifying moment.

"No," I say. "No, thank you." I pull a receipt and a pen out of my purse and write my phone number on the back. He could, I guess, just get the number from Colt, but I don't even want to bring him up. And for all I know, Colt has deleted my phone number. "If you can, call me when you've decided if you can help?"

"Will do," he says. "It was nice to see you." He takes the receipt from me and slips it into his pocket. I can't read his expression.

"Thanks," I say. "Well, bye." I turn quickly and leave without looking back. My heart is beating hard in my chest to the rhythm of *ohmygod ohmygod ohmygod*. I have been trying not to think about the fact that Colt probably told Seth the things that I said about him, but it breaks over me like a wave, and I am so embarrassed when I get to my car that I am immobilized. I just sit in the driver's seat and stare at the aloe planted in front of my car.

What the hell was I thinking?

I shake my head and slowly pull out of the parking lot, and I try to ignore the sad, heavy feeling in my stomach.

I guess I was really hoping I would see Colt.

Chapter Nine

Shotgun

"Fucking bastard," I say to the dishwasher. I'm crouched behind the bar at the Clubhouse with Constantine, and the piece of shit is refusing to cooperate. Both of us have soaked jeans from kneeling in the water. We've given up trying to mop it up, though wearing wet jeans is probably the only thing more comfortable than walking on tacks. He isn't a mechanic, and I only have one good arm, so between the two of us we're trying to get the thing working again.

"Normally there would be a service tech on leased equipment in a bar," Constantine told me when we started. "But this thing was bought secondhand. No service contract."

"Lucky us," I replied.

I hear footsteps, but I don't look up from what I'm doing. Constantine stands up beside me and says, "Heya."

"Kid brother," Seth says to me over the bar.

I look up at him. "Yeah? Kinda busy."

"Almost as busy as a one-armed man in an ass-kicking contest," Seth says. "But dishwashers aren't quite as taxing."

"Very funny," I say and scowl at him. "What's up?"

He glances at Constantine and says, "Let's take a little walk."

I glance at Constantine too and then back at my brother. I raise my eyebrow at him, but decide it's best not to argue. Is it me he's giving privacy to or Constantine?

"I'll be back," I say to Constantine, I wipe my hand on the white bar towel hanging from my pocket and loop around the bar. I follow my brother out onto the landing and say again, "What's up?"

"A little bird just came by to ask for some help," he says. He holds a small piece of paper out to me and I take it from him, rubbing it between my fingers to open it with my one good hand. My heart gives a hard *thunk*, and my throat is immediately dry.

"M—Erica?" I say. I almost say *my* Erica, but I bite my tongue so hard I'm surprised that it doesn't bleed. I have too many questions. "When? Why? What happened?"

"Just now," he says, cocking his thumb toward the door. "It's a long story, but those *Los Brujos* thugs are giving her some trouble too, and the cops aren't doing shit about it. Talk about a coincidence, huh?"

"What do you mean trouble?" My blood starts to simmer. I crumble the piece of paper in my hand. Those fucking bastards. It's one thing to shoot *me*, but what fucking business do they have bullying a harmless, lovely creature like Erica? "What have they done to her?"

"It's a long story," he says. "I didn't even get all of it. But I'm sure she'll be happy to tell you herself. The thing is that she came by here to ask if she could hire us to deal with this problem. I told her I couldn't make the call, that Nick has to make the call. Especially because this means warfare with another MC. But I didn't want to bring it to him until I cleared this with you."

"With me?" I say.

"I mean," Seth says, "you have history with her. And as much as Holly and I have encouraged you to reach out to her, you've shown no interest in re-establishing ties. I didn't want to bring it to Nick until I knew that you're okay with us getting mixed up in her business." He pauses. "It sounds like pretty bad business, so I vote yes."

"Why didn't you tell me she was here?" Now it's Seth that's making me angry, but he is unmoved by this. Still cool as a cucumber.

"Didn't want to put you on the spot, I guess," says Seth.

"When did she leave?" I look past his shoulder at the door, as if she might still be standing there.

"Just a couple of minutes—" he was saying, but I'm past him, taking the stairs two at a time.

"Where are you going, Romeo?" Seth calls from the second level, but I ignore him. I rip the sling off of my arm and throw it. "Holly's going to kill you," he adds. I give him a look as I reach the door. He looks too pleased with himself.

"She definitely will after I kill *you*," I tell him. And then I'm out the door. But I stop, surprised, when I recognize Erica's little Toyota getting ready to turn right out of the parking lot. I wave to her, but I guess she doesn't see me. I'm going to hope that's why she isn't acknowledging me.

I fumble in my pocket for my keys and have them in my hand before I get to my bike. I've had the stupid sling on for two weeks now at Holly's insistence, and I think I can get away with a few minutes without it. I swing my leg over and mount my bike. I have a moment of absolute bliss. I've missed the hell out of this thing. My arm is, admittedly, very sore and feeling pretty weak when I lift it to grip the handlebars, but I ignore that. I look over my shoulder at where Erica turned out of the parking lot, but there's no sign of her. Heart racing, I back out and rev the engine, getting ready to shoot after her like a blast from a shotgun. The sound of the engine roaring makes my blood tick up a whole lot of notches and I hit the gas. I stop briefly at the turn out to make sure I won't collide with any cars and then I turn right, just like she did.

My eyes are searching for that little Toyota, and I'm weaving around cars, hoping I don't get myself killed playing the hero.

My mind is fucking rioting while I ride. Why the hell didn't she call *me*? And I thought she had a whole lot against the Knights, but here she is, asking them for help instead of coming to me directly. That fucking stings, but I guess I can't complain about it entirely. At least she came here. And what was Seth thinking, not telling me she was there? After all of the nagging he and Holly have done to get me to call her. Now I have to chase her down like a fox after a rabbit. I have to admit this is a bit fun, though it would be a lot more fun if my arm didn't hurt like a bitch.

My heart gives a thump when I see a little Toyota with a decal sticker on the back window ahead of me. I'm not close enough yet to see the decal sticker, but I already know what it says: *Love Your Mother*, on a cutesy little planet Earth sticker. I used to give her a hell of a hard time about it, and she always took my teasing well and gave it back to me with twice the spice.

Jesus *Christ*, I miss her.

I'm so busy missing her, apparently, that I don't mind getting myself killed. The sound of a horn shocks me back into the present, and I see a car out of my peripheral vision swiping into my lane. I can't move over because there's a concrete barrier, so I brake and turn, praying that I don't flip my bike, and also that I don't clip the back end of the car coming at me.

Miraculously, neither occur. I look over at the car that almost hits me and I give the asshole driving my middle finger, which he returns like I'm the one who almost killed *him*. Whatever, I don't have time for this. I rev my engine again and take off.

I'm closing in on her and my heart is racing. I'm realizing that I didn't even think about what I was going to do when I finally caught up with her. All I know is that she was there, I missed her, and I wanted to see her. I feel kind of fucking foolish to be honest, but it doesn't even occur to me to stop what I'm doing now. I give my bike a little more gas and feel a big rush as I pull up alongside her. I glimpse her profile, the glimmer of her golden hair sitting on her shoulder, and my heart stops for a minute that lasts an eternity. Her head turns, and I see her hand snap up to push her shades up onto her head. Her eyes are wide as her head swivels back and forth between me and the road. I'm doing the same bobble-headed dance.

"Pull over," I shout, pointing to the shoulder ahead. "Pull over," I say again, for good measure because she cannot possibly hear me. She's going to have to read my lips.

She gets the message, I guess, because she slows and pulls her car off to the shoulder on the right. I pull in after her and slowly bring my bike to a halt about ten feet behind her. My hands are shaking as I kill the engine. Is it adrenaline or am I that nervous? How can *I* be that nervous? Over a woman? I'll never tell anyone on pain of death.

I realize my shoulder is aching as I climb off of my bike, but my adrenaline has subdued the pain to a mild, buzzing annoyance. I ignore it as I walk toward her car. She hasn't opened the door yet, and my heart is flipping and flopping, hitting the floor of my belly and the ceiling of my rib cage as I close the gap between us. I'm a few steps away when her car door slowly opens and I see one luscious leg, tanned golden from days in the sun slip out of the car, followed by the other. I keep my eyes fixed on them, drinking them down, filling myself up with the sight of her skin. One of her hands, and a forearm that I know is as soft as a petal, push the car door open even further. And then, in a moment that lasts an eternity, she leans out of the car and looks at me with those green eyes that have haunted my days and nights for months. She stays in the driver's seat, crossing her ankles. She gives me a small smile, just a quirk at the corner of her lips that I remember so well that it seems burned into my memory.

"Hi," she says. My God, I forgot how beautiful her voice is. Just that one word echoes through me like a golden note.

"Hey," I say. I put my hand on her door, instantly regretting it when a surge of pain shoots through my arm. I hope she doesn't notice me wince, that would kill my suave move.

She raises her eyebrows at me, looking too amused for my comfort. "Fancy meeting you here" She says it shyly, despite the look on her face, and it's almost enough to bring me to my knees.

"Heard you came by the Clubhouse," I say. "I missed you."

I realize the double entendre of what I just said, though I was referring specifically to missing her at the Clubhouse. But it's also true that I *missed* her, so I don't make any corrections to the statement.

Unless I'm mistaken, she's blushing under her tan. Her smile grows a bit. God, was she always this beautiful? Did I make myself forget so that it hurt less? Or has she just grown more beautiful since the last time I saw her? Mysteries of the universe.

"Um, yeah," she says. "I did... come by the Clubhouse."

I shake myself out of my head. "Right," I say. Some of the smoldering anger I felt earlier comes back into the pit of my stomach. "Seth said you have some dickheads giving you some trouble."

She nods and some of the light goes out of her eyes. I realize how tired she actually looks.

"A whole lot of trouble," she says. Are those tears sparkling in her eyes? She blinks hard and looks away before letting out a big breath.

"Tell me," I say.

"My mom bought this ranch," she starts. "And these people have been trying to intimidate us into selling it to them. I don't know why it's such a big deal, but they won't take no for an answer."

"My brother said they're another motorcycle club, *Los Brujos*?" I say. remembering the way the Sergeant at Arms sneered at me and wishing I could put my fist through his teeth.

"Yes," Erica says. "I don't know what they want with it. But they started threatening us. First it was letters in the mail, then they killed some of our chickens and left us a note that said, 'You're next.' And last night, they tried to kill the dogs."

"Christ," I say. Because I don't trust myself to say anything else. Rage is moving through me like caffeine, turning up the dials on everything in my system. I'm gritting my teeth so hard that my jaw is starting to ache. I don't want to scare Erica, so I don't move or say anything.

"The sheriff's department won't do anything," she adds. "I don't understand. They said it was a coyote that attacked the dogs and the chickens. They said the letters and the animal attacks are unrelated."

"*What?*" I mean, I already have beef with the sheriff's department after those dickheads arrested me for disturbing the peace, which was a massive pile of horseshit. But this is something else entirely. This is gross neglect.

"I don't understand it." Erica gets out of the car, slowly unfurling into the desert sun like an oasis. Her shoulders gleam in the afternoon light and I want to press my lips to each of them.

I fold my arms in case I can't resist the temptation to reach out and touch her. *Not yet*, I say to myself. *Not yet*.

"That's fucked up," I say. She covers her face with her hands and exhales long and slow.

"So I came to you guys," she says. "Because I don't know what else to do. No one will help us. And we shouldn't have to leave our home, there's no good reason for this. These people are dangerous and I think it's only a matter of time until something—something serious happens."

"As if dog murder and death threats aren't serious."

"My mom is really scared," she says. "I'm just really worried about her, I don't care about me as much, it's her I'm worried about."

She's blinking away tears, but this time she can't stop them. One of them escapes and slips down her cheek, more precious than all of the diamonds in the world. Her bottom lip is trembling. I forgot how pretty she is when she cries. My chest feels tight. I reach out and collect the falling tear with my forefinger. She looks up at me and I can't quite read her expression. Surprise? Relief?

I lick the tear off of my finger and smile at her. Then I reach for her, whispering, "Hey, no tears. Everything is going to be all right."

She reaches for me too, and her arms come around my rib cage while I loop mine around her shoulders. I press my lips to her temple and breathe in the scent of her hair. It smells just the way I remember it, a rich, sensual combination of jasmine and vanilla. She told me the name of the shampoo once, but I forgot.

I would never have described Erica as fragile, but right now she's as fragile as gossamer. Her hands grip my shirt, and I can feel her body shaking in my arms from her effort not to sob.

"I'll talk to the Knights," I say, stroking her hair. "We'll take care of everything."

"Thank you," she says. Her voice is muffled against my T-shirt, which is starting to feel wet from her tears, but I didn't mind one bit. "I'm sorry." She looks up at me. The redness of her eyes makes her irises look radiant and intensely green. "I'm sorry for everything. I'm so sorry. I missed you."

"I missed you, too," I tell her. I smile and, despite her tears, she smiles too.

I can't resist anymore. I lean in and press my lips against hers. I just meant to kiss her a little, just a taste, but it seizes me like a fever and I draw her tightly against me. Her lips open under mine and I caress her tongue with mine. Her arms are around my neck and mine wrap around her waist. I have her pressed against the car, pinned with my hips, and I have no idea how we got there. There's no way she *isn't* aware that I'm very happy to see her.

I pull away, breathing a bit heavily, and she's doing the same. Her cheeks are flushed and she's smiling just a little—a quirk of the lips that she tries to hide. Which makes me have to kiss her again. I pull away, feeling like I'm going to explode if I don't hit the brakes now, and I'm definitely not going to fuck her in her little Toyota on the side of the road, not after I've waited this long.

This boy can be patient. Sometimes.

"Okay," I gasp. "Okay. Uncle."

She giggles and presses her face into my neck.

"Let's get out of here so I can go talk to Nick," I say. I boop her lightly on the nose with my finger, which makes her laugh again. Then her face grows serious.

"Thanks," she says. "I mean it."

"Don't thank me," I say. And I just can't help but kiss her again.

Chapter Ten

Shotgun

Now that I actually have to ask him, I've never been more afraid of anything in my life. I think of all the brownie points I've worked hard to rack up and wonder how much they *really* count for when the cookie crumbles.

I really respect Nick. I am honored to be riding with the Knights, and I don't want to do anything to make him regret patching me in. I don't see how this could go wrong. Nick is a sensible guy. He's a caring person, even if he's a fucking hard ass. He takes care of his people. And I'm sort of one of his people. And Erica is sort of one of mine, so I think everything will work out. Not many people make me nervous. He may, in fact, be the only one. It's kind of embarrassing, like I'm a kid who wants to impress his dad or something. Guess I have my own set of daddy issues.

He's playing darts with Bullet and Bucky when I get to the Clubhouse. He's sitting back, elbow resting on the high-top pub stable he's sitting at, beer in hand while he watches Bucky miss the target wildly.

"Can't have everything," he shouts to Bucky. Rumor has it that Bucky has a fucking huge, ah, *package*, and what can you do but give a man a hard time about it?

"Heya," I say to Nick. "Mind if I join you?"

"Kid, you do whatever the hell you want," Nick says, amiably. "How's that shoulder of yours?"

"Oh, it's good, it's good," I say. It's back in the sling where it belongs and, from the way it's throbbing, I can tell I haven't done myself any favors today by galivanting off to save the damsel in distress on my trusty steed. I just hope Seth doesn't tattle to Holly. Nick may be the only person who makes me nervous, but Holly is the only person who scares me. With good reason.

"That's what I like to hear," he says. "What kinda MC member are you if you can't ride a bike?" He gives me a grin and for a minute I entirely forget why I even came in here. I feel like St. Peter has called me to the gates and told me it's almost time to come in. I can practically hear angelic singing, motorcycle engines throbbing in the background. Then I shake myself.

"More motivation than ever to get back on," I say. Then I clear my throat. "There was something I wanted to ask you about, Nick. If you don't mind."

"Sure, kid," he says. He turns to me, eyebrows raised. "You can ask. What's up?"

"There's a situation," I say. "You remember that girl, Erica? I was, ah, hanging out with her for a while. She did the landscaping for the Clubhouse?"

"Yeah," Nick said. "Sure, I remember her. Nice little gal. Haven't seen her around in a hot minute, so I take it you two aren't...?"

"Well, we haven't been," I say. "But she came by today. To the Clubhouse. Seems like she's having some trouble, and she asked for our help."

"Did she?" Nick takes a sip of his beer and puts it carefully back on the table. "And what kind of help did she ask for?"

"Her mother just bought this place," I say. "Just a little ways outside of town and this bike gang, *Los Brujos*, showed up from out of town. They want to buy the place and they're not taking no for an answer. They've resorted to death threats, and she said last night they tried to kill the dogs."

"Well, that's fucked up," Nick says. "Who the fuck kills a dog?" I happen to know Nick has three of his very own spoiled, precious pit bull babies so I can imagine this offends him on a particularly personal level. "It's one thing if you've got a beef with somebody, but leave the dogs out of it."

"Right you are," I say. "But things have been escalating and the sheriff's department isn't doing anything about it. Vet says the dog was stabbed. sheriff's department is insisting that coyotes attacked them. They're refusing to take the matter seriously."

"So," Nick says, "she wants us to get involved?"

"Well," I say, "yeah. They're offering to pay us, I don't know how much. I didn't want to get involved with that, the numbers thing is outside of my jurisdiction. But this matters to me a lot—*she* matters to me a lot, and it would mean a lot to me if this is something we could handle."

Nick stares off into space so long that I worry he's had a stroke and didn't hear a word I said. Then he begins to stroke his mustache. He's frowning to himself.

"Kid," he says. "I appreciate your position. I really do. But what it comes down to is the fact that this club is first and foremost my responsibility."

My heart is already sinking down into my stomach.

"And what that means," he continues, "is that I have to keep my people safe. *Los Brujos* are some mean motherfuckers. Ruthless, if you ask me. You remember the news story from the other day? We were just talking about these assholes. They hunted down ol' Johnny and shot him behind the dumpster over a year later."

Well, they threatened to cut bits off him before he shot himself to avoid the exciting fun of being tortured to death, but I don't mention that.

"My point is," Nick says, "if they're riding in, wearing their colors, and we ride out wearing our colors, this could bring down the hammer. And you do not, and I do not, want to tangle with those assholes. I mean, I've heard some sick shit about what they do to people they've got beef with."

I think he sees something in my face, because he changes direction. "What I would tell that sweet, little gal of yours, honestly, is to just give 'em what they want. It's not worth it." He shakes his head. "It is not worth it to tangle with those guys, Colt. And unless I'm mistaken, that property must have a very direct connection with the fact that they just shot and killed their old vice president here in town. I'd bet a good, fat load of money that your little gal and her mother just happened on that property because its owner has very recently perished under very unfortunate circumstances."

That connection had not even occurred to me before this moment. I can't believe I didn't think of it. "After that pirate treasure, you think?" I ask.

"Oh, definitely," Nick says. "At least, they're doing what they can to try to recoup what they lost, and I guess the best place they can start is seizing his property the best way they can—with money. That won't help them, of course, if the new owners won't sell."

I nod. I feel a very heavy dread creeping into my chest. I wasn't expecting this, honestly. I was expecting an emphatic yes. It didn't occur to me that Nick wouldn't agree in some way, shape, or form.

"It won't be good for us, kid," he says, kindly. "And it won't be good for them, either, even if we *do* get involved. And those guys have a lot bigger numbers than us. A lot. If you count their hang-arounds, they're probably in the three digits. They'll just keep coming at us. Won't do none of us any good. So, like I say, tell her the best thing is to just walk away. Take their money and walk away."

"Thanks," I say. "I'll let them know."

Nick offers me his hand and I take it, smiling at him and feeling grateful that he's good enough to let me down easily.

"I wish them the best," says Nick.

"I appreciate that," I say. I lift a hand to Bullet and Bucky. "See you guys later."

"See you," says Bucky. Bullet is too busy trying to land a dart to pay attention to what's happening.

"I'll walk you out," says Bullet. "I left something in my saddlebag."

I can't think of anything to say because I'm too fucking distracted, trying to figure out what the fuck to do now. Bullet slings his arm around my shoulders.

"Really sorry about that," says Bullet. "I see his point, but it seems wrong not to do something. But, he's the boss, you know?"

"Yeah," I say. "I do."

When we get outside, he gives me a hard clap on the back. "Good luck, Shotgun."

"Thanks," I say, not feeling like I have even an ounce of the stuff.

I chew my lip as I walk to my car. What the hell am I going to tell Erica?

I gave her the key to my apartment. I figured she'd be more comfortable there while I went and had this conversation with Nick, rather than sitting awkwardly in the foyer. And, frankly, I was picturing it like this: I would sweep in the door and announce that the Knights would be doing whatever it took to protect them, then she would fall into my arms and we would fuck like crazy all night. And then in the morning, waffles.

I am having a feeling there might not be any waffles. There might not even be any fucking. This plan is definitely backfiring. Thinking about fucking her is also not helping. That was the worst part of splitting up, honestly. The sexual chemistry between us is just *real*. I don't know what it is about that woman, but when I get around her I'm always half-hard. It's probably a pheromone thing, but it's also that she's fucking beautiful and funny and smart and—

What the hell am I going to tell her? I guess all I can do is say what Nick suggested. He's been around a long time, I respect him enough to believe him when he tells me that *Los Brujos* are bad people that none of us want to tangle with. I believe it. I tangled with those dipshits for five minutes, and I got shot in the arm and another guy ended up dead.

The walk feels much longer than usual, but I finally reach my place. I'm sweating under the cotton of my T-shirt and my arm is dripping with sweat inside the sling. Very attractive, if you ask me. I ease the door open when I arrive and hear music playing softly in the background. Some sort of oldie music that makes me smile. Erica is not one to listen to today's top hits and I've always liked that about her.

I follow the sound of the music and the smell of her shampoo out to a little patch of sun in front of the sliding glass door of my apartment balcony. She's looking out the window at the dying plants that I so haphazardly water that it's a miracle there's even a grain of life left in them at all.

"Hey," she says with a smile. It's so effortlessly sexy that I'm at half-mast already when I kneel on the carpet beside her. She looks at my arm and furrows her brow. "What the hell did you do to your arm?"

"Hurt it at work," I say, automatically. Then I realize telling her the truth may ease us into what I have to say about Nick's answer. "That's a lie." I smother a laugh. "I've been telling everyone that so I don't get in trouble. I got shot."

"You got shot," she says, and she is so alarmed that she moves from her sexy butt to her beautiful, perfect knees. I have a hard time not staring down at the way her cut-offs are straining around her thighs. "When the hell did you have time to get shot?"

"Not today," I say. "This was a couple of weeks ago."

"What *happened*?"

"Well," I say. "Now that you mention it, I had a run in with some friends of yours."

"Friends of mine?" she asks with her eyebrows raised. I've never seen her look more confused, and I am trying not to enjoy it so much. I failed.

"Those *Los Brujos* motherfuckers," I say. "I met them at a bar. It's a whole thing, but they dragged this guy outside, and I went to see what they were doing. They were threatening him behind the dumpster so I jumped in. He ended shooting himself and they got away, but not before plugging me with my own share of lead."

"What the fuck," she says. "Are you all right? I mean, I guess you are, you're here. But in your head? I'm so sorry that happened to you, that's just awful." And she looks like she really means it. Her green eyes are burning with empathy and anger. "God, those guys are—they're *shitbags*."

"I'd say so," I say, and I find my fingers in her hair, pushing it behind her ear and toying with her earring while she talks. Despite the gravity of the subject matter, I'm entirely distracted.

"But I don't get it," she says. "That's really weird. What are the odds of you having a run in with them, too?"

"I think Johnny—the guy who died—has something they're looking for," I say. "A whole lot of something they're looking for. And I think that they think they'll find it at his house. A house that I think your mother just happened to buy."

"What do you mean?" she says. She covers her hand with mine. She seems to be able to focus better than I can at the moment. All I can do is watch her lips while she talks.

"I mean," I say, "according to Nick, those guys stole a bunch of gold bars and bags of cocaine from the FBI. And Johnny, he made off with all of it and let a bunch of other guys take the fall. So our guess is that they've come to get their pound of flesh and as many pounds of gold they can find."

"Gold?" she laughs. "Like pirate's gold?"

"Like bars of gold," I say. "Apparently it's a thing. And Bullet says it's hard to get rid of, especially for a guy on the run from the FBI *and* his outlaw MC."

I can't wait anymore. I lean in and kiss her, pulling her body against mine with my palm on her lower back. Her mouth softens against mine and her arms come around my shoulders. Her mouth tastes so delicious, as sweet as golden honey. She nibbles on my lower lip and it pulls a soft groan from me. She starts to pull me toward her, and I realize she wants me on top of her. I am simultaneously the happiest man on earth and also the guiltiest. I pull my mouth away from hers and look at her.

"What is it?" she asks, opening her green eyes. She looks anxious suddenly, and I kiss her again, just a quick one to try to take that look away.

"It's not anything—" I straighten up and sit back on my heels. I stare down at the carpet.

"Colt," she says. "You're scaring me."

"I just haven't told you the part about what Nick said," I say. What I don't say is that I don't feel right fucking her because I know it's going to upset her. That just doesn't seem very nice, even if it's taking everything in me not to tear her panties off and do unspeakable things to her with my mouth.

"What did Nick say?" She sits up straight. She has a serious look on her face now, and I wish the sweet, sexy smile would come back.

"He says that we can't help you," I say.

She starts to open her mouth, but I hold up my hand. "I'm sorry, babe, I am. But I also just want to tell you what he said. He says that *Los Brujos* are really fucked up dudes. He says that even if we tangle with them, we're all going to get hurt. It wouldn't be to anyone's benefit. He says that he thinks you and your mother should just give them what they want. It's not worth it to do anything otherwise."

She gets to her feet, and I follow her. I can't quite read her expression, but I don't like it: anger, fear, disbelief, grief. I try to take her into my arms, but she stops me. She shakes her head.

"You said you would help me," she says. Her voice cracks slightly, and she won't look at me.

"It's not that I—" I start to say, but she interrupts me.

"I don't understand why no one will help us," she says, more to herself than to me. She sweeps her hair behind her ears, an angry gesture that I remember from the old days. I try to take her arm gently, but she shakes me off. She still won't look at me.

"Erica," I say. "We'll figure something out. I just don't want something to happen to you. You can stay here if you need to. Hell, your mom and her boyfriend too, whatever you need. I just think Nick is right."

"Yeah," she says. "I'm sure you do." And she sounds so bitter that I can almost taste it in my mouth.

"Will you stop?" I say. I'm getting a bit heated now, but I'm trying to keep it from escalating. I take a breath. "Just think about it. Okay? I'm here for you."

"No," she says. She finally looks at me. Her eyes are full of angry tears. "You're not."

Then she opens the door and tries to snap it shut behind her, but I grab it and hold it open. She turns to look at me again.

"I'm sorry," I say again. I try to sound soft, but my voice comes out a sort of hoarse grumble. "Let me come with you, it's the least I can do."

"No," she says.

"Why not?" I ask, trying not to feel irritated at her stubborn ass ways.

"I don't want you to," she says. "Leave me alone."

Then, she lets go of the door and walks away. I'd be lying if I say I don't feel like I just got knifed in the fucking heart. I slam the door shut and pace around my apartment. I realize I'm gritting my teeth so hard that they feel like they might crumble in my mouth.

"*Goddammit*," I say out loud. I scrub my hand through my hair, and then I go to the door. I yank it open and take the stairs two at a time. But by the time I get down to the parking lot, she's already pulling out. I wave at her, but she peels out and hardly stops to look for traffic before she shoots out of the driveway.

This time, I don't have a bike to gallantly chase her down with.

"*Fuck*," I say. "Fuck."

I stare down the road at the spot where her car disappeared, feeling like I might fall apart.

Chapter Eleven

Erica

My chest hurts, and my arms feel leaden while I hold the steering wheel and try to concentrate on the road. Everything feels like it's moving in slow motion around me, and I can't remember how long I've been driving. My head is too busy spinning.

I keep telling myself that I shouldn't feel this upset. Why on Earth should I feel upset? But thinking this just makes the pain in the center of me surge. *Why* do I feel this upset?

Because I thought he was going to be there for me. Because I have to go home now and tell my mother no one is coming. No one is going to help us. My throat hurts and my eyes are stinging, but I wrinkle my nose and stare at the road. I will *not* cry.

But the fact is inescapable: no one is going to help us. And now we have to figure it out on our own. And what was I expecting from Colt, anyway? That I was just going to walk back into his life after all this time, and he'd drop everything that matters to him, everything that he's worked so hard to earn for himself, and rush to my side? I mean, that's not reasonable.

Reasonable or not, it hurts. It hurts that I thought I would have him to lean into, that I could stop pining for him. And now that's not going to happen. I guess it bothers me most that he isn't willing to be there for me, even if the rest of them want nothing to do with the situation. I get it, it's not their fight, and it doesn't have to be his either. But it's the principle of it. It really all comes back down to what broke us up in the first place—I just can't get my head around him being part of a group of people who have that much hold over his life. I try to understand, but I can't. And I worry that they will always take priority over me. I don't know anyone who wants to play second fiddle in a relationship, whether it's to another person or an organization.

I mean, yeah, I thought it was sexy when we first started dating. The whole bike-gang thing. He looks too yummy in that black leather vest, too cool to be real on his bike. I used to stand outside in the heat to wait for him to ride up just so I could see him pull in, watch him come to a slow stop on his bike. Watching him ride is an aphrodisiac. But the reality of the situation is a different story, and here it is again, biting me in the ass.

And now I don't know what to tell my mother. I didn't tell her where I was going or what I was doing. Not that I worry of her disapproving or anything like that. I just couldn't stand to get her hopes up and have them totally shattered like mine have been. But more than anything, I'd been hoping I would come home and be able to tell her that help was on the way, and we didn't have to lay awake at night anymore.

Underneath all of this is the cold fury at the assholes who are doing this to us. Which makes me think of the sheriff's department again, and then the Knights, and it keeps spinning around and around in a circle of shitty bullshit until my head aches.

I need to go back to the ranch and dig in the dirt for a while. That's what I need to do. I turn up the radio and roll down the windows and let the scorched desert air into the car to blow my poor braid to smithereens. Janis Joplin serenades me as I drive, and I try to ignore the ache in my chest.

Instead of going home though, I decide to take a little drive. I can't go home and sit at the ranch and just stew in my thoughts about all of this stuff. Seems like a miserable, sad thing to do.

Why did I leave California, again?

I absent-mindedly pull into a spot at the gas station. The tank is half full—see, I'm not *totally* pessimistic—but I might as well put some juice in it, anyway. I could do any number of other errands right now, but I'm feeling blank. All of my energy is going into not thinking about Colt.

But I can't help it. I just need to admit to myself for just ten seconds how good it felt to have his lips on mine, to taste his mouth again. His hands felt just as strong and reassuring as they ever had. I flush with embarrassment when I think of how close I was to fucking him when he walked back into his apartment. I just can't help it, he walks into the room, and my brain turns to goo. I press my hands over my face and take a deep breath. My bottom lip is starting to ache in my effort not to cry.

Jesus, I'm not going to cry at the gas station.

I kick open the door and climb out, checking to make sure my sunglasses are in place before I climb out of the car. I'm the only one here, which is kind of nice. I wander inside to pay for my gas and browse the snacks for a minute. I linger for a while, soaking up the cool air before I head back out to my car.

I stop dead a few steps from the door when I spot a motorcycle sitting directly in front of my car.

My heart stops and then does a flip-flop for a second—

Then it stops again and drops down into the pit of my stomach.

It isn't Colt, it's one of *them*. My pushy friend from the restaurant, as a matter of fact. Why am I surprised?

I can't move for what seems like eternity. I'm rooted to the spot with shock and, frankly, fear. He followed me here? I turn my head slowly to scan for his friends, but he seems to be alone.

He's leaning against my driver's side door with his arms folded while he watches me with what I can only call amusement. There's something dark in his look that makes my skin crawl, and I want to get into my car and run him over.

I probably look like a frightened rabbit standing here. It makes my stomach boil with anger, that he looks so amused because he feels like the cat who got the canary. Not like him and his shitbag friends are terrorizing us. Leta flashes into my head, whimpering and covered in her own blood. And the sound of Hector vanishing into the night. The look on my mother's face.

And I'm *way* more angry than scared now.

"*Hola*," he says to me softly.

"What the fuck do *you* want?" I ask. Which is a pretty childish way to begin, but I'm so upset I can't really think of anything snappy and clever.

"You wound me," he says, pressing a hand encased in a black leather glove against his heart. "I just happened to be driving by."

"Following me," I say.

"Not at all," he says. Then he smiles, and it makes me feel cold. "Not this time."

That makes me stop. I swallow hard. It hasn't occurred to me that they would be following us. And he's probably just trying to scare me, but it makes me feel very, very helpless.

I think of what Colt told me, about the stuff they're looking for. Frankly, knowing *why* they're doing what they're doing has taken the edge off the fear in a strange way. Not knowing why someone is tormenting you is somehow more frightening. The fact that I know what their agenda is has made them seem less like boogeymen. But I'm not at all comforted by the facts brought into the light either. They're after what we've got, and they're willing to kill people for it.

And to put the cherry on top of that god-awful sundae, this guy has taken a real shine to me. How did I get so lucky?

"Want to go for a spin?" he asks, tilting his head toward his motorcycle. But there is *definitely* a double entendre in the question.

"Maybe in hell," I say.

"I could make that happen," he says. It's kind of mind-boggling. He's coming onto me and threatening to kill me in the same breath—with a relaxed, easy smile on his face.

I want to ask him if this tactic works on all the girls, but I don't. As much as I want to heckle this fucking jerk, I don't need any more trouble from him than we've already got. And, frankly, there probably *are* women out there who are into that kind of thing. Different strokes for different folks, I guess.

"Can you get the fuck away from my car so I can go home?" I spit. I don't want to get any closer to him. He's already made it apparent in every way, shape, and form from the moment that we met that he has absolutely no respect for my personal boundaries. He probably doesn't even know the word *boundaries*.

"Why don't we go together?" he asks with his lascivious smile that makes me want to roll my eyes. Really, being handsome only gets you so far. Being a truly evil *asshole* kind of ruins the effect.

Somehow, standing outside in the middle of a gas station talking to this guy makes him seem more like a pesky mosquito instead of a truly frightening gang member, capable of doing terrible things to people. And dogs. I have to remind myself of the things Colt told me about their gang. Even if he's about as intimidating as a strutting turkey right this minute. I remind myself not to underestimate him.

"Get away from my car or I'm going to call the police," I say. I'm trying to be as dignified as I can. I'm trying to keep him from seeing how upset I am, how ridiculous I find him. Men don't like it when you can see through their shit, and I don't want to give him any reasons to add to his list for tormenting me or my mother.

"Go ahead," he says. "They've been so helpful to you so far, I don't know why you haven't called them already."

My whole body goes still, and I shiver in the brutal heat. "Wha-what do you know about that?"

"It pays to have good friends," he says. "Good friends in convenient places. So I know a lot, baby girl. A lot about what happens. And what doesn't happen."

"You've bought them," I whisper. And suddenly everything makes *extreme* sense. The dismissiveness, the refusal to do a legitimate investigation. But this knowledge does not bring any sort of comfort with it. In fact, I feel like I might cry again.

He holds up his hands and says, "Not sure what you're talking about, *lindacita*." There's a glitter in his dark eyes. "But I *do* know that everything has its price." And now we're back to innuendos.

I feel tired, suddenly. Tired of this whole thing. Especially tired of him. I find myself aching for Colt for one intense moment, but I shove that away too. I'm tired of men.

"All right, I guess I'll walk home," I say. And I mean it. I'll leave that car here if I have to, I'm not playing chicken with him.

"You sure love to play hard to get," he says.

"I'm impossible to get," I reassure him.

"My kind of lady." He straightens up, stretches his arms over his head and pivots toward his motorcycle. Looking at me over his shoulder, he gives me one of his smiles. "I'll be seeing you."

The thought is not comforting.

He starts his engine and pulls out, taking care to circle around behind me like a shark. He says nothing else but guns it out of the gas station with one more unsettling look back over his shoulder. Then he's gone, a glimmer of chrome and black leather in the sun.

"Jesus fucking Christ" My knees suddenly feel so weak that they might knock together. I somehow make it to my car without falling over. My hands are shaking so hard that I'm having a hard time extracting the keys from my purse. I feel so cold that I don't even start the AC right away, which is normally a must when climbing into the car.

He may be ridiculous, but the situation isn't. The sheriff's department isn't massively incompetent—or if they are that isn't why they're not coming to help us. They're looking the other way on purpose. It's the kind of thing you hear about on the news, or see in movies. But for that to be the reality of what's happening…

He could be lying. He could be grandstanding. But somehow, I don't think so. He seems like the type to take a lot of satisfaction from bragging. He doesn't need to grandstand about anything. Things just are how they are. He's comfortable in the knowledge that he has all the power. He doesn't have to do anything to exert that power, and that's not a comforting thought.

I'm so distracted on the drive home that I blow through a stoplight and nearly cause an accident. I'm more shaken than ever, and I just want to get out of this stupid car and to climb into my bed, but the drive takes an eternity.

When I park in the driveway, I pause inside the car to look at my phone. I've got a new message. A lightning bolt goes through me when I see who it's from. Colt. I stare at his name with the little red arrow next to it, feeling like I can't move a muscle. I hate the feeling of levity that suddenly comes into the middle of me. With slightly shaking hands, I open the message. *I'm sorry*, is all it says. The light feeling is suddenly gone again, and it's replaced by a cold feeling, like an ice cube dropping into my stomach. I shove my phone in my purse and kick the car door open. Bet he's *real* sorry. Sorry doesn't help anything.

My eyes are burning again, and I sit in the car until I blink them away, double checking in the rearview mirror that they aren't too red.

Another text comes through on my phone. *Give me your address, I'll come out.*

But it's too late for that now. My pride is hurt. My feelings are hurt. My heart is hurt. I don't want his stupid help. I think of that whole, hideous scene at the gas station. He should have been there with me. Or if he wasn't physically there, I should have been comfortable with the knowledge that he had my back.

As it is, I can't seem to find comfort in anything. The whole world is just a big, soggy, wet blanket right now. I feel the urge to sob again, but instead I gather up my gummy worms and trek into the house.

"How'd it go?" Mom asks over some herbs she's chopping at the kitchen counter.

"Oh, fine," I say. "Just fine."

Even though I haven't responded to Colt, I keep checking my phone. Pretty unreasonable of me to think he's going to keep hounding me when I left in a huff, and I didn't respond to his texts. My pride is too wounded for me to reply, but it doesn't stop me from wanting the reassurance of his messages.

I've been playing this game with myself for hours since I got home. My mind is starting to feel like it's been scraped raw. My mother, Ted, and I are all sitting around in the living room. It's past bedtime, but none of us have moved. I think we're all afraid to go to bed after last night. Like, if we don't go to sleep we can be on alert. We finished our movie at least a half hour ago, but we're all still sitting, playing on our phones or staring off into space while we all start to droop. My mother is nursing a second glass of red wine and chewing at her fingernails while she stares at the carpet. There's a deep line between her brows.

"Well," Ted says. He slaps his legs and then climbs slowly to his feet. "Better make sure everyone's tucked in for the night."

He means the animals outside. We all know they're already tucked in, but I don't blame him for wanting to make another round and double check everything, try to regain some sense of security. Maybe see if Hector has wandered home. He goes out quietly, shutting the door firmly behind him.

I haven't told them what that asshole at the gas station said to me about the sheriff. Maybe I should, but I can't bring myself to make this situation any worse for them. But I'm starting to get worn down—I'm wondering if maybe Colt is right.

"Maybe we should just sell the house," I say after a long stretch of silence.

"I don't want to do that," my mother says, shaking her head. "That's just not reasonable. To be bullied into selling your house."

"It's just—" I say. I don't even know what to say to her that will make her hear me. I guess you can't make anyone listen. Lead a horse to water and all that. "Things just keep getting worse. And you look like you haven't slept in days. I just don't know if this is worth it anymore."

"I'm not going to do it," she says. "People like that do things like this because they think they can get away with it. And they do because no one stands up to them."

"I really don't think that's how it works," I say. "I think they get away with it because they're willing to do things sane, law-abiding, good people are not willing to do."

"They're just trying to intimidate us," she says. She drains her wine glass before getting up off the couch.

"And it's working," I say. "I don't think they're playing around, Mom."

"I don't want to talk about it anymore," she says.

I throw up my hands because I don't know what else to do. I certainly don't want to be here anymore. We haven't had a day's peace since we moved to this house. But I'm also really unwilling to go off and leave my mom and Ted alone out here.

What I don't get is why this is the hill she's willing to die on. On the one hand, I understand not wanting someone to push you around, to feel like you're conceding unfairly. But this is kind of drifting outside the limit of reason. There's just no point in discussing this more tonight though. She's tired and cranky and, lord, she can be such a stubborn lady when she's feeling moody.

I get up and go to my room. I'm tired but somehow also on edge. I wish we could just pack up and go. Instead, I crawl into my bed and unlock my phone. I stare at Colt's messages and think very seriously about texting him. No matter how upset I am right now, I'd give almost anything for him to just hold me while I sleep and make me feel safe. It's probably too late now though.

I don't realize that I've drifted off until my mother shakes me awake.

"Erica." She sounds breathless and frightened, and I am immediately on high alert.

"What?" I say, sitting up and looking around. The light in my room is off. "What's going on?"

"Ted hasn't come back," she says. Her voice is high, breathy, like a girl's.

"What do you mean Ted hasn't come back?" I slowly push the covers back with shaking hands. They feel slick with cold sweat already, and I feel like someone just tossed a bowling ball into my stomach. "What time is it?"

"It's almost midnight," she says. "He's been gone for 45 minutes. I've been trying to call him, and he isn't answering. The truck is still in the driveway."

"Oh my God," I say. I stand up too quickly and the head rush nearly gets me, but I steady myself.

"I don't know what to do," she says. She grabs at my elbow, and I can hear her holding back tears. "I don't know what to do," she says again. "I'm afraid to go out there, but we can't just leave him..."

"It's going to be all right," I say. Even though I am by no means an authority on the subject, and if things are the way they seem, they are most definitely *not* going to be all right. I walk down the hallway to her room, feeling like I'm floating out of my body. I check Ted's bedside table for his pistol. I push things around a bit, but all I find is the extra clip. He took it with him, but I didn't hear any shots fired. Somehow that makes me feel worse.

"What are you doing?" my mom asks. "What are you looking for?

"Ted bought that gun," I say. "I can't find it, he must have it."

"Right. The gun," she says, sounding more frightened than ever. "Oh my god."

"Well, it's not an unreasonable response to this situation," I say. Her stress is starting to amplify my own. I have to remind myself to breathe. "I'm going to go look outside. If anything happens, call Colt. Don't call the sheriff, call Colt." I hand her my phone, unlocked, so she can pull up his contact information if she needs to.

"Why can't I call the sheriff?" she says, looking down at the phone.

"They're useless," I say. And it's true. I pick up one of the walking sticks stashed in the closet by the door. Unfortunately, we don't have as much as a baseball bat, because none of us play baseball, but this stick is hefty and solid. It would hurt if I managed to land it on somebody. Not that it's much good against a gun or a very bad man with a very sharp knife.

"What are you doing?" she asks.

"Going out to look for Ted," I say. "Can't go empty-handed."

She rummages around the closet and comes up with another walking stick. "Okay," she says. "I'm ready."

We creep toward the door like two terrified, albeit determined, mice. The door, thank god, is well-maintained and doesn't squeak when we open it. Outside, the moon is half-full and there isn't a cloud in the sky. It's bright enough to light our way as we move slowly across the porch. My heart is pounding in my chest, and it occurs to me that we just might be about to die.

I am in way over my fucking head. I should have called Colt. I should have just called him. He would know what to do. I would feel so much better if he were here. Why was I being so fucking stubborn again?

I'm trying not to think about Ted, or Leta. Or about finding Ted like we found Leta, stabbed and bleeding out onto the sunbaked dirt.

There is hardly a sound at all. The chickens are silent. There isn't so much as a breeze in the suffocatingly hot night. I can't see anyone in the dim light of the moon, but I grip my walking stick so hard that my hands are getting slick.

We walk to the edge of the porch and then we stop. I look around slowly, searching for any sign of a human or movement or anything else suspicious. And there's nothing.

Until we hear it. A soft sound. I freeze, totally immobilized by my fear. Until I realize that it's a groaning sound. A person is making that sound. And it's not a sound someone makes if they're in great shape.

"Ted?" Mom says behind me, sort of whisper-shouting.

I step down off the porch and follow the sound.

"Ted?" I say, echoing my mother. I hear the sound again, louder this time, and I follow it. My mother is right on my heels. We round the corner around the chicken coop and my mother, who sees Ted before I do, has to smother a scream. I nearly trip over him.

He's lying on his side. We crouch down next to him, and it takes me a minute to realize that I can't see his face because it's totally obscured by blood.

"We have to get him to the hospital," I say. I'm no expert, but I know this is bad. Really bad.

"Get the keys," my mom says. "I'll stay with him."

"Give me my phone," I say.

She hands it to me and before I'm even to the porch I'm texting him. I should have just done it in the first goddamn place.

Chapter Twelve

Shotgun

"I don't want to talk about it," I say for the thousandth time. Holly keeps giving me these meaningful looks while she and Seth exchange glances. It's enough to make a guy crazy. So what if I'm so depressed that I can't even stand to go out to the bar for a drink? So what if I'm so depressed that I'd rather stay here with Holly and Seth and play Clue, for fuck's sake.

Holly was kind enough to get me a cold Coors Light from the refrigerator and pour it into a nice frosty glass from the freezer for esteemed company like myself, but I can hardly even stand the taste. Everything turns to ash in my mouth. I would cry if I wasn't so damn manly.

I guess I shouldn't have come over here and expected not to be interrogated. Seth tried to ask me about what happened with Erica and I refused to say a word about it. I'm sure he went home and told Holly all about us lovebirds. They finished planning their own stupid wedding so long ago that they were probably halfway done planning *our* wedding when I got here. In fact, they look more upset than I feel right now. That's saying something.

Holly waits until Seth gets up to go to the bathroom to finally pounce.

"Just tell me what happened," she says. No sugar coating it or anything. I guess I appreciate that about Holly. It's probably one of the things my brother likes most about her, I would be willing to bet. Seth is a straight shooter. Doesn't surprise me that his lady is too.

"I don't want to—"

"—talk about it," she finishes for me with a big ol' sigh. "Fine. *Fine*. But I know you're going to break down and tell Seth eventually, so you might as well do it now. Maybe we can help."

"Not unless you are able to perform a frontal lobe lobotomy on Nick," I say. "Not sure where that falls in terms of doctor ethics."

Holly frowns at me and looks kind of surprised. "Nick?" she asks. "What does Nick have to do with any of this?"

"It's just... it's a long story," I say and stare down into my beer. It's probably a shade too warm to drink now with real gusto, but I take a sip anyway. Just so I can avoid looking at Holly. I don't want her to read my face.

"I have a whole lot of time," she s, leaning back against the couch. Seth chooses this moment to come back from the bathroom.

"What are you guys on about?" he says, sitting down next to her. He puts his hand on her leg in the most proprietary—yet comfortable—fashion, and she puts her hand right on top of his. Like neither of them even thought about it. It's such a *couple* thing to do that I nearly vomit. Not because I'm grossed out, but because I'm in agony over the shit that went down with Erica today.

"Colt was about to tell us what's bothering him," she says.

I exhale long and slow. "Fine. Fine."

"Spit it out," He says. "I've already aged a decade waiting to hear what the fuck happened today."

I look down at my hands. "It didn't go well."

"Well, that much I gather," he says.

"What happened?" Holly asks for the millionth time.

"I went to ask Nick if he'd help her out," I say. I look at Seth. "I don't know if you told Holly about all of this."

Seth nods. They look at each other and smile. Seriously, gag me with a spoon. They're a hair's breadth from being a Hallmark commercial.

"Okay, so you know," I say. "I went to ask Nick if he would consider offering her family protection. And I guess I kind of just assumed that he would say yes. I didn't think about the bigger picture. I was just thinking..."

"With your dick," Seth offers.

"Rude," I say. "Very rude. And only partially true." He knows it's more than that, but I sure as shit am not about to say that out loud. "*Anyway*, he said no. Put the big fat kibosh on it. He says that he isn't willing to tangle with *Los Brujos* because they're basically way too fucking dangerous. He isn't willing to put the rest of the Knights, and their families, in harm's way like that. He says that they should give up the house to *Los Brujos* and find another one."

"Jesus," says Seth. "Really? Shit must be really fucked up for Nick to say no way."

"That and he's trying to salvage our reputation right now," I say.

"So, what?" says Holly. "She got mad that he said no?"

"Basically, yes," I say. "She went to my apartment to wait for me to have this conversation, and I went back and told her what he said. And she got really hurt and left. I didn't say the right stuff, I guess. I tried to text her and tell her that I would be there for her, but she hasn't gotten back to me." I stare into my beer, feeling queasy just thinking about it. "I guess I shouldn't be surprised. This is the same shit that came up before. They say it's insane to be doing the same shit over and over again and expecting a different result, or something like that."

"I'm so sorry," Holly says. And she looks like she is. I'd be sorry too, if I was that excited to plan someone else's wedding.

"Really," Seth says. "That fucking blows."

"I just thought... I thought that we were going to work everything out. I thought that things were going to be okay."

"I know," says Holly. She's excellent at being sympathetic. I bet her bedside manners are great. I start to say this, but then I realize that this will probably provoke some sort of disgusting joke from my brother that I do not want to hear.

"Anyway," I say. "That's it. That's the whole thing."

"It's a drag," Seth says. He puts his hand on my shoulder and gives me a friendly shake. "You can't say you didn't try."

"I just feel like shit about it," I say. "I feel like shit that she thought she could count on me to handle this for her, and I can't."

"It was never your decision to begin with," Seth says.

"I know." I take another big swig of my lukewarm Coors Light. "But I still can't help it."

"I know," says Seth. "It's hard on a guy when you can't be there for your lady." Thankfully, he spares me and doesn't turn to Holly to make this a sappy moment.

"It really fucking is," I say. "What the hell else am I good for?"

"Not much," he says and grins at me.

"Thanks a whole lot."

A phone alarm starts to beep and Holly silences it. "Dinner's ready. I'll grab it." She disentangles herself from my brother and heads to the kitchen.

"Well," he says. "If it's really the end, we've got to move you into the recovery phase."

"What's the rush?" I say. "I'm wallowing."

"Well," he says, giving me a slap on the leg. "You can't wallow forever."

"Oh my god," I say. "It just happened. Where is your humanity?"

This makes my otherwise stoic brother chuckle. "I'm just giving you a hard time. Of course, you can wallow."

"She's just..." I look into my beer again like I might find the proper word there. "She's just *perfect*. And I refuse to believe that I have been thrown into her path, shown the gates of Heaven, just to have it all snatched away."

"What kind of gates are you talking about?" he asks.

"Don't be terrible," I say. The smell of dinner is hitting the air, and I wish I was hungry. Broccoli, cheese, and chicken casserole. Normally, I'm not one for casseroles. My aunt used to make this bland, awful slop that reminded me of something you'd scrape out of the garbage disposal in a sink and call it a casserole. Just thinking about it makes me want to gag. But Seth is a pretty good cook. It took some persuading the first time to get me to try the broccoli cheese concoction, I admit. But now I'm hooked. It might be my favorite.

My phone dings, and I pull it out of my pocket. "Wh—" I start to say, but whatever it was goes completely out of my head. My mouth goes instantly dry. "Oh my god," I say. "It's from Erica."

"What did she say?" Holly says behind me.

I almost drop my phone in my haste to open the text message. *Ted's in the hospital. They beat him up badly.*

"Oh my god," I say again. "It's her, uh, step-dad. Or whatever. He's in the hospital." My heart feels like it's slowing to a halt, and I can't stop staring at my phone.

"What happened?" Seth says. I look up at him, and he's watching me intently. Holly has come around the side of the couch.

I swallow hard and look back at the phone. "They beat the shit out of him, I guess."

"*Los Brujos?*" He asks. And I see right away that the fuse has been lit. The look on his face must be reflecting my own.

"Those motherfuckers," I say. But I don't have the privilege of feeling only anger like my brother. I am also drowning in fucking guilt, and it's like pouring gasoline on the anger. "Those fucking motherfuckers." I realize that my hand hurts, and I look down to see that I've been making such a tight fist that my palm has little lines of blood from my fingernails.

"Colt," Holly says. Her voice sounds like it's far away, somewhere beyond the heavy haze that's settled over my mind. "Don't do anything stupid."

"I'm not going to do anything stupid." I get to my feet. "I'm going to do the smartest thing I can think of."

"And what's that?" Seth says. "You're not doing shit with that bum arm of yours, kid. You're going to get your stupid ass killed." He looks like he's trying to decide if he's going to have to tie me to a chair.

"I'm going to the hospital to be with her," I say. "Like I fucking should have been all along."

"I'll drive you," Seth says.

"Fine," I say after a pause. Only because I'm so mad that I think I might wreck the car before I can get to the hospital and I'll be letting Erica down yet again. Not an option.

The hospital is pretty quiet. I figure she'll be easy to find. I don't want to tell her that I'm here, I want it to be a surprise.

"Name of the patient?" the lady behind the front desk asks.

"Uh..." I actually have no fucking idea. "I'm not familiar with the patient," I say. "I'm familiar with the patient's family."

"Well, I can't find the patient unless you tell me their name," the lady says. It's probably the most polite "fuck off" I've ever heard in my life. She doesn't seem like she could give a single, flying fuck one way or the other.

This is really interfering with my plan of surprise. But who the fuck cares. I send her a text, *Which room are you guys in?* And we move away from the front desk, and the very apathetic lady, to stand near the wall. Seth crosses his arms, leaning his shoulder against the wall while he watches me.

"What now?"

"I just asked her which room they're in," I say. "Fuck it. My gallant effort has been foiled, but I don't give a fuck."

I wait and I stare at my phone. She shoots me back a message: *302. Are you here?*

Sure am, I answer.

I consult the map near the elevator and lead the way inside, punching the button for the third floor.

"I'll wait in the waiting area," Seth tells me. "Let you two get reacquainted."

"You're so very thoughtful," I say. And then, with less sarcasm, I add, "Thanks for bringing me though. You didn't have to come." It means a lot actually. Now that I'm in a better thinking space, it means a lot that he's doing what he can for me. I may be all grown-up and the past is the past, but it's really nice to know that my big brother has my back.

"You think I'd miss this?" Seth says. "Holly would never forgive me."

"I'm so glad my life is such quality entertainment," I grumble as we step off the elevator and into a waiting area.

Seth says, "I'll hang here and watch the Buffy reruns. Maybe read a Life magazine if I'm feeling really crazy."

"Maybe you'll even find a bridal magazine, or two," I say. "You guys might have forgotten one or two details you'd like to throw in."

"You're right," Seth says. "I don't think my man of honor looks *quite* uncomfortable enough. The magazines might give me some good inspiration."

"Man of honor," I say, giving him a look of disgust.

"Go on," he says, giving me a little push. "She's waiting for you."

I *am* stalling. I don't know why really. She told me she was here. She wanted me to come, right? Something else occurs to me. She might have sent that message to let me know what a giant sack of shit I am. I mean I already feel that way, but what if that's all she intended? And what if she doesn't want to see me?

Well. I guess there's only one way to find out. She *did* give me the room number. I run a hand through my hair and wish that I didn't have to wear this ridiculous sling. It occurs to me suddenly that I haven't met her family. What a shitty way to make that happen. I'd take just about any other circumstance over this.

Outside the door, I pause, take a deep breath, and knock. I wish I wasn't so nervous. Why does this woman make me so nervous? I don't think anyone has ever made me feel so nervous. I'm usually the one that's calm, cool, all dialed in. But I'm caught hook, line, and sinker. And now that I've just had the smallest taste of her again, I'm like a dope fiend who's relapsed. I can't stop thinking about her, and I know for a fact I will never get enough.

I hear soft footsteps walking toward me, and I step back a bit. The door glides inward quietly, and there she is. So beautiful that my heart stops, even with the dark circles under her eyes and the grim look tightening her jaw.

"Hi," I say softly.

She pauses a long minute before she says, "Hey." She has her shoulder and her cheek resting against the door.

"Want to take a little walk?" I offer. I look past her into the room. The lights are off except for a lamp, but I can't see more than the foot of the bed. I feel very weird intruding on her mom and... *Ted*, that's his name. If someone had just beat the shit out of me, I wouldn't want some punk rolling into my hospital room.

"I guess," she says. "I need to run to the store in a bit."

I can feel the frost coming off of her, but I'm not going to be put off by it. I don't blame her for being upset with me.

"I'll be right back," she says. She leaves the door open when she walks back into the room. I hear her talking softly to someone before she comes back out and closes the door behind her. "Come on." She wraps her arms around herself and walks to the elevator bay. She doesn't turn her head, so I don't think she sees my brother. He gives me a nod, and I nod back. I mouth, *I'll be back*.

"What are you going to the store for?" I ask her once we're neatly tucked inside the elevator and headed back to the first floor. I'm just trying to make casual conversation, and I think I probably sound like a babbling idiot. Being this close to her and not touching her is making my brain hurt. I study her face and wait for a flash of her green eyes. I get it when she glances up at me, but I'm worried by the look I see on her face.

"Snacks. Hospital food is miserable."

"Good point," I say. We get off the elevator, and I walk slowly with her, not sure where we're going, but being with her is like a balm on my aching soul. We're alone in the lobby area. This time of night the hospital is really quiet. We wander into the foyer, and then she slowly comes to a stop. We sort of just stand there, her with her arms folded, avoiding looking at me. While I stare at her, eating her down with my eyes and wishing like hell I could just take her into my arms and kiss away the worry that's settled over her.

"I was really scared," she says really quietly, so quietly that I almost don't hear her. "I *am* really scared."

"Oh," I say, softly. "I'm so sorry. I should have been there." I reach out to touch her, but she shrugs me off. That fucking stings, but I guess I probably deserve it.

"He could have been killed," she says. "Any of us could have been killed." There are tears escaping her eyes now, slipping down her cheeks like crystals. Her face crumples, and she brings the neck of her shirt up to cover it. She chokes down a sob. "I'm so tired of all of this. And no one is doing anything to help us."

"I'm so sorry," I say again. "I'm sorry I wasn't there."

"You should have been," she says. And I can't tell if it's an accusation or just a statement.

"I should have gotten into your car and gone home with you," I say.

"It's just the same old story," she says. And she looks so sad that my heart feels like it might crack. "It's the Knights that are important to you. They're the most important thing. There's no room for me in your life."

"That's not—" I start to say, but she interrupts me.

"It *is* true," she says. "If it wasn't, you would have been with me tonight. Nothing would have stopped you."

"It's not that simple," I say. But she turns away from me.

"I just kept thinking about you," she says. "Wanting you, hoping you'd call me or text me. But I think I just sort of forgot about this stuff, forgot what it meant to be with you. It's the Knights first and nothing else."

"They're my family," I say. I'm starting to feel anger boiling in my belly. I don't want to get upset, but it's starting to happen anyway.

"I get that," she says. "But it doesn't change the fact that they come before anything else."

"Well," I say. "What do you want me to say? Would I ask you to put me before your mother? Hell no, I wouldn't."

She's silent, staring at the ground. I watch a single tear fall off her upper eyelashes. "No, of course not." She lets out a long breath. "I have to go. I just—I need to go to the store."

"Do you want me to go with you?" I ask.

"No," she says softly. "I'll go by myself."

I feel like someone hollowed me out with an ice cream scooper, but I just nod. Jesus Christ, this woman is stubborn. I can't help but feel really fucking frustrated.

"I'll wait for you," I say.

"No," she says. "That's okay."

"Erica—" I start to say, but she holds up her hand. She still won't look at me.

"I just need some time," she says. "Everything fucking sucks right now, and I can't make any sense of any of it."

"Okay," I say. She looks so fragile and alone standing there. I can't help myself. I put my arm around her and pull her into me. She softens against me for one blissful moment, pressing her face into my shoulder and gripping my T-shirt. But then she's pulling away.

"Call me," I say. "I'm serious. Even if you're calling me to tell me what a miserable fucking asshole I am. Call me."

"Okay," she says. She nods. Her demeanor is slightly softer, slightly lighter.

"I'll walk you out." I inform her, with no intention of budging this time.

"I have to go up and get my purse," she says. "I'll be okay."

"Well," I say. "At least let me walk you up. I have to go up and get my brother."

"Oh," she says, wiping at her cheek with her wrist. "I didn't realize he was here."

"He's in the waiting area." We climb back into the elevator and neither of us say anything. The silence is thick between us, but I refuse to think of it as awkward. There's just a lot that is going unsaid, but sometimes I think you just have to know when to say it and when not to say it.

"See you," she says and walks back up the hallway. I watch her go and even with all the shit flying right now, I am entirely distracted by the way her denim cut offs sit around her thighs. At the door to Ted's room, she stops and looks at me. But she says nothing before she disappears in the room.

Well, it's not the scenario I would have hoped for, but it's going to have to be enough for now. My stomach aches while I stare at the spot where she disappeared.

I don't realize Seth has walked up to me until he repeats my name for the third time.

"All good?" he says, raising his eyebrows when I finally snap out of it.

"I don't know," I say. "Maybe? I think so?"

"What happened?" he asks.

"You know," I say. "We didn't really talk about that."

"Some kind of lover boy you are," he says. "You gonna stay here?"

"No," I say, swallowing hard. "She wants me to go."

"Ouch," Seth says. He puts a hand on my shoulder, and I try to laugh.

"You're not helping," I say, jabbing him with my elbow.

"I'm not trying to," he says, giving my shoulder a painful squeeze. "Come on, let's get you out of here. I'm sure Holly's waiting up to hear all the news. And, frankly, I'm pretty fucking hungry."

"Yeah." I look back over my shoulder, hoping to catch a glimpse of her again before we go, but all I see is nurses in scrubs, not one of them half as pretty as the girl who just vanished through the door. "She said not to wait for her, but I just hate leaving her like this. I think she's just being fucking stubborn."

"I don't blame you," says Seth. "This has really gotten out of hand."

We climb into the elevator while we talk.

"No fucking shit," I say. "I don't want them going back to that fucking house. They could have killed him. They could have killed all of them."

"I didn't see the cops around," says Seth. "Did they end up showing up or...?"

"We didn't get that far," I say. And now that I'm thinking about it, I'm frustrated that the conversation got off the rails so quickly. I didn't even have a chance to ask how Ted was doing. Obviously he's not dead, but beyond that, I have no idea.

We step out into the hot night and walk to my brother's car. I start sweating almost immediately.

"Jesus fucking Christ," I say. "Why did we move to Arizona again?"

"I ask myself that every single day March through October," he says. "But I'm gettin' hitched, so there's definitely no getting out of it now."

"Anyway," I say, "it's getting pretty fucking suspicious that the cops aren't doing shit about this."

"It *is* pretty fucking suspicious."

We climb in the car, and Seth starts the engine to get the AC going.

"But it's maybe a bit of a stretch to start up a conspiracy theory," I say. "Crooked cops are a real thing, but we don't have much to go on."

"No," says Seth. "We don't. But something tells me it's not all clean cut."

"Maybe," I say. The doors to the building open, and Erica steps out into the night.

"There's your girl," says Seth, as if I might be blind. "Where's she off to?"

"The grocery store," I say.

"Oh yeah," says Seth. "Hospital food fucking sucks."

We both fall silent while we watch her walk to her car. She has her arms wrapped around herself and seems to be totally lost in her thoughts. I want to get out of the car and insist that she let me go with her to the grocery store. She's so fucking precious, and I am more and more scared of something bad happening to her. But we're just getting things back on track, and I don't want to let my stubborn shit get me into trouble. I've waited too long to get things working between us again. I'll be patient.

She gets into her car and slowly pulls out of the parking spot. I try to wave to her, but she either doesn't see me as she goes to pull out of the parking lot. Seth starts the car so we can head home, but I hear the familiar rumble of motorcycle engines. Three of them at least.

"The fuck is that," I say. I turn around in my seat, searching the parking lot. It's pretty dark, the outer edges are not well-lit at all, so I don't see them until they creep out of the shadows. One, two, three, four of them.

"Jesus fucking Christ," I say.

They wait until Erica has pulled out of the parking lot and turned left before they follow, kicking into high gear as they rip out of the parking lot after her.

"*Go!*" I say. Seth doesn't need to be told, he's already putting the pedal to the metal and tearing out after the motorcycles.

"Fuck!" I hit my fist on the dash so hard it fucking hurts. "The nerve of these fucking assholes"

As we pull out onto the highway, we can see the bikes flanking Erica's car on either side.

"Speed up," I say. The bikes are maneuvering around her like gnats, and I realize that these fucking assholes are trying to run her off the road. I also realize that they're not *Los Brujos*. "Holy shit, I say. It's the *Dogs*."

"Jesus, fuck, you're right," says Seth. "What the fuck do they want with her?"

"If I had one guess," I say, "it's that *Los Brujos* have made friends while they're in town." I'm gripping the handle on the passenger seat door so hard that it's making my hand ache.

"Busy boys," Seth says under his breath.

"Run them off the fucking road," I say. But it's like he's read my mind because he's already riding up on one of them. The rider looks surprised to see us so close to him and swerves dangerously. I wouldn't give a single flying fuck if we ran right over the top of him, but he manages to right himself. He slows down though, making room for us to pull up alongside Erica's car.

I dial Erica's number. She locks eyes with me, and my heart lurches when I see how frightened she looks. She picks up her cell phone after nearly dropping it twice.

"They're trying to push me off the road," she says, and she does not sound calm.

"We've got this," I say. "Just keep driving. I won't let anything happen to you." And this time, I'd better make good on that because if I don't, I'll be three strikes in, and I don't think I could forgive myself for that.

Seth accelerates hard, and I roll down my window. There's a six-pack of diet soda in the back of the car that I'm going to put to good goddamn use. I pull one of the cans free. "Pull up a little ahead of this fucking shithead."

Seth maneuvers the car expertly. The rider is trying to keep his eyes on the road while also trying to keep an eye on me, but he can't do both. I hurl the soda can at him as hard as I can, and it clips him on the shoulder. It's not enough to knock him over, but he wobbles so hard that he has to swerve to a stop. The other two bikes have left their post on the other side of Erica's car, and they've come up on either side of us. I chuck another can of soda out the window at the bike on my side of the car, but he ducks and accelerates toward me. Seth swerves into him and, finally, he goes down on the concrete. It doesn't look fun. He should probably see a chiropractor for the next few months.

The last asshole seems to get the hint and falls back. I'm kind of disappointed, because I would've liked to give him his fucking dose of medicine too, but Erica is more important. We pull up alongside her and I motion to her, mouthing *pull over*.

She nods, and when we come up to a shoulder a minute later, she slows and pulls her car off the side of the road. Seth follows her. I'm opening my door before the car has even come to a complete stop.

"Hey, you can just drop me," I say. "I'll see you later. Thanks."

"If anything else happens, call," he says. He keeps glancing in the rearview mirror.

"Will do," I say. "I'm going to get her out of here, and then we're going to start talking about how to kick some serious ass. Time for a motherfucking shotgun blast."

This makes Seth chuckle. "I'm down for that."

I give him a wave and close the door. He pulls off of the shoulder and back onto the road. I don't quite run to Erica's car, I make myself walk. But it's hard. My heart is still pounding, and I guess I don't realize just how jacked up on adrenaline I've been. I go straight to the driver's side door and open it.

"You all right?" I ask. "Are you hurt?"

I haven't even finished talking before she's clambering out of the driver's seat and throwing herself against me. I put my arm around her and hold her so tightly that I'm afraid I might hurt her. She holds me just as tightly. She's shaking against me.

"It's okay," I say softly. "I'm not going to let anything happen to you."

"Don't leave me," she says.

"Don't worry," I say. I press my lips to her temple and breathe in the scent of her. Even after all of that fucking bullshit, I feel so peaceful standing here, holding onto her, like I've come into the eye of the storm. Everything here is quiet. "I won't leave you again."

Chapter Thirteen

Erica

Everything is a blur from the time I leave the hospital to the time Colt maneuvers me gently to the passenger seat of my car.

"Do you want me to take you back to the hospital?" he asks, studying my face intently.

"No," I say. "I don't want to upset my mother." I feel frozen. In shock. I can't even begin to comprehend what just happened to me.

"My place?" he says. He's already putting the car into drive and checking the rearview mirror.

"Yes." And while I'm still shaking, still feeling like I might vomit, I feel calmer. Clearer. Like everything is going to be all right. I let out a breath that I didn't even realize I was holding and some of the tension leaves my body. I feel too tired to even cry. And thank God because I am so fucking tired of crying.

"It's going to be okay," he says. He takes his one good hand off the steering wheel for a second and puts it on my leg before he takes it back. His voice is a soothing, beautiful rumble, and it sure makes me feel like everything is going to be okay. "We'll get you somewhere safe. I'll make you a cup of tea and we'll get you all fixed up."

I can't help but laugh. "Tea?" I ask. Colt is definitely not the type I would have pegged for liking tea.

"Holly got Seth stuck on the stuff, and now they've both got me stuck on the stuff," he says. He seems pleased with himself, and this is inexplicably adorable. "Lemon and honey, it's just the best."

"Even when it's hot outside?" I say.

"Peppermint has menthol on it," he says. "Cools you down. In Morocco, they drink hot peppermint in the heat to cool down."

I'm betting that information also came from Holly. Bless her. I always liked her.

"Well," I say. "I'll give it a try."

We're at his apartment in almost no time at all. I can't help but notice that he's been glancing in the rearview mirror during the whole drive, but no one followed us here.

When Colt puts the car into park, he says, "I'll get your door."

I stay put and smother another laugh. While I am perfectly capable of opening my own door, I forgot that Colt is very cavalier about this sort of thing. Makes him feel like a gentleman, he said, the first time that I did it. Who am I to tell him no when he wants to feel like a gentleman? Sometimes it's nice to do things the old-fashioned way.

He opens my door and holds his hand out to me, which I take. I was about to make a cheeky comment about how I can stand on my own two feet, thank you very much, but my knees are actually quite shaky. I zip my lips and keep my sass to myself.

He smiles at me and puts his arm around my shoulders. "Let's get you inside."

That smile is nearly enough to make me melt. Honestly, it's not a lie. How is it allowed for a man to be so charming, so cocky, so sure of himself, but also be so sweet and attentive? The two sides are incongruous. He should be one of those guys your mother tells you to stay far, far away from. And in a lot of ways, I guess he is. The bad-boy, motorcycle guy with smoldering eyes and a smile that feels like a caress.

I'm suddenly very aware that we are on our way up to his apartment. Alone. Just the two of us. When he asked me if I wanted to come to his place, my automatic answer was yes. Of course. Of course, I want to go and be with him. He's the only thing in the entire world right now that feels right. And I know that I've been unfair to him. That he would have been there for me if I had let him. And now my family has suffered for it, and I'm suffering for it. And he's still here after I've pushed him away.

But I didn't think about what being *alone* would entail. I wasn't in the head space for that. But now that the incident is wearing off a little, now that my head is getting back in the right place, I'm more than aware of his arm around me and the way his hip keeps glancing off mine while we walk. He stops when we reach the bottom of the stairs and gestures for me to go ahead of him. I would like to think that this is so he can have an advantageous position for admiring my figure while we go up the stairs, but I'll keep that to myself. I make my way to his apartment door on legs that are still slightly shaky. There are lots of butterflies batting around in my stomach, and most of them have nothing at all to do with the incident that just happened.

He smiles at me again when he draws up next to me. He fumbles in his pocket for his apartment key and leans his shoulder into mine while he unlocks the door.

"Make yourself comfortable," he says in his low rumble when the door swings open. How is it fair for a man's voice alone to have such an impact on a woman like me? Really, I feel at a massive disadvantage.

"Thanks," I say. I give a smile that I'm sure comes across as extra shy, and I hurry inside before he can see that I'm blushing.

I've always liked his apartment. It's really tidy, especially for a man's place. You would think a guy like him, living on his own, would have trouble picking up his socks or keeping up with the dishes. I've seen it and heard about it enough to think that it's a pretty common state that young bachelors live in. But here, everything has a place and there are nice touches, like framed pictures on the walls, and a rack to put shoes on by the door. A man who can keep a tidy house is a sexy man.

He's so nearly perfect.

But, is *anyone* perfect? Am I just being really fucking unreasonable, holding him to a standard that isn't actually achievable or realistic?

I hug myself while I stand in his living room, looking around the tidy space. He's in the kitchen behind me, rustling around.

"I feel like I should be making the tea," I say. "With your arm and all." I turn to watch him, catching glimpses of his firm butt in the jeans he's wearing and the way his T-shirt stretches over his arm muscles. I bite down on my finger while I watch him and hope he doesn't happen to glance at me right this minute. I might need some smelling salts if I don't get myself under control.

He scoffs from the kitchen. "You just put your pretty butt down and get comfortable," he says. "I'm injured, not out of commission."

"Whatever you say." I sit on the couch and pull my knees up. I'm impatient for him to finish, but I'm also savoring this. I don't think a man has ever made me a cup of tea before. And it may be hot outside, but it's actually pretty cool in his apartment right now with the air conditioning blowing. Tea sounds just fine.

"Here you go," he says. He walks around the couch and hands me a mug with Snoopy on it—which makes me laugh a little.

"Nice choice," I say, holding it up.

"Can't go wrong with Snoopy," he says over his shoulder as he walks back toward the kitchen. Music comes on, soft acoustic stuff. He returns a moment later with a mug of his own. He sits down on the couch next to me, close but with a little bit of room between us.

"Nice tunes," I say, giving him a small smile.

"Some Pandora station," he says, waving his hand.

"I like it," I say.

"I remember," he said. "You like the acoustic stuff."

I smile at him and then look down at my tea. Looking at him for too long feels too intense, like holding your hand close to the fire. But unlike fire, this doesn't hurt. It feels too good. But it *does* make me feel like I might go up in flames if I'm not careful enough.

And Colt, damn him, seems to be aware of the effect that he's having on me, and if I were pressed, I would say that he's enjoying it.

"Feel better?" he asks quietly. He says it kindly, even with that twinkle in his eye that promises many, many things, none of which are mentionable in polite company.

"Yeah," I say. "Thanks for the tea." I realize I haven't even tried it, so I sip it to show him that I'm glad to have it. Just enough honey. I give him a smile.

He reaches out and touches my knee with his finger, just tracing a small line back and forth. A simple gesture, but it has my heart thrashing in my chest, and my whole body comes alive in a way that only seems to happen in response to him. I feel myself blush again, and I give him another smile, which does the job it's meant to. He puts his whole hand on my leg and runs his fingers up and down the top of my thigh.

He watches his hand move, completely absorbed in his task, and I watch his face while he touches me. It suddenly feels very warm in his apartment.

I put my mug of tea on the little table next to the couch, and I reach out and run my finger along his jaw. There's just a little roughness there, and the texture is enough to make my stomach flip-flop. How is he *so* fucking handsome?

He puts his hand over mine, pressing my fingers against his cheek.

"I was really fucking worried about you," he says softly. His eyes find mine, and he looks at me so intently that I feel like he's seeing into me. The connection between us hums and shivers like a live powerline. The air is thick with the electric current that's been building between us, and I can almost hear it and see it sparking around us. The rest of the world is falling away and it's just us, here and now. "I would never have forgiven myself if something happened to you."

"Shhhh," I say. I press my other hand to his cheek so that I'm holding his beautiful face. And like we're both following an unspoken cue, we lean into each other until our noses and foreheads are pressed together. I close my eyes and just breathe in the scent of him, and it's enough to make me dizzy.

"You are so beautiful," he whispers against my lips. "It fucking hurts me how beautiful you are."

I can't even think of what to say to that. It's enough to send me up, past cloud nine. Our lips meet, and I feel a surge of that electricity. It crackles now, sparking brightly, and I feel like we're in serious danger of combusting. His mouth tastes so good, a warm and luscious taste with a hint of honey and peppermint. His tongue caresses mine. He kisses me over and over, long lingering kisses that begin to turn into more rugged, demanding kisses. I am totally helpless.

He pulls away from me suddenly and begins to yank at the sling that his arm is in. I help him pull the strap over his head, and he tosses the thing away with disgust. And then he turns to look at me with that twinkle in his eye. He gives me the smallest smile before he puts both hands on my waist and presses me back against the couch's armrest. His hands find their way under my shirt and squeeze before they move up and down, caressing my skin. Goosebumps come up all over my body, and I shiver, which makes him laugh.

I stick my tongue out at him, and then pull him down on top of me, fitting him perfectly between my legs.

"Oh my," he breathes, smiling at me wickedly. "Fancy meeting you here, Miss Peters."

"Fancy," I whisper against his lips, and then kiss him again. This time he doesn't hold back at all. He kisses me hungrily, ardently, until my lips feel swollen, but I don't want him to stop. It's like we've broken a dam, and there's no stopping any of it now. All of the time we've spent apart, all of this energy has just been building, waiting for the moment when we would come together again.

He sits up and I sit up too, helping him get his shirt over his head. He winces a bit when he lifts his hurt arm, but when I open my mouth to ask him if he's all right, he sees my face and says, "I'm fine, don't worry." And then he gives me another one of those smiles and says, "Your turn." His fingers slip under my shirt and pull it up over my head. He dips his head to press his lips to my collar bone, to taste my neck with his tongue. His mouth moves down, across my chest, and over the swell of my breasts until he comes to the top of my bra. He slips his fingers just under the cup, breathing deeply while he keeps eyes fixed on the soft, rounded flesh there.

He looks up at me, and his eyes are nearly glowing, the color of pine. He straightens up and slips his hands over my shoulders and over my back.

"This thing sure looks awfully uncomfortable," he whispers against my ear while his fingers fumble with my bra clasp. "Allow me to help you with that."

"Oh, you think so?" I answer, but I lean into him, smiling against his shoulder while he unhooks my bra. He sits back again, and I let it slowly fall into my hands. Watching his face is nearly enough to make me come. He stares intently at my breasts and then looks at my face again. He slips his hands around my ribcage and squeezes so tightly that the breath goes out of me. He pulls me up onto my knees and then into his lap. His fingers caress the curve of my breasts, and I can feel his hot breath against my skin. He looks up and locks eyes with me while he tastes my nipples with his tongue, one at a time. Then he closes his eyes and takes one of them into his mouth, drawing on it hard enough to make me gasp. I run my hands through his hair and press my hand against the back of his head.

He moves his mouth to my other breast, sucking hard.

"Oh my God," I whisper.

I can feel him through his jeans, rock hard, pressing against the ache between my legs. I move against him, grinding slowly. It's just enough to feel good and drive me fucking nuts. I hope it does the same for him. The sound he makes tells me that it probably comes close to hitting the mark. His hands slide down the swell of my hips and grabs my ass, squeezing hard. He frees my breast from his mouth and looks up at me with those beautiful, intense eyes. Then he renews his grip on my ass and stands so suddenly that I have to grab onto him to keep from toppling out of his arms. I wrap my legs around his waist and my arms around his neck. Our mouths find each other again and we kiss deeply, urgently.

Somehow he manages to steer us to his bedroom without crashing into anything, and he spills us onto his bed, pinning me beneath him with his hips. He kisses me again and then he gets to his feet, leaving me laying on the bed. He picks up one of my feet and presses it against his chest with his hand. He caresses my calf, and his eyes follow the line of my leg up to the tattered hem of my cutoff jeans. He kisses my foot and then moves my leg aside. He hooks his fingers into the waistband of my shorts.

"These," he says, "just have to come off."

"If you insist," I say, giving him a look that I hope conveys just how much I want him to insist.

"Oh, I do," he says. And he makes quick work of the button and the zipper. He hooks his fingers into them and has them down around my thighs in one quick motion, leaving my panties on. He goes to his knees, pulling them all the way down my legs and then he tosses them aside. He turns to face me again and then he grabs onto my calves, tugging my butt all the way to the edge of the bed.

"Now I have you," he says, "right where I want you."

He slips his hands up my thighs and over my hips to my waist, which he gives a hungry squeeze again. He brings his fingers back down to the hook into my panties, but he leaves them there. He brings his mouth to the edge of the lace and then drags his tongue along the flesh there, making me shiver with anticipation. He moves his fingers like he's going to pull my panties off and stops.

I make a sound of protest, but he just smiles at me. Then he presses his mouth against the most sensitive part of me through the cloth, and it's enough to make me nearly fly apart.

"Tease," I accuse him. And he just smiles at me angelically and does it again, licking me through the thin fabric. I think I probably swore at him for being so terrible, but I don't know if the words actually made it out of my mouth. My eyes are nearly rolling around my skull, it feels so good.

"Please," I say when I just can't take it anymore. "Colt, *please*."

He yanks my panties off in a quick jerk, and then puts his lips against my flesh. He kisses me as hungrily there as he did my mouth, and then he slides his tongue against me until I'm seeing stars. And when I can't imagine being any closer to the edge of oblivion, he slips his fingers inside of me.

He moves his tongue in long, slow strokes and it's enough to make me close my eyes. He's somehow keeping me at this point of absolute pleasure while preventing me from having an orgasm. I have never, ever been with a man who has managed to do this, and I would be impressed if I had the capacity right now. As it is, I'm lost in what he's doing to me with his mouth and his hands. And then, suddenly, he stops. It's enough to almost make me wail in protest.

I'm a panting mound of Jell-O, but I still manage to sit up all the way and loop my arms around his neck. We kiss deeply, and his fingers are gripping my waist so tightly that I think I might bruise. I can't even begin to care.

We kiss again until I'm so worked up that I push him away from me. "Stand up," I say.

"As the lady wishes," he says, and he gets to his feet.

"I always return a favor," I say, slipping my fingers into his belt loops. I pull him so close to me that I can kiss the soft trail of hair that disappears into the waistband of his jeans. I slip my hand up his thigh and across the front of his jeans until I find the shape of him under the denim, so hard that I can't imagine how he hasn't lost control yet. I press my lips against him through the fabric, and he lets out a sharp breath. His fingers are twining through my hair, letting the long tresses fall through his fingers like water.

I unbutton his jeans and peel them slowly over his hips and push them down until they fall around his ankles. I take a moment to fully appreciate how fucking delicious he looks in his sky blue boxer briefs—the hard planes of his stomach, the beautiful solid muscles of his thighs and of course, the thick shape of him covered by the thin cloth.

I'm too impatient to appreciate the view for long. I tug his underwear down, releasing him, and I wrap my hand around his shaft, giving it a squeeze. It's like granite in my hand. I want him inside of me so bad that I could scream, but I caress him and slowly work him into my mouth.

"*Jesus*," he says. He grips my hair and moans. I take him as far into my mouth as I can and stroke him with my hand while my tongue caresses the silky, wet head of his cock. I take him as far back into my throat as I can handle. This is no mean feat because he is anything but small.

"That feels so fucking good," he says, stroking my hair.

I look up at him and the look on his face while I have him in my mouth is almost enough to finish the job he started. Giving head is one of those things that can be so good or so awful. And I absolutely love going down on Colt. I work him in and out of my mouth, stroking the shaft while I lick the head. I can feel his body starting to shake and, unless I'm mistaken, his knees might just be ready to give out. I don't stop until he's breathing fast, and his body is tensing. Then I release him and wrap my arms around his hips and smile up at him innocently.

"*You're* the tease," he says. "You are."

"I'm not sorry," I say.

"I hope to make you sorry," he says, giving me a very wicked look. "Very, very sorry."

His hand closes in my hair, and I allow him to pull me slowly to my feet. He kisses me again, slow and deep, and then he lifts me by the ass and tosses me back onto the bed. I giggle helplessly and he chuckles a little, too. Then he's fitting himself between my thighs. He rests his forehead against mine and begins to press himself against my opening. It's been so long since we've done this that it aches when he moves into me, but it's a delicious sort of ache, and I'm so wet that it's not difficult for him. When he's inside of me he stops for a moment, and we just hold each other. The intensity of the moment, and the sensation of him inside of me, is almost more than I can bear.

"Colt," I say softly. "God."

He laughs a little and kisses. And then he begins to move, slowly and steadily, and it is the best fucking thing. I think I must have forgotten how good this was because I can't remember it ever being so good. He moves his hand up and down my thigh and then presses my legs back so he can enter me more deeply. My eyes are literally rolling again, but he's not satisfied until he can sense that I'm this close to coming. Then, he stops.

"No," I moan. "Fuck me. Please, fuck me."

"Roll over," he commands, and he begins to shift my hips with my hands. I do what he says, happily. He pulls my ass toward him, putting me on all fours. He grips my hips and then caresses them. He bends over me to kiss my shoulder, and he begins to stroke the hot, velvet wetness between my legs. Then, I feel him pressing his cock into me again, and it feels so good to have him inside of me that it takes my breath away. He holds my hips firmly, and he pulls almost all the way out and waits until I start moaning impatiently before he pushes back in. He does this until I think I'm going to go insane. Then, as if he read my mind, he starts to move faster and harder. I try to tell him how fucking good it is, but I can't even speak. He's moving faster and the pleasure is starting to build and spill over. And then the bastard stops again.

"You are so evil," I say to him. My body is literally trembling, I'm so close to having an orgasm. He actually has the nerve to chuckle at me as settles back on the bed.

"I want to watch you," he says. "I want to watch you ride me."

He doesn't have to tell me twice. I straddle him and lean forward to tangle my mouth with his as I guide his cock toward my opening. But he's not the only one who can be evil. Instead of slipping it inside of me, I use it to stroke my clit until I'm panting and nearly at the edge again.

"Fuck me," he moans, grabbing me by the hips and pushing up against me. His look is hazy with desire, and I can't take it anymore either. I slowly ease the head against my opening and allow myself to sit down on it slowly, loving the way he feels as he enters me.

"Oh God," I say.

I lift myself until he's almost all the way out of me before I ease him back inside of me. His eyes are moving between my face and watching himself slip in and out of me—and the look on his face is the hottest fucking thing I've ever seen. But I'm losing my own patience, I can't wait anymore. I begin to move faster, bending toward him and opening my mouth for his tongue. He grips one of my hips with his hand and tangles the other in my hair. His hips are moving up to meet mine, and I'm breathless with pleasure.

"I want to watch you make yourself come," he says.

I lean back again and this time, I stroke my clit while I ride him. The pleasure is so intense that it's only a matter of seconds before I can feel my orgasm approaching.

"That's so fucking hot," he says.

"I'm going to come," I moan, and I can't even see his face anymore because I'm drowning in the feeling.

But he says, "Me too." I explode, my orgasm rolls through me, and I practically scream. He stifles a moan and grips my hips so hard that I *know* he's going to leave a mark there too.

We stay like that for what feels like an eternity—me straddling his lap, with my hands resting against his chest, and him inside of me with his hands gently caressing my hips. Then, he slips out of me and patters away to the bathroom to get us a towel to clean ourselves up with. When that's done, he lays down next to me and pulls me against him, pressing a series of tender kisses against my forehead and my temple.

"Jesus Christ," he says. He looks so happy in his rumpled, sexy way. I can't help but match his smile. "*That* was beyond overdue."

"Couldn't agree more," I say. I tease the end of his nose with a lock of my hair and he swipes at it like a cat.

"It's good to see you," he whispers. And I think he's actually only being partially facetious.

"I missed you," I say, risking being frank.

"I missed you too," he says, and he's perfectly serious now. "I really did. I've never stopped thinking about you."

"Same," I say. "You annoying man."

"*Me?*" he says and laughs again. "*I'm* the annoying one?"

"Absolutely," I say, primly.

"Well, *you* are stubborn, missy," he says. And he tickles me a little, making me giggle.

"Is that supposed to be an insult?" I ask him, which makes him laugh.

"So much for that tea," he says. "It's probably stone cold by now."

"Ah, well," I say, trailing my fingers down his chest. "I guess I'll just have to come over for another cup of tea."

"Oh, *please* do," he says, and the facetiousness is back.

I lean in and press my lips against his. I feel his lips curve against mine as he laces his fingers in my hair and gives me several more delicious kisses.

"You gonna stay the night?" he says, softly.

I pause, thinking it over. Then I sigh. "I don't think so. I should be with my mother. She gets worked up pretty easily. In fact…" I look over my shoulder at the bedside clock. "I should probably be getting back."

The man actually pouts. And is more adorable than he has a right to be while he does it. He should look absurd, but he doesn't. I laugh and tickle the end of his nose with my hair again.

"I'll come with you," he says.

"I'm going to take a cab," I say. "I don't want to be driving my car. Even with you in it."

He pauses for a while, running his fingertips up and down my arm.

"All right," he says. "But I'm going to pay for your cab." And when I open my mouth to argue, he points at me and says, "No arguing." And he has that look in his eye that tells me that he means business.

"Fine," I say.

"We're going to get this all taken care of," he says, softly. "I promise."

I look into his eyes, searching for sincerity, and I find it. It's enough to make me feel warm inside. "Okay," I say. And I believe him.

We kiss again, a long, lingering kiss, and then I peel myself away from him. I don't want to be in a hurry to escape this beautiful dream, but truthfully I'm starting to get really tired. I'm afraid I'll fall asleep if I don't get out of here.

He's kind enough to call a cab for me while I get dressed. He pulls his jeans over his beautiful naked body, and I can't help but grab his butt. He's just so yummy. I'm almost ready to start all over again. I loop my arms around him and press my face into his back. He presses his hand over mine and then picks one of them up and presses my palm against his lips.

"I'm really glad you came over," he says in a rough, tender voice.

"Me too," I say. I kiss his shoulder blades, and we stand there like that, rocking slightly, until my phone rings. It's the cab company.

"I'll be right down," I tell the driver.

Colt walks me down to the taxi.

"Let me know when you get there safely," he says. We kiss again, and he pulls me into his arms, hugging me so tightly that I can't breathe. "Be safe," he whispers into my hair.

"Promise," I say. Then he kisses me on the head once more and lets me go. I climb into the back of the taxi and blow him a kiss through the window as it pulls away from the curb.

I am soaring in the clouds all the way to the hospital. I'm so distracted that I almost forgot to thank the driver. I hurry inside, throwing a glance over my shoulder to make sure that no one is following me. But even the dark events that preceded my visit to Colt's house aren't enough to take the air out of my balloon for long.

I'm here, I text him. Almost immediately, he sends me back a kissy face. I smile and head into the elevator bay. I hardly see where I'm going. I hope my mother doesn't notice that I'm in such a good mood. The reason why we're at the hospital in the first place pushes in on my happy feeling.

I step off the elevator and walk down the hallway, feeling a lot more somber. It also occurs to me that I left quite some time ago to get snacks from the store, and I have returned without any. I wasn't going to tell my mother what happened, but I don't really know how to explain this without telling at least some of the truth.

I push the door open to Ted's room.

"Hi," I say. But I walk in, and it's just Ted. My mother's nowhere to be seen. The bathroom door is ajar, and the light is off. Huh. She must have gone to find her own snacks, seeing as I took so long.

"Hi," Ted says. His voice is very strained and gravelly. I walk to his side and put my hand on his shoulder.

"Hey," I say. I give him a smile. Jesus, he's in bad shape. His face is so bruised and swollen he's almost unrecognizable. "How you feeling?"

"Like dog shit," he says. Which makes me laugh a little. "Where's your mother?"

"Not sure," I say. "I just got back."

"I thought she was with you," he says. "I've been waiting for her to come back since I woke up an hour ago."

My heart thumps in my chest. I don't want to alarm Ted though.

"I'll just give her a call," I say. I dial her number, but the phone goes straight to voicemail. I try again. And again. I swallow hard. "It's going to voicemail. Maybe she left her charger at home." I try to smile, and I give his shoulder a squeeze. "I'll just go ask the nurse. I'm sure they'll know something."

I leave the room and make the short trip down the hall to the desk, but my knees are almost knocking together. I have a really, really horrible feeling about this.

"Have you seen my mother?" I ask the redheaded nurse that's been coming through to check on Ted. "Did she say anything to you?"

The red headed nurse frowns and looks at the clock. "She said she was going to get some fresh air. But honestly, that was quite a while ago. I haven't seen her since."

The floor feels like it's falling away. "I can't get a hold of her."

"I'll call security and let them know to call us if they see her," the nurse says.

"I'm going to go down and look around for her," I say. "Her phone just might be dead."

I fumble with my phone while I walk toward the elevators. I try calling her again, three more times, and it goes to voicemail each time.

"Oh my god," I say under my breath. My mouth is so dry that it feels like it's going to crack. I dial Colt with shaking hands and hold the phone against my ear, aching to hear his voice tell me that he's on his way. But it rings to voicemail. Normally I wouldn't back-to-back dial, but this is not a normal situation. I redial, but he doesn't pick up again.

Mom's been missing for at least an hour, I text him.

Nothing.

I walk out the front doors and look around. "Mom?" I call. "Mom?"

I hear nothing.

I'm alone outside of the hospital and neither of the two people I need to talk to are answering their fucking phones.

I take a deep breath and dial Colt again.

Chapter Fourteen

Shotgun

I put down my phone and breathe a sigh of relief after it pings with a message from her telling me that she made it okay to the hospital. I wasn't *super* worried about her making it in the taxi—in fact, I think it was a really smart idea. But these guys have been pulling some really ballsy shit. I'm confident she'll be okay at the hospital. There are people constantly there on watch. Trying to pull something there would just carry way too much risk.

I wish she had stayed. I understand that she had to go, I do. But I also crave her, like a smoker fiends for a cigarette. It's like I don't even realize how much tension I carry around in my body until we come together and it's all released. I don't know if I've ever felt better in my life. I'm coming down from that state of pure bliss a bit, but the glow is still there.

I look over to the other side of my bed and try to picture her lying there. I used to love spending the night with her. She holds onto me like she's going to be swept away when she's sleeping. It was a bit strange at first, but I got used to it. And by the time I got used to it, it was gone.

The reality that I have to contend with now is that I *do* have every intention of handling shit with these *Los Brujos* dickheads. But I don't know where to start. I need a plan. I'm glad Nick knows stuff, I'm glad he was able to give me some background on these guys so I'm not going in blind. It's good to know how far they're willing to go and that they're a big organization. But I kind of feel like David facing down Goliath. But I don't know what to put in my slingshot, and I can't just let this go. No fucking way. Even if Erica and her mother just handed that house over. These guys have actively tried to harm my girl, and her family, and that's not going to stand. There's no fucking way.

I sit up and groan slightly. The ache in my arm is back. The lovely endorphin kick I got from fucking the most beautiful woman in the world is all but gone, and the pain is coming back in full force. Granted, it's not nearly as bad as it was in the beginning, but it still gets grumpy when I jostle it around a bunch. Needless to say, I just did a hell of a lot of jostling.

I'm tired, but I'm feeling restless. I sit up in bed and swing my legs over the edge. I think I'll take a shower. I sure fucking wish she was here to take a shower with me. My mind immediately seizes on the image of her body, slicked down with soap and I'm half-hard again already. Jesus Christ, this woman must have some magic power over me. I'm not opposed to that, honestly. Whatever this hold she has, I'm happy with it.

I get to my feet and start to walk down the hallway to get to the bathroom when there's a knock on my door. A very firm, solid knock.

I hold very still for a minute. There are only two types of people who would show up at my door and pound like that without at least trying to call first: cops or assholes. And I don't like either of those options. I have a shotgun leaning in the closet right by the door, but if there are cops at my door, I don't want them to catch me with it anywhere near me. I'm not trying to get shot. Again.

Whoever is at the door pounds again. I walk as softly as I can across the living to the door and peer through the peephole. Uh-huh. The boys in brown, our friends from the sheriff's department. I'm not exactly sure why they're knocking on my door, but I can guess that it's probably nothing I want anything to do with. I don't really have a choice, though.

I open the door. "Good evening, deputies," I say to the two in front of me. I recognize the woman, she came by the Clubhouse and was grilling us about what happened with Johnny. Her name tag reads Deputy Wilson. The other dickhead I haven't met before. Deputy Round, his name tag informs me.

"Colt Hardy," says Deputy Round. "You are under arrest for the murder of Jesus Rafael Blanco."

"What?" I say. Because I honestly feel like I just walked into the Twilight zone.

Wilson has handcuffs, and she gestures at me to come toward her. "Turn around, please."

"You have the right to remain silent," Round continues in one long monotonous breath, like he's bored and annoyed with the fact that he should have to notify anyone of their rights. "Anything you say can and will be used against you in a court of law. You have the right to have a lawyer, if you can't afford one we will appoint one for you, you have the right to exercise any of these rights at any time. Do you understand your rights?"

I can't say I didn't think they would eventually come knocking at my door. I was there at the crime scene. The truth usually comes out one way or another, and I wasn't prepared to be there. It's not like I premeditated the whole thing and had a strategic exit plan. But after the media was blathering about a robbery, I guess I started to relax. On the other hand, Deputy Wilson came snooping around, asking questions. I shouldn't be surprised that she's here while all of this is going down. I look at her and try to read her face, but she's as blank as an empty canvas.

I stare at the petite woman holding the handcuffs. One of her hands is on her gun. It's still in its holster, but the holster has been unsnapped. I seriously consider what my options are, but decide not to be a fucking idiot. I turn around, rolling my eyes and putting my hands behind him.

"Could I at least finish getting dressed?" I ask over my shoulder.

The horribly painful crack of those steel cuffs against my wrist bones is my answer, I guess. I grit my teeth, and it takes everything I have not to make a sound. My wrists aren't broken, but that is sure as shit going to be a bone bruise. I'm starting to think Deputy Wilson might be one of those all-bite-and-no-bark kinda cops. She grabs me by the arm and turns me toward the stairs.

I sigh inwardly. I have had two too many encounters with the cops this month. I swear to God my wrists just recovered from the last time they slapped those fucking cuffs on me. I don't care how big and tough a man thinks he is, getting cracked on the wrists with cuffs hurts every fucking time.

I don't think about the fact that my phone is sitting on my bed at home until we're halfway down the street. *Fuck.* Erica's not going to be able to get a hold of me at all if something comes up. But I need to chill the fuck out. These assholes have nothing on me. They're probably just trying to scare me into giving them answers that they want. They won't be able to keep me long, and this shit definitely isn't going to stick once they get down to the nuts and bolts of it. Johnny died from a self-inflicted gunshot wound. Case closed. I'll be in and out, no problem. I feel bad that I won't be able to get back to Erica quickly if she needs me though. But I reassure myself that Erica and her family are at the hospital. What can possibly happen to them at the hospital?

The station is not a far drive from my house, but because I'm impatient for this whole stupid thing to be over it seems to be taking an exceptionally long time. When we pull into the parking lot, they both get out of the car. And instead of letting me out, they let me sit in the back for a good few minutes. It's not objectively super long, but it's long enough that I feel pissed off, especially considering that I am sitting in a really fucking uncomfortable position with my hands cuffed behind me.

Deputy Wilson finally opens the door for me and motions for me to step out of the car, which I do awkwardly in my bare feet. The ground is still shockingly warm, even this late at night. She takes me by the upper arm and marches me toward the building, like a stern school teacher directing a student to the principal's office.

"This way," she says and off we go, like a really stupid parade. It occurs to me then, as we enter the building and we make our way to one of their interrogation rooms, that I have never been in one of these rooms before. I've been in the holding cell. I've definitely been arrested and brought down here a few times, but nothing has ever stuck. And I've certainly never been implicated or questioned about anything as serious as murder. It's not something I particularly want to be connected to. But the bottom line is that Johnny wasn't actually murdered. He died from a deliberately self-inflicted gunshot wound. There's a world of difference there. I mean, the circumstances seemed to force his hand. But there's got to be some sort of proof in the ballistics.

The more I think about it though, the more nervous I get. What if I'm wrong? And what if this is some kind of set up? My mouth is a bit dry when I follow Deputy Round into the interrogation room. He gestures to a plastic chair for me to sit in—the kind that is not meant to conform to *anyone's* ass comfortably. I sit and he remains standing. I know from watching enough bits and pieces of police procedurals over the years that he's trying to intimidate me. Set the tone. He's in charge, and I'm the small guy. He's going to ask the questions, and I'm going to answer them. But he's got me all wrong. Nothing about him is intimidating. He looks like a pig in an ugly pair of brown trousers. What about that could possibly be considered intimidating?

"Don't mind if I do," I say. "You got any coffee?"

Deputy Round stares hard at me for a moment. "Deputy Wilson," he says in a most condescending voice. "Would you be so kind as to get Mr. Hardy some coffee?"

I see her eyes flicker to him ever so slightly, and then she leaves the room. That look is the first trace of anything human behind her mask. And I'm sure that look means she would like to get coffee—and dump the whole scalding pot in his big, stupid face. He's probably always ordering her to get the coffee, and it's probably because she's a woman. And I'm also willing to bet that Deputy Wilson is really tired of that.

"Appreciate it," I say to Deputy Round.

"If you'll just wait here," he says. And then he goes out and shuts the door behind him. And I'm willing to bet this is more mind-fucking bullshit. They're going to make me sit here while they watch me through the glass and they hope I'm sweating, wondering what on Earth is going to happen now.

A couple of minutes later, the door opens and Deputy Wilson comes in with a tiny white Styrofoam cup full of steaming black coffee. She puts it at the edge of the table I'm sitting at, just out of my comfortable reach.

"Turn around," she says. And I swivel in the chair. I feel her fiddling with the cuffs and then one of my wrists is free. "Back this way," she instructs, and I turn back toward her. She cuffs my wrist again, but at least my hands are in front of me now.

"Thanks," I say to her.

She doesn't acknowledge me, just turns on her heel and closes the door behind her with a snap. Yeah, I bet she's *really* tired of getting the coffee. But hell, I would be too if I were her. I reach for the coffee and awkwardly use both hands to bring the tiny cup to my mouth. More time passes, and I sip at the coffee. It's not the worst, but it's not the best either. I look around discreetly and realize that there isn't a goddamn clock in the room. Those fucking bastards. I have no idea how long I've been sitting here. The main thing about that that makes me nervous is that I've left my phone at home like an idiot, and I'm worried about Erica trying to get ahold of me.

Well, if these fucking clowns would stop playing mind games and commence the questioning, I could get out of here a whole hell of a lot faster.

After what seems like a goddamn year, the door finally opens. Deputy Round steps in with a file tucked under his arm and a big mug of steaming coffee. The difference between his cup size and my cup size is not lost on me. He probably also has the good stuff in his cup. Starbucks French Roast or something, not some off brand stuff that tastes like a boiled tire the longer it sits.

Deputy Wilson follows him into the room. She has declined to indulge in a cup of coffee, and I can't say I blame her. Deputy Round makes a big show of getting settled in his chair, pulling at his tie. He opens the file and shuffles things around. Clears his throat. Shuffles things some more. I glance at Deputy Wilson, who has not taken a seat in the chair next to Deputy Round. Instead, she's watching me. I would peg her look as curiosity more than anything else, which is kind of surprising. But when she glances at Deputy Round, I would bet some good money that what I'm detecting there is the smallest hint of hostility. She doesn't like him an ounce. And that's pretty good to know.

The shit head finally clears his throat one last time and says, "Where were you on the evening of June eighteenth at approximately 9 PM?"

"I was at Mike's Cellar with my boss," I say. The best way to tell a good lie is to stick nearly to the truth. And, frankly, there's not *too* much I need to lie about. It's more about omitting information really. And that's only sort of lying.

"And what were you doing there?" Round asks, squinting his piggy eyes at me.

"Having a few drinks after work," I say.

"And where is it that you work?" he asks, flipping through the pages in his file like he's doing something important. He's probably not.

"Kyle's Garage," I say.

I watch Deputy Round flip back to the front of the folder and pick up a glossy picture. He pushes it across the table to me. It's a mugshot of Johnny.

"Do you recognize this man?" asks Deputy Round, tapping Johnny's face with his sausage fingers.

"Sure," I say. "I don't go into Mike's Cellar much—I'm a Hoppa Taphouse guy myself—but he always seemed to be in there when I would go in. My boss, Kyle, goes in more often. He was on friendly terms with this guy. Called himself Johnny."

"Are you aware that he was killed at Mike's Cellar on the night of June eighteenth?" says Deputy Round.

"I saw something on the news about it," I say. I glance down at Johnny's picture again and hope that my face is as blank as I think it is. "Nice guy. It's a shame."

Deputy Round snorts. "You," he points his finger in my direction, "were seen at Mike's Cellar on the night of June eighteenth. The bartender tells me that you left just after he did." He jabs his finger at Johnny's picture. Jesus, everyone knows that pointing is fucking rude.

"The party was breaking up," I say. "He left with a few other guys. I didn't see where they went."

"I have reason to believe that isn't true," says Deputy Round.

I resist the urge to lick my lips. It's an indication of worry. My mouth is dry as hell, but I'm not giving this asshole even a crumb.

"Wish I could help you," I say.

Deputy Round flicks through his folder and pulls out another picture. This time, it's a picture of me. A mug shot. I have to keep myself from laughing at the pissed off look on my face. I'd give anything to be able to snap a photo of this and send it to the rest of the Knights. Makes me wonder what their mugshots look like.

"You were arrested," he says. "Just the week before for gang violence outside of Hoppa Taphouse."

"Gang violence," I say, and this time I can't help but laugh.

"Are you or are you not a member of the motorcycle club the Steel Knights?" he asks. He doesn't seem happy that I laughed at him. That makes me want to laugh again, but I keep it under wraps.

"I am," I say. "I was just voted in."

"Hooray for you," he says. Rude *and* porcine, Officer Round. He sniffs and refers back to his file. "You had an altercation outside of Hoppa Taphouse with another local motorcycle club called the Unchained Dogs."

"Perhaps," I say.

"You were arrested," says Office Round, flicking me a look of disdain. "And charged with disturbing the peace."

"I was," I say. "I can't say I expected to be back here at the station to visit so soon." I wish I knew what time it was. It's hard to tell how long I've been here. I think of my phone, sitting back at my apartment, and hope to God Erica hasn't been trying to get ahold of me. I'm sure it's all fine, but the last thing I want to do is drop the ball on the whole situation with her.

"You guys think this is your territory, don't you?" says Round. He slurps coffee out of his mug, watching me with his piggy eyes. I glance at Deputy Wilson, but she's standing with arms folded, watching me with a totally unreadable expression. I can't really tell who's supposed to be the bad cop.

"There are common courtesies that motorcycle clubs adhere to," I say.

"And they weren't adhering?" says Round. "The Unchained Dogs?"

"You could say that," I say.

"I don't think it's a coincidence that this guy," he taps Johnny's picture and nearly sloshes coffee all over his brown uniform, "happened to be the founder of another bike gang."

"Was he?" I say, raising my eyebrows.

"Don't play stupid," says Deputy Round. I think by the triumphant look in his eye that he thinks he's coming in for the kill. "You tell me this guy shows up at Mike's Cellar, and ya'll leave nearly at the same time, and you don't know a thing about what happened to him."

He shuffles through his folder again and pushes a photograph toward me. It's a picture of Johnny lying by the dumpster, dead. The blood looks particularly red in the photo, like it's paint. I feel a pang of sadness for Johnny, but I don't let my expression change. I look up at Deputy Round.

"Like I said," I say. "He was a nice guy. It's a shame what happened to him. But maybe you should be talking to the three guys he left with. They were from a different club from out of town. *Los Brujos?*"

"Bullshit," says Deputy Round. "He left the bar alone. You followed him outside and shot him behind that dumpster, Hardy."

"I did no such thing," I say. I'm distracted by how amazed I am by what's happening. Three key players have just been totally erased from the narrative. The bartender claims he left alone? Or Deputy Round is spinning it that way to suit his own purposes?

"Deputy Wilson here saw you the morning after the murder," says Deputy Round, nodding over his shoulder at the cop behind him. "She says your arm was in a sling. Hurt yourself, did you?"

"Sure did," I say. "At work. I'm all better now."

"You hurt yourself at work that morning?" Deputy Round asks. "On a Saturday morning?"

I see his point and try to back track smoothly. "The day before," I say.

"But you weren't wearing your sling at the bar," says Deputy Round.

"Don't like wearing the thing," I say. "I'll lose my street cred, wearing that thing at the bar. " I give him an innocent smile. "Don't tell my doctor. She'll kill me."

"Your doctor," says Deputy Round. He snorts. "And just who is your doctor?"

"My brother's fiancée," I say. "It's nice to have an MD in the family."

"I'm sure it is," he says, narrowing his eyes at me.

He falls silent, and I say nothing. He stares at me, and I stare right back. I don't know if I've engaged in a real staring contest since elementary school, but I'm sure as shit not going to lose this one. He's spared humiliation by a knock on the door, so he has an excuse to break eye contact. He opens it, but I can't really see who's standing there. I catch a glimpse of a brown uniform. I don't know if it has to do with me, but I'm starting to sweat a little bit. It's beginning to occur to me that they're really spinning this whole thing. What do they mean by denying that *Los Brujos* were at that bar? If they talked to Kyle like he said they did, he told them about what happened. The bartender wasn't the only person in that bar.

For the first time, it occurs to me that they could really get away with something. I've heard about this kind of thing happening in small towns. The cops and the judges decide how it's going to go and they can ignore all the facts they want to.

"I'd like to speak to a lawyer," I say as Deputy Round comes back and settles his bulk into the chair. I've never had to ask for a lawyer, but it's really starting to sink in to me that I might be in some deep shit.

"Sure," says Deputy Round with a truly unpleasant gleam in his eye. He leans back in chair and drums his fingers on the file laid out in front of him. "But you know." He leans forward now, dropping his voice in a conspiratorial whisper. "I'll make that call just as soon as you admit to killing Jesus Rafael Blanco."

I glance at Deputy Wilson. She's not looking at me, she's looking at Round. It's hard to read her expression, but for just a moment, I think I see shock. Maybe anger. And then the look vanishes and she regains her composure.

"You just read me my fucking rights," I say. "Before you dragged my ass down here. And you told me very clearly, as is the law, that I have the right to a lawyer at any time. So I'm lawyering up. I'm not answering anymore of your fucking questions until I get a lawyer."

"Well, fella," says Deputy Round. He gets slowly to his feet and makes a big show of shuffling those papers and tidying them up carefully like he has all the time in the world. He tucks the file under his arm and picks up his coffee mug. He takes a leisurely sip. "I'll just give you a little bit of time to really think about this. Seems like maybe a little time on your own might help you clarify things. Wilson," he says, glancing at her. The tone he uses might normally be reserved for a senile dog, not a person. "Come on."

Chapter Fifteen

Erica

"Come on. Come on. Come on," I say under my breath for the thousandth time.

"You've reached Colt—" the voicemail message starts to say, but I hang up the phone.

"*God*," I say, and I have to resist throwing my phone against the wall. My throat hurts so much from trying not to sob that I don't think I'm going to talk right for a week. Where the fuck is he? Maybe he fell asleep. I'm drowning in such a strong, shitty swirl of emotions that it's hard for me to think clearly about everything that's happening here. It's perfectly normal for him to fall asleep and not wake up to the ringer. But I've been trying to call him for an hour and nothing. All kinds of thoughts are racing through my mind. Is he out at the bar? Hanging out with the Knights? Getting drunk, even though he told me that all I need to do is call, and he would be here for me? It's the most hideous feeling to think that he would say that so flippantly and then not back it up.

But something tells me that there's more going on. I have this horrible feeling in the pit of my stomach. My mother has officially been missing for almost two hours and no one knows where she is. The nice, red-headed nurse called security, they've reviewed the cameras, but all they can see is my mother walking out of the range. The most they've been able to catch is the flash of what looks like tail lights whipping by, but it's so dark that it's impossible to tell if they belong to a motorcycle or a car, let alone anything as specific as make or model.

I'm trying not to get fucking hysterical, and it's like bobbing in the waves of a ferocious storm. I go up and down, up and down. I have to keep breathing deeply and slowly to keep myself from hyperventilating. The last thing I need to do is work myself up into a panic attack. I've hyperventilated so badly that I made myself pass out before, and it wasn't fun. Me being unconscious right now wouldn't help my mother.

The club. I suddenly remember that I have the number for the club. And even if Colt isn't there, maybe his brother is. At the very least, one of the Knights might know where he is or what's happened to him. I mean, he just texted me, and now he's not responding. I have to ride a wave of panic and guilt—what if something happened to him and it's my fault? What if *Los Brujos* tracked him down and did something to him? I still have the club's number from back in the day when I did the landscape design for them. I shuffle through my contacts and dial.

"Pick up," I beg. "Someone please pick up."

It rings a couple of times while my heart thunders in my chest, until—

"Hello?" A man's voice answers.

"Oh, thank God," I say because I can't help it. "This is Erica Peters. Is Colt there?"

"Nah, haven't seen him," says the guy on the other line. "Or talked to him. I thought his brother said he was at home tonight."

"His brother?" I say. My heart jumps into my throat. "Is Seth there?"

"Yeah, he's here," says the guy on the phone.

"Can I talk to him, please?" I say.

"Let me see if he can come to the phone," the guy says.

"Thanks," I say. "Thank you." But he's already put me on hold. I wait there for what feels like an eternity, heart beating so hard that it hurts. I wonder if it's possible to die of a stress overdose. Probably.

"This is Seth." He sounds so much like Colt on the phone that I want to cry.

"Seth," I say, breathless. "I can't get a hold of Colt. My mother went missing from the hospital two hours ago, and Colt said I could call and he isn't picking up."

"He hasn't answered me, either," says Seth. "I figured you two were... you know, hanging out." *Hanging out* sounds strongly like a euphemism to me, but I'm not in the mood to reprimand him.

"No," I say. "I left his place more than an hour ago, and I texted him when I got to the hospital. He texted back immediately, but from the time it took me to go upstairs and figure out that no one had seen my mother in almost an hour. I called him, and he stopped answering his phone."

"I mean, maybe he fell asleep?" says Seth.

"Maybe," I say. "But it seems a bit early. And, I don't know, he made a point to tell me to call if anything happened. I just don't think he would drop off like that."

"True," says Seth. "I'm really sorry to hear about your mother."

"I don't know what to do," I say. I'm getting so choked up that it's hard to talk. "One of those *Brujos* assholes all but told me the cops are in their pocket. I don't know who to call. I don't know what to do."

"Okay," says Seth. In a soothing way. The way someone would talk to a nutty horse. "Okay, I'm going to go over to Colt's house right now to check it out. And then when I get there, I'll call you. Or, ideally, have him call you. I'll be there in ten minutes."

"Thank you," I say. "Oh my God, thank you so much."

"Stay put," he says. "Don't go anywhere alone. And keep trying to call the little bastard. Maybe he's taking a really long shower."

"Okay," I say. The line goes dead, and I feel a little less like I'm drowning in panic. I also feel a horrible fucking knot of guilt in my stomach for all of the effort I've put into disliking Seth. I'm kind of fucking stunned at the way he's jumping in like this. How kind he's being to me. He's really not a bad guy. In fact, he's been a pretty good one.

I pace the hospital like a lunatic, wandering all over the floor while I wait for Seth's phone calls. I'm sure I'm totally in the way, and the nurses are sick of me, but I cannot possibly sit still.

And Ted is trying to rest in his room, as he deserves to after the ordeal he's had. And on top of that, now he has to fucking worry about my mother. No, I don't want to add to his stress by being in there and stirring it up with my anxious energy. I asked the nurse if it was possible to give him something that might help him relax a little bit. I normally don't go in for pharmaceuticals, but I nearly asked her to give me something too. I'm wound tighter than a spring.

My phone rings, and I nearly jump out of my skin trying to get it out of my pocket. My heart lurches when I see that it's Seth, not Colt. "Hello?" I say.

"I'm at his apartment," says Seth. "The door is unlocked, and he isn't here. His phone is by his bed. His wallet is on the counter."

"Oh my God," I say. And then I press a hand over my mouth to keep my lips from trembling. My eyes are burning, and I think I might vomit.

"I'm going to come down there," says Seth. "Sit tight."

And before I can answer, the line goes dead. I finally stumble to one of the hideous green chairs in the empty waiting room and just kind of stare at the floor while I sit there. All of the strength has gone out of me. My knees literally will not hold me.

Colt. What in God's name could have happened to him? And how is it that he goes missing so soon after my mother does? What the fuck is going on?

I stare at the wall, at the television, at the ugly carpet while I wait for Seth to arrive.

"Any luck?" a voice asks. I look up. It's the nice, red-headed nurse. She has a jacket on and a bag over her shoulder.

"No," I say and realize the word didn't even come out. I clear my throat and try again. "No."

"I'm really sorry to hear that," says the woman, and she looks like she means it. "I wish you the best of luck."

"Thank you," I say. Her kindness is nearly enough to make me cry again, but I honestly don't know if I have any tears left in me. I'm starting to feel numb.

"Hey." I look up, and Seth is standing there. He's wearing his heavy, patched vest over a T-shirt and seems a bit out of place in the waiting room, but I don't even give a shit right now.

"I don't know what to do," I say.

"Let's think about this," he says. "You said the *Brujos* have the cops in their pocket." He sits on the coffee table in front of my chair.

"Yeah." I rub my eyes. I suddenly realize that I'm exhausted, but I'm so wired I couldn't possibly sleep even if I wanted to.

"So that's dead," says Seth.

"Wait," I say. I slowly lower my hands and frown at the carpet.

"What?" he says. He's looking at me with a frown of concern.

"There was one cop..." I stand up. "Wait here."

"Uh," says Seth. "Okay." But I'm already walking away. I hurry down the hall to Ted's room, where my purse is. I creep inside, not wanting to disturb Ted. But he's passed out, snoring softly. I grab my purse and creep back out, closing the door silently behind me.

"What about this cop?" Seth says. I have a moment of appreciation of the similarities between the brothers, just in the way Seth is sitting there and the way he's frowning at me. It's enough to almost produce a nervous giggle from me. Jesus, I must be losing it.

"She was different," I say. I'm rummaging through my purse now. It's where I shoved her card after she handed it to me back at the ranch. "When the thing happened with the dogs, she gave me her card after Deputy Round walked away. And she made this point to tell me to call *her* if anything else happened, not the department."

"You think she's onto them?" he asks. He looks a bit surprised now and intrigued.

"I think it's starting to make sense," I say. I finally find the card, shoved into one of the zippered inner pockets. "I didn't know why she said that at the time. It seemed a bit weird to me. But I had a feeling about her. So I kept her card."

"Can I see?" says Seth. He holds out his hand for it before he's even finished asking, and I find myself handing it over before I even have time to think about it. Both of the Hardy boys share that commanding quality.

"Deputy Wilson," he says slowly. "She came by the Clubhouse."

"Why?" I say.

"After that guy got shot a couple weeks ago," says Seth. "She came by to ask if any of us knew anything about it. I thought it was weird because on the news they were saying the cops thought it was a robbery. But she was asking questions like she had her own ideas about it."

"I wonder if we can trust her," I say. And I'm almost asking for permission to do what I think I'm about to do. Because I don't know if I have the nerve to make the decision on my own.

Seth stares hard at the card. "I don't know what else we have to lose. If she's bought and paid for, the worst she can do is be unhelpful."

"You're right," I say. I hold out my hand for the card, and he gives it to me. I punch the number into my phone and find that I'm so nervous that I'm shaking. Not sure why I'm nervous. I want so much for this to lead to something. I'm so tired of dead ends and frustrations and no answers and no help.

The phone rings so long that I start to pull my phone away from my ear to hang up. But the line clicks, and I hear a woman's voice on the other end of the phone. "This is Deputy Wilson."

"Deputy Wilson," I say. "This is Erica Peters. You gave me your card when you came out to my house because of the dogs—"

"I remember you," says Deputy Wilson. "How can I help you, Ms. Peters?"

"Well," I say. I swallow hard. "You gave me your card and told me to call you if anything else happened. My mother's boyfriend was attacked outside of our home earlier this evening. We brought him to the hospital. And I stepped out for a couple of hours, and now my mother is missing."

"Missing?" says Deputy Wilson. "Can you tell me what happened?"

"No one's seen her for two hours," I say. "Security pulled the footage and all they have is her exiting the camera's field of vision. Deputy Wilson, I feel like no one in the department has wanted to hear our concerns about these people harassing us, but now my bo—uh friend, Colt Hardy, is missing too, and—"

"Colt Hardy is here in our custody," says Deputy Wilson.

"What?" I say. I look at Seth, confused. He frowns and mouths, *what?* "Why is he in your custody?" Seth's look shifts to one of shock and then consternation.

"He's been arrested for murder," says Deputy Wilson. "What is your connection to Colt Hardy?"

"He's my—I mean, we're kind of dating," I say. I feel like a babbling idiot. I'm picturing this competent, tough police woman listening to me over the line, and I'm so embarrassed I want to die. "I mean we were. And then we stopped. But we just started sort of—sorry, *whose* murder has been arrested for?"

"Jesus Rafael Blanco," says Deputy Wilson. "Went by the name Johnny. Did he ever mention this man to you?"

"He told me that he knew him," I say. "It came up because it turns out this guy was the founder of *Los Brujos*. The guys that have been after me and my mother. Why was Colt arrested for the murder when these guys are doing this to us? They're bad people. He said they were at the bar that night. Why aren't you talking to them?"

Deputy Wilson is silent so long on the other end of the line that I think for a minute that the connection has gone dead. I'm about to speak when she says, "I'd really like to know that, myself."

I'm surprised by this admission, but before I have time to say anything, she cuts me off. "I have to get going, Ms. Peters. Please call me if anything else comes up."

"Will you tell him that I called? Will you tell him what happened?" I say.

"Thanks for calling," she says. And the line goes dead.

I pull the phone away from my ear slowly and stare at it. Then I look at Seth.

"They arrested him for *murder?*" And while he's quiet and calm, I can see the flame of rage burning in his eyes. It's almost enough to make me take a step back.

"Yes," I say, and I feel sick. Not because I think Colt did it, but because I *know* he didn't. "They're trying to frame him." And there is a really big part of me that's fucking terrified that they might just get away with it.

"Time to go," he says. "No one fucks with my kid brother. Badge or no badge."

"Go where?" I say.

"The Clubhouse, for starters," he says. "It's the Knights' problem now, whether or not Nick wants to hear it."

"I'm coming with you," I say.

"I brought my bike," he says. "Normally I'd say only my old lady rides on the back of the bike, but in this case, I think she will be *very* understanding."

"Okay," I say. "I'll thank her, myself."

As we walk outside, I work up the nerve to say, "Thank you. For all of this."

"Of course," says Seth. "You mean an awful lot to my brother. Therefore, you mean a lot to me and Holly."

"I misjudged you," I say. I don't feel right unless I tell him this. "I really thought you were a—a bad influence on him. But you really care about him, and I'm sorry."

"Oh, I *am* a bad influence," says Seth. And he gives me a rare smile. I can't help but laugh.

"Still," I say. "Thank you. It means a lot."

"I want him to be happy," says Seth. He leads me to his bike and slings his leg over. "Climb aboard."

I do so, and he rolls the bike off of its kickstand and starts the engine.

"Hold on tight," he says.

And we're off like the blast of a shotgun.

Chapter Sixteen

Shotgun

I have no idea how long I've been in this fucking room. My wrists are sore from rubbing against the cuffs, I'm cold sitting here without my shirt or my shoes on in the AC, and I'm fucking starving to death. And above all, I can't stop thinking about Erica. What if she needs me? What if she needs me, and I'm sitting here like an idiot with my thumb up my ass?

And, not to mention, I have a few troubles of my own. Like the fact that I've been arrested for a murder that I did not commit and instead of evaluating any of the actual evidence that shows a pretty clear link to *Los Brujos*, they're hounding me and trying to force me to confess to something that I didn't do. It's starting to look bad for ol' Shotgun Hardy. I guess it always seemed like a possibility to me that I might do some actual time for something, but I never thought it would be murder. And I'm definitely not prepared to go away for a murder I didn't commit. And it wasn't a murder in the first place, it was goddamn suicide. Hell if I'm going to tell them that. Hell if I'll admit to being anywhere near what went down.

I'm frankly still stunned by the lack of proper procedure. There is protocol to this shit, and even low-life working class biker trash like me knows that. I know my rights. I knew them before the pig in the brown uniform read them to me. And what is happening here is a concrete miscarriage of justice. Deputy Round doesn't seem to be troubled by that. Wilson is hard to read so I can't be sure about her, but it seems to me like she might have salty feelings about it.

As if on cue, the door opens. I sit back, ready for more verbal sparring with the industrious and aptly named Deputy Round, but it's Wilson.

"I want my lawyer," I say. "I'm not saying another fucking word to you pigs until you get me a lawyer."

She stops and looks at me. She really studies me. I can't read her expression, and it's starting to make me crazy.

"Come with me," she says.

"Ah, the lovely holding cells," I say. "I was starting to think I'd never make it there."

But she doesn't lead me to a holding cell. She leads me out down a hallway and out a door directly into the night.

"Where are we going?" I say.

"Deputy Round was called away for the night," she says. "I am in charge of this situation now. I'll need those back." She gestures to my wrists.

"What?" I say and I'm sure I look like a slack-jawed idiot, standing there with my mouth hanging open and my eyebrows nearly hitting my hairline.

"The handcuffs," she says. "I'll need to have those back."

For once, I'm nearly speechless. "Uh," I say. "Okay?"

I hold my hands up and watch her suspiciously. I've been thinking she might be the *worse* cop—as in bad cop/worse cop—and maybe this is the part where she beats the shit out of me. Or she'll tell me some scary-accurate, fucked-up shit about myself and my childhood and spook me into confessing in order to unburden myself from lifelong shame. But instead, she just takes the cuffs off and backs away.

"Your friend Erica called," says Deputy Wilson. "Her mother is missing."

"Missing?" I say, rubbing at my wrists. "What the fuck do you mean missing?"

"Don't know the details," says Deputy Wilson. "Get going. I'll deal with them here."

"Why are you helping me?" I say.

"Because I'm tired of not doing the right thing," she says. And then closes the door, leaving me out in the night on my own. I stand there for a minute, in a sort of shock over what just happened. It feels like it must be a trick of some kind. But I can't afford to stand here and wonder about it like an idiot. If they catch me again, I won't be so lucky.

I move along the side of the building and try to stay in the shadows until I'm a block away from the sheriff's department building, and then I start to run. It's not that far to my apartment, and I run often to keep myself fit. But with my legs feeling like Jell-O, and my head full of miserable thoughts, it seems like ten miles.

I'm a sweaty, disgusting, panting mess by the time I reach my apartment. I stumble inside and pound water until my stomach is so full that I might vomit. Then I go straight to my phone. There are a million missed calls and texts from Erica and Seth both. I rifle through them quickly, feeling queasy, and it has nothing to do with drinking water.

Erica's mother is missing. How the fuck is that possible? They were at the hospital. And of all the times for some shit like this to happen, it's when the cops slap cuffs on me and haul me away.

I dial her number and she picks up almost instantly. "Hello?"

"Hey," I say. It's a fucking relief to hear her voice. "Are you all right?"

"No," she says. "Are you?"

"I am now," I say.

"What happened?" she says.

"They picked me up for murder," I say. "Johnny's murder. Deputy Wilson says that you called her. How did you know they arrested me?"

"I didn't," she says. "When they came out after the dogs were attacked, she gave me her card. She told me to call *her* directly if anything happened. Not the department. I think now that I know they're all fucking crooked that perhaps she's the only one who's not."

"I'd bet my life on that," I say. "She just let me go while the others were off stuffing donuts in their faces."

"She let you go?" says Erica.

I put the phone on speaker phone so I can pull on a T-shirt, some socks, and then shoes. "Yeah. She literally walked me out of the building, took cuffs off me, and told me that you called. And then told me to fuck off before I get caught."

"Are you serious?" She sounds a little like she might laugh.

"Weird, huh?" I say. "Where are you now?"

"I'm at the Clubhouse," she says.

"What the hell are you doing at the Clubhouse?" I chuckle a bit at my clever girl.

"I called and got a hold of Seth," she says. "I couldn't reach you, and I had a feeling something was wrong. I called here to see if I could reach him or someone who might know something."

"You sly minx," I say. "I'm sorry about your mom. I'm on my way right now, and we are going to get her back if we have to burn the whole fucking town to the ground."

"Let's hope it doesn't come to that," she says. "But if it does, I'll be handing you the gasoline."

"My kinda woman," I say.

"Hurry."

"I will." And I hang up, even though I would love to keep talking to her. The faster I get out of here, the faster I can take her into my arms. I grab my keys, wallet, and throw my vest over my T-shirt. I'm riding with my colors tonight—full Shotgun mode. I'll be wearing them proudly when I destroy those fucking bastards for hurting my girl and her family.

I don't even notice if my arm hurts as I ride over to the Clubhouse, and I nearly wipe out pulling into the parking lot, 'cause I'm in so much of a hurry to get to her. I blow through the front door.

"Hello?" I shout. I take the stairs two at a time up to the bar, and they're all in there. Nick, Bullet, Wildfire, Bullseye, Bucky, my brother Dynamite and, of course, Erica. The boys are all seated at the bar, and Constantine is standing behind it with his arms crossed. Erica is sitting off by herself while the Knights talk. My heart fucking surges with pride when I see them sitting there, all in their vests. My family. My friends.

"About time," says Seth.

"I was a bit tied up," I say. "Or cuffed up, however you want to look at it."

"The cops get you, eh?" says Nick.

"Fucking dickheads," Bullseye adds.

I ignore their jabs and walk straight to Erica. She stands up from the barstool her cute butt has been sitting on, and I pull her into a hug so tight that I hope I don't break her. She looks miserable, exhausted, and totally beat down, but she's still the most beautiful woman in the entire world. I decide right here and now that I'm not going to rest until we get married. I can't possibly risk losing her again.

"You okay?" I whisper into her hair.

"I am now," she says just as softly into my shoulder. Her voice is muffled. I take a deep breath of her lovely scent, and then I let her go. A guy can only get a pass for being so gooey with his old lady in front of the other guys.

I turn around and walk toward the Knights. I look at Nick and realize I don't think I've ever been more nervous in my life, but I have to go for it. I take a deep breath and say, "Nick—"

But he holds up his hand to cut me off. "No need," he says. "We're in."

"What?" I say. "Really?"

Nick sighs. "I tried to avoid this," he says. "Getting us pulled in with these assholes. But the way things are playing out, it's unavoidable. They're buddies with the Dogs now, they're putting their roots down in town, and I know for a fact this won't be the end of this. But even if we did nothing, things aren't looking too good for us. So let's help out this nice, little gal and remind these motherfuckers whose territory they're shitting all over."

"Thank you," I say. "That really—thanks, Nick."

"Don't thank me just yet," he says. "You can thank me after we put their asses through the wood chipper."

I give him a big grin and salute him. "Yes, sir."

"What do you know about how these guys are operating around here?" Nick asks. "Know where they're based in town?"

"The only clue I have," I say, "is the Dogs. So, with your permission, I think we should start there."

"That seems reasonable to me," says Nick. "And I never say no to riling up some rabid mutts."

Bullseye laughs. "This is going to be fun."

I glance at Erica, and she's watching me anxiously. Though, admittedly, she looks a lot more relieved than she did earlier. I shoot her a small smile and she returns it.

"I'll take you back to the hospital," I say.

"Absolutely not," she says, and she says it fiercely.

It's enough to make the Knights laugh and whoop at me.

Erica flushes with embarrassment, but she doesn't back down. "I can't sit there and do nothing while you are all out there risking yourselves for me and my mother."

"Sure you can," I say.

"I want to go," she says. "It's my family. I have to do my part to protect them."

"I respect the shit out of that, girl," Nick says.

Erica gives him a tiny smile, and he nods to her. Then he slaps his thighs and stands up. "Well then, to the Doghouse, shall we?"

The Knights all get to their feet and holler an eclectic mix of *fuck yeah*s and *let's fucking do it*. My blood surges, and I feel the good kind of adrenaline go through me. Erica walks to me, and I sling my arm around her shoulders. I see Bullet, Bullseye, and Bucky checking their pistols for ammo and making sure the safeties are on. Bullet and Bucky wear their guns in hip holsters, but Bullseye has his at the shoulder. I kind of envy how fucking cool he looks. I ought to get me one of those.

"I don't want anything to happen to you," I say as we all head down the stairs and out of the Clubhouse.

"Don't worry about me," she says. "Let's worry about my mother."

"Oh, I do," I say. "We'll make them real fucking sorry for this shit. We can't let these fucking punks be coming around here, getting away with this shit." I shake my head. "Bad people. And they're hanging out with the Dogs? Pfft, that alone tells you something about what sort of guys they are."

"I don't think I've ever seen you like this," she says, laughing a little as I sling one leg over my bike.

"Like what?" I say. I pat the seat behind me and give her a playful smile.

"Like *Shotgun*," she says. "You look like you're out for blood and, you're going to enjoy getting it."

"You're catching on nicely," I say.

"I should tell you," she says. "I rode on the back of your brother's bike."

I gasp, feigning horror and disgust. "How could you?"

"I'm a terrible woman," she says. And I chuckle as I start my bike's engine. All of the engines come to life, creating an insane cacophony of noise. It gives me another huge kick of adrenaline. We all start revving our engines, and backing out of our parking spots so we're in a neat line, waiting to ride out behind Nick.

"Hold on, baby," I say to Erica over my shoulder. I feel her squeeze me around the ribs. And even though I'm about to put her in a shit load of danger, I can't help but feel proud and excited that she's riding out with us. I also feel a little smug and vindicated that she's getting a taste of my world, the world she showed so much disdain for, and from what I can tell she actually might be enjoying herself. I just wish it was under different circumstances. But that's life.

We rip out of the parking lot and follow the Knights, weaving in and out of cars like the fucking hooligans we are. We finally ride up to the Dogs' clubhouse, like the Hosts of Hell, but I know right away there's nothing going on here. There aren't any bikes parked out front, and all of the windows are dark.

All of us circle up and kill our engines so we can hear one another.

"What now?" says Bullet, looking at Nick.

"They're up to some shit," he says.

"Awful big coincidence no one is home," says Seth.

"The ranch," says Erica behind me. "They could be at the ranch."

"That makes sense," I say. "It's rural, out of the way. No one to keep them from doing whatever evil shit they're trying to get up to."

"The ranch it is," says Nick.

"It's showtime," I say to Erica over my shoulder as I start the engine again.

"I'm ready." She wraps her arms around me again.

Chapter Seventeen

Shotgun

We all ride together in perfect synchronicity, like we're all on the same wavelength. A single unit of roaring fury ready to kick some serious ass. I only hope that we're correct in our suspicion that they've taken Therese and gone back out to the ranch with her. If they didn't, then we were running out of time. I certainly don't think they nabbed her to have her over for a cup of tea, a muffin, and some nice conversation about the weather and the neighbors. They keep escalating their behavior and after what they did to Ted, I just hope we make it in time. I don't want to have to kill anyone, but I fucking will.

As if Erica is reading my mind, she tightens her arms around my waist. I take a hand off of the bike just long enough to give her arm a squeeze of reassurance, before I put it back on the handlebar.

It's a clear night and the moon is bright, lighting our way down the long, empty road to the ranch. We haven't passed a single car, or seen a single pair of headlights. I scan the shadows continuously as we ride, searching for the shape of deer or coyote trying to cross the road. I've nearly flipped my bike over animals crossing the road at night, and the last thing we need on our way to war is an accident because a deer decided she needed to get from one side to the other just as we happened to be passing by.

Up ahead something in the shadows moves, and I squeeze my breaks. More than one shape is moving, breaking apart the darkness, and then headlights come on. The roar of more motorcycles adds to our own symphony of chaos. They pull out into the middle of the road and face us, creating a blockade. We all hit the brakes and slow in unison, and I pray that no one wipes out. Bucky comes close, but he slides around to the left and manages to plant his foot to keep himself from going under his bike.

"*Fuck.*" I hear him say. "Fucking *assholes.*"

"Stay back," I tell Erica as I flip down the kick stand. "There could be bullets."

She slips off the bike behind me and I dismount too. I pull a pair of brass knuckles from the saddle bag of my bike and fit them snugly onto my fingers. We fall into line with each other as we walk toward the assholes blocking the road. It doesn't surprise me at all that we're facing down the Dogs, instead of *Los Brujos* themselves. Bitch work seems like the appropriate thing for a bunch of dickless idiots that don't know their armpits from their assholes. They're a bunch of toothless hounds.

"Road's closed," one of them says. He's actually wearing sunglasses, even though it's been dark for hours. I hate him even more than I would have just for being a Dog.

"We're going to need a pass," Nick says.

"Like fuck you do," the sunglasses idiot says.

Bucky still seems to be feeling salty about nearly wiping out, because he's the first one to break the line and throw a punch. And boy, does he fucking land it. I hear the solid thud and the Dog that he hit staggers, nearly going down. That moment hangs for a long stretch of silence. And then we all move toward each other. I find my dance partner, and he's bringing something out of his pocket. The little sound it makes announces that he's brought a switchblade to the party. He slashes at me, and I dodge him. I bring up my fists, and we circle each other. I have a knife in my pocket too, but I'd rather pummel the shit out of this dirtbag with my bare hands. I'm a clean fighter, not like these fucking mutts.

He's not very good with the knife. He keeps slashing at me crudely, and I'll bet he probably hasn't ever taken anyone down with a blade. He's also doing it in a predictable rhythm, so I wait until he does it one more time before I step forward and slam my brass knuckles into his jaw. He makes a horrible sound and drops the knife to hold his face. He starts to spit, and I think I see at least one tooth exit his mouth in the dark.

"More?" I say.

He roars at me and lunges, this time with his fists. I dodge him and then circle around him. He throws another punch at me, and I block it with my forearm. It hurts like a fucking bitch, and it sends a shockwave through me. That'll leave a mark for sure. He takes the chance to throw another punch my way. I nearly get out of the way, but he clips my ear. And it fucking hurts. I throw another punch at him, and I catch him on the nose. More blood spurts and he screams.

"You broke my fucking nose," he chokes out.

"Can't say I'm sorry," I say to him and I have the craziest urge to laugh.

I kick him in the stomach hard, and send him toppling over. Before I have the chance to gauge what's happening around me or to celebrate my small victory, I'm going sideways. I tumble onto the asphalt with a big, meaty Dog that smells so strongly of BO that I have to hold my breath. He knocks the wind out of me when his bulk slams me into the ground. I think maybe one of my ribs is broken, but worrying about an injury is the least of my concerns right now.

"Jesus Christ," I gasp.

He straddles me and throws a punch at my face. I bring up my arms to protect myself, and he pounds the shit out of them. He's not giving me time between blows to land a counterstrike. All I can do is try not to get *my* nose broken as well.

Suddenly, he freezes.

"Get up," says a voice.

I slowly lower my arms, at risk of getting my face smashed in. But Bullet is standing over us, and he has a pistol pressed against the Dog's head.

"Get up," he says again. "Slowly."

I feel the bulk start to ease off of me. The Dog nearly topples over as he tries to get up, and I hear him grunt with the effort. He needs to do more squats.

"Thanks, buddy," I say to Bullet.

"No thanks needed," says Bullet. He keeps the pistol trained on the Dog who has slowly brought his hands up in the air. I look around and of the handful of mutts here, only two are standing and both of them have guns pointed at them.

Nick walks toward us, eyes on the Dog. "Where's the woman?" he asks.

"I don't know what you're talking about," mumbles the Dog.

"Shotgun," he says to me. I sock the fucker on the side of his head. Hard, but not hard enough to send him sideways or knock him unconscious.

"*Jesus*," says the Dog and holds the side of his head with hand.

"We know you jackasses are riding with *Los Brujos*," says Nick. "Where are they?"

The Dog mutters something unintelligible.

"What was that?" says Nick. "Maybe you need a bit more encouragement."

"No," says the Dog. He holds up both hands, looking from me to Bullet. "I—They'll kill me if I talk."

"Well, we'll kill you if you don't," says Bullet.

"They took her up the road," he says.

"Why did they take her?" says Nick.

"I don't know," he says. "Blackmail or somethin'. They don't tell me nothin'. I just do what I'm told."

"Good boy," says Nick.

"Is she alive?" I say.

"I—I don't know."

I punch him again.

"*Christ*," he says. "What was that for?"

"Because I'm fucking mad," I say.

"What's their plan?" says Nick.

"Man, I don't fuckin' know," says the Dog. There's a trickle of blood down the side of his face from where my fist split the skin.

"You're fucking useless," I say. Then I glance over at Erica, who is lingering uncertainly by my bike. "We've got to get going. I'm worried that..." I let the sentence trail off and Nick puts a hand on my shoulder.

"Let's go," he shouts. He walks away from us, back to his bike.

"*Arf arf*," says Bullet to the Dog. "Run along."

The Dog begins to lower his hands.

"Keep 'em where I can see 'em," says Bullet. The Dog raises his hands again and backs away. Bullet keeps the pistol trained on him while we step away. I doubt he's armed since he used his grubby fists to attack me, but it's not worth taking the chance. Bullet doesn't put up his pistol until we're back at our bikes, with a good bit of distance between us and the two Dogs still standing.

"Here," he says. He pulls a pistol out of the waistband of his jeans and hands it to me. "Picked it up from one of the others. It's not a shotgun, but it'll have to do." He chuckles.

"Thanks," I say. I check to make sure the safety is on before I tuck it into my jeans.

"All right, kid brother?" Seth says, suddenly at my elbow. He has a split eyebrow, but his eyes are burning in a way that tells me he just had a hell of a good time.

"Sure am," I say.

Erica is on the other side of me, putting her arm through mine. "Oh my god," she says. "I thought for a minute—"

"I'm all right," I say to her with a smile. "Let's get going."

Seth walks to his own bike as I mount mine and let Erica climb up right behind me. She's a natural. Even sore and tired from fighting, I have the capacity to feel super fucking proud right now.

"On we go," I say. And the roar of our engines starts up again in unison, like a mighty demon from hell.

Nick pulls out first, and the rest of us follow him. We're getting close now and the turn off for the ranch is up ahead in what seems like a blink. In the light of the moon, I can read the sign above the gate: *Escondido Ranch*. I think of Johnny suddenly, think of him riding this road night after night to come out to Mike's Cellar for some warm gin and friendly conversation. Poor guy.

The ranch is dark as we head up the long driveway to the house. I'm getting a nasty feeling as we head in, and I'm not quite sure why. The shit that just went down with the Dogs on the road seems like a warm up. A small appetizer. A palate teaser for what we're about to deal with. Nick slows his bike to a stop far from the house. We all stop behind him in the driveway and kill our engines.

"Let's walk up," he says.

Erica climbs off behind me, and I climb off after her. I loop my arm around her shoulder and press a kiss to her temple.

"If anything happens to me," I say, "run. If they start shooting, duck and cover."

"Okay," she says. And I can hear the fear in her voice.

"You can stay here with the bike," I say, but I already know it's futile.

"No," she says, sounding less afraid. "I'm coming with you. I'm not going to sit here while you all get shot at and fight for my mother."

I can't help but grin. I don't know if she can see it, but I give her a soft squeeze.

"At least get behind me," I say. I pull the pistol out of the waistband of my jeans and pull her behind me by the hand.

"Okay," she says.

The night is eerily silent while we walk the rest of the way up the long, dirt driveway. Not so much as a coyote cackling, or a small rodent rustling around in the sagebrush.

"It's too quiet," Seth says to my right as we cautiously approach a truck and a small Honda parked in the driveway near the house.

We pause in unison around the cars, looking toward the house.

"I'll go up," says Wildfire.

"Like hell you will," says Bullseye. "I'll go."

I don't have to see her face to know that she just rolled her eyes at him, but I don't blame him. She's one tough chick that can definitely hold her own, but if she was my old lady, I wouldn't let her go either.

"I'll go," I say. And before any of them can argue, I begin to walk toward the house. Slowly. Carefully. My ears and my eyes are sharpened for any tiny movement or sound. I'm holding the pistol in front of me, ready to fire if I need to. The door is slightly ajar as I approach. I edge up to it, holding my gun steadily. I look through the crack as best I can without moving the door. I can't see much in the darkness of the interior of the house. I glance over my shoulder at the Knights, who are watching, ready to move into action at a moment's notice.

I carefully nudge the door open with my shoulder and bring the pistol up. There's no one there. I move into the house, moving as quietly as I could. I pause to listen for even the tiniest sound. I hear nothing. I see nothing.

Well, not nothing. I'm realizing as my eyes adjust that the house is a fucking wreck. It's been totally torn apart. And I mean, totally. There are holes in the walls. The rugs have been pulled up. Anything and everything that could have been moved has been. I walk through the house as quietly as I can, holding the pistol in front of me and trying not trip over the chaos and the debris scattered all over the fucking floor. In the bedrooms, the mattresses have been flipped off the beds and torn open. I don't want Erica to see this, but I guess we don't really have a choice.

"Jesus Christ," I say out loud. I go back to the door and silently gesture for the rest of the Knights to follow me inside.

"Holy shit," says Nick when he enters the house.

"Oh," Erica whines, looking around. The look on her face actually makes my chest hurt. She hugs herself and walks slowly to the back of the house. I follow her to the doorway of the room I'd suspected was hers to begin with.

"Unbelievable," she says to herself more than to me. And unless I'm mistaken, she sounds kind of fucking pissed off.

"They're sure fucking determined."

She starts to say something else, but she's interrupted by the very distinct sound of gunfire.

"Fuck," I say. "Hide!"

I press my shoulder to the doorjamb and look down the hallway to the living room.

"Is there a back door?" I say.

"Yes, but—" she says.

"I want you to use it," I say. "Go. Go, I'll meet you outside."

"I don't want to leave you here," she says, gripping the sleeve of my T-shirt.

"I'll be all right," I say with a smile. "But I won't be if anything happens to you. Go on."

She kisses my cheek and then slips down the hallway. I risk a glance her way, but all I see is the moonlight spilling onto the ground and her shadow being swallowed up by light as she slips out into the night.

I raise my pistol and press my shoulder against the wall as I move down the hallway. As soon as I step into view of the living room, a Dog comes into my line of sight. I fire, hitting him in the shoulder, and he goes down. The pistol he was holding goes flying. I move further into the living room, adrenaline slamming through me. I look around for more Dogs, but that seems to have been the last one standing. The Knights are all gathered in a circle, and I move over to them.

"What's...?" I start to say, but I stop cold. My brother is on the ground. Nick is on one side of him and Wildfire is on the other. She's gripping his hand tightly, and Nick is pressing a blanket to his abdomen.

"Oh my God." The others make room for me to kneel next to him.

"Hey, kid brother," he says. "I'm okay, swear."

"Well, you don't fucking look okay," I say. "Jesus Christ, Holly is going to kill me."

"That makes two of us," he says. I take his hand, and it's fucking clammy.

"Oh Jesus," I say.

"I'll be all right."

"We've got to get him to the hospital," Nick says.

"I'll take him," says Wildfire. "There's a truck out there. The keys must be around here somewhere."

"There's some here," says Bucky. He's standing by a key holder by the door.

"Let's get him loaded in," says Bullseye.

"I'll come with you," I say.

"No," says Seth. "You stay here and finish what you started. I'll be all right. Holly will meet us at the hospital. I'm in the best of hands."

"I—I—" I can't find the words. I'm fucking stuck in the worst possible dilemma of my life.

"You're not allowed to come," says Seth. "You're not invited. Stay here and rescue the lady. Be a hero."

"I'll come," says Bullseye. "Someone's got to make sure you don't bleed to death while Seneca drives."

Wildfire gets the keys for the truck and goes outside to get it opened up. We lift Seth very carefully, but he still groans when we move him. I stare at the dark pool of blood on the ground where he was laying. I realize that this means the bullet went clean through him. I don't know much about medical nonsense, but I have some hazy notion that's supposed to be a good thing.

We get him into the back of the truck.

"Drive like the Devil is at your heels," I tell Wildfire. I'm fucking nauseous with worry, but I'm not going to let that show. But more than that, my vision is red with rage. If my brother dies, there will be fucking hell to pay. I can't even comprehend a world where he isn't alive.

"Go," he says to me. "You're running out of time."

"You'd better be fucking all right," I say. "Or I'll kill you myself."

I realize as the truck starts to pull away that I sent Erica out into the night. I look around for her, but she's not here with us. I'm so shaken now that it's hard to get my bearings straight. Casualties are a given in these situations, but this is my fucking brother we're talking about.

I swallow hard. "Erica?" I say. I walk around the side of the house to where the back door is. The door is slightly ajar, but there is no Erica to be found. I stick my head into the house. "Erica?" No answer.

I turn around and scan the night. Yards away I see what I realize is a small light. Probably the flashlight on her cell phone. What the hell is she doing out there? I almost call her name, but think better of it. We still haven't found the hornet's nest, and it won't do any good to go kicking around and accidentally bring them down on us out in the open.

I take one deep breath. I have to trust that my brother will be all right. Holly won't let anything happen to him. I let the breath out and start after Erica at a dead run.

I hope we're not too late.

Chapter Eighteen

Shotgun

I can see the shape of her as I close the gap between us. And I can also see a large structure in the moonlight ahead of her. She's almost to it by the time she can hear me. She freezes and turns around to face me, looking for all the world like she's ready to fight to the death. But she sees that it's me and puts a hand on her chest.

"Jesus Christ, Colt," she hisses at me. "You scared the shit out of me."

"Sorry about that," I say and after a pause I add, "Seth is on his way to the hospital."

"Oh my God," she whispers. "Why aren't you with him? What are you doing here? I can handle this, go and be with your brother!"

I snort. "No offense, little lady, but I sincerely doubt you can handle this."

"Your brother is more important than the mess I've dragged you into," she says.

"He doesn't seem to think so," I say. "Holly is going to take care of him." It's like a mantra I keep repeating to myself because I have to believe that it's true.

"She's going to kill us," Erica whispers. She sure catches on quickly.

"Yeah, these bastards have nothing on her," I say. "But right now they're here and she's not, so let's deal with this. I'd rather focus on this and not think of everything that could be going wrong with my brother. We're here to rescue your mother, and we're going to do that. If Seth—If things don't go well, I'd rather know it was for a reason."

I can see her nod in the moonlight, but I can't see her expression. She reaches out and takes my hand. "I'm sorry," she says. "I can't tell you how much it means to me that you're here. It's not your fight."

"Erica," I say, "your fight *is* my fight."

"Thank you," she whispers.

I can't help myself. I pull her into my arms and kiss her, forcing her mouth open with my tongue so I can taste her completely. Her arms come around my neck, and she's kissing me back. I release her and she presses a hand to my cheek, then she turns away from me and looks toward the old barn ahead of us. I can see a low light coming through the window and from underneath the doors. "I think they're in here."

"Let's see if we can get a look through the windows," I say.

"This way," she says. "Watch your step." I follow her around the barn, impressed at how silently and effortlessly she moves like a cat.

I can hear voices from inside the barn, but I can't make out any of the words they're saying. As we round a corner, I see a small square of light on the dirt ahead of us. I move ahead of Erica and put my shoulder against the wall of the barn. I begin to edge toward the window.

Slowly, very slowly, I move my head until I can see into the barn. Some jackass wearing a Dogs vest is standing in my way, but when I curse at him under my breath he moves like magic. Presto. Directly in my line of sight, I can see Therese. She's huddled on the ground with her back to the opposite wall and her hands are tied to her ankles. There's a gag tied around her mouth. My heart stops for a minute while I stare at her. She must be alive if they've bothered to tie her up. She must be. Relief sweeps through me when I see her move her head slightly.

"Do you see her?" says Erica behind me. "Is she in there?" Her hand grips the back of my vest.

"Yes," I say. I feel her release me. "They've got her tied up and gagged. Those fucking motherfuckers." I dare to move my head for a slightly better view. The three *Los Brujos* assholes are standing in the corner talking. And holy shit, if I'm not mistaken, there's two men in brown uniforms in there. And if I'm not *further* mistaken, I recognize the bulging silhouette of one of them. He turns his head slightly, and I can just make out his porcine profile.

Fucking Deputy Round is in on it. On the one hand, I am totally gratified by this information. I knew he was a real piece of shit. Not that I am a fan of cops in general, but dirty cops are even worse than the usual ones. They've got no honor, and I don't stand for that.

I see the men turn and look toward the door.

"Holy shit," I say to Erica. "You wouldn't fucking believe this, but the cop that arrested me earlier is there, cozy as a thief in a den. He's the fucking worst. I guess those dickheads weren't kidding. They are *real* friendly with the cops."

She doesn't answer me. "You okay?" I say over my shoulder.

Nothing. I turn around slowly, expecting the worst. And it's just shy of that. She's no longer standing behind me.

"Erica?" I say, scanning the darkness for her mane of blonde hair. "Erica, where are you?"

I turn slowly back toward the window, stomach sinking. The door to the barn is open now. The men are all standing around it in a semicircle, and they've got their guns out. Turns out the reason they were all looking there is that someone evidently knocked. That someone is Erica.

"Are you fucking kidding me," I say. What the fuck is she *thinking*? I don't know if I've ever been this close to panic. It takes everything I have not to slam my fist into the side of the barn. I don't need to draw attention to the fact that I'm standing right here spying on them. Erica is gesturing between herself and her mother.

One of *Los Brujos* walks toward her, and I watch with speechless rage as he puts his hand into her hair and tilts her face up toward his. She spits at him, which is very gratifying, but only until he uses her hair to throw her on the ground in front of her mother. One of the Dogs pushes the barn door shut, and I can hear them laughing at her.

I am blind with rage as I move around the side of the building. I don't even know what the fuck I'm about to do, but I'm not going to stand there and watch that fucking punk put his hands all over my woman or throw her around like a bag of trash. I'm going to fucking kill him. I'm going to take him apart, piece by piece. There are going to be more piece of his dick scattered around the desert than there are states in America by the time I'm fucking done with him.

I remind myself to think clearly. Going in there shooting is just going to get us all killed, and if Seth fucking dies, it sure as shit won't be because his shithead brother did something fucking stupid because he lost his temper. I pause at the corner and take a deep breath. I pull my phone out of my pocket and send Bullet a text: *We're out at the barn, they have her mother here. Don't do anything until you hear from me.* Then I round the corner, walk straight to the door and knock. I back up and toss away my pistol and put my hands in the air. The door opens slowly and the first thing I see is the barrel of a shotgun pointed at me.

Very appropriate.

The barn is bigger than it looks on the outside, and the beams holding up the old ceiling look pretty close to collapsing. Heavy, ancient-looking chains hang from the ceiling. There are Dogs scattered throughout, smoking cigarettes and doing their best to look like hot shit. I crane my neck to try to get a good look at Erica and Therese, but all I can see is part of Erica's long, beautiful legs off to the left. They're blocked by a giant old hunk of rusty machinery and a couple of Dogs who move in closer to get a better look at me. I reassure myself of her safety with the knowledge that she was still okay when I last saw her through the window a minute ago.

The whole scene looks like the beginning of a redneck, torture porn. Not my cup of tea.

"Well, look who it is," says a voice that I very unfortunately recognize. Deputy Round steps around the corner with the other brown uniform and puts his hands on his hips. He sounds puzzled, annoyed, and just slightly amused. "How the fuck did you slip the cuffs?" Then he waves his hand in the air. "I knew we couldn't trust Wilson. Something needs to be done about her, Deputy Chief."

"We'll take care of that as soon as we get back to the station," says the man who is presumably the Deputy Chief. "One bad apple spoils the bunch, as they say."

Los Brujos come around the corner and stand next to the dirty cops. The asshole Sergeant at Arms that plugged a bullet into my arm actually laughs when he sees me. "What the fuck are you doing here, *cabron*? Come for your revenge?"

"Well," I say, "that too."

"I'm guessing this is his little girlfriend," says Deputy Round, looking over his shoulder at where Erica is laying on the ground. The idea sends another wave of rage through me, but I remind myself to stay calm. If I just manage to stay calm and keep myself from unloading on these motherfuckers I will be able to get us out of this. I know it.

"I want you to let them go," I say.

They all laugh at me. No, they don't just laugh. They howl.

"Sure," says the Sergeant at Arms. "Want a ride home too?"

"I know where the gold is," I say. They all stop laughing immediately, like someone threw a switch.

"What did you say?" says the Sergeant at Arms.

"The gold," I say. "The gold he stole from you. He told me where he hid it."

Los Brujos exchange glances. Then they begin talking rapidly in Spanish. I can't understand what they're saying, but I'm fucking hoping that whatever it is, it's working in my favor.

"The cocaine is all gone," I say. I realize my T-shirt is soaked with sweat, but I've never felt more steady in my life. I don't even know what's coming out of my mouth, I'm just saying anything that could possibly get them to listen to me. "He told me about the heist. How he took the shit and ran, let you guys take the fall for it."

"Oh yeah?" says the Sergeant at Arms. He's looking at me with a frown. He's trying to decide if he can believe me. "And why would he tell a nobody like you what he did with that kind of shit?"

"He told me about the heist ages ago," I say. "But he told me all of the stuff was gone. But after he shot himself and you assholes ran off to leave him to bleed to death, he told me where it's hidden."

The Sergeant at Arms starts to laugh like I just said the funniest fucking thing in the entire world. He slaps his leg. "*Dios mio*, so you came sniffing around that sweet, little honey to get in good with her. Just to get your hands on some ass and some gold?"

"Exactly," I say. "You guys have been really fucking that up for me."

"My pleasure," says the Sergeant at Arms. "Okay, *guey*, take us to the gold."

"Only if you let them go first," I say.

"You don't make the orders here," says the Sergeant, his face darkening. "I do."

"I happen to believe that you're going to kill me either way," I say. "Whether or not I tell you shit. So you can let them go, and I can tell you. Or you can kill me, and I won't say anything at all."

"Oh," says one of the other *Los Brujos*. "We definitely know how to make you talk." He walks toward me, and he's almost toe to toe with me. He opens a switchblade so close to my face that I think he might have grazed my nose. Fucking bastard. This is the asshole who was pawing at Erica. I make a mental note to kill him as slowly as humanly possible when I manage to get my hands on him.

The Sergeant at Arms says something in Spanish. The asshole with the blade in my face looks even angrier for a moment. Then he steps away from me, cursing. He spits on my boot and walks back to where his friends are standing. He looks at me very meaningfully, and I'm sure it's an exact reflection of the look I'm wearing on my face: *I'll fucking kill you.*

They talk amongst themselves again.

"We can't let the women go," says Deputy Round. "They've seen us."

"Who're they gonna tell?" says the Sergeant at Arms. "The police?" He laughs.

"Seems like more trouble than it's worth," he grumbles.

"Maybe you should think about how badly you want your cut of the money," says the Sergeant, squaring off with Deputy Round. "And then multiply that by keeping your fucking mouth shut." He looks him up and down with disgust. I actually find it obviously satisfying that he seems to hate Deputy Round as much as I do. So we have that in common.

"Hey now," says the other one, the Chief Deputy. He steps between them. "Deputy Round, these are friends of mine. And we'll treat them that way. Let's defer to the good

Sergeant's wishes in this case."

Deputy Round just shakes his head and looks very sullen. I'm still just standing here like a fucking deer in the headlights with my hands in the air, sweating like a fucking pig in a barnyard while I listen to them debate whether they're going to kill the woman that I love. Between that and my brother on the way to the hospital, this is definitely not the best day I've ever had.

"All right," says the Sergeant at Arms after a bit more conversation with his men. "Let the bitches go. I don't like killing women unless I have to."

I really don't think it's going to be that easy. There's a trick here. And even if they let them get away tonight, they're going to come back for them. But we will cross that bridge when we get there. In the meantime, I have just stepped squarely into a pile of shit that I need to figure out how to maneuver my way out of. I may not make it out of this alive, but at least I can give Erica and her mother a head start.

"Now, tell us where that shit is," says the Sergeant. "And if you're playing tricks with me, I *will* make you sorry."

"I want to see them," I say.

"Yeah, yeah," he says. He gestures to them in the barn and a minute later, I see them drag Erica and her mother outside. Therese is *not* in good shape. The gag has rubbed her cheeks raw and she has a black eye. The rope has also rubbed her wrists and her ankles raw. She's leaning on Erica and limping as they walk out into the night. The look on Erica's face will stay with me forever—a curious combination of terror and fierce determination. Jesus Christ, I am actually in love with this woman.

"It was nice having you," says the Sergeant at Arms to the women. "Perhaps next time we'll get to know each other better." They laugh and whoop at the women. Erica looks at me and stops in her tracks. She looks from her mother to me. I give her the smallest nod. So she knows I'll be okay. Whether or not that's true remains to be seen.

She breaks away from her mother and runs to me, putting her arms around me.

"Hey, hey, hey," say the men standing around us. They raise their guns and point them at us.

I keep my hands in the air so they don't have more cause to shoot at us.

"There's a ravine just North of here," she whispers in my ear. "It'll give you a chance."

"Come now," says the switchblade asshole, coming toward us. "Enough of that."

He grabs Erica by the arm and drags her away from me roughly. She turns and looks at me, holding her hand in a tight fist. I think for a second she might punch him. He sees it too, and smiles at her. He leans in slowly and stops with his face an inch away from hers. He says something that I can't hear, but she loses the battle with her self-control. Her expression changes from mere anger to outrage. Her hand flies up toward his face, but his reflexes are too good. He catches her wrist and laughs at her. Then, the shitbag kisses her. She leans away from him, and her body goes rigid with fury. It's an exact mirror of my own. It's taking everything I have in me to not kill him where he stands. But I just did an awful lot of hard work to give Erica a chance to walk away, and I'm not going to spoil it now. I'll deal with him later.

He finally releases her arm and gives her a little push. "Nice to see you again, hot stuff," he says to her. "Call me." He looks right at me when he says this, and it takes everything I have not to punch him to death. Erica says nothing and walks away from him. She takes her mother by the hand, and they move away from the men. She stops just for a moment to throw me a look over her shoulder. And then they walk away into the night, Erica strongly holding up her mother while she limps along beside her.

I look back at the assholes with the guns pointed at me.

"So tell us," says the Sergeant. "Where did Johnny hide the money?"

"Just North of here," I say. I consult the sky and find the North Star. I point in the corresponding direction. "There's a cave. He said the cave just North of the barn."

"We'll see, won't we?" says the Sergeant. "We'll just see about that." He tilts his head to the Dogs standing nearby. "Bring him along for the ride."

One of them comes toward me and grabs me by the vest.

"Hey, hey," I say. "Don't fuck with my colors."

The asshole grunts at me and shoves me in front of him. I feel the shotgun jab into my back. It occurs to me that I very well may be about to die. And being blown away by a shotgun is probably the most appropriate death I can think of. It's not the death I would *like* to have, but at least it's pretty fucking legendary. My mouth is totally fucking dry, but I am not about to start getting scared. Now is not the time to feel afraid. When they fucking shoot me, that's about the time to feel afraid. And anyway, I reassure myself, I've already been shot once before. That was apparently just a warm up call for this sort of thing. A foreshadowing for what was to come.

I look over my shoulder as we walk to see if I can spot Erica in the darkness. Even with the light of the moon I can't make out the shape of her. My heart thumps hard, and I hope that they didn't just trick me. There's not much I can do if they did, but I want to die knowing that at least I set them free.

"Move along," says the guy behind me, giving a shove so hard that it nearly topples me over. I want to punch him in his stupid fucking face, but I keep my cool. I train my eyes ahead toward the slope of the hills that I see and search along the landscape for any sign of the ravine that Erica just mentioned to me. I look over my shoulder to see if there's anyone else approaching us. I told Bullet not to do anything until they've heard from me, but I hope he's smart enough not to listen. He outranks me, after all. He gets to make the decisions.

But really, it probably isn't going to come around to that until it's too late. Because I don't have much time. The hills are getting closer to us, and I still haven't figured out what I'm going to do. Up ahead I see darkness growing against the desert floor, and I realize it's the ravine opening up in my field of vision. I keep my eyes fixed on the thing while we walk like one little happy family out into the night, looking for treasure that is absolutely not where I said it was. While we approach both the foothills and the ravine, I'm calculating how close I need to be in order to get over the edge before they might end up shooting me. This is a crazy, fucked up fool's errand, but I just might be able to buy myself some time. The one thing I have going for me is that even with the moon high in the sky it might be too dark outside to aim true.

I'm going to lose my nerve. It's now or never. I don't even remember telling myself to run, but I do. I split off to the left and run straight for the ravine. I've never run so fast or so hard in my goddamn life. I can hear them firing their weapons after me, and the bullets are whizzing through the air. The adrenaline in me is so high right now that I can say with certainty that I don't think I would be able to tell if I *was* shot. I can hear them running after me, shouting and yelling. Most of the Dogs don't strike me as fit enough for a long distance chase on foot, but a couple of those *Los Brujos* motherfuckers look like they definitely work out. In all ways, they're the most dangerous ones that I need to look out for. I spare a glance over my shoulder and, sure enough, they're the three that have the closest tail on me. As I turn my head, I see one of them raise a pistol and fire it at me, and I hear the bullet travel dangerously close to my ear.

In the distance, I can hear a roar start up. The sound of motorcycle engines. I can't tell if it's the Knights or these assholes and I can't spare another look behind me. One of them is gaining on me, I can hear him. The sound of the engines is coming closer and out of the corner of my eye I can see headlights coming up on us in the night. I can't hear the asshole behind me anymore, but I hear the gunfire behind me divert. The sound of more guns joins the party, and my heart gives a giant leap. The Knights have come to my rescue, how appropriate.

As I reach the edge of the ravine, I hit my knees and slide. I'm going so fast that I think for one horrible moment that I'm going to go sailing over the edge, but I stop just short of it. Breathing hard, I find myself staring down into a deep, black abyss. Something tells me that would have *really* hurt. I'm too lost in my shock at coming so close to death that I didn't realize that the *Brujo* that's been chasing me is all but on top of me now. I feel an arm come around my throat, and I instantly recognize this as the sleeper hold. He's pressing so hard that the world immediately starts to get fuzzy around the edges. I grip his arm and try to break the hold but he's strong. I lift my heavy boots and try to stamp on his feet, but he's also wearing heavy motorcycle boots—the kind that are designed to keep your feet from getting crushed. *Goddammit.*

I throw my elbow back, trying to catch him in the stomach, to do anything that will loosen his grip even a little bit. I don't even want to think about all of the cells rupturing in my brain right now while the world around fades a little at a time. Sounds are becoming muffled and while I'm still trying to fight him off, I'm starting to lose the battle. I realize, with my last flash of good sense, that if I just pretend to pass out, that he'll relax the hold. I go limp like a fish and after a moment, he starts to ease the grip. It's just enough to let me suck air into my lungs and simultaneously throw my head backward, praying it will make contact with his stupid fucking face. I'm honestly almost surprised when it works.

"Fuck," he hollers. Or that's what I think he says because his hands are cupped around his nose, which I'm certain I've probably broken.

I wasn't anticipating it to work, and the blow nearly makes me pass out. The world swings sideways, and I stagger but I manage to right myself. I begin to cough and gag so hard that it makes me tear up. After the number he just did on my windpipe, I can't stop myself from doing it. It's not ideal when he steps forward and takes a swing at me. I dance backward, out of his reach and don't realize until it's too late that I'm right at the edge of the ravine. My heels are hanging off and for one horrible fucking minute, the world slows down. I bring my arms up to balance myself. I regain my footing. He obviously realizes the advantage of his position because he moves toward me like he's going to give me a hard push. I throw myself at him, and we tumble to the cracked earth. He grabs the front of my vest and rolls hard, like a goddamn crocodile until we're dangerously close to the edge of the ravine again. He's on top of me, and the blood from his nose is dripping down into my face. Fucking gross.

"*Adios*, asshole," he says in my ear, and then heaves his entire weight again like he's going to pitch me over the edge. But as we roll, I bring my leg up and shove him as hard as I can toward the edge of the ravine. I've caught him by surprise, and he tries to grab at me for purchase, but he can't get a grip. He vanishes over the edge and judging by the crashing I hear as he falls, he's not doing too great. Panting and coughing, I stand up and rub my throat. It hurts like hell. I'm so tired that I just want to stretch out on the hard desert ground and go right to sleep. But instead, I pivot until I can see the chaos going on behind me.

I set off toward them at a pace that can only be described as a mild jog. A three-legged dog could go faster than me in this state. But when I get closer, my adrenaline starts up again, and it roars like a motorcycle engine. The first thing I see is one of the Dogs holding Bullet by the car. He's landing blow after blow, and I see blood spurt from Bullet's lip as it splits against his teeth. *Jesus*. It's not his fault, Bullet can kick as much ass as anybody else, but this guy is particularly huge. At least 6'5" and he looks like a WWE wrestler. I take a deep breath and steel myself, then I run up behind that big motherfucker and punch him in the back of the head as hard as I can. Which, admittedly, is not as hard as I like, but the height difference and the angle make it difficult to get a good shot.

But it's enough to startle him into letting go of Bullet, who staggers backward and spits out a mouthful of blood—and probably a tooth or two. The giant wheels on me, and I put up my fists and almost laugh because if he lands one good blow, I'm going to go sideways like a Jenga tower.

Crack. The big bastard suddenly goes over, and Nick is standing there, holding a baseball bat and breathing hard. But goddammit if he isn't looking like he's having the time of his fucking life. He turns to Bullet.

"You okay, man?" Nick says.

"Just dandy," says Bullet. "My girl isn't going to like my new face though."

Now that I'm getting a look at the situation, there aren't very many people still standing, and there are a whole lot of guys scattered on the ground. A pistol goes off, and I hear a bullet go whizzing dangerously close. We all dive behind a bike parked nearby.

"I'm glad you have the sense not to listen to me," I say to Bullet as I very carefully move my head to peek over the bike.

"I outrank you," he says. "I only take orders from Nick."

"Pfft, only when you feel like, you little bastard," says Nick affectionately.

"Where the hell is Bucky?" I say, looking around.

"They knocked him out cold," says Bullet.

"Shit," I say. I try to get another look over the seat of the bike, but this invites more gunfire. I can't see who's shooting. They're out of the circle of light cast by the motorcycle headlights.

"Sore losers," Nick says. "We've cleaned their fucking clocks."

"I think it's those sheriff assholes," says Bullet.

"Got a lot to lose if they let us walk away," says Nick.

"I've got three left," says Bullet, pulling his pistol out of its holster. "But being a good shot doesn't mean shit if I can't see who I'm firing at."

I open my mouth to say something, but the thought vanishes from my head when I hear sirens in the distance.

"Ah, fuck," I say. "Might as well use those three bullets to put us all out of our fucking misery, because they called in calvary." I'll die defending the Knights and trying to get back to Seth and Erica if I have to, but let's not have it come to that. It occurs to me that we could try to run, but I can already see the blue and red of the lights flashing through the night.

A fucking fleet of cops are suddenly on top of us. I count six police cars, all marked Arizona State Police. Before they even come to a stop, the doors are opening and cops are pointing Glocks and shotguns at us.

"Drop your weapons," says a voice over a loudspeaker. "I repeat, drop your weapons or we *will* open fire. Put your hands in the air where we can see them."

We climb to our feet with our hands in the air. Slowly, I might add, while we all groan from our injuries. Buncha old men.

I realize as I'm assessing the situation, that Deputy Wilson is one of the cops, holding a gun pointed at the rest of us. I'm very satisfied to see that her gun is pointed specifically at Deputy Round, who is being illuminated by the bright headlights of the car. She's the only brown uniform. The rest of them are classic boys in blue.

"Holy shit," I say. "Unless I'm totally fucking mistaken, it's not the calvary. They're in deep shit." And I can't help but laugh.

"What do you mean?" Bullet asks.

"That's Deputy Wilson," I say. "She's the one who busted me out."

I slowly move around the bike and begin to walk toward Deputy Wilson.

"Freeze!" one of the cops yells to me and I obey. I feel very exposed, out in the open with a dozen state troopers staring me down. But I see Deputy Wilson turn toward me. I can't see her face, but she must recognize me. She steps out in front of the headlights and holsters her gun.

"It's all right, officer," she says. She gestures for me to come closer.

I walk toward Deputy Wilson, who looks me over. "What the hell happened to you?" she says.

"Long story," I say, and I think I probably sound as exhausted as I feel.

"Looks like we got here right on time," she says.

"What took you so long?" I say and have the crazy urge to laugh.

"Had to call in a favor," she says. And for the first time, she smiles.

"Got sick of these assholes?" I say, nodding toward Deputy Round and Chief Deputy Wilkes.

"Forever ago," she said. "I've suspected a lot of corruption going on in the department, but it's taken me a while to put together enough compelling evidence. Cops have a nasty habit of looking the other way where other cops are concerned."

"I don't think I've ever been so happy to see a cop in my life," I say.

"Thank you?" she says, and it's definitely a question.

"But Deputy Wilson, my brother is in the hospital," I say. "And I have to find Erica."

"What do you mean find her?" she says, sounding a little alarmed. "She's missing?"

"No," I say. "I mean, I don't think so. They let her and Therese go. They probably went back to the hospital."

"Okay, get going" she says, looking at me hard. "But I expect you at the station tomorrow, or I *will* arrest you for a whole lot more than disturbing the peace."

"What about these guys?" I say, nodding over my shoulder to Nick and Harry.

"Don't push it," she says.

"It was all self-defense," I say.

"I believe you," she says. "But I gotta take them in. If everything squares away, they'll be out in no time."

I sigh. "I'm going to tell them goodbye." Wilson nods, and I turn to go back to Harry and Nick.

"She's letting me off the hook for the night," I say to them, "but she says you guys have to go down to the station."

"Ah, fuck," Nick says this time.

"Just where I want to spend the night after getting the shit beat out of me," says Bullet.

"She says she's going to get you out as fast she can," I say. "I have to come down and turn myself in tomorrow.

"I wonder if they serve Danish with the continental breakfast," says Nick and chuckles at his own joke.

"All right, all right, Shotgun," says Bullet. "Beat it, kid."

I put my hand on his shoulder and give it a slight squeeze. "I can't thank you guys enough."

"Get going," says Nick. "Call Wilson when you find out how your brother is doing, see if she can get the message to us."

"Yes, sir," I say. I give them both a grin, and then I turn back to the cops. They're in the process of arresting the stragglers. I scan for Wilson and spot her *slamming* Deputy Round into the hood of a state trooper car. Best sight of the night. I pass close enough that I can give her a nod and a wave.

And I wish I could say that I run off into the night, but instead, I limp steadily toward the house to get on my bike.

I don't think I've ever been happier to be alive.

Chapter Nineteen

Shotgun

I have been at the hospital too many times in the last couple of days if you ask me. And I would have liked to have brought my bike, but I had to leave it at the ranch. It's not practical to try to fit yourself, your girl, *and* your girl's mother on the back of your bike. I'm driving though, because Erica is sitting in the back of the car with her arm around her mother. I keep glancing in the rearview mirror. Our eyes meet once or twice, and she gives me a gentle smile, before she goes back to tending to her mother. I'm so tired that I feel like it's very possible I could wreck the car on the drive back into town, but I grip the steering wheel and keep shaking myself.

We need to get Therese to the hospital, but I also desperately need to know what's going on with Seth. I texted Holly as soon as I got back to the house, and she told me that he was going in for surgery. That's all I know, and I'm sure that's all she knows too. It's like the world's most fucked up question mark—is he, or isn't he?

At least he made it to the hospital alive. So there's that.

I pull through the turnaround in front of the hospital to let the girls out, and then I park the car in the lot. I hurry inside and pass them checking in at the front desk. I walk to Erica and take her hand, giving her a brief kiss on the cheek.

"I'll see you soon," I say, and then I keep walking. I run to the elevator and jab the arrow pointing up with my finger until the elevator bell dings, and I can step inside the elevator. I'm not normally and anxious person, but holy shit, am I anxious right this fucking minute. Maybe if I ask nicely one of the nurses will shoot me with a tranquilizer gun. The elevator crawls up to the second floor, and I burst out of the doors as soon as they open. I rush into the waiting area and look around.

Holly is sitting there, hands clasped between her knees, staring at the floor. She looks how I feel right now. Wildfire and Bullseye are sitting across from her. Wildfire is staring at the floor intently, and Bullseye is leafing aimlessly through a LIFE magazine.

"Holly Berry," I say, sitting down in the chair next to her.

"Colt," she says. I can see that she's been crying. She's very composed, but her eyes are red-rimmed. Her look of grief is replaced by one of shock. "Holy shit, what happened to you?"

"Just a little slap and tickle," I say, giving her a tired grin.

"Have you looked in a fucking mirror?" she asks.

"Should I?" I say, suddenly feeling concerned.

She manages to smile. "Nothing permanent. But I can see that someone tried to smother you to death because there are broken blood vessels in your eyes."

"*Gross*," I say. My vanity rears its ugly—or rather, beautiful—head. "How long does that take to go awake? Never mind, never mind. How is he? Any news?"

She shakes her head.

"Do you know…" I start to say, and then I swallow hard. "What are the chances? What are the odds?"

She shrugs. "I don't know. A gunshot wound to the abdomen…" She shakes her head. "I mean, it's not good."

I sit back in my chair and swallow again, feeling like I might be sick. "How long does this sort of thing take?"

"It depends on how bad the injury is," she says. "If the bullet is still inside of him. How many major…"

"He was bleeding out the back," I say. "Seems like it went clear through him."

She looks a bit relieved. "That's good to hear. But if he's lost too much blood or if it hit his liver…"

"Let's just wait to hear," I say. I take her hand. It's as shaky and clammy as my own.

"I would just feel a lot better if I was the one operating on him," she says. And then her composure crumples, and she starts to cry. She covers her mouth like she's embarrassed about it, and I'd bet a lot of money that it's her inner doctor fighting with her inner human. I'm too numb with fear and exhaustion to even think about crying. "I just want him to make it through this. He has to make it through this. Colt, I'm pregnant."

"*What?*" I say. I nearly jump to my feet.

"That's amazing," Wildfire says, perking up a tiny bit. "I'm so happy for you." I can't help but notice that she gives Bullseye a subtle but meaningful look that nearly makes me laugh.

"Holly, that's—I mean, that's wonderful!" I say. "Why haven't you said anything?"

"I was going to tell him this weekend," she says. "I had this whole thing planned. I mean, we want children, but we weren't counting on this happening so soon. It's kind of a happy accident."

"I'll say." There's a big balloon filling up in my chest. I've never been an uncle before. I'm really fucking excited about the idea. I mean, I've heard them go on and on about their disgusting plans to have a family until I thought I'd drown myself in a pool of my own vomit, but now that it's happening, I'm really happy for them. And for me. Uncle Colt, the greatest uncle in the fucking universe. Even while I'm feeling exceptionally happy about this, there's a distinct bitterness to the moment. I look down the hall to the doors that are closed, and my heart gives a thump.

Seth had better fucking come out of there. He has no choice. He's about to be a father.

"How'd it go?" says Bullseye.

"Not as bad as it could have," I say. "We kicked their asses, but the cops showed up before we could finish the job. The sheriff's deputies were in on the whole thing."

Bullseye gives a low whistle.

"Are you serious?" Wildfire says. A line appears between her eyebrows. "So, if the cops showed up..."

"Different cops," I say. "One of the Deputies brought in the state police to hem their asses up."

"Uh, lucky for us?" says Wildfire.

"I guess," I say. "Nick and Bullet weren't too happy about getting arrested. Deputy Wilson said I have to go turn myself in tomorrow."

"Looks like we made out well, babe," says Bullseye with a laugh.

"I guess you guys did," I say with a laugh.

I'm really fucking grateful they're here. It makes me feel better, and the light humor is helping to ease the aching sense of dread that is gnawing at the pit of my stomach.

Time stretches on and I really think I might go fucking crazy. And then, at last, there's a doctor in scrubs coming through the doors.

We all jump to our feet like we sat on hot pokers. "Doctor?" Holly prompts.

"Seth Hardy's family?" the doctor asks, looking back and forth between us.

"Yes, yes," I say, already wanting to throttle the doctor for not just spitting it out. How is he? Is he—?"

"He's stable," says the doctor. And I don't think there's ever been a bigger sigh of relief than the one that I hear come out of Holly. She actually staggers a bit and presses her hand to her stomach. I catch her by the arm and keep her from toppling over. I'll never tell anyone, but I actually have to blink hard a couple of times to keep tears from escaping. I take a deep breath.

"Can we see him?" I say.

"He's resting for a bit in post-op," says the doctor. "He's just coming out of the anesthesia. You're welcome to go to his room, but I don't think he's much for conversation right now. He'll be transferred to the third floor soon."

I grab the doctor's hand and shake it so hard that I'm sure I hurt the poor man, but I can't help myself. "Thank you," I say. "Thank you, Doctor."

"No problem," he says. I think I see him give his hand a small shake when he releases himself from my grip.

"Now that we know he's going to be okay, I'm going to go check on Erica while he comes out from the drugs," I say to Holly. "I'll meet you in his room on the third floor?"

She nods, smiling. She's still dabbing tears off of her face with a Kleenex.

"I'll take you to him," says the doctor.

"We'll wait here," Bullseye says and Wildfire nods along with him. They're just as anxious to see him, I'm sure, but it's nice of them to want to give Holly her privacy with him.

"Thank you," says Holly. I watch them walk away for just a moment before I turn and go to the elevator. I'm so happy right now that I feel like I might do a fucking jig. I feel a bit shitty that several of the Knights are sitting in jail right now, but at least Wildfire and Bullseye manage to keep out of the clank. Everyone made it out alive. It wasn't a total fucking failure of a night.

I take the elevator down to the first floor, to the ER, and I approach the desk.

"Peters. Therese?" I say.

"Room four," she says, after consulting a clipboard. "That way."

"Thank you," I say and follow the direction she's indicated. When I get to the appropriate room, I knock lightly on the door.

Erica opens it and smiles at me. Despite how exhausted she looks, it's a dazzling smile.

"Hey," she says. "Seth, is he—?"

"He's stable," I say. And I sweep her into my arms, gripping her as tightly as I dare without crushing her precious ribs. Over her shoulder, I can see her mother looking at us and smiling. She looks *more* tired than I feel and I can't say I blame her. I release Erica and go to Therese.

"Happy to see you made it out okay," I say.

"Thank you so much," she says. Her voice is pretty raspy. "I can't thank you enough." She reaches for my hand, and I give it to her awkwardly. I'm really not good with this touchy feely stuff with people I don't know super well.

"No need," I say. I actually feel embarrassed. I'm this close to saying, *aw shucks*, and scuffing the ground with the boot. "I'm just glad everyone is okay."

"Mom, we're going to let you rest while we wait for the doctor to come back," Erica says, taking me by the elbow. She seems to sense my distress and is coming to my rescue.

"Be safe," her mother says.

"I've got Colt," says Erica. "I'm as safe as I can be."

And if that's not enough to make a man's heart swell, I don't know what is. We step out into the hallway, and Erica closes the door quietly behind her. She turns to me and smiles again. There's this air of relief around her, like she's been carrying a heavy load that she's finally been able to put aside. She comes to me and puts her arms around my neck.

"What do you say we get my mother settled in with Ted and go back to your place?" she whispers into my neck.

"That's the best idea I've heard all goddamn day," I say. I put my arms around her waist and lift her up off of the floor. It makes her giggle. Things are starting to feel right in the world again.

She steps back and looks at me. "You really look like hell," she says. "I think you need a bath." And if I'm not mistaken, there is a gleam of mischief in her eye.

"Nurse Erica," I say, "I submit to all of your ministrations."

"I was hoping you would say that," she says. And there's no mistaking it this time. There is *definitely* a mischievous look in her eye.

After we get her mother settled and we stop off to see Seth, who is hilariously loopy from the anesthesia, we finally hit the road. And thank God, because I was starting to get impatient. Mainly because if I waited too much longer, I'd be too goddamn tired to do the things that I'm very much hoping to do once we get alone.

"I'm driving," she says as we reach the car.

"Absolutely not," I say. "You're going to cripple my masculinity."

"Nurse Erica insists," she says. "And you said you would submit to *all* of my ministrations." She looks at me meaningfully. "And I'm an *all* or nothing kind of gal, if you follow my meaning."

I think about this for about two seconds then say, "Yep, whatever you want." And I climb into the passenger seat of her mother's car. Secretly, I'm grateful. I'm so exhausted that I might have killed us if she hadn't taken over and sexually blackmailed me into submitting to her demands.

On the drive over, she keeps her right hand on my inner thigh, massaging my leg in the cruelest way a woman can.

I try to return the favor, but she clicks her tongue and says, "I'm trying to concentrate on the road." And then she gives me a smile that is too angelic to be believable.

When we get to the apartment, I have to work hard not to limp. My body is starting to get really stiff, but I refuse to abandon my present course of action. I need my bruised and battered limbs tangled up with Erica's, and I need it more than anything else in the world right now. When we get inside, I go to remove my leather vest and I can't stifle a groan.

"Here," she says. "Let me help you." And she does, slipping the heavy leather off of my shoulders. She folds it neatly and lays it on the back of my couch. Then she walks around in front of me and tugs at my T-shirt. "Arms up."

I do as she says, but I groan louder this time. I might be playing the baby thing up just a tiny bit, but even the biggest, toughest dudes love the care of a good woman after a rough fucking day. And for her part, she seems to be enjoying herself.

She pulls her shirt off, and I think I nearly drool on myself.

"Come on," she says, and she takes me by the hand and leads me down the hallway to the bathroom. She pulls off her cut offs and leans over the bathtub, giving me a beautifully gratuitous look at her ass while she starts the water. She looks over her shoulder at me and smiles when she straightens up. Then she brings her hands around her back and unhooks her bra.

"Let me help you with that," I say, bringing her into the circle of my arms. I slip her bra off and then run my hands over her ribs, enjoying in the beautiful smoothness of her skin. Then I bring my hands up, over her breasts, and tease nipples lightly.

Jesus Christ, I'm already as hard as a rock.

"I can think of a thing or two to do while the bathtub fills," she whispers. Then she turns around and kisses me deeply. I get lost in the texture of lips and tongue, and the taste of her, until she pulls away and gives me her impish smile. Then, she slowly lowers herself down the front of my body until she's kneeling on the floor in front of me. "Don't mind me," she says.

"Wouldn't dream of it," I say, and my eyes nearly roll out of my fucking skull when she takes me all the way into her mouth. She works the shaft of my dick with her hand while she licks the head. Her other hand cups my balls and massages them softly while she does these insane things to me with her mouth. I put my hand in her hair and gently pull her head back, forcing her to release my dick from her mouth.

"I want to finish you like this," she says. And the look she gives me with her green eyes is almost enough to do the job. She keeps her hand moving up and down my shaft while she's talking and it's very distracting.

"No way," I say. I reach down and circle my hands around her waist, lifting her until our faces are even, and she can put her legs around me. "I want to fuck you. I *need* to fuck you."

She takes my face between her hands and kisses me, a deep, delicious kiss. Her tongue eases into my mouth and caresses mine. I walk a couple of steps until I can put her ass down on the bathroom counter, which is just the right height for my purposes.

I slip my fingers inside of her and she moans softly. I'm amazed at how wet she already is. "Oh my God," I whisper against her lips and she laughs.

"I can't help it," she says.

I work my fingers in and out of her, massaging her g-spot and rubbing her clit softly with my thumb. I watch her face while I do it, and my knees are starting to get shaky. She grips me tightly and digs her fingernails into me. I don't mind, I like it when she gets a little freaky.

But Jesus Christ, I can't take it anymore. I cover her lips with mine and replace my fingers with my dick, slipping inside of her tight, wet opening.

"Jesus," she says, holding onto me for dear life.

"No," I say. "It's Colt."

She laughs. "You're ridiculous."

"You have no idea," I say and grin at her. I kiss her again, tasting her tongue and mouth, drinking down the taste of her like a greedy kid in a candy store. I hold her hips while I push into her slowly and pull myself back out. The slow, sensual rhythm is fucking amazing, and the sound of her moans is enough to make me crazy. I force myself to stop, breathing hard, and lean down to take her breast in my mouth. Her nipples are hard and delicious, like candies. She grips my hair and moans while I tease her nipple with my tongue, and when I think she just can't take it anymore, I move my mouth to the other one and start all over.

"Fuck me," she moans. "Fuck me, Colt."

"Only if you ask nicely," I say. I stroke her clit with my thumb again and watch her face, totally transformed by her need.

"Please," she says. She squeezes me with her thighs. "*Please?*"

I put my hands on her hips and slide inside of her again, so slowly that I make *myself* crazy. Then I pull almost all the way out and wait just a moment before I enter her again, just as slowly. It's a horrible game to play, to tease us both like this, but it's just fucking wasteful to rush through it. She's too sexy and delicious. I wouldn't deserve to fuck her if I didn't take my time.

"More," she whispers against my lips. "More."

I can't help myself, my desire for her is too strong. I tighten my grip on her hips and begin to move faster.

"Harder," she says.

And who am I to deny a lady. I thrust a little harder every time, working up to a rhythm that leaves us both moaning and totally swept away in the moment. Her fingers comb through my hair and she pulls my mouth toward hers. She kisses me hard and moans into my mouth while I grip her tightly and fuck her like the world is about to end. In the back of my mind, it occurs to me that the bathtub might overflow, but I can't be bothered to stop and check. I pick up her thighs and lift her knees so I can watch my dick moving in and out of her. It's the best fucking thing I've ever seen.

"Jesus fucking Christ," I say. She smiles at me with her sexy bedroom eyes and slips her fingers in between her legs to stroke herself while I move in and out of her. I could pass out, I'm so turned on by her. Maybe I should run the other way. This could be dangerous, bad for my health or something. She could make me die of a heart attack if we carry on like this. But right now, I can't stop. It could kill me to stop.

Watching her is working me into a frenzy. I grab her hips again and pull her closer. She pulls my head toward hers and kisses me again, biting and licking my lips like a madwoman.

"I'm going to come," she says breathily, and I pull my head back far enough to watch her face. A moment later, her face twists into the most delicious expression of pleasure, and she starts to scream like I'm murdering her. I don't mind, I just hope the neighbors don't call the cops. Her eyes are literally rolling in the back of her head, and I don't think I've ever felt prouder of myself.

I want to laugh, but I'm at the threshold myself. "Holy fucking shit," I breath out, and I thrust faster and faster until I'm coming so hard that I think I actually black out for a minute and somehow manage to stay standing.

"I can't feel my fucking face," I gasp.

Erica giggles and pulls me close to put a long, sweet kiss on my lips.

"That was fucking unreal," I say.

"Again?" she says, giving me a wicked smile.

"Woman, you're going to be the death of me," I say.

She laughs and then looks over my shoulder. "Oh Shit! The bathtub!"

I look over my shoulder and see that it's actually just beginning to overflow.

"Fuck," I say and reluctantly disentangle from Erica. I shut the water off and nearly slip and fall to my death on the wet tile. Erica is laughing, and I can't help but join.

This must be what happiness is.

After our bath, we lay in my bed and hold each other. Both of us are totally exhausted, both from orgasms and from the worst day ever.

"I keep thinking," I say to Erica. "About this thing that Johnny said to me right before he died."

"What did he say?" she asks, shifting her head off my chest so she can look at my face.

"He said 'it' was in the bear." I frown at the ceiling. "I can't figure out what '*it*' was."

"A bear?" she says. She sits up. "He didn't say what he was referring to?"

"No," I shake my head. I heave myself up into a sitting position, despite how sore my body is. "I mean, it's kind of a crazy thought, but maybe he was talking about the stuff that he stole from *Los Brujos*."

"Thousands of bricks of gold?" she says. "Hidden in a bear?" She laughs. "Doesn't seem likely."

"Yeah," I say. "I don't really know how it fits. But that's what he said. I mean, he *was* dying."

"Well," says Erica, frowning at me, then at the blanket. "There *is* a bear in the house."

"What sort of bear?" I say, sitting up a little straighter.

"I mean, it's just a dumb clock," she says. "But it's carved into the frame above the kitchen door. It's a bear, and his belly is the clock."

"Seems like a long shot," I say. "But I kind of want to go look at it. I don't know if '*it*' is anything of value, but that was his house, and he did mention the bear. And so far, it's the only bear we know about."

Erica smiles at me. And I smile back.

Before I can go anywhere, I have to go to the police station. But Wilson gives me a solid break, takes my statement, and doesn't put cuffs on me. And she lets Bullet and Nick go. They're particularly salty about the fact that they're the only ones who had to sit in the clink, but I reassure them that I will do an excellent job cleaning both of their motorcycles.

"For the next month," Nick grumbles. And I can't argue with that.

Erica and I get to the house early after another stop at the hospital with flowers for Therese and Holly. Seth grumbled that we didn't bring *him* flowers, but you know, he would have grumbled about being emasculated if we had. Lose-lose sort of situation.

After that, we hit the road back out to the ranch. I'm tired. Probably because we woke up to fuck two more times through the night, but also because it's just been a long goddamn few weeks. In the back of my mind, I keep thinking about the fact that this is not the end of *Los Brujos* coming after this property. But I think Erica and Therese are pretty set on putting the thing back on the market now. I haven't confirmed this with them, but I'm sure it will come up soon.

Walking back into the house is pretty depressing. The destruction in the daylight is even more shocking than it was last night. Erica pauses at the door, and I watch her face as her green eyes flick around, taking everything in.

"We'll make it right," I say, rubbing her back.

She takes a deep breath, and then walks toward the kitchen. I follow her. She turns around as we enter and points above her head.

"There," she says. "See?"

And there it is, a bear carved into the door frame, just like she said there was. There's a little clock in its belly. I reach up to see if I can fuck with the thing, but it's just a bit far for me.

"Here," she says. And she walks away to grab a chair that's been toppled in the other room. She puts it down in front of the bear, trying to avoid putting the feet on any shards of glass or scattered food. She climbs up on the chair and straightens up to face the bear.

She fiddles with it for a moment and then with a soft click, the belly opens and the clock face swings outward.

"Holy shit," I say.

"There's something in here," she says.

"Bricks of gold?" I ask, grinning up at her and running a hand up her leg. She swats at me.

"No," she says. "But there's a piece of paper." She pulls it out and looks around in the hole. "That's it, that's all."

I offer my hand to help her down off the chair and look over her shoulder while she unfolds the piece of paper.

"It's a diagram?" I say, frowning while I look it over.

"It's the ranch," she says. "It's a map of the ranch." Toward the middle of the property, there is a big fat X drawn and circled in Sharpie.

"Oh my god," I say.

She looks up at me, looking stunned. "You don't think—?"

"There's only one way to find out," I say, and I can't help but smile. "Let's go hunt some treasure."

"I've already found my treasure," she says and puts a tender kiss on my lips.

"Well, when you put it like that," I say. "I guess I have too. But a little gold never hurt anybody."

We smile at each other and head out into the sunlight.

Your Free Gifts

Wow I hope that satisfied your MC itch...at least for now. If you've enjoyed reading about these gritty bikers, please take a minute to leave a review.

Are you craving more bad boy bikers? Don't forget to claim your FREE exclusive access to the prequel by joining my VIP newsletter.

You'll also be the first to hear about upcoming new releases, giveaways, future discounts, and much more.

Click here to sign up and get your FREE access to the Steel Knights Prequel now! www.BookHip.com/NXQBZZ

See you on the inside,
Ivy Black

Printed in Great Britain
by Amazon